D1423691

THE PRICE WAS HIGH

The Last Uncollected Stories of

F. Scott Fitzgerald

I have asked a lot of my emotions—one hundred and twenty stories. The price was high, right up with Kipling, because there was one little drop of something not blood, not a tear, not my seed, but me more intimately than these, in every story, it was the extra I had. Now it has gone and I am just like you now.

"Our April Letter,"
The Notebooks of F. Scott Fitzgerald

THE PRICE WAS HIGH

The Last Uncollected Stories of

F. Scott Fitzgerald

edited by Matthew J. Bruccoli

QUARTET BOOKS

LONDON MELBOURNE NEW YORK

First published in Great Britain by Quartet Books Limited 1979
A member of the Namara Group
27 Goodge Street, London W1P 1FD

First published in the United States of America by Harcourt Brace
Jovanovich Bruccoli Clark, New York, 1979

ISBN 0 7043 2233 1

Printed and bound by The Garden City Press Limited, Letchworth,
Hertfordshire SG6 1JS

Contents

Contents

Illustrations are grouped between pages 364 and 365.

$106,585

Fitzgerald was a better just plain writer than all of us put together. Just words writing.

—John O'Hara

The stories in *The Price Was High* were written for money. They brought F. Scott Fitzgerald $106,585 from the mass-circulation magazines—less agent's commissions. His stories provided most of his income before he went to Hollywood in 1937, and he expended a major part of his talent on them. In 1925 he received $11,025 for five stories, whereas *The Great Gatsby* earned $1981.85 beyond the $4264 advance. In 1934, the year *Tender Is the Night* was published, his total income from eight books was $58.35; but eight stories—even at reduced Depression prices—brought $12,475.

Fitzgerald lived off his stories. His intention was to write stories only to finance his novels. Like so many of his practical plans, it did not work out. Instead of getting financially ahead from his stories, Fitzgerald was often in debt to his literary agent, Harold Ober, for an unwritten story as he borrowed against future magazine sales.

One hundred sixty-four of Fitzgerald's stories were published in magazines.[1] He collected forty-six in his four story volumes: *Flappers and Philosophers* (1920), *Tales of the Jazz Age* (1922), *All the Sad Young Men* (1926), and *Taps at Reveille* (1935). Each of these collections followed publication of a novel. Since story volumes are notoriously poor sellers, the 14,000-16,000 sales for the first three collections were more than respectable. After his death in 1940, sixty-one previously uncollected stories were included in six volumes: *The Stories of F. Scott Fitzgerald* (1951), *Afternoon of an Author* (1957), *The Pat Hobby Stories* (1962), *The Apprentice Fiction of F. Scott Fitzgerald* (1965), *The Basil and Josephine Stories* (1973), and *Bits of Paradise* (1974). Of the remaining fifty-seven published stories, forty-nine are in *The Price Was High*. Eight stories remain

---

[1]This figure includes Fitzgerald's school publications and the plays and parodies he published in his story collections. It excludes the stories by-lined "F. Scott and Zelda Fitzgerald," which were mostly her work. See Bruccoli, *F. Scott Fitzgerald: A Descriptive Bibliography* (Pittsburgh: University of Pittsburgh Press, 1972).

uncollected because Scottie Fitzgerald Smith feels that they are so far below her father's standards that they should be left in oblivion.[2] At least ten of Fitzgerald's unpublished stories survive. The best of these, "On Your Own," is included in this volume.

It would be desirable to have "The Complete Stories of F. Scott Fitzgerald" available in a uniform edition, but the present arrangement will serve. By supplementing the volumes published by Charles Scribner's Sons with *The Price Was High*, readers have access to the Fitzgerald story canon without recourse to microfilms of old magazines.

The stories in this volume are not Fitzgerald's best. They are worth collecting because he wrote them. Dorothy Parker commented that although he could write a bad story, he could not write badly. Even his weak stories are redeemed by glimpses of what can be conveniently called "the Fitzgerald touch"—wit, sharp observations, dazzling descriptions, or the felt emotion. Even the most predictably plotted of the Twenties stories have a spontaneity (which is not the same as facility) that differentiates them from other writers' work. Above all, Fitzgerald's style shines through: the colors and rhythms of his prose.

After a quarter of a century of intensive Fitzgerald criticism, the significance of the stories in his career is still not generally understood. Many critics have accepted his frequent disparagement of his stories, as when he wrote Hemingway in 1929 that "the *Post* now pays the old whore $4000 a screw. But now it's because she's mastered the 40 positions—in her youth one was enough." This self-abnegating remark makes the point that after a decade he had become an expert story technician. Fitzgerald bitterly resented the work that went into stories because it was work taken away from novels. Most of the stories were admittedly pot-boilers; but they required a good deal of sweat and—until 1935—were the best work Fitzgerald was capable of for that market. They show him as a professional writer earning his living in a highly competitive market by meeting a certain standard of quality and satisfying commercial requirements. They were not just

---

[2]"Shaggy's Morning," *Esquire*, III (May 1935); "The Count of Darkness," *Redbook*, LXV (June 1935); "The Passionate Eskimo," *Liberty*, XII (8 June 1935); "The Kingdom in the Dark," *Redbook*, LXV (August 1935); " 'Send Me In, Coach,' " *Esquire*, VI (November 1936); "The Honor of the Goon," *Esquire*, VII (June 1937); "Strange Sanctuary," *Liberty*, XVI (9 December 1939); "Gods of Darkness," *Redbook*, LXXVIII (November 1941).

hack-work. In 1935 when he was finding it increasingly difficult to write commercial fiction he explained to Harold Ober: "—all my stories are conceived like novels, require a special emotion, a special experience—so that my readers, if such there be, know that each time it'll be something new, not in form but in substance. (It'd be better for me if I could do pattern stories but the pencil just goes dead on me.)"[3] Fitzgerald's magazine stories required structural discipline, as well as emotion and style. He commented in his *Notebooks*: "In a short story you have only so much money to buy just one costume. Not the parts of many. One mistake in the shoes or tie, and you're gone." Moreover, he customarily polished his stories through layers of revision. The price was high because Fitzgerald delivered what nobody else could provide. When he tried to be a hack in 1936-1937, he couldn't grind out formula stories.

Fitzgerald's principal showcase was *The Saturday Evening Post*, the top story market in America. Because of its circulation and pay scale, most of the top American writers—including Faulkner and Wolfe—were glad to sell stories to the *Post*. Sixty-six Fitzgerald stories appeared in the *Post* from 1920 to 1937. Between 1929 and 1931 he received his peak *Post* price—$4000 per story, the equivalent in purchasing power of perhaps $10,000 today.

Readers for whom the old *Saturday Evening Post* is not even a memory may be surprised by the contents of the 8 October 1927 issue (2,750,000 circulation), which had 226 pages and sold for 5¢: the first part of a serial by Sir Arthur Conan Doyle, an historical article by Joseph Hergesheimer, Fitzgerald's "The Love Boat," an article on the *Uncle Tom* plays, a story by Ben Ames Williams, a travel article by Cornelius Vanderbilt, Jr., a story by Nunnally Johnson, a story by Horatio Winslow, an article on foreign policy by Henry L. Stimson, an animal story by Hal G. Evarts, a story by Thomas Beer, an article about Caruso by his daughter, a story by Octavus Roy Cohen, an article about German recovery by Isaac Marcosson, the continuation of a serial by Donn Byrne, the continuation of a serial by Frances Noyes Hart, an article on international affairs by Alonzo E. Taylor, a story by F. Britton Austin, and an article on crime by Kenneth Roberts—in addition to regular departments. Most of these names mean little now, but in their day Hergesheimer, Williams, Johnson,

---

[3] *As Ever, Scott Fitz—*, ed. Bruccoli and Jennifer Atkinson (Philadelphia & New York: Lippincott), p. 221.

Beer, Cohen, and Roberts were highly successful writers. The amount of fiction is noteworthy—eight stories and three serials as against eight articles. Magazine readers had a large appetite for fiction in those days, and the mass-circulation magazines competed for story writers.

Although the *Post* was the most successful of the magazines offering a mixture of fiction and articles, others served the same readership—*Collier's, Liberty, Metropolitan, International, Scribner's, Red Book, Smart Set,* and *Woman's Home Companion.* Fitzgerald appeared in all of these. Newspapers also published a good deal of fiction—usually reprinted from magazines or books. Several of Fitzgerald's stories and two of his novels were syndicated to newspapers. Syndication brought him very little money, but it extended his exposure. In the Twenties Fitzgerald may have been the most widely known living American writer of quality stories. Unfortunately, his reputation as a magazinist did not correlate with the sales of his books. There was some overlap, but in general his magazine and book audiences were discrete. Most of Fitzgerald's readers probably knew him only as a writer of magazine stories.

The magazine readers of the time expected illustrated stories. The artwork for Fitzgerald's stories contributed to their flavor and to his image as a writer—or to the image that the magazines were trying to promote. A sampling of illustrations has been included here to convey an impression of what readers saw when they found one of his stories in a magazine.

Although Fitzgerald became typed as a writer of "young-love stories," they were not regarded as callow or conventional in their own time. It may surprise readers born after 1940, when he died, that in the Twenties he was regarded as a radical writer who announced the existence of new social values and new sexual roles. Fitzgerald's girls are not dumb dolls. At their best they are courageous and self-reliant, determined to make the best of their assets in a man's world. They are frankly sensual, though chaste—warm and promising. At an extreme there are Fitzgerald's man-eating women who dominate or destroy men, though this condition is unusual in his short stories.

It remains an open question whether Fitzgerald compromised or diluted his stories to make them acceptable to the *Post* and other popular magazines. "May Day" and "The Rich Boy" were declined by the *Post* because they were too "realistic"; but the *Post* later published "Babylon Revisited" and "One Trip Abroad," two of his least conventional stories. While Fitzgerald had to observe *Post* strictures against profanity and adultery in stories, there is no evidence that he felt constrained by these prohibitions; he was fastidious about his material and puritanical by today's literary standards. Nonetheless, it would be foolish to claim that his awareness of the *Post*'s expectations did not exert an influence on his material or that he did not to some extent tailor his stories to his best market. He was writing stories that were supposed to free him from the necessity of writing more stories; therefore he wanted the top price for his servitude. He wrote stories that he expected the *Post* or its competitors to buy; but they were stories into which he put his own deep feelings about love, youth, ambition, and success. Fitzgerald's *Post* stories represented a marriage between the writer and the magazine. For more than a decade they needed and suited each other.

Fitzgerald's stories often served as testing-places for material and themes that were subsequently developed in his novels. There are clusters of stories connected with *The Great Gatsby* and *Tender Is the Night*. Reading these uncollected stories one frequently recognizes passages or phrases that were later incorporated into his novels. Indeed, he refused to collect some of the stories because he had a firm rule against repeating anything between book covers. A story, even a published one, that had been scrapped for a novel was classified as "stripped and permanently buried." Fitzgerald's *Notebooks* and story tearsheets show how carefully he conducted his salvage and banking operation.[4]

Fitzgerald's attitude toward publication of his uncollected stories is shown in his 1935 "Preface" (which he later designated as a memo for his Scribners editor) for a projected posthumous volume:

---

[4]The story strippings are identified in *The Notebooks of F. Scott Fitzgerald*, ed. Bruccoli (New York: Harcourt Brace Jovanovich/Bruccoli Clark, 1978).

Dear Max:
You aught file this
Scott Fitzgerald

March 26, 1935.

To Maxwell Perkins

P R E F A C E

This collection will be published only in case of
my sudden death. It contains many stories that have been
chosen for anthologies but, though it is the winnowing
from almost fifty stories, none that I have seen fit to
reprint in book form—~~sate for a few recent ones~~. This
is in some measure because the best of these stories have
been stripped of their high spots which were woven into
novels—but it is also because each story contains some
special fault—sentimentality, faulty construction, confusing change of pace—or else was too obviously made
for the trade.

~~Lastly~~ But, readers of my other books will find whole
passages here and there which I have used elsewhere—so
I should prefer that this collection should be allowed
to run what course it may have, and die with its season.

~~NOTE TO EDITOR~~: If the Mediaeval stories are six
or more they should be in a small book of their own. If
less than six they should be in one section in this book.
Note date above—there may be other good ones after this
date.

CHOOSE FROM THESE	THESE ARE SCRAPPED

Not More Than 16

	1919 Myra Meets His Family
	The Smilers
1921 Two for a Cent	**1921** The Popular Girl
	1923 Dice Brass Knuckles and Guitar
1924 One of My Oldest Friends	**1924** John Jackson's Arcady
The Pusher in the Face	The Unspeakable Egg
	The Third Casket
	Love in the Night
1925 Presumption	**1925** Not in the Guide Book
Adolescent Marriage	A Penny Spent
1926 The Dance	**1926** Your Way and Mine
1927 Jacob's Ladder	**1927** The Love Boat
The Bowl	Magnetism
Outside the Cabinet Makers	
	1928 A Night at the Fair
1929 The Rough Crossing	**1929** Forging Ahead
At Your Age	Basil and Cleopatra
	The Swimmers
1930 One Trip Abroad	**1930** The Bridal Party
The Hotel Child	A Snobbish Story
1931 A New Leaf	**1931** Indecision
Emotional Bankruptcy	Flight and Pursuit
Between Three and Four	Half a Dozen of the Others
A Change of Class	Diagnosis
A Freeze Out	
	1932 What a Handsome Pair
	The Rubber Check
	On Schedule
1933 More than Just a House	
I Got Shoes	
The Family Bus	
1934 No Flowers	**1934** New Types
Her Last Case	
1935 The Intimate Strangers	**1935** Shaggy's Morning

And, to date, four
mediaval stories

xvii

The stories in *The Price Was High* fall into two groups—dividing at 1935, when Fitzgerald largely lost his ability to produce *Post*-type stories reliably. His commercial stories became forced and padded as he struggled to simulate emotions that he no longer felt. He had anticipated this change in a 1933 essay, "One Hundred False Starts"—which, by one of the precise ironies that abound in Fitzgerald, appeared in *The Saturday Evening Post*:

> Mostly, we authors must repeat ourselves—that's the truth. We have two or three great and moving experiences in our lives—experiences so great and so moving that it doesn't seem at the time that anyone else has been so caught up and pounded and dazzled and astonished and beaten and broken and rescued and illuminated and rewarded and humbled in just that way ever before.
>
> Then we learn our trade, well or less well, and we tell our two or three stories—each time in a new disguise—maybe ten times, maybe a hundred, as long as people will listen.
>
> Whether it's something that happened twenty years ago or only yesterday, I must start out with an emotion—one that's close to me and that I can understand.

Even for his commercial or slick stories Fitzgerald required emotional capital to draw upon. The blows that struck commencing with his wife's breakdown in 1930—and followed by his worsening alcoholism, illness, and loss of confidence—caused him to characterize himself as a cracked plate in 1936. It was not true, as he feared, that he was emotionally bankrupt. But the emotions of 1935-1940 were not convertible into *Post* stories. In 1935 Fitzgerald found an alternate market at *Esquire*, a new magazine which paid only $250. He began selling to *Esquire* stories that had been declined by the high-paying magazines; but after 1937 Fitzgerald was writing only for *Esquire* and developed a special short-short story format for that magazine.

When Zelda Fitzgerald suggested that he resume writing *Post* stories, Fitzgerald replied in May 1940:

> It's hard to explain about the *Saturday Evening Post* matter. It isn't that I haven't tried, but the trouble with

them goes back to the time of Lorimer's retirement in 1935. I wrote them three stories that year[5] and sent them about three others which they didn't like. The last story they bought they published last in the issue[6] and my friend, Adelaide Neil [Neall] on the staff implied to me that they didn't want to pay that big price for stories unless they could use them in the beginning of the issue. Well, that was the time of my two-year sickness, T.B., the shoulder, etc., and you were at a most crucial point and I was foolishly trying to take care of Scottie and for one reason or another I lost the knack of writing the particular kind of stories they wanted.

As you should know from your own attempts, high-priced commercial writing for the magazines is a very definite trick. The rather special things that I brought to it, the intelligence and the good writing and even the radicalism all appealed to old Lorimer who had been a writer himself and liked style. The man who runs the magazine now [Wesley Stout] is an up-and-coming young Republican who gives not a damn about literature and who publishes almost nothing except escape stories about the brave frontiersmen, etc., or fishing, or football captains—nothing that would even faintly shock or disturb the reactionary bourgeois. Well, I simply can't do it and, as I say, I've tried not once but twenty times.

As soon as I feel I am writing to a cheap specification my pen freezes and my talent vanishes over the hill, and I honestly don't blame them for not taking the things that I ve offered to them from time to time in the past three or four years. An explanation of their new attitude is that you no longer have a chance of selling a story with an unhappy ending (in the old days many of mine *did* have unhappy endings—if you remember).[7]

---

[5]The *Post* published two Fitzgerald stories in 1935: "Zone of Accident" and "Too Cute for Words." Both are in this collection.

[6] " 'Trouble' " was the third story in the 6 March 1937 issue; it is included in this collection.

[7]*The Letters of F. Scott Fitzgerald*, ed. Andrew Turnbull (New York: Scribners, 1963), pp. 117-118.

In the introduction to *The Portable F. Scott Fitzgerald* John O'Hara decreed that Fitzgerald was "our best novelist, one of our best novella-ists, and one of our finest writers of short stories." It seemed like an example of O'Haraesque eccentricity in 1945. Now it is a sound judgment, though perhaps a bit cautious. Fitzgerald was, along with O'Hara and Hemingway, one of our three best short story writers. Indeed, it is becoming fashionable to claim that Fitzgerald was better as a short story writer than as a novelist. This truly eccentric notion does not have as many adherents as the familiar dismissal of his stories as trivial pot-boilers. Most critics would still prefer to rescue a few stories—"May Day," "Rich Boy," "The Diamond as Big as the Ritz," "Babylon Revisited"—and inter the rest.

It has been justly held that a writer deserves to be judged by his best work. Nonetheless, a writer's best work must be assessed in terms of his total work. By making an additional fifty stories available, *The Price Was High* should aid in a sounder evaluation of Fitzgerald's career. Sometimes an unsuccessful work provides a gauge for an excellent one. Moreover, these stories correct the popular assumption that Fitzgerald squandered his energy in dissipation. Much of his energy went into writing 164 commercial stories in twenty years. (Hemingway published fifty-odd stories in forty years.) Fitzgerald's name now connotes alcoholic excess; but, as he reminded Maxwell Perkins, "even Post stories must be done in a state of sobriety."

There are no masterpieces in *The Price Was High*. Certainly it would be preferable for Fitzgerald to have written another novel instead of the stories collected here. But he never really had that option. With regret and disappointment and gratitude and pleasure we take what he did write. There isn't anymore now. F. Scott Fitzgerald's stories are all used up.

THE PRICE WAS HIGH

The Last Uncollected Stories of

F. Scott Fitzgerald

The Smilers

(*The Smart Set*, June 1920)

"The Smilers" was written in St. Paul in September 1919 as "A Smile for Sylvo." After failing at his attempt to make a fast success as an advertising writer in New York, Fitzgerald returned to St. Paul to rewrite his first novel. *This Side of Paradise* was accepted by Scribners in September, and Fitzgerald devoted the rest of the year to writing short stories for ready money. He submitted "The Smilers" to *Scribner's Magazine*, which rejected it. After Harold Ober, his literary agent, was unable to place the story in one of the magazines that paid well, Fitzgerald sold it to *The Smart Set* for $35: "I want to keep in right with Menken + Nathan as they're the most powerful critic in the country." Although *The Smart Set* under editors H. L. Mencken and George Jean Nathan was an influential magazine among literary people, its limited circulation did not allow for generous payment. Fitzgerald sold stories to *The Smart Set* when they were unplaceable in the mass-circulation magazines—including two of his masterpieces, "The Diamond as Big as the Ritz" and "May Day."

Although "The Smilers" was written soon after acceptance of *This Side of Paradise*, it is still very much a college literary magazine piece—self-conscious and blatantly ironic. This story shows the didactic streak that marked several of Fitzgerald's early stories, such as "The Four Fists" and "The Cut-Glass Bowl." The moralizing quality in his work—especially the stories—has been obscured by Fitzgerald's image as the Boswell of the Jazz Age. Near the end of his life he noted that he sometimes wishes he had gone into musical comedy, "but I guess I am too much a moralist at heart and really want to preach at people in some acceptable form rather than to entertain them."

I

We all have that exasperated moment!

There are times when you almost tell the harmless old lady next door what you really think of her face—that it ought to be on a night-nurse in a house for the blind; when you'd like to ask the man you've been waiting ten minutes for if he isn't all over-heated from racing the postman down the block; when you nearly say to the waiter that if they deducted a cent from the bill for every degree the soup was below tepid the hotel would owe you half a dollar; when—and this is the infallible earmark of true exasperation—a smile affects you as an oil-baron's undershirt affects a cow's husband.

But the moment passes. Scars may remain on your dog or your collar or your telephone receiver, but your soul has slid gently back into its place between the lower edge of your heart and the upper edge of your stomach, and all is at peace.

But the imp who turns on the shower-bath of exasperation apparently made it so hot one time in Sylvester Stockton's early youth that he never dared dash in and turn it off—in consequence no first old man in an amateur production of a Victorian comedy was ever more pricked and prodded by the daily phenomena of life than was Sylvester at thirty.

Accusing eyes behind spectacles—suggestion of a stiff neck—this will have to do for his description, since he is not the hero of this story. He is the plot. He is the factor that makes it one story instead of three stories. He makes remarks at the beginning and end.

The late afternoon sun was loitering pleasantly along Fifth Avenue when Sylvester, who had just come out of that hideous public library where he had been consulting some ghastly book, told his impossible chauffeur (it is true that I am following his movements through his own spectacles) that he wouldn't need his stupid, incompetent services any longer. Swinging his cane (which he found too short) in his left hand (which he should have cut off long ago since it was constantly offending him), he began walking slowly down the Avenue.

When Sylvester walked at night he frequently glanced behind and on both sides to see if anyone was sneaking up on him. This had become a constant mannerism. For this reason he was unable to pretend that he didn't see Betty Tearle sitting in her machine in front of Tiffany's.

Back in his early twenties he had been in love with Betty Tearle. But he had depressed her. He had misanthropically dissected every meal, motor trip and musical comedy that they attended together, and on the few occasions when she had tried to be especially nice to him—from a mother's point of view he had been rather desirable—he had suspected hidden motives and fallen into a deeper gloom than ever. Then one day she told him that she would go mad if he ever again parked his pessimism in her sun-parlour.

And ever since then she had seemed to be smiling—uselessly, insultingly, charmingly smiling.

"Hello, Sylvo," she called.

"Why—how do, Betty." He wished she wouldn't call him Sylvo—it sounded like a—like a darn monkey or something.

"How goes it?" she asked cheerfully. "Not very well, I suppose."

"Oh, yes," he answered stiffly, "I manage."

"Taking in the happy crowd?"

"Heavens, yes." He looked around him. "Betty, why are they happy? What are they smiling at? What do they find to smile at?"

Betty flashed at him a glance of radiant amusement.

"The women may smile because they have pretty teeth, Sylvo."

"You smile," continued Sylvester cynically, "because you're comfortably married and have two children. You imagine you're happy, so you suppose everyone else is."

Betty nodded.

"You may have hit it, Sylvo—" The chauffeur glanced around and she nodded at him. "Good-bye."

Sylvo watched with a pang of envy which turned suddenly to exasperation as he saw she had turned and smiled at him once more. Then her car was out of sight in the traffic; and with a voluminous sigh he galvanized his cane into life and continued his stroll.

At the next corner he stopped in at a cigar store and there he ran into Waldron Crosby. Back in the days when Sylvester had been a prize pigeon in the eyes of debutantes he had also been a game partridge from the point of view of promoters. Crosby, then a young bond salesman, had given him much safe and sane advice and saved him many dollars. Sylvester liked Crosby as much as he could like anyone. Most people did like Crosby.

"Hello, you old bag of 'nerves,' " cried Crosby genially, "come and have a big gloom-dispelling Corona."

Sylvester regarded the cases anxiously. He knew he wasn't going to like what he bought.

"Still out at Larchmont, Waldron?" he asked.

"Right-o."

"How's your wife?"

"Never better."

"Well," said Sylvester suspiciously, "you brokers always look as if you're smiling at something up your sleeve. It must be a hilarious profession."

Crosby considered.

"Well," he admitted, "it varies—like the moon and the price of soft drinks—but it has its moments."

"Waldron," said Sylvester earnestly, "you're a friend of mine—please do me the favour of not smiling when I leave you. It seems like a—like a mockery."

A broad grin suffused Crosby's countenance.

"Why, you crabbed old son-of-a-gun!"

But Sylvester with an irate grunt had turned on his heel and disappeared.

He strolled on. The sun finished its promenade and began calling in the few stray beams it had left among the westward streets. The Avenue darkened with black bees from the department stores; the traffic swelled in to an interlaced jam; the busses were packed four deep like platforms above the thick crowd; but Sylvester, to whom the daily shift and change of the city was a matter only of sordid monotony, walked on, taking only quick sideward glances through his frowning spectacles.

He reached his hotel and was elevated to his four-room suite on the twelfth floor.

"If I dine down-stairs," he thought, "the orchestra will play either 'Smile, Smile, Smile' or 'The Smiles That You Gave To Me.' But then if I go to the Club I'll meet all the cheerful people I know, and if I go somewhere else where there's no music, I won't get anything fit to eat."

He decided to have dinner in his rooms.

An hour later, after disparaging some broth, a squab and a salad, he tossed fifty cents to the room-waiter, and then held up his hand warningly.

"Just oblige me by not smiling when you say thanks?"

He was too late. The waiter had grinned.

"Now, will you please tell me," asked Sylvester peevishly, "what on earth you have to smile about?"

The waiter considered. Not being a reader of the magazines he was not sure what was characteristic of waiters, yet he supposed something characteristic was expected of him.

"Well, Mister," he answered, glancing at the ceiling with all the ingenuousness he could muster in his narrow, sallow countenance, "it's just something my face does when it sees four bits comin'."

Sylvester waved him away.

"Waiters are happy because they've never had anything better," he thought. "They haven't enough imagination to want anything."

At nine o'clock from sheer boredom he sought his expressionless bed.

II

As Sylvester left the cigar store, Waldron Crosby followed him out, and turning off Fifth Avenue down a cross street entered a brokerage office. A plump man with nervous hands rose and hailed him.

"Hello, Waldron."

"Hello, Potter—I just dropped in to hear the worst."

The plump man frowned.

"We've just got the news," he said.

"Well, what is it? Another drop?"

"Closed at seventy-eight. Sorry, old boy."

"Whew!"

"Hit pretty hard?"

"Cleaned out!"

The plump man shook his head, indicating that life was too much for him, and turned away.

Crosby sat there for a moment without moving. Then he rose, walked into Potter's private office and picked up the phone.

"Gi'me Larchmont 838."

In a moment he had his connection.

"Mrs. Crosby there?"

A man's voice answered him.

"Yes; this you, Crosby? This is Doctor Shipman."

"Dr. Shipman?" Crosby's voice showed sudden anxiety.

"Yes—I've been trying to reach you all afternoon. The situation's changed and we expect the child tonight."

"Tonight?"

"Yes. Everything's O. K. But you'd better come right out."

"I will. Good-bye."

He hung up the receiver and started out the door, but paused as an idea struck him. He returned, and this time called a Manhattan number.

"Hello, Donny, this is Crosby."

"Hello, there, old boy. You just caught me; I was going—"

"Say, Donny, I want a job right away, quick."

"For whom?"

"For me."

"Why, what's the—"

"Never mind. Tell you later. Got one for me?"

"Why, Waldron, there's not a blessed thing here except a clerkship. Perhaps next—"

"What salary goes with the clerkship?"

"Forty—say forty-five a week."

"I've got you. I start tomorrow."

"All right. But say, old man—"

"Sorry, Donny, but I've got to run."

Crosby hurried from the brokerage office with a wave and a smile at Potter. In the street he took out a handful of small change and after surveying it critically hailed a taxi.

"Grand Central—quick!" he told the driver.

III

At six o'clock Betty Tearle signed the letter, put it into an envelope and wrote her husband's name upon it. She went into his room and after a moment's hesitation set a black cushion on the bed and laid the white letter on it so that it could not fail to attract his attention when he came in. Then with a quick glance around the room she walked into the hall and upstairs to the nursery.

"Clare," she called softly.

"Oh, Mummy!" Clare left her doll's house and scurried to her mother.

"Where's Billy, Clare?"

Billy appeared eagerly from under the bed.

"Got anything for me?" he inquired politely.

His mother's laugh ended in a little catch and she caught both her children to her and kissed them passionately. She found that she was crying quietly and their flushed little faces seemed cool against the sudden fever racing through her blood.

"Take care of Clare—always—Billy darling—"

Billy was puzzled and rather awed.

"You're crying," he accused gravely.

"I know—I know I am—"

Clare gave a few tentative sniffles, hesitated, and then clung to her mother in a storm of weeping.

"I d-don't feel good, Mummy—I don't feel good."

Betty soothed her quietly.

"We won't cry any more, Clare dear—either of us."

But as she rose to leave the room her glance at Billy bore a mute appeal, too vain, she knew, to be registered on his childish consciousness.

Half an hour later as she carried her travelling bag to a taxi-cab at the door she raised her hand to her face in mute admission that a veil served no longer to hide her from the world.

"But I've chosen," she thought dully.

As the car turned the corner she wept again, resisting a temptation to give up and go back.

"Oh, my God!" she whispered. "What am I doing? What have I done? What have I done?"

IV

When Jerry, the sallow, narrow-faced waiter, left Sylvester's rooms he reported to the head-waiter, and then checked out for the day.

He took the subway south and alighting at Williams Street walked a few blocks and entered a billiard parlour.

An hour later he emerged with a cigarette drooping from his bloodless lips, and stood on the sidewalk as if hesitating before making a decision. He set off eastward.

As he reached a certain corner his gait suddenly increased and then quite as suddenly slackened. He seemed to want to pass by, yet some magnetic attraction was apparently exerted on him, for with a sudden face-about he turned in at the door of a cheap restaurant—half-cabaret, half chop-suey parlour—where a miscellaneous assortment gathered nightly.

Jerry found his way to a table situated in the darkest and most obscure corner. Seating himself with a contempt for his surroundings that betokened familiarity rather than superiority he ordered a glass of claret.

The evening had begun. A fat woman at the piano was expelling the last jauntiness from a hackneyed foxtrot, and a lean, dispirited male was assisting her with lean, dispirited notes from a violin. The attention of the patrons was directed at a dancer wearing soiled stockings and done largely in peroxide and rouge who was about to step upon a small platform, meanwhile exchanging pleasantries with a fat, eager person at the table beside her who was trying to capture her hand.

Over in the corner Jerry watched the two by the platform and, as he gazed, the ceiling seemed to fade out, the walls growing into tall buildings and the platform becoming the top of a Fifth Avenue bus on a breezy spring night three years ago. The fat, eager person disappeared, the short skirt of the dancer rolled down and the rouge faded from her cheeks—and he was beside her again in an old delirious ride, with the lights blinking kindly at them from the tall buildings beside and the voices of the street merging into a pleasant somnolent murmur around them.

"Jerry," said the girl on top of the bus, "I've said that when you were gettin' seventy-five I'd take a chance with you. But, Jerry, I can't wait forever."

Jerry watched several street numbers sail by before he answered.

"I don't know what's the matter," he said helplessly, "they won't raise me. If I can locate a new job—"

"You better hurry, Jerry," said the girl; "I'm gettin' sick of just livin' along. If I can't get married I got a couple of chances to work in a cabaret—get on the stage maybe."

"You keep out of that," said Jerry quickly. "There ain't no need, if you just wait about another month or two."

"I can't wait forever, Jerry," repeated the girl. "I'm tired of stayin' poor alone."

"It won't be so long," said Jerry clenching his free hand, "I can make it somewhere, if you'll just wait."

But the bus was fading out and the ceiling was taking shape and the murmur of the April streets was fading into the rasping whine of the violin—for that was all three years before and now he was sitting here.

The girl glanced up on the platform and exchanged a metallic impersonal smile with the dispirited violinist, and Jerry shrank farther back in his corner watching her with burning intensity.

"Your hands belong to anybody that wants them now," he cried silently and bitterly. "I wasn't man enough to keep you out of that— not man enough, by God, by God!"

But the girl by the door still toyed with the fat man's clutching fingers as she waited for her time to dance.

V

Sylvester Stockton tossed restlessly upon his bed. The room, big as it was, smothered him, and a breeze drifting in and bearing with it a rift of moon seemed laden only with the cares of the world he would have to face next day.

"They don't understand," he thought. "They don't see, as I do, the underlying misery of the whole damn thing. They're hollow optimists. They smile because they think they're always going to be happy.

"Oh, well," he mused drowsily, "I'll run up to Rye tomorrow and endure more smiles and more heat. That's all life is—just smiles and heat, smiles and heat."

Myra Meets His Family

(*The Saturday Evening Post*, 20 March 1920)

"Myra Meets His Family" was rewritten in St. Paul in December 1919 from an abandoned story called "Lilah Meets His Family."

When Fitzgerald submitted "Myra" to Harold Ober, he admitted: "I'm afraid its no good and if you agree with me don't hesitate to send it back. Perhaps if you give me an idea what the matter with it is I'll be able to rewrite it." Ober had no trouble selling it to the *Post* for $400; it was Fitzgerald's second *Post* appearance. In 1919-1920 Fitzgerald wrote a string of excellent *Saturday Evening Post* stories, including "Head and Shoulders," "The Ice Palace," "The Camel's Back," "Bernice Bobs Her Hair," and "The Offshore Pirate." Fox studios bought "Myra" in 1920 for $1000—a good price at that time—and made it into *The Husband Hunter* with Eileen Percy.

Its popular appeal did not alter Fitzgerald's feelings about the story. In 1921 he wrote Ober about English magazine rights: "I believe you have disposed of . . . *Myra Meets His Family* which story, however, I never have liked, + do not intend ever republishing in book form." The reasons for his rejection of the story are not clear. It relies on unlikely plotting, but so do a number of his other commercial stories. Perhaps he saw too great a contrast between "Myra" and "The Ice Palace," one of his finest stories, which was written during the same month.

"Myra Meets His Family" is a representative early Fitzgerald story in terms of its material and characters. It stakes out the territory of the Eastern rich; and Myra is a readily recognizable Fitzgerald heroine who reappears under a dozen other names in later stories.

Probably every boy who has attended an Eastern college in the last ten years has met Myra half a dozen times, for the Myras live on the Eastern colleges, as kittens live on warm milk. When Myra is young, seventeen or so, they call her a "wonderful kid"; in her prime—say, at nineteen—she is tendered the subtle compliment of being referred to by her name alone; and after that she is a "prom trotter" or "the famous coast-to-coast Myra."

You can see her practically any winter afternoon if you stroll through the Biltmore lobby. She will be standing in a group of sophomores just in from Princeton or New Haven, trying to decide whether to dance away the mellow hours at the Club de Vingt or the Plaza Red Room. Afterward one of the sophomores will take her to the theater and ask her down to the February prom—and then dive for a taxi to catch the last train back to college.

Invariably she has a somnolent mother sharing a suite with her on one of the floors above.

When Myra is about twenty-four she thinks over all the nice boys she might have married at one time or other, sighs a little and does the best she can. But no remarks, please! She has given her youth to you; she has blown fragrantly through many ballrooms to the tender tribute of many eyes; she has roused strange surges of romance in a hundred pagan young breasts; and who shall say she hasn't counted?

The particular Myra whom this story concerns will have to have a paragraph of history. I will get it over with as swiftly as possible.

When she was sixteen she lived in a big house in Cleveland and attended Derby School in Connecticut, and it was while she was still there that she started going to prep-school dances and college proms. She decided to spend the war at Smith College, but in January of her freshman year, falling violently in love with a young infantry officer, she failed all her midyear examinations and retired to Cleveland in disgrace. The young infantry officer arrived about a week later.

Just as she had about decided that she didn't love him after all he was ordered abroad, and in a great revival of sentiment she rushed down to the port of embarkation with her mother to bid him good-by. She wrote him daily for two months, and then weekly for two months, and then once more. This last letter he never got, for a machine-gun bullet ripped through his head one rainy July morning. Perhaps this was just as well, for the letter informed him that it had all been a mistake, and that something told her they would never be happy together, and so on.

The "something" wore boots and silver wings and was tall and dark. Myra was quite sure that it was the real thing at last, but as an engine went through his chest at Kelly Field in mid-August she never had a chance to find out.

Instead she came East again, a little slimmer, with a becoming pallor and new shadows under her eyes, and throughout armistice year she left the ends of cigarettes all over New York on little china trays marked "Midnight Frolic" and "Coconut Grove" and "Palais Royal." She was twenty-one now, and Cleveland people said that her mother ought to take her back home—that New York was spoiling her.

You will have to do your best with that. The story should have started long ago.

It was an afternoon in September when she broke a theater date in order to have tea with young Mrs. Arthur Elkins, once her roommate at school.

"I wish," began Myra as they sat down exquisitely, "that I'd been a señorita or a mademoiselle or something. Good grief! What is there to do over here once you're out, except marry and retire!"

Lilah Elkins had seen this form of ennui before.

"Nothing," she replied coolly; "do it."

"I can't seem to get interested, Lilah," said Myra, bending forward earnestly. "I've played round so much that even while I'm kissing the man I just wonder how soon I'll get tired of him. I never get carried away like I used to."

"How old are you, Myra?"

"Twenty-one last spring."

"Well," said Lilah complacently, "take it from me, don't get married unless you're absolutely through playing round. It means giving up an awful lot, you know."

"Through! I'm sick and tired of my whole pointless existence. Funny, Lilah, but I do feel ancient. Up at New Haven last spring men danced with me that seemed like little boys—and once I overheard a girl say in the dressing room, 'There's Myra Harper! She's been coming up here for eight years.' Of course she was about three years off, but it did give me the calendar blues."

"You and I went to our first prom when we were sixteen—five years ago."

"Heavens!" sighed Myra. "And now some men are afraid of me. Isn't that odd? Some of the nicest boys. One man dropped me like a hotcake after coming down from Morristown for three straight weekends. Some kind friend told him I was husband hunting this year, and he was afraid of getting in too deep."

"Well, you are husband hunting, aren't you?"

"I suppose so—after a fashion." Myra paused and looked about her rather cautiously. "Have you ever met Knowleton Whitney? You know what a wiz he is on looks, and his father's worth a fortune, they say. Well, I noticed that the first time he met me he started when he heard my name and fought shy—and, Lilah darling, I'm not so ancient and homely as all that, am I?"

"You certainly are not!" laughed Lilah. "And here's my advice: Pick out the best thing in sight—the man who has all the mental, physical, social and financial qualities you want, and then go after him hammer and tongs—the way we used to. After you've got him don't say to yourself 'Well, he can't sing like Billy,' or 'I wish he played better golf.' You can't have everything. Shut your eyes and turn off your sense of humor, and then after you're married it'll be very different and you'll be mighty glad."

"Yes," said Myra absently; "I've had that advice before."

"Drifting into romance is easy when you're eighteen," continued Lilah emphatically; "but after five years of it your capacity for it simply burns out."

"I've had such nice times," sighed Myra, "and such sweet men. To tell you the truth I have decided to go after someone."

"Who?"

"Knowleton Whitney. Believe me, I may be a bit blasé, but I can still get any man I want."

"You really want him?"

"Yes—as much as I'll ever want anyone. He's smart as a whip, and shy—rather sweetly shy—and they say his family have the best-looking place in Westchester County."

Lilah sipped the last of her tea and glanced at her wrist watch. "I've got to tear, dear."

They rose together and, sauntering out on Park Avenue, hailed taxicabs.

"I'm awfully glad, Myra; and I know you'll be glad too."

Myra skipped a little pool of water and, reaching her taxi, balanced on the running board like a ballet dancer.

" 'By, Lilah. See you soon."

"Good-by, Myra. Good luck!"

And knowing Myra as she did, Lilah felt that her last remark was distinctly superfluous.

II

That was essentially the reason that one Friday night six weeks later Knowleton Whitney paid a taxi bill of seven dollars and ten cents and with a mixture of emotions paused beside Myra on the Biltmore steps.

The outer surface of his mind was deliriously happy, but just below that was a slowly hardening fright at what he had done. He, protected since his freshman year at Harvard from the snares of fascinating fortune hunters, dragged away from several sweet young things by the acquiescent nape of his neck, had taken advantage of his family's absence in the West to become so enmeshed in the toils that it was hard to say which was toils and which was he.

The afternoon had been like a dream: November twilight along Fifth Avenue after the matinee, and he and Myra looking out at the swarming crowds from the romantic privacy of a hansom cab—quaint device—then tea at the Ritz and her white hand gleaming on the arm of a chair beside him; and suddenly quick broken words. After that had come the trip to the jeweler's and a mad dinner in some little Italian restaurant where he had written "Do you?" on the back of the bill of fare and pushed it over for her to add the ever-miraculous "You know I do!" And now at the day's end they paused on the Biltmore steps.

"Say it," breathed Myra close to his ear.

He said it. Ah, Myra, how many ghosts must have flitted across your memory then!

"You've made me so happy, dear," she said softly.

"No—you've made me happy. Don't you know—Myra——"

"I know."

"For good?"

"For good. I've got this, you see." And she raised the diamond solitaire to her lips. She knew how to do things, did Myra.

"Good night."

"Good night. Good night."

Like a gossamer fairy in shimmering rose she ran up the wide stairs and her cheeks were glowing wildly as she rang the elevator bell.

At the end of a fortnight she got a telegraph from him saying that his family had returned from the West and expected her up in Westchester County for a week's visit. Myra wired her train time, bought three new evening dresses and packed her trunk.

It was a cool November evening when she arrived, and stepping from the train in the late twilight she shivered slightly and looked eagerly round for Knowleton. The station platform swarmed for a moment with men returning from the city; there was a shouting medley of wives and chauffeurs, and a great snorting of automobiles as they backed and turned and slid away. Then before she realized it the platform was quite deserted and not a single one of the luxurious cars remained. Knowleton must have expected her on another train.

With an almost inaudible "Damn!" she started toward the Elizabethan station to telephone, when suddenly she was accosted by a very dirty, dilapidated man who touched his ancient cap to her and addressed her in a cracked, querulous voice.

"You Miss Harper?"

"Yes," she confessed, rather startled. Was this unmentionable person by any wild chance the chauffeur?

"The chauffeur's sick," he continued in a high whine. "I'm his son."

Myra gasped.

"You mean Mr. Whitney's chauffeur?"

"Yes; he only keeps just one since the war. Great on

economizin'—regelar Hoover.'' He stamped his feet nervously and smacked enormous gauntlets together. "Well, no use waitin' here gabbin' in the cold. Le's have your grip."

Too amazed for words and not a little dismayed, Myra followed her guide to the edge of the platform, where she looked in vain for a car. But she was not left to wonder long, for the person led her steps to a battered old flivver, wherein was deposited her grip.

"Big car's broke," he explained. "Have to use this or walk."

He opened the front door for her and nodded.

"Step in."

"I b'lieve I'll sit in back if you don't mind."

"Surest thing you know," he cackled, opening the back door. "I thought the trunk bumpin' round back there might make you nervous."

"What trunk?"

"Yourn."

"Oh, didn't Mr. Whitney—can't you make two trips?"

He shook his head obstinately.

"Wouldn't allow it. Not since the war. Up to rich people to set 'n example; that's what Mr. Whitney says. Le's have your check, please."

As he disappeared Myra tried in vain to conjure up a picture of the chauffeur if this was his son. After a mysterious argument with the station agent he returned, gasping violently, with the trunk on his back. He deposited it in the rear seat and climbed up front beside her.

It was quite dark when they swerved out of the road and up a long dusky driveway to the Whitney place, whence lighted windows flung great blots of cheerful, yellow light over the gravel and grass and trees. Even now she could see that it was very beautiful, that its blurred outline was Georgian Colonial and that great shadowy garden parks were flung out at both sides. The car plumped to a full stop before a square stone doorway and the chauffeur's son climbed out after her and pushed open the outer door.

"Just go right in," he cackled; and as she passed the threshold she heard him softly shut the door, closing out himself and the dark.

Myra looked round her. She was in a large somber hall paneled in old English oak and lit by dim shaded lights clinging like luminous yellow turtles at intervals along the wall. Ahead of her was a broad staircase and on both sides there were several doors, but there was no sight or sound of life, and an intense stillness seemed to rise ceaselessly from the deep crimson carpet.

She must have waited there a full minute before she began to have that unmistakable sense of someone looking at her. She forced herself to turn casually round.

A sallow little man, bald and clean shaven, trimly dressed in a frock coat and white spats, was standing a few yards away regarding her quizzically. He must have been fifty at the least, but even before he moved she had noticed a curious alertness about him—something in his pose which promised that it had been instantaneously assumed and would be instantaneously changed in a moment. His tiny hands and feet and the odd twist to his eyebrows gave him a faintly elfish expression, and she had one of those vague transient convictions that she had seen him before, many years ago.

For a minute they stared at each other in silence and then she flushed slightly and discovered a desire to swallow.

"I suppose you're Mr. Whitney." She smiled faintly and advanced a step toward him. "I'm Myra Harper."

For an instant longer he remained silent and motionless, and it flashed across Myra that he might be deaf; then suddenly he jerked into spirited life exactly like a mechanical toy started by the pressure of a button.

"Why, of course—why, naturally. I know—ah!" he exclaimed excitedly in a high-pitched elfin voice. Then raising himself on his toes in a sort of attenuated ecstasy of enthusiasm and smiling a wizened smile, he minced toward her across the dark carpet.

She blushed appropriately.

"That's awfully nice of——"

"Ah!" he went on. "You must be tired; a rickety, cindery, ghastly trip, I know. Tired and hungry and thirsty, no doubt, no doubt!" He looked round him indignantly. "The servants are frightfully inefficient in this house!"

Myra did not know what to say to this, so she made no answer. After an instant's abstraction Mr. Whitney crossed over with his furious energy and pressed a button; then almost as if he were dancing he was by her side again, making thin, disparaging gestures with his hands.

"A little minute," he assured her, "sixty seconds, scarcely more. Here!"

He rushed suddenly to the wall and with some effort lifted a great carved Louis Fourteenth chair and set it down carefully in the geometrical center of the carpet.

"Sit down—won't you? Sit down! I'll go get you something. Sixty seconds at the outside."

She demurred faintly, but he kept on repeating "Sit down!" in such an aggrieved yet hopeful tone that Myra sat down. Instantly her host disappeared.

She sat there for five minutes and a feeling of oppression fell over her. Of all the receptions she had ever received this was decidedly the oddest—for though she had read somewhere that Ludlow Whitney was considered one of the most eccentric figures in the financial world, to find a sallow, elfin little man who, when he walked, danced was rather a blow to her sense of form. Had he gone to get Knowleton! She revolved her thumbs in interminable concentric circles.

Then she started nervously at a quick cough at her elbow. It was Mr. Whitney again. In one hand he held a glass of milk and in the other a blue kitchen bowl full of those hard cubical crackers used in soup.

"Hungry from your trip!" he exclaimed compassionately. "Poor girl, poor little girl, starving!" He brought out this last word with such emphasis that some of the milk plopped gently over the side of the glass.

Myra took the refreshments submissively. She was not hungry, but it had taken him ten minutes to get them so it seemed ungracious to refuse. She sipped gingerly at the milk and ate a cracker, wondering vaguely what to say. Mr. Whitney, however, solved the problem for her by disappearing again—this time by way of the wide stairs—four steps at a hop—the back of his bald head gleaming oddly for a moment in the half dark.

Minutes passed. Myra was torn between resentment and bewilderment that she should be sitting on a high comfortless chair in the middle of this big hall munching crackers. By what code was a visiting fiancée ever thus received!

Her heart gave a jump of relief as she heard a familiar whistle on the stairs. It was Knowleton at last, and when he came in sight he gasped with astonishment.

"Myra!"

She carefully placed the bowl and glass on the carpet and rose, smiling.

"Why," he exclaimed, "they didn't tell me you were here!"

"Your father—welcomed me."

"Lordy! He must have gone upstairs and forgotten all about it. Did he insist on your eating this stuff? Why didn't you just tell him you didn't want any?"

"Why—I don't know."

"You musn't mind father, dear. He's forgetful and a little unconventional in some ways, but you'll get used to him."

He pressed a button and a butler appeared.

"Show Miss Harper to her room and have her bag carried up—
and her trunk if it isn't there already." He turned to Myra. "Dear, I'm
awfully sorry I didn't know you were here. How long have you been
waiting?"

"Oh, only a few minutes."

It had been twenty at the least, but she saw no advantage in
stressing it. Nevertheless it had given her an oddly uncomfortable
feeling.

Half an hour later as she was hooking the last eye on her dinner
dress there was a knock on the door.

"It's Knowleton, Myra; if you're about ready we'll go in and see
mother for a minute before dinner."

She threw a final approving glance at her reflection in the mirror
and turning out the light joined him in the hall. He led her down a
central passage which crossed to the other wing of the house, and
stopping before a closed door he pushed it open and ushered Myra
into the weirdest room upon which her young eyes had ever rested.

It was a large luxurious boudoir, paneled, like the lower hall, in
dark English oak and bathed by several lamps in a mellow orange
glow that blurred its every outline into misty amber. In a great
armchair piled high with cushions and draped with a curiously
figured cloth of silk reclined a very sturdy old lady with bright white
hair, heavy features, and an air about her of having been there for
many years. She lay somnolently against the cushions, her eyes half
closed, her great bust rising and falling under her black negligee.

But it was something else that made the room remarkable, and
Myra's eyes scarcely rested on the woman, so engrossed was she in
another feature of her surroundings. On the carpet, on the chairs and
sofas, on the great canopied bed and on the soft Angora rug in front of
the fire sat and sprawled and slept a great army of white poodle dogs.
There must have been almost two dozen of them, with curly hair
twisting in front of their wistful eyes and wide yellow bows flaunting
from their necks. As Myra and Knowleton entered a stir went over the
dogs; they raised one-and-twenty cold black noses in the air and from
one-and-twenty little throats went up a great clatter of staccato barks
until the room was filled with such an uproar that Myra stepped back
in alarm.

But at the din the somnolent fat lady's eyes trembled open and in
a low husky voice that was in itself oddly like a bark she snapped out:
"Hush that racket!" and the clatter instantly ceased. The two or three
poodles round the fire turned their silky eyes on each other
reproachfully, and lying down with little sighs faded out on the white
Angora rug; the tousled ball on the lady's lap dug his nose into the
crook of an elbow and went back to sleep, and except for the patches of

white wool scattered about the room Myra would have thought it all a dream.

"Mother," said Knowleton after an instant's pause, "this is Myra."

From the lady's lips flooded one low husky word: "Myra?"

"She's visiting us, I told you."

Mrs. Whitney raised a large arm and passed her hand across her forehead wearily.

"Child!" she said—and Myra started, for again the voice was like a low sort of growl—"you want to marry my son Knowleton?"

Myra felt that this was putting the tonneau before the radiator, but she nodded. "Yes, Mrs. Whitney."

"How old are you?" This very suddenly.

"I'm twenty-one, Mrs. Whitney."

"Ah—and you're from Cleveland?" This was in what was surely a series of articulate barks.

"Yes, Mrs. Whitney."

"Ah——"

Myra was not certain whether this last ejaculation was conversation or merely a groan, so she did not answer.

"You'll excuse me if I don't appear downstairs," continued Mrs. Whitney; "but when we're in the East I seldom leave this room and my dear little doggies."

Myra nodded and a conventional health question was trembling on her lips when she caught Knowleton's warning glance and checked it.

"Well," said Mrs. Whitney with an air of finality, "you seem like a very nice girl. Come in again."

"Good night, mother," said Knowleton.

" 'Night!" barked Mrs. Whitney drowsily, and her eyes sealed gradually up as her head receded back again into the cushions.

Knowleton held open the door and Myra feeling a bit blank left the room. As they walked down the corridor she heard a burst of furious sound behind them; the noise of the closing door had again roused the poodle dogs.

When they went downstairs they found Mr. Whitney already seated at the dinner table.

"Utterly charming, completely delightful!" he exclaimed, beaming nervously. "One big family, and you the jewel of it, my dear."

Myra smiled, Knowleton frowned and Mr. Whitney tittered.

"It's been lonely here," he continued; "desolate, with only us three. We expect you to bring sunlight and warmth, the peculiar radiance and efflorescence of youth. It will be quite delightful. Do you sing?"

"Why—I have. I mean, I do, some."

He clapped his hands enthusiastically.

"Splendid! Magnificent! What do you sing? Opera? Ballads? Popular music?"

"Well, mostly popular music."

"Good; personally I prefer popular music. By the way, there's a dance to-night."

"Father," demanded Knowleton sulkily, "did you go and invite a crowd here?"

"I had Monroe call up a few people—just some of the neighbors," he explained to Myra. "We're all very friendly hereabouts; give informal things continually. Oh, it's quite delightful."

Myra caught Knowleton's eye and gave him a sympathetic glance. It was obvious that he had wanted to be alone with her this first evening and was quite put out.

"I want them to meet Myra," continued his father. "I want them to know this delightful jewel we've added to our little household."

"Father," said Knowleton suddenly, "eventually of course Myra and I will want to live here with you and mother, but for the first two or three years I think an apartment in New York would be more the thing for us."

Crash! Mr. Whitney had raked across the tablecloth with his fingers and swept his silver to a jangling heap on the floor.

"Nonsense!" he cried furiously, pointing a tiny finger at his son. "Don't talk that utter nonsense! You'll live here, do you understand me? Here! What's a home without children?"

"But, father——"

In his excitement Mr. Whitney rose and a faint unnatural color crept into his sallow face.

"Silence!" he shrieked. "If you expect one bit of help from me you can have it under my roof—nowhere else! Is that clear? As for you, my exquisite young lady," he continued, turning his wavering finger on Myra, "you'd better understand that the best thing you can do is to decide to settle down right here. This is my home, and I mean to keep it so!"

He stood then for a moment on his tiptoes, bending furiously indignant glances first on one, then on the other, and then suddenly he turned and skipped from the room.

"Well," gasped Myra, turning to Knowleton in amazement, "what do you know about that!"

III

Some hours later she crept into bed in a great state of restless discontent. One thing she knew—she was not going to live in this house. Knowleton would have to make his father see reason to the extent of giving them an apartment in the city. The sallow little man made her nervous; she was sure Mrs. Whitney's dogs would haunt her dreams; and there was a general casualness in the chauffeur, the butler, the maids and even the guests she had met that night, that did not in the least coincide with her ideas on the conduct of a big estate.

She had lain there an hour perhaps when she was startled from a slow reverie by a sharp cry which seemed to proceed from the adjoining room. She sat up in bed and listened, and in a minute it was repeated. It sounded exactly like the plaint of a weary child stopped summarily by the placing of a hand over its mouth. In the dark silence her bewilderment shaded gradually off into uneasiness. She waited for the cry to recur, but straining her ears she heard only the intense crowded stillness of three o'clock. She wondered where Knowleton slept, remembered that his bedroom was over in the other wing just beyond his mother's. She was alone over here—or was she?

With a little gasp she slid down into bed again and lay listening. Not since childhood had she been afraid of the dark, but the unforeseen presence of someone next door startled her and sent her imagination racing through a host of mystery stories that at one time or another had whiled away a long afternoon.

She heard the clock strike four and found she was very tired. A curtain drifted slowly down in front of her imagination, and changing her position she fell suddenly to sleep.

Next morning, walking with Knowleton under starry frosted bushes in one of the bare gardens, she grew quite light-hearted and wondered at her depression of the night before. Probably all families seemed odd when one visited them for the first time in such an intimate capacity. Yet her determination that she and Knowleton were going to live elsewhere than with the white dogs and the jumpy little man was not abated. And if the near-by Westchester County society was typified by the chilly crowd she had met at the dance——

"The family," said Knowleton, "must seem rather unusual. I've been brought up in an odd atmosphere, I suppose, but mother is really quite normal outside of her penchant for poodles in great quantities, and father in spite of his eccentricities seems to hold a secure position in Wall Street."

"Knowleton," she demanded suddenly, "who lives in the room next door to me?"

Did he start and flush slightly—or was that her imagination?

"Because," she went on deliberately, "I'm almost sure I heard someone crying in there during the night. It sounded like a child, Knowleton."

"There's no one in there," he said decidedly. "It was either your imagination or something you ate. Or possibly one of the maids was sick."

Seeming to dismiss the matter without effort he changed the subject.

The day passed quickly. At lunch Mr. Whitney seemed to have forgotten his temper of the previous night; he was as nervously enthusiastic as ever; and watching him Myra again had that impression that she had seen him somewhere before. She and Knowleton paid another visit to Mrs. Whitney—and again the poodles stirred uneasily and set up a barking, to be summarily silenced by the harsh throaty voice. The conversation was short and of inquisitional flavor. It was terminated as before by the lady's drowsy eyelids and a pæan of farewell from the dogs.

In the evening she found that Mr. Whitney had insisted on organizing an informal neighborhood vaudeville. A stage had been erected in the ballroom and Myra sat beside Knowleton in the front row and watched proceedings curiously. Two slim and haughty ladies sang, a man performed some ancient card tricks, a girl gave impersonations, and then to Myra's astonishment Mr. Whitney appeared and did a rather effective buck-and-wing dance. There was something inexpressibly weird in the motion of the well-known financier flitting solemnly back and forth across the stage on his tiny feet. Yet he danced well, with an effortless grace and an unexpected suppleness, and he was rewarded with a storm of applause.

In the half dark the lady on her left suddenly spoke to her.

"Mr. Whitney is passing the word along that he wants to see you behind the scenes."

Puzzled, Myra rose and ascended the side flight of stairs that led to the raised platform. Her host was waiting for her anxiously.

"Ah," he chuckled, "splendid!"

He held out his hand, and wonderingly she took it. Before she realized his intention he had half led, half drawn her out on to the stage. The spotlight's glare bathed them, and the ripple of conversation washing the audience ceased. The faces before her were pallid splotches on the gloom and she felt her ears burning as she waited for Mr. Whitney to speak.

"Ladies and gentlemen," he began, "most of you know Miss Myra Harper. You had the honor of meeting her last night. She is a delicious girl, I assure you. I am in a position to know. She intends to become the wife of my son."

He paused and nodded and began clapping his hands. The audience immediately took up the clapping and Myra stood there in motionless horror, overcome by the most violent confusion of her life.

The piping voice went on: "Miss Harper is not only beautiful but talented. Last night she confided to me that she sang. I asked whether she preferred the opera, the ballad or the popular song, and she confessed that her taste ran to the latter. Miss Harper will now favor us with a popular song."

And then Myra was standing alone on the stage, rigid with embarrassment. She fancied that on the faces in front of her she saw critical expectation, boredom, ironic disapproval. Surely this was the height of bad form—to drop a guest unprepared into such a situation.

In the first hush she considered a word or two explaining that Mr. Whitney had been under a misapprehension—then anger came to her assistance. She tossed her head and those in front saw her lips close together sharply.

Advancing to the platform's edge she said succinctly to the orchestra leader: "Have you got 'Wave That Wishbone'?"

"Lemme see. Yes, we got it."

"All right. Let's go!"

She hurriedly reviewed the words, which she had learned quite by accident at a dull house party the previous summer. It was perhaps not the song she would have chosen for her first public appearance, but it would have to do. She smiled radiantly, nodded at the orchestra leader and began the verse in a light clear alto.

As she sang a spirit of ironic humor slowly took possession of her—a desire to give them all a run for their money. And she did. She injected an East Side snarl into every word of slang; she ragged; she shimmied; she did a tickle-toe step she had learned once in an amateur musical comedy; and in a burst of inspiration finished up in an Al Jolson position, on her knees with her arms stretched out to her audience in syncopated appeal.

Then she rose, bowed and left the stage.

For an instant there was silence, the silence of a cold tomb; then perhaps half a dozen hands joined in a faint, perfunctory applause that in a second had died completely away.

"Heavens!" thought Myra. "Was it as bad as all that? Or did I shock 'em?"

Mr. Whitney, however, seemed delighted. He was waiting for her in the wings and seizing her hand shook it enthusiastically.

"Quite wonderful!" he chuckled. "You are a delightful little actress—and you'll be a valuable addition to our little plays. Would you like to give an encore?"

"No!" said Myra shortly, and turned away.

In a shadowy corner she waited until the crowd had filed out, with an angry unwillingness to face them immediately after their rejection of her effort.

When the ballroom was quite empty she walked slowly up the stairs, and there she came upon Knowleton and Mr. Whitney alone in the dark hall, evidently engaged in a heated argument.

They ceased when she appeared and looked toward her eagerly.

"Myra," said Mr. Whitney, "Knowleton wants to talk to you."

"Father," said Knowleton intensely, "I ask you——"

"Silence!" cried his father, his voice ascending testily. "You'll do your duty—now."

Knowleton cast one more appealing glance at him, but Mr. Whitney only shook his head excitedly and, turning, disappeared phantomlike up the stairs.

Knowleton stood silent a moment and finally with a look of dogged determination took her hand and led her toward a room that opened off the hall at the back. The yellow light fell through the door after them and she found herself in a dark wide chamber where she could just distinguish on the walls great square shapes which she took to be frames. Knowleton pressed a button, and immediately forty portraits sprang into life—old gallants from colonial days, ladies with floppity Gainsborough hats, fat women with ruffs and placid clasped hands.

She turned to Knowleton inquiringly, but he led her forward to a row of pictures on the side.

"Myra," he said slowly and painfully, "there's something I have to tell you. These"—he indicated the pictures with his hand—"are family portraits."

There were seven of them, three men and three women, all of them of the period just before the Civil War. The one in the middle, however, was hidden by crimson-velvet curtains.

"Ironic as it may seem," continued Knowleton steadily, "that frame contains a picture of my great-grandmother."

Reaching out, he pulled a little silken cord and the curtains parted, to expose a portrait of a lady dressed as a European but with the unmistakable features of a Chinese.

"My great-grandfather, you see, was an Australian tea importer. He met his future wife in Hong-Kong."

Myra's brain was whirling. She had a sudden vision of Mr. Whitney's yellowish face, peculiar eyebrows and tiny hands and feet—she remembered ghastly tales she had heard of reversions to type—of Chinese babies—and then with a final surge of horror she thought of that sudden hushed cry in the night. She gasped, her knees seemed to crumple up and she sank slowly to the floor.

In a second Knowleton's arms were round her.

"Dearest, dearest!" he cried. "I shouldn't have told you! I shouldn't have told you!"

As he said this Myra knew definitely and unmistakably that she could never marry him, and when she realized it she cast at him a wild pitiful look, and for the first time in her life fainted dead away.

IV

When she next recovered full consciousness she was in bed. She imagined a maid had undressed her, for on turning up the reading lamp she saw that her clothes had been neatly put away. For a minute she lay there, listening idly while the hall clock struck two, and then her overwrought nerves jumped in terror as she heard again that child's cry from the room next door. The morning seemed suddenly infinitely far away. There was some shadowy secret near her—her feverish imagination pictured a Chinese child brought up there in the half dark.

In a quick panic she crept into a negligee and, throwing open the door, slipped down the corridor toward Knowleton's room. It was very dark in the other wing, but when she pushed open his door she could see by the faint hall light that his bed was empty and had not been slept in. Her terror increased. What could take him out at this hour of the night? She started for Mrs. Whitney's room, but at the thought of the dogs and her bare ankles she gave a little discouraged cry and passed by the door.

Then she suddenly heard the sound of Knowleton's voice issuing from a faint crack of light far down the corridor, and with a glow of joy she fled toward it. When she was within a foot of the door she found she could see through the crack—and after one glance all thought of entering left her.

Before an open fire, his head bowed in an attitude of great dejection, stood Knowleton, and in the corner, feet perched on the table, sat Mr. Whitney in his shirt sleeves, very quiet and calm, and pulling contentedly on a huge black pipe. Seated on the table was a part of Mrs. Whitney—that is, Mrs. Whitney without any hair. Out of the familiar great bust projected Mrs. Whitney's head, but she was bald; on her cheeks was the faint stubble of a beard, and in her mouth was a large black cigar, which she was puffing with obvious enjoyment.

"A thousand," groaned Knowleton as if in answer to a question. "Say twenty-five hundred and you'll be nearer the truth. I got a bill from the Graham Kennels to-day for those poodle dogs. They're soaking me two hundred and saying that they've got to have 'em back tomorrow."

"Well," said Mrs. Whitney in a low barytone voice, "send 'em back. We're through with 'em."

"That's a mere item," continued Knowleton glumly. "Including your salary, and Appleton's here, and that fellow who did the chauffeur, and seventy supes for two nights, and an orchestra—that's nearly twelve hundred, and then there's the rent on the costumes and that darn Chinese portrait and the bribes to the servants. Lord! There'll probably be bills for one thing or another coming in for the next month."

"Well, then," said Appleton, "for pity's sake pull yourself together and carry it through to the end. Take my word for it, that girl will be out of the house by twelve noon."

Knowleton sank into a chair and covered his face with his hands. "Oh——"

"Brace up! It's all over. I thought for a minute there in the hall that you were going to balk at that Chinese business."

"It was the vaudeville that knocked the spots out of me," groaned Knowleton. "It was about the meanest trick ever pulled on any girl, and she was so darned game about it!"

"She had to be," said Mrs. Whitney cynically.

"Oh, Kelly, if you could have seen the girl look at me to-night just before she fainted in front of that picture. Lord, I believe she loves me! Oh, if you could have seen her!"

Outside Myra flushed crimson. She leaned closer to the door, biting her lip until she could taste the faintly bitter savor of blood.

"If there was anything I could do now," continued Knowleton— "anything in the world that would smooth it over I believe I'd do it."

Kelly crossed ponderously over, his bald shiny head ludicrous above his feminine negligee, and put his hand on Knowleton's shoulder.

"See here, my boy—your trouble is just nerves. Look at it this way: You undertook somep'n to get yourself out of an awful mess. It's a cinch the girl was after your money—now you've beat her at her own game an' saved yourself an unhappy marriage and your family a lot of suffering. Ain't that so, Appleton?"

"Absolutely!" said Appleton emphatically. "Go through with it."

"Well," said Knowleton with a dismal attempt to be righteous, "if she really loved me she wouldn't have let it all affect her this much. She's not marrying my family."

Appleton laughed.

"I thought we'd tried to make it pretty obvious that she is."

"Oh, shut up!" cried Knowleton miserably.

Myra saw Appleton wink at Kelly.

" 'At's right," he said; "she's shown she was after your money. Well, now then, there's no reason for not going through with it. See here. On one side you've proved she didn't love you and you're rid of her and free as air. She'll creep away and never say a word about it— and your family never the wiser. On the other side twenty-five hundred thrown to the bow-wows, miserable marriage, girl sure to hate you as soon as she finds out, and your family all broken up and probably disownin' you for marryin' her. One big mess, I'll tell the world."

"You're right," admitted Knowleton gloomily. "You're right, I suppose—but oh, the look in that girl's face! She's probably in there now lying awake, listening to the Chinese baby——"

Appleton rose and yawned.

"Well——" he began.

But Myra waited to hear no more. Pulling her silk kimono close about her she sped like lightning down the soft corridor, to dive headlong and breathless into her room.

"My heavens!" she cried, clenching her hands in the darkness. "My heavens!"

V

Just before dawn Myra drowsed into a jumbled dream that seemed to act on through interminable hours. She awoke about seven and lay listlessly with one blue-veined arm hanging over the side of the bed. She who had danced in the dawn at many proms was very tired.

A clock outside her door struck the hour, and with her nervous start something seemed to collapse within her—she turned over and began to weep furiously into her pillow, her tangled hair spreading like a dark aura round her head. To her, Myra Harper, had been done this cheap vulgar trick by a man she had thought shy and kind.

Lacking the courage to come to her and tell her the truth he had gone into the highways and hired men to frighten her.

Between her fevered broken sobs she tried in vain to comprehend the workings of a mind which could have conceived this in all its subtlety. Her pride refused to let her think of it as a deliberate plan of Knowleton's. It was probably an idea fostered by this little actor Appleton or by the fat Kelly with his horrible poodles. But it was all unspeakable—unthinkable. It gave her an intense sense of shame.

But when she emerged from her room at eight o'clock and, disdaining breakfast, walked into the garden she was a very self-possessed young beauty, with dry cool eyes only faintly shadowed. The ground was firm and frosty with the promise of winter, and she found gray sky and dull air vaguely comforting and one with her mood. It was a day for thinking and she needed to think.

And then turning a corner suddenly she saw Knowleton seated on a stone bench, his head in his hands, in an attitude of profound dejection. He wore his clothes of the night before and it was quite evident that he had not been to bed.

He did not hear her until she was quite close to him, and then as a dry twig snapped under her heel he looked up wearily. She saw that the night had played havoc with him—his face was deathly pale and his eyes were pink and puffed and tired. He jumped up with a look that was very like dread.

"Good morning," said Myra quietly.

"Sit down," he began nervously. "Sit down; I want to talk to you! I've got to talk to you."

Myra nodded and taking a seat beside him on the bench clasped her knees with her hands and half closed her eyes.

"Myra, for heaven's sake have pity on me!"

She turned wondering eyes on him.

"What do you mean?"

He groaned.

"Myra, I've done a ghastly thing—to you, to me, to us. I haven't a word to say in favor of myself—I've been just rotten. I think it was a sort of madness that came over me."

"You'll have to give me a clew to what you're talking about."

"Myra—Myra"—like all large bodies his confession seemed difficult to imbue with momentum—"Myra—Mr. Whitney is not my father."

"You mean you were adopted?"

"No; I mean—Ludlow Whitney is my father, but this man you've met isn't Ludlow Whitney."

"I know," said Myra coolly. "He's Warren Appleton, the actor."

Knowleton leaped to his feet.

"How on earth——"

"Oh," lied Myra easily, "I recognized him the first night. I saw him five years ago in *The Swiss Grapefruit*."

At this Knowleton seemed to collapse utterly. He sank down limply on to the bench.

"You knew?"

"Of course! How could I help it? It simply made me wonder what it was all about."

With a great effort he tried to pull himself together.

"I'm going to tell you the whole story, Myra."

"I'm all ears."

"Well, it starts with my mother—my real one, not the woman with those idiotic dogs; she's an invalid and I'm her only child. Her one idea in life has always been for me to make a fitting match, and her idea of a fitting match centers round social position in England. Her greatest disappointment was that I wasn't a girl so I could marry a title; instead she wanted to drag me to England—marry me off to the sister of an earl or the daughter of a duke. Why, before she'd let me stay up here alone this fall she made me promise I wouldn't go to see any girl more than twice. And then I met you."

He paused for a second and continued earnestly: "You were the first girl in my life whom I ever thought of marrying. You intoxicated me, Myra. It was just as though you were making me love you by some invisible force."

"I was," murmured Myra.

"Well, that first intoxication lasted a week, and then one day a letter came from mother saying she was bringing home some wonderful English girl, Lady Helena Something-or-Other. And the same day a man told me that he'd heard I'd been caught by the most famous husband hunter in New York. Well, between these two things I went half crazy. I came into town to see you and call it off—got as far as the Biltmore entrance and didn't dare. I started wandering down Fifth Avenue like a wild man, and then I met Kelly. I told him the whole story—and within an hour we'd hatched up this ghastly plan. It was his plan—all the details. His histrionic instinct got the better of him and he had me thinking it was the kindest way out."

"Finish," commanded Myra crisply.

"Well, it went splendidly, we thought. Everything—the station meeting, the dinner scene, the scream in the night, the vaudeville— though I thought that was a little too much—until—until——Oh, Myra, when you fainted under that picture and I held you there in my arms, helpless as a baby, I knew I loved you. I was sorry then, Myra."

There was a long pause while she sat motionless, her hands still clasping her knees—then he burst out with a wild plea of passionate sincerity.

"Myra!" he cried. "If by any possible chance you can bring yourself to forgive and forget I'll marry you when you say, let my family go to the devil, and love you all my life."

For a long while she considered, and Knowleton rose and began pacing nervously up and down the aisle of bare bushes, his hands in his pockets, his tired eyes pathetic now, and full of dull appeal. And then she came to a decision.

"You're perfectly sure?" she asked calmly.

"Yes."

"Very well, I'll marry you to-day."

With her words the atmosphere cleared and his troubles seemed to fall from him like a ragged cloak. An Indian summer sun drifted out from behind the gray clouds and the dry bushes rustled gently in the breeze.

"It was a bad mistake," she continued, "but if you're sure you love me now, that's the main thing. We'll go to town this morning, get a license, and I'll call up my cousin, who's a minister in the First Presbyterian Church. We can go West to-night."

"Myra!" he cried jubilantly. "You're a marvel and I'm not fit to tie your shoe strings. I'm going to make up to you for this, darling girl."

And taking her supple body in his arms he covered her face with kisses.

The next two hours passed in a whirl. Myra went to the telephone and called her cousin, and then rushed upstairs to pack. When she came down a shining roadster was waiting miraculously in the drive and by ten o'clock they were bowling happily toward the city.

They stopped for a few minutes at the City Hall and again at the jeweler's, and then they were in the house of the Reverend Walter Gregory on Sixty-ninth Street, where a sanctimonious gentleman with twinkling eyes and a slight stutter received them cordially and urged them to a breakfast of bacon and eggs before the ceremony.

On the way to the station they stopped only long enough to wire Knowleton's father, and then they were sitting in their compartment on the Broadway Limited.

"Darn!" exclaimed Myra. "I forgot my bag. Left it at Cousin Walter's in the excitement."

"Never mind. We can get a whole new outfit in Chicago."

She glanced at her wrist watch.

"I've got time to telephone him to send it on."

She rose.

"Don't be long, dear."

She leaned down and kissed his forehead.

"You know I couldn't. Two minutes, honey."

Outside Myra ran swiftly along the platform and up the steel stairs to the great waiting room, where a man met her—a twinkly-eyed man with a slight stutter.

"How d-did it go, M-myra?"

"Fine! Oh, Walter, you were splendid! I almost wish you'd join the ministry so you could officiate when I do get married."

"Well—I r-rehearsed for half an hour after I g-got your telephone call."

"Wish we'd had more time. I'd have had him lease an apartment and buy furniture."

"H'm," chuckled Walter. "Wonder how far he'll go on his honeymoon."

"Oh, he'll think I'm on the train till he gets to Elizabeth." She shook her little fist at the great contour of the marble dome. "Oh, he's getting off too easy—far too easy!"

"I haven't f-figured out what the f-fellow did to you, M-myra."

"You never will, I hope."

They had reached the side drive and he hailed her a taxicab.

"You're an angel!" beamed Myra. "And I can't thank you enough."

"Well, any time I can be of use t-to you——By the way, what are you going to do with all the rings?"

Myra looked laughingly at her hand.

"That's the question," she said. "I may send them to Lady Helena Something-or-Other—and—well, I've always had a strong penchant for souvenirs. Tell the driver 'Biltmore,' Walter."

Two For a Cent

(*Metropolitan Magazine*, April 1922)

"Two For a Cent" was written at White Bear Lake, Minnesota, in September 1921 while the Fitzgeralds were awaiting the birth of their child. It was a measure of Fitzgerald's popularity as a magazinist that *Metropolitan* (which serialized *The Beautiful and Damned*) had signed him to an option on his story output at $900 per story at a time when *The Saturday Evening Post* was paying him $500. Four of his stories appeared in *Metropolitan* before it went into receivership.

Fitzgerald explained to Harold Ober in November: "I am not very fond of *Two for a Penny*. It is a fair story with an O. Henry twist but it is neither 1st class nor popular because it has no love interest. My heart wasn't in it so I know it lacks vitality. Perhaps you'd better return it to me so I can fix it up." Revision was not necessary, and it became one of his most popular stories. It was included in *The Best Short Stories of 1922*; it was syndicated by the Metropolitan Newspaper Service; and it brought what appears to have been Fitzgerald's first textbook appearance, in *Short Stories for Class Reading* (1925).

"Two For a Cent" was the first of Fitzgerald's stories in which successful men make pilgrimages to their home towns (see "John Jackson's Arcady" and "Diagnosis" in this collection), seeking their personal identities. It is noteworthy that Fitzgerald, a Midwesterner, wrote so much about the South—including "The Ice Palace," "The Jelly Bean," "The Dance," "Family in the Wind," and "The Last of the Belles." The South was associated with his own love story; nevertheless Fitzgerald was ambivalent about it—seeing it both as a place of romance and as a land in which the climate saps vitality. In 1940 he commented to his daughter: "It is a grotesquely pictorial country as I found out long ago, and as Mr. Faulkner has since abundantly demonstrated."

When the rain was over the sky became yellow in the west and the air was cool. Close to the street, which was of red dirt and lined with cheap bungalows dating from 1910, a little boy was riding a big bicycle along the sidewalk. His plan afforded a monotonous fascination. He rode each time for about a hundred yards, dismounted, turned the bicycle around so that it adjoined a stone step and getting on again, not without toil or heat, retraced his course. At one end this was bounded by a colored girl of fourteen holding an anemic baby, and at the other by a scarred, ill-nourished kitten, squatting dismally on the curb. These four were the only souls in sight.

The little boy had accomplished an indefinite number of trips oblivious alike to the melancholy advances of the kitten at one end and to the admiring vacuousness of the colored girl at the other when he swerved dangerously to avoid a man who had turned the corner into the street and recovered his balance only after a moment of exaggerated panic.

But if the incident was a matter of gravity to the boy, it attracted scarcely an instant's notice from the newcomer, who turned suddenly from the sidewalk and stared with obvious and peculiar interest at the house before which he was standing. It was the oldest house in the street, built with clapboards and a shingled roof. It was a *house*—in the barest sense of the word: the sort of house that a child would draw on a blackboard. It was of a period, but of no design, and its exterior had obviously been made only as a decent cloak for what was within. It antedated the stucco bungalows by about thirty years and except for the bungalows, which were reproducing their species with prodigious avidity as though by some monstrous affiliation with the guinea-pig, it was the most common type of house in the country. For thirty years such dwellings had satisfied the canons of the middle class; they had satisfied its financial canons by being cheap, they had satisfied its aesthetic canons by being hideous. It was a house built by a race whose more energetic complement hoped either to move up or move on, and it was the more remarkable that its instability had survived so many summers and retained its pristine hideousness and discomfort so obviously unimpaired.

The man was about as old as the house, that is to say, about forty-five. But unlike the house, he was neither hideous nor cheap. His clothes were too good to have been made outside of a metropolis—moreover, they were so good that it was impossible to tell in which metropolis they were made. His name was Abercrombie and the most important event of his life had taken place in the house before which he was standing. He had been born there.

It was one of the last places in the world where he should have been born. He had thought so within a very few years after the event and he thought so now—an ugly home in a third-rate Southern town where his father had owned a partnership in a grocery store. Since then Abercrombie had played golf with the President of the United States and sat between two duchesses at dinner. He had been bored with the President, he had been bored and not a little embarrassed with the duchesses—nevertheless, the two incidents had pleased him and still sat softly upon his naive vanity. It delighted him that he had gone far.

He had looked fixedly at the house for several minutes before he perceived that no one lived there. Where the shutters were not closed it was because there were no shutters to be closed and in these vacancies, blind vacuous expanses of grey window looked unseeingly down at him. The grass had grown wantonly long in the yard and faint green mustaches were sprouting facetiously in the wide cracks of the walk. But it was evident that the property had been recently occupied for upon the porch lay half a dozen newspapers rolled into cylinders for quick delivery and as yet turned only to a faint resentful yellow.

They were not nearly so yellow as the sky when Abercrombie walked up on the porch and sat down upon an immemorial bench, for the sky was every shade of yellow, the color of tan, the color of gold, the color of peaches. Across the street and beyond a vacant lot rose a rampart of vivid red brick houses and it seemed to Abercrombie that the picture they rounded out was beautiful—the warm earthy brick and the sky fresh after the rain, changing and grey as a dream. All his life when he had wanted to rest his mind he had called up into it the image those two things had made for him when the air was clear just at this hour. So Abercrombie sat there thinking about his young days.

Ten minutes later another man turned the corner of the street, a different sort of man, both in the texture of his clothes and the texture of his soul. He was forty-six years old and he was a shabby drudge, married to a woman, who, as a girl, had known better days. This latter fact, in the republic, may be set down in the red italics of misery.

His name was Hemmick—Henry W. or George D. or John F.— the stock that produced him had had little imagination left to waste either upon his name or his design. He was a clerk in a factory which made ice for the long Southern Summer. He was responsible to the man who owned the patent for canning ice, who, in his turn was responsible only to God. Never in his life had Henry W. Hemmick discovered a new way to advertise canned ice nor had it transpired that by taking a diligent correspondence course in ice canning he had secretly been preparing himself for a partnership. Never had he rushed home to his wife, crying: "You can have that servant now, Nell, I have been made General Superintendent." You will have to take him as you take Abercrombie, for what he is and will always be. This is a story of the dead years.

When the second man reached the house he turned in and began to mount the tipsy steps, noticed Abercrombie, the stranger, with a tired surprise, and nodded to him.

"Good evening," he said.

Abercrombie voiced his agreement with the sentiment.

"Cool"—The newcomer covered his forefinger with his handkerchief and sent the swatched digit on a complete circuit of his collar band. "Have you rented this?" he asked.

"No, indeed, I'm just—resting. Sorry if I've intruded—I saw the house was vacant——"

"Oh, you're not intruding!" said Hemmick hastily. "I don't reckon anybody *could* intrude in this old barn. I got out two months ago. They're not ever goin' to rent it any more. I got a little girl about this high—" he held his hand parallel to the ground and at an indeterminate distance "—and she's mighty fond of an old doll that got left here when we moved. Began hollerin' for me to come over and look it up."

"You used to live here?" inquired Abercrombie with interest.

"Lived here eighteen years. Came here'n I was married, raised four children in this house. Yes, *sir*. I know this old fellow." He struck the door-post with the flat of his hand. "I know every leak in her roof and every loose board in her old floor."

Abercrombie had been good to look at for so many years that he knew if he kept a certain attentive expression on his face his companion would continue to talk—indefinitely.

"You from up North?" inquired Hemmick politely, choosing with habituated precision the one spot where the anemic wooden railing would support his weight. "I thought so," he resumed at Abercrombie's nod. "Don't take long to tell a Yankee."

"I'm from New York."

"So?" The man shook his head with inappropriate gravity. "Never have got up there, myself. Started to go a couple of times, before I was married, but never did get to go."

He made a second excursion with his finger and handkerchief and then, as though having come suddenly to a cordial decision, he replaced the handkerchief in one of his bumpy pockets and extended the hand toward his companion.

"My name's Hemmick."

"Glad to know you." Abercrombie took the hand without rising. "Abercrombie's mine."

"I'm mighty glad to know you, Mr. Abercrombie."

Then for a moment they both hesitated, their two faces assumed oddly similar expressions, their eyebrows drew together, their eyes looked far away. Each was straining to force into activity some minute cell long sealed and forgotten in his brain. Each made a little noise in his throat, looked away, looked back, laughed. Abercrombie spoke first.

"We've met."

"I know," agreed Hemmick, "but whereabouts? That's what's got me. You from New York you say?"

"Yes, but I was born and raised in this town. Lived in this house till I left here when I was about seventeen. As a matter of fact, I remember you—you were a couple of years older."

Again Hemmick considered.

"Well," he said vaguely, "I sort of remember, too. I *begin* to remember—I got your name all right and I guess maybe it was your daddy had this house before I rented it. But all I can recollect about you is, that there was a boy named Abercrombie and he went away."

In a few moments they were talking easily. It amused them both to have come from the same house—amused Abercrombie especially, for he was a vain man, rather absorbed, that evening, in his own early poverty. Though he was not given to immature impulses, he found it necessary somehow to make it clear in a few sentences that five years after he had gone away from the house and the town he had been able to send for his father and mother to join him in New York.

Hemmick listened with that exaggerated attention which men who have not prospered generally render to men who have. He would have continued to listen had Abercrombie become more expansive, for he was beginning faintly to associate him with an Abercrombie who had figured in the newspapers for several years at the head of shipping boards and financial committees. But Abercrombie, after a moment, made the conversation less personal.

"I didn't realize you had so much heat here, I guess I've forgotten a lot in twenty-five years."

"Why, this is a *cool* day," boasted Hemmick, "this is *cool*. I was just sort of overheated from walking when I came up."

"It's too hot," insisted Abercrombie with a restless movement; then he added abruptly, "I don't like it here. It means nothing to me—nothing—I've wondered if it did, you know, that's why I came down. And I've decided.

"You see," he continued hesitantly, "up to recently the North was still full of professional Southerners, some real, some by sentiment, but all given to flowery monologues on the beauty of their old family plantations and all jumping up and howling when the band played Dixie. You know what I mean,"—he turned to Hemmick,—"it got to be a sort of a national joke. Oh, I was in the game, too, I suppose, I used to stand up and perspire and cheer, and

I've given young men positions for no particular reason except that they claimed to come from South Carolina or Virginia—" again he broke off and became suddenly abrupt—"but I'm through, I've been here six hours and I'm through!"

"Too hot for you?" inquired Hemmick, with mild surprise.

"Yes! I've felt the heat and I've seen the men—those two or three dozen loafers standing in front of the stores on Jackson Street—in thatched straw hats"—then he added, with a touch of humor, "they're what my son calls 'slash-pocket, belted-back boys.' Do you know the ones I mean?"

"Jelly-beans," Hemmick nodded gravely, "we call 'em Jelly-beans. No-account lot of boys all right. They got signs up in front of most of the stores asking 'em not to stand there."

"They ought to!" asserted Abercrombie, with a touch of irascibility. "That's my picture of the South now, you know—a skinny, dark-haired young man with a gun on his hip and a stomach full of corn liquor or Dope Dola, leaning up against a drug store waiting for the next lynching."

Hemmick objected, though with apology in his voice.

"You got to remember, Mr. Abercrombie, that we haven't had the money down here since the war——"

Abercrombie waved this impatiently aside.

"Oh, I've heard all that," he said, "and I'm tired of it. And I've heard the South lambasted till I'm tired of that, too. It's not taking France and Germany fifty years to get on their feet, and their war made your war look like a little fracas up an alley. And it's not your fault and it's not anybody's fault. . . ."*

Hemmick nodded, thoughtfully, though without thought. He had never thought; for over twenty years he had seldom ever held opinions, save the opinions of the local press or of some majority made articulate through passion. There was a certain luxury in thinking that he had never been able to afford. When cases were set before him he either accepted them outright if they were comprehensible to him or rejected them if they required a modicum of concentration. Yet he was not a stupid man. He was poor and busy and tired and there were no ideas at large in his community, even had he been capable of grasping them. The idea that he did not think would have been equally incomprehensible to him. He was a closed book, half full of badly printed, uncorrelated trash.

Just now, his reaction to Abercrombie's assertion was exceedingly simple. Since the remarks proceeded from a man who was a Southerner by birth, who was successful—moreover, who was

---

*Forty-one words have been omitted.

confident and decisive and persuasive and suave—he was inclined to accept them without suspicion or resentment.

He took one of Abercrombie's cigars and pulling on it, still with a stern imitation of profundity upon his tired face, watched the color glide out of the sky and the grey veils come down. The little boy and his bicycle, the baby, the nursemaid, the forlorn kitten, all had departed. In the stucco bungalows pianos gave out hot weary notes that inspired the crickets to competitive sound, and squeaky graphophones filled in the intervals with patches of whining ragtime until the impression was created that each living room in the street opened directly out into the darkness.

"What *I* want to find out," Abercrombie was saying with a frown, "is why I didn't have sense enough to *know* that this was a worthless town. It was entirely an accident that I left here, an utterly blind chance, and as it happened, the very train that took me away was full of luck for me. The man I sat beside gave me my start in life." His tone became resentful. "But I thought this was all right. I'd have stayed except that I'd gotten into a scrape down at the High School—I got expelled and my daddy told me he didn't want me at home any more. Why didn't I know the place wasn't any good? Why didn't I *see?*"

"Well, you'd probably never known anything better?" suggested Hemmick mildly.

"That wasn't any excuse," insisted Abercrombie. "If I'd been any good I'd have known. As a matter of fact—as—a—matter—of—fact," he repeated slowly, "I think that at heart I was the sort of boy who'd have lived and died here happily and never known there was anything better." He turned to Hemmick with a look almost of distress. "It worries me to think that my—that what's happened to me can be ascribed to chance. But that's the sort of boy I think I was. I didn't start off with the Dick Whittington idea—I started off by accident."

After this confession, he stared out into the twilight with a dejected expression that Hemmick could not understand. It was impossible for the latter to share any sense of the importance of such a distinction—in fact from a man of Abercrombie's position it struck him as unnecessarily trivial. Still, he felt that some manifestation of acquiescence was only polite.

"Well," he offered, "it's just that some boys get the bee to get up and go North and some boys don't. I happened to have the bee to go North. But I didn't. That's the difference between you and me."

Abercrombie turned to him intently.

"You did?" he asked, with unexpected interest, "you wanted to get out?"

"At one time." At Abercrombie's eagerness Hemmick began to

attach a new importance to the subject. "At one time," he repeated, as though the singleness of the occasion was a thing he had often mused upon.

"How old were you?"

"Oh—'bout twenty."

"What put it into your head?"

"Well, let me see—" Hemmick considered. "—I don't know whether I remember sure enough but it seems to me that when I was down to the University—I was there two years—one of the professors told me that a smart boy ought to go North. He said, business wasn't going to amount to much down here for the next fifty years. And I guessed he was right. My father died about then, so I got a job as runner in the bank here, and I didn't have much interest in anything except saving up enough money to go North. I was bound I'd go."

"Why didn't you? Why didn't you?" insisted Abercrombie in an aggrieved tone.

"Well," Hemmick hesitated. "Well, I right near did but—things didn't work out and I didn't get to go. It was a funny sort of business. It all started about the smallest thing you can think of. It all started about a penny."

"A penny?"

"That's what did it—one little penny. That's why I didn't go 'way from here and all, like I intended."

"Tell me about it, man," exclaimed his companion. He looked at his watch impatiently. "I'd like to hear the story."

Hemmick sat for a moment, distorting his mouth around the cigar.

"Well, to begin with," he said at length, "I'm going to ask you if you remember a thing that happened here about twenty-five years ago. A fellow named Hoyt, the cashier of the Cotton National Bank, disappeared one night with about thirty thousand dollars in cash. Say, man, they didn't talk about anything else down here at the time. The whole town was shaken up about it, and I reckin you can imagine the disturbance it caused down at all the banks and especially at the Cotton National."

"I remember."

"Well, they caught him, and they got most of the money back, and by and by the excitement died down, except in the bank where the thing had happened. Down there it seemed as if they'd never get used to it. Mr. Deems, the First Vice-President, who'd always been pretty kind and decent, got to be a changed man. He was suspicious of the clerks, the tellers, the janitor, the watchman, most of the officers, and yes, by Golly, I guess he got so he kept an eye on the President himself.

"I don't mean he was just watchful—he was downright hipped on the subject. He'd come up and ask you funny questions when you were going about your business. He'd walk into the teller's cage on tip-toe and watch him without saying anything. If there was any mistake of any kind in the book-keeping, he'd not only fire a clerk or so, but he'd raise such a riot that he made you want to push him into a vault and slam the door on him.

"He was just about running the bank then, and he'd affected the other officers, and—oh, you can imagine the havoc a thing like that could work on any sort of an organization. Everybody was so nervous that they made mistakes whether they were careful or not. Clerks were staying downtown until eleven at night trying to account for a lost nickel. It was a thin year, anyhow, and everything financial was pretty rickety, so one thing worked on another until the crowd of us were as near craziness as anybody can be and carry on the banking business at all.

"I was a runner—and all through the heat of one God-forsaken Summer I ran. I ran and I got mighty little money for it, and that was the time I hated that bank and this town, and all I wanted was to get out and go North. I was getting ten dollars a week, and I'd decided that when I'd saved fifty out of it I was going down to the depot and buy me a ticket to Cincinnati. I had an uncle in the banking business there, and he said he'd give me an opportunity with him. But he never offered to pay my way, and I guess he thought if I was worth having I'd manage to get up there by myself. Well, maybe I wasn't worth having because, anyhow, I never did.

"One morning on the hottest day of the hottest July I ever knew—and you know what that means down here—I left the bank to call on a man named Harlan and collect some money that'd come due on a note. Harlan had the cash waiting for me all right, and when I counted it I found it amounted to three hundred dollars and eighty-six cents, the change being in brand new coin that Harlan had drawn from another bank that morning. I put the three one-hundred-dollar bills in my wallet and the change in my vest pocket, signed a receipt and left. I was going straight back to the bank.

"Outside the heat was terrible. It was enough to make you dizzy, and I hadn't been feeling right for a couple of days, so, while I waited in the shade for a street car, I was congratulating myself that in a month or so I'd be out of this and up where it was some cooler. And then as I stood there it occurred to me all of a sudden that outside of the money which I'd just collected, which, of course, I couldn't touch, I didn't have a cent in my pocket. I'd have to walk back to the bank, and it was about fifteen blocks away. You see, on the night before, I'd found that my change came to just a dollar, and I'd traded it for a bill at the corner store and added it to the roll in the bottom of my trunk. So there was no help for it—I took off my coat and I stuck my handkerchief into my collar and struck off through the suffocating heat for the bank.

"Fifteen blocks—you can imagine what that was like, and I was sick when I started. From away up by Juniper Street—you remember where that is; the new Mieger Hospital's there now—all the way down to Jackson. After about six blocks I began to stop and rest whenever I found a patch of shade wide enough to hold me, and as I got pretty near I could just keep going by thinking of the big glass of iced tea my mother'd have waiting beside my plate at lunch. But after that I began getting too sick to even want the iced tea—I wanted to get rid of that money and then lie down and die.

"When I was still about two blocks away from the bank I put my hand into my watch pocket and pulled out that change; was sort of jingling it in my hand; making myself believe that I was so close that it was convenient to have it ready. I happened to glance into my hand, and all of a sudden I stopped up short and reached down quick into my watch pocket. The pocket was empty. There was a little hole in the bottom, and my hand held only a half dollar, a quarter and a dime. I had lost one cent.

"Well, sir, I can't tell you, I can't express to you the feeling of discouragement that this gave me. One penny, mind you—but think: just the week before a runner had lost his job because he was a little bit shy twice. It was only carelessness; but there you were! They were all in a panic that they might get fired themselves, and the best thing to do was to fire some one else—first.

"So you can see that it was up to me to appear with that penny.

"Where I got the energy to care as much about it as I did is more than I can understand. I was sick and hot and weak as a kitten, but it never occurred to me that I could do anything except find or replace that penny, and immediately I began casting about for a way to do it. I looked into a couple of stores, hoping I'd see some one I knew, but while there were a few fellows loafing in front, just as you saw them today, there wasn't one that I felt like going up to and saying: 'Here! You got a penny?' I thought of a couple of offices where I could have gotten it without much trouble, but they were some distance off, and besides being pretty dizzy, I hated to go out of my route when I was carrying bank money, because it looked kind of strange.

"So what should I do but commence walking back along the street toward the Union Depot where I last remembered having the penny. It was a brand new penny, and I thought maybe I'd see it shining where it dropped. So I kept walking, looking pretty carefully at the sidewalk and thinking what I'd better do. I laughed a little, because I felt sort of silly for worrying about a penny, but I didn't enjoy laughing, and it really didn't seem silly to me at all.

"Well, by and by I got back to the Union Depot without having either seen the old penny or having thought what was the best way to get another. I hated to go all the way home, 'cause we lived a long distance out; but what else was I to do? So I found a piece of shade close to the depot, and stood there considering, thinking first one thing and then another, and not getting anywhere at all. One little penny, just *one*—something almost any man in sight would have given me; something even the nigger baggage-smashers were jingling around in their pockets. . . . I must have stood there about five minutes. I remember there was a line of about a dozen men in front of an army recruiting station they'd just opened, and a couple of them began to yell: 'Join the Army!' at me. That woke me up, and I moved on back toward the bank, getting worried now, getting mixed up and sicker and sicker and knowing a million ways to find a penny and not one that seemed convenient or right. I was exaggerating the importance of losing it, and I was exaggerating the difficulty of finding another, but you just have to believe that it seemed about as important to me just then as though it were a hundred dollars.

"Then I saw a couple of men talking in front of Moody's soda place, and recognized one of them—Mr. Burling—who'd been a friend of my father's. That was relief, I can tell you. Before I knew it I was chattering to him so quick that he couldn't follow what I was getting at.

" 'Now,' he said, 'you know I'm a little deaf and can't understand when you talk that fast! What is it you want, Henry? Tell me from the beginning.'

" 'Have you got any change with you?' I asked him just as loud as I dared. 'I just want—' Then I stopped short; a man a few feet away had turned around and was looking at us. It was Mr. Deems, the First Vice-President of the Cotton National Bank."

Hemmick paused, and it was still light enough for Abercrombie to see that he was shaking his head to and fro in a puzzled way. When he spoke his voice held a quality of pained surprise, a quality that it might have carried over twenty years.

"I never *could* understand what it was that came over me then. I must have been sort of crazy with the heat—that's all I can decide. Instead of just saying, 'Howdy' to Mr. Deems, in a natural way, and telling Mr. Burling I wanted to borrow a nickel for tobacco, because I'd left my purse at home, I turned away quick as a flash and began walking up the street at a great rate, feeling like a criminal who had come near being caught.

"Before I'd gone a block I was sorry. I could almost hear the conversation that must've been taking place between those two men:

" 'What do you reckon's the matter with that young man?' Mr. Burling would say without meaning any harm. 'Came up to me all excited and wanted to know if I had any money, and then he saw you and rushed away like he was crazy.'

"And I could almost see Mr. Deems' big eyes get narrow with suspicion and watch him twist up his trousers and come strolling along after me. I was in a real panic now, and no mistake. Suddenly I saw a one-horse surrey going by, and recognized Bill Kennedy, a friend of mine, driving it. I yelled at him, but he didn't hear me. Then I yelled again, but he didn't pay any attention, so I started after him at a run, swaying from side to side, I guess, like I was drunk, and calling his name every few minutes. He looked around once, but he didn't see me; he kept right on going and turned out of sight at the next corner. I stopped then because I was too weak to go any farther. I was just about to sit down on the curb and rest when I looked around, and the first thing I saw was Mr. Deems walking after me as fast as he could come. There wasn't any of my imagination about it this time—the look in his eyes showed he wanted to know what was the matter with *me*!

"Well, that's about all I remember clearly until about twenty minutes later, when I was at home trying to unlock my trunk with fingers that were trembling like a tuning fork. Before I could get it open, Mr. Deems and a policeman came in. I began talking all at once about not being a thief and trying to tell them what had happened, but I guess I was sort of hysterical, and the more I said the worse matters were. When I managed to get the story out it seemed sort of crazy, even to me—and it was true—it was true, true as I've told you—every word!—that one penny that I lost somewhere down by the station—" Hemmick broke off and began laughing grotesquely—as though the excitement that had come over him as he finished his tale was a weakness of which he was ashamed. When he resumed it was with an affectation of nonchalance.

"I'm not going into the details of what happened because nothing much did—at least not on the scale you judge events by up North. It cost me my job, and I changed a good name for a bad one. Somebody tattled and somebody lied, and the impression got around that I'd lost a lot of the bank's money and had been tryin' to cover it up.

"I had an awful time getting a job after that. Finally I got a statement out of the bank that contradicted the wildest of the stories that had started, but the people who were still interested said it was just because the bank didn't want any fuss or scandal—and the rest had forgotten: that is they'd forgotten what had happened, but they remembered that somehow I just wasn't a young fellow to be trusted——"

Hemmick paused and laughed again, still without enjoyment, but bitterly, uncomprehendingly, and with a profound helplessness.

"So, you see, that's why I didn't go to Cincinnati," he said slowly; "my mother was alive then, and this was a pretty bad blow to her. She had an idea—one of those old-fashioned Southern ideas that stick in people's heads down here—that somehow I ought to stay here in town and prove myself honest. She had it on her mind, and she wouldn't hear of my going. She said that the day I went'd be the day she'd die. So I sort of had to stay till I'd got back my—my reputation."

"How long did that take?" asked Abercrombie quietly.

"About—ten years."

"Oh——"

"Ten years," repeated Hemmick, staring out into the gathering darkness. "This is a little town you see: I say ten years because it was about ten years when the last reference to it came to my ears. But I was married long before that; had a kid. Cincinnati was out of my mind by that time."

"Of course," agreed Abercrombie.

They were both silent for a moment—then Hemmick added apologetically:

"That was sort of a long story, and I don't know if it could have interested you much. But you asked me——"

"It *did* interest me," answered Abercrombie politely. "It interested me tremendously. It interested me much more than I thought it would."

It occurred to Hemmick that he himself had never realized what a curious, rounded tale it was. He saw dimly now that what had seemed to him only a fragment, a grotesque interlude was really significant, complete. It was an interesting story; it was the story upon which turned the failure of his life. Abercrombie's voice broke in upon his thoughts.

"You see, it's so different from my story," Abercrombie was saying. "It was an accident that you stayed—and it was an accident that I went away. You deserve more actual—actual credit, if there is such a thing in the world, for your intention of getting out and getting on. You see, I'd more or less gone wrong at seventeen. I was—well, what you call a Jelly-bean. All I wanted was to take it easy through life—and one day I just happened to see a sign up above my head that had on it: 'Special rate to Atlanta, three dollars and forty-two cents.' So I took out my change and counted it——"

Hemmick nodded. Still absorbed in his own story, he had forgotten the importance, the comparative magnificence of Abercrombie. Then suddenly he found himself listening sharply:

"I had just three dollars and forty-one cents in my pocket. But, you see, I was standing in line with a lot of other young fellows down by the Union Depot about to enlist in the army for three years. And I saw that extra penny on the walk not three feet away. I saw it because it was brand new and shining in the sun like gold."

The Alabama night had settled over the street, and as the blue drew down upon the dust the outlines of the two men had become less distinct, so that it was not easy for any one who passed along the walk to tell that one of these men was of the few and the other of no importance. All the detail was gone—Abercrombie's fine gold wrist watch, his collar, that he ordered by the dozen from London, the dignity that sat upon him in his chair—all faded and were engulfed with Hemmick's awkward suit and preposterous humped shoes into that pervasive depth of night that, like death, made nothing matter, nothing differentiate, nothing remain. And a little later on a passerby saw only the two glowing disks about the size of a penny that marked the rise and fall of their cigars.

Dice, Brassknuckles & Guitar

(*Hearst's International Magazine*, May 1923)*

"Dice, Brassknuckles & Guitar" was written in Great Neck, Long Island, in January 1923. The Fitzgeralds had moved East from St. Paul in October 1922 because they missed New York and because he wanted to be near Broadway for the production of his ill-starred comedy, *The Vegetable*. "Dice" was the first story submitted under an option with the Hearst magazines for his 1923 story output. *International* paid $1500 for it—a $600 increase over what *Metropolitan* had paid Fitzgerald the year before. The story was printed with the headline "A Typical Fitzgerald Story."

"Dice" is one of the *Gatsby* cluster of stories written in 1922-1923 in which Fitzgerald can be seen trying out material that would be developed in the novel, written in 1924. Although treated comically, the subject of "Dice" is the familiar Fitzgerald theme of the hardness of the rich. Amanthis's comment to the outsider—"You're better than all of them put together, Jim."—prefigures Nick Carraway's recognition that Gatsby is "worth the whole damn bunch put together." Another recurring Fitzgerald theme in "Dice" is the cultural conflict between the South and the North.

Parts of New Jersey, as you know, are under water, and other parts are under continual surveillance by the authorities. But here and there lie patches of garden country dotted with old-fashioned frame mansions, which have wide shady porches and a red swing on the lawn. And perhaps, on the widest and shadiest of the porches there is even a hammock left over from the hammock days, stirring gently in a mid-Victorian wind.

When tourists come to such last-century landmarks they stop their cars and gaze for a while and then mutter: "Well, thank God this age is joined on to *some*thing" or else they say: "Well, of course, that house is mostly halls and has a thousand rats and one bathroom, but there's an atmosphere about it——"

The tourist doesn't stay long. He drives on to his Elizabethan

---

*"Dice, Brassknuckles & Guitar" is the only story in this volume which has appeared in a collection. It was added to the paperback edition of *Bits of Paradise* (New York: Pocket Books, [1976]). This story is included here to make it permanently available in a clothbound edition.

villa of pressed cardboard or his early Norman meat-market or his medieval Italian pigeon-coop—because this is the twentieth century and Victorian houses are as unfashionable as the works of Mrs. Humphry Ward.

He can't see the hammock from the road—but sometimes there's a girl in the hammock. There was this afternoon. She was asleep in it and apparently unaware of the esthetic horrors which surrounded her, the stone statue of Diana, for instance, which grinned idiotically under the sunlight on the lawn.

There was something enormously yellow about the whole scene—there was this sunlight, for instance, that was yellow, and the hammock was of the particularly hideous yellow peculiar to hammocks, and the girl's yellow hair was spread out upon the hammock in a sort of invidious comparison.

She slept with her lips closed and her hands clasped behind her head, as it is proper for young girls to sleep. Her breast rose and fell slightly with no more emphasis than the sway of the hammock's fringe.

Her name, Amanthis, was as old-fashioned as the house she lived in. I regret to say that her mid-Victorian connections ceased abruptly at this point.

Now if this were a moving picture (as, of course, I hope it will some day be) I would take as many thousand feet of her as I was allowed—then I would move the camera up close and show the yellow down on the back of her neck where her hair stopped and the warm color of her cheeks and arms, because I like to think of her sleeping there, as you yourself might have slept, back in your young days. Then I would hire a man named Israel Glucose to write some idiotic line of transition, and switch thereby to another scene that was taking place at no particular spot far down the road.

In a moving automobile sat a southern gentleman accompanied by his body-servant. He was on his way, after a fashion, to New York but he was somewhat hampered by the fact that the upper and lower portions of his automobile were no longer in exact juxtaposition. In fact from time to time the two riders would dismount, shove the body on to the chassis, corner to corner, and then continue onward, vibrating slightly in involuntary unison with the motor.

Except that it had no door in back the car might have been built early in the mechanical age. It was covered with the mud of eight states and adorned in front by an enormous but defunct motometer and behind by a mangy pennant bearing the legend "Tarleton, Ga." In the dim past someone had begun to paint the hood yellow but unfortunately had been called away when but half through the task.

As the gentleman and his body-servant were passing the house where Amanthis lay beautifully asleep in the hammock, something happened—the body fell off the car. My only apology for stating this so suddenly is that it happened very suddenly indeed. When the noise had died down and the dust had drifted away master and man arose and inspected the two halves.

"Look-a-there," said the gentleman in disgust, "the doggone thing got all separated that time."

"She bust in two," agreed the body-servant.

"Hugo," said the gentleman, after some consideration, "we got to get a hammer an' nails an' *tack* it on."

They glanced up at the Victorian house. On all sides faintly irregular fields stretched away to a faintly irregular unpopulated horizon. There was no choice, so the black Hugo opened the gate and followed his master up a gravel walk, casting only the blasé glances of a confirmed traveler at the red swing and the stone statue of Diana which turned on them a storm-crazed stare.

At the exact moment when they reached the porch Amanthis awoke, sat up suddenly and looked them over.

The gentleman was young, perhaps twenty-four, and his name was Jim Powell. He was dressed in a tight and dusty readymade suit which was evidently expected to take flight at a moment's notice, for it was secured to his body by a line of six preposterous buttons.

There were supernumerary buttons upon the coat-sleeves also and Amanthis could not resist a glance to determine whether or not more buttons ran up the side of his trouser leg. But the trouser bottoms were distinguished only by their shape, which was that of a bell. His vest was cut low, barely restraining an amazing necktie from fluttering in the wind.

He bowed formally, dusting his knees with a thatched straw hat. Simultaneously he smiled, half shutting his faded blue eyes and displaying white and beautifully symmetrical teeth.

"Good evenin'," he said in abandoned Georgian. "My automobile has met with an accident out yonder by your gate. I wondered if it wouldn't be too much to ask you if I could have the use of a hammer and some tacks—nails, for a little while."

Amanthis laughed. For a moment she laughed uncontrollably. Mr. Jim Powell laughed, politely and appreciatively, with her. His body-servant, deep in the throes of colored adolescence, alone preserved a dignified gravity.

"I better introduce who I am, maybe," said the visitor. "My name's Powell. I'm a resident of Tarleton, Georgia. This here nigger's my boy Hugo."

"Your *son!*" The girl stared from one to the other in wild fascination.

"No, he's my body-servant, I guess you'd call it. We call a nigger a boy down yonder."

At this reference to the finer customs of his native soil the boy Hugo put his hands behind his back and looked darkly and superciliously down the lawn.

"Yas'm," he muttered, "I'm a body-servant."

"Where you going in your automobile," demanded Amanthis.

"Goin' north for the summer."

"Where to?"

The tourist waved his hand with a careless gesture as if to indicate the Adirondacks, the Thousand Islands, Newport—but he said:

"We're tryin' New York."

"Have you ever been there before?"

"Never have. But I been to Atlanta lots of times. An' we passed through all kinds of cities this trip. Man!"

He whistled to express the enormous spectacularity of his recent travels.

"Listen," said Amanthis intently, "you better have something to eat. Tell your—your body-servant to go 'round in back and ask the cook to send us out some sandwiches and lemonade. Or maybe you don't drink lemonade—very few people do any more."

Mr. Powell by a circular motion of his finger sped Hugo on the designated mission. Then he seated himself gingerly in a rocking-chair and began revolving his thatched straw hat rapidly in his hands.

"You cer'nly are mighty kind," he told her. "An' if I wanted anything stronger than lemonade I got a bottle of good old corn out in the car. I brought it along because I thought maybe I wouldn't be able to drink the whisky they got up here."

"Listen," she said, "my name's Powell too. Amanthis Powell."

"Say, is that right?" He laughed ecstatically. "Maybe we're kin to each other. I come from mighty good people," he went on. "Pore though. I got some money because my aunt she was using it to keep her in a sanitarium and she died." He paused, presumably out of respect to his late aunt. Then he concluded with brisk nonchalance, "I ain't touched the principal but I got a lot of the income all at once so I thought I'd come north for the summer."

At this point Hugo reappeared on the veranda steps and became audible.

"White lady back there she asked me don't I want eat some too. What I tell her?"

"You tell her yes mamm if she be so kind," directed his master. And as Hugo retired he confided to Amanthis: "That boy's got no sense at all. He don't want to do nothing without I tell him he can. I brought him up," he added, not without pride.

When the sandwiches arrived Mr. Powell stood up. He was unaccustomed to white servants and obviously expected an introduction.

"Are you a married lady?" he inquired of Amanthis, when the servant was gone.

"No," she answered, and added from the security of eighteen, "I'm an old maid."

Again he laughed politely.

"You mean you're a society girl."

She shook her head. Mr. Powell noted with embarrassed enthusiasm the particular yellowness of her yellow hair.

"Does this old place look like it?" she said cheerfully. "No, you perceive in me a daughter of the countryside. Color—one hundred percent spontaneous—in the daytime anyhow. Suitors—promising young barbers from the neighboring village with somebody's late hair still clinging to their coat-sleeves."

"Your daddy oughtn't to let you go with a country barber," said the tourist disapprovingly. He considered——"You ought to be a New York society girl."

"No." Amanthis shook her head sadly. "I'm too good-looking. To be a New York society girl you have to have a long nose and projecting teeth and dress like the actresses did three years ago."

Jim began to tap his foot rhythmically on the porch and in a moment Amanthis discovered that she was unconsciously doing the same thing.

"Stop!" she commanded, "Don't make me do that."

He looked down at his foot.

"Excuse me," he said humbly. "I don't know—it's just something I do."

This intense discussion was now interrupted by Hugo who appeared on the steps bearing a hammer and a handful of nails.

Mr. Powell arose unwillingly and looked at his watch.

"We got to go, daggone it," he said, frowning heavily. "See here. Wouldn't you *like* to be a New York society girl and go to those dances an' all, like you read about, where they throw gold pieces away?"

She looked at him with a curious expression.

"Don't your folks know some society people?" he went on.

"All I've got's my daddy—and, you see, he's a judge."

"That's too bad," he agreed.

She got herself by some means from the hammock and they went down toward the road, side by side.

"Well, I'll keep my eyes open for you and let you know," he persisted. "A pretty girl like you ought to go around in society. We may be kin to each other, you see, and us Powells ought to stick together."

"What are you going to do in New York?"

They were now almost at the gate and the tourist pointed to the two depressing sectors of his automobile.

"I'm goin' to drive a taxi. This one right here. Only it's got so it busts in two all the time."

"You're going to drive *that* in New York?"

Jim looked at her uncertainly. Such a pretty girl should certainly control the habit of shaking all over upon no provocation at all.

"Yes mamm," he said with dignity.

Amanthis watched while they placed the upper half of the car upon the lower half and nailed it severely into place. Then Mr. Powell took the wheel and his body-servant climbed in beside him.

"I'm cer'nly very much obliged to you indeed for your hospitality. Convey my respects to your father."

"I will," she assured him. "Come back and see me, if you don't mind barbers in the room."

He dismissed this unpleasant thought with a gesture.

"Your company would always be charming." He put the car into gear as though to drown out the temerity of his parting speech. "You're the prettiest girl I've seen up north—by far."

Then with a groan and a rattle Mr. Powell of southern Georgia with his own car and his own body-servant and his own ambitions and his own private cloud of dust continued on north for the summer.

She thought she would never see him again. She lay in her hammock, slim and beautiful, opened her left eye slightly to see June come in and then closed it and retired contentedly back into her dreams.

But one day when the midsummer vines had climbed the precarious sides of the red swing in the lawn, Mr. Jim Powell of Tarleton, Georgia, came vibrating back into her life. They sat on the wide porch as before.

"I've got a great scheme," he told her.

"Did you drive your taxi like you said?"

"Yes mamm, but the business was right bad. I waited around in front of all those hotels and theaters an' nobody ever got in."

"*Nobody?*"

"Well, one night there was some drunk fellas they got in, only just as I was gettin' started my automobile came apart. And another night it was rainin' and there wasn't no other taxis and a lady got in because she said she had to go a long ways. But before we got there she made me stop and she got out. She seemed kinda mad and she went walkin' off in the rain. Mighty proud lot of people they got up in New York."

"And so you're going home?" asked Amanthis sympathetically.

"No *mamm*. I got an idea." His blue eyes grew narrow. "Has that barber been around here—with hair on his sleeves?"

"No. He's—he's gone away."

"Well, then, first thing is I want to leave this car of mine here with you, if that's all right. It ain't the right color for a taxi. To pay for its keep I'd like to have you drive it just as much as you want. 'Long as you got a hammer an' nails with you there ain't much bad that can happen——"

"I'll take care of it," interrupted Amanthis, "but where are *you* going?"

"Southampton. It's about the most aristocratic watering trough—watering-place there is around here, so that's where I'm going."

She sat up in amazement.

"What are you going to do there?"

"Listen." He leaned toward her confidentially. "Were you serious about wanting to be a New York society girl?"

"Deadly serious."

"That's all I wanted to know," he said inscrutably. "You just wait here on this porch a couple of weeks and—and sleep. And if any barbers come to see you with hair on their sleeves you tell 'em you're too sleepy to see 'em."

"What then?"

"Then you'll hear from me. Just tell your old daddy he can do all the judging he wants but you're goin' to do some *dancin'*. Mamm," he continued decisively, "you talk about society! Before one month I'm goin' to have you in more society than you ever saw."

Further than this he would say nothing. His manner conveyed that she was going to be suspended over a perfect pool of gaiety and violently immersed, to an accompaniment of: "Is it gay enough for you, mamm? Shall I let in a little more excitement, mamm?"

"Well," answered Amanthis, lazily considering, "there are few things for which I'd forego the luxury of sleeping through July and August—but if you'll write me a letter I'll—I'll run up to Southampton.

Jim snapped his fingers ecstatically.

"More society," he assured her with all the confidence at his command, "than anybody ever saw."

Three days later a young man wearing a straw hat that might have been cut from the thatched roof of an English cottage rang the doorbell of the enormous and astounding Madison Harlan house at Southampton. He asked the butler if there were any people in the house between the ages of sixteen and twenty. He was informed that Miss Genevieve Harlan and Mr. Ronald Harlan answered that description and thereupon he handed in a most peculiar card and requested in fetching Georgian that it be brought to their attention.

As a result he was closeted for almost an hour with Mr. Ronald Harlan (who was a student at the Hillkiss School) and Miss Genevieve Harlan (who was not uncelebrated at Southampton dances). When he left he bore a short note in Miss Harlan's handwriting which he presented together with his peculiar card at the next large estate. It happened to be that of the Clifton Garneaus. Here, as if by magic, the same audience was granted him.

He went on—it was a hot day, and men who could not afford to do so were carrying their coats on the public highway, but Jim, a native of southernmost Georgia, was as fresh and cool at the last house as at the first. He visited ten houses that day. Anyone following him in his course might have taken him to be some curiously gifted book-agent with a much sought-after volume as his stock in trade.

There was something in his unexpected demand for the adolescent members of the family which made hardened butlers lose their critical acumen. As he left each house a close observer might have seen that fascinated eyes followed him to the door and excited voices whispered something which hinted at a future meeting.

The second day he visited twelve houses. Southampton has grown enormously—he might have kept on his round for a week and never seen the same butler twice—but it was only the palatial, the amazing houses which intrigued him.

On the third day he did a thing that many people have been told to do and few have done—he hired a hall. Perhaps the sixteen-to-twenty-year-old people in the enormous houses had told him to. The hall he hired had once been "Mr. Snorkey's Private Gymnasium for Gentlemen." It was situated over a garage on the south edge of Southampton and in the days of its prosperity had been, I regret to say, a place where gentlemen could, under Mr. Snorkey's direction, work off the effects of the night before. It was now abandoned—Mr. Snorkey had given up and gone away and died.

We will now skip three weeks during which time we may assume that the project which had to do with hiring a hall and visiting the two dozen largest houses in Southampton got under way.

The day to which we will skip was the July day on which Mr. James Powell sent a wire to Miss Amanthis Powell saying that if she still aspired to the gaiety of the highest society she should set out for Southampton by the earliest possible train. He himself would meet her at the station.

Jim was no longer a man of leisure, so when she failed to arrive at the time her wire had promised he grew restless. He supposed she was coming on a later train, turned to go back to his—his project—and met her entering the station from the street side.

"Why, how did you——"

"Well," said Amanthis, "I arrived this morning instead, and I didn't want to bother you so I found a respectable, not to say dull, boarding-house on the Ocean Road."

She was quite different from the indolent Amanthis of the porch hammock, he thought. She wore a suit of robins' egg blue and a rakish young hat with a curling feather—she was attired not unlike those young ladies between sixteen and twenty who of late were absorbing his attention. Yes, she would do very well.

He bowed her profoundly into a taxicab and got in beside her.

"Isn't it about time you told me your scheme?" she suggested.

"Well, it's about these society girls up here." He waved his hand airily. "I know 'em all."

"Where are they?"

"Right now they're with Hugo. You remember—that's my body-servant."

"With Hugo!" Her eyes widened. "Why? What's it all about?"

"Well, I got—I got sort of a school, I guess you'd call it."

"A school?"

"It's a sort of Academy. And I'm the head of it. I invented it."

He flipped a card from his case as though he were shaking down a thermometer.

"Look."

She took the card. In large lettering it bore the legend

JAMES POWELL; J. M.
"Dice, Brassknuckles and Guitar"

She stared in amazement.

"Dice, Brassknuckles and Guitar?" she repeated in awe.

"Yes mamm."

"What does it mean? What——do you *sell* 'em?"

"No mamm, I teach 'em. It's a profession."

"Dice, Brassknuckles and Guitar? What's the J. M.?"

"That stands for Jazz Master."

"But what *is* it? What's it about?"

"Well, you see, it's like this. One night when I was in New York I got talkin' to a young fella who was drunk. He was one of my fares. And he'd taken some society girl somewhere and lost her."

"*Lost* her?"

"Yes mamm. He forgot her, I guess. And he was right worried. Well, I got to thinkin' that these girls nowadays—these society girls— they lead a sort of dangerous life and my course of study offers a means of protection against these dangers."

"You teach 'em to use brassknuckles?"

"Yes mamm, if necessary. Look here, you take a girl and she goes into some cafe where she's got no business to go. Well then, her escort he gets a little too much to drink an' he goes to sleep an' then some other fella comes up and says 'Hello, sweet mamma' or whatever one of those mashers says up here. What does she do? She can't scream, on account of no real lady'll scream nowadays—no—She just reaches down in her pocket and slips her fingers into a pair of Powell's defensive brassknuckles, debutante's size, executes what I call the Society Hook, and *Wham*! that big fella's on his way to the cellar."

"Well—what—what's the guitar for?" whispered the awed Amanthis. "Do they have to knock somebody over with the guitar?"

"No, *mamm*!" exclaimed Jim in horror. "No mamm. In my course no lady would be taught to raise a guitar against anybody. I teach 'em to play. Shucks! you ought to hear 'em. Why, when I've given 'em two lessons you'd think some of 'em was colored."

"And the dice?"

"Dice? I'm related to a dice. My grandfather was a dice. I teach 'em how to make those dice perform. I protect pocketbook as well as person."

"Did you——Have you got any pupils?"

"Mamm I got all the really nice, rich people in the place. What I told you ain't all. I teach lots of things. I teach 'em the jellyroll—and the Mississippi Sunrise. Why, there was one girl she came to me and said she wanted to learn to snap her fingers. I mean *real*ly snap 'em— like they do. She said she never could snap her fingers since she was little. I gave her two lessons and now *Wham*! Her daddy says he's goin' to leave home."

"When do you have it?" demanded the weak and shaken Amanthis.

"Three times a week. We're goin' there right now."

"And where do I fit in?"

"Well, you'll just be one of the pupils. I got it fixed up that you come from very high-tone people down in New Jersey. I didn't tell 'em your daddy was a judge——I told 'em he was the man that had the patent on lump sugar."

She gasped.

"So all you got to do," he went on, "is to pretend you never saw no barber."

They were now at the south end of the village and Amanthis saw a row of cars parked in front of a two-story building. The cars were all low, long, rakish and of a brilliant hue. They were the sort of car that is manufactured to solve the millionaire's problem on his son's eighteenth birthday.

Then Amanthis was ascending a narrow stairs to the second story. Here, painted on a door from which came the sounds of music and laughter were the words:

JAMES POWELL; J. M.
"Dice, Brassknuckles and Guitar"
Mon.—Wed.—Fri.
Hours 3-5 P.M.

"Now if you'll just step this way——" said the Principal, pushing open the door.

Amanthis found herself in a long, bright room, populated with girls and men of about her own age. The scene presented itself to her at first as a sort of animated afternoon tea but after a moment she began to see, here and there, a motive and a pattern to the proceedings.

The students were scattered into groups, sitting, kneeling, standing, but all rapaciously intent on the subjects which engrossed them. From six young ladies gathered in a ring around some indistinguishable objects came a medley of cries and exclamations— plaintive, pleading, supplicating, exhorting, imploring and lamenting—their voices serving as tenor to an undertone of mysterious clatters.

Next to this group, four young men were surrounding an adolescent black, who proved to be none other than Mr. Powell's late body-servant. The young men were roaring at Hugo apparently unrelated phrases, expressing a wide gamut of emotion. Now their voices rose to a sort of clamor, now they spoke softly and gently, with mellow implication. Every little while Hugo would answer them with words of approbation, correction or disapproval.

"What are they doing?" whispered Amanthis to Jim.

"That there's a course in southern accent. Lot of young men up here want to learn southern accent—so we teach it—Georgia, Florida, Alabama, Eastern Shore, Ole Virginian. Some of 'em even want straight nigger—for song purposes."

They walked around among the groups. Some girls with metal knuckles were furiously insulting two punching bags on each of which was painted the leering, winking face of a "masher." A mixed group, led by a banjo tom-tom, were rolling harmonic syllables from their guitars. There were couples dancing flat-footed in the corner to a phonograph record made by Rastus Muldoon's Savannah Band; there were couples stalking a slow Chicago with a Memphis Side-swoop solemnly around the room.

"Are there any rules?" asked Amanthis.

Jim considered.

"Well," he answered finally, "they can't smoke unless they're over sixteen, and the boys have got to shoot square dice and I don't let 'em bring liquor into the Academy."

"I see."

"And now, Miss Powell, if you're ready I'll ask you to take off your hat and go over and join Miss Genevieve Harlan at that punching bag in the corner." He raised his voice. "Hugo," he called, "there's a new student here. Equip her with a pair of Powell's Defensive Brassknuckles—debutante size."

I regret to say that I never saw Jim Powell's famous Jazz School in action nor followed his personally conducted tours into the mysteries of Dice, Brassknuckles and Guitar. So I can give you only such details as were later reported to me by one of his admiring pupils. During all the discussion of it afterwards no one ever denied that it was an enormous success, and no pupil ever regretted having received its degree—Bachelor of Jazz.

The parents innocently assumed that it was a sort of musical and dancing academy, but its real curriculum was transmitted from Santa Barbara to Biddeford Pool by that underground associated press which links up the so-called younger generation. Invitations to visit Southampton were at a premium—and Southampton generally is almost as dull for young people as Newport.

The Academy branched out with a small but well-groomed Jazz Orchestra.

"If I could keep it dark," Jim confided to Amanthis, "I'd have up Rastus Muldoon's Band from Savannah. That's the band I've always wanted to lead."

He was making money. His charges were not exorbitant—as a rule his pupils were not particularly flush—but he moved from his boarding-house to the Casino Hotel where he took a suite and had Hugo serve him his breakfast in bed.

The establishing of Amanthis as a member of Southampton's younger set was easier than he had expected. Within a week she was known to everyone in the school by her first name. Miss Genevieve Harlan took such a fancy to her that she was invited to a sub-deb dance at the Harlan house—and evidently acquitted herself with tact, for thereafter she was invited to almost every such entertainment in Southampton.

Jim saw less of her than he would have liked. Not that her manner toward him changed—she walked with him often in the mornings, she was always willing to listen to his plans—but after she was taken up by the fashionable her evenings seemed to be monopolized. Several times Jim arrived at her boarding-house to find her out of breath, as if she had just come in at a run, presumably from some festivity in which he had no share.

So as the summer waned he found that one thing was lacking to complete the triumph of his enterprise. Despite the hospitality shown to Amanthis, the doors of Southampton were closed to him. Polite to, or rather, fascinated by him as his pupils were from three to five, after that hour they moved in another world.

His was the position of a golf professional who, though he may fraternize, and even command, on the links, loses his privileges with the sun-down. He may look in the club window but he cannot dance. And, likewise, it was not given to Jim to see his teachings put into effect. He could hear the gossip of the morning after—that was all.

But while the golf professional, being English, holds himself proudly below his patrons, Jim Powell, who "came from a right good family down there—pore though," lay awake many nights in his hotel bed and heard the music drifting into his window from the Katzbys' house or the Beach Club, and turned over restlessly and wondered what was the matter. In the early days of his success he had bought himself a dress-suit, thinking that he would soon have a chance to wear it—but it still lay untouched in the box in which it had come from the tailor's.

Perhaps, he thought, there was some real gap which separated him from the rest. It worried him. One boy in particular, Martin Van Vleck, son of Van Vleck the ash-can King, made him conscious of the gap. Van Vleck was twenty-one, a tutoring-school product who still hoped to enter Yale. Several times Jim had heard him make remarks not intended for Jim's ear—once in regard to the suit with multiple buttons, again in reference to Jim's long, pointed shoes. Jim had passed these over.

He knew that Van Vleck was attending the school chiefly to monopolize the time of little Martha Katzby, who was just sixteen and too young to have attention of a boy of twenty-one—especially the attention of Van Vleck, who was so spiritually exhausted by his educational failures that he drew on the rather exhaustible innocence of sixteen.

It was late in September, two days before the Harlan dance which was to be the last and biggest of the season for this younger crowd. Jim, as usual, was not invited. He had hoped that he would be. The two young Harlans, Ronald and Genevieve, had been his first patrons when he arrived at Southampton—and it was Genevieve who had taken such a fancy to Amanthis. To have been at their dance—the most magnificent dance of all—would have crowned and justified the success of the waning summer.

His class, gathering for the afternoon, was loudly anticipating the next day's revel with no more thought of him than if he had been the family butler. Hugo, standing beside Jim, chuckled suddenly and remarked:

"Look yonder that man Van Vleck. He paralyzed. He been havin' powerful lotta corn this evenin'."

Jim turned and stared at Van Vleck, who had linked arms with little Martha Katzby and was saying something to her in a low voice. Jim saw her try to draw away.

He put his whistle to his mouth and blew it.

"All right," he cried, "Le's go! Group one tossin' the drumstick, high an' zig-zag, group two, test your mouth organs for the Riverfront Shuffle. Promise 'em sugar! Flatfoots this way! Orchestra—let's have the Florida Drag-Out played as a dirge."

There was an unaccustomed sharpness in his voice and the exercises began with a mutter of facetious protest.

With his smoldering grievance directing itself toward Van Vleck, Jim was walking here and there among the groups when Hugo tapped him suddenly on the arm. He looked around. Two participants had withdrawn from the mouth organ institute—one of them was Van Vleck and he was giving a drink out of his flask to fifteen-year-old Ronald Harlan.

Jim strode across the room. Van Vleck turned defiantly as he came up.

"All right," said Jim, trembling with anger, "you know the rules. You get out!"

The music died slowly away and there was a sudden drifting over in the direction of the trouble. Somebody snickered. An atmosphere of anticipation formed instantly. Despite the fact that they all liked Jim their sympathies were divided—Van Vleck was one of them.

"Get out!" repeated Jim, more quietly.

"Are you talking to me?" inquired Van Vleck coldly.

"Yes."

"Then you better say 'sir.' "

"I wouldn't say 'sir' to anybody that'd give a little boy whisky! You get out!"

"Look here!" said Van Vleck furiously. "You've butted in once too much. I've known Ronald since he was two years old. Ask *him* if he wants *you* to tell him what he can do!"

Ronald Harlan, his dignity offended, grew several years older and looked haughtily at Jim.

"Mind your own business!" he said defiantly, albeit a little guiltily.

"Hear that?" demanded Van Vleck. "My God, can't you see you're just a servant? Ronald here'd no more think of asking you to his party than he would his bootlegger."

"Youbettergetout!" cried Jim incoherently.

Van Vleck did not move. Reaching out suddenly, Jim caught his wrist and jerking it behind his back forced his arm upward until Van Vleck bent forward in agony. Jim leaned and picked the flask from the floor with his free hand. Then he signed Hugo to open the hall-door, uttered an abrupt "You *step!*" and marched his helpless captive out into the hall where he literally *threw* him downstairs, head over heels bumping from wall to banister, and hurled his flask after him.

Then he reentered his academy, closed the door behind him and stood with his back against it.

"It—it happens to be a rule that nobody drinks while in this Academy." He paused, looking from face to face, finding there sympathy, awe, disapproval, conflicting emotions. They stirred uneasily. He caught Amanthis's eye, fancied he saw a faint nod of encouragement and, with almost an effort, went on:

"I just *had* to throw that fella out an' you-all know it." Then he concluded with a transparent affectation of dismissing an unimportant matter——"All right, let's go! Orchestra——!"

But no one felt exactly like going on. The spontaneity of the proceedings had been violently disturbed. Someone made a run or two on the sliding guitar and several of the girls began whamming at the leer on the punching bags, but Ronald Harlan, followed by two other boys, got their hats and went silently out the door.

Jim and Hugo moved among the groups as usual until a certain measure of routine activity was restored but the enthusiasm was unrecapturable and Jim, shaken and discouraged, considered discontinuing school for the day. But he dared not. If they went home in this mood they might not come back. The whole thing depended on a mood. He must recreate it, he thought frantically—now, at once!

But try as he might, there was little response. He himself was not happy—he could communicate no gaiety to them. They watched his efforts listlessly and, he thought, a little contemptuously.

Then the tension snapped when the door burst suddenly open, precipitating a brace of middle-aged and excited women into the room. No person over twenty-one had ever entered the Academy before—but Van Vleck had gone direct to headquarters. The women were Mrs. Clifton Garneau and Mrs. Poindexter Katzby, two of the most fashionable and, at present, two of the most flurried women in Southampton. They were in search of their daughters as, in these days, so many women continually are.

The business was over in about three minutes.

"And as for you!" cried Mrs. Clifton Garneau in an awful voice, "your idea is to run a bar and—and *opium* den for children! You ghastly, horrible, unspeakable man! I can smell morphin fumes! Don't tell me I can't smell morphin fumes. I can smell morphin fumes!"

"And," bellowed Mrs. Poindexter Katzby, "you have colored men around! You have colored girls hidden! I'm going to the police!"

Not content with herding their own daughters from the room, they insisted on the exodus of their friends' daughters. Jim was not a little touched when several of them—including even little Martha Katzby, before she was snatched fiercely away by her mother—came up and shook hands with him. But they were all going, haughtily, regretfully or with shame-faced mutters of apology.

"Good-by," he told them wistfully. "In the morning I'll send you the money that's due you."

And, after all, they were not sorry to go. Outside, the sound of their starting motors, the triumphant put-put of their cut-outs cutting the warm September air, was a jubilant sound—a sound of youth and hopes high as the sun. Down to the ocean, to roll in the waves and forget—forget him and their discomfort at his humiliation.

They were gone—he was alone with Hugo in the room. He sat down suddenly with his face in his hands.

"Hugo," he said huskily. "They don't want us up here."

"Don't you care," said a voice.

He looked up to see Amanthis standing beside him.

"You better go with them," he told her. "You better not be seen here with me."

"Why?"

"Because you're in society now and I'm no better to those people than a servant. You're in society—I fixed that up. You better go or they won't invite you to any of their dances."

"They won't anyhow, Jim," she said gently. "They didn't invite me to the one tomorrow night."

He looked up indignantly.

"They *did*n't?"

She shook her head.

"I'll *make* 'em!" he said wildly. "I'll tell 'em they got to. I'll— I'll——"

She came close to him with shining eyes.

"Don't you mind, Jim," she soothed him. "Don't you mind. They don't matter. We'll have a party of our own tomorrow—just you and I."

"I come from right good folks," he said, defiantly. "Pore though."

She laid her hand softly on his shoulder.

"I understand. You're better than all of them put together, Jim."

He got up and went to the window and stared out mournfully into the late afternoon.

"I reckon I should have let you sleep in that hammock."

She laughed.

"I'm awfully glad you didn't."

He turned and faced the room, and his face was dark.

"Sweep up and lock up, Hugo," he said, his voice trembling. "The summer's over and we're going down home."

Autumn had come early. Jim Powell woke next morning to find his room cool, and the phenomenon of frosted breath in September absorbed him for a moment to the exclusion of the day before. Then the lines of his face drooped with unhappiness as he remembered the humiliation which had washed the cheery glitter from the summer. There was nothing left for him except to go back where he was known, where under no provocation were such things said to white people as had been said to him here.

After breakfast a measure of his customary light-heartedness returned. He was a child of the South—brooding was alien to his nature. He could conjure up an injury only a certain number of times before it faded into the great vacancy of the past.

But when, from force of habit, he strolled over to his defunct establishment, already as obsolete as Snorkey's late sanitarium, melancholy again dwelt in his heart. Hugo was there, a specter of despair, deep in the lugubrious blues amidst his master's broken hopes.

Usually a few words from Jim were enough to raise him to an inarticulate ecstasy, but this morning there were no words to utter. For two months Hugo had lived on a pinnacle of which he had never dreamed. He had enjoyed his work simply and passionately, arriving before school hours and lingering long after Mr. Powell's pupils had gone.

The day dragged toward a not-too-promising night. Amanthis did not appear and Jim wondered forlornly if she had not changed her mind about dining with him that night. Perhaps it would be better if she were not seen with them. But then, he reflected dismally, no one would see them anyhow—everybody was going to the big dance at the Harlans' house.

When twilight threw unbearable shadows into the school hall he locked it up for the last time, took down the sign "James Powell; J. M., Dice, Brassknuckles and Guitar," and went back to his hotel. Looking over his scrawled accounts he saw that there was another month's rent to pay on his school and some bills for windows broken and new equipment that had hardly been used. Jim had lived in state, and he realized that financially he would have nothing to show for the summer after all.

When he had finished he took his new dress-suit out of its box and inspected it, running his hand over the satin of the lapels and lining. This, at least, he owned and perhaps in Tarleton somebody would ask him to a party where he could wear it.

"Shucks!" he said scoffingly. "It was just a no account old academy, anyhow. Some of those boys round the garage down home could of beat it all hollow."

Whistling "Jeanne of Jelly-bean Town" to a not-dispirited rhythm Jim encased himself in his first dress-suit and walked downtown.

"Orchids," he said to the clerk. He surveyed his purchase with some pride. He knew that no girl at the Harlan dance would wear anything lovelier than these exotic blossoms that leaned languorously backward against green ferns.

In a taxi-cab, carefully selected to look like a private car, he drove to Amanthis's boarding-house. She came down wearing a rose-colored evening dress into which the orchids melted like colors into a sunset.

"I reckon we'll go to the Casino Hotel," he suggested, "unless you got some other place——"

At their table, looking out over the dark ocean, his mood became a contented sadness. The windows were shut against the cool but the orchestra played "Kalula" and "South Sea Moon" and for awhile, with her young loveliness opposite him, he felt himself to be a romantic participant in the life around him. They did not dance, and he was glad—it would have reminded him of that other brighter and more radiant dance to which they could not go.

After dinner they took a taxi and followed the sandy roads for an hour, glimpsing the now starry ocean through the casual trees.

"I want to thank you," she said, "for all you've done for me, Jim."

"That's all right—we Powells ought to stick together."

"What are you going to do?"

"I'm going to Tarleton tomorrow."

"I'm sorry," she said softly. "Are you going to drive down?"

"I got to. I got to get the car south because I couldn't get what she was worth by sellin' it. You don't suppose anybody's stole my car out of your barn?" he asked in sudden alarm.

She repressed a smile.

"No."

"I'm sorry about this—about you," he went on huskily, "and—and I would like to have gone to just one of their dances. You shouldn't of stayed with me yesterday. Maybe it kept 'em from asking you."

"Jim," she suggested eagerly, "let's go and stand outside and listen to their old music. We don't care."

"They'll be coming out," he objected.

"No, it's too cold. Besides there's nothing they could do to you any more than they *have* done."

She gave the chauffeur a direction and a few minutes later they stopped in front of the heavy Georgian beauty of the Madison Harlan house whence the windows cast their gaiety in bright patches on the lawn. There was laughter inside and the plaintive wind of fashionable horns, and now and again the slow, mysterious shuffle of dancing feet.

"Let's go up close," whispered Amanthis in an ecstatic trance, "I want to hear."

They walked toward the house, keeping in the shadow of the great trees. Jim proceeded with awe—suddenly he stopped and seized Amanthis's arm.

"Man!" he cried in an excited whisper. "Do you know what that is?"

"A night watchman?" Amanthis cast a startled look around.

"It's Rastus Muldoon's Band from Savannah! I heard 'em once, and I *know*. It's Rastus Muldoon's Band!"

They moved closer till they could see first pompadours, then slicked male heads, and high coiffures and finally even bobbed hair pressed under black ties. They could distinguish chatter below the ceaseless laughter. Two figures appeared on the porch, gulped something quickly from flasks and returned inside. But the music had bewitched Jim Powell. His eyes were fixed and he moved his feet like a blind man.

Pressed in close behind some dark bushes they listened. The number ended. A breeze from the ocean blew over them and Jim shivered slightly. Then, in a wistful whisper:

"I've always wanted to lead that band. Just once." His voice grew listless. "Come on. Let's go. I reckon I don't belong around here."

He held out his arm to her but instead of taking it she stepped suddenly out of the bushes and into a bright patch of light.

"Come on, Jim," she said startlingly. "Let's go inside."

"What——?"

She seized his arm and though he drew back in a sort of stupefied horror at her boldness she urged him persistently toward the great front door.

"Watch out!" he gasped. "Somebody's coming out of that house and see us."

"No, Jim," she said firmly. "Nobody's coming out of that house—but two people are going in."

"Why?" he demanded wildly, standing in full glare of the porte-cochere lamps. "Why?"

"Why?" she mocked him. "Why, just because this dance happens to be given for me."

He thought she was mad.

"Come home before they see us," he begged her.

The great doors swung open and a gentleman stepped out on the porch. In horror Jim recognized Mr. Madison Harlan. He made a movement as though to break away and run. But the man walked down the steps holding out both hands to Amanthis.

"Hello at last," he cried. "Where on earth have you two been? Cousin Amanthis——" He kissed her, and turned cordially to Jim. "And for you, Mr. Powell," he went on, "to make up for being late you've got to promise that for just one number you're going to lead that band."

New Jersey was warm, all except the part that was under water, and that mattered only to the fishes. All the tourists who rode through the long green miles stopped their cars in front of a spreading old-fashioned country house and looked at the red swing on the lawn and the wide, shady porch, and sighed and drove on—swerving a little to avoid a jet-black body-servant in the road. The body-servant was applying a hammer and nails to a decayed flivver which flaunted from its rear the legend, "Tarleton, Ga."

A girl with yellow hair and a warm color to her face was lying in the hammock looking as though she could fall asleep any moment. Near her sat a gentleman in an extraordinarily tight suit. They had come down together the day before from the fashionable resort at Southampton.

"When you first appeared," she was explaining, "I never thought I'd see you again so I made that up about the barber and all. As a matter of fact, I've been around quite a bit—with or without brassknuckles. I'm coming out this autumn."

"I reckon I had a lot to learn," said Jim.

"And you see," went on Amanthis, looking at him rather anxiously, "I'd been invited up to Southampton to visit my cousins— and when you said you were going, I wanted to see what you'd do. I always slept at the Harlans' but I kept a room at the boarding-house so you wouldn't know. The reason I didn't get there on the right train was because I had to come early and warn a lot of people to pretend not to know me."

Jim got up, nodding his head in comprehension.

"I reckon I and Hugo had better be movin' along. We got to make Baltimore by night."

"That's a long way."

"I want to sleep south tonight," he said simply.

Together they walked down the path and past the idiotic statue of Diana on the lawn.

"You see," added Amanthis gently, "you don't have to be rich up here in order to—to go around, any more than you do in Georgia——" She broke off abruptly, "Won't you come back next year and start another Academy?"

"No mamm, not me. That Mr. Harlan told me I could go on with the one I had but I told him no."

"Haven't you——didn't you make money?"

"No mamm," he answered. "I got enough of my own income to just get me home. I didn't have my principal along. One time I was way ahead but I was livin' high and there was my rent an' apparatus and those musicians. Besides, there at the end I had to pay what they'd advanced me for their lessons."

"You shouldn't have done that!" cried Amanthis indignantly.

"They didn't want me to, but I told 'em they'd have to take it."

He didn't consider it necessary to mention that Mr. Harlan had tried to present him with a check.

They reached the automobile just as Hugo drove in his last nail. Jim opened a pocket of the door and took from it an unlabeled bottle containing a whitish-yellow liquid.

"I intended to get you a present," he told her awkwardly, "but my money got away before I could, so I thought I'd send you something from Georgia. This here's just a personal remembrance. It won't do for you to drink but maybe after you come out into society you might want to show some of those young fellas what good old corn tastes like."

She took the bottle.

"Thank you, Jim."

"That's all right." He turned to Hugo. "I reckon we'll go along now. Give the lady the hammer."

"Oh, you can have the hammer," said Amanthis tearfully. "Oh, won't you promise to come back?"

"Someday—maybe."

He looked for a moment at her yellow hair and her blue eyes misty with sleep and tears. Then he got into his car and as his foot found the clutch his whole manner underwent a change.

"I'll say good-by mamm," he announced with impressive dignity, "we're goin' south for the winter."

The gesture of his straw hat indicated Palm Beach, St. Augustine, Miami. His body-servant spun the crank, gained his seat and became part of the intense vibration into which the automobile was thrown.

"South for the winter," repeated Jim, and then he added softly, "You're the prettiest girl I ever knew. You go back up there and lie down in that hammock, and sleep—sle-eep——"

It was almost a lullaby, as he said it. He bowed to her, magnificently, profoundly, including the whole North in the splendor of his obeisance——

Then they were gone down the road in quite a preposterous cloud of dust. Just before they reached the first bend Amanthis saw them come to a full stop, dismount and shove the top part of the car on to the bottom part. They took their seats again without looking around. Then the bend—and they were out of sight, leaving only a faint brown mist to show that they had passed.

Diamond Dick
and the First Law of Woman

(*Hearst's International Magazine*, April 1924)

"Diamond Dick and the First Law of Woman" was written in Great Neck in December 1923. *International* bought it for $1500.

Fitzgerald had been counting on his play, *The Vegetable*, to solve his money problems. After *The Vegetable* failed at its Atlantic City tryout in November 1923, he was compelled to write himself out of debt with stories. Between November 1923 and April 1924 he wrote ten stories (of which six are included in this collection): "The Sensible Thing," "Rags Martin-Jones and the Pr-nce of W-les," "Diamond Dick and the First Law of Woman," "Gretchen's Forty Winks," "The Baby Party," "The Third Casket," "One of My Oldest Friends," "The Pusher-in-the-Face," "The Unspeakable Egg," and "John Jackson's Arcady." These were competent commercial stories which paid off Fitzgerald's debts and financed the writing of *The Great Gatsby* on the Riviera in the summer of 1924.

When Diana Dickey came back from France in the spring of 1919, her parents considered that she had atoned for her nefarious past. She had served a year in the Red Cross and she was presumably engaged to a young American ace of position and charm. They could ask no more; of Diana's former sins only her nickname survived——

Diamond Dick!—she had selected it herself, of all the names in the world, when she was a thin, black-eyed child of ten.

"Diamond Dick," she would insist, "that's my name. Anybody that won't call me that's a double darn fool."

"But that's not a nice name for a little lady," objected her governess. "If you want to have a boy's name why don't you call yourself George Washington?"

"Be-cause my name's Diamond Dick," explained Diana patiently. "Can't you understand? I got to be named that be-cause if I don't I'll have a fit and upset the family, see?"

She ended by having the fit—a fine frenzy that brought a disgusted nerve specialist out from New York—and the nickname too. And once in possession she set about modeling her facial expression on that of a butcher boy who delivered meats at Greenwich back doors. She stuck out her lower jaw and parted her lips on one side, exposing sections of her first teeth—and from this alarming aperture there issued the harsh voice of one far gone in crime.

"Miss Caruthers," she would sneer crisply, "what's the idea of no jam? Do you wanta whack the side of the head?"

"*Diana*! I'm going to call your mother *this minute*!"

"Look at here!" threatened Diana darkly. "If you call her you're liable to get a bullet the side of the head."

Miss Caruthers raised her hand uneasily to her bangs. She was somewhat awed.

"Very well," she said uncertainly, "if you want to act like a little ragamuffin——"

Diana did want to. The evolutions which she practiced daily on the sidewalk and which were thought by the neighbors to be some new form of hop-scotch were in reality the preliminary work on an Apache slouch. When it was perfected, Diana lurched forth into the streets of Greenwich, her face violently distorted and half obliterated by her father's slouch hat, her body reeling from side to side, jerked hither and yon by the shoulders, until to look at her long was to feel a faint dizziness rising to the brain.

At first it was merely absurd, but when Diana's conversation commenced to glow with weird rococo phrases, which she imagined to be the dialect of the underworld, it became alarming. And a few years later she further complicated the problem by turning into a beauty—a dark little beauty with tragedy eyes and a rich voice stirring in her throat.

Then America entered the war and Diana on her eighteenth birthday sailed with a canteen unit to France.

The past was over; all was forgotten. Just before the armistice was signed, she was cited in orders for coolness under fire. And—this was the part that particularly pleased her mother—it was rumored that she was engaged to be married to Mr. Charley Abbot of Boston and Bar Harbor, "a young aviator of position and charm."

But Mrs. Dickey was scarcely prepared for the changed Diana who landed in New York. Seated in the limousine bound for Greenwich, she turned to her daughter with astonishment in her eyes.

"Why, everybody's proud of you, Diana," she cried, "the house is simply bursting with flowers. Think of all you've seen and done, at *nineteen*!"

Diana's face, under an incomparable saffron hat, stared out into Fifth Avenue, gay with banners for the returning divisions.

"The war's over," she said in a curious voice, as if it had just occurred to her this minute.

"Yes," agreed her mother cheerfully, "and we won. I knew we would all the time."

She wondered how to best introduce the subject of Mr. Abbot.

"You're quieter," she began tentatively. "You look as if you were more ready to settle down."

"I want to come out this fall."

"But I thought——" Mrs. Dickey stopped and coughed—"Rumors had led me to believe——"

"Well, go on, Mother. What did you hear?"

"It came to my ears that you were engaged to that young Charles Abbot."

Diana did not answer and her mother licked nervously at her veil. The silence in the car became oppressive. Mrs. Dickey had always stood somewhat in awe of Diana—and she began to wonder if she had gone too far.

"The Abbots are such nice people in Boston," she ventured uneasily. "I've met his mother several times—she told me how devoted——"

"Mother!" Diana's voice, cold as ice, broke in upon her loquacious dream. "I don't care what you heard or where you heard it, but I'm not engaged to Charley Abbot. And please don't ever mention the subject to me again."

In November Diana made her debut in the ball room of the Ritz. There was a touch of irony in this "introduction to life"—for at nineteen Diana had seen more of reality, of courage and terror and pain, than all the pompous dowagers who peopled the artificial world.

But she was young and the artificial world was redolent of orchids and pleasant, cheerful snobbery and orchestras which set the rhythm of the year, summing up the sadness and suggestiveness of life in new tunes. All night the saxophones wailed the hopeless comment of the "Beale Street Blues," while five hundred pairs of gold and silver slippers shuffled the shining dust. At the gray tea hour there were always rooms that throbbed incessantly with this low sweet fever, while fresh faces drifted here and there like rose petals blown by the sad horns around the floor.

In the center of this twilight universe Diana moved with the season, keeping half a dozen dates a day with half a dozen men, drowsing asleep at dawn with the beads and chiffon of an evening dress tangled among dying orchids on the floor beside her bed.

The year melted into summer. The flapper craze startled New York, and skirts went absurdly high and the sad orchestras played new tunes. For a while Diana's beauty seemed to embody this new fashion as once it had seemed to embody the higher excitement of the war; but it was noticeable that she encouraged no lovers, that for all her popularity her name never became identified with that of any one man. She had had a hundred "chances," but when she felt that an interest was becoming an infatuation she was at pains to end it once and for all.

A second year dissolved into long dancing nights and swimming trips to the warm south. The flapper movement scattered to the winds and was forgotten; skirts tumbled precipitously to the floor and there were fresh songs from the saxophones for a new crop of girls. Most of those with whom she had come out were married now—some of them had babies. But Diana, in a changing world, danced on to newer tunes.

With a third year it was hard to look at her fresh and lovely face and realize that she had once been in the war. To the young generation it was already a shadowy event that had absorbed their older brothers in the dim past—ages ago. And Diana felt that when its last echoes had finally died away her youth, too, would be over. It was only occasionally now that anyone called her "Diamond Dick." When it happened, as it did sometimes, a curious, puzzled expression would come into her eyes as though she could never connect the two pieces of her life that were broken sharply asunder.

Then, when five years had passed, a brokerage house failed in Boston and Charley Abbot, the war hero, came back from Paris, wrecked and broken by drink and with scarcely a penny to his name.

Diana saw him first at the Restaurant Mont Mihiel, sitting at a side table with a plump, indiscriminate blonde from the half-world. She excused herself unceremoniously to her escort and made her way toward him. He looked up as she approached and she felt a sudden faintness, for he was worn to a shadow and his eyes, large and dark like her own, were burning in red rims of fire.

"Why, Charley——"

He got drunkenly to his feet and they shook hands in a dazed way. He murmured an introduction, but the girl at the table evinced her displeasure at the meeting by glaring at Diana with cold blue eyes.

"Why, Charley——" said Diana again, "you've come home, haven't you."

"I'm here for good."

"I want to see you, Charley. I—I want to see you as soon as possible. Will you come out to the country tomorrow?"

"Tomorrow?" He glanced with an apologetic expression at the blonde girl. "I've got a date. Don't know about tomorrow. Maybe later in the week——"

"Break your date."

His companion had been drumming with her fingers on the cloth and looking restlessly around the room. At this remark she wheeled sharply back to the table.

"Charley," she ejaculated, with a significant frown.

"Yes, I know," he said to her cheerfully, and turned to Diana. "I can't make it tomorrow. I've got a date."

"It's absolutely necessary that I see you tomorrow," went on Diana ruthlessly. "Stop looking at me in that idiotic way and say you'll come out to Greenwich."

"What's the idea?" cried the other girl in a slightly raised voice. "Why don't you stay at your own table? You must be tight."

"Now Elaine!" said Charley, turning to her reprovingly.

"I'll meet the train that gets to Greenwich at six," Diana went on coolly. "If you can't get rid of this—this woman——" she indicated his companion with a careless wave of her hand—"send her to the movies."

With an exclamation the other girl got to her feet and for a moment a scene was imminent. But nodding to Charley, Diana turned from the table, beckoned to her escort across the room and left the cafe.

"I don't like her," cried Elaine querulously when Diana was out of hearing. "Who is she anyhow? Some old girl of yours?"

"That's right," he answered, frowning. "Old girl of mine. In fact, my only old girl."

"Oh, you've known her all your life."

"No." He shook his head. "When I first met her she was a canteen worker in the war."

"*She* was!" Elaine raised her brows in surprise. "Why she doesn't look——"

"Oh, she's not nineteen any more—she's nearly twenty-five." He laughed. "I saw her sitting on a box at an ammunition dump near Soissons one day with enough lieutenants around her to officer a regiment. Three weeks after that we were engaged!"

"Then what?" demanded Elaine sharply.

"Usual thing," he answered with a touch of bitterness. "She broke it off. Only unusual part of it was that I never knew why. Said good-by to her one day and left for my squadron. I must have said something or done something then that started the big fuss. I'll never know. In fact I don't remember anything about it very clearly because a few hours later I had a crash and what happened just before has always been damn dim in my head. As soon as I was well enough to care about anything I saw that the situation was changed. Thought at first that there must be another man."

"Did she break the engagement?"

"She cern'ly did. While I was getting better she used to sit by my bed for hours looking at me with the funniest expression in her eyes. Finally I asked for a mirror—I thought I must be all cut up or something. But I wasn't. Then one day she began to cry. She said she'd been thinking it over and perhaps it was a mistake and all that sort of thing. Seemed to be referring to some quarrel we'd had when we said good-by just before I got hurt. But I was still a pretty sick man and the whole thing didn't seem to make any sense unless there was another man in it somewhere. She said that we both wanted our freedom, and then she looked at me as if she expected me to make some explanation or apology—and I couldn't think what I'd done. I remember leaning back in the bed and wishing I could die right then and there. Two months later I heard she'd sailed for home."

Elaine leaned anxiously over the table.

"Don't go to the country with her, Charley," she said. "Please don't go. She wants you back—I can tell by looking at her."

He shook his head and laughed.

"Yes she does," insisted Elaine, "I can tell. I hate her. She had you once and now she wants you back. I can see it in her eyes. I wish you'd stay in New York with me."

"No," he said stubbornly. "Going out and look her over. Diamond Dick's an old girl of mine."

Diana was standing on the station platform in the late afternoon, drenched with golden light. In the face of her immaculate freshness Charley Abbot felt ragged and old. He was only twenty-nine, but four wild years had left many lines around his dark, handsome eyes. Even his walk was tired—it was no longer a demonstration of fitness and physical grace. It was a way of getting somewhere, failing other forms of locomotion; that was all.

"Charley," Diana cried, "where's your bag?"

"I only came out to dinner—I can't possibly spend the night."

He was sober, she saw, but he looked as if he needed a drink badly. She took his arm and guided him to a red-wheeled coupe parked in the street.

"Get in and sit down," she commanded. "You walk as if you were about to fall down anyhow."

"Never felt better in my life."

She laughed scornfully.

"Why do you have to get back tonight?" she demanded.

"I promised—you see I had an engagement——"

"Oh, let her wait!" exclaimed Diana impatiently. "She didn't look as if she had much else to do. Who is she anyhow?"

"I don't see how that could possibly interest you, Diamond Dick."

She flushed at the familiar name.

"Everything about you interests me. Who is that girl?"

"Elaine Russel. She's in the movies—sort of."

"She looked pulpy," said Diana thoughtfully. "I keep thinking of her. You look pulpy too. What are you doing with yourself—waiting for another war?"

They turned into the drive of a big rambling house on the Sound. Canvas was being stretched for dancing on the lawn.

"Look!" She was pointing at a figure in knickerbockers on a side veranda. "That's my brother Breck. You've never met him. He's home from New Haven for the Easter holidays and he's having a dance tonight."

A handsome boy of eighteen came down the veranda steps toward them.

"He thinks you're the greatest man in the world," whispered Diana. "Pretend you're wonderful."

There was an embarrassed introduction.

"Done any flying lately?" asked Breck immediately.

"Not for some years," admitted Charley.

"I was too young for the war myself," said Breck regretfully, "but I'm going to try for a pilot's license this summer. It's the only thing, isn't it—flying I mean."

"Why, I suppose so," said Charley somewhat puzzled. "I hear you're having a dance tonight."

Breck waved his hand carelessly.

"Oh, just a lot of people from around here. I should think anything like that'd bore you to death—after all you've seen."

Charley turned helplessly to Diana.

"Come on," she said, laughing, "we'll go inside."

Mrs. Dickey met them in the hall and subjected Charley to a polite but somewhat breathless scrutiny. The whole household seemed to treat him with unusual respect, and the subject had a tendency to drift immediately to the war.

"What are you doing now?" asked Mr. Dickey. "Going into your father's business?"

"There isn't any business left," said Charley frankly. "I'm just about on my own."

Mr. Dickey considered for a moment.

"If you haven't made any plans why don't you come down and see me at my office some day this week. I've got a little proposition that may interest you."

It annoyed Charley to think that Diana had probably arranged all this. He needed no charity. He had not been crippled, and the war was over five years. People did not talk like this any more.

The whole first floor had been set with tables for the supper that would follow the dance, so Charley and Diana had dinner with Mr. and Mrs. Dickey in the library upstairs. It was an uncomfortable meal at which Mr. Dickey did the talking and Diana covered up the gaps with nervous gaiety. He was glad when it was over and he was standing with Diana on the veranda in the gathering darkness.

"Charley——" She leaned close to him and touched his arm gently. "Don't go to New York tonight. Spend a few days down here with me. I want to talk to you and I don't feel that I can talk tonight with this party going on."

"I'll come out again—later in the week," he said evasively.

"Why not stay tonight?"

"I promised I'd be back at eleven."

"At eleven?" She looked at him reproachfully. "Do you have to account to that girl for your evenings?"

"I like her," he said defiantly. "I'm not a child, Diamond Dick, and I rather resent your attitude. I thought you closed out your interest in my life five years ago."

"You won't stay?"

"No."

"All right—then we only have an hour. Let's walk out and sit on the wall by the Sound."

Side by side they started through the deep twilight where the air was heavy with salt and roses.

"Do you remember the last time we walked somewhere together?" she whispered.

"Why—no. I don't think I do. Where was it?"

"It doesn't matter—if you've forgotten."

When they reached the shore she swung herself up on the low wall that skirted the water.

"It's spring, Charley."

"Another spring."

"No—just spring. If you say 'another spring' it means you're getting old." She hesitated. "Charley——"

"Yes, Diamond Dick."

"I've been waiting to talk to you like this for five years."

Looking at him out of the corner of her eye she saw he was frowning and changed her tone.

"What kind of work are you going into, Charley?"

"I don't know. I've got a little money left and I won't have to do anything for awhile. I don't seem to fit into business very well."

"You mean like you fitted into the war."

"Yes." He turned to her with a spark of interest. "I belonged to the war. It seems a funny thing to say but I think I'll always look back to those days as the happiest in my life."

"I know what you mean," she said slowly. "Nothing quite so intense or so dramatic will ever happen to our generation again."

They were silent for a moment. When he spoke again his voice was trembling a little.

"There are things lost in it—parts of me—that I can look for and never find. It was my war in a way, you see, and you can't quite hate what was your own." He turned to her suddenly. "Let's be frank, Diamond Dick—we loved each other once and it seems—seems rather silly to be stalling this way with you."

She caught her breath.

"Yes," she said faintly, "let's be frank."

"I know what you're up to and I know you're doing it to be kind. But life doesn't start all over again when a man talks to an old love on a spring night."

"I'm not doing it to be kind."

He looked at her closely.

"You lie, Diamond Dick. But—even if you loved me now it wouldn't matter. I'm not like I was five years ago—I'm a different person, can't you see? I'd rather have a drink this minute than all the moonlight in the world. I don't even think I could love a girl like you any more."

She nodded.

"I see."

"Why wouldn't you marry me five years ago, Diamond Dick?"

"I don't know," she said after a minute's hesitation, "I was wrong."

"Wrong!" he exclaimed bitterly. "You talk as if it had been guesswork, like betting on white or red."

"No, it wasn't guesswork."

There was a silence for a minute—then she turned to him with shining eyes.

"Won't you kiss me, Charley?" she asked simply.

He started.

"Would it be so hard to do?" she went on. "I've never asked a man to kiss me before."

With an exclamation he jumped off the wall.

"I'm going to the city," he said.

"Am I—such bad company as all that?"

"Diana." He came close to her and put his arms around her knees and looked into her eyes. "You know that if I kiss you I'll have to stay. I'm afraid of you—afraid of your kindness, afraid to remember anything about you at all. And I couldn't go from a kiss of yours to—another girl."

"Good-by," she said suddenly.

He hesitated for a moment then he protested helplessly.

"You put me in a terrible position."

"Good-by."

"Listen Diana——"

"Please go away."

He turned and walked quickly toward the house.

Diana sat without moving while the night breeze made cool puffs and ruffles on her chiffon dress. The moon had risen higher now, and floating in the Sound was a triangle of silver scales, trembling a little to the stiff, tinny drip of the banjos on the lawn.

Alone at last—she was alone at last. There was not even a ghost left now to drift with through the years. She might stretch out her arms as far as they could reach into the night without fear that they would brush friendly cloth. The thin silver had worn off from all the stars.

She sat there for almost an hour, her eyes fixed upon the points of light on the other shore. Then the wind ran cold fingers along her silk stockings so she jumped off the wall, landing softly among the bright pebbles of the sand.

"Diana!"

Breck was coming toward her, flushed with the excitement of his party.

"Diana! I want you to meet a man in my class at New Haven. His brother took you to a prom three years ago."

She shook her head.

"I've got a headache; I'm going upstairs."

Coming closer Breck saw that her eyes were glittering with tears.

"Diana, what's the matter?"

"Nothing."

"Something's the matter."

"Nothing, Breck. But oh, take care, take care! Be careful who you love."

"Are you in love with—Charley Abbot?"

She gave a strange, hard little laugh.

"Me? Oh, God, no, Breck! I don't love anybody. I wasn't made for anything like love. I don't even love myself any more. It was you I was talking about. That was advice, don't you understand?"

She ran suddenly toward the house, holding her skirts high out of the dew. Reaching her own room she kicked off her slippers and threw herself on the bed in the darkness.

"I should have been careful," she whispered to herself. "All my life I'll be punished for not being more careful. I wrapped all my love up like a box of candy and gave it away."

Her window was open and outside on the lawn the sad, dissonant horns were telling a melancholy story. A blackamoor was two-timing the lady to whom he had pledged faith. The lady warned him, in so many words, to stop fooling 'round Sweet Jelly-Roll, even though Sweet Jelly-Roll was the color of pale cinnamon——

The 'phone on the table by her bed rang imperatively. Diana took up the receiver.

"Yes."

"One minute please, New York calling."

It flashed through Diana's head that it was Charley—but that was impossible. He must be still on the train.

"Hello." A woman was speaking. "Is this the Dickey residence?"

"Yes."

"Well, is Mr. Charles Abbot there?"

Diana's heart seemed to stop beating as she recognized the voice—it was the blonde girl of the cafe.

"What?" she asked dazedly.

"I would like to speak to Mr. Abbot at once please."

"You—you can't speak to him. He's gone."

There was a pause. Then the girl's voice, suspiciously:

"He isn't gone."

Diana's hands tightened on the telephone.

"I know who's talking," went on the voice, rising to a hysterical note, "and I want to speak to Mr. Abbot. If you're not telling the truth, and he finds out, there'll be trouble."

"Be quiet!"

"If he's gone, where did he go?"

"I don't know."

"If he isn't at my apartment in half an hour I'll know you're lying and I'll——"

Diana hung up the receiver and tumbled back on the bed—too weary of life to think or care. Out on the lawn the orchestra was singing and the words drifted in her window on the breeze.

Lis-sen *while I—get you tole:*
Stop foolin' 'roun' sweet—Jelly-Roll——

She listened. The Negro voices were wild and loud—life was in that key, so harsh a key. How abominably helpless she was! Her appeal was ghostly, impotent, absurd, before the barbaric urgency of this other girl's desire.

Just treat me pretty, just treat me sweet
Cause I possess a fo'ty-fo' that don't repeat.

The music sank to a weird, threatening minor. It reminded her of something—some mood in her own childhood—and a new atmosphere seemed to open up around her. It was not so much a definite memory as it was a current, a tide setting through her whole body.

Diana jumped suddenly to her feet and groped for her slippers in the darkness. The song was beating in her head and her little teeth set together in a click. She could feel the tense golf-muscles rippling and tightening along her arms.

Running into the hall she opened the door to her father's room, closed it cautiously behind her and went to the bureau. It was in the top drawer—black and shining among the pale anaemic collars. Her hand closed around the grip and she drew out the bullet clip with steady fingers. There were five shots in it.

Back in her room she called the garage.

"I want my roadster at the side entrance right away!"

Wriggling hurriedly out of her evening dress to the sound of breaking snaps she let it drop in a soft pile on the floor, replacing it with a golf sweater, a checked sport-skirt and an old blue and white blazer which she pinned at the collar with a diamond bar. Then she pulled a tam-o-shanter over her dark hair and looked once in the mirror before turning out the light.

"Come on, Diamond Dick!" she whispered aloud.

With a short exclamation she plunged the automatic into her blazer pocket and hurried from the room.

Diamond Dick! The name had jumped out at her once from a lurid cover, symbolizing her childish revolt against the softness of life. Diamond Dick was a law unto himself, making his own judgments with his back against the wall. If justice was slow he vaulted into his saddle and was off for the foothills, for in the unvarying rightness of his instincts he was higher and harder than the law. She had seen in him a sort of deity, infinitely resourceful, infinitely just. And the commandment he laid down for himself in the cheap, ill-written pages was first and foremost to keep what was his own.

An hour and a half from the time when she had left Greenwich, Diana pulled up her roadster in front of the Restaurant Mont Mihiel. The theaters were already dumping their crowds into Broadway and half a dozen couples in evening dress looked at her curiously as she slouched through the door. A moment later she was talking to the head waiter.

"Do you know a girl named Elaine Russel?"

"Yes, Miss Dickey. She comes here quite often."

"I wonder if you can tell me where she lives."

The head waiter considered.

"Find out," she said sharply, "I'm in a hurry."

He bowed. Diana had come there many times. with many men. She had never asked him a favor before.

His eyes roved hurriedly around the room.

"Sit down," he said.

"I'm all right. You hurry."

He crossed the room and whispered to a man at a table—in a minute he was back with the address, an apartment on Forty-Ninth Street.

In her car again she looked at her wrist watch—it was almost midnight, the appropriate hour. A feeling of romance, of desperate and dangerous adventure thrilled her, seemed to flow out of the electric signs and the rushing cabs and the high stars. Perhaps she was only one out of a hundred people bound on such an adventure tonight—for her there had been nothing like this since the war.

Skidding the corner into East Forty-Ninth Street she scanned the apartments on both sides. There it was—"The Elkson"—a wide mouth of forbidding yellow light. In the hall a Negro elevator boy asked her name.

"Tell her it's a girl with a package from the moving picture company."

He worked a plug noisily.

"Miss Russel? There's a lady here says she's got a package from the moving picture company."

A pause.

"That's what she says. . . . All right." He turned to Diana. "She wasn't expecting no package but you can bring it up." He looked at her, frowned suddenly. "You ain't got no package."

Without answering she walked into the elevator and he followed, shoving the gate closed with maddening languor. . . .

"First door to your right."

She waited until the elevator door had started down again. Then she knocked, her fingers tightening on the automatic in her blazer pocket.

Running footsteps, a laugh; the door swung open and Diana stepped quickly into the room.

It was a small apartment, bedroom, bath and kitchenette, furnished in pink and white and heavy with last week's smoke. Elaine Russel had opened the door herself. She was dressed to go out and a green evening cape was over her arm. Charley Abbot sipping at a highball was stretched out in the room's only easy chair.

"What is it?" cried Elaine quickly.

With a sharp movement Diana slammed the door behind her and Elaine stepped back, her mouth falling ajar.

"Good evening," said Diana coldly, and then a line from a forgotten nickel novel flashed into her head, "I hope I don't intrude."

"What do you want?" demanded Elaine. "You've got your nerve to come butting in here!"

Charley who had not said a word set down his glass heavily on the arm of the chair. The two girls looked at each other with unwavering eyes.

"Excuse me," said Diana slowly, "but I think you've got my man."

"I thought you were supposed to be a lady!" cried Elaine in rising anger. "What do you mean by forcing your way into this room?"

"I mean business. I've come for Charley Abbot."

Elaine gasped.

"Why, you must be crazy!"

"On the contrary, I've never been so sane in my life. I came here to get something that belongs to me."

Charley uttered an exclamation but with a simultaneous gesture the two women waved him silent.

"All right," cried Elaine, "we'll settle this right now."

"I'll settle it myself," said Diana sharply. "There's no question or argument about it. Under other circumstances I might feel a certain pity for you—in this case you happen to be in my way. What is there between you two? Has he promised to marry you?"

"That's none of your business!"

"You'd better answer," Diana warned her.

"I won't answer."

Diana took a sudden step forward, drew back her arm and with all the strength in her slim hard muscles, hit Elaine a smashing blow in the cheek with her open hand.

Elaine staggered up against the wall. Charley uttered an exclamation and sprang forward to find himself looking into the muzzle of a forty-four held in a small determined hand.

"Help!" cried Elaine wildly. "Oh, she's hurt me! She's hurt me!"

"Shut up!" Diana's voice was hard as steel. "You're not hurt. You're just pulpy and soft. But if you start to raise a row I'll pump you full of tin as sure as you're alive. Sit down! Both of you. Sit *down!*"

Elaine sat down quickly, her face pale under her rouge. After an instant's hesitation Charley sank down again into his chair.

"Now," went on Diana, waving the gun in a constant arc that included them both. "I guess you know I'm in a serious mood. Understand this first of all. As far as I'm concerned neither of you have any rights whatsoever and I'd kill you both rather than leave this room without getting what I came for. I asked if he'd promised to marry you."

"Yes," said Elaine sullenly.

The gun moved toward Charley.

"Is that so?"

He licked his lips, nodded.

"My God!" said Diana in contempt. "And you admit it. Oh, it's funny, it's absurd—if I didn't care so much I'd laugh."

"Look here!" muttered Charley, "I'm not going to stand much of this, you know."

"Yes you are! You're soft enough to stand anything now." She turned to the girl, who was trembling. "Have you any letters of his?"

Elaine shook her head.

"You lie," said Diana. "Go and get them! I'll give you three. One——"

Elaine rose nervously and went into the other room. Diana edged along the table, keeping her constantly in sight.

"Hurry!"

Elaine returned with a small package in her hand which Diana took and slipped into her blazer pocket.

"Thanks. You had 'em all carefully preserved I see. Sit down again and we'll have a little talk."

Elaine sat down. Charley drained off his whisky and soda and leaned back stupidly in his chair.

"Now," said Diana, "I'm going to tell you a little story. It's about a girl who went to a war once and met a man who she thought was the finest and bravest man she had ever known. She fell in love with him and he with her and all the other men she had ever known became like pale shadows compared with this man that she loved. But one day he was shot down out of the air, and when he woke up into the world he'd changed. He didn't know it himself but he'd forgotten things and become a different man. The girl felt sad about this—she saw that she wasn't necessary to him any more, so there was nothing to do but say good-by.

"So she went away and every night for a while she cried herself to sleep but he never came back to her and five years went by. Finally word came to her that this same injury that had come between them was ruining his life. He didn't remember anything important any more—how proud and fine he had once been, and what dreams he had once had. And then the girl knew that she had the right to try and save what was left of his life because she was the only one who knew all the things he'd forgotten. But it was too late. She couldn't approach him any more—she wasn't coarse enough and gross enough to reach him now—he'd forgotten so much.

"So she took a revolver, very much like this one here, and she came after this man to the apartment of a poor, weak, harmless rat of a girl who had him in tow. She was going to either bring him to himself—or go back to the dust with him where nothing would matter any more."

She paused. Elaine shifted uneasily in her chair. Charley was leaning forward with his face in his hands.

"Charley!"

The word, sharp and distinct, startled him. He dropped his hands and looked up at her.

"Charley!" she repeated in a thin clear voice. "Do you remember Fontenay in the late fall?"

A bewildered look passed over his face.

"Listen, Charley. Pay attention. Listen to every word I say. Do you remember the poplar trees at twilight, and a long column of French infantry going through the town? You had on your blue uniform, Charley, with the little numbers on the tabs and you were going to the front in an hour. Try and remember, Charley!"

He passed his hand over his eyes and gave a funny little sigh. Elaine sat bolt upright in her chair and gazed from one to the other of them with wide eyes.

"Do you remember the poplar trees?" went on Diana. "The sun was going down and the leaves were silver and there was a bell ringing. Do you remember, Charley? Do you remember?"

Again silence. Charley gave a curious little groan and lifted his head.

"I can't—understand," he muttered hoarsely. "There's something funny here."

"Can't you remember?" cried Diana. The tears were streaming

from her eyes. "Oh God! Can't you remember? The brown road and the poplar trees and the yellow sky." She sprang suddenly to her feet. "Can't you remember?" she cried wildly. "Think, think—there's time. The bells are ringing—the bells are ringing, Charley! And there's just one hour!"

Then he too was on his feet, reeling and swaying.

"Oh-h-h-h!" he cried.

"Charley," sobbed Diana, "remember, remember, remember!"

"I see!" he said wildly. "I can see now—I remember, oh I remember!"

With a choking sob his whole body seemed to wilt under him and he pitched back senseless into his chair.

In a minute the two girls were beside him.

"He's fainted!" Diana cried—"get some water quick."

"You devil!" screamed Elaine, her face distorted. "Look what's happened! What right have you to do this? What right? What right?"

"What right?" Diana turned to her with black, shining eyes. "Every right in the world. I've been married to Charley Abbot for five years."

Charley and Diana were married again in Greenwich early in June. After the wedding her oldest friends stopped calling her Diamond Dick—it had been a most inappropriate name for some years, they said, and it was thought that the effect on her children might be unsettling, if not distinctly pernicious.

Yet perhaps if the occasion should arise Diamond Dick would come to life again from the colored cover and, with spurs shining and buckskin fringes fluttering in the breeze, ride into the lawless hills to protect her own. For under all her softness Diamond Dick was always hard as steel—so hard that the years knew it and stood still for her and the clouds rolled apart and a sick man, hearing those untiring hoofbeats in the night, rose up and shook off the dark burden of the war.

The Third Casket

(*The Saturday Evening Post*, 31 May 1924)

"The Third Casket" was written in Great Neck in March 1924. The *Post* paid $1750 for it. After the expiration of the story options with *Metropolitan* and *International*, Fitzgerald became virtually a *Post* author for the next decade. All of his best stories were offered there first, and the *Post* steadily raised his story price to a peak of $4000 in 1929. The *Post* obviously regarded Fitzgerald as a star author. His name regularly appeared on the cover, and his stories were prominently positioned. "Casket" was the lead story in the issue, following a serial.

Like most of the stories Fitzgerald wrote in 1924, "The Third Casket" depends on plot rather than character. Here he adapted an episode from *The Merchant of Venice*—which Shakespeare had borrowed from somebody else. "The Third Casket" was tailored to the business values of the *Post*. The simple message is that work is more rewarding than leisure.

When you come into Cyrus Girard's office suite on the thirty-second floor you think at first that there has been a mistake, that the elevator instead of bringing you upstairs has brought you uptown, and that you are walking into an apartment on Fifth Avenue where you have no business at all. What you take to be the sound of a stock ticker is only a businesslike canary swinging in a silver cage overhead, and while the languid debutante at the mahogany table gets ready to ask you your name you can feast your eyes on etchings, tapestries, carved panels and fresh flowers.

Cyrus Girard does not, however, run an interior-decorating establishment, though he has, on occasion, run almost everything else. The lounging aspect of his ante-room is merely an elaborate camouflage for the wild clamor of affairs that goes on ceaselessly within. It is merely the padded glove over the mailed fist, the smile on the face of the prize fighter.

No one was more intensely aware of this than the three young men who were waiting there one April morning to see Mr. Girard. Whenever the door marked Private trembled with the pressure of enormous affairs they started nervously in unconscious unison. All three of them were on the hopeful side of thirty, each of them had just got off the train, and they had never seen one another before. They had been waiting side by side on a Circassian leather lounge for the best part of an hour.

Once the young man with the pitch-black eyes and hair had pulled out a package of cigarettes and offered it hesitantly to the two others. But the two others had refused in such a politely alarmed way that the dark young man, after a quick look around, had returned the package unsampled to his pocket. Following this disrespectful incident a long silence had fallen, broken only by the clatter of the canary as it ticked off the bond market in bird land.

When the Louis XIII clock stood at noon the door marked Private swung open in a tense, embarrassed way, and a frantic secretary demanded that the three callers step inside. They stood up as one man.

"Do you mean—all together?" asked the tallest one in some embarrassment.

"All together."

Falling unwillingly into a sort of lock step and glancing neither to left nor right, they passed through a series of embattled rooms and marched into the private office of Cyrus Girard, who filled the position of Telamonian Ajax among the Homeric characters of Wall Street.

He was a thin, quiet-mannered man of sixty, with a fine, restless face and the clear, fresh, trusting eyes of a child. When the procession of young men walked in he stood up behind his desk with an expectant smile.

"Parrish?" he said eagerly.

The tall young man said "Yes, sir," and was shaken by the hand.

"Jones?"

This was the young man with the black eyes and hair. He smiled back at Cyrus Girard and announced in a slightly Southern accent that he was mighty glad to meet him.

"And so you must be Van Buren," said Girard, turning to the third. Van Buren acknowledged as much. He was obviously from a large city—unflustered and very spick-and-span.

"Sit down," said Girard, looking eagerly from one to the other. "I can't tell you the pleasure of this minute."

They all smiled nervously and sat down.

"Yes, sir," went on the older man, "if I'd had any boys of my own I don't know but what I'd have wanted them to look just like you three." He saw that they were all growing pink, and he broke off with a laugh. "All right, I won't embarrass you any more. Tell me about the health of your respective fathers and we'll get down to business."

Their fathers, it seemed, were very well; they had all sent congratulatory messages by their sons for Mr. Girard's sixtieth birthday.

"Thanks. Thanks. Now that's over." He leaned back suddenly in his chair. "Well, boys, here's what I have to say. I'm retiring from business next year. I've always intended to retire at sixty, and my wife's always counted on it, and the time's come. I can't put it off any longer. I haven't any sons and I haven't any nephews and I haven't any cousins and I have a brother who's fifty years old and in the same boat I am. He'll perhaps hang on for ten years more down here; after that it looks as if the house, Cyrus Girard, Incorporated, would change its name.

"A month ago I wrote to the three best friends I had in college, the three best friends I ever had in my life, and asked them if they had any sons between twenty-five and thirty years old. I told them I had room for just one young man here in my business, but he had to be about the best in the market. And as all three of you arrived here this morning I guess your fathers think you are. There's nothing complicated about my proposition. It'll take me three months to find out what I want to know, and at the end of that time two of you'll be disappointed; the other one can have about everything they used to give away in the fairy tales, half my kingdom and, if she wants him, my daughter's hand." He raised his head slightly. "Correct me, Lola, if I've said anything wrong."

At these words the three young men started violently, looked behind them, and then jumped precipitately to their feet. Reclining lazily in an armchair not two yards away sat a gold-and-ivory little beauty with dark eyes and a moving, childish smile that was like all the lost youth in the world. When she saw the startled expressions on their faces she gave vent to a suppressed chuckle in which the victims after a moment joined.

"This is my daughter," said Cyrus Girard, smiling innocently. "Don't be so alarmed. She has many suitors come from far and near— and all that sort of thing. Stop making these young men feel silly, Lola, and ask them if they'll come to dinner with us tonight."

Lola got to her feet gravely and her gray eyes fell on them one after another.

"I only know part of your names," she said.

"Easily arranged," said Van Buren. "Mine's George."

The tall young man bowed.

"I respond to John Hardwick Parrish," he confessed, "or anything of that general sound."

She turned to the dark-haired Southerner, who had volunteered no information. "How about Mr. Jones?"

"Oh, just—Jones," he answered uneasily.

She looked at him in surprise.

"Why, how partial!" she exclaimed, laughing. "How—I might even say how fragmentary."

Mr. Jones looked around him in a frightened way.

"Well, I tell you," he said finally, "I don't guess my first name is much suited to this sort of thing."

"What is it?"

"It's Rip."

"Rip!"

Eight eyes turned reproachfully upon him.

"Young man," exclaimed Girard, "you don't mean that my old friend in his senses named his son that!"

Jones shifted defiantly on his feet.

"No, he didn't," he admitted. "He named me Oswald."

There was a ripple of sympathetic laughter.

"Now you four go along," said Girard, sitting down at his desk. "Tomorrow at nine o'clock sharp you report to my general manager, Mr. Galt, and the tournament begins. Meanwhile if Lola has her coupe-sport-limousine-roadster-landaulet, or whatever she drives now, she'll probably take you to your respective hotels."

After they had gone Girard's face grew restless again and he stared at nothing for a long time before he pressed the button that started the long-delayed stream of traffic through his mind.

"One of them's sure to be all right," he muttered, "but suppose it turned out to be the dark one. Rip Jones, Incorporated!"

II

As the three months drew to an end it began to appear that not one, but all of the young men were going to turn out all right. They were all industrious, they were all possessed of that mysterious ease known as personality and, moreover, they all had brains. If Parrish, the tall young man from the West, was a little the quicker in sizing up the market; if Jones, the Southerner, was a bit the most impressive in his relations with customers, then Van Buren made up for it by spending his nights in the study of investment securities. Cyrus Girard's mind was no sooner drawn to one of them by some exhibition of shrewdness or resourcefulness than a parallel talent appeared in one of the others. Instead of having to enforce upon himself a strict neutrality he found himself trying to concentrate upon the individual merits of first one and then another—but so far without success.

Every week-end they all came out to the Girard place at Tuxedo Park, where they fraternized a little self-consciously with the young and lovely Lola, and on Sunday mornings tactlessly defeated her father at golf. On the last tense week-end before the decision was to be made Cyrus Girard asked them to meet him in his study after dinner. On their respective merits as future partners in Cyrus Girard, Inc., he had been unable to decide, but his despair had evoked another plan, on which he intended to base his decision.

"Gentlemen," he said, when they had convoked in his study at the appointed hour, "I have brought you here to tell you that you're all fired."

Immediately the three young men were on their feet, with shocked, reproachful expressions in their eyes.

"Temporarily," he added, smiling good-humoredly. "So spare a decrepit old man your violence and sit down."

They sat down, with short relieved smiles.

"I like you all," he went on, "and I don't know which one I like better than the others. In fact—this thing hasn't come out right at all. So I'm going to extend the competition for two more weeks—but in an entirely different way."

They all sat forward eagerly in their chairs.

"Now my generation," he went on, "have made a failure of our leisure hours. We grew up in the most hard-boiled commercial age any country ever knew, and when we retire we never know what to do with the rest of our lives. Here I am, getting out at sixty, and miserable about it. I haven't any resources—I've never been much of a reader, I can't stand golf except once a week, and I haven't got a hobby in the world. Now some day you're going to be sixty too. You'll see other men taking it easy and having a good time, and you'll want to do the same. I want to find out which one of you will be the best sort of man after his business days are over."

He looked from one to the other of them eagerly. Parrish and Van Buren nodded at him comprehendingly. Jones after a puzzled half moment nodded too.

"I want you each to take two weeks and spend them as you think you'll spend your time when you're too old to work. I want you to solve my problem for me. And whichever one I think has got the most out of his leisure—he'll be the man to carry on my business. I'll know it won't swamp him like it's swamped me."

"You mean you want us to enjoy ourselves?" inquired Rip Jones politely. "Just go out and have a big time?"

Cyrus Girard nodded.

"Anything you want to do."

"I take it Mr. Girard doesn't include dissipation," remarked Van Buren.

"Anything you want to do," repeated the older man. "I don't bar anything. When it's all done I'm going to judge of its merits."

"Two weeks of travel for me," said Parrish dreamily. "That's what I've always wanted to do. I'll——"

"Travel!" interrupted Van Buren contemptuously. "When there's so much to do here at home? Travel, perhaps, if you had a year; but for two weeks——I'm going to try and see how the retired business man can be of some use in the world."

"I said travel," repeated Parrish sharply. "I believe we're all to employ our leisure in the best——"

"Wait a minute," interrupted Cyrus Girard. "Don't fight this out in talk. Meet me in the office at 10:30 on the morning of August first—that's two weeks from tomorrow—and then let's see what you've done." He turned to Rip Jones. "I suppose you've got a plan too."

"No, sir," admitted Rip Jones with a puzzled look; "I'll have to think this over."

But though he thought it over for the rest of the evening Rip Jones went to bed still uninspired. At midnight he got up, found a pencil and wrote out a list of all the good times he had ever had. But all his holidays now seemed unprofitable and stale, and when he fell asleep at five his mind still threshed disconsolately on the prospect of hollow useless hours.

Next morning as Lola Girard was backing her car out of the garage she saw him hurrying toward her over the lawn.

"Ride in town, Rip?" she asked cheerfully.

"I reckon so."

"Why do you only reckon so? Father and the others left on the nine-o'clock train."

He explained to her briefly that they had all temporarily lost their jobs and there was no necessity of getting to the office today.

"I'm kind of worried about it," he said gravely. "I sure hate to leave my work. I'm going to run in this afternoon and see if they'll let me finish up a few things I had started."

"But you better be thinking how you're going to amuse yourself."

He looked at her helplessly.

"All I can think of doing is maybe take to drink," he confessed. "I come from a little town, and when they say leisure they mean hanging round the corner store." He shook his head. "I don't want any leisure. This is the first chance I ever had, and I want to make good."

"Listen, Rip," said Lola on a sudden impulse. "After you finish up at the office this afternoon you meet me and we'll fix up something together."

He met her, as she suggested, at five o'clock, but the melancholy had deepened in his dark eyes.

"They wouldn't let me in," he said. "I met your father in there, and he told me I had to find some way to amuse myself or I'd be just a bored old man like him."

"Never mind. We'll go to a show," she said consolingly; "and after that we'll run up on some roof and dance."

It was the first of a week of evenings they spent together. Sometimes they went to the theater, sometimes to a cabaret; once they spent most of an afternoon strolling in Central Park. But she saw that from having been the most light-hearted and gay of the three young men, he was now the most moody and depressed. Everything whispered to him of the work he was missing.

Even when they danced at teatime, the click of bracelets on a hundred women's arms only reminded him of the busy office sound on Monday morning. He seemed incapable of inaction.

"This is mighty sweet of you," he said to her one afternoon, "and if it was after business hours I can't tell you how I'd enjoy it. But my mind is on all the things I ought to be doing. I'm—I'm right sad."

He saw then that he had hurt her, that by his frankness he had rejected all she was trying to do for him. But he was incapable of feeling differently.

"Lola, I'm mighty sorry," he said softly, "and maybe some day it'll be after hours again, and I can come to you——"

"I won't be interested," she said coldly. "And I see I was foolish ever to be interested at all."

He was standing beside her car when this conversation took place, and before he could reply she had thrown it into gear and started away.

He stood there looking after her sadly, thinking that perhaps he would never see her any more and that she would remember him always as ungrateful and unkind. But there was nothing he could have said. Something dynamic in him was incapable of any except a well-earned rest.

"If it was only after hours," he muttered to himself as he walked slowly away. "If it was only after hours."

III

At ten o'clock on the morning of August first a tall, bronzed young man presented himself at the office of Cyrus Girard, Inc., and sent in his card to the president. Less than five minutes later another young man arrived, less blatantly healthy, perhaps, but with the light of triumphant achievement blazing in his eyes. Word came out through the palpitating inner door that they were both to wait.

"Well, Parrish," said Van Buren condescendingly, "how did you like Niagara Falls?"

"I couldn't tell you," answered Parrish haughtily. "You can determine that on your honeymoon."

"My honeymoon!" Van Buren started. "How—what made you think I was contemplating a honeymoon?"

"I merely meant that when you do contemplate it you will probably choose Niagara Falls."

They sat for a few minutes in stony silence.

"I suppose," remarked Parrish coolly, "that you've been making a serious study of the deserving poor."

"On the contrary, I have done nothing of the kind." Van Buren looked at his watch. "I'm afraid that our competitor with the rakish name is going to be late. The time set was 10:30; it now lacks three minutes of the half hour."

The private door opened, and at a command from the frantic secretary they both arose eagerly and went inside. Cyrus Girard was standing behind his desk waiting for them, watch in hand.

"Hello!" he exclaimed in surprise. "Where's Jones?"

Parrish and Van Buren exchanged a smile. If Jones were snagged somewhere so much the better.

"I beg your pardon, sir," spoke up the secretary, who had been lingering near the door; "Mr. Jones is in Chicago."

"What's he doing there?" demanded Cyrus Girard in astonishment.

"He went out to handle the matter of those silver shipments. There wasn't anyone else who knew much about it, and Mr. Galt thought——"

"Never mind what Mr. Galt thought," broke in Girard impatiently. "Mr. Jones is no longer employed by this concern. When he gets back from Chicago pay him off and let him go." He nodded curtly. "That's all."

The secretary bowed and went out. Girard turned to Parrish and Van Buren with an angry light in his eyes.

"Well, that finishes him," he said determinedly. "Any young man who won't even attempt to obey my orders doesn't deserve a good chance." He sat down and began drumming with his fingers on the arm of his chair.

"All right, Parrish, let's hear what you've been doing with your leisure hours."

Parrish smiled ingratiatingly.

"Mr. Girard," he began, "I've had a bully time. I've been traveling."

"Traveling where? The Adirondacks? Canada?"

"No, sir. I've been to Europe."

Cyrus Girard sat up.

"I spent five days going over and five days coming back. That left me two days in London and a run over to Paris by aeroplane to spend the night. I saw Westminster Abbey, the Tower of London and the Louvre, and spent an afternoon at Versailles. On the boat I kept in wonderful condition—swam, played deck tennis, walked five miles every day, met some interesting people and found time to read. I came back after the greatest two weeks of my life, feeling fine and knowing more about my own country since I had something to compare it with. That, sir, is how I spent my leisure time and that's how I intend to spend my leisure time after I'm retired."

Girard leaned back thoughtfully in his chair.

"Well, Parrish, that isn't half bad," he said. "I don't know but what the idea appeals to me—take a run over there for the sea voyage and a glimpse of the London Stock Ex——I mean the Tower of London. Yes, sir, you've put an idea in my head." He turned to the other young man, who during this recital had been shifting uneasily in his chair. "Now, Van Buren, let's hear how you took your ease."

"I thought over the travel idea," burst out Van Buren excitedly, "and I decided against it. A man of sixty doesn't want to spend his time running back and forth between the capitals of Europe. It might fill up a year or so, but that's all. No, sir, the main thing is to have some strong interest—and especially one that'll be for the public good, because when a man gets along in years he wants to feel that he's leaving the world better for having lived in it. So I worked out a plan—it's for a historical and archaeological endowment center, a thing that'd change the whole face of public education, a thing that any man would be interested in giving his time and money to. I've spent my whole two weeks working out the plan in detail, and let me tell you it'd be nothing but play work—just suited to the last years of an active man's life. It's been fascinating, Mr. Girard. I've learned more from doing it than I ever knew before—and I don't think I ever had a happier two weeks in my life."

When he had finished, Cyrus Girard nodded his head up and down many times in an approving and yet somehow dissatisfied way.

"Found an institute, eh?" he muttered aloud. "Well, I've always thought that maybe I'd do that some day—but I never figured on running it myself. My talents aren't much in that line. Still, it's certainly worth thinking over."

He got restlessly to his feet and began walking up and down the carpet, the dissatisfied expression deepening on his face. Several times he took out his watch and looked at it as if hoping that perhaps Jones had not gone to Chicago after all, but would appear in a few moments with a plan nearer his heart.

"What's the matter with me?" he said to himself unhappily. "When I say a thing I'm used to going through with it. I must be getting old."

Try as he might, however, he found himself unable to decide. Several times he stopped in his walk and fixed his glance first on one and then on the other of the two young men, trying to pick out some attractive characteristic to which he could cling and make his choice. But after several of these glances their faces seemed to blur together and he couldn't tell one from the other. They were twins who had told him the same story—of carrying the stock exchange by aeroplane to London and making it into a moving-picture show.

"I'm sorry, boys," he said haltingly. "I promised I'd decide this morning, and I will, but it means a whole lot to me and you'll have to give me a little time."

They both nodded, fixing their glances on the carpet to avoid encountering his distraught eyes.

Suddenly he stopped by the table and picking up the telephone called the general manager's office.

"Say, Galt," he shouted into the mouthpiece, "you sure you sent Jones to Chicago?"

"Positive," said a voice on the other end. "He came in here couple of days ago and said he was half crazy for something to do. I told him it was against orders, but he said he was out of the competition anyhow and we needed somebody who was competent to handle that silver. So I——"

"Well, you shouldn't have done it, see? I wanted to talk to him about something, and you shouldn't have done it."

Clack! He hung up the receiver and resumed his endless pacing up and down the floor. Confound Jones, he thought. Most ungrateful thing he ever heard of after he'd gone to all this trouble for his father's sake. Outrageous! His mind went off on a tangent and he began to wonder whether Jones would handle that business out in Chicago. It was a complicated situation—but then, Jones was a trustworthy fellow. They were all trustworthy fellows. That was the whole trouble.

Again he picked up the telephone. He would call Lola; he felt vaguely that if she wanted to she could help him. The personal element had eluded him here; her opinion would be better than his own.

"I have to ask your pardon, boys," he said unhappily; "I didn't mean there to be all this fuss and delay. But it almost breaks my heart when I think of handing this shop over to anybody at all, and when I try to decide, it all gets dark in my mind." He hesitated. "Have either one of you asked my daughter to marry him?"

"I did," said Parrish; "three weeks ago."

"So did I," confessed Van Buren; "and I still have hopes that she'll change her mind."

Girard wondered if Jones had asked her also. Probably not; he never did anything he was expected to do. He even had the wrong name.

The phone in his hand rang shrilly and with an automatic gesture he picked up the receiver.

"Chicago calling, Mr. Girard."

"I don't want to talk to anybody."

"It's personal. It's Mr. Jones."

"All right," he said, his eyes narrowing. "Put him on."

A series of clicks—then Jones' faintly Southern voice over the wire.

"Mr. Girard?"

"Yeah."

"I've been trying to get you since ten o'clock in order to apologize."

"I should think you would!" exploded Girard. "Maybe you know you're fired."

"I knew I would be," said Jones gloomily. "I guess I must be pretty dumb, Mr. Girard, but I'll tell you the truth—I can't have a good time when I quit work."

"Of course you can't!" snapped Girard. "Nobody can——" He corrected himself. "What I mean is, it isn't an easy matter."

There was a pause at the other end of the line.

"That's exactly the way I feel," came Jones' voice regretfully. "I guess we understand each other, and there's no use my saying any more."

"What do you mean—we understand each other?" shouted Girard. "That's an impertinent remark, young man. We don't understand each other at all."

"That's what I meant," amended Jones; "I don't understand you and you don't understand me. I don't want to quit working, and you—you do."

"Me quit work!" cried Girard, his face reddening. "Say, what are you talking about? Did you say I wanted to quit work?" He shook the telephone up and down violently. "Don't talk back to me, young man! Don't tell me I want to quit! Why—why, I'm not going to quit work at all! Do you hear that? I'm not going to quit work at all!"

The transmitter slipped from his grasp and bounced from the table to the floor. In a minute he was on his knees, groping for it wildly.

"Hello!" he cried. "Hello—hello! Say get Chicago back! I wasn't through!"

The two young men were on their feet. He hung up the receiver and turned to them, his voice husky with emotion.

"I've been an idiot," he said brokenly. "Quit work at sixty! Why—I must have been an idiot! I'm a young man still—I've got twenty good years in front of me! I'd like to see anybody send me home to die!"

The phone rang again and he took up the receiver with fire blazing in his eyes.

"Is this Jones? No, I want Mr. Jones; Rip Jones. He's—he's my partner." There was a pause. "No, Chicago, that must be another party. I don't know any Mrs. Jones—I want Mr.——"

He broke off and the expression on his face changed slowly. When he spoke again his husky voice had grown suddenly quiet.

"Why—why, Lola——"

The Pusher-in-the-Face

(*Woman's Home Companion*, February 1925)

"The Pusher-in-the-Face" was written in Great Neck in March 1924. It was bought for $1750 by *Woman's Home Companion*, which featured fiction as well as household articles. Although this story is an extended gag and does not display the qualities of Fitzgerald's best magazine fiction, it was very popular. "Pusher" was syndicated by the Metro Newspaper Service; it was included in *The Cream of the Jug*, a 1927 humor anthology; and it was made into a movie in 1929.

Though many—perhaps most—of Fitzgerald's stories rely on wit, he was not a comic writer. His infrequent attempts at straight comedy—as in "Pusher"—rely heavily on slapstick. This story reads like a movie scenario, and maybe it was intended as one.

The last prisoner was a man—his masculinity was not much in evidence, it is true; he would perhaps better be described as a "person," but he undoubtedly came under that general heading and was so classified in the court record. He was a small, somewhat shriveled, somewhat wrinkled American who had been living along for probably thirty-five years.

His body looked as if it had been left by accident in his suit the last time it went to the tailor's and pressed out with hot, heavy irons to its present sharpness. His face was merely a face. It was the kind of face that makes up crowds, gray in color with ears that shrank back against the head as if fearing the clamor of the city, and with the tired, tired eyes of one whose forebears have been underdogs for five thousand years.

Brought into the dock between two towering Celts in executive blue he seemed like the representative of a long extinct race, a very fagged out and shriveled elf who had been caught poaching on a buttercup in Central Park.

"What's your name?"

"Stuart."

"Stuart what?"

"Charles David Stuart."

The clerk recorded it without comment in the book of little crimes and great mistakes.

"Age?"

"Thirty."

"Occupation?"

"Night cashier."

The clerk paused and looked at the judge. The judge yawned. "Wha's charge?" he asked.

"The charge is"—the clerk looked down at the notation in his hand—"the charge is that he pushed a lady in the face."

"Pleads guilty?"

"Yes."

The preliminaries were now disposed of. Charles David Stuart, looking very harmless and uneasy, was on trial for assault and battery.

The evidence disclosed, rather to the judge's surprise, that the lady whose face had been pushed was not the defendant's wife.

On the contrary the victim was an absolute stranger—the prisoner had never seen her before in his life. His reasons for the assault had been two: first, that she talked during a theatrical performance; and, second, that she kept joggling the back of his chair with her knees. When this had gone on for some time he had turned around and without any warning pushed her severely in the face.

"Call the plaintiff," said the judge, sitting up a little in his chair. "Let's hear what she has to say."

The courtroom, sparsely crowded and unusually languid in the hot afternoon, had become suddenly alert. Several men in the back of the room moved into benches near the desk and a young reporter leaned over the clerk's shoulder and copied the defendant's name on the back of an envelope.

The plaintiff arose. She was a woman just this side of fifty with a determined, rather overbearing face under yellowish white hair. Her dress was a dignified black and she gave the impression of wearing glasses; indeed the young reporter, who believed in observation, had so described her in his mind before he realized that no such adornment sat upon her thin, beaked nose.

It developed that she was Mrs. George D. Robinson of 1219 Riverside Drive. She had always been fond of the theater and sometimes she went to the matinee. There had been two ladies with her yesterday, her cousin, who lived with her, and a Miss Ingles—both ladies were in court.

This is what had occurred:

As the curtain went up for the first act a woman sitting behind had asked her to remove her hat. Mrs. Robinson had been about to do so anyhow, and so she was a little annoyed at the request and had remarked as much to Miss Ingles and her cousin. At this point she had first noticed the defendant who was sitting directly in front, for he had turned around and looked at her quickly in a most insolent way. Then she had forgotten his existence until just before the end of the act when she made some remark to Miss Ingles—when suddenly he had stood up, turned around and pushed her in the face.

"Was it a hard blow?" asked the judge at this point.

"A hard blow!" said Mrs. Robinson indignantly, "I should say it was. I had hot and cold applications on my nose all night."

—"on her nose all night."

This echo came from the witness bench where two faded ladies were leaning forward eagerly and nodding their heads in corroboration.

"Were the lights on?" asked the judge.

No, but everyone around had seen the incident and some people had taken hold of the man right then and there.

This concluded the case for the plaintiff. Her two companions gave similar evidence and in the minds of everyone in the courtroom the incident defined itself as one of unprovoked and inexcusable brutality.

The one element which did not fit in with this interpretation was the physiognomy of the prisoner himself. Of any one of a number of minor offenses he might have appeared guilty—pickpockets were notoriously mild-mannered, for example—but of this particular assault in a crowded theater he seemed physically incapable. He did not have the kind of voice or the kind of clothes or the kind of mustache that went with such an attack.

"Charles David Stuart," said the judge, "you've heard the evidence against you?"

"Yes."

"And you plead guilty?"

"Yes."

"Have you anything to say before I sentence you?"

"No." The prisoner shook his head hopelessly. His small hands were trembling.

"Not one word in extenuation of this unwarranted assault?"

The prisoner appeared to hesitate.

"Go on," said the judge. "Speak up—it's your last chance."

"Well," said Stuart with an effort, "she began talking about the plumber's stomach."

There was a stir in the courtroom. The judge leaned forward.

"What do you mean?"

"Why, at first she was only talking about her own stomach to—to those two ladies there"—he indicated the cousin and Miss Ingles—

"and that wasn't so bad. But when she began talking about the plumber's stomach it got different."

"How do you mean—different?"

Charles Stuart looked around helplessly.

"I can't explain," he said, his mustache wavering a little, "but when she began talking about the plumber's stomach you—you had to listen."

A snicker ran about the courtroom. Mrs. Robinson and her attendant ladies on the bench were visibly horrified. The guard took a step nearer as if at a nod from the judge he would whisk off this criminal to the dingiest dungeon in Manhattan.

But much to his surprise the judge settled himself comfortably in his chair.

"Tell us about it, Stuart," he said not unkindly. "Tell us the whole story from the beginning."

This request was a shock to the prisoner and for a moment he looked as though he would have preferred the order of condemnation. Then after one nervous look around the room he put his hands on the edge of the desk, like the paws of a fox-terrier just being trained to sit up, and began to speak in a quivering voice.

"Well, I'm a night cashier, your honor, in T. Cushmael's restaurant on Third Avenue. I'm not married"—he smiled a little, as if he knew they had all guessed *that*—"and so on Wednesday and Saturday afternoons I usually go to the matinee. It helps to pass the time till dinner. There's a drug store, maybe you know, where you can get tickets for a dollar sixty-five to some of the shows and I usually go there and pick out something. They got awful prices at the box office now." He gave out a long silent whistle and looked feelingly at the judge. "Four or five dollars for one seat—"

The judge nodded his head.

"Well," continued Charles Stuart, "when I pay even a dollar sixty-five I expect to see my money's worth. About two weeks ago I went to one of these here mystery plays where they have one fella that did the crime and nobody knows who it was. Well, the fun at a thing like that is to guess who did it. And there was a lady behind me that'd been there before and she gave it all away to the fella with her. Gee"— his face fell and he shook his head from side to side—"I like to died right there. When I got home to my room I was so mad that they had to come and ask me to stop walking up and down. Dollar sixty-five of my money gone for nothing.

"Well, Wednesday came around again, and this show was one show I wanted to see. I'd been wanting to see it for months, and every time I went into the drug store I asked them if they had any tickets. But they never did." He hesitated. "So Tuesday I took a chance and went over to the box office and got a seat. Two seventy-five it cost me." He nodded impressively. "Two seventy-five. Like throwing money away. But I wanted to see that show."

Mrs. Robinson in the front row rose suddenly to her feet.

"I don't see what all this story has to do with it," she broke out a little shrilly. "I'm sure I don't care—"

The judge brought his gavel sharply down on the desk.

"Sit down, please," he said.

"This is a court of law, not a matinee."

Mrs. Robinson sat down, drawing herself up into a thin line and sniffing a little as if to say she'd see about this after a while. The judge pulled out his watch.

"Go on," he said to Stuart. "Take all the time you want."

"I got there first," continued Stuart in a flustered voice. "There wasn't anybody in there but me and the fella that was cleaning up. After awhile the audience came in, and it got dark and the play started, but just as I was all settled in my seat and ready to have a good time I heard an awful row directly behind me. Somebody had asked this lady"—he pointed directly to Mrs. Robinson—"to remove her hat like she should of done anyhow and she was sore about it. She kept telling the two ladies that was with her how she'd been at the theater before and knew enough to take off her hat. She kept that up for a long time, five minutes maybe, and then every once in a while she'd think of something new and say it in a loud voice. So finally I turned around and looked at her because I wanted to see what a lady looked like that could be so inconsiderate as that. Soon as I turned back she began on me. She said I was insolent and then she said 'Tchk! Tchk! Tchk!' a lot with her tongue and the two ladies that was with her said 'Tchk! Tchk! Tchk!' until you could hardly hear yourself think, much less listen to the play. You'd have thought I'd done something terrible.

"By and by, after they calmed down and I began to catch up with what was doing on the stage, I felt my seat sort of creak forward and then creak back again and I knew the lady had her feet on it and I was in for a good rock. Gosh!" he wiped his pale, narrow brow on which the sweat had gathered thinly, "it was awful. I hope to tell you I wished I'd never come at all. Once I got excited at a show and rocked a man's chair without knowing it and I was glad when he asked me to stop. But I knew this lady wouldn't be glad if I asked her. She'd of just rocked harder than ever."

Some time before, the population of the courtroom had begun

stealing glances at the middle-aged lady with yellowish-white hair. She was of a deep, life-like lobster color with rage.

"It got to be near the end of the act," went on the little pale man, "and I was enjoying it as well as I could, seeing that sometimes she'd push me toward the stage and sometimes she'd let go, and the seat and me would fall back into place. Then all of a sudden she began to talk. She said she had an operation or something—I remember she said she told the doctor that she guessed she knew more about her own stomach than he did. The play was getting good just then—the people next to me had their handkerchiefs out and was weeping—and I was feeling sort of that way myself. And all of a sudden this lady began to tell her friends what she told the plumber about his indigestion. Gosh!" Again he shook his head from side to side; his pale eyes fell involuntarily on Mrs. Robinson—then looked quickly away. "You couldn't help but hear some and I begun missing things and then missing more things and then everybody began laughing and I didn't know what they were laughing at and, as soon as they'd leave off, her voice would begin again. Then there was a great big laugh that lasted for a long time and everybody bent over double and kept laughing and laughing, and I hadn't heard a word. First thing I knew the curtain came down and then I don't know what happened. I must of been a little crazy or something because I got up and closed my seat, and reached back and pushed the lady in the face."

As he concluded there was a long sigh in the courtroom as though everyone had been holding in his breath waiting for the climax. Even the judge gasped a little and the three ladies on the witness bench burst into a shrill chatter and grew louder and louder and shriller and shriller until the judge's gavel rang out again upon his desk.

"Charles Stuart," said the judge in a slightly raised voice, "is this the only extenuation you can make for raising your hand against a woman of the plaintiff's age?"

Charles Stuart's head sank a little between his shoulders, seeming to withdraw as far as it was able into the poor shelter of his body.

"Yes, sir," he said faintly.

Mrs. Robinson sprang to her feet.

"Yes, judge," she cried shrilly, "and there's more than that. He's a liar too, a dirty little liar. He's just proclaimed himself a dirty little—"

"Silence!" cried the judge in a terrible voice. "I'm running this court, and I'm capable of making my own decisions!" He paused. "I will now pronounce sentence upon Charles Stuart," he referred to the register, "upon Charles David Stuart of 212½ West 22nd St."

The courtroom was silent. The reporter drew nearer—he hoped the sentence would be light—just a few days on the Island in lieu of a fine.

The judge leaned back in his chair and hid his thumbs somewhere under his black robe.

"Assault justified," he said. "Case dismissed."

The little man Charles Stuart came blinking out into the sunshine, pausing for a moment at the door of the court and looking furtively behind him as if he half expected that it was a judicial error. Then, sniffling once or twice, not because he had a cold but for those dim psychological reasons that make people sniff, he moved slowly south with an eye out for a subway station.

He stopped at a news-stand to buy a morning paper; then entering the subway was borne south to Eighteenth Street where he disembarked and walked east to Third Avenue. Here he was employed in an all-night restaurant built of glass and plaster white tile. Here he sat at a desk from curfew until dawn, taking in money and balancing the books of T. Cushmael, the proprietor. And here, through the interminable nights, his eyes, by turning a little to right or left, could rest upon the starched linen uniform of Miss Edna Schaeffer.

Miss Edna Schaeffer was twenty-three, with a sweet mild face and hair that was a living example of how henna should not be applied. She was unaware of this latter fact, because all the girls she knew used henna just this way, so perhaps the odd vermilion tint of her coiffure did not matter.

Charles Stuart had forgotten about the color of her hair long ago—if he had ever noticed its strangeness at all. He was much more interested in her eyes, and in her white hands which, as they moved deftly among piles of plates and cups, always looked as if they should be playing the piano. He had almost asked her to go to a matinee with him once, but when she had faced him her lips half-parted in a weary, cheerful smile, she had seemed so beautiful that he had lost courage and mumbled something else instead.

It was not to see Edna Schaeffer, however, that he had come to the restaurant so early in the afternoon. It was to consult with T. Cushmael, his employer, and discover if he had lost his job during his night in jail. T. Cushmael was standing in the front of the restaurant looking gloomily out the plate-glass window, and Charles Stuart approached him with ominous forebodings.

"Where've you been?" demanded T. Cushmael.

"Nowhere," answered Charles Stuart discreetly.

"Well, you're fired."

Stuart winced.

"Right now?"

Cushmael waved his hands apathetically.

"Stay two or three days if you want to, till I find somebody. Then"—he made a gesture of expulsion—"outside for you."

Charles Stuart assented with a weary little nod. He assented to everything. At nine o'clock, after a depressed interval during which he brooded upon the penalty of spending a night among the police, he reported for work.

"Hello, Mr. Stuart," said Edna Schaeffer, sauntering curiously toward him as he took his place behind the desk. "What became of you last night? Get pinched?"

She laughed, cheerfully, huskily, charmingly he thought, at her joke.

"Yes," he answered on a sudden impulse, "I was in the Thirty-fifth Street jail."

"Yes, you were," she scoffed.

"That's the truth," he insisted, "I was arrested."

Her face grew serious at once.

"Go *on*. What did you do?"

He hesitated.

"I pushed somebody in the face."

Suddenly she began to laugh, at first with amusement and then immoderately.

"It's a fact," mumbled Stuart, "I almost got sent to prison account of it."

Setting her hand firmly over her mouth Edna turned away from him and retired to the refuge of the kitchen. A little later, when he was pretending to be busy at the accounts, he saw her retailing the story to the two other girls.

The night wore on. The little man in the grayish suit with the grayish face attracted no more attention from the customers than the whirring electric fan over his head. They gave him their money and his hand slid their change into a little hollow in the marble counter. But to Charles Stuart the hours of this night, this last night, began to assume a quality of romance. The slow routine of a hundred other nights unrolled with a new enchantment before his eyes. Midnight was always a sort of a dividing point—after that the intimate part of the evening began. Fewer people came in, and the ones that did seemed depressed and tired: a casual ragged man for coffee, the beggar from the street corner who ate a heavy meal of cakes and a beefsteak, a few nightbound street-women and a watchman with a red face who exchanged warning phrases with him about his health.

Midnight seemed to come early tonight and business was brisk until after one. When Edna began to fold napkins at a nearby table he was tempted to ask her if she too had not found the night unusually short. Vainly he wished that he might impress himself on her in some way, make some remark to her, some sign of his devotion that she would remember forever.

She finished folding the vast pile of napkins, loaded it onto the stand and bore it away, humming to herself. A few minutes later the door opened and two customers came in. He recognized them immediately, and as he did so a flush of jealousy went over him. One of them, a young man in a handsome brown suit, cut away rakishly from his abdomen, had been a frequent visitor for the last ten days. He came in always at about this hour, sat down at one of Edna's tables, and drank two cups of coffee with lingering ease. On his last two visits he had been accompanied by his present companion, a swarthy Greek with sour eyes who ordered in a loud voice and gave vent to noisy sarcasm when anything was not to his taste.

It was chiefly the young man, though, who annoyed Charles Stuart. The young man's eyes followed Edna wherever she went, and on his last two visits he had made unnecessary requests in order to bring her more often to his table.

"Good evening, girlie," Stuart heard him say to-night. "How's tricks?"

"O. K.," answered Edna formally. "What'll it be?"

"What have you?" smiled the young man. "Everything, eh? Well, what'd you recommend?"

Edna did not answer. Her eyes were staring straight over his head into some invisible distance.

He ordered finally at the urging of his companion. Edna withdrew and Stuart saw the young man turn and whisper to his friend, indicating Edna with his head.

Stuart shifted uncomfortably in his seat. He hated that young man and wished passionately that he would go away. It seemed as if his last night here, his last chance to watch Edna, and perhaps even in some blessed moment to talk to her a little, was marred by every moment this man stayed.

Half a dozen more people had drifted into the restaurant—two or three workmen, the newsdealer from over the way—and Edna was too busy for a few minutes to be bothered with attentions. Suddenly Charles Stuart became aware that the sour-eyed Greek had raised his hand and was beckoning him. Somewhat puzzled he left his desk and approached the table.

"Say, fella," said the Greek, "what time does the boss come in?"

"Why—two o'clock. Just a few minutes now."

"All right. That's all. I just wanted to speak to him about something."

Stuart realized that Edna was standing beside the table; both men turned toward her.

"Say, girlie," said the young man, "I want to talk to you. Sit down."

"I can't."

"Sure you can. The boss don't mind." He turned menacingly to Stuart. "She can sit down, can't she?"

Stuart did not answer.

"I say she can sit down, can't she?" said the young man more intently, and added, "Speak up, you little dummy."

Still Stuart did not answer. Strange blood currents were flowing all over his body. He was frightened; anything said determinedly had a way of frightening him. But he could not move.

"Sh!" said the Greek to his companion.

But the younger man was angered.

"Say," he broke out, "some time somebody's going to take a paste at you when you don't answer what they say. Go on back to your desk!"

Still Stuart did not move.

"Go on away!" repeated the young man in a dangerous voice. "Hurry up! *Run!*"

Then Stuart ran. He ran as hard as he was able. But instead of running away from the young man he ran *toward* him, stretching out his hands as he came near in a sort of straight arm that brought his two palms, with all the force of his hundred and thirty pounds, against his victim's face. With a crash of china the young man went over backward in his chair and, his head striking the edge of the next table, lay motionless on the floor.

The restaurant was in a small uproar. There was a terrified scream from Edna, an indignant protest from the Greek, and the customers arose with exclamations from their tables. Just at this moment the door opened and Mr. Cushmael came in.

"Why you little fool!" cried Edna wrathfully. "What are you trying to do? Lose me my job?"

"What's this?" demanded Mr. Cushmael, hurrying over. "What's the idea?"

"Mr. Stuart pushed a customer in the face!" cried a waitress, taking Edna's cue. "For no reason at all!"

The population of the restaurant had now gathered around the prostrate victim. He was doused thoroughly with water and a folded tablecloth was placed under his head.

"Oh, he did, did he?" shouted Mr. Cushmael in a terrible voice, seizing Stuart by the lapels of his coat.

"He's raving crazy!" sobbed Edna. "He was in jail last night for pushing a lady in the face. He told me so himself!"

A large laborer reached over and grasped Stuart's small trembling arm. Stuart gazed around dumbly. His mouth was quivering.

"Look what you done!" shouted Mr. Cushmael. "You like to kill a man."

Stuart shivered violently. His mouth opened and he fought the air for a moment. Then he uttered a half-articulate sentence:

"Only meant to push him in the face."

"Push him in the face?" ejaculated Cushmael in a frenzy. "So you got to be a pusher-in-the-face, eh? Well, we'll push your face right into jail!"

"I—I couldn't help it," gasped Stuart. "Sometimes I can't help it." His voice rose unevenly. "I guess I'm a dangerous man and you better take me and lock me up!" He turned wildly to Cushmael, "I'd push you in the face if he'd let go my arm. Yes, I would! I'd push you—right-in-the-*face!*"

For a moment an astonished silence fell, broken by the voice of one of the waitresses who had been groping under the table.

"Some stuff dropped out of this fella's back pocket when he tipped over," she explained, getting to her feet. "It's—why, it's a revolver and—"

She had been about to say handkerchief, but as she looked at what she was holding her mouth fell open and she dropped the thing quickly on the table. It was a small black mask about the size of her hand.

Simultaneously the Greek, who had been shifting uneasily upon his feet ever since the accident, seemed to remember an important engagement that had slipped his mind. He dashed suddenly around the table and made for the front door, but it opened just at that moment to admit several customers who, at the cry of "Stop him!" obligingly spread out their arms. Barred in that direction, he jumped an overturned chair, vaulted over the delicatessen counter, and set out for the kitchen, collapsing precipitately in the firm grasp of the chef in the doorway.

"Hold him! Hold him!" screamed Mr. Cushmael, realizing the turn of the situation. "They're after my cash drawer!"

Willing hands assisted the Greek over the counter, where he stood panting and gasping under two dozen excited eyes.

"After my money, hey?" shouted the proprietor, shaking his fist under the captive's nose.

The stout man nodded, panting.

"We'd of got it too!" he gasped, "if it hadn't been for that little pusher-in-the-face."

Two dozen eyes looked around eagerly. The little pusher-in-the-face had disappeared.

The beggar on the corner had just decided to tip the policeman and shut up shop for the night when he suddenly felt a small, somewhat excited hand fall on his shoulder.

"Help a poor man get a place to sleep—" he was beginning automatically when he recognized the little cashier from the restaurant. "Hello, brother," he added, leering up at him and changing his tone.

"You know what?" cried the little cashier in a strangely ominous tone. "I'm going to push you in the face!"

"What do you mean?" snarled the beggar. "Why, you Ga—"

He got no farther. The little man seemed to run at him suddenly, holding out his hands, and there was a sharp, smacking sound as the beggar came in contact with the sidewalk.

"You're a fakir!" shouted Charles Stuart wildly. "I gave you a dollar when I first came here, before I found out you had ten times as much as I had. And you never gave it back!"

A stout, faintly intoxicated gentlemen who was strutting expansively along the other sidewalk had seen the incident and came running benevolently across the street.

"What does this mean!" he exclaimed in a hearty, shocked voice. "Why, poor fellow—" He turned indignant eyes on Charles Stuart and knelt unsteadily to raise the beggar.

The beggar stopped cursing and assumed a piteous whine.

"I'm a poor man, Cap'n—"

"This is—this is *horrible!*" cried the Samaritan, with tears in his eyes. "It's a disgrace! Police! *Pol—!*"

He got no farther. His hands, which he was raising for a megaphone, never reached his face—other hands reached his face, however, hands held stiffly out from a one-hundred-and-thirty-pound body! He sank down suddenly upon the beggar's abdomen, forcing out a sharp curse which faded into a groan.

"This beggar'll take you home in his car!" shouted the little man who stood over him. "He's got it parked around the corner."

Turning his face toward the hot strip of sky which lowered over the city the little man began to laugh, with amusement at first, then loudly and triumphantly until his high laughter ran out in the quiet street with a weird, elfish sound, echoing up the sides of the tall buildings, growing shriller and shriller until people blocks away heard its eerie cadence on the air and stopped to listen.

Still laughing the little man divested himself of his coat and then of his vest and hurriedly freed his neck of tie and collar. Then he spat upon his hands and with a wild, shrill, exultant cry began to run down the dark street.

He was going to clean up New York, and his first objective was the disagreeable policeman on the corner!

They caught him at two o'clock, and the crowd which had joined in the chase were flabbergasted when they found that the ruffian was only a weeping little man in his shirt sleeves. Someone at the station house was wise enough to give him an opiate instead of a padded cell, and in the morning he felt much better.

Mr. Cushmael, accompanied by an anxious young lady with crimson hair, called at the jail before noon.

"I'll get you out," cried Mr. Cushmael, shaking hands excitedly through the bars. "One policeman, he'll explain it all to the other."

"And there's a surprise for you too," added Edna softly, taking his other hand. "Mr. Cushmael's got a big heart and he's going to make you his day man now."

"All right," agreed Charles Stuart calmly. "But I can't start till to-morrow."

"Why not?"

"Because this afternoon I got to go to a matinee—with a friend."

He relinquished his employer's hand but kept Edna's white fingers twined firmly in his.

"One more thing," he went on in a strong, confident voice that was new to him, "if you want to get me off don't have the case come up in the Thirty-fifth Street court."

"Why not?"

"Because," he answered with a touch of swagger in his voice, "that's the judge I had when I was arrested last time."

"Charles," whispered Edna suddenly, "what would you do if I refused to go with you this afternoon?"

He bristled. Color came into his cheeks and he rose defiantly from his bench.

"Why, I'd—I'd—"

"Never mind," she said, flushing slightly. "You'd do nothing of the kind."

One of My Oldest Friends

(*Woman's Home Companion*, September 1925)

"One of My Oldest Friends" was written in Great Neck in March 1924. When Fitzgerald sent it to Ober he noted, "Here's the revised story. I don't know what to think of it but I'd rather *not* offer it to the Post. The ending is effective but a little sensational." *Woman's Home Companion* paid $1750 for it and used it as the lead piece.

Fitzgerald's reservations about the story were well-founded. The use of a crucifix at the end represents one of his rare excursions into forced religious symbolism. Nonetheless, "One of My Oldest Friends" was a popular story. It was included in *The World's Best Short Stories of 1926* and was probably syndicated in newspapers, as short stories often were at that time.

All afternoon Marion had been happy. She wandered from room to room of their little apartment, strolling into the nursery to help the nurse-girl feed the children from dripping spoons, and then reading for a while on their new sofa, the most extravagant thing they had bought in their five years of marriage.

When she heard Michael's step in the hall she turned her head and listened; she liked to hear him walk, carefully always as if there were children sleeping close by.

"Michael."

"Oh—hello." He came into the room, a tall, broad, thin man of thirty with a high forehead and kind black eyes.

"I've got some news for you," he said immediately. "Charley Hart's getting married."

"No!"

He nodded.

"Who's he marrying?"

"One of the little Lawrence girls from home." He hesitated. "She's arriving in New York to-morrow and I think we ought to do something for them while she's here. Charley's about my oldest friend."

"Let's have them up for dinner—"

"I'd like to do something more than that," he interrupted. "Maybe a theater party. You see—" Again he hesitated. "It'd be a nice courtesy to Charley."

"All right," agreed Marion, "but we musn't spend much—and I don't think we're under any obligation."

He looked at her in surprise.

"I mean," went on Marion, "we—we hardly see Charley any more. We hardly ever see him at all."

"Well, you know how it is in New York," explained Michael apologetically. "He's just as busy as I am. He has made a big name for himself and I suppose he's pretty much in demand all the time."

They always spoke of Charley Hart as their oldest friend. Five years before, when Michael and Marion were first married, the three of them had come to New York from the same Western city. For over a year they had seen Charley nearly every day and no domestic adventure, no uprush of their hopes and dreams, was too insignificant for his ear. His arrival in times of difficulty never failed to give a pleasant, humorous cast to the situation.

Of course Marion's babies had made a difference, and it was several years now since they had called up Charley at midnight to say that the pipes had broken or the ceiling was falling in on their heads; but so gradually had they drifted apart that Michael still spoke of Charley rather proudly as if he saw him every day. For a while Charley dined with them once a month and all three found a great deal to say; but the meetings never broke up any more with, "I'll give you a ring to-morrow." Instead it was, "You'll have to come to dinner more often," or even, after three or four years, "We'll see you soon."

"Oh, I'm perfectly willing to give a little party," said Marion now, looking speculatively about her. "Did you suggest a definite date?"

"Week from Saturday." His dark eyes roamed the floor vaguely. "We can take up the rugs or something."

"No." She shook her head. "We'll have a dinner, eight people, very formal and everything, and afterwards we'll play cards."

She was already speculating on whom to invite. Charley of course, being an artist, probably saw interesting people every day.

"We could have the Willoughbys," she suggested doubtfully. "She's on the stage or something—and he writes movies."

"No—that's not it," objected Michael. "He probably meets that crowd at lunch and dinner every day until he's sick of them. Besides, except for the Willoughbys, who else like that do we know? I've got a better idea. Let's collect a few people who've drifted down here from home. They've all followed Charley's career and they'd probably enjoy seeing him again. I'd like them to find out how natural and unspoiled he is after all."

After some discussion they agreed on this plan and within an hour Marion had her first guest on the telephone:

"It's to meet Charley Hart's fiancée," she explained. "Charley Hart, the artist. You see, he's one of our oldest friends."

As she began her preparations her enthusiasm grew. She rented a serving-maid to assure an impeccable service and persuaded the neighborhood florist to come in person and arrange the flowers. All the "people from home" had accepted eagerly and the number of guests had swollen to ten.

"What'll we talk about, Michael?" she demanded nervously on the eve of the party. "Suppose everything goes wrong and everybody gets mad and goes home?"

He laughed.

"Nothing will. You see, these people all know each other—"

The phone on the table asserted itself and Michael picked up the receiver.

"Hello . . . why, hello, Charley."

Marion sat up alertly in her chair.

"Is that so? Well, I'm very sorry. I'm very, very sorry . . . I hope it's nothing serious."

"Can't he come?" broke out Marion.

"Sh!" Then into the phone, "Well, it certainly is too bad, Charley. No, it's no trouble for us at all. We're just sorry you're ill."

With a dismal gesture Michael replaced the receiver.

"The Lawrence girl had to go home last night and Charley's sick in bed with grip."

"Do you mean he can't come?"

"He can't come."

Marion's face contracted suddenly and her eyes filled with tears.

"He says he's had the doctor all day," explained Michael dejectedly. "He's got fever and they didn't even want him to go to the telephone."

"I don't care," sobbed Marion. "I think it's terrible. After we've invited all these people to meet him."

"People can't help being sick."

"Yes they *can*," she wailed illogically, "they can help it some way. And if the Lawrence girl was going to leave last night why didn't he let us know *then*?"

"He said she left unexpectedly. Up to yesterday afternoon they both intended to come."

"I don't think he c-cares a bit. I'll bet he's glad he's sick. If he'd cared he'd have brought her to see us long ago."

She stood up suddenly.

"I'll tell you one thing," she assured him vehemently, "I'm just going to telephone everybody and call the whole thing off."

"Why, Marion—"

But in spite of his half-hearted protests she picked up the phone book and began looking for the first number.

They bought theater tickets next day hoping to fill the hollowness which would invest the evening. Marion had wept when the unintercepted florist arrived at five with boxes of flowers and she felt that she must get out of the house to avoid the ghosts who would presently people it. In silence they ate an elaborate dinner composed of all the things that she had bought for the party.

"It's only eight," said Michael afterwards, "I think it'd be sort of nice if we dropped in on Charley for a minute, don't you?"

"Why, no," Marion answered, startled, "I wouldn't think of it."

"Why not? If he's seriously sick I'd like to see how well he's being taken care of."

She saw that he had made up his mind, so she fought down her instinct against the idea and they taxied to a tall pile of studio apartments on Madison Avenue.

"You go on in," urged Marion nervously, "I'd rather wait out here."

"Please come in."

"Why? He'll be in bed and he doesn't want any women around."

"But he'd like to see you—it'd cheer him up. And he'd know that we understood about to-night. He sounded awfully depressed over the phone."

He urged her from the cab.

"Let's only stay a minute," she whispered tensely as they went up in the elevator. "The show starts at half past eight."

"Apartment on the right," said the elevator man.

They rang the bell and waited. The door opened and they walked directly into Charley Hart's great studio room.

It was crowded with people; from end to end ran a long lamp-lit dinner table strewn with ferns and young roses, from which a gay murmur of laughter and conversation arose into the faintly smoky air. Twenty women in evening dress sat on one side in a row chatting across the flowers at twenty men, with an elation born of the sparkling Burgundy which dripped from many bottles into thin chilled glass. Up on the high narrow balcony which encircled the room a string quartet was playing something by Stravinski in a key that was pitched just below the women's voices and filled the air like an audible wine.

The door had been opened by one of the waiters, who stepped back deferentially from what he thought were two belated guests—and immediately a handsome man at the head of the table started to his feet, napkin in hand, and stood motionless, staring toward the newcomers. The conversation faded into half silence and all eyes followed Charley Hart's to the couple at the door. Then, as if the spell was broken, conversation resumed, gathering momentum word by word—the moment was over.

"Let's get out!" Marion's low, terrified whisper came to Michael out of a void and for a minute he thought he was possessed by an illusion, that there was no one but Charley in the room after all. Then his eyes cleared and he saw that there were many people here—he had never seen so many! The music swelled suddenly into the tumult of a great brass band and a wind from the loud horns seemed to blow against them; without turning he and Marion each made one blind step backward into the hall, pulling the door to after them.

"Marion—!"

She had run toward the elevator, stood with one finger pressed hard against the bell which rang through the hall like a last high note from the music inside. The door of the apartment opened suddenly and Charley Hart came out into the hall.

"Michael!" he cried, "Michael and Marion, I want to explain! Come inside. I want to *explain*, I tell you."

He talked excitedly—his face was flushed and his mouth formed a word or two that did not materialize into sound.

"Hurry up, Michael," came Marion's voice tensely from the elevator.

"Let me explain," cried Charley frantically. "I want—"

Michael moved away from him—the elevator came and the gate clanged open.

"You act as if I'd committed some crime." Charley was following Michael along the hall. "Can't you understand that this is all an accidental situation?"

"It's all right," Michael muttered, "I understand."

"No, you don't." Charley's voice rose with exasperation. He was working up anger against them so as to justify his own intolerable position. "You're going away mad and I asked you to come in and join the party. Why did you come up here if you won't come in? Did you—?"

Michael walked into the elevator.

"Down, please!" cried Marion. "Oh, I want to go down, *please!*"

The gates clanged shut.

They told the taxi-man to take them directly home—neither of them could have endured the theater. Driving uptown to their apartment, Michael buried his face in his hands and tried to realize that the friendship which had meant so much to him was over. He saw now that it had been over for some time, that not once during the past year had Charley sought their company and the shock of the discovery far outweighed the affront he had received.

When they reached home, Marion, who had not said a word in the taxi, led the way into the living-room and motioned for her husband to sit down.

"I'm going to tell you something that you ought to know," she said. "If it hadn't been for what happened to-night I'd probably never have told you—but now I think you ought to hear the whole story." She hesitated. "In the first place, Charley Hart wasn't a friend of yours at all."

"What?" He looked up at her dully.

"He wasn't your friend," she repeated. "He hasn't been for years. He was a friend of mine."

"Why, Charley Hart was—"

"I know what you're going to say—that Charley was a friend to both of us. But it isn't true. I don't know how he considered you at first but he stopped being your friend three or four years ago."

"Why—" Michael's eyes glowed with astonishment. "If that's true, why was he with us all the time?"

"On account of me," said Marion steadily. "He was in love with me."

"What?" Michael laughed incredulously. "You're imagining things. I know how he used to pretend in a kidding way—"

"It wasn't kidding," she interrupted, "not underneath. It began that way—and it ended by his asking me to run away with him."

Michael frowned.

"Go on," he said quietly, "I suppose this is true or you wouldn't be telling me about it—but it simply doesn't seem real. Did he just suddenly begin to—to—"

He closed his mouth suddenly, unable to say the words.

"It began one night when we three were out dancing," Marion hesitated. "And at first I thoroughly enjoyed it. He had a faculty for noticing things—noticing dresses and hats and the new ways I'd do my hair. He was good company. He could always make me feel important, somehow, and attractive. Don't get the idea that I preferred his company to yours—I didn't. I knew how completely selfish he was, and what a will-o'-the-wisp. But I encouraged him, I suppose—I thought it was fine. It was a new angle on Charley, and he was amusing at it just as he was at everything he did."

"Yes—" agreed Michael with an effort, "I suppose it was—hilariously amusing."

"At first he liked you just the same. It didn't occur to him that he was doing anything treacherous to you. He was just following a natural impulse—that was all. But after a few weeks he began to find you in the way. He wanted to take me to dinner without you along—and it couldn't be done. Well, that sort of thing went on for over a year."

"What happened then?"

"Nothing happened. That's why he stopped coming to see us any more."

Michael rose slowly to his feet.

"Do you mean—"

"Wait a minute. If you'll think a little you'll see it was bound to turn out that way. When he saw that I was trying to let him down easily so that he'd be simply one of our oldest friends again, he broke away. He didn't want to be one of our oldest friends—that time was over."

"I see."

"Well—" Marion stood up and began biting nervously at her lip, "that's all. I thought this thing to-night would hurt you less if you understood the whole affair."

"Yes," Michael answered in a dull voice, "I suppose that's true."

Michael's business took a prosperous turn, and when summer came they went to the country, renting a little old farmhouse where the children played all day on a tangled half acre of grass and trees. The subject of Charley was never mentioned between them and as the months passed he receded to a shadowy background in their minds. Sometimes, just before dropping off to sleep, Michael found himself thinking of the happy times the three of them had had together five years before—then the reality would intrude upon the illusion and he would be repelled from the subject with almost physical distaste.

One warm evening in July he lay dozing on the porch in the twilight. He had had a hard day at his office and it was welcome to rest here while the summer light faded from the land.

At the sound of an automobile he raised his head lazily. At the end of the path a local taxicab had stopped and a young man was getting out. With an exclamation Michael sat up. Even in the dusk he recognized those shoulders, that impatient walk—

"Well, I'm damned," he said softly.

As Charley Hart came up the gravel path Michael noticed in a glance that he was unusually disheveled. His handsome face was drawn and tired, his clothes were out of press and he had the unmistakable look of needing a good night's sleep.

He came up on the porch, saw Michael and smiled in a wan, embarrassed way.

"Hello, Michael."

Neither of them made any move to shake hands but after a moment Charley collapsed abruptly into a chair.

"I'd like a glass of water," he said huskily, "it's hot as hell."

Without a word Michael went into the house—returned with a glass of water which Charley drank in great noisy gulps.

"Thanks," he said, gasping, "I thought I was going to pass away."

He looked about him with eyes that only pretended to take in his surroundings.

"Nice little place you've got here," he remarked; his eyes returned to Michael. "Do you want me to get out?"

"Why—no. Sit and rest if you want to. You look all in."

"I am. Do you want to hear about it?"

"Not in the least."

"Well, I'm going to tell you anyhow," said Charley defiantly. "That's what I came out here for. I'm in trouble, Michael, and I haven't got anybody to go to except you."

"Have you tried your friends?" asked Michael coolly.

"I've tried about everybody—everybody I've had time to go to. God!" He wiped his forehead with his hand. "I never realized how hard it was to raise a simple two thousand dollars."

"Have you come to me for two thousand dollars?"

"Wait a minute, Michael. Wait till you hear. It just shows you what a mess a man can get into without meaning any harm. You see, I'm the treasurer of a society called the Independent Artists' Benefit— a thing to help struggling students. There was a fund, thirty-five hundred dollars, and it's been lying in my bank for over a year. Well, as you know, I live pretty high—make a lot and spend a lot—and about a month ago I began speculating a little through a friend of mine—"

"I don't know why you're telling me all this," interrupted Michael impatiently, "I—"

"Wait a minute, won't you—I'm almost through." He looked at Michael with frightened eyes. "I used that money sometimes without even realizing that it wasn't mine. I've always had plenty of my own,

you see. Till this week," he hesitated, "this week there was a meeting
of this society and they asked me to turn over the money. Well, I went
to a couple of men to try and borrow it and as soon as my back was
turned one of them blabbed. There was a terrible blow-up last night.
They told me unless I handed over the two thousand this morning
they'd send me to jail—" His voice rose and he looked around wildly.
"There's a warrant out for me now—and if I can't get the money I'll
kill myself, Michael; I swear to God I will; I won't go to prison. I'm an
artist—not a business man. I—"

He made an effort to control his voice.

"Michael," he whispered, "you're my oldest friend. I haven't got
anyone in the world but you to turn to."

"You're a little late," said Michael uncomfortably, "you didn't
think of me four years ago when you asked my wife to run away with
you."

A look of sincere surprise passed over Charley's face.

"Are you mad at me about that?" he asked in a puzzled way. "I
thought you were mad because I didn't come to your party."

Michael did not answer.

"I supposed she'd told you about that long ago," went on
Charley. "I couldn't help it about Marion I was lonesome and you
two had each other. Every time I went to your house you'd tell me
what a wonderful girl Marion was and finally I—I began to agree
with you. How could I help falling in love with her, when for a year
and a half she was the only decent girl I knew?" He looked defiantly at
Michael. "Well, you've got her, haven't you. I didn't take her away. I
never so much as kissed her—do you have to rub it in?"

"Look here," said Michael sharply, "just why should I lend you
this money?"

"Well—" Charley hesitated, laughed uneasily, "I don't know
any exact reason. I just thought you would."

"Why should I?"

"No reason at all, I suppose, from your way of looking at it."

"That's the trouble. If I gave it to you it would just be because I
was slushy and soft. I'd be doing something that I don't want to do."

"All right," Charley smiled unpleasantly, "that's logical. Now
that I think, there's no reason why you should lend it to me. Well—"
he shoved his hands into his coat pocket and throwing his head back
slightly seemed to shake the subject off like a cap, "I won't go to
prison—and maybe you'll feel differently about it to-morrow."

"Don't count on that."

"Oh, I don't mean I'll ask you again. I mean something—quite
different."

He nodded his head, turned quickly and walking down the gravel path was swallowed up in the darkness. Where the path met the road Michael heard his footsteps cease as if he were hesitating. Then they turned down the road toward the station a mile away.

Michael sank into his chair, burying his face in his hands. He heard Marion come out the door.

"I listened," she whispered, "I couldn't help it. I'm glad you didn't lend him anything."

She came close to him and would have sat down in his lap but an almost physical repulsion came over him and he got up quickly from his chair.

"I was afraid he'd work on your sentiment and make a fool of you," went on Marion. She hesitated. "He hated you, you know. He used to wish you'd die. I told him that if he ever said so to me again I'd never see him any more."

Michael looked up at her darkly.

"In fact, you were very noble."

"Why, Michael—"

"You let him say things like that to you—and then when he comes here, down and out, without a friend in the world to turn to, you say you're glad I sent him away."

"It's because I love you, dear—"

"No, it isn't!" He interrupted savagely. "It's because hate's cheap in this world. Everybody's got it for sale. My God! What do you suppose I think of myself now?"

"He's not worth feeling that way about."

"Please go away!" cried Michael passionately. "I want to be alone."

Obediently she left him and he sat down again in the darkness of the porch, a sort of terror creeping over him. Several times he made a motion to get up but each time he frowned and remained motionless. Then after another long while he jumped suddenly to his feet, cold sweat starting from his forehead. The last hour, the months just passed, were washed away and he was swept years back in time. Why, they were after Charley Hart, his old friend. Charley Hart who had come to him because he had no other place to go. Michael began to run hastily about the porch in a daze, hunting for his hat and coat.

"Why Charley!" he cried aloud.

He found his coat finally and, struggling into it, ran wildly down the steps. It seemed to him that Charley had gone out only a few minutes before.

"Charley!" he called when he reached the road, "Charley, come back here. There's been a mistake!"

He paused, listening. There was no answer. Panting a little he began to run doggedly along the road through the hot night.

It was only half past eight o'clock but the country was very quiet and the frogs were loud in the strip of wet marsh that ran along beside the road. The sky was salted thinly with stars and after a while there would be a moon, but the road ran among dark trees and Michael could scarcely see ten feet in front of him. After a while he slowed down to a walk, glancing at the phosphorous dial of his wrist watch—the New York train was not due for an hour. There was plenty of time.

In spite of this he broke into an uneasy run and covered the mile between his house and the station in fifteen minutes. It was a little station, crouched humbly beside the shining rails in the darkness. Beside it Michael saw the lights of a single taxi waiting for the next train.

The platform was deserted and Michael opened the door and peered into the dim waiting-room. It was empty.

"That's funny," he muttered.

Rousing a sleepy taxi driver, he asked if there had been anyone waiting for the train. The taxi driver considered—yes, there had been a young man waiting, about twenty minutes ago. He had walked up and down for a while, smoking a cigarette, and then gone away into the darkness.

"That's funny," repeated Michael. He made a megaphone of his hands and facing toward the wood across the track shouted aloud.

"Charley!"

There was no answer. He tried again. Then he turned back to the driver.

"Have you any idea what direction he went?"

The man pointed vaguely down the New York road which ran along beside the railroad track.

"Down there somewhere."

With increasing uneasiness Michael thanked him and started swiftly along the road which was white now under the risen moon. He knew now as surely as he knew anything that Charley had gone off by himself to die. He remembered the expression on his face as he had turned away and the hand tucked down close in his coat pocket as if it clutched some menacing thing.

"Charley!" he called in a terrible voice.

The dark trees gave back no sound. He walked on past a dozen fields bright as silver under the moon, pausing every few minutes to shout and then waiting tensely for an answer.

It occurred to him that it was foolish to continue in this

direction—Charley was probably back by the station in the woods somewhere. Perhaps it was all imagination, perhaps even now Charley was pacing the station platform waiting for the train from the city. But some impulse beyond logic made him continue. More than that—several times he had the sense that someone was in front of him, someone who just eluded him at every turning, out of sight and earshot, yet leaving always behind him a dim, tragic aura of having passed that way. Once he thought he heard steps among the leaves on the side of the road but it was only a piece of vagrant newspaper blown by the faint hot wind.

It was a stifling night—the moon seemed to be beating hot rays down upon the sweltering earth. Michael took off his coat and threw it over his arm as he walked. A little way ahead of him now was a stone bridge over the tracks and beyond that an interminable line of telephone poles which stretched in diminishing perspective toward an endless horizon. Well, he would walk to the bridge and then give up. He would have given up before except for this sense he had that someone was walking very lightly and swiftly just ahead.

Reaching the stone bridge he sat down on a rock, his heart beating in loud exhausted thumps under his dripping shirt. Well, it was hopeless—Charley was gone, perhaps out of range of his help forever. Far away beyond the station he heard the approaching siren of the nine-thirty train.

Michael found himself wondering suddenly why he was here. He despised himself for being here. On what weak chord in his nature had Charley played in those few minutes, forcing him into this senseless, frightened run through the night? They had discussed it all and Charley had been unable to give a reason why he should be helped.

He got to his feet with the idea of retracing his steps but before turning he stood for a minute in the moonlight looking down the road. Across the track stretched the line of telephone poles and, as his eyes followed them as far as he could see, he heard again, louder now and not far away, the siren of the New York train which rose and fell with musical sharpness on the still night. Suddenly his eyes, which had been traveling down the tracks, stopped and were focused suddenly upon one spot in the line of poles, perhaps a quarter of a mile away. It was a pole just like the others and yet it was different— there was something about it that was indescribably different.

And watching it as one might concentrate on some figure in the pattern of a carpet, something curious happened in his mind and instantly he saw everything in a completely different light. Something had come to him in a whisper of the breeze, something that changed the whole complexion of the situation. It was this: He remembered having read somewhere that at some point back in the dark ages a man named Gerbert had all by himself summed up the whole of European civilization. It became suddenly plain to Michael that he himself had just now been in a position like that. For one minute, one spot in time, all the mercy in the world had been vested in him.

He realized all this in the space of a second with a sense of shock and instantly he understood the reason why he should have helped Charley Hart. It was because it would be intolerable to exist in a world where there was no help—where any human being could be as alone as Charley had been alone this afternoon.

Why, that was it, of course—he had been trusted with that chance. Someone had come to him who had no other place to go— and he had failed.

All this time, this moment, he had been standing utterly motionless staring at the telephone pole down the track, the one that his eye had picked out as being different from the others. The moon was so bright now that near the top he could see a white bar set crosswise on the pole and as he looked the pole and the bar seemed to have become isolated as if the other poles had shrunk back and away.

Suddenly a mile down the track he heard the click and clamor of the electric train when it left the station, and as if the sound had startled him into life he gave a short cry and set off at a swaying run down the road, in the direction of the pole with the crossed bar.

The train whistled again. Click—click—click—it was nearer now, six hundred, five hundred yards away and as it came under the bridge he was running in the bright beam of its searchlight. There was no emotion in his mind but terror—he knew only that he must reach that pole before the train, and it was fifty yards away, struck out sharp as a star against the sky.

There was no path on the other side of the tracks under the poles but the train was so close now that he dared wait no longer or he would be unable to cross at all. He darted from the road, cleared the tracks in two strides and with the sound of the engine at his heels raced along the rough earth. Twenty feet, thirty feet—as the sound of the electric train swelled to a roar in his ears he reached the pole and threw himself bodily on a man who stood there close to the tracks, carrying him heavily to the ground with the impact of his body.

There was the thunder of steel in his ear, the heavy clump of the wheels on the rails, a swift roaring of air, and the nine-thirty train had gone past.

"Charley," he gasped incoherently, "Charley."

A white face looked up at him in a daze. Michael rolled over on his back and lay panting. The hot night was quiet now—there was no sound but the far-away murmur of the receding train.

"Oh, God!"

Michael opened his eyes to see that Charley was sitting up, his face in his hands.

"S'all right," gasped Michael, "s'all right, Charley. You can have the money. I don't know what I was thinking about. Why—why, you're one of my oldest friends."

Charley shook his head.

"I don't understand," he said brokenly. "Where did you come from—how did you get here?"

"I've been following you. I was just behind."

"I've been here for half an hour."

"Well, it's good you chose this pole to—to wait under. I've been looking at it from down by the bridge. I picked it out on account of the crossbar."

Charley had risen unsteadily to his feet and now he walked a few steps and looked up the pole in the full moonlight.

"What did you say?" he asked after a minute, in a puzzled voice. "Did you say this pole had a crossbar?"

"Why, yes. I was looking at it a long time. That's how—"

Charley looked up again and hesitated curiously before he spoke.

"There isn't any crossbar," he said.

The Unspeakable Egg

(*The Saturday Evening Post*, 12 July 1924)

"The Unspeakable Egg" was written in Great Neck in April 1924. The *Post* paid $1750 for it.

Most of the 1924 stories depend on trick plots; and "Egg" employs the concealed identity gimmick that Fitzgerald had used effectively before. It seems probable that some of these stories were written with the hope of a movie sale, since three of his stories had been made into movies. There were no takers for "Egg."

Fitzgerald has been criticized for the facility of his *Post* stories—which was what he was being paid for. He was writing entertainment for the 2,750,000 customers who bought the magazine in the Twenties. But what seemed like facility was not the result of easy writing. His stories had a finish or polish that was achieved with painstaking care. Even the commercial stories were distinctive because of the deft touches that made them recognizable as Fitzgerald stories. One such passage in "Egg" is the description of the newspaper report of a society wedding.

When Fifi visited her Long Island aunts the first time she was only ten years old, but after she went back to New York the man who worked around the place said that the sand dunes would never be the same again. She had spoiled them. When she left, everything on Montauk Point seemed sad and futile and broken and old. Even the gulls wheeled about less enthusiastically, as if they missed the brown, hardy little girl with big eyes who played barefoot in the sand.

The years bleached out Fifi's tan and turned her a pale-pink color, but she still managed to spoil many places and plans for many hopeful men. So when at last it was announced in the best newspapers that she had concentrated on a gentleman named Van Tyne everyone was rather glad that all the sadness and longing that followed in her wake should become the responsibility of one self-sacrificing individual; not better for the individual, but for Fifi's little world very much better indeed.

The engagement was not announced on the sporting page, nor even in the help-wanted column, because Fifi's family belonged to the Society for the Preservation of Large Fortunes; and Mr. Van Tyne was descended from the man who accidentally founded that society, back before the Civil War. It appeared on the page of great names and was illustrated by a picture of a cross-eyed young lady holding the hand of a savage gentleman with four rows of teeth. That was how their pictures came out, anyhow, and the public was pleased to know that they were ugly monsters for all their money, and everyone was satisfied all around. The society editor set up a column telling how Mrs. Van Tyne started off in the *Aquitania* wearing a blue traveling dress of starched felt with a round square hat to match; and so far as human events can be prophesied, Fifi was as good as married; or, as not a few young men considered, as bad as married.

"An exceptionally brilliant match," remarked Aunt Cal on the eve of the wedding, as she sat in her house on Montauk Point and clipped the notice for the cousins in Scotland, and then she added abstractedly, "All is forgiven."

"Why, Cal!" cried Aunt Josephine. "What do you mean when you say all is forgiven? Fifi has never injured you in any way."

"In the past nine years she has not seen fit to visit us here at Montauk Point, though we have invited her over and over again."

"But I don't blame her," said Aunt Josephine, who was only thirty-one herself. "What would a young pretty girl do down here with all this sand?"

"We like the sand, Jo."

"But we're old maids, Cal, with no vices except cigarettes and double-dummy mah-jongg. Now Fifi, being young, naturally likes exciting, vicious things—late hours, dice playing, all the diversions we read about in these books."

She waved her hand vaguely.

"I don't blame her for not coming down here. If I were in her place——"

What unnatural ambitions lurked in Aunt Jo's head were never disclosed, for the sentence remained unfinished. The front door of the house opened in an abrupt, startled way, and a young lady walked into the room in a dress marked "Paris, France."

"Good evening, dear ladies," she cried, smiling radiantly from one to the other. "I've come down here for an indefinite time in order to play in the sand."

"Fifi!"

"Fifi!"

"Aunts!"

"But, my dear child," cried Aunt Jo, "I thought this was the night of the bridal dinner."

"It is," admitted Fifi cheerfully. "But I didn't go. I'm not going to the wedding either. I sent in my regrets today."

It was all very vague; but it seemed, as far as her aunts could gather, that young Van Tyne was too perfect—whatever that meant. After much urging Fifi finally explained that he reminded her of an advertisement for a new car.

"A new car?" inquired Aunt Cal, wide eyed. "What new car?"

"Any new car."

"Do you mean——"

Aunt Cal blushed.

"I don't understand this new slang, but isn't there some part of a car that's called the—the clutch?"

"Oh, I like him physically," remarked Fifi coolly. Her aunts started in unison. "But he was just——Oh, too perfect, too new; as if they'd fooled over him at the factory for a long time and put special curtains on him——"

Aunt Jo had visions of a black-leather sheik.

"——and balloon tires and a permanent shave. He was too civilized for me, Aunt Cal." She sighed. "I must be one of the rougher girls, after all."

She was as immaculate and dainty sitting there as though she were the portrait of a young lady and about to be hung on the wall. But underneath her cheerfulness her aunts saw that she was in a state of hysterical excitement, and they persisted in suspecting that something more definite and shameful was the matter.

"But it isn't," insisted Fifi. "Our engagement was announced three months ago, and not a single chorus girl has sued George for breach of promise. Not one! He doesn't use alcohol in any form except as hair tonic. Why, we've never even quarreled until today!"

"You've made a serious mistake," said Aunt Cal.

Fifi nodded.

"I'm afraid I've broken the heart of the nicest man I ever met in my life, but it can't be helped. Immaculate! Why, what's the use of being immaculate when, no matter how hard you try, you can't be half so immaculate as your husband? And tactful? George could introduce Mr. Trotzky to Mr. Rockefeller and there wouldn't be a single blow. But after a certain point, I want to have all the tact in my family, and I told him so. I've never left a man practically at the church door before, so I'm going to stay here until everyone has had a chance to forget."

And stay she did—rather to the surprise of her aunts, who expected that next morning she would rush wildly and remorsefully back to New York. She appeared at breakfast very calm and fresh and cool, and as though she had slept soundly all night, and spent the day reclining under a red parasol beside the sunny dunes, watching the Atlantic roll in from the east. Her aunts intercepted the evening paper and burnt it unseen in the open fire, under the impression that Fifi's flight would be recorded in red headlines across the front page. They accepted the fact that Fifi was here, and except that Aunt Jo was inclined to go mah-jongg without a pair when she speculated on the too perfect man, their lives went along very much the same. But not quite the same.

"What's the matter with that niece of yourn?" demanded the yardman gloomily of Aunt Josephine. "What's a young pretty girl want to come and hide herself down here for?"

"My niece is resting," declared Aunt Josephine stiffly.

"Them dunes ain't good for wore-out people," objected the yardman, soothing his head with his fingers. "There's a monotoness about them. I seen her yesterday take her parasol and like to beat one down, she got so mad at it. Some day she's going to notice how many of them there are, and all of a sudden go loony." He sniffed. "And then what kind of a proposition we going to have on our hands?"

"That will do, Percy," snapped Aunt Jo. "Go about your business. I want ten pounds of broken-up shells rolled into the front walk."

"What'll I do with that parasol?" he demanded. "I picked up the pieces."

"It's not my parasol," said Aunt Jo tartly. "You can take the pieces and roll them into the front walk too."

And so the June of Fifi's abandoned honeymoon drifted away, and every morning her rubber shoes left wet footprints along a desolate shore at the end of nowhere. For a while she seemed to thrive on the isolation, and the sea wind blew her cheeks scarlet with health; but after a week had passed, her aunts saw that she was noticeably restless and less cheerful even than when she came.

"I'm afraid it's getting on your nerves, my dear," said Aunt Cal one particularly wild and windy afternoon. "We love to have you here, but we hate to see you looking so sad. Why don't you ask your mother to take you to Europe for the summer?"

"Europe's too dressed up," objected Fifi wearily. "I like it here where everything's rugged and harsh and rude, like the end of the world. If you don't mind, I'd like to stay longer."

She stayed longer, and seemed to grow more and more melancholy as the days slipped by to the raucous calls of the gulls and the flashing tumult of the waves along the shore. Then one afternoon she returned at twilight from the longest of her long walks with a strange derelict of a man. And after one look at him her aunts thought that the gardener's prophecy had come true and that solitude had driven Fifi mad at last.

II

He was a very ragged wreck of a man as he stood in the doorway on that summer evening, blinking into Aunt Cal's eyes; rather like a beachcomber who had wandered accidentally out of a movie of the South Seas. In his hands he carried a knotted stick of a brutal, treacherous shape. It was a murderous-looking stick, and the sight of it caused Aunt Cal to shrink back a little into the room.

Fifi shut the door behind them and turned to her aunts as if this were the most natural occasion in the world.

"This is Mr. Hopkins," she announced, and then turned to her companion for corroboration. "Or is it Hopwood?"

"Hopkins," said the man hoarsely. "Hopkins."

Fifi nodded cheerfully.

"I've asked Mr. Hopkins to dinner," she said.

There was some dignity which Aunt Cal and Aunt Josephine had acquired, living here beside the proud sea, that would not let them show surprise. The man was a guest now; that was enough. But in their hearts all was turmoil and confusion. They would have been no more surprised had Fifi brought in a many-headed monster out of the Atlantic.

"Won't you—won't you sit down, Mr. Hopkins?" said Aunt Cal nervously.

Mr. Hopkins looked at her blankly for a moment, and then made a loud clicking sound in the back of his mouth. He took a step toward a chair and sank down on its gilt frailty as though he meant to annihilate it immediately. Aunt Cal and Aunt Josephine collapsed rather weakly on the sofa.

"Mr. Hopkins and I struck up an acquaintance on the beach," explained Fifi. "He's been spending the summer down here for his health."

Mr. Hopkins fixed his eyes glassily on the two aunts.

"I come down for my health," he said.

Aunt Cal made some small sound; but recovering herself quickly, joined Aunt Jo in nodding eagerly at the visitor, as if they deeply sympathized.

"Yeah," he repeated cheerfully.

"He thought the sea air would make him well and strong again," said Fifi eagerly. "That's why he came down here. Isn't that it, Mr. Hopkins?"

"You said it, sister," agreed Mr. Hopkins, nodding.

"So you see, Aunt Cal," smiled Fifi, "you and Aunt Jo aren't the only two people who believe in the medicinal quality of this location."

"No," agreed Aunt Cal faintly. "There are—there are three of us now."

Dinner was announced.

"Would you—would you"—Aunt Cal braced herself and looked Mr. Hopkins in the eye—"would you like to wash your hands before dinner?"

"Don't mention it." Mr. Hopkins waved his fingers at her carelessly.

They went in to dinner, and after some furtive backing and bumping due to the two aunts trying to keep as far as possible from Mr. Hopkins, sat down at table.

"Mr. Hopkins lives in the woods," said Fifi. "He has a little house all by himself, where he cooks his own meals and does his own washing week in and week out."

"How fascinating!" said Aunt Jo, looking searchingly at their guest for some signs of the scholarly recluse. "Have you been living near here for some time?"

"Not so long," he answered with a leer. "But I'm stuck on it, see? I'll maybe stay here till I rot."

"Are you—do you live far away?" Aunt Cal was wondering what price she could get for the house at a forced sale, and how she and her sister could ever bear to move.

"Just a mile down the line. . . . This is a pretty gal you got here," he added, indicating their niece with his spoon.

"Why—yes." The two ladies glanced uneasily at Fifi.

"Some day I'm going to pick her up and run away with her," he added pleasantly.

Aunt Cal, with a heroic effort, switched the subject away from their niece. They discussed Mr. Hopkins' shack in the woods. Mr. Hopkins liked it well enough, he confessed, except for the presence of minute animal life, a small fault in an otherwise excellent habitat.

After dinner Fifi and Mr. Hopkins went out to the porch, while her aunts sat side by side on the sofa turning over the pages of magazines and from time to time glancing at each other with stricken eyes. That a savage had a few minutes since been sitting at their dinner table, that he was now alone with their niece on the dark veranda—no such terrible adventure had ever been allotted to their prim, quiet lives before.

Aunt Cal determined that at nine, whatever the consequences, she would call Fifi inside; but she was saved this necessity, for after half an hour the young lady strolled in calmly and announced that Mr. Hopkins had gone home. They looked at her, speechless.

"Fifi!" groaned Aunt Cal. "My poor child! Sorrow and loneliness have driven you insane!"

"We understand, my dear," said Aunt Jo, touching her handkerchief to her eyes. "It's our fault for letting you stay. A few weeks in one of those rest-cure places, or perhaps even a good cabaret, will——"

"What do you mean?" Fifi looked from one to the other in surprise. "Do you mean you object to my bringing Mr. Hopkins here?"

Aunt Cal flushed a dull red and her lips shut tight together.

" 'Object' is not the word. You find some horrible, brutal roustabout along the beach——"

She broke off and gave a little cry. The door had swung open suddenly and a hairy face was peering into the room.

"I left my stick."

Mr. Hopkins discovered the unpleasant weapon leaning in the corner and withdrew as unceremoniously as he had come, banging the door shut behind him. Fifi's aunt sat motionless until his footsteps left the porch. Then Aunt Cal went swiftly to the door and pulled down the latch.

"I don't suppose he'll try to rob us tonight," she said grimly, "because he must know we'll be prepared. But I'll warn Percy to go around the yard several times during the night."

"Rob you!" cried Fifi incredulously.

"Don't excite yourself, Fifi," commanded Aunt Cal. "Just rest quietly in that chair while I call up your mother."

"I don't want you to call up my mother."

"Sit calmly and close your eyes and try to—try to count sheep jumping over a fence."

"Am I never to see another man unless he has a cutaway coat on?" exclaimed Fifi with flashing eyes. "Is this the Dark Ages, or the century of—of illumination? Mr. Hopkins is one of the most attractive eggs I've ever met in my life."

"Mr. Hopkins is a savage!" said Aunt Cal succinctly.

"Mr. Hopkins is a very attractive egg."

"A very attractive what?"

"A very attractive egg."

"Mr. Hopkins is a—a—an unspeakable egg," proclaimed Aunt Cal, adopting Fifi's locution.

"Just because he's natural," cried Fifi impatiently. "All right, I don't care; he's good enough for me."

The situation, it seemed, was even worse than they thought. This was no temporary aberration; evidently Fifi, in the reaction from her recent fiancé, was interested in this outrageous man. She had met him several days ago, she confessed, and she intended to see him tomorrow. They had a date to go walking.

The worst of it was that after Fifi had gone scornfully to bed, Aunt

Cal called up her mother—and found that her mother was not at home; her mother had gone to White Sulphur Springs and wouldn't be home for a week. It left the situation definitely in the hands of Aunt Cal and Aunt Jo, and the situation came to a head the next afternoon at teatime, when Percy rushed in upon them excitedly through the kitchen door.

"Miss Marsden," he exclaimed in a shocked, offended voice, "I want to give up my position!"

"Why, Percy!"

"I can't help it. I lived here on the Point for more'n forty-five years, and I never seen such a sight as I seen just now."

"What's the matter?" cried the two ladies, springing up in wild alarm.

"Go to the window and look for yourself. Miss Fifi is kissing a tramp in broad daylight, down on the beach!"

III

Five minutes later two maiden ladies were making their way across the sand toward a couple who stood close together on the shore, sharply outlined against the bright afternoon sky. As they came closer Fifi and Mr. Hopkins, absorbed in the contemplation of each other, perceived them and drew lingeringly apart. Aunt Cal began to speak when they were still thirty yards away.

"Go into the house, Fifi!" she cried.

Fifi looked at Mr. Hopkins, who touched her hand reassuringly and nodded. As if under the influence of a charm, Fifi turned away from him, and with her head lowered walked with slender grace toward the house.

"Now, my man," said Aunt Cal, folding her arms, "what are your intentions?"

Mr. Hopkins returned her glare rudely. Then he gave a low hoarse laugh.

"What's that to you?" he demanded.

"It's everything to us. Miss Marsden is our niece, and your attentions are unwelcome—not to say obnoxious."

Mr. Hopkins turned half away.

"Aw, go on and blab your mouth out!" he advised her.

Aunt Cal tried a new approach.

"What if I were to tell you that Miss Marsden were mentally deranged?"

"What's that?"

"She's—she's a little crazy."

He smiled contemptuously.

"What's the idea? Crazy 'cause she likes me?"

"That merely indicates it," answered Aunt Cal bravely. "She's had an unfortunate love affair and it's affected her mind. Look here!" She opened the purse that swung at her waist. "If I give you fifty—a hundred dollars right now in cash, will you promise to move yourself ten miles up the beach?"

"Ah-h-h-h!" he exclaimed, so venomously that the two ladies swayed together.

"Two hundred!" cried Aunt Cal, with a catch in her voice.

He shook his finger at them.

"You can't buy me!" he growled. "I'm as good as anybody. There's chauffeurs and such that marry millionaires' daughters every day in the week. This is Umerica, a free country, see?"

"You won't give her up?" Aunt Cal swallowed hard on the words. "You won't stop bothering her and go away?"

He bent over suddenly and scooped up a large double handful of sand, which he threw in a high parabola so that it scattered down upon the horrified ladies, enveloping them for a moment in a thick mist. Then laughing once again in his hoarse, boorish way, he turned and set off at a loping run along the sand.

In a daze the two women brushed the casual sand from their shoulders and walked stiffly toward the house.

"I'm younger than you are," said Aunt Jo firmly when they reached the living room. "I want a chance now to see what I can do."

She went to the telephone and called a New York number.

"Doctor Roswell Gallup's office? Is Doctor Gallup there?" Aunt Cal sat down on the sofa and gazed tragically at the ceiling. "Doctor Gallup? This is Miss Josephine Marsden, of Montauk Point. . . . Doctor Gallup, a very curious state of affairs has arisen concerning my niece. She has become entangled with a—a—an unspeakable egg." She gasped as she said this, and went on to explain in a few words the uncanny nature of the situation.

"And I think that perhaps psychoanalysis might clear up what my sister and I have been unable to handle."

Doctor Gallup was interested. It appeared to be exactly his sort of a case.

"There's a train in half an hour that will get you here at nine o'clock," said Aunt Jo. "We can give you dinner and accommodate you overnight."

She hung up the receiver.

"There! Except for our change from bridge to mah-jongg, this will be the first really modern step we've ever taken in our lives."

The hours passed slowly. At seven Fifi came down to dinner, as unperturbed as though nothing had happened; and her aunts played up bravely to her calmness, determined to say nothing until the doctor had actually arrived. After dinner Aunt Jo suggested mahjongg, but Fifi declared that she would rather read, and settled on the sofa with a volume of the encyclopedia. Looking over her shoulder, Aunt Cal noted with alarm that she had turned to the article on the Australian bush.

It was very quiet in the room. Several times Fifi raised her head as if listening, and once she got up and went to the door and stared out for a long time into the night. Her aunts were both poised in their chairs to rush after her if she showed signs of bolting, but after a moment she closed the door with a sigh and returned to her chair. It was with relief that a little after nine they heard the sound of automobile wheels on the shell drive and knew that Doctor Gallup had arrived at last.

He was a short, stoutish man, with alert black eyes and an intense manner. He came in, glancing eagerly about him, and his eye brightened as it fell on Fifi like the eye of a hungry man when he sees prospective food. Fifi returned his gaze curiously, evidently unaware that his arrival had anything to do with herself.

"Is this the lady?" he cried, dismissing her aunts with a perfunctory handshake and approaching Fifi at a lively hop.

"This gentleman is Doctor Gallup, dear," beamed Aunt Jo, expectant and reassured. "He's an old friend of mine who's going to help you."

"Of course I am!" insisted Doctor Gallup, jumping around her cordially. "I'm going to fix her up just fine."

"He understands everything about the human mind," said Aunt Jo.

"Not everything," admitted Doctor Gallup, smiling modestly. "But we often make the regular doctors wonder." He turned roguishly to Fifi. "Yes, young lady, we often make the regular doctors wonder."

Clapping his hands together decisively, he drew up a chair in front of Fifi.

"Come," he cried, "let us see what can be the matter. We'll start by having you tell me the whole story in your own way. Begin."

"The story," remarked Fifi, with a slight yawn, "happens to be none of your business."

"None of my business!" he exclaimed incredulously. "Why, my girl, I'm trying to help you! Come now, tell old Doctor Gallup the whole story."

"Let my aunts tell you," said Fifi coldly. "They seem to know more about it than I do."

Doctor Gallup frowned.

"They've already outlined the situation. Perhaps I'd better begin by asking you questions."

"You'll answer the doctor's questions, won't you, dear?" coaxed Aunt Jo. "Doctor Gallup is one of the most modern doctors in New York."

"I'm an old-fashioned girl," objected Fifi maliciously. "And I think it's immoral to pry into people's affairs. But go ahead and I'll try to think up a comeback for everything you say."

Doctor Gallup overlooked the unnecessary rudeness of this remark and mustered a professional smile.

"Now, Miss Marsden, I understand that about a month ago you came out here for a rest."

Fifi shook her head.

"No, I came out to hide my face."

"You were ashamed because you had broken your engagement?"

"Terribly. If you desert a man at the altar you brand him for the rest of his life."

"Why?" he demanded sharply.

"Why not?"

"You're not asking me. I'm asking you. . . . However, let that pass. Now, when you arrived here, how did you pass your time?"

"I walked mostly—walked along the beach."

"It was on one of these walks that you met the—ah—person your aunt told me of over the telephone?"

Fifi pinkened slightly.

"Yes."

"What was he doing when you first saw him?"

"He was looking down at me out of a tree."

There was a general exclamation from her aunts, in which the word "monkey" figured.

"Did he attract you immediately?" demanded Doctor Gallup.

"Why, not especially. At first I only laughed."

"I see. Now, as I understand, this man was very—ah—very originally clad."

"Yes," agreed Fifi.

"He was unshaven?"

"Yes."

"Ah!" Doctor Gallup seemed to go through a sort of convolution like a medium coming out of a trance. "Miss Fifi," he cried out triumphantly, "did you ever read *The Sheik*?"

"Never heard of it."

"Did you ever read any book in which a girl was wooed by a so-called sheik or cave man?"

"Not that I remember."

"What, then, was your favorite book when you were a girl?"

"*Little Lord Fauntleroy.*"

Doctor Gallup was considerably disappointed. He decided to approach the case from a new angle.

"Miss Fifi, won't you admit that there's nothing behind this but some fancy in your head?"

"On the contrary," said Fifi startlingly, "there's a great deal more behind it than any of you suspect. He's changed my entire attitude on life."

"What do you mean?"

She seemed on the point of making some declaration, but after a moment her lovely eyes narrowed obstinately and she remained silent.

"Miss Fifi"—Doctor Gallup raised his voice sharply—"the daughter of C. T. J. Calhoun, the biscuit man, ran away with a taxi driver. Do you know what she's doing now?"

"No."

"She's working in a laundry on the East Side, trying to keep her child's body and soul together."

He looked at her keenly; there were signs of agitation in her face.

"Estelle Holliday ran away in 1920 with her father's second man!" he cried. "Shall I tell you where I heard of her last? She stumbled into a charity hospital, bruised from head to foot, because her drunken husband had beaten her to within an inch of her life!"

Fifi was breathing hard. Her aunts leaned forward. Doctor Gallup sprang suddenly to his feet.

"But they were playing safe compared to you!" he shouted. "They didn't woo an ex-convict with blood on his hands."

And now Fifi was on her feet, too, her eyes flashing fire.

"Be careful!" she cried. "Don't go too far!"

"I can't go too far!" He reached in his pocket, plucked out a folded evening paper and slapped it down on the table.

"Read that, Miss Fifi!" he shouted. "It'll tell you how four man-killers entered a bank in West Crampton three weeks ago. It'll tell you how they shot down the cashier in cold blood, and how one of them, the most brutal, the most ferocious, the most inhuman, got away. And it will tell you that that human gorilla is now supposed to be hiding in the neighborhood of Montauk Point!"

There was a short stifled sound as Aunt Jo and Aunt Cal, who had always done everything in complete unison, fainted away together. At the same moment there was loud, violent knocking, like the knocking of a heavy club, upon the barred front door.

IV

"Who's there?" cried Doctor Gallup, starting. "Who's there—or I'll shoot!"

His eyes roved quickly about the room, looking for a possible weapon.

"Who are you?" shouted a voice from the porch. "You better open up or I'll blow a hole through the door."

"What'll we do?" exclaimed Doctor Gallup, perspiring freely.

Fifi, who had been sprinkling water impartially upon her aunts, turned around with a scornful smile.

"It's just Percy, the yardman," she explained. "He probably thinks that you're a burglar."

She went to the door and lifted the latch. Percy, gun in hand, peered cautiously into the room.

"It's all right, Percy. This is just an insane specialist from New York."

"Everything's a little insane tonight," announced Percy in a frightened voice. "For the last hour I've been hearing the sound of oars."

The eyes of Aunt Jo and Aunt Cal fluttered open simultaneously.

"There's a fog all over the Point," went on Percy dazedly, "and it's got voices in it. I couldn't see a foot before my face, but I could swear there was boats offshore, and I heard a dozen people talkin' and callin' to each other, just as if a lot of ghosts was havin' a picnic supper on the beach."

"What was that noise?" cried Aunt Jo, sitting upright.

"The door was locked," explained Percy, "so I knocked on it with my gun."

"No, I mean now!"

They listened. Through the open door came a low, groaning sound, issuing out of the dark mist which covered shore and sea alike.

"We'll go right down and find out!" cried Doctor Gallup, who had recovered his shattered equilibrium; and, as the moaning sound drifted in again, like the last agony of some monster from the deep, he added, "I think you needed more than a psychoanalyst here tonight. Is there another gun in the house?"

Aunt Cal got up and took a small pearl-mounted revolver from the desk drawer.

"You can't leave us in this house alone," she declared emphatically. "Wherever you go we're going too!"

Keeping close together, the four of them, for Fifi had suddenly disappeared, made their way outdoors and down the porch steps, where they hesitated a moment, peering into the impenetrable haze, more mysterious than darkness upon their eyes.

"It's out there," whispered Percy, facing the sea.

"Forward we go!" muttered Doctor Gallup tensely. "I'm inclined to think this is all a question of nerves."

They moved slowly and silently along the sand, until suddenly Percy caught hold of the doctor's arm.

"Listen!" he whispered sharply.

They all became motionless. Out of the neighboring darkness a dim, indistinguishable figure had materialized, walking with unnatural rigidity along the shore. Pressed against his body he carried some long, dark drape that hung almost to the sand. Immediately he disappeared into the mist, to be succeeded by another phantom walking at the same military gait, this one with something white and faintly terrible dangling from his arm. A moment later, not ten yards away from them, in the direction in which the figure had gone, a faint dull glow sprang into life, proceeding apparently from behind the largest of the dunes.

Huddled together, they advanced toward the dune, hesitated, and then, following Doctor Gallup's example, dropped to their knees and began to crawl cautiously up its shoreward side. The glow became stronger as they reached the top, and at the same moment their heads popped up over the crest. This is what they saw:

In the light of four strong pocket flash lights, borne by four sailors in spotless white, a gentleman was shaving himself, standing clad only in athletic underwear upon the sand. Before his eyes an irreproachable valet held a silver mirror which gave back the soapy reflection of his face. To right and left stood two additional men-servants, one with a dinner coat and trousers hanging from his arm and the other bearing a white stiff shirt whose studs glistened in the glow of the electric lamps. There was not a sound except the dull scrape of the razor along its wielder's face and the intermittent groaning sound that blew in out of the sea.

But it was not the bizarre nature of the ceremony, with its dim, weird surroundings under the unsteady light, that drew from the two women a short, involuntary sigh. It was the fact that the face in the mirror, the unshaven half of it, was terribly familiar, and in a moment they knew to whom that half face belonged—it was the countenance of their niece's savage wooer who had lately prowled half naked along the beach.

Even as they looked he completed one side of his face, whereupon a valet stepped forward and with a scissors sheared off the exterior growth on the other, disclosing, in its entirety now, the symmetrical visage of a young, somewhat haggard but not unhandsome man. He lathered the bearded side, pulled the razor quickly over it and then applied a lotion to the whole surface, and inspected himself with considerable interest in the mirror. The sight seemed to please him, for he smiled. At a word one of the valets held forth the trousers in which he now incased his likely legs. Diving into his open shirt, he procured the collar, flipped a proper black bow with a practiced hand and slipped into the waiting dinner coat. After a transformation which had taken place before their very eyes, Aunt Cal and Aunt Jo found themselves gazing upon as immaculate and impeccable a young man as they had ever seen.

"Walters!" he said suddenly, in a clear, cultured voice.

One of the white-clad sailors stepped forward and saluted.

"You can take the boats back to the yacht. You ought to be able to find it all right by the foghorn."

"Yes, sir."

"When the fog lifts you'd better stand out to sea. Meanwhile, wireless New York to send down my car. It's to call for me at the Marsden house on Montauk Point."

As the sailor turned away, his torch flashed upward accidentally wavering upon the four amazed faces which were peering down at the curious scene.

"Look there, sir!" he exclaimed.

The four torches picked out the eavesdropping party at the top of the hill.

"Hands up, there!" cried Percy, pointing his rifle down into the glare of light.

"Miss Marsden!" called the young man eagerly. "I was just coming to call."

"Don't move!" shouted Percy; and then to the doctor, "Had I better fire?"

"Certainly not!" cried Doctor Gallup. "Young man, does your name happen to be what I think it is?"

The young man bowed politely.

"My name is George Van Tyne."

A few minutes later the immaculate young man and two completely bewildered ladies were shaking hands. "I owe you more apologies than I can ever make," he confessed, "for having sacrificed you to the strange whim of a young girl."

"What whim?" demanded Aunt Cal.

"Why"—he hesitated—"you see, all my life I have devoted much attention to the so-called niceties of conduct; niceties of dress, of manners, of behavior——"

He broke off apologetically.

"Go on," commanded Aunt Cal.

"And your niece has too. She always considered herself rather a model of—of civilized behavior"—he flushed—"until she met me."

"I see," Doctor Gallup nodded. "She couldn't bear to marry anyone who was more of a—shall we say, a dandy?—than herself."

"Exactly," said George Van Tyne, with a perfect eighteenth-century bow. "It was necessary to show her what a—what an——"

"——unspeakable egg," supplied Aunt Josephine.

"——what an unspeakable egg I could be. It was difficult, but not impossible. If you know what's correct, you must necessarily know what's incorrect; and my aim was to be as ferociously incorrect as possible. My one hope is that some day you'll be able to forgive me for throwing the sand—I'm afraid that my impersonation ran away with me."

A moment later they were all walking toward the house.

"But I still can't believe that a gentleman could be so—so unspeakable," gasped Aunt Jo. "And what will Fifi say?"

"Nothing," answered Van Tyne cheerfully. "You see, Fifi knew about it all along. She even recognized me in the tree that first day. She begged me to—to desist until this afternoon; but I refused until she had kissed me tenderly, beard and all."

Aunt Cal stopped suddenly.

"This is all very well, young man," she said sternly; "but since you have so many sides to you, how do we know that in one of your off moments you aren't the murderer who's hiding out on the Point?"

"The murderer?" asked Van Tyne blankly. "What murderer?"

"Ah, I can explain that, Miss Marsden." Doctor Gallup smiled apologetically. "As a matter of fact, there wasn't any murderer."

"No murderer?" Aunt Cal looked at him sharply.

"No, I invented the bank robbery and the escaped murderer and all. I was merely applying a form of strong medicine to your niece."

Aunt Cal looked at him scornfully and turned to her sister. "All your modern ideas are not so successful as mah-jongg," she remarked significantly.

The fog had blown back to sea, and as they came in sight of the house the lamps were glowing out into the darkness. On the porch waited an immaculate girl in a gleaming white dress, strung with beads which glistened in the new moonlight.

"The perfect man," murmured Aunt Jo, flushing, "is, of course, he who will make any sacrifice."

Van Tyne did not answer; he was engaged in removing some imperceptible flaw, less visible than a hair, from his elbow, and when he had finished he smiled. There was now not the faintest imperfection anywhere about him, except where the strong beating of his heart disturbed faintly the satin facing of his coat.

John Jackson's Arcady

(*The Saturday Evening Post*, 26 July 1924)

"John Jackson's Arcady" was written in April 1924—the last story Fitzgerald wrote in Great Neck before moving to the Riviera. The *Post* paid $1750 for it. The departure for France was motivated by Fitzgerald's wish to escape the interruptions of metropolitan life, which had delayed work on *The Great Gatsby*, as well as by a desire to economize. Fitzgerald treated his financial problems humorously in two 1924 *Post* articles—"How to Live on $36,000 a Year" and "How to Live on Practically Nothing a Year."

Although this story is marred by its patently sentimental ending, it is interesting as a treatment of Fitzgerald's roots-pilgrimage theme—reflecting his increasing sense of deracination and estrangement from his midwestern values.

In 1928 "John Jackson's Arcady" was re-published as a pamphlet for public reading contests.

The first letter, crumpled into an emotional ball, lay at his elbow, and it did not matter faintly now what this second letter contained. For a long time after he had stripped off the envelope, he still gazed up at the oil painting of slain grouse over the sideboard, just as though he had not faced it every morning at breakfast for the past twelve years. Finally he lowered his eyes and began to read:

"*Dear Mr. Jackson*: This is just a reminder that you have consented to speak at our annual meeting Thursday. We don't want to dictate your choice of a topic, but it has occurred to me that it would be interesting to hear from you on What Have I Got Out of Life. Coming from you this should be an inspiration to everyone.

"We are delighted to have you anyhow, and we appreciate the honor that you confer on us by coming at all.

"Most cordially yours,
"ANTHONY ROREBACK,
"Sec. Civic Welfare League."

"What have I got out of life?" repeated John Jackson aloud, raising up his head.

He wanted no more breakfast, so he picked up both letters and went out on his wide front porch to smoke a cigar and lie about for a lazy half hour before he went downtown. He had done this each morning for ten years—ever since his wife ran off one windy night and gave him back the custody of his leisure hours. He loved to rest on this porch in the fresh warm mornings and through a porthole in the green vines watch the automobiles pass along the street, the widest, shadiest, pleasantest street in town.

"What have I got out of life?" he said again, sitting down on a creaking wicker chair; and then, after a long pause, he whispered, "Nothing."

The word frightened him. In all his forty-five years he had never said such a thing before. His greatest tragedies had not embittered him, only made him sad. But here beside the warm friendly rain that tumbled from his eaves onto the familiar lawn, he knew at last that life had stripped him clean of all happiness and all illusion.

He knew this because of the crumpled ball which closed out his hope in his only son. It told him what a hundred hints and indications had told him before; that his son was weak and vicious, and the language in which it was conveyed was no less emphatic for being polite. The letter was from the dean of the college at New Haven, a gentleman who said exactly what he meant in every word:

"*Dear Mr. Jackson*: It is with much regret that I write to tell you that your son, Ellery Hamil Jackson, has been requested to withdraw from the university. Last year largely, I am afraid, out of personal feeling toward you, I yielded to your request that he be allowed another chance. I see now that this was a mistake, and I should be failing in my duty if I did not tell you that he is not the sort of boy we want here. His conduct at the sophomore dance was such that several undergraduates took it upon themselves to administer violent correction.

"It grieves me to write you this, but I see no advantage in presenting the case otherwise than as it is. I have requested that he leave New Haven by the day after tomorrow. I am, sir,   "Yours very sincerely,
                                        "AUSTIN SCHEMMERHORN
                                        "Dean of the College."

What particularly disgraceful thing his son had done John Jackson did not care to imagine. He knew without any question that what the dean said was true. Why, there were houses already in this town where his son, John Jackson's son, was no longer welcome! For a while Ellery had been forgiven because of his father, and he had been more than forgiven at home, because John Jackson was one of those rare men who can forgive even their own families. But he would never be forgiven any more. Sitting on his porch this morning beside the gentle April rain, something had happened in his father's heart.

"What have I had out of life?" John Jackson shook his head from side to side with quiet, tired despair. "Nothing!"

He picked up the second letter, the civic-welfare letter, and read it over; and then helpless, dazed laughter shook him physically until he trembled in his chair. On Wednesday, at the hour when his delinquent boy would arrive at the motherless home, John Jackson would be standing on a platform downtown, delivering one hundred resounding platitudes of inspiration and cheer. "Members of the association"—their faces, eager, optimistic, impressed, would look up at him like hollow moons—"I have been requested to try to tell you in a few words what I have had from life——"

Many people would be there to hear, for the clever young secretary had hit upon a topic with the personal note—what John Jackson, successful, able and popular, had found for himself in the tumultuous grab bag. They would listen with wistful attention, hoping that he would disclose some secret formula that would make their lives as popular and successful and happy as his own. They believed in rules; all the young men in the city believed in hard-and-fast rules, and many of them clipped coupons and sent away for little booklets that promised them the riches and good fortune they desired.

"Members of the association, to begin with, let me say that there is so much in life that if we don't find it, it is not the fault of life, but of ourselves."

The ring of the stale, dull words mingled with the patter of the rain went on and on endlessly, but John Jackson knew that he would never make that speech, or any speeches ever again. He had dreamed his last dream too long, but he was awake at last.

"I shall not go on flattering a world that I have found unkind," he whispered to the rain. "Instead, I shall go out of this house and out of this town and somewhere find again the happiness that I possessed when I was young."

Nodding his head, he tore both letters into small fragments and dropped them on the table beside him. For half an hour longer he sat there, rocking a little and smoking his cigar slowly and blowing the blue smoke out into the rain.

II

Down at his office, his chief clerk, Mr. Fowler, approached him with his morning smile.

"Looking fine, Mr. Jackson. Nice day if it hadn't rained."

"Yeah," agreed John Jackson cheerfully. "Clear up in an hour. Anybody outside?"

"A lady named Mrs. Ralston."

Mr. Fowler raised his grizzled eyebrows in facetious mournfulness.

"Tell her I can't see her," said John Jackson, rather to his clerk's surprise. "And let me have a pencil memorandum of the money I've given away through her these twenty years."

"Why—yes, sir."

Mr. Fowler had always urged John Jackson to look more closely into his promiscuous charities; but now, after these two decades, it rather alarmed him.

When the list arrived—its preparation took an hour of burrowing through old ledgers and check stubs—John Jackson studied it for a long time in silence.

"That woman's got more money than you have," grumbled Fowler at his elbow. "Every time she comes in she's wearing a new hat. I bet she never hands out a cent herself—just goes around asking other people."

John Jackson did not answer. He was thinking that Mrs. Ralston had been one of the first women in town to bar Ellery Jackson from her house. She did quite right, of course; and yet perhaps back there when Ellery was sixteen, if he had cared for some nice girl——

"Thomas J. MacDowell's outside. Do you want to see him? I said I didn't think you were in, because on second thoughts, Mr. Jackson, you look tired this morning——"

"I'll see him," interrupted John Jackson.

He watched Fowler's retreating figure with an unfamiliar expression in his eyes. All that cordial diffuseness of Fowler's—he wondered what it covered in the man's heart. Several times, without Fowler's knowledge, Jackson had seen him giving imitations of the boss for the benefit of the other employes; imitations with a touch of malice in them that John Jackson had smiled at then, but that now crept insinuatingly into his mind.

"Doubtless he considers me a good deal of a fool," murmured John Jackson thoughtfully, "because I've kept him long after his usefulness was over. It's a way men have, I suppose, to despise anyone they can impose on."

Thomas J. MacDowell, a big barn door of a man with huge white hands, came boisterously into the office. If John Jackson had gone in for enemies he must have started with Tom MacDowell. For twenty years they had fought over every question of municipal affairs, and back in 1908 they had once stood facing each other with clenched hands on a public platform, because Jackson had said in print what everyone knew—that MacDowell was the worst political influence that the town had ever known. That was forgotten now; all that was remembered of it went into a peculiar flash of the eye that passed between them when they met.

"Hello, Mr. Jackson," said MacDowell with full, elaborate cordiality. "We need your help and we need your money."

"How so?"

"Tomorrow morning, in the *Eagle*, you'll see the plan for the new Union Station. The only thing that'll stand in the way is the question of location. We want your land."

"My land?"

"The railroad wants to build on the twenty acres just this side of the river, where your warehouse stands. If you'll let them have it cheap we get our station; if not, we can just whistle into the air."

Jackson nodded.

"I see."

"What price?" asked MacDowell mildly.

"No price."

His visitor's mouth dropped open in surprise.

"That from you?" he demanded.

John Jackson got to his feet.

"I've decided not to be the local goat any more," he announced steadily. "You threw out the only fair, decent plan because it interfered with some private reservations of your own. And now that there's a snag, you'd like the punishment to fall on me. I tear down my warehouse and hand over some of the best property in the city for a song because you made a little 'mistake' last year!"

"But last year's over now," protested MacDowell. "Whatever happened then doesn't change the situation now. The city needs the station, and so"—there was a faint touch of irony in his voice—"and so naturally I come to its leading citizen, counting on his well-known public spirit."

"Go out of my office, MacDowell," said John Jackson suddenly. "I'm tired."

MacDowell scrutinized him severely.

"What's come over you today?"

Jackson closed his eyes.

"I don't want to argue," he said after a while.

MacDowell slapped his fat upper leg and got to his feet.

"This is a funny attitude from you," he remarked. "You better think it over."

"Good-by."

Perceiving, to his astonishment, that John Jackson meant what he said, MacDowell took his monstrous body to the door.

"Well, well," he said, turning and shaking his finger at Jackson as if he were a bad boy, "who'd have thought it from you after all?"

When he had gone Jackson rang again for his clerk.

"I'm going away," he remarked casually. "I may be gone for some time—perhaps a week, perhaps longer. I want you to cancel every engagement I have and pay off my servants at home and close up my house."

Mr. Fowler could hardly believe his ears.

"Close up your house?"

Jackson nodded.

"But why—why is it?" demanded Fowler in amazement.

Jackson looked out the high window upon the gray little city drenched now by slanting, slapping rain—his city, he had felt sometimes, in those rare moments when life had lent him time to be happy. That flash of green trees running up the main boulevard—he had made that possible, and Children's Park, and the white dripping buildings around Courthouse Square over the way.

"I don't know," he answered, "but I think I ought to get a breath of spring."

When Fowler had gone he put on his hat and raincoat and, to avoid anyone who might be waiting, went through an unused filing room that gave access to the elevator. The filing room was actively inhabited this morning, however; and, rather to his surprise, by a young boy about nine years old, who was laboriously writing his initials in chalk on the steel files.

"Hello!" exclaimed John Jackson.

He was accustomed to speak to children in a tone of interested equality.

"I didn't know this office was occupied this morning."

The little boy looked at him steadily.

"My name's John Jackson Fowler," he announced.

"What?"

"My name's John Jackson Fowler."

"Oh, I see. You're—you're Mr. Fowler's son?"

"Yeah, he's my father."

"I see." John Jackson's eyes narrowed a little. "Well, I bid you good morning."

He passed on out the door, wondering cynically what particular ax Fowler hoped to grind by this unwarranted compliment. John Jackson Fowler! It was one of his few sources of relief that his own son did not bear his name.

A few minutes later he was writing on a yellow blank in the telegraph office below:

"ELLERY JACKSON, CHAPEL STREET, NEW HAVEN, CONNECT-ICUT.

"THERE IS NOT THE SLIGHTEST REASON FOR COMING HOME, BECAUSE YOU HAVE NO HOME TO COME TO ANY MORE. THE MAMMOTH TRUST COMPANY OF NEW YORK WILL PAY YOU FIFTY DOLLARS A MONTH FOR THE REST OF YOUR LIFE, OR FOR AS LONG AS YOU CAN KEEP YOURSELF OUT OF JAIL.

"JOHN JACKSON."

"That's—that's a long message, sir," gasped the dispatcher, startled. "Do you want it to go straight?"

"Straight," said John Jackson, nodding.

III

He rode seventy miles that afternoon, while the rain dried up into rills of dust on the windows of the train and the country became green with vivid spring. When the sun was growing definitely crimson in the west he disembarked at a little lost town named Florence, just over the border of the next state. John Jackson had been born in this town; he had not been back here for twenty years.

The taxi driver, whom he recognized, silently, as a certain George Stirling, playmate of his youth, drove him to a battered hotel, where, to the surprise of the delighted landlord, he engaged a room. Leaving his raincoat on the sagging bed, he strolled out through a deserted lobby into the street.

It was a bright, warm afternoon, and the silver sliver of a moon riding already in the east promised a clear, brilliant night. John Jackson walked along a somnolent Main Street, where every shop and hitching post and horse fountain made some strange thing happen inside him, because he had known these things for more than inanimate objects as a little boy. At one shop, catching a glimpse of a familiar face through the glass, he hesitated; but changing his mind, continued along the street, turning off at a wide road at the corner. The road was lined sparsely by a row of battered houses, some of them repainted a pale unhealthy blue and all of them set far back in large plots of shaggy and unkempt land.

He walked along the road for a sunny half mile—a half mile shrunk up now into a short green aisle crowded with memories. Here, for example, a careless mule had stamped permanently on his thigh the mark of an iron shoe. In that cottage had lived two gentle old maids, who gave brown raisin cakes every Thursday to John Jackson and his little brother—the brother who had died as a child.

As he neared the end of his pilgrimage his breath came faster and the house where he was born seemed to run up to him on living feet. It was a collapsed house, a retired house, set far back from the road and sunned and washed to the dull color of old wood.

One glance told him it was no longer a dwelling. The shutters that remained were closed tight, and from the tangled vines arose, as a single chord, a rich shrill sound of a hundred birds. John Jackson left the road and stalked across the yard knee-deep in abandoned grass. When he came near, something choked up his throat. He paused and sat down on a stone in a patch of welcome shade.

This was his own house, as no other house would ever be; within these plain walls he had been incomparably happy. Here he had known and learned that kindness which he had carried into life. Here he had found the secret of those few simple decencies, so often invoked, so inimitable and so rare, which in the turmoil of competitive industry had made him to coarser men a source of half-scoffing, half-admiring surprise. This was his house, because his honor had been born and nourished here; he had known every hardship of the country poor, but no preventable regret.

And yet another memory, a memory more haunting than any other, and grown strong at this crisis in his life, had really drawn him back. In this yard, on this battered porch, in the very tree over his head, he seemed still to catch the glint of yellow hair and the glow of bright childish eyes that had belonged to his first love, the girl who had lived in the long-vanished house across the way. It was her ghost who was most alive here, after all.

He got up suddenly, stumbling through the shrubbery, and followed an almost obliterated path to the house, starting at the whirring sound of a blackbird which rose out of the grass close by. The front porch sagged dangerously at his step as he pushed open the door. There was no sound inside, except the steady slow throb of silence; but as he stepped in a word came to him, involuntary as his breath, and he uttered it aloud, as if he were calling to someone in the empty house.

"Alice," he cried; and then louder, "Alice!"

From a room at the left came a short, small, frightened cry. Startled, John Jackson paused in the door, convinced that his own imagination had evoked the reality of the cry.

"Alice!" he called doubtfully.

"Who's there?"

There was no mistake this time. The voice, frightened, strange, and yet familiar, came from what had once been the parlor, and as he listened John Jackson was aware of a nervous step within. Trembling a little, he pushed open the parlor door.

A woman with alarmed bright eyes and reddish gold hair was standing in the center of the bare room. She was of that age that trembles between the enduring youth of a fine, unworried life and the imperative call of forty years, and there was that indefinable loveliness in her face that youth gives sometimes just before it leaves a dwelling it has possessed for long. Her figure, just outside of slenderness, leaned with dignified grace against the old mantel on which her white hand rested, and through a rift in the shutter a shaft of late sunshine fell through upon her gleaming hair.

When John Jackson came in the doorway her large gray eyes closed and then opened again, and she gave another little cry. Then a curious thing happened; they stared at each other for a moment without a word, her hand dropped from the mantel and she took a swaying step toward him. And, as if it were the most natural thing in the world, John Jackson came forward, too, and took her into his arms and kissed her as if she were a little child.

"Alice!" he said huskily.

She drew a long breath and pushed herself away from him.

"I've come back here," he muttered unsteadily, "and find you waiting in this room where we used to sit, just as if I'd never been away."

"I only dropped in for a minute," she said, as if that was the most important thing in the world. "And now, naturally, I'm going to cry."

"Don't cry."

"I've got to cry. You don't think"—she smiled through wet eyes—"you don't think that things like this hap—happen to a person every day."

John Jackson walked in wild excitement to the window and threw it open to the afternoon.

"What were you doing here?" he cried, turning around. "Did you just come by accident today?"

"I come every week. I bring the children sometimes, but usually I come alone."

"The children!" he exclaimed. "Have you got children?"

She nodded.

"I've been married for years and years."

They stood there looking at each other for a moment; then they both laughed and glanced away.

"I kissed you," she said.

"Are you sorry?"

She shook her head.

"And the last time I kissed you was down by that gate ten thousand years ago."

He took her hand, and they went out and sat side by side on the broken stoop. The sun was painting the west with sweeping bands of peach bloom and pigeon blood and golden yellow.

"You're married," she said. "I saw in the paper—years ago."

He nodded.

"Yes, I've been married," he answered gravely. "My wife went away with someone she cared for many years ago."

"Ah, I'm sorry." And after another long silence—"It's a gorgeous evening, John Jackson."

"It's a long time since I've been so happy."

There was so much to say and to tell that neither of them tried to talk, but only sat there holding hands, like two children who had wandered for a long time through a wood and now came upon each other with unimaginable happiness in an accidental glade. Her husband was poor, she said; he knew that from the worn, unfashionable dress which she wore with such an air. He was George Harland—he kept a garage in the village.

"George Harland—a red-headed boy?" he asked wonderingly.

She nodded.

"We were engaged for years. Sometimes I thought we'd never marry. Twice I postponed it, but it was getting late to just be a girl—I was twenty-five, and so finally we did. After that I was in love with him for over a year."

When the sunset fell together in a jumbled heap of color in the bottom of the sky, they strolled back along the quiet road, still hand in hand.

"Will you come to dinner? I want you to see the children. My oldest boy is just fifteen."

She lived in a plain frame house two doors from the garage, where two little girls were playing around a battered and ancient but occupied baby carriage in the yard.

"Mother! Oh, mother!" they cried.

Small brown arms swirled around her neck as she knelt beside them on the walk.

"Sister says Anna didn't come, so we can't have any dinner."

"Mother'll cook dinner. What's the matter with Anna?"

"Anna's father's sick. She couldn't come."

A tall, tired man of fifty, who was reading a paper on the porch, rose and slipped a coat over his suspenders as they mounted the steps.

"Anna didn't come," he said in a noncommittal voice.

"I know. I'm going to cook dinner. Who do you suppose this is here?"

The two men shook hands in a friendly way, and with a certain deference to John Jackson's clothes and his prosperous manner, Harland went inside for another chair.

"We've heard about you a great deal, Mr. Jackson," he said as Alice disappeared into the kitchen. "We heard about a lot of ways you made them sit up and take notice over yonder."

John nodded politely, but at the mention of the city he had just left a wave of distaste went over him.

"I'm sorry I ever left here," he answered frankly. "And I'm not just saying that either. Tell me what the years have done for you, Harland. I hear you've got a garage."

"Yeah—down the road a ways. I'm doing right well, matter of fact. Nothing you'd call well in the city," he added in hasty depreciation.

"You know, Harland," said John Jackson, after a moment, "I'm very much in love with your wife."

"Yeah?" Harland laughed. "Well, she's a pretty nice lady, I find."

"I think I always have been in love with her, all these years."

"Yeah?" Harland laughed again. That someone should be in love with his wife seemed the most casual pleasantry. "You better tell her about it. She don't get so many nice compliments as she used to in her young days."

Six of them sat down at table, including an awkward boy of fifteen, who looked like his father, and two little girls whose faces shone from a hasty toilet. Many things had happened in the town, John discovered; the factitious prosperity which had promised to descend upon it in the late 90's had vanished when two factories had closed up and moved away, and the population was smaller now by a few hundred than it had been a quarter of a century ago.

After a plentiful plain dinner they all went to the porch, where the children silhouetted themselves in silent balance on the railing and unrecognizable people called greeting as they passed along the dark, dusty street. After a while the younger children went to bed, and the boy and his father arose and put on their coats.

"I guess I'll run up to the garage," said Harland. "I always go up about this time every night. You two just sit here and talk about old times."

As father and son moved out of sight along the dim street John

Jackson turned to Alice and slipped his arm about her shoulder and looked into her eyes.

"I love you, Alice."

"I love you."

Never since his marriage had he said that to any woman except his wife. But this was a new world tonight, with spring all about him in the air, and he felt as if he were holding his own lost youth in his arms.

"I've always loved you," she murmured. "Just before I go to sleep every night, I've always been able to see your face. Why didn't you come back?"

Tenderly he smoothed her hair. He had never known such happiness before. He felt that he had established dominance over time itself, so that it rolled away for him, yielding up one vanished springtime after another to the mastery of his overwhelming emotion.

"We're still young, we two people," he said exultantly. "We made a silly mistake a long, long time ago, but we found out in time."

"Tell me about it," she whispered.

"This morning, in the rain, I heard your voice."

"What did my voice say?"

"It said, 'Come home.' "

"And here you are, my dear."

"Here I am."

Suddenly he got to his feet.

"You and I are going away," he said. "Do you understand that?"

"I always knew that when you came for me I'd go."

Later, when the moon had risen, she walked with him to the gate.

"Tomorrow!" he whispered.

"Tomorrow!"

His heart was going like mad, and he stood carefully away from her to let footsteps across the way approach, pass and fade out down the dim street. With a sort of wild innocence he kissed her once more and held her close to his heart under the April moon.

IV

When he awoke it was eleven o'clock, and he drew himself a cool bath, splashing around in it with much of the exultation of the night before.

"I have thought too much these twenty years," he said to himself. "It's thinking that makes people old."

It was hotter than it had been the day before, and as he looked out the window the dust in the street seemed more tangible than on the night before. He breakfasted alone downstairs, wondering with the incessant wonder of the city man why fresh cream is almost unobtainable in the country. Word had spread already that he was home, and several men rose to greet him as he came into the lobby. Asked if he had a wife and children, he said no, in a careless way, and after he had said it he had a vague feeling of discomfort.

"I'm all alone," he went on, with forced jocularity. "I wanted to come back and see the old town again."

"Stay long?" They looked at him curiously.

"Just a day or so."

He wondered what they would think tomorrow. There would be excited little groups of them here and there along the street with the startling and audacious news.

"See here," he wanted to say, "you think I've had a wonderful life over there in the city, but I haven't. I came down here because life had beaten me, and if there's any brightness in my eyes this morning it's because last night I found a part of my lost youth tucked away in this little town."

At noon, as he walked toward Alice's house, the heat increased and several times he stopped to wipe the sweat from his forehead. When he turned in at the gate he saw her waiting on the porch, wearing what was apparently a Sunday dress and moving herself gently back and forth in a rocking-chair in a way that he remembered her doing as a girl.

"Alice!" he exclaimed happily.

Her finger rose swiftly and touched her lips.

"Look out!" she said in a low voice.

He sat down beside her and took her hand, but she replaced it on the arm of her chair and resumed her gentle rocking.

"Be careful. The children are inside."

"But I can't be careful. Now that life's begun all over again, I've forgotten all the caution that I learned in the other life, the one that's past."

"Sh-h-h!"

Somewhat irritated, he glanced at her closely. Her face, unmoved and unresponsive, seemed vaguely older than it had yesterday; she was white and tired. But he dismissed the impression with a low, exultant laugh.

"Alice, I haven't slept as I slept last night since I was a little boy, except that several times I woke up just for the joy of seeing the same moon we once knew together. I'd got it back."

"I didn't sleep at all."

"I'm sorry."

"I realized about two o'clock or three o'clock that I could never go away from my children—even with you."

He was struck dumb. He looked at her blankly for a moment, and then he laughed—a short, incredulous laugh.

"Never, never!" she went on, shaking her head passionately. "Never, never, never! When I thought of it I began to tremble all over, right in my bed." She hesitated. "I don't know what came over me yesterday evening, John. When I'm with you, you can always make me do or feel or think just exactly what you like. But this is too late, I guess. It doesn't seem real at all; it just seems sort of crazy to me, as if I'd dreamed it, that's all."

John Jackson laughed again, not incredulously this time, but on a menacing note.

"What do you mean?" he demanded.

She began to cry and hid her eyes behind her hand because some people were passing along the road.

"You've got to tell me more than that," cried John Jackson, his voice rising a little. "I can't just take that and go away."

"Please don't talk so loud," she implored him. "It's so hot and I'm so confused. I guess I'm just a small-town woman, after all. It seems somehow awful to be talking here with you, when my husband's working all day in the dust and heat."

"Awful to be talking here?" he repeated.

"Don't look that way!" she cried miserably. "I can't bear to hurt you so. You have children, too, to think of—you said you had a son."

"A son." The fact seemed so far away that he looked at her, startled. "Oh, yes, I have a son."

A sort of craziness, a wild illogic in the situation had communicated itself to him; and yet he fought blindly against it as he felt his own mood of ecstasy slipping away. For twenty hours he had recaptured the power of seeing things through a mist of hope—hope in some vague, happy destiny that lay just over the hill—and now with every word she uttered the mist was passing, the hope, the town, the memory, the very face of this woman before his eyes.

"Never again in this world," he cried with a last despairing effort, "will you and I have a chance at happiness!"

But he knew, even as he said this, that it had never been a chance; simply a wild, desperate sortie from two long-beleaguered fortresses by night.

He looked up to see that George Harland had turned in at the gate.

"Lunch is ready," called Alice, raising her head with an expression of relief. "John's going to be with us too."

"I can't," said John Jackson quickly. "You're both very kind."

"Better stay." Harland, in oily overalls, sank down wearily on the steps and with a large handkerchief polished the hot space beneath his thin gray hair. "We can give you some iced tea." He looked up at John. "I don't know whether these hot days make you feel your age like I feel mine."

"I guess—it affects all of us alike," said John Jackson with an effort. "The awful part of it is that I've got to go back to the city this afternoon."

"Really?" Harland nodded with polite regret.

"Why, yes. The fact is I promised to make a speech."

"Is that so? Speak on some city problem, I suppose."

"No; the fact is"—the words, forming in his mind to a senseless rhythm, pushed themselves out—"I'm going to speak on What Have I Got Out of Life."

Then he became conscious of the heat indeed; and still wearing that smile he knew so well how to muster, he felt himself sway dizzily against the porch rail. After a minute they were walking with him toward the gate.

"I'm sorry you're leaving," said Alice, with frightened eyes. "Come back and visit your old town again."

"I will."

Blind with unhappiness, he set off up the street at what he felt must be a stumble; but some dim necessity made him turn after he had gone a little way and smile back at them and wave his hand. They were still standing there, and they waved at him and he saw them turn and walk together into their house.

"I must go back and make my speech," he said to himself as he walked on, swaying slightly, down the street. "I shall get up and ask aloud 'What have I got out of life?' And there before them all I shall answer, 'Nothing.' I shall tell them the truth; that life has beaten me at every turning and used me for its own obscure purposes over and over; that everything I have loved has turned to ashes, and that every time I have stooped to pat a dog I have felt his teeth in my hand. And so at last they will learn the truth about one man's heart."

V

The meeting was at four, but it was nearly five when he dismounted from the sweltering train and walked toward the Civic Club hall. Numerous cars were parked along the surrounding streets, promising an unusually large crowd. He was surprised to find that even the rear of the hall was thronged with standing people, and that there were recurrent outbursts of applause at some speech which was being delivered upon the platform.

"Can you find me a seat near the rear?" he whispered to an attendant. "I'm going to speak later, but I don't—I don't want to go upon the platform just now."

"Certainly, Mr. Jackson."

The only vacant chair was half behind a pillar in a far corner of the hall, but he welcomed its privacy with relief; and settling himself, looked curiously around him. Yes, the gathering was large, and apparently enthusiastic. Catching a glimpse of a face here and there, he saw that he knew most of them, even by name; faces of men he had lived beside and worked with for twenty years. All the better. These were the ones he must reach now, as soon as that figure on the platform there ceased mouthing his hollow cheer.

His eyes swung back to the platform, and as there was another ripple of applause he leaned his face around the corner to see. Then he uttered a low exclamation—the speaker was Thomas MacDowell. They had not been asked to speak together in several years.

"I've had many enemies in my life," boomed the loud voice over the hall, "and don't think I've had a change of heart, now that I'm fifty and a little gray. I'll go on making enemies to the end. This is just a little lull when I want to take off my armor and pay a tribute to an enemy—because that enemy happens to be the finest man I ever knew."

John Jackson wondered what candidate or protégé of MacDowell's was in question. It was typical of the man to seize any opportunity to make his own hay.

"Perhaps I wouldn't have said what I've said," went on the booming voice, "were he here today. But if all the young men in this city came up to me and asked me 'What is being honorable?' I'd answer them, 'Go up to that man and look into his eyes.' They're not happy eyes. I've often sat and looked at him and wondered what went on back of them that made those eyes so sad. Perhaps the fine, simple hearts that spend their hours smoothing other people's troubles never find time for happiness of their own. It's like the man at the soda fountain who never makes an ice-cream soda for himself."

There was a faint ripple of laughter here, but John Jackson saw wonderingly that a woman he knew just across the aisle was dabbing with a handkerchief at her eyes.

His curiosity increased.

"He's gone away now," said the man on the platform, bending his head and staring down for a minute at the floor: "gone away suddenly, I understand. He seemed a little strange when I saw him yesterday; perhaps he gave in at last under the strain of trying to do many things for many men. Perhaps this meeting we're holding here comes a little too late now. But we'll all feel better for having said our say about him.

"I'm almost through. A lot of you will think it's funny that I feel this way about a man who, in fairness to him, I must call an enemy. But I'm going to say one thing more"—his voice rose defiantly—"and it's a stranger thing still. Here, at fifty, there's one honor I'd like to have more than any honor this city ever gave me, or ever had it in its power to give. I'd like to be able to stand up here before you and call John Jackson my friend."

He turned away and a storm of applause rose like thunder through the hall. John Jackson half rose to his feet, and then sank back again in a stupefied way, shrinking behind the pillar. The applause continued until a young man arose on the platform and waved them silent.

"Mrs. Ralston," he called, and sat down.

A woman rose from the line of chairs and came forward to the edge of the stage and began to speak in a quiet voice. She told a story about a man whom—so it seemed to John Jackson—he had known once, but whose actions, repeated here, seemed utterly unreal, like something that had happened in a dream. It appeared that every year many hundreds of babies in the city owed their lives to something this man had done five years before; he had put a mortgage upon his own house to assure the children's hospital on the edge of town. It told how this had been kept secret at the man's own request, because he wanted the city to take pride in the hospital as a community affair, when but for the man's effort, made after the community attempt had failed, the hospital would never have existed at all.

Then Mrs. Ralston began to talk about the parks; how the town had baked for many years under the midland heat; and how this man, not a very rich man, had given up land and time and money for many months that a green line of shade might skirt the boulevards, and that the poor children could leave the streets and play in fresh grass in the center of town.

That was only the beginning, she said; and she went on to tell how, when any such plan tottered, or the public interest lagged, word was brought to John Jackson, and somehow he made it go and seemed to give it life out of his own body, until there was scarcely anything in this city that didn't have a little of John Jackson's heart in it, just as there were few people in this city that didn't have a little of their hearts for John Jackson.

Mrs. Ralston's speech stopped abruptly at this point. She had been crying a little for several moments, but there must have been many people there in the audience who understood what she meant—a mother or a child here and there who had been the recipients of some of that kindness—because the applause seemed to fill the whole room like an ocean, and echoed back and forth from wall to wall.

Only a few people recognized the short grizzled man who now got up from his chair in the rear of the platform, but when he began to speak silence settled gradually over the house.

"You didn't hear my name," he said in a voice which trembled a little, "and when they first planned this surprise meeting I wasn't expected to speak at all. I'm John Jackson's head clerk. Fowler's my name, and when they decided they were going to hold the meeting, anyhow, even though John Jackson had gone away, I thought perhaps I'd like to say a few words"—those who were closest saw his hands clench tighter—"say a few words that I couldn't say if John Jackson was here.

"I've been with him twenty years. That's a long time. Neither of us had gray hair when I walked into his office one day just fired from somewhere and asked him for a job. Since then I can't tell you, gentlemen, I can't tell you what his—his presence on this earth has meant to me. When he told me yesterday, suddenly, that he was going away, I thought to myself that if he never came back I didn't—I didn't want to go on living. That man makes everything in the world seem all right. If you knew how we felt around the office——" He paused and shook his head wordlessly. "Why, there's three of us there—the janitor and one of the other clerks and me—that have sons named after John Jackson. Yes, sir. Because none of us could think of anything better than for a boy to have that name or that example before him through life. But would we tell him? Not a chance. He wouldn't even know what it was all about. Why"—he sank his voice to a hushed whisper—"he'd just look at you in a puzzled way and say, 'What did you wish that on the poor kid for?' "

He broke off, for there was a sudden and growing interruption. An epidemic of head turning had broken out and was spreading rapidly from one corner of the hall until it had affected the whole assemblage. Someone had discovered John Jackson behind the post in the corner, and first an exclamation and then a growing mumble that mounted to a cheer swept over the auditorium.

Suddenly two men had taken him by the arms and set him on his feet, and then he was pushed and pulled and carried toward the platform, arriving somehow in a standing position after having been lifted over many heads.

They were all standing now, arms waving wildly, voices filling the hall with tumultuous clamor. Someone in the back of the hall began to sing "For he's a jolly good fellow," and five hundred voices took up the air and sang it with such feeling, with such swelling emotion, that all eyes were wet and the song assumed a significance far beyond the spoken words.

This was John Jackson's chance now to say to these people that he had got so little out of life. He stretched out his arms in a sudden gesture and they were quiet, listening, every man and woman and child.

"I have been asked——" His voice faltered. "My dear friends, I have been asked to—to tell you what I have got out of life——"

Five hundred faces, touched and smiling, every one of them full of encouragement and love and faith, turned up to him.

"What have I got out of life?"

He stretched out his arms wide, as if to include them all, as if to take to his breast all the men and women and children of this city. His voice rang in the hushed silence.

"Everything!"

At six o'clock, when he walked up his street alone, the air was already cool with evening. Approaching his house, he raised his head and saw that someone was sitting on the outer doorstep, resting his face in his hands. When John Jackson came up the walk, the caller— he was a young man with dark, frightened eyes—saw him and sprang to his feet.

"Father," he said quickly, "I got your telegram, but I—I came home."

John Jackson looked at him and nodded.

"The house was locked," said the young man in an uneasy way.

"I've got the key."

John Jackson unlocked the front door and preceded his son inside.

"Father," cried Ellery Jackson quickly, "I haven't any excuse to make—anything to say. I'll tell you all about it if you're still interested—if you can stand to hear——"

John Jackson rested his hand on the young man's shoulder.

"Don't feel too badly," he said in his kind voice. "I guess I can always stand anything my son does."

This was an understatement. For John Jackson could stand anything now forever—anything that came, anything at all.

Not in the Guidebook

(*Woman's Home Companion*, November 1925)

"Not in the Guidebook" was written in Rome's Hotel des Princes in December 1924, just after *The Great Gatsby* had been sent to Scribners. The Fitzgeralds had gone to Rome from the Riviera, planning to spend the winter of 1924-1925 there, but were unhappy and moved on to Capri in February. When Fitzgerald reread this story, he decided to rewrite it, which he did at the Hotel Tiberio in Capri. Although he doubted whether it would be saleable, *Woman's Home Companion* paid $1750.

"Not in the Guidebook" was the second story Fitzgerald wrote with a European setting. Whereas the first, "Love in the Night," is distinguished by rich descriptions of the Riviera, "Not in the Guidebook" depends on a predictable plot trick. Part of the problem may have been that at this time Fitzgerald did not know Paris well—having spent only a few days there.

Fitzgerald was ashamed of his 1924 story output and wrote John Peale Bishop: "I've done about 10 pieces of horrible junk in the last year tho that I can never republish or bear to look at—cheap and without the spontaneity of my first work."

This story began three days before it got into the papers. Like many other news-hungry Americans in Paris this spring, I opened the *Franco-American Star* one morning, and having skimmed the hackneyed headlines (largely devoted to reporting the sempiternal "Lafayette-love-Washington" bombast of French and American orators) I came upon something of genuine interest.

"Look at that!" I exclaimed, passing it over to the twin bed. But the occupant of the twin bed immediately found an article about Leonora Hughes, the dancer, in another column, and began to read it. So of course I demanded the paper back.

"You don't realize—" I began.

"I wonder," interrupted the occupant of the twin bed, "if she's a real blonde."

However, when I issued from the domestic suite a little later I found other men in various cafes saying, "Look at that!" as they pointed to the Item of Interest. And about noon I found another writer (whom I have since bribed with champagne to hold his peace) and together we went down into Franco-American officialdom to see.

It began on a boat, and with a young woman who, though she wasn't even faintly uneasy, was leaning over the rail. She was watching the parallels of longitude as they swam beneath the keel, and trying to read the numbers on them, but of course the *S. S. Olympic* travels too fast for that, and all that the young woman could see was the agate-green, foliage-like spray, changing and complaining around the stern. Though there was little to look at except the spray and a dismal Scandinavian tramp in the distance and the admiring millionaire who was trying to catch her eye from the first-class deck above, Milly Cooley was perfectly happy. For she was beginning life over.

Hope is a usual cargo between Naples and Ellis Island, but on ships bound east for Cherbourg it is noticeably rare. The first-class passengers specialize in sophistication and the steerage passengers go in for disillusion (which is much the same thing) but the young woman by the rail was going in for hope raised to the ultimate power. It was not her own life she was beginning over, but someone else's, and this is a much more dangerous thing to do.

Milly was a frail, dark, appealing girl with the spiritual, haunted eyes that so frequently accompany South European beauty. By birth her mother and father had been respectively Czech and Roumanian, but Milly had missed the overshort upper lip and the pendulous, pointed nose that disfigure the type; her features were regular and her skin was young and olive-white and clear.

The good-looking, pimply young man with eyes of a bright marbly blue who was asleep on a dunnage bag a few feet away was her husband—it was his life that Milly was beginning over. Through the six months of their marriage he had shown himself to be shiftless and dissipated, but now they were getting off to a new start. Jim Cooley deserved a new start, for he had been a hero in the war. There was a thing called "shell shock" which justified anything unpleasant in a war hero's behavior—Jim Cooley had explained that to her on the second day of their honeymoon when he had gotten abominably drunk and knocked her down with his open hand.

"I get crazy," he said emphatically next morning, and his marbly eyes rolled back and forth realistically in his head. "I get started, thinkin' I'm fightin' the war, an' I take a poke at whatever's in front of me, see?"

He was a Brooklyn boy, and he had joined the marines. And on a June twilight he had crawled fifty yards out of his lines to search the body of a Bavarian captain that lay out in plain sight. He found a copy of German regimental orders, and in consequence his own brigade attacked much sooner than would otherwise have been possible, and perhaps the war was shortened by so much as a quarter of an hour. The fact was appreciated by the French and American races in the form of engraved slugs of precious metal which Jim showed around for four years before it occurred to him how nice it would be to have a permanent audience. Milly's mother was impressed with his martial achievement, and a marriage was arranged. Milly didn't realize her mistake until twenty-four hours after it was too late.

At the end of several months Milly's mother died and left her daughter two hundred and fifty dollars. The event had a marked effect on Jim. He sobered up and one night came home from work with a plan for turning over a new leaf, for beginning life over. By the aid of his war record he had obtained a job with a bureau that took care of American soldier graves in France. The pay was small but then, as everyone knew, living was dirt cheap over there. Hadn't the forty a month that he drew in the war looked good to the girls and the wine-sellers of Paris? Especially when you figured it in French money.

Milly listened to his tales of the land where grapes were full of champagne and then thought it all over carefully. Perhaps the best use for her money would be in giving Jim his chance, the chance that he had never had since the war. In a little cottage in the outskirts of Paris they could forget this last six months and find peace and happiness and perhaps even love as well.

"Are you going to try?" she asked simply.

"Of course I'm going to try, Milly."

"You're going to make me think I didn't make a mistake?"

"Sure I am, Milly; it'll make a different person out of me. Don't you believe it?"

She looked at him. His eyes were bright with enthusiasm, with determination. A warm glow had spread over him at the prospect—he had never really had his chance before.

"All right," she said finally. "We'li go."

They were there. The Cherbourg breakwater, a white stone snake, glittered along the sea at dawn; behind it red roofs and steeples and then small, neat hills traced with a warm, orderly pattern of toy farms. "Do you like this French arrangement?" it seemed to say. "It's considered very charming, but if you don't agree just shift it about—set this road here, this steeple there. It's been done before, and it always comes out lovely in the end!"

It was Sunday morning, and Cherbourg was in flaring collars and high lace hats. Donkey carts and diminutive automobiles moved to the sound of incessant bells. Jim and Milly went ashore on a tugboat and were inspected by customs officials and immigration authorities. Then they were free with an hour before the Paris train, and they moved out into the bright thrilling world of French blue. At a point of vantage, a pleasant square that continually throbbed with soldiers and innumerable dogs and the clack of wooden shoes, they sat down at a cafe.

"Du vaah," said Jim to the waiter. He was a little disappointed when the answer came in English. After the man went for the wine he took out his two war medals and pinned them to his coat. The waiter returned with the wine, seemed not to notice the medals, made no remark. Milly wished Jim hadn't put them on—she felt vaguely ashamed.

After another glass of wine it was time for the train. They got into the strange little third-class carriage, an engine that was out of some boy's playroom began to puff and, in a pleasant, informal way, jogged them leisurely south through the friendly lived-over land.

"What are we going to do first when we get there?" asked Milly.

"First?" Jim looked at her abstractedly and frowned. "Why, first I got to see about the job, see?" The exhilaration of the wine had passed and left him surly. "What do you want to ask so many questions for? Buy yourself a guidebook, why don't you?"

Milly felt a slight sinking of the heart; he hadn't grumbled at her like this since the trip was first proposed.

"It didn't cost as much as we thought, anyhow," she said cheerfully. "We must have over a hundred dollars left anyway."

He grunted. Outside the window Milly's eyes were caught by the sight of a dog drawing a legless man.

"Look!" she exclaimed, "how funny!"

"Aw, dry up. I've seen it all before."

An encouraging idea occurred to her: it was in France that Jim's nerves had gone to pieces, it was natural that he should be cross and uneasy for a few hours.

Westward through Caen, Lisieux and the rich green plains of Calvados. When they reached the third stop Jim got up and stretched himself.

"Going out on the platform," he said gloomily. "I need to get a breath of air; hot in here."

It was hot, but Milly didn't mind. Her eyes were excited with all she saw—a pair of little boys in black smocks began to stare at her curiously through the windows of the carriage.

"American?" cried one of them suddenly.

"Hello," said Milly, "what place is this?"

"Pardon?"

They came closer.

"What's the name of this place?"

Suddenly the two boys poked each other in the stomach and went off into roars of laughter. Milly didn't see that she had said anything funny.

There was an abrupt jerk as the train started. Milly jumped up in alarm and put her head out the carriage window.

"Jim!" she called.

She looked up and down the platform. He wasn't there. The boys, seeing her distraught face, ran along beside the train as it moved from the station. He must have jumped for one of the rear cars. But—

"Jim!" she cried wildly. The station slid past. "Jim!"

Trying desperately to control her fright, she sank back into her seat and tried to think. Her first supposition was that he had gone to a cafe for a drink and missed the train—in that case she should have got off too while there was still time, for otherwise there was no telling what would happen to him. If this were one of his spells he might just go on drinking, until he had spent every cent of their money. It was unbelievably awful to imagine—but it was possible.

She waited, gave him ten, fifteen minutes to work his way up to this car—then she admitted to herself that he wasn't on the train. A dull panic began. The sudden change in her relations to the world was so startling that she thought neither of his delinquency nor of what must be done, but only of the immediate fact that she was alone. Erratic as his protection had been, it was something. Now—why, she might sit in this strange train until it carried her to China and there was no one to care!

After a long while it occurred to her that he might have left part of the money in one of the suitcases. She took them down from the rack and went feverishly through all the clothes. In the bottom of an old pair of pants that Jim had worn on the boat she found two bright American dimes. The sight of them was somehow comforting and she clasped them tight in her hand. The bags yielded up nothing more.

An hour later, when it was dark outside, the train slid in under the yellow misty glow of the Gare du Nord. Strange, incomprehensible station cries fell on her ears, and her heart was beating loudly as she wrenched at the handle of the door. She took her own bag with one hand and picked up Jim's suitcase in the other, but it was heavy and she couldn't get out the door with both, so in a rush of anger she left the suitcase in the carriage.

On the platform she looked left and right with the forlorn hope that he might appear, but she saw no one except a Swedish brother and sister from the boat whose tall bodies, straight and strong under the huge bundles they both carried, were hurrying out of sight. She took a quick step after them and then stopped, unable to tell them of the shameful thing that had happened to her. They had worries of their own.

With the two dimes in one hand and her suitcase in the other, Milly walked slowly along the platform. People hurried by her, baggage-smashers under forests of golf sticks, excited American girls full of the irrepressible thrill of arriving in Paris, obsequious porters from the big hotels. They were all walking and talking very fast, but Milly walked slowly because ahead of her she saw only the yellow arc of the waiting-room and the door that led out of it and after that she did not know where she would go.

By 10 P.M. Mr. Bill Driscoll was usually weary, for by that time he had a full twelve-hour day behind him. After that he only went out with the most celebrated people. If someone had tipped off a multi-millionaire or a moving-picture director—at that time American directors were swarming over Europe looking for new locations—about Bill Driscoll, he would fortify himself with two cups of coffee, adorn his person with his new dinner-coat and show them the most dangerous dives of Montmartre in the very safest way.

Bill Driscoll looked well in his new dinner-coat, with his reddish brown hair soaked in water and slicked back from his attractive forehead. Often he regarded himself admiringly in the mirror, for it was the first dinner-coat he had ever owned. He had earned it himself, with his wits, as he had earned the swelling packet of American bonds which awaited him in a New York bank. If you have been in Paris during the past two years you must have seen his large white auto-bus with the provoking legend on the side:

WILLIAM DRISCOLL

HE SHOWS YOU THINGS NOT IN THE GUIDEBOOK

When he found Milly Cooley it was after three o'clock and he had just left Director and Mrs. Claude Peebles at their hotel after escorting them to those celebrated apache dens, Zelli's and *Le Rat Mort* (which are about as dangerous, all things considered, as the Biltmore Hotel at noon), and he was walking homeward toward his pension on the left bank. His eye was caught by two disreputable-looking parties under the lamp-post who were giving aid to what was apparently a drunken girl. Bill Driscoll decided to cross the street—he was aware of the tender affection which the French police bore toward embattled Americans, and he made a point of keeping out of trouble. Just at that moment Milly's subconscious self came to her aid and she called out, "Let me go!" in an agonized moan.

The moan had a Brooklyn accent. It was a Brooklyn moan.

Driscoll altered his course uneasily and, approaching the group, asked politely what was the matter; whereat one of the disreputable parties desisted in his attempt to open Milly's tightly clasped left hand.

The man answered quickly that she had fainted. He and his friend were assisting her to the gendarmery. They loosened their hold on her and she collapsed gently to the ground.

Bill came closer and bent over her, being careful to choose a position where neither man was behind him. He saw a young, frightened face that was drained now of the color it possessed by day.

"Where did you find her?" he inquired in French.

"Here. Just now. She looked to be so tired—"

Billy put his hand in his pocket and when he spoke he tried very hard to suggest by his voice that he had a revolver there.

"She is American," he said. "You leave her to me."

The man made a gesture of acquiescence and took a step backward, his hand going with a natural movement to his coat as if he intended buttoning it. He was watching Bill's right hand, the one in his coat-pocket, and Bill happened to be left-handed. There is nothing much faster than an untelegraphed left-hand blow—this one traveled less than eighteen inches and the recipient staggered back against a lamp-post, embraced it transiently and regretfully and settled to the ground. Nevertheless Bill Driscoll's successful career might have ended there, ended with the strong shout of *"Voleurs!"* which he raised into the Paris night, had the other man had a gun. The other man indicated that he had no gun by retreating ten yards down the street. His prostrate companion moved slightly on the sidewalk and, taking a step toward him, Billy drew back his foot and kicked him full in the head as a football player kicks a goal from placement. It was not a pretty gesture, but he had remembered that he was wearing his new dinner-coat and he didn't want to wrestle on the ground for the piece of poisonous hardware.

In a moment two gendarmes in a great hurry came running down the moonlit street.

Two days after this it came out in the papers—*"War hero deserts wife en route to Paris,"* I think, or *"American bride arrives penniless, husbandless at Gare du Nord."* The police were informed, of course, and word was sent out to the provincial departments to seek an American named James Cooley who was without *carte d'identité*. The newspapers learned the story at the American Aid Society, and made a neat, pathetic job of it, because Milly was young and pretty and curiously loyal to her husband. Almost her first words were to explain that it was all because his nerves had been shattered in the war.

Young Driscoll was somewhat disappointed to find that she was married. Not that he had fallen in love at first sight—on the contrary, he was unusually level-headed—but after the moonlight rescue, which rather pleased him, it didn't seem appropriate that she should have a heroic husband wandering over France. He had carried her to his own pension that night, and his landlady, an American widow named Mrs. Horton, had taken a fancy to Milly and wanted to look after her, but before eleven o'clock on the day the paper appeared, the office of the American Aid Society was literally jammed with Samaritans. They were mostly rich old ladies from America who were tired of the Louvre and the Tuileries, and anxious for something to do. Several eager but sheepish Frenchmen, inspired by a mysterious and unfathomable gallantry, hung about outside the door.

The most insistent of the ladies was a Mrs. Coots, who considered that Providence had sent her Milly as a companion. If she had heard Milly's story in the street she wouldn't have listened to a word, but print makes things respectable. After it got into the *Franco-American Star*, Mrs. Coots was sure Milly wouldn't make off with her jewels.

"I'll pay you well, my dear," she insisted shrilly. "Twenty-five a week. How's that?"

Milly cast an anxious glance at Mrs. Horton's faded, pleasant face.

"I don't know—" she said hesitantly.

"I can't pay you anything." Mrs. Horton was confused by Mrs. Coots' affluent, positive manner. "You do as you like. I'd love to have you."

"You've certainly been kind," said Milly, "but I don't want to impose—"

Driscoll, who had been walking up and down with his hands in his pockets, stopped and turned toward her quickly.

"I'll take care of that," he said quickly. "You don't have to worry about that."

Mrs. Coots' eyes flashed at him indignantly.

"She's better with me," she insisted. "Much better." She turned to the secretary and remarked in a pained, disapproving stage whisper, "Who is this forward young man?"

Again Milly looked appealingly at Mrs. Horton.

"If it's not too much trouble I'd rather stay with you," she said. "I'll help you all I can—"

It took another half hour to get rid of Mrs. Coots, but finally it was arranged that Milly was to stay at Mrs. Horton's pension, until some trace of her husband was found. Later the same day they ascertained that the American Bureau of Military Graves had never heard of Jim Cooley—he had no job promised him in France.

However distressing her situation, Milly was young and she was in Paris in mid-June. She decided to enjoy herself. At Mr. Bill Driscoll's invitation she went on an excursion to Versailles next day in his rubberneck wagon. She had never been on such a trip before. She sat among garment buyers from Sioux City and school-teachers from California and honeymoon couples from Japan, and was whirled through fifteen centuries of Paris, while their guide stood up in front with the megaphone pressed to his voluble and original mouth.

"Building on your left is the Louvre, ladies and gentlemen. Excursion number twenty-three leaving to-morrow at ten sharp takes you inside. Sufficient to remark now that it contains fifteen thousand works of art of every description. The oil used in its oil paintings would lubricate all the cars in the state of Oregon over a period of two years. The frames alone if placed end to end—"

Milly watched him, believing every word. It was hard to remember that he had come to her rescue that night. Heroes weren't like that—she knew; she had lived with one. They brooded constantly on their achievements and retailed them to strangers at least once a day. When she had thanked this young man he told her gravely that Mr. Carnegie had been trying to get him on the ouija board all that day.

After a dramatic stop before the house in which Landru, the Bluebeard of France, had murdered his fourteen wives, the expedition proceeded to Versailles. There, in the great hall of mirrors, Bill Driscoll delved into the forgotten scandal of the eighteenth century as he described the meeting between "Louie's girl and Louie's wife."

"Du Barry skipped in, wearing a creation of mauve georgette, held out by bronze hoops over a tablier of champagne lace. The gown had a ruched collarette of Swedish fox, lined with yellow satin fulgurante which matched the hansom that brought her to the party. She was nervous, ladies. She didn't know how the queen was going to take it. After a while the queen walked in, wearing an oxidized silver gown with collar, cuffs and flounces of Russian ermine and strappings of dentist's gold. The bodice was cut with a very long waistline and the skirt arranged full in front and falling in picot-edged points tipped with the crown jewels. When Du Barry saw her she leaned over to King Louie and whispered: 'Royal Honey-boy, who's that lady with all the laundry on that just came in the door?'

" 'That isn't a lady,' said Louie, 'that's my wife.' "

That was the first of many trips that Milly took in the rubberneck wagon—to Malmaison, to Passy, to St. Cloud. The weeks passed, three of them, and still there was no word from Jim Cooley, who seemed to have stepped off the face of the earth when he vanished from the train.

In spite of a sort of dull worry that possessed her when she thought of her situation, Milly was happier than she had ever been. It was a relief to be rid of the incessant depression of living with a morbid and broken man. Moreover, it was thrilling to be in Paris when it seemed that all the world was there, when each arriving boat dumped a new thousand into the pleasure ground, when the streets were so clogged with sight-seers that Billy Driscoll's busses were reserved for days ahead. And it was pleasantest of all to stroll down to the corner and watch the blood-red sun sink like a slow penny into the Seine while she sipped coffee with Bill Driscoll at a cafe.

"How would you like to go to Château-Thierry with me to-morrow?" he asked her one evening.

The name struck a chord in Milly. It was at Château-Thierry that Jim Cooley, at the risk of his life, had made his daring expedition between the lines.

"My husband was there," she said proudly.

"So was I," he remarked. "And I didn't have any fun at all."

He thought for a moment.

"How old are you?" he asked suddenly.

"Eighteen."

"Why don't you get a divorce?"

The suggestion shocked Milly.

"I think you'd better," he continued, looking down. "It's easier here than anywhere else. Then you'd be free."

"I couldn't," she said, frightened. "It wouldn't be fair. You see, he doesn't—"

"I know," he interrupted. "But I'm beginning to think that you're spoiling your life with this man. Is there anything except his war record to his credit?"

"Isn't that enough?" answered Milly gravely.

"Milly—" He raised his eyes. "Won't you think it over carefully?"

She got up uneasily. He looked very honest and safe and cool sitting there, and for a moment she was tempted to do what he said, to put the whole thing in his hands. But looking at him she saw now what she hadn't seen before, that the advice was not disinterested—there was more than an impersonal care for her future in his eyes. She turned away with a mixture of emotions.

Side by side and in silence they walked back toward the pension. From a high window the plaintive wail of a violin drifted down into the street, mingling with practice chords from an invisible piano and a shrill incomprehensible quarrel of French children over the way. The twilight was fast dissolving into a starry blue Parisian evening, but it was still light enough for them to make out the figure of Mrs. Horton standing in front of the pension. She came toward them swiftly, talking as she came.

"I've got some news for you," she said. "The secretary of the American Aid Society just telephoned. They've located your husband, and he'll be in Paris the day after to-morrow."

When Jim Cooley, the war hero, left the train at the small town of Evreux, he walked very fast until he was several hundred yards from the station. Then, standing behind a tree, he watched until the train pulled out and the last puff of smoke burst up behind a little hill. He stood for several minutes, laughing and looking after the train, until abruptly his face resumed his normal injured expression and he turned to examine the place in which he had chosen to be free.

It was a sleepy provincial village with two high lines of silver sycamores along its principal street, at the end of which a fine fountain purred crystal water from a cat's mouth of cold stone. Around the fountain was a square and on the sidewalks of the square several groups of small iron tables indicated open-air cafes. A farm wagon drawn by a single white ox was toiling toward the fountain and several cheap French cars, together with an ancient American one, were parked along the street.

"It's a hick town," he said to himself with some disgust. "Reg'lar hick town."

But it was peaceful and green, and he caught sight of two stockingless ladies entering the door of a shop; and the little tables by the fountain were inviting. He walked up the street and at the first cafe sat down and ordered a large beer.

"I'm free," he said to himself. "Free, by God!"

His decision to desert Milly had been taken suddenly—in Cherbourg, as they got on the train. Just at that moment he had seen a little French girl who was the real thing and he realized that he didn't want Milly "hanging on him" any more. Even on the boat he had played with the idea, but until Cherbourg he had never quite made up his mind. He was rather sorry now that he hadn't thought to leave Milly a little money, enough for one night—but then somebody would be sure to help her when she got to Paris. Besides, what he didn't know didn't worry him, and he wasn't going ever to hear about her again.

"Cognac this time," he said to the waiter.

He needed something strong. He wanted to forget. Not to forget Milly, that was easy, she was already behind him; but to forget himself. He felt that he had been abused. He felt that it was Milly who had deserted him, or at least that her cold mistrust was responsible for driving him away. What good would it have done if he had gone on to Paris anyways? There wasn't enough money left to keep two people for very long, and he had invented the job on the strength of a vague rumor that the American Bureau of Military Graves gave jobs to veterans who were broke in France. He shouldn't have brought Milly, wouldn't have if he had had the money to get over. But, though he was not aware of it, there was another reason why he had brought Milly. Jim Cooley hated to be alone.

"Cognac," he said to the waiter. "A big one. *Tres grand.*"

He put his hand in his pocket and fingered the blue notes that had been given him in Cherbourg in exchange for his American money. He took them out and counted them. Crazy-looking kale. It was funny you could buy things with it just like you could do with the real mazuma.

He beckoned to the waiter.

"Hey!" he remarked conversationally. "This is funny money you got here, ain't it?"

But the waiter spoke no English, and was unable to satisfy Jim Cooley's craving for companionship. Never mind. His nerves were at rest now—body was glowing triumphantly from top to toe.

"This is the life," he muttered to himself. "Only live once. Might as well enjoy it." And then aloud to the waiter, " 'Nother one of those big cognacs. Two of them. I'm set to go."

He went—for several hours. He awoke at dawn in a bedroom of a small inn, with red streaks in his eyes and fever pounding his head. He was afraid to look in his pockets until he had ordered and swallowed another cognac, and then he found that his worst fears were justified. Of the ninety-odd dollars with which he had got off the train only six were left.

"I must have been crazy," he whispered.

There remained his watch. His watch was large and methodical, and on the outer case two hearts were picked out in diamonds from the dark solid gold. It had been part of the booty of Jim Cooley's heroism, for when he had located the paper in the German officer's pocket he had found it clasped tight in the dead hand. One of the diamond hearts probably stood for some human grief back in Friedland or Berlin, but when Jim married he told Milly that the diamond hearts stood for their hearts and would be a token of their everlasting love. Before Milly fully appreciated this sentimental suggestion their enduring love had been tarnished beyond repair and the watch went back into Jim's pocket where it confined itself to marking time instead of emotion.

But Jim Cooley had loved to show the watch, and he found that parting with it would be much more painful than parting with Milly—so painful, in fact, that he got drunk in anticipation of the sorrow. Late that afternoon, already a reeling figure at which the town boys jeered along the streets, he found his way into the shop of a *bijouterie*, and when he issued forth into the street he was in possession of a ticket of redemption and a note for two thousand francs which, he figured dimly, was about one hundred and twenty dollars. Muttering to himself, he stumbled back to the square.

"One American can lick three Frenchmen!" he remarked to three small stout bourgeois drinking their beer at a table.

They paid no attention. He repeated his jeer.

"One American—" tapping his chest, "can beat up three dirty frogs, see?"

Still they didn't move. It infuriated him. Lurching forward, he seized the back of an unoccupied chair and pulled at it. In what seemed less than a minute there was a small crowd around him and the three Frenchmen were all talking at once in excited voices.

"Aw, go on, I meant what I said!" he cried savagely. "One American can wipe up the ground with three Frenchmen!"

And now there were two men in uniform before him—two men with revolver holsters on their hips, dressed in red and blue.

"You heard what I said," he shouted, "I'm a hero—I'm not afraid of the whole damn French army!"

A hand fell on his arm, but with blind passion he wrenched it free and struck at the black mustached face before him. Then there was a rushing, crashing noise in his ears as fists and then feet struck at him, and the world seemed to close like water over his head.

When they located him and, after a personal expedition by one of the American vice consuls, got him out of jail Milly realized how much these weeks had meant to her. The holiday was over. But even though Jim would be in Paris tomorrow, even though the dreary round of her life with him was due to recommence, Milly decided to take the trip to Château-Thierry just the same. She wanted a last few hours of happiness that she could always remember. She supposed they would return to New York—what chance Jim might have had of obtaining a position had vanished now that he was marked by a fortnight in a French prison.

The bus, as usual, was crowded. As they approached the little village of Château-Thierry, Bill Driscoll stood up in front with his megaphone and began to tell his clients how it had looked to him when his division went up to the line five years before.

"It was nine o'clock at night," he said, "and we came out of a wood and there was the western front. I'd read about it for three years back in America, and here it was at last—it looked like the line of a forest fire at night except that fireworks were blazing up instead of grass. We relieved a French regiment in new trenches that weren't three feet deep. At that, most of us were too excited to be scared until the top sergeant was blown to pieces with shrapnel about two o'clock in the morning. That made us think. Two days later we went over and the only reason I didn't get hit was that I was shaking so much they couldn't aim at me."

The listeners laughed and Milly felt a faint thrill of pride. Jim hadn't been scared—she'd heard him say so, many times. All he'd thought about was doing a little more than his duty. When others were in the comparative safety of the trenches he had gone into no-man's land alone.

After lunch in the village the party walked over the battlefield, changed now into a peaceful undulating valley of graves. Milly was glad she had come—the sense of rest after a struggle soothed her. Perhaps after the bleak future her life might be quiet as this peaceful land. Perhaps Jim would change some day. If he had risen once to such a height of courage there must be something deep inside him that was worth while, that would make him try once more.

Just before it was time to start home Driscoll, who had hardly spoken to her all day, suddenly beckoned her aside.

"I want to talk to you for the last time," he said.

The last time! Milly felt a flutter of unexpected pain. Was to-morrow so near?

"I'm going to say what's in my mind," he said, "and please don't be angry. I love you, and you know it; but what I'm going to say isn't because of that—it's because I want you to be happy."

Milly nodded. She was afraid she was going to cry.

"I don't think your husband's any good," he said.

She looked up.

"You don't know him," she exclaimed quickly. "You can't judge."

"I can judge from what he did to you. I think this shell-shock business is all a plain lie. And what does it matter what he did five years ago?"

"It matters to me," cried Milly. She felt herself growing a little angry. "You can't take that away from him. He acted brave."

Driscoll nodded.

"That's true. But other men were brave."

"You weren't," she said scornfully; "you just said you were scared to death—and when you said it all the people laughed. Well, nobody laughed at Jim—they gave him a medal because he wasn't afraid."

When Milly had said this she was sorry, but it was too late now. At his next words she leaned forward in surprise.

"That was a lie too," said Bill Driscoll slowly. "I told it because I wanted them to laugh. I wasn't even in the attack."

He stared silently down the hill.

"Well, then," said Milly contemptuously, "how can you sit here and say things about my husband when—when you didn't even—"

"It was only a professional lie," he said impatiently. "I happened to be wounded the night before."

He stood up suddenly.

"There's no use," he said. "I seem to have made you hate me, and that's the end. There's no use saying any more."

He stared down the hill with haunted eyes.

"I shouldn't have talked to you here," he cried. "There's no luck here for me. Once before I lost something I wanted, not a hundred yards from this hill. And now I've lost you."

"What was it you lost?" demanded Milly bitterly. "Another girl?"

"There's never been any other girl but you."

"What was it then?"

He hesitated.

"I told you I was wounded," he said. "I was. For two months I didn't know I was alive. But the worst of it was that some dirty sneak thief had been through my pockets, and I guess he got the credit for a copy of German orders that I'd just brought in. He took a gold watch too. I'd pinched them both off the body of a German officer out between the lines."

Mr. and Mrs. William Driscoll were married the following spring and started off on their honeymoon in a car that was much larger than the king of England's. There were two dozen vacant places in it, so they gave many rides to tired pedestrians along the white poplar-lined roads of France. The wayfarers, however, always sat in the back seat as the conversation in front was not for profane ears. The tour progressed through Lyons, Avignon, Bordeaux, and smaller places not in the guidebook.

Presumption

(*The Saturday Evening Post*, 9 January 1926)

"Presumption" was written in Paris in November 1925. The *Post* paid
$2500—a raise of $500—and printed it as the lead piece.

The Great Gatsby had been published in April 1925, but its
disappointing sale (23,000 copies) compelled Fitzgerald to resume writing
stories instead of concentrating on a new novel. This story has obvious
connections with *Gatsby* in its treatment of the poor boy who falls in love
with a rich girl and sets out to win her by becoming financially worthy of her.
Because "Presumption" was written for the *Post*, it has a happy ending
through one of the reversals of fortune that frequently occur in Fitzgerald's
commercial fiction. "Rich girls can't live on air." Neither Fitzgerald nor their
suitors expected them to.

Sitting by the window and staring out into the early autumn dusk,
San Juan Chandler remembered only that Noel was coming
tomorrow; but when, with a romantic sound that was half gasp, half
sigh, he turned from the window, snapped on the light and looked at
himself in the mirror, his expression became more materially
complicated. He leaned closer. Delicacy balked at the abominable
word "pimple," but some such blemish had undoubtedly appeared
on his cheek within the last hour, and now formed, with a pair from
last week, a distressing constellation of three. Going into the
bathroom adjoining his room—Juan had never possessed a bathroom
to himself before—he opened a medicine closet, and, after peering
about, carefully extracted a promising-looking jar of black ointment
and covered each slight protuberance with a black gluey mound.
Then, strangely dotted, he returned to the bedroom, put out the light
and resumed his vigil over the shadowy garden.

He waited. That roof among the trees on the hill belonged to
Noel Garneau's house. She was coming back to it tomorrow; he
would see her there. . . . A loud clock on the staircase inside struck
seven. Juan went to the glass and removed the ointment with a
handkerchief. To his chagrin, the spots were still there, even slightly
irritated from the chemical sting of the remedy. That settled it—no
more chocolate malted milks or eating between meals during his visit
to Culpepper Bay. Taking the lid from the jar of talcum he had
observed on the dressing table, he touched the laden puff to his cheek.
Immediately his brows and lashes bloomed with snow and he

coughed chokingly, observing that the triangle of humiliation was still observable upon his otherwise handsome face.

"Disgusting," he muttered to himself. "I never saw anything so disgusting." At twenty, such childish phenomena should be behind him.

Downstairs three gongs, melodious and metallic, hummed and sang. He listened for a moment, fascinated. Then he wiped the powder from his face, ran a comb through his yellow hair and went down to dinner.

Dinner at Cousin Cora's he had found embarrassing. She was so stiff and formal about things like that, and so familiar about Juan's private affairs. The first night of his visit he had tried politely to pull out her chair and bumped into the maid; the second night he remembered the experience—but so did the maid, and Cousin Cora seated herself unassisted. At home Juan was accustomed to behave as he liked; like all children of deferent and indulgent mothers, he lacked both confidence and good manners.

Tonight there were guests.

"This is San Juan Chandler, my cousin's son—Mrs. Holyoke—and Mr. Holyoke."

The phrase "my cousin's son" seemed to explain him away, seemed to account for his being in Miss Chandler's house: "You understand—we must have our poor relations with us occasionally." But a tone which implied that would be rude—and certainly Cousin Cora, with all her social position, couldn't be rude.

Mr. and Mrs. Holyoke acknowledged the introduction politely and coolly, and dinner was served. The conversation, dictated by Cousin Cora, bored Juan. It was about the garden and about her father, for whom she lived and who was dying slowly and unwillingly upstairs. Toward the salad Juan was wedged into the conversation by a question from Mr. Holyoke and a quick look from his cousin.

"I'm just staying for a week," he answered politely; "then I've got to go home because college opens pretty soon."

"Where are you at college?"

Juan named his college, adding almost apologetically, "You see, my father went there."

He wished that he could have answered that he was at Yale or Princeton, where he had wanted to go. He was prominent at Henderson and belonged to a good fraternity, but it annoyed him when people occasionally failed to recognize his alma mater's name.

"I suppose you've met all the young people here," supposed Mrs. Holyoke—"my daughter?"

"Oh, yes"—her daughter was the dumpy, ugly girl with the thick spectacles—"oh, yes." And he added, "I knew some people who lived here before I came."

"The little Garneau girl," explained Cousin Cora.

"Oh, yes. Noel Garneau," agreed Mrs. Holyoke. "Her mother's a great beauty. How old is Noel now? She must be——"

"Seventeen," supplied Juan; "but she's old for her age."

"Juan met her on a ranch last summer. They were on a ranch together. What is it that they call those ranches, Juan?"

"Dude ranches."

"Dude ranches. Juan and another boy worked for their board." Juan saw no reason why Cousin Cora should have supplied this information; she continued on an even more annoying note: "Noel's mother sent her out there to keep her out of mischief, but Juan says the ranch was pretty gay itself."

Mr. Holyoke supplied a welcome change of subject.

"Your name is——" he inquired, smiling and curious.

"San Juan Chandler. My father was wounded in the battle of San Juan Hill and so they called me after it—like Kenesaw Mountain Landis."

He had explained this so many times that the sentences rolled off automatically—in school he had been called Santy, in college he was Don.

"You must come to dinner while you're here," said Mrs. Holyoke vaguely.

The conversation slipped away from him as he realized freshly, strongly, that Noel would arrive tomorrow. And she was coming because he was here. She had cut short a visit in the Adirondacks on receipt of his letter. Would she like him now—in this place that was so different from Montana? There was a spaciousness, an air of money and pleasure about Culpepper Bay for which San Juan Chandler—a shy, handsome, spoiled, brilliant, penniless boy from a small Ohio city—was unprepared. At home, where his father was a retired clergyman, Juan went with the nice people. He didn't realize until this visit to a fashionable New England resort that where there are enough rich families to form a self-sufficient and exclusive group, such a group is invariably formed. On the dude ranch they had all dressed alike; here his ready-made Prince of Wales suit seemed exaggerated in style, his hat correct only in theory—an imitation hat—his very ties only projections of the ineffable Platonic ties which were worn here at Culpepper Bay. Yet all the differences were so small that he was unable quite to discern them.

But from the morning three days ago when he had stepped off the train into a group of young people who were waiting at the station for some friend of their own, he had been uneasy; and Cousin Cora's introductions, which seemed to foist him horribly upon whomever he was introduced to, did not lessen his discomfort. He thought mechanically that she was being kind, and considered himself lucky that her invitation had coincided with his wild desire to see Noel Garneau again. He did not realize that in three days he had come to hate Cousin Cora's cold and snobbish patronage.

Noel's fresh, adventurous voice on the telephone next morning made his own voice quiver with nervous happiness. She would call for him at two and they would spend the afternoon together. All morning he lay in the garden, trying unsuccessfully to renew his summer tan in the mild lemon light of the September sun, sitting up quickly whenever he heard the sound of Cousin Cora's garden shears at the end of a neighboring border. He was back in his room, still meddling desperately with the white powder puff, when Noel's roadster stopped outside and she came up the front walk.

Noel's eyes were dark blue, almost violet, and her lips, Juan had often thought, were like very small, very soft, red cushions—only cushions sounded all wrong, for they were really the most delicate lips in the world. When she talked they parted to the shape of "Oo!" and her eyes opened wide as though she was torn between tears and laughter at the poignancy of what she was saying. Already, at seventeen, she knew that men hung on her words in a way that frightened her. To Juan, her most indifferent remarks assumed a highly ponderable significance and begot an intensity in him—a fact which Noel had several times found somewhat of a strain.

He ran downstairs, down the gravel path toward her.

"Noel, my dear," he wanted so much to say, "you are the loveliest thing—the loveliest thing. My heart turns over when I see your beautiful face and smell that sweet fresh smell you have around you." That would have been the precious, the irreplaceable truth. Instead he faltered, "Why, hello, Noel! How are you? . . . Well, I certainly am glad. Well, is this your car? What kind is it? Well, you certainly look fine."

And he couldn't look at her, because when he did his face seemed to him to be working idiotically—like someone else's face. He got in, they drove off and he made a mighty effort to compose himself; but as her hand left the steering wheel to fall lightly on his, a perverse instinct made him jerk his hand away. Noel perceived the embarrassment and was puzzled and sorry.

They went to the tennis tournament at the Culpepper Club. He was so little aware of anything except Noel that later he told Cousin Cora they hadn't seen the tennis, and believed it himself.

Afterward they loitered about the grounds, stopped by innumerable people who welcomed Noel home. Two men made him uneasy—one a small handsome youth of his own age with shining brown eyes that were bright as the glass eyes of a stuffed owl; the other a tall, languid dandy of twenty-five who was introduced to her, Juan rightly deduced, at his own request.

Wher. they were in a group of girls he was more comfortable. He was able to talk, because being with Noel gave him confidence before these others, and his confidence before others made him more confident with Noel. The situation improved.

There was one girl, a sharp, pretty blonde named Holly Morgan, with whom he had spent some facetiously sentimental hours the day before, and in order to show Noel that he had been able to take care of himself before her return he made a point of talking aside to Holly Morgan. Holly was not responsive. Juan was Noel's property, and though Holly liked him, she did not like him nearly well enough to annoy Noel.

"What time do you want me for dinner, Noel?" she asked.

"Eight o'clock," said Noel. "Billy Harper'll call for you."

Juan felt a twinge of disappointment. He had thought that he and Noel were to be alone for dinner; that afterward they would have a long talk on the dark veranda and he would kiss her lips as he had upon that never-to-be-forgotten Montana night, and give her his D. K. E. pin to wear. Perhaps the others would leave early—he had told Holly Morgan of his love for Noel; she should have sense enough to know.

At twilight Noel dropped him at Miss Chandler's gate, lingered for a moment with the engine cut off. The promise of the evening— the first lights in the houses along the bay, the sound of a remote piano, the little coolness in the wind—swung them both up suddenly into that paradise which Juan, drunk with ecstasy and terror, had been unable to evoke.

"Are you glad to see me?" she whispered.

"Am I glad?" The words trembled on his tongue. Miserably he struggled to bend his emotion into a phrase, a look, a gesture, but his mind chilled at the thought that nothing, nothing, nothing could express what he felt in his heart.

"You embarrass me," he said wretchedly. "I don't know what to say."

Noel waited, attuned to what she expected, sympathetic, but too young quite to see that behind the mask of egotism, of moody childishness, which the intensity of Juan's devotion compelled him to wear, there was a tremendous emotion.

"Don't be embarrassed," Noel said. She was listening to the music now, a tune they had danced to in the Adirondacks. The wings of a trance folded about her and the inscrutable someone who waited always in the middle distance loomed down over her with passionate words and dark romantic eyes. Almost mechanically, she started the engine and slipped the gear into first.

"At eight o'clock," she said, almost abstractedly. "Good-by, Juan."

The car moved off down the road. At the corner she turned and waved her hand and Juan waved back, happier than he had ever been in his life, his soul dissolved to a sweet gas that buoyed up his body like a balloon. Then the roadster was out of sight and, all unaware, he had lost her.

II

Cousin Cora's chauffeur took him to Noel's door. The other male guest, Billy Harper, was, he discovered, the young man with the bright brown eyes whom he had met that afternoon. Juan was afraid of him; he was on such familiar, facetious terms with the two girls— toward Noel his attitude seemed almost irreverent—that Juan was slighted during the conversation at dinner. They talked of the Adirondacks and they all seemed to know the group who had been there. Noel and Holly spoke of boys at Cambridge and New Haven and of how wonderful it was that they were going to school in New York this winter. Juan meant to invite Noel to the autumn dance at his college, but he thought that he had better wait and do it in a letter, later on. He was glad when dinner was over.

The girls went upstairs. Juan and Billy Harper smoked.

"She certainly is attractive," broke out Juan suddenly, his repression bursting into words.

"Who? Noel?"

"Yes."

"She's a nice girl," agreed Harper gravely.

Juan fingered the D. K. E. pin in his pocket.

"She's wonderful," he said. "I like Holly Morgan pretty well—I was handing her a sort of line yesterday afternoon—but Noel's really the most attractive girl I ever knew."

Harper looked at him curiously, but Juan, released from the enforced and artificial smile of dinner, continued enthusiastically: "Of course it's silly to fool with two girls. I mean, you've got to be careful not to get in too deep."

Billy Harper didn't answer. Noel and Holly came downstairs. Holly suggested bridge, but Juan didn't play bridge, so they sat talking by the fire. In some fashion Noel and Billy Harper became involved in a conversation about dates and friends, and Juan began boasting to Holly Morgan, who sat beside him on the sofa.

"You must come to a prom at college," he said suddenly. "Why don't you? It's a small college, but we have the best bunch in our house and the proms are fun."

"I'd love it."

"You'd only have to meet the people in our house."

"What's that?"

"D. K. E." He drew the pin from his pocket. "See?"

Holly examined it, laughed and handed it back.

"I wanted to go to Yale," he went on, "but my family always go to the same place."

"I love Yale," said Holly.

"Yes," he agreed vaguely, half hearing her, his mind moving between himself and Noel. "You must come up. I'll write you about it."

Time passed. Holly played the piano. Noel took a ukulele from the top of the piano, strummed it and hummed. Billy Harper turned the pages of the music. Juan listened, restless, unamused. Then they sauntered out into the dark garden, and finding himself beside Noel at last, Juan walked her quickly ahead until they were alone.

"Noel," he whispered, "here's my Deke pin. I want you to have it."

She looked at him expressionlessly.

"I saw you offering it to Holly Morgan," she said.

"Noel," he cried in alarm, "I wasn't offering it to her. I just showed it to her. Why, Noel, do you think——"

"You invited her to the prom."

"I didn't. I was just being nice to her."

The others were close behind. She took the Deke pin quickly and put her finger to his lips in a facile gesture of caress.

He did not realize that she had not been really angry about the pin or the prom, and that his unfortunate egotism was forfeiting her interest.

At eleven o'clock Holly said she must go, and Billy Harper drove his car to the front door.

"I'm going to stay a few minutes if you don't mind," said Juan, standing in the door with Noel. "I can walk home."

Holly and Billy Harper drove away. Noel and Juan strolled back into the drawing-room, where she avoided the couch and sat down in a chair.

"Let's go out on the veranda," suggested Juan uncertainly.

"Why?"

"Please, Noel."

Unwillingly she obeyed. They sat side by side on a canvas settee and he put his arm around her.

"Kiss me," he whispered. She had never seemed so desirable to him before.

"No."

"Why not?"

"I don't want to. I don't kiss people any more."

"But—me?" he demanded incredulously.

"I've kissed too many people. I'll have nothing left if I keep on kissing people."

"But you'll kiss me, Noel?"

"Why?"

He could not even say, "Because I love you." But he could say it, he knew that he could say it, when she was in his arms.

"If I kiss you once, will you go home?"

"Why, do you want me to go home?"

"I'm tired. I was traveling last night and I can never sleep on a train. Can you? I can never——"

Her tendency to leave the subject willingly made him frantic.

"Then kiss me once," he insisted.

"You promise?"

"You kiss me first."

"No, Juan, you promise first."

"Don't you want to kiss me?"

"Oh-h-h!" she groaned.

With gathering anxiety Juan promised and took her in his arms. For one moment at the touch of her lips, the feeling of her, of Noel, close to him, he forgot the evening, forgot himself—rather became the inspired, romantic self that she had known. But it was too late. Her hands were on his shoulders, pushing him away.

"You promised."

"Noel——"

She got up. Confused and unsatisfied, he followed her to the door.

"Noel——"

"Good night, Juan."

As they stood on the doorstep her eyes rose over the line of dark trees toward the ripe harvest moon. Some glowing thing would happen to her soon, she thought, her mind far away. Something that would dominate her, snatch her up out of life, helpless, ecstatic, exalted.

"Good night, Noel. Noel, please——"

"Good night, Juan. Remember we're going swimming tomorrow. It's wonderful to see you again. Good night."

She closed the door.

III

Toward morning he awoke from a broken sleep, wondering if she had not kissed him because of the three spots on his cheek. He turned on the light and looked at them. Two were almost invisible. He went into the bathroom, doused all three with the black ointment and crept back into bed.

Cousin Cora greeted him stiffly at breakfast next morning.

"You kept your great-uncle awake last night," she said. "He heard you moving around in your room."

"I only moved twice," he said unhappily. "I'm terribly sorry."

"He has to have his sleep, you know. We all have to be more considerate when there's someone sick. Young people don't always think of that. And he was so unusually well when you came."

It was Sunday, and they were to go swimming at Holly Morgan's house, where a crowd always collected on the bright easy beach. Noel called for him, but they arrived before any of his half-humble remarks about the night before had managed to attract her attention. He spoke to those he knew and was introduced to others, made ill at ease again by their cheerful familiarity with one another, by the correct informality of their clothes. He was sure they noticed that he had worn only one suit during his visit to Culpepper Bay, varying it with white flannel trousers. Both pairs of trousers were out of press now, and after keeping his great-uncle awake, he had not felt like bothering Cousin Cora about it at breakfast.

Again he tried to talk to Holly, with the vague idea of making Noel jealous, but Holly was busy and she eluded him. It was ten minutes before he extricated himself from a conversation with the obnoxious Miss Holyoke. At the moment he managed this he perceived to his horror that Noel was gone.

When he last saw her she had been engaged in a light but somehow intent conversation with the tall well-dressed stranger she had met yesterday. Now she wasn't in sight. Miserable and horribly alone, he strolled up and down the beach, trying to look as if he were having a good time, seeming to watch the bathers, but keeping a sharp eye out for Noel. He felt that his self-conscious perambulations were attracting unbearable attention, and sat down unhappily on a sand dune beside Billy Harper. But Billy Harper was neither cordial nor communicative, and after a minute hailed a man across the beach and went to talk to him.

Juan was desperate. When, suddenly, he spied Noel coming down from the house with the tall man, he stood up with a jerk, convinced that his features were working wildly.

She waved at him.

"A buckle came off my shoe," she called. "I went to have it put on. I thought you'd gone in swimming."

He stood perfectly still, not trusting his voice to answer. He understood that she was through with him; there was someone else. Immediately he wanted above all things to be away. As they came nearer, the tall man glanced at him negligently and resumed his vivacious, intimate conversation with Noel. A group suddenly closed around them.

Keeping the group in the corner of his eye, Juan began to move carefully and steadily toward the gate that led to the road. He started when the casual voice of a man behind him said "Going?" and he answered "Got to" with what purported to be a reluctant nod. Once behind the shelter of the parked cars, he began to run, slowed down as several chauffeurs looked at him curiously. It was a mile and a half to the Chandler house and the day was broiling, but he walked fast lest Noel, leaving the party—"with that man," he thought bitterly— should overtake him trudging along the road. That would be more than he could bear.

There was the sound of a car behind him. Immediately Juan left the road and sought concealment behind a convenient hedge. It was no one from the party, but thereafter he kept an eye out for available cover, walking fast, or even running, over unpromising open spaces.

He was within sight of his cousin's house when it happened. Hot and disheveled, he had scarcely flattened himself against the back of a tree when Noel's roadster, with the tall man at the wheel, flashed by down the road. Juan stepped out and looked after them. Then, blind with sweat and misery, he continued on toward home.

IV

At luncheon, Cousin Cora looked at him closely.

"What's the trouble?" she inquired. "Did something go wrong at the beach this morning?"

"Why, no," he exclaimed in simulated astonishment. "What made you think that?"

"You have such a funny look. I thought perhaps you'd had some trouble with the little Garneau girl."

He hated her.

"No, not at all."

"You don't want to get any idea in your head about her," said Cousin Cora.

"What do you mean?" He knew with a start what she meant.

"Any ideas about Noel Garneau. You've got your own way to make." Juan's face burned. He was unable to answer. "I say that in all kindness. You're not in any position to think anything serious about Noel Garneau."

Her implications cut deeper than her words. Oh, he had seen well enough that he was not essentially of Noel's sort, that being nice in Akron wasn't enough at Culpepper Bay. He had that realization that comes to all boys in his position that for every advantage—that was what his mother called this visit to Cousin Cora's—he paid a harrowing price in self-esteem. But a world so hard as to admit such an intolerable state of affairs was beyond his comprehension. His mind rejected it all completely, as it had rejected the dictionary name for the three spots on his face. He wanted to let go, to vanish, to be home. He determined to go home tomorrow, but after this heart-rending conversation he decided to put off the announcement until tonight.

That afternoon he took a detective story from the library and retired upstairs to read on his bed. He finished the book by four o'clock and came down to change it for another. Cousin Cora was on the veranda arranging three tables for tea.

"I thought you were at the club," she exclaimed in surprise. "I thought you'd gone up to the club."

"I'm tired," he said. "I thought I'd read."

"Tired!" she exclaimed. "A boy your age! You ought to be out in the open air playing golf—that's why you have that spot on your cheek"—Juan winced; his experiments with the black salve had irritated it to a sharp redness—"instead of lying around reading on a day like this."

"I haven't any clubs," said Juan hurriedly.

"Mr. Holyoke told you you could use his brother's clubs. He spoke to the caddie master. Run on now. You'll find lots of young people up there who want to play. I'll begin to think you're not having a good time."

In agony Juan saw himself dubbing about the course alone—seeing Noel coming under his eye. He never wanted to see Noel again except out in Montana—some bright day, when she would come saying, "Juan, I never knew—never understood what your love was."

Suddenly he remembered that Noel had gone into Boston for the afternoon. She would not be there. The horror of playing alone suddenly vanished.

The caddie master looked at him disapprovingly as he displayed his guest card, and Juan nervously bought a half dozen balls at a dollar each in an effort to neutralize the imagined hostility. On the first tee he glanced around. It was after four and there was no one in sight except two old men practicing drives from the top of a little hill. As he addressed his ball he heard someone come up on the tee behind him, and he breathed easier at the sharp crack that sent his ball a hundred and fifty yards down the fairway.

"Playing alone?"

He looked around. A stout man of fifty, with a huge face, high forehead, long wide upper lip and great undershot jaw, was taking a driver from a bulging bag.

"Why—yes."

"Mind if I go round with you?"

"Not at all."

Juan greeted the suggestion with a certain gloomy relief. They were evenly matched, the older man's steady short shots keeping pace with Juan's occasional brilliancy. Not until the seventh hole did the conversation rise above the fragmentary boasting and formalized praise which forms the small talk of golf.

"Haven't seen you around before."

"I'm just visiting here," Juan explained, "staying with my cousin, Miss Chandler."

"Oh, yes—know Miss Chandler very well. Nice old snob."

"What?" inquired Juan.

"Nice old snob, I said. No offense. . . . Your honor, I think."

Not for several holes did Juan venture to comment on his partner's remark.

"What do you mean when you say she's a nice old snob?" he inquired with interest.

"Oh, it's an old quarrel between Miss Chandler and me,"

answered the older man brusquely. "She's an old friend of my wife's. When we were married and came out to Culpepper Bay for the summer, she tried to freeze us out. Said my wife had no business marrying me. I was an outsider."

"What did you do?"

"We just let her alone. She came round, but naturally I never had much love for her. She even tried to put her oar in before we were married." He laughed. "Cora Chandler of Boston—how she used to boss the girls around in those days! At twenty-five she had the sharpest tongue in Back Bay. They were old people there, you know—Emerson and Whittier to dinner and all that. My wife belonged to that crowd too. I was from the Middle West. . . . Oh, too bad. I should have stopped talking. That makes me two up again."

Suddenly Juan wanted to present his case to this man—not quite as it was, but adorned with a dignity and significance it did not so far possess. It began to round out in his mind as the sempiternal struggle of the poor young man against a snobbish, purse-proud world. This new aspect was comforting, and he put out of his mind the less pleasant realization that, superficially at least, money hadn't entered into it. He knew in his heart that it was his unfortunate egotism that had repelled Noel, his embarrassment, his absurd attempt to make her jealous with Holly. Only indirectly was his poverty concerned; under different circumstances it might have given a touch of romance.

"I know exactly how you must have felt," he broke out suddenly as they walked toward the tenth tee. "I haven't any money and I'm in love with a girl who has—and it just seems as if every busybody in the world is determined to keep us apart."

For a moment Juan believed this. His companion looked at him sharply.

"Does the girl care about you?" he inquired.

"Yes."

"Well, go after her, young man. All the money in this world hasn't been made by a long shot."

"I'm still in college," said Juan, suddenly taken aback.

"Won't she wait for you?"

"I don't know. You see, the pressure's pretty strong. Her family want her to marry a rich man"—his mind visualized the tall well-dressed stranger of this morning and invention soared—"an Easterner that's visiting here, and I'm afraid they'll all sweep her off her feet. If it's not this man, it's the next."

His friend considered.

"You can't have everything, you know," he said presently. "I'm the last man to advise a young man to leave college, especially when I don't know anything about him or his abilities; but if it's going to break you up not to get her, you better think about getting to work."

"I've been considering that," said Juan, frowning. The idea was ten seconds old in his mind.

"All the girls are crazy now, anyhow," broke out the older man. "They begin to think of men at fifteen, and by the time they're seventeen they run off with the chauffeur next door."

"That's true," agreed Juan absently. He was absorbed in the previous suggestion. "The trouble is that I don't live in Boston. If I left college I'd want to be near her, because it might be a few months before I'd be able to support her. And I don't know how I'd go about getting a position in Boston."

"If you're Cora Chandler's cousin, that oughtn't to be difficult. She knows everybody in town. And the girl's family will probably help you out, once you've got her—some of them are fools enough for anything in these crazy days."

"I wouldn't like that."

"Rich girls can't live on air," said the older man grimly.

They played for a while in silence. Suddenly, as they approached a green, Juan's companion turned to him frowning.

"Look here, young man," he said, "I don't know whether you are really thinking of leaving college or whether I've just put the idea in your head. If I have, forget it. Go home and talk it over with your family. Do what they tell you to."

"My father's dead."

"Well, then ask your mother. She's got your best interest at heart."

His attitude had noticeably stiffened, as if he were sorry he had become even faintly involved in Juan's problem. He guessed that there was something solid in the boy, but he suspected his readiness to confide in strangers and his helplessness about getting a job. Something was lacking—not confidence, exactly—"It might be a few months before I was able to support her"—but something stronger, fiercer, more external. When they walked together into the caddie house he shook hands with him and was about to turn away, when impulse impelled him to add one word more.

"If you decide to try Boston come and see me," he said. He pressed a card into Juan's hand. "Good-by. Good luck. Remember, a woman's like a street car——"

He walked into the locker room. After paying his caddie, Juan glanced down at the card which he still held in his hand.

"Harold Garneau," it read, "23-27 State Street."

A moment later Juan was walking nervously and hurriedly from the grounds of the Culpepper Club, casting no glance behind.

V

One month later San Juan Chandler arrived in Boston and took an inexpensive room in a small downtown hotel. In his pocket was two hundred dollars in cash and an envelope full of Liberty Bonds aggregating fifteen hundred dollars more—the whole being a fund which had been started by his father when he was born, to give him his chance in life. Not without argument had he come into possession of this—not without tears had his decision to abandon his last year at college been approved by his mother. He had not told her everything; simply that he had an advantageous offer of a position in Boston; the rest she guessed and was tactfully silent. As a matter of fact, he had neither a position nor a plan, but he was twenty-one now, with the blemishes of youth departed forever. One thing Juan knew—he was going to marry Noel Garneau. The sting and hurt and shame of that Sunday morning ran through his dreams, stronger than any doubts he might have felt, stronger even than the romantic boyish love for her that had blossomed one dry, still Montana night. That was still there, but locked apart; what had happened later overlay it, muffled it. It was necessary now to his pride, his self-respect, his very existence, that he have her, in order to wipe out his memory of the day on which he had grown three years.

He hadn't seen her since. The following morning he had left Culpepper Bay and gone home.

Yes, he had a wonderful time. Yes, Cousin Cora had been very nice.

Nor had he written, though a week later a surprised but somehow flippant and terrible note had come from her, saying how pleasant it was to have seen him again and how bad it was to leave without saying good-by.

"Holly Morgan sends her best," it concluded, with kind, simulated reproach. "Perhaps she ought to be writing instead of me. I always thought you were fickle, and now I know it."

The poor effort which she had made to hide her indifference made him shiver. He did not add the letter to a certain cherished package tied with blue ribbon, but burned it up in an ash tray—a tragic gesture which almost set his mother's house on fire.

So he began his life in Boston, and the story of his first year there is a fairy tale too immoral to be told. It is the story of one of those mad, illogical successes upon whose substantial foundations ninety-nine failures are later reared. Though he worked hard, he deserved no special credit for it—no credit, that is, commensurate with the reward he received. He ran into a man who had a scheme, a preposterous scheme, for the cold storage of sea food which he had been trying to finance for several years. Juan's inexperience allowed him to be responsive and he invested twelve hundred dollars. In the first year this appalling indiscretion paid him 400 per cent. His partner attempted to buy him out, but they reached a compromise and Juan kept his shares.

The inner sense of his own destiny which had never deserted him whispered that he was going to be a rich man. But at the end of that year an event took place which made him think that it didn't matter after all.

He had seen Noel Garneau twice—once entering a theater and once riding through a Boston street in the back of her limousine, looking, he thought afterward, bored and pale and tired. At the time he had thought nothing; an overwhelming emotion had seized his heart, held it helpless, suspended, as though it were in the grasp of material fingers. He had shrunk back hastily under the awning of a shop and waited trembling, horrified, ecstatic, until she went by. She did not know he was in Boston—he did not want her to know until he was ready. He followed her every move in the society columns of the papers. She was at school, at home for Christmas, at Hot Springs for Easter, coming out in the fall. Then she was a debutante, and every day he read of her at dinners and dances and assemblies and balls and charity functions and theatricals of the Junior League. A dozen blurred newspaper unlikenesses of her filled a drawer of his desk. And still he waited. Let Noel have her fling.

When he had been sixteen months in Boston, and when Noel's first season was dying away in the hum of the massed departure for Florida, Juan decided to wait no longer. So on a raw, damp February day, when children in rubber boots were building dams in the snow-filled gutters, a blond, handsome, well-dressed young man walked up the steps of the Garneau's Boston house and handed his card to the maid. With his heart beating loud, he went into a drawing-room and sat down.

A sound of a dress on the stairs, light feet in the hall, an exclamation—Noel!

"Why, Juan," she exclaimed, surprised, pleased, polite, "I didn't know you were in Boston. It's so good to see you. I thought you'd thrown me over forever."

In a moment he found voice—it was easier now than it had been.

Whether or not she was aware of the change, he was a nobody no longer. There was something solid behind him that would prevent him ever again from behaving like a self-centered child.

He explained that he might settle in Boston, and allowed her to guess that he had done extremely well; and, though it cost him a twinge of pain, he spoke humorously of their last meeting, implying that he had left the swimming party on an impulse of anger at her. He could not confess that the impulse had been one of shame. She laughed. Suddenly he grew curiously happy.

Half an hour passed. The fire glowed in the hearth. The day darkened outside and the room moved into that shadowy twilight, that weather of indoors, which is like a breathless starshine. He had been standing; now he sat down beside her on the couch.

"Noel——"

Footsteps sounded lightly through the hall as the maid went through to the front door. Noel reached up quickly and turned up the electric lamp on the table behind her head.

"I didn't realize how dark it was growing," she said, rather quickly, he thought. Then the maid stood in the doorway.

"Mr. Templeton," she announced.

"Oh, yes," agreed Noel.

Mr. Templeton, with a Harvard-Oxford drawl, mature, very much at home, looked at him with just a flicker of surprise, nodded, mumbled a bare politeness and took an easy position in front of the fire. He exchanged several remarks with Noel which indicated a certain familiarity with her movements. Then a short silence fell. Juan rose.

"I want to see you soon," he said. "I'll phone, shall I, and you tell me when I can call?"

She walked with him to the door.

"So good to talk to you again," she told him cordially. "Remember, I want to see a lot of you, Juan."

When he left he was happier than he had been for two years. He ate dinner alone at a restaurant, almost singing to himself; and then, wild with elation, walked along the water front till midnight. He awoke thinking of her, wanting to tell people that what had been lost was found again. There had been more between them than the mere words said—Noel's sitting with him in the half darkness, her slight but perceptible nervousness as she came with him to the door.

Two days later he opened the *Transcript* to the society page and read down to the third item. There his eyes stopped, became like china eyes:

"Mr. and Mrs. Harold Garneau announce the engagement of their daughter Noel to Mr. Brooks Fish Templeton. Mr. Templeton graduated from Harvard in the class of 1912 and is a partner in——"

VI

At three o'clock that afternoon Juan rang the Garneaus' doorbell and was shown into the hall. From somewhere upstairs he heard girls' voices, and another murmur came from the drawing-room on the right, where he had talked to Noel only the week before.

"Can you show me into some room that isn't being used?" he demanded tensely of the maid. "I'm an old friend—it's very important—I've got to see Miss Noel alone."

He waited in a small den at the back of the hall. Ten minutes passed—ten minutes more; he began to be afraid she wasn't coming. At the end of half an hour the door bounced open and Noel came hurriedly in.

"Juan!" she cried happily. "This is wonderful! I might have known you'd be the first to come." Her expression changed as she saw his face, and she hesitated. "But why were you shown in here?" she went on quickly. "You must come and meet everyone. I'm rushing around today like a chicken without a head."

"Noel!" he said thickly.

"What?"

Her hand was on the door knob. She turned, startled.

"Noel, I haven't come to congratulate you," Juan said, his face white and firm, his voice harsh with his effort at self-control. "I've come to tell you you're making an awful mistake."

"Why—Juan!"

"And you know it," he went on. "You know no one loves you as I love you, Noel. I want you to marry me."

She laughed nervously.

"Why, Juan, that's silly! I don't understand your talking like this. I'm engaged to another man."

"Noel, will you come here and sit down?"

"I can't, Juan—there're a dozen people outside. I've got to see them. It wouldn't be polite. Another time, Juan. If you come another time I'd love to talk to you."

"Now!" The word was stark, unyielding, almost savage. She hesitated. "Ten minutes," he said.

"I've really got to go, Juan."

She sat down uncertainly, glancing at the door. Sitting beside her, Juan told her simply and directly everything that had happened to him since they had met, a year and a half before. He told her of his family, his Cousin Cora, of his inner humiliation at Culpepper Bay. Then he told her of coming to Boston and of his success, and how at last, having something to bring to her, he had come only to find he was too late. He kept back nothing. In his voice, as in his mind, there was no pretense now, no self-consciousness, but only a sincere and overmastering emotion. He had no defense for what he was doing, he said, save this—that he had somehow gained the right to present his case, to have her know how much his devotion had inspired him, to have her look once, if only in passing, upon the fact that for two years he had loved her faithfully and well.

When Juan finished, Noel was crying. It was terrible, she said, to tell her all this—just when she had decided about her life. It hadn't been easy, yet it was done now, and she was really going to marry this other man. But she had never heard anything like this before—it upset her. She was—oh, so terribly sorry, but there was no use. If he had cared so much he might have let her know before.

But how could he let her know? He had had nothing to offer her except the fact that one summer night out West they had been overwhelmingly drawn together.

"And you love me now," he said in a low voice. "You wouldn't cry, Noel, if you didn't love me. You wouldn't care."

"I'm—I'm sorry for you."

"It's more than that. You loved me the other day. You wanted me to sit beside you in the dark. Didn't I feel it—didn't I know? There's something between us, Noel—a sort of pull. Something you always do to me and I to you—except that one sad time. Oh, Noel, don't you know how it breaks my heart to see you sitting there two feet away from me, to want to put my arms around you and know you've made a senseless promise to another man?"

There was a knock outside the door.

"Noel!"

She raised her head, putting a handkerchief quickly to her eyes. "Yes?"

"It's Brooks. May I come in?" Without waiting for an answer, Templeton opened the door and stood looking at them curiously. "Excuse me," he said. He nodded brusquely at Juan. "Noel, there are lots of people here——"

"In a minute," she said lifelessly.

"Aren't you well?"

"Yes."

He came into the room, frowning.

"What's been upsetting you, dear?" He glanced quickly at Juan, who stood up, his eyes blurred with tears. A menacing note crept into Templeton's voice. "I hope no one's been upsetting you."

For answer, Noel flopped down over a hill of pillows and sobbed aloud.

"Noel"—Templeton sat beside her and put his arm on her shoulder—"Noel." He turned again to Juan. "I think it would be best if you left us alone, Mr.——" The name escaped his memory. "Noel's a little tired."

"I won't go," said Juan.

"Please wait outside then. We'll see you later."

"I won't wait outside. I want to speak to Noel. It was you who interrupted."

"And I have a perfect right to interrupt." His face reddened angrily. "Just who the devil are you, anyhow?"

"My name is Chandler."

"Well, Mr. Chandler, you're in the way here—is that plain? Your presence here is an intrusion and a presumption."

"We look at it in different ways."

They glared at each other angrily. After a moment Templeton raised Noel to a sitting posture.

"I'm going to take you upstairs, dear," he said. "This has been a strain today. If you lie down till dinnertime——"

He helped her to her feet. Not looking at Juan, and still dabbing her face with her handkerchief, Noel suffered herself to be persuaded into the hall. Templeton turned in the doorway.

"The maid will give you your hat and coat, Mr. Chandler."

"I'll wait right here," said Juan.

VII

He was still there at half past six, when, following a quick knock, a large broad bulk which Juan recognized as Mr. Harold Garneau came into the room.

"Good evening, sir," said Mr. Garneau, annoyed and peremptory. "Just what can I do for you?"

He came closer and a flicker of recognition passed over his face. "Oh!" he muttered.

"Good evening, sir," said Juan.

"It's you, is it?" Mr. Garneau appeared to hesitate. "Brooks Templeton said that you were—that you insisted on seeing Noel"— he coughed—"that you refused to go home."

"I want to see Noel, if you don't mind."

"What for?"

"That's between Noel and me, Mr. Garneau."

"Mr. Templeton and I are quite entitled to represent Noel in this case," said Mr. Garneau patiently. "She has just made the statement before her mother and me that she doesn't want to see you again. Isn't that plain enough?"

"I don't believe it," said Juan stubbornly.

"I'm not in the habit of lying."

"I beg your pardon. I meant——"

"I don't want to discuss this unfortunate business with you," broke out Garneau contemptuously. "I just want you to leave right now—and not come back."

"Why do you call it an unfortunate business?" inquired Juan coolly.

"Good night, Mr. Chandler."

"You call it an unfortunate business because Noel's broken her engagement."

"You are presumptuous, sir!" cried the older man. "Unbearably presumptuous."

"Mr. Garneau, you yourself were once kind enough to tell me——"

"I don't give a damn what I told you!" cried Garneau. "You get out of here now!"

"Very well, I have no choice. I wish you to be good enough to tell Noel that I'll be back tomorrow afternoon."

Juan nodded, went into the hall and took his hat and coat from a chair. Upstairs, he heard running footsteps and a door opened and closed—not before he had caught the sound of impassioned voices and a short broken sob. He hesitated. Then he continued on along the hall toward the front door. Through a portiere of the dining room he caught sight of a manservant laying the service for dinner.

He rang the bell the next afternoon at the same hour. This time the butler, evidently instructed, answered the door.

Miss Noel was not at home. Could he leave a note? It was no use; Miss Noel was not in the city. Incredulous but anxious, Juan took a taxicab to Harold Garneau's office.

"Mr. Garneau can't see you. If you like, he will speak to you for a moment on the phone."

Juan nodded. The clerk touched a button on the waiting-room switchboard and handed an instrument to Juan.

"This is San Juan Chandler speaking. They told me at your

residence that Noel had gone away. Is that true?"

"Yes." The monosyllable was short and cold. "She's gone away for a rest. Won't be back for several months. Anything else?"

"Did she leave any word for me?"

"No! She hates the sight of you."

"What's her address?"

"That doesn't happen to be your affair. Good morning."

Juan went back to his apartment and mused over the situation. Noel had been spirited out of town—that was the only expression he knew for it. And undoubtedly her engagement to Templeton was at least temporarily broken. He had toppled it over within an hour. He must see her again—that was the immediate necessity. But where? She was certainly with friends, and probably with relatives. That latter was the first clew to follow—he must find out the names of the relatives she had most frequently visited before.

He phoned Holly Morgan. She was in the South and not expected back in Boston till May.

Then he called the society editor of the *Boston Transcript*. After a short wait, a polite, attentive, feminine voice conversed with him on the wire.

"This is Mr. San Juan Chandler," he said, trying to intimate by his voice that he was a distinguished leader of cotillions in the Back Bay. "I want to get some information, if you please, about the family of Mr. Harold Garneau."

"Why don't you apply directly to Mr. Garneau?" advised the society editor, not without suspicion.

"I'm not on speaking terms with Mr. Garneau."

A pause; then—"Well, really, we can't be responsible for giving out information in such a peculiar way."

"But there can't be any secret about who Mr. and Mrs. Garneau's relations are!" protested Juan in exasperation.

"But how can we be sure that you——"

He hung up the receiver. Two other papers gave no better results, a third was willing, but ignorant. It seemed absurd, almost like a conspiracy, that in a city where the Garneaus were so well known he could not obtain the desired names. It was as if everything had tightened up against his arrival on the scene. After a day of fruitless and embarrassing inquiries in stores, where his questions were looked upon with the suspicion that he might be compiling a sucker list, and of poring through back numbers of the *Social Register*, he saw that there was but one resource—that was Cousin Cora. Next morning he took the three-hour ride to Culpepper Bay.

It was the first time he had seen her for a year and a half, since the disastrous termination of his summer visit. She was offended—that he knew—especially since she had heard from his mother of the unexpected success. She greeted him coldly and reproachfully; but she told him what he wanted to know, because Juan asked his questions while she was still startled and surprised by his visit. He left Culpepper Bay with the information that Mrs. Garneau had one sister, the famous Mrs. Morton Poindexter, with whom Noel was on terms of great intimacy. Juan took the midnight train for New York.

The Morton Poindexters' telephone number was not in the New York phone book, and Information refused to divulge it; but Juan procured it by another reference to the *Social Register*. He called the house from his hotel.

"Miss Noel Garneau—is she in the city?" he inquired, according to his plan. If the name was not immediately familiar, the servant would reply that he had the wrong number.

"Who wants to speak to her, please?"

That was a relief; his heart sank comfortably back into place.

"Oh—a friend."

"No name?"

"No name."

"I'll see."

The servant returned in a moment.

No, Miss Garneau was not there, was not in the city, was not expected. The phone clicked off suddenly.

Late that afternoon a taxi dropped him in front of the Morton Poindexters' house. It was the most elaborate house that he had ever seen, rising to five stories on a corner of Fifth Avenue and adorned even with that ghost of a garden which, however minute, is the proudest gesture of money in New York.

He handed no card to the butler, but it occurred to him that he must be expected, for he was shown immediately into the drawing-room. When, after a short wait, Mrs. Poindexter entered he experienced for the first time in five days a touch of uncertainty.

Mrs. Poindexter was perhaps thirty-five, and of that immaculate fashion which the French describe as *bien soignée*. The inexpressible loveliness of her face was salted with another quality which for want of a better word might be called dignity. But it was more than dignity, for it wore no rigidity, but instead a softness so adaptable, so elastic, that it would withdraw from any attack which life might bring against it, only to spring back at the proper moment, taut, victorious and complete. San Juan saw that even though his guess was correct as to Noel's being in the house, he was up against a force with which he had no contact before. This woman seemed to be not entirely of America, to possess resources which the American woman lacked or handled ineptly.

She received him with a graciousness which, though it was largely external, seemed to conceal no perturbation underneath. Indeed, her attitude appeared to be perfectly passive, just short of encouraging. It was with an effort that he resisted the inclination to lay his cards on the table.

"Good evening." She sat down on a stiff chair in the center of the room and asked him to take an easy-chair near by. She sat looking at him silently until he spoke.

"Mrs. Poindexter, I am very anxious to see Miss Garneau. I telephoned your house this morning and was told that she was not here." Mrs. Poindexter nodded. "However, I know she is here," he continued evenly. "And I'm determined to see her. The idea that her father and mother can prevent me from seeing her, as though I had disgraced myself in some way—or that you, Mrs. Poindexter, can prevent me from seeing her"—his voice rose a little—"is preposterous. This is not the year 1500—nor even the year 1910."

He paused. Mrs. Poindexter waited for a moment to see if he had finished. Then she said, quietly and unequivocally, "I quite agree with you."

Save for Noel, Juan thought he had never seen anyone so beautiful before.

"Mrs. Poindexter," he began again, in a more friendly tone, "I'm sorry to seem rude. I've been called presumptuous in this matter, and perhaps to some extent I am. Perhaps all poor boys who are in love with wealthy girls are presumptuous. But it happens that I am no longer a poor boy, and I have good reason to believe that Noel cares for me."

"I see," said Mrs. Poindexter attentively. "But of course I knew nothing about all that."

Juan hesitated, again disarmed by her complaisance. Then a surge of determination went over him.

"Will you let me see her?" he demanded. "Or will you insist on keeping up this farce a little longer?"

Mrs. Poindexter looked at him as though considering.

"Why should I let you see her?"

"Simply because I ask you. Just as, when someone says 'Excuse me,' you step aside for him in a doorway."

Mrs. Poindexter frowned.

"But Noel is concerned in this matter as much as you. And I'm not like a person in a crowd. I'm more like a bodyguard, with instructions to let no one pass, even if they say 'Excuse me' in a most appealing voice."

"You have instructions only from her father and mother," said Juan, with rising impatience. "She's the person concerned."

"I'm glad you begin to admit that."

"Of course I admit it," he broke out. "I want you to admit it."

"I do."

"Then what's the point of all this absurd discussion?" he demanded heatedly.

She stood up suddenly.

"I bid you good evening, sir."

Taken aback, Juan stood up too.

"Why, what's the matter?"

"I will not be spoken to like that," said Mrs. Poindexter, still in a low cool voice. "Either you can conduct yourself quietly or you can leave this house at once."

Juan realized that he had taken the wrong tone. The words stung at him and for a moment he had nothing to say—as though he were a scolded boy at school.

"This is beside the question," he stammered finally. "I want to talk to Noel."

"Noel doesn't want to talk to you."

Suddenly Mrs. Poindexter held out a sheet of note paper to him. He opened it. It said:

"*Aunt Jo:* As to what we talked about this afternoon: If that intolerable bore calls, as he will probably do, and begins his presumptuous whining, please speak to him frankly. Tell him I never loved him, that I never at any time claimed to love him and that his persistence is revolting to me. Say that I am old enough to know my own mind and that my greatest wish is never to see him again in this world."

Juan stood there aghast. His universe was suddenly about him. Noel did not care, she had never cared. It was all a preposterous joke on him, played by those to whom the business of life had been such jokes from the beginning. He realized now that fundamentally they were all akin—Cousin Cora, Noel, her father, this cold, lovely woman here—affirming the prerogative of the rich to marry always within their caste, to erect artificial barriers and standards against those who could presume upon a summer's philandering. The scales fell from his eyes and he saw his year and a half of struggle and effort not as progress toward a goal but only as a little race he had run by himself, outside, with no one to beat except himself—no one who cared.

Blindly he looked about for his hat, scarcely realizing it was in the hall. Blindly he stepped back when Mrs. Poindexter's hand moved toward him half a foot through the mist and Mrs. Poindexter's voice said softly, "I'm sorry." Then he was in the hall, the note still clutched in the hand that struggled through the sleeve of his overcoat, the words which he felt he must somehow say choking through his lips.

"I didn't understand. I regret very much that I've bothered you. It wasn't clear to me how matters stood—between Noel and me——"

His hand was on the door knob.

"I'm sorry, too," said Mrs. Poindexter. "I didn't realize from what Noel said that what I had to do would be so hard—Mr. Templeton."

"Chandler," he corrected her dully. "My name's Chandler."

She stood dead still; suddenly her face went white.

"What?"

"My name—it's Chandler."

Like a flash she threw herself against the half-open door and it bumped shut. Then in a flash she was at the foot of the staircase.

"Noel!" she cried in a high, clear call. "Noel! Noel! Come down, Noel!" Her lovely voice floated up like a bell through the long high central hall. "Noel! Come down! It's Mr. Chandler! It's Chandler!"

The Adolescent Marriage

(*The Saturday Evening Post*, 6 March 1926)

"The Adolescent Marriage" was written in Paris in December 1925 and was almost lost. Fitzgerald entrusted the typescript to someone who was returning to America but who failed to deliver it to Harold Ober; then the carbon was ruined. However, the typist had kept the manuscript, and Fitzgerald rewrote the story from that. The *Post* bought it for $2500 but annoyed Fitzgerald by cutting it. He wrote Ober: "They have a right to be silly at 2500. a story but when two very clever paragraphs disappear of which I have no duplicate or record it makes me angry.... Could you get me the ms. or an uncut proof of it so I can clip the uncut pps. for my files? Especially the one about a church with car-cards in the pews or something."*

Chauncey Garnett, the architect, once had a miniature city constructed, composed of all the buildings he had ever designed. It proved to be an expensive and somewhat depressing experiment; for the toy did not result in a harmonious whole. Garnett found it depressing to be reminded that he himself had often gone in for monstrosities, and even more depressing to realize that his architectural activities had extended over half a century. In disgust, he distributed the tiny houses to his friends and they ended up as the residences of undiscriminating dolls.

Garnett had never—at least not yet—been called a nice old man; yet he was both old and nice. He gave six hours a day to his offices in Philadelphia or to his branch in New York, and during the remaining time demanded only a proper peace in which to brood quietly over his crowded and colorful past. In several years no one had demanded a favor that could not be granted with pen and check book, and it seemed that he had reached an age safe from the intrusion of other people's affairs. This calm, however, was premature, and it was violently shattered one afternoon in the summer of 1925 by the shrill clamor of a telephone bell.

George Wharton was speaking. Could Chauncey come to his house at once on a matter of the greatest importance?

On the way to Chestnut Hill, Garnett dozed against the gray duvetyn cushions of his limousine, his sixty-eight-year-old body

---

*This material has not been found.

warmed by the June sunshine, his sixty-eight-year-old mind blank
save for some vivid, unsubstantial memory of a green branch
overhanging green water. Reaching his friend's house, he awoke
placidly and without a start. George Wharton, he thought, was
probably troubled by some unexpected surplus of money. He would
want Garnett to plan one of these modern churches, perhaps. He was
of a younger generation than Garnett—a modern man.

Wharton and his wife were waiting in the gilt-and-morocco
intimacy of the library.

"I couldn't come to your office," said Wharton immediately. "In
a minute you'll understand why."

Garnett noticed that his friend's hands were slightly trembling.

"It's about Lucy," Wharton added.

It was a moment before Garnett placed Lucy as their daughter.

"What's happened to Lucy?"

"Lucy's married. She ran up to Connecticut about a month ago
and got married." A moment's silence. "Lucy's only sixteen,"
continued Wharton. "The boy's twenty."

"That's very young," said Garnett considerately; "but then my
grandmother married at sixteen and no one thought much about it.
Some girls develop much quicker than others."

"We know all that, Chauncey." Wharton waved it aside
impatiently. "The point is, these young marriages don't work
nowadays. They're not normal. They end in a mess."

Again Garnett hesitated.

"Aren't you a little premature in looking ahead for trouble? Why
don't you give Lucy a chance? Why not wait and see if it's going to
turn out a mess?"

"It's a mess already," cried Wharton passionately. "And Lucy's
life's a mess. The one thing her mother and I cared about—her
happiness—that's a mess, and we don't know what to do—what to
do."

His voice trembled and he turned away to the window—came
back again impulsively.

"Look at us, Chauncey. Do we look like the kind of parents who
would drive a child into a thing like this? She and her mother have
been like sisters—just like sisters. She and I used to go on parties
together—football games and all that sort of thing—ever since she
was a little kid. She's all we've got, and we always said we'd try to steer
a middle course with her—give her enough liberty for her self-respect
and yet keep an eye on where she went and who she went with, at least
till she was eighteen. Why, Chauncey, if you'd told me six weeks ago
that this thing could happen——" He shook his head helplessly.

Then he continued in a quieter voice. "When she came and told us what she'd done it just about broke our hearts, but we tried to make the best of it. Do you know how long the marriage—if you can call it that—lasted? Three weeks. It lasted three weeks. She came home with a big bruise on her shoulder where he'd hit her."

"Oh, dear!" said Mrs. Wharton in a low tone. "Please——"

"We talked it over," continued her husband grimly, "and she decided to go back to this—this young"—again he bowed his head before the insufficiency of expletives—"and try to make a go of it. But last night she came home again, and now she says it's definitely over."

Garnett nodded. "Who's the man?" he inquired.

"Man!" cried Wharton. "It's a boy. His name's Llewellyn Clark."

"What's that?" exclaimed Garnett in surprise. "Llewellyn Clark? Jesse Clark's son? The young fellow in my office?"

"Yes."

"Why, he's a nice young fellow," Garnett declared. "I can't believe he'd——"

"Neither could I," interrupted Wharton quietly. "I thought he was a nice young fellow too. And what's more, I rather suspected that my daughter was a pretty decent young girl."

Garnett was astonished and annoyed. He had seen Llewellyn Clark not an hour before in the small drafting room he occupied in the Garnett & Linquist offices. He understood now why Clark wasn't going back to Boston Tech this fall. And in the light of this revelation he remembered that there had been a change in the boy during the past month—absences, late arrivals, a certain listlessness in his work.

Mrs. Wharton's voice broke in upon the ordering of his mind. "Please do something, Chauncey," she said. "Talk to him. Talk to them both. She's only sixteen and we can't bear to see her life ruined by a divorce. It isn't that we care what people will say; it's only Lucy we care about, Chauncey."

"Why don't you send her abroad for a year?"

Wharton shook his head.

"That doesn't solve the problem. If they have an ounce of character between them they'll make an attempt to live together."

"But if you think so badly of him——"

"Lucy's made her choice. He's got some money—enough. And there doesn't seem to be anything vicious in his record so far."

"What's his side of it?"

Wharton waved his hands helplessly.

"I'm damned if I know. Something about a hat. Some bunch of rubbish. Elsie and I have no idea why they ran away, and now we can't get a clear idea why they won't stick together. Unfortunately, his father and mother are dead." He paused. "Chauncey, if you could see your way clear——"

An unpleasant prospect began to take shape before Garnett's eyes. He was an old man with one foot, at least, in the chimney corner. From where he stood, this youngest generation was like something infinitely distant, and perceived through the large end of a telescope.

"Oh, of course," he heard himself saying vaguely. So hard to think back to that young time. Since his youth such a myriad of prejudices and conventions had passed through the fashion show and died away with clamor and acrimony and commotion. It would be difficult even to communicate with these children. How hollowly and fatuously his platitudes would echo on their ears. And how bored he would be with their selfishness and with their shallow confidence in opinions manufactured day before yesterday.

He sat up suddenly. Wharton and his wife were gone, and a slender, dark-haired girl whose body hovered delicately on the last edge of childhood had come quietly into the room. She regarded him for a moment with a shadow of alarm in her intent brown eyes; then sat down on a stiff chair near him.

"I'm Lucy," she said. "They told me you wanted to talk to me."

She waited. It occurred to Garnett that he must say something, but the form his speech should take eluded him.

"I haven't seen you since you were ten years old," he began uneasily.

"Yes," she agreed, with a small, polite smile.

There was another silence. He must say something to the point before her young attention slipped utterly away.

"I'm sorry you and Llewellyn have quarreled," he broke out. "It's silly to quarrel like that. I'm very fond of Llewellyn, you know."

"Did he send you here?"

Garnett shook his head. "Are you—in love with him?" he inquired.

"Not any more."

"Is he in love with you?"

"He says so, but I don't think he is—any more."

"You're sorry you married him?"

"I'm never sorry for anything that's done."

"I see."

Again she waited.

"Your father tells me this is a permanent separation."

"Yes."

"May I ask why?"

"We just couldn't get along," she answered simply. "I thought he was terribly selfish and he thought the same about me. We fought all the time, from almost the first day."

"He hit you?"

"Oh, that!" She dismissed that as unimportant.

"How do you mean—selfish?"

"Just selfish," she answered childishly. "The most selfish thing I ever saw in my life. I never saw anything so selfish in my life."

"What did he do that was selfish?" persisted Garnett.

"Everything. He was so stingy—gosh!" Her eyes were serious and sad. "I can't stand anybody to be so stingy—about money," she explained contemptuously. "Then he'd lose his temper and swear at me and say he was going to leave me if I didn't do what he wanted me to." And she added, still very gravely, "Gosh!"

"How did he happen to hit you?"

"Oh, he didn't mean to hit me. I was trying to hit him on account of something he did, and he was trying to hold me and so I bumped into a still."

"A still!" exclaimed Garnett, startled.

"The woman had a still in our room because she had no other place to keep it—down on Beckton Street, where we lived."

"Why did Llewellyn take you to such a place?"

"Oh, it was a perfectly good place except that the woman had this still. We looked around two or three days and it was the only apartment we could afford." She paused reminiscently and then added, "It was very nice and quiet."

"H'm—you never really got along at all?"

"No." She hesitated. "He spoiled it all. He was always worrying about whether we'd done the right thing. He'd get out of bed at night and walk up and down worrying about it. I wasn't complaining. I was perfectly willing to be poor if we could get along and be happy. I wanted to go to cooking school, for instance, and he wouldn't let me. He wanted me to sit in the room all day and wait for him."

"Why?"

"He was afraid that I wanted to go home. For three weeks it was one long quarrel from morning till night. I couldn't stand it."

"It seems to me that a lot of this quarreling was over nothing," ventured Garnett.

"I haven't explained it very well, I guess," she said with sudden weariness. "I knew a lot of it was silly and so did Llewellyn. Sometimes we'd apologize to each other, and be in love like we were before we were married. That's why I went back to him. But it wasn't any use." She stood up. "What's the good of talking about it any more? You wouldn't understand."

Garnett wondered if he could get back to his office before Llewellyn Clark went home. He could talk to Clark, while the girl only confused him as she teetered disconcertingly between adolescence and disillusion. But when Clark reported to him just as the five o'clock bell rang, the same sensation of impotence stole over Garnett, and he stared at his apprentice blankly for a moment, as if he had never seen him before.

Llewellyn Clark looked older than his twenty years—a tall, almost thin, young man with dark-red hair of a fine, shiny texture, and auburn eyes. He was of a somewhat nervous type, talented and impatient, but Garnett could find little of the egotist in his reserved, attentive face.

"I hear you've been getting married," Garnett began abruptly.

Clark's cheeks deepened to the color of his hair.

"Who told you that?" he demanded.

"Lucy Wharton. She told me the whole story."

"Then you know it, sir," said Clark almost rudely. "You know all there is to know."

"What do you intend to do?"

"I don't know." Clark stood up, breathing quickly. "I can't talk about it. It's my affair, you see. I——"

"Sit down, Llewellyn."

The young man sat down, his face working. Suddenly it crinkled uncontrollably and two great tears, stained faintly with the dust of the day's toil, gushed from his eyes.

"Oh, hell!" he said brokenly, wiping his eyes with the back of his hand.

"I've been wondering why you two can't make a go of it, after all." Garnett looked down at his desk. "I like you, Llewellyn, and I like Lucy. Why not fool everybody and——"

Llewellyn shook his head emphatically.

"Not me," he said. "I don't care a snap of my finger about her. She can go jump in the lake for all I care."

"Why did you take her away?"

"I don't know. We'd been in love for almost a year and marriage seemed a long way off. It came over us all of a sudden."

"Why couldn't you get along?"

"Didn't she tell you?"

"I want your version."

"Well, it started one afternoon when she took all our money and threw it away."

"Threw it away?"

"She took it and bought a new hat. It was only thirty-five dollars, but it was all we had. If I hadn't found forty-five cents in an old suit we wouldn't have had any dinner."

"I see," said Garnett dryly.

"Then—oh, one thing happened after another. She didn't trust me, she didn't think I could take care of her, she kept saying she was going home to her mother. And finally we began to hate each other. It was a great mistake, that's all, and I'll probably spend a good part of my life paying for it. Wait till it leaks out!" He laughed bitterly.

"Aren't you thinking about yourself a little too much?" suggested Garnett coldly.

Llewellyn looked at him in unfeigned surprise.

"About myself?" he repeated. "Mr. Garnett, I'll give you my word of honor, this is the first time I've ever thought about that side of it. Right now I'd do anything in the world to save Lucy any pain—except live with her. She's got great things in her, Mr. Garnett." His eyes filled again with tears. "She's just as brave and honest, and sweet sometimes. I'll never marry anybody else, you can bet your life on that, but—we were just poison to each other. I never want to see her any more."

After all, thought Garnett, it was only the old human attempt to get something for nothing—neither of them had brought to the marriage any trace of tolerance or moral experience. However trivial the reasons for their incompatibility, it was firmly established now in both their hearts, and perhaps they were wise in realizing that the wretched voyage, too hastily embarked upon, was over.

That night, Garnett had a long and somewhat painful talk with George Wharton, and on the following morning he went to New York, where he spent several days. When he returned to Philadelphia, it was with the information that the marriage of Lucy and Llewellyn Clark had been annulled by the state of Connecticut on the grounds of their minority. They were free.

II

Almost everyone who knew Lucy Wharton liked her, and her friends rose rather valiantly to the occasion. There was a certain element, of course, who looked at her with averted eyes; there were slights, there were the stares of the curious; but since it was wisely given out, upon Chauncey Garnett's recommendation, that the Whartons themselves had insisted upon the annulment, the burden of the affair fell less heavily upon Lucy than upon Llewellyn. He became not exactly a pariah—cities live too quickly to linger long over any single scandal—but he was cut off entirely from the crowd in which he had grown up, and much bitter and unpleasant comment reached his ears.

He was a boy who felt things deeply, and in the first moment of depression he contemplated leaving Philadelphia. But gradually a mood of defiant indifference took possession of him; try as he might, he wasn't able to feel in his heart that he had done anything morally wrong. He hadn't thought of Lucy as being sixteen, but only as the girl whom he loved beyond understanding. What did age matter? Hadn't people married as children, almost, one hundred—two hundred years ago? The day of his elopement with Lucy had been like an ecstatic dream; he the young knight, scorned by her father, the baron, as a mere youth, bearing her away, and all willing, on his charger, in the dead of the night.

And then the realization, almost before his eyes had opened from their romantic vision, that marriage meant the complicated adjustment of two lives to each other, and that love is a small part only of the long, long marriage day. Lucy was a devoted child whom he had contracted to amuse—an adorable and somewhat frightened child, that was all.

As suddenly as it had begun, it was over. Doggedly Llewellyn went his way, along with his mistake. And so quickly had his romance bloomed and turned to dust that after a month a merciful unreality began to clothe it as if it were something vaguely sad that had happened long ago.

One day in July he was summoned to Chauncey Garnett's private office. Few words had passed between them since their conversation the month before, but Llewellyn saw that there was no hostility in the older man's attitude.

He was glad of that, for now that he felt himself utterly alone, cut off from the world in which he had grown up, his work had come to be the most important thing in his life.

"What are you doing, Llewellyn?" asked Garnett, picking up a yellow pamphlet from the litter of his desk.

"Helping Mr. Carson with the Municipal Country Club."

"Take a look at this." He handed the pamphlet to Llewellyn. "There isn't a gold mine in it, but there's a good deal of this gilt-edge hot air they call publicity. It's a syndicate of twenty papers, you see. The best plans for—what is it?—a neighborhood store—you know, a small drug store or grocery store that could fit into a nice street without being an eyesore. Or else for a suburban cottage—that'll be the regular thing. Or thirdly for a small factory recreation house."

Llewellyn read over the specifications.

"The last two aren't so interesting," he said. "Suburban cottage—that'll be the usual thing, as you say—recreation house, no. But I'd like to have a shot at the first, sir—the store."

Garnett nodded. "The best part is that the plan which wins each competition materializes as a building right away, and therein lies the prize. The building is yours. You design it, it's put up for you, then you sell it and the money goes into your own pocket. Matter of six or seven thousand dollars—and there won't be more than six or seven hundred other young architects trying."

Llewellyn read it over again carefully.

"I like it," he said. "I'd like to try the store."

"Well, you've got a month. I wouldn't mind it a bit, Llewellyn, if that prize came into this office."

"I can't promise you that." Again Llewellyn ran his eyes over the conditions, while Garnett watched him with quiet interest.

"By the way," he asked suddenly, "what do you do with yourself all the time, Llewellyn?"

"How do you mean, sir?"

"At night—over the week-ends. Do you ever go out?"

Llewellyn hesitated.

"Well, not so much—now."

"You mustn't let yourself brood over this business, you know."

"I'm not brooding."

Mr. Garnett put his glasses carefully away in their case.

"Lucy isn't brooding," he said suddenly. "Her father told me that she's trying to live just as normal a life as possible."

Silence for a moment.

"I'm glad," said Llewellyn in an expressionless voice.

"You must remember that you're free as air now," said Garnett. "You don't want to let yourself dry up and get bitter. Lucy's father and mother are encouraging her to have callers and go to dances—behave just as she did before."

"Before Rudolf Rassendyll* came along," said Llewellyn grimly. He held up the pamphlet. "May I keep this, Mr. Garnett?"

"Oh, yes." His employer's hand gave him permission to retire. "Tell Mr. Carson that I've taken you off the country club for the present."

"I can finish that too," said Llewellyn promptly. "In fact——"

His lips shut. He had been about to remark that he was doing

---

*The hero of *The Prisoner of Zenda*—ed.

practically the whole thing himself anyhow.

"Well?"

"Nothing, sir. Thank you very much."

Llewellyn withdrew, excited by his opportunity and relieved by the news of Lucy. She was herself again, so Mr. Garnett had implied; perhaps her life wasn't so irrevocably wrecked after all. If there were men to come and see her, to take her out to dances, then there were men to care for her. He found himself vaguely pitying them—if they knew what a handful she was, the absolute impossibility of dealing with her, even of talking to her. At the thought of those desolate weeks he shivered, as though recalling a nightmare.

Back in his room that night, he experimented with a few tentative sketches. He worked late, his imagination warming to the set task, but next day the result seemed "arty" and pretentious—like a design for a tea shop. He scrawled "Ye Olde-Fashioned Butcher Shoppe—Veree Unsanitaree," across the face of it and tore it into pieces, which he tossed into the wastebasket.

During the first weeks in August he continued his work on the plans for the country club, trusting that for the more personal venture some burst of inspiration would come to him toward the end of the allotted time. An then one day occurred an incident which he had long dreaded in the secret corners of his mind—walking home along Chestnut Street he ran unexpectedly into Lucy.

It was about five o'clock, when the crowds were thickest. Suddenly they found themselves in an eddy facing each other, and then borne along side by side as if fate had pressed into service all these swarming hundreds to throw them together.

"Why, Lucy!" he exclaimed, raising his hat automatically. She stared at him with startled eyes. A woman laden with bundles collided with her and a purse slipped from Lucy's hand.

"Thank you very much," she said as he retrieved it. Her voice was tense, breathless. "That's all right. Give it to me. I have a car right here."

Their eyes joined for a moment, cool, impersonal, and he had a vivid memory of their last meeting—of how they had stood, like this, hating each other with a cold fury.

"Are you sure I can't help you?"

"Quite sure. Our car's at the curb."

She nodded quickly. Llewellyn caught a glimpse of an unfamiliar limousine and a short smiling man of forty who helped her inside.

He walked home—for the first time in weeks he was angry, excited, confused. He must get away tomorrow. It was all too recent for any such casual encounter as this; the wounds she had left on him were raw and they opened easily.

"The little fool!" he said to himself bitterly. "The selfish little fool! She thought I wanted to walk along the street with her as if nothing had ever happened. She dares to imagine that I'm made of the same flimsy stuff as herself!"

He wanted passionately to spank her, to punish her in some way like an insolent child. Until dinnertime he paced up and down in his room, going over in his mind the forlorn and useless arguments, reproaches, imprecations, furies, that had made up their short married life. He rehearsed every quarrel from its trivial genesis down to the time when a merciful exhaustion intervened and brought them, almost hysterical, into each other's arms. A brief moment of peace— then again the senseless, miserable human battle.

"Lucy," he heard himself saying, "listen to me. It isn't that I want you to sit here waiting for me. It's your hands, Lucy. Suppose you went to cooking school and burned your pretty hands. I don't want your hands coarsened and roughened, and if you'll just have patience till next week when my money comes in——I won't stand it! Do you hear? I'm not going to have my wife doing that! No use of being stubborn."

Wearily, just as he had been made weary by those arguments in reality, he dropped into a chair and reached listlessly for his drawing materials. Laying them out, he began to sketch, crumpling each one into a ball before a dozen lines marred the paper. It was her fault, he whispered to himself, it was all her fault. "If I'd been fifty years old I couldn't have changed her."

Yet he could not rid himself of her dark young face set sharp and cool against the August gloaming, against the hot hurrying crowds of that afternoon.

"Quite sure. Our car's at the curb."

Llewellyn nodded to himself and tried to smile grimly.

"Well, I've got one thing to be thankful for," he told himself. "My responsibility will be over before long."

He had been sitting for a long while, looking at a blank sheet of drawing paper; but presently his pencil began to move in light strokes at the corner. He watched it idly, impersonally, as though it were a motion of his fingers imposed on him from outside. Finally he looked at the result with disapproval, scratched it out and then blocked it in again in exactly the same way.

Suddenly he chose a new pencil, picked up his ruler and made a measurement on the paper, and then another. An hour passed. The sketch took shape and outline, varied itself slightly, yielded in part to an eraser and appeared in an improved form. After two hours, he raised his head, and catching sight of his tense, absorbed face he started with surprise. There were a dozen half-smoked cigarettes in the tray beside him.

When he turned out his light at last it was half-past five. The milk wagons were rumbling through the twilit streets outside, and the first sunshine streaming pink over the roofs of the houses across the way fell upon the board which bore his night's work. It was the plan of a suburban bungalow.

III

As the August days passed, Llewellyn continued to think of Lucy with a certain anger and contempt. If she could accept so lightly what had happened just two months ago, he had wasted his emotion upon a girl who was essentially shallow. It cheapened his conception of her, of himself, of the whole affair. Again the idea came to him of leaving Philadelphia and making a new start farther west, but his interest in the outcome of the competition decided him to postpone his departure for a few weeks more.

The blue prints of his design were made and dispatched. Mr. Garnett cautiously refused to make any prophecies, but Llewellyn knew that everyone in the office who had seen the drawing felt a vague excitement about it. Almost literally he had drawn a bungalow in the air—a bungalow that had never been lived in before. It was neither Italian, Elizabethan, New England or California Spanish, nor a mongrel form with features from each one. Someone dubbed it the tree house, and there was a certain happiness in the label; but its charm proceeded less from any bizarre quality than from the virtuosity of the conception as a whole—an unusual length here and there, an odd, tantalizingly familiar slope of the roof, a door that was like the door to the secret places of a dream. Chauncey Garnett remarked that it was the first skyscraper he had ever seen built with one story, but he recognized that Llewellyn's unquestionable talent had matured overnight. Except that the organizers of the competition were probably seeking something more adapted to standardization, it might have had a chance for the award.

Only Llewellyn was sure. When he was reminded that he was only twenty-one, he kept silent, knowing that, whatever his years, he would never again be twenty-one at heart. Life had betrayed him. He had squandered himself on a worthless girl and the world had punished him for it, as ruthlessly as though he had spent spiritual coin other than his own. Meeting Lucy on the street again, he passed her without a flicker of his eye—and returned to his room, his day spoiled by the sight of that young distant face, the insincere reproach of those dark haunting eyes.

A week or so later arrived a letter from New York informing him that from four hundred plans submitted the judges of the competition had chosen his for the prize. Llewellyn walked into Mr. Garnett's office without excitement, but with a strong sense of elation, and laid the letter on his employer's desk.

"I'm especially glad," he said, "because before I go away I wanted to do something to justify your belief in me."

Mr. Garnett's face assumed an expression of concern.

"It's this business of Lucy Wharton, isn't it?" he demanded. "It's still on your mind?"

"I can't stand meeting her," said Llewellyn. "It always makes me feel—like the devil."

"But you ought to stay till they put up your house for you."

"I'll come back for that, perhaps. I want to leave tonight."

Garnett looked at him thoughtfully.

"I don't like to see you go away," he said. "I'm going to tell you something I didn't intend to tell you. Lucy needn't worry you a bit any more—your responsibility is absolutely over."

"Why's that?" Llewellyn felt his heart quicken.

"She's going to marry another man."

"Going to marry another man!" repeated Llewellyn mechanically.

"She's going to marry George Hemmick, who represents her father's business in Chicago. They're going out there to live."

"I see."

"The Whartons are delighted," continued Garnett. "I think they've felt this thing pretty deeply—perhaps more deeply than it deserves. And I've been sorry all along that the brunt of it fell on you. But you'll find the girl you really want one of these days, Llewellyn, and meanwhile the sensible thing for everyone concerned is to forget that it happened at all."

"But I can't forget," said Llewellyn in strained voice. "I don't understand what you mean by all that—you people—you and Lucy and her father and mother. First it was such a tragedy, and now it's something to forget! First I was this vicious young man and now I'm to go ahead and find the girl I want. Lucy's going to marry somebody and live in Chicago. Her father and mother feel fine because our elopement didn't get in the newspapers and hurt their social position. It came out 'all right'!"

Llewellyn stood there speechless, aghast and defeated by this manifestation of the world's indifference. It was all about nothing—his very self-reproaches had been pointless and in vain.

"So that's that," he said finally in a new, hard voice. "I realize now that from beginning to end I was the only one who had any conscience in this affair after all."

IV

The little house, fragile yet arresting, all aglitter like a toy in its fresh coat of robin's-egg blue, stood out delicately against the clear sky. Set upon new-laid sod between two other bungalows, it swung the eye sharply toward itself, held your glance for a moment, then turned up the corners of your lips with the sort of smile reserved for children. Something went on in it, you imagined; something charming and not quite real. Perhaps the whole front opened up like the front of a doll's house; you were tempted to hunt for the catch because you felt an irresistible inclination to peer inside.

Long before the arrival of Llewellyn Clark and Mr. Garnett a small crowd had gathered—the constant efforts of two policemen were required to keep people from breaking through the strong fence and trampling the tiny garden. When Llewellyn's eye first fell upon it, as their car rounded a corner, a lump rose in his throat. That was his own—something that had come alive out of his mind. Suddenly he realized that it was not for sale, that he wanted it more than anything in the world. It could mean to him what love might have meant, something always bright and warm where he could rest from whatever disappointments life might have in store. And unlike love, it would set no traps for him. His career opened up before him in a shining path and for the first time in months he was radiantly happy.

The speeches, the congratulations, passed in a daze. When he got up to make a stumbling but grateful acknowledgment, even the sight of Lucy standing close to another man on the edge of the crowd failed to send a pang through him, as it would have a month before. That was the past, and only the future counted. He hoped with all his heart, without reservations now, or bitterness, that she would be happy.

Afterward, when the crowd melted away, he felt the necessity of being alone. Still in a sort of trance, he went inside the house again and wandered from room to room, touching the walls, the furniture, the window casements, with almost a caress. He pulled aside curtains and gazed out; he stood for a while in the kitchen and seemed to see the fresh bread and butter on the white boards of the table, and hear the kettle, murmurous on the stove. Then back through the dining room—he remembered planning that the evening light should fall through the window just so—and into the bedroom, where he watched a breeze ruffle the edge of a curtain faintly, as if someone already lived here. He would sleep in this room tonight, he thought. He would buy things for a cold supper from a corner store. He was sorry for everyone who was not an architect, who could not make their own houses; he wished he could have set up every stick and stone with his own hands.

The September dusk fell. Returning from the store, he set out his purchases on the dining-room table—cold roast chicken, bread and jam, and a bottle of milk. He ate lingeringly, then he sat back in his chair and smoked a cigarette, his eyes wandering about the walls. This was home. Llewellyn, brought up by a series of aunts, scarcely remembered ever having had a home before—except, of course, where he had lived with Lucy. Those barren rooms in which they were so miserable together had been, nevertheless, a sort of home. Poor children—he looked back on them both, himself as well as her, from a great distance. Little wonder their love had made a faint, frail effort, a gesture, and then, unprepared for the oppression of those stifling walls, starved quickly to death.

Half an hour passed. Outside, the silence was heavy except for the complaint of some indignant dog far down the street. Llewellyn's mind, detached by the unfamiliar, almost mystical surroundings, drifted away from the immediate past; he was thinking of the day when he had first met Lucy, a year before. Little Lucy Wharton—how touched he had been by her trust in him, by her confidence that, at twenty, he was experienced in the ways of the world.

He got to his feet and began to walk slowly up and down the room—starting suddenly as the front doorbell pealed through the house for the first time. He opened the door and Mr. Garnett stepped inside.

"Good evening, Llewellyn," he said. "I came back to see if the king was happy in his castle."

"Sit down," said Llewellyn tensely. "I've got to ask you something. Why is Lucy marrying this man? I want to know."

"Why, I think I told you that he's a good deal older," answered Garnett quietly. "She feels that he understands."

"I want to see her!" Llewellyn cried. He leaned miserably against the mantelpiece. "I don't know what to do. Mr. Garnett, we're in love with each other, don't you realize that? Can you stay in this house and not realize it? It's her house and mine. Why, every room in it is haunted with Lucy! She came in when I was at dinner and sat with me—just now I saw her in front of the mirror in the bedroom, brushing her hair——"

"She's out on the porch," interrupted Garnett quietly. "I think she wants to talk to you. In a few months she's going to have a child."

For a few minutes Chauncey Garnett moved about the empty room, looking at this feature or that, here and there, until the walls seemed to fade out and melt into the walls of the little house where he had brought his own wife more than forty years ago. It was long gone, that house—the gift of his father-in-law; it would have seemed an atrocity to this generation. Yet on many a forgotten late afternoon when he had turned in at its gate, and the gas had flamed out at him cheerfully from its windows, he had got from it a moment of utter peace that no other house had given him since.

Until this house. The same quiet secret thing was here. Was it that his old mind was confusing the two, or that love had built this out of the tragedy in Llewellyn's heart? Leaving the question unanswered he found his hat and walked out on the dark porch, scarcely glanced at the single shadow on the porch chair a few yards away.

"You see, I never bothered to get that annulment, after all," he said as if he were talking to himself. "I thought it over carefully and I saw that you two were good people. And I had an idea that eventually you'd do the right thing. Good people—so often do."

When he reached the curb he looked back at the house. Again his mind—or his eyes—blurred and it seemed to him that it was that other house of forty years ago. Then, feeling vaguely ineffectual and a little guilty because he had meddled in other people's affairs, he turned and walked off hastily down the street.

Your Way and Mine

(*Woman's Home Companion*, May 1927)

"Your Way and Mine" was written in February 1926 at Salies-de-Bearn, a spa in the French Pyrenees where the Fitzgeralds spent two months while Zelda was taking a cure for digestive problems. In his cover letter Fitzgerald informed Harold Ober:

> This is one of the lowsiest stories I've ever written Just *terrible*! I lost interest in the middle (by the way the last part is typed triple space because I thought I could fix it—but I couldn't)
>
> *Please*—and I mean this—don't offer it to the *Post*. I think that as things are now it would be wretched policy. Nor to the *Red Book*. It hasn't *one* redeeming touch of my usual spirit in it. I was desparate to begin a story + invented a business plot—the kind I can't handle. I'd rather have $1000, for it from some obscure place than twice that + have it seen. *I feel very strongly about this*!

Woman's Home Companion paid $1750, featuring it on the cover; and it was syndicated by the Metro Newspaper Service.

One spring afternoon in the first year of the present century a young man was experimenting with a new typewriter in a brokerage office on lower Broadway. At his elbow lay an eight-line letter and he was endeavoring to make a copy on the machine but each attempt was marred by a monstrous capital rising unexpectedly in the middle of a word or by the disconcerting intrusion of some symbol such as $ or % into an alphabet whose membership was set at twenty-six many years ago. Whenever he detected a mistake he made a new beginning with a fresh sheet but after the fifteenth try he was aware of a ferocious instinct to cast the machine from the window.

The young man's short blunt fingers were too big for the keys. He was big all over; indeed his bulky body seemed to be in the very process of growth for it had ripped his coat at the back seam, while his trousers clung to thigh and calf like skin tights. His hair was yellow and tousled—you could see the paths of his broad fingers in it—and his eyes were of a hard brilliant blue but the lids drooping a little over them reinforced an impression of lethargy that the clumsy body conveyed. His age was twenty-one.

"What do you think the eraser's for, McComas?"

The young man looked around.

"What's that?" he demanded brusquely.

"The eraser," repeated the short alert human fox who had come in the outer door and paused behind him. "That there's a good copy except for one word. Use your head or you'll be sitting there until tomorrow."

The human fox moved on into his private office. The young man sat for a moment, motionless, sluggish. Suddenly he grunted, picked up the eraser referred to and flung it savagely out of the window.

Twenty minutes later he opened the door of his employer's office. In his hand was the letter, immaculately typed, and the addressed envelope.

"Here it is, sir," he said, frowning a little from his late concentration.

The human fox took it, glanced at it and then looked at McComas with a peculiar smile.

"You didn't use the eraser?"

"No, I didn't, Mr. Woodley."

"You're one of those thorough young men, aren't you?" said the fox sarcastically.

"What?"

"I said 'thorough' but since you weren't listening I'll change it to 'pig-headed.' Whose time did you waste just to avoid a little erasure that the best typists aren't too proud to make? Did you waste your time or mine?"

"I wanted to make one good copy," answered McComas steadily. "You see, I never worked a typewriter before."

"Answer my question," snapped Mr. Woodley. "When you sat there making two dozen copies of that letter were you wasting your time or mine?"

"It was mostly my lunch time," McComas replied, his big face flushing to an angry pink. "I've got to do things my own way or not at all."

For answer Mr. Woodley picked up the letter and envelope, folded them, tore them once and again and dropped the pieces into the wastepaper basket with a toothy little smile.

"That's my way," he announced. "What do you think of that?"

Young McComas had taken a step forward as if to snatch the fragments from the fox's hand.

"By golly," he cried. "By golly. Why, for two cents I'd spank you!"

With an angry snarl Mr. Woodley sprang to his feet, fumbled in his pocket and threw a handful of change upon his desk.

Ten minutes later the outside man coming in to report perceived that neither young McComas nor his hat were in their usual places. But in the private office he found Mr. Woodley, his face crimson and foam bubbling between his teeth, shouting frantically into the telephone. The outside man noticed to his surprise that Mr. Woodley was in daring dishabille and that there were six suspender buttons scattered upon the office floor.

In 1902 Henry McComas weighed 196 pounds. In 1905 when he journeyed back to his home town, Elmira, to marry the love of his boyhood he tipped accurate beams at 210. His weight remained constant for two years but after the panic of 1907 it bounded to 220, about which comfortable figure it was apparently to hover for the rest of his life.

He looked mature beyond his years—under certain illuminations his yellow hair became a dignified white—and his bulk added to the impression of authority that he gave. During his first five years off the farm there was never a time when he wasn't scheming to get into business for himself.

For a temperament like Henry McComas', which insisted on running at a pace of its own, independence was an utter necessity. He must make his own rules, willy-nilly, even though he join the ranks of those many abject failures who have also tried. Just one week after he had achieved his emancipation from other people's hierarchies he was moved to expound his point to Theodore Drinkwater, his partner—this because Drinkwater had wondered aloud if he intended never to come downtown before eleven.

"I doubt it," said McComas.

"What's the idea?" demanded Drinkwater indignantly. "What do you think the effect's going to be on our office force?"

"Does Miss Johnston show any sign of being demoralized?"

"I mean after we get more people. It isn't as if you were an old man, Mac, with your work behind you. You're only twenty-eight, not a day older than I. What'll you do at forty?"

"I'll be downtown at eleven o'clock," said McComas, "every working day of my life."

Later in the week one of their first clients invited them to lunch at a celebrated business club; the club's least member was a rajah of the swelling, expanding empire.

"Look around, Ted," whispered McComas as they left the dining-room. "There's a man looks like a prize-fighter, and there's one who looks like a ham actor. That's a plumber there behind you; there's a coal heaver and a couple of cowboys—do you see? There's a chronic invalid and a confidence man, a pawn-broker—that one on the right. By golly, where are all the big business men we came to see?"

The route back to their office took them by a small restaurant where the clerks of the district flocked to lunch.

"Take a look at them, Ted, and you'll find the men who know the rules—and think and act and look like just what they are."

"I suppose if they put on pink mustaches and came to work at five in the afternoon they'd get to be great men," scoffed Drinkwater.

"Posing is exactly what I don't mean. Just accept yourself. We're brought up on fairy stories about the new leaf, but who goes on believing them except those who have to believe and have to hope or else go crazy. I think America will be a happier country when the individual begins to look his personal limitations in the face. Anything that's in your character at twenty-one is usually there to stay."

In any case what was in Henry McComas' was there to stay. Henry McComas wouldn't dine with a client in a bad restaurant for a proposition of three figures, wouldn't hurry his luncheon for a proposition of four, wouldn't go without it for a proposition of five. And in spite of these peculiarities the exporting firm in which he owned forty-nine per cent of the stock began to pepper South America with locomotives, dynamos, barb wire, hydraulic engines, cranes, mining machinery, and other appurtenances of civilization. In 1913 when Henry McComas was thirty-four he owned a house on Ninety-second Street and calculated that his income for the next year would come to thirty thousand dollars. And because of a sudden and unexpected demand from Europe which was not for pink lemonade, it came to twice that. The buying agent for the British Government arrived, followed by the buying agents for the French, Belgian, Russian and Serbian Governments, and a share of the commodities required were assembled under the stewardship of Drinkwater and McComas. There was a chance that they would be rich men. Then suddenly this eventually began to turn on the woman Henry McComas had married.

Stella McComas was the daughter of a small hay and grain dealer of upper New York. Her father was unlucky and always on the verge of failure, so she grew up in the shadow of worry. Later, while Henry McComas got his start in New York, she earned her living by teaching physical culture in the public schools of Utica. In consequence she brought to her marriage a belief in certain stringent rules for the care of the body and an exaggerated fear of adversity.

For the first years she was so impressed with her husband's rapid rise and so absorbed in her babies that she accepted Henry as something infallible and protective, outside the scope of her provincial wisdom. But as her little girl grew into short dresses and hair ribbons, and her little boy into the custody of an English nurse she had more time to look closely at her husband. His leisurely ways, his corpulency, his sometimes maddening deliberateness, ceased to be the privileged idiosyncrasies of success, and became only facts.

For a while he paid no great attention to her little suggestions as to his diet, her occasional crankiness as to his hours, her invidious comparisons between his habits and the fancied habits of other men. Then one morning a peculiar lack of taste in his coffee precipitated the matter into the light.

"I can't drink the stuff—it hasn't had any taste for a week," he complained. "And why is it brought in a cup from the kitchen? I like to put the cream and sugar in myself."

Stella avoided an answer but later he reverted to the matter.

"About my coffee. You'll remember—won't you?—to tell Rose."

Suddenly she smiled at him innocently.

"Don't you feel better, Henry?" she asked eagerly.

"What?"

"Less tired, less worried?"

"Who said I was tired and worried? I never felt better in my life."

"There you are." She looked at him triumphantly. "You laugh at my theories but this time you'll have to admit there's something in them. You feel better because you haven't had sugar in your coffee for over a week."

He looked at her incredulously.

"What have I had?"

"Saccharine."

He got up indignantly and threw his newspaper on the table.

"I might have known it," he broke out. "All that bringing it out from the kitchen. What the devil is saccharine?"

"It's a substitute, for people who have a tendency to run to fat."

For a moment he hovered on the edge of anger, then he sat down shaking with laughter.

"It's done you good," she said reproachfully.

"Well, it won't do me good any more," he said grimly. "I'm thirty-four years old and I haven't been sick a day in ten years. I've forgotten more about my constitution than you'll ever know."

"You don't live a healthy life, Henry. It's after forty that things begin to tell."

"Saccharine!" he exclaimed, again breaking into laughter. "Saccharine! I thought perhaps it was something to keep me from drink. You know they have these—"

Suddenly she grew angry.

"Well why not? You ought to be ashamed to be so fat at your age. You wouldn't be if you took a little exercise and didn't lie around in bed all morning."

Words utterly failed her.

"If I wanted to be a farmer," said her husband quietly, "I wouldn't have left home. This saccharine business is over today—do you see?"

Their financial situation rapidly improved. By the second year of the war they were keeping a limousine and chauffeur and began to talk vaguely of a nice summer house on Long Island Sound. Month by month a swelling stream of materials flowed through the ledgers of Drinkwater and McComas to be dumped on the insatiable bonfire across the ocean. Their staff of clerks tripled and the atmosphere of the office was so charged with energy and achievement that Stella herself often liked to wander in on some pretext during the afternoon.

One day early in 1916 she called to learn that Mr. McComas was out and was on the point of leaving when she ran into Ted Drinkwater coming out of the elevator.

"Why, Stella," he exclaimed, "I was thinking about you only this morning."

The Drinkwaters and the McComases were close if not particularly spontaneous friends. Nothing but their husbands' intimate association would have thrown the two women together, yet they were "Henry, Ted, Mollie, and Stella" to each other and in ten years scarcely a month had passed without their partaking in a superficially cordial family dinner. The dinner being over, each couple indulged in an unsparing post-mortem over the other without, however, any sense of disloyalty. They were used to each other—so Stella was somewhat surprised by Ted Drinkwater's personal eagerness at meeting her this afternoon.

"I want to see you," he said in his intent direct way. "Have you got a minute, Stella? Could you come into my office?"

"Why, yes."

As they walked between rows of typists toward the glassed privacy of THEODORE DRINKWATER, PRESIDENT, Stella could not help thinking that he made a more appropriate business figure than her husband. He was lean, terse, quick. His eye glanced keenly from right to left as if taking the exact measure of every clerk and stenographer in sight.

"Sit down, Stella."

She waited, a feeling of vague apprehension stealing over her.

Drinkwater frowned.

"It's about Henry," he said.

"Is he sick?" she demanded quickly.

"No. Nothing like that." He hesitated. "Stella, I've always thought you were a woman with a lot of common sense."

She waited.

"This is a thing that's been on my mind for over a year," he continued. "He and I have battled it out so often that—that a certain coldness has grown up between us."

"Yes?" Stella's eyes blinked nervously.

"It's about the business," said Drinkwater abruptly. "A coldness with a business partner is a mighty unpleasant thing."

"What's the matter?"

"The old story, Stella. These are big years for us and he thinks business is going to wait while he carries on in the old country-store way. Down at eleven, hour and a half for lunch, won't be nice to a man he doesn't like for love or money. In the last six months he's lost us about three sizable orders by things like that."

Instinctively she sprang to her husband's defense.

"But hasn't he saved money too by going slow? On that thing about the copper, you wanted to sign right away and Henry—"

"Oh, that—" He waved it aside a little hurriedly. "I'm the last man to deny that Henry has a wonderful instinct in certain ways—"

"But it was a great big thing," she interrupted. "It would have practically ruined you if he hadn't put his foot down. He said—"

She pulled herself up short.

"Oh, I don't know," said Drinkwater with an expression of annoyance, "perhaps not so bad as that. Anyway, we all make mistakes and that's aside from the question. We have the opportunity right now of jumping into Class A. I mean it. Another two years of this kind of business and we can each put away our first million dollars. And, Stella, whatever happens, I am determined to put away mine. Even—" He considered his words for a moment. "Even if it comes to breaking with Henry."

"Oh!" Stella exclaimed. "I hope—"

"I hope not too. That's why I wanted to talk to you. Can't you do something, Stella? You're about the only person he'll listen to. He's so darn pig-headed he can't understand how he disorganizes the office. Get him up in the morning. No man ought to lie in bed till eleven."

"He gets up at half past nine."

"He's down here at eleven. That's what counts. Stir him up. Tell him you want more money. Orders are more money and there are lots of orders around for anyone who goes after them."

"I'll see what I can do," she said anxiously. "But I don't know—Henry's difficult—very set in his ways."

"You'll think of something. You might—" He smiled grimly. "You might give him a few more bills to pay. Sometimes I think an extravagant wife's the best inspiration a man can have. We need more pep down here. I've got to be the pep for two. I mean it, Stella, I can't carry this thing alone."

Stella left the office with her mind in a panic. All the fears and uncertainties of her childhood had been brought suddenly to the surface. She saw Henry cast off by Ted Drinkwater and trying unsuccessfully to run a business of his own. With his easy-going ways! They would slide down hill, giving up the servants one by one, the car, the house. Before she reached home her imagination had envisaged poverty, her children at work—starvation. Hadn't Ted Drinkwater just told her that he himself was the life of the concern—that he kept things moving? What would Henry do alone?

For a week she brooded over the matter, guarding her secret but looking with a mixture of annoyance and compassion at Henry over the dinner table. Then she mustered up her resolution. She went to a real estate agent and handed over her entire bank account of nine thousand dollars as the first payment on a house they had fearfully coveted on Long Island. . . . That night she told Henry.

"Why, Stella, you must have gone crazy," he cried aghast. "You must have gone crazy. Why didn't you ask me?"

He wanted to take her by the shoulders and shake her.

"I was afraid, Henry," she answered truthfully.

He thrust his hands despairingly through his yellow hair.

"Just at this time, Stella. I've just taken out an insurance policy that's more than I can really afford—we haven't paid for the new car—we've had a new front put on this house—last week your sable coat. I was going to devote tonight to figuring just how close we were running on money."

"But can't you—can't you take something out of the business until things get better?" she demanded in alarm.

"That's just what I can't do. It's impossible. I can't explain because you don't understand the situation down there. You see Ted and I—can't agree on certain things—"

Suddenly a new light dawned on her and she felt her body flinch. Supposing that by bringing about this situation she had put her husband into his partner's hands. Yet wasn't that what she wanted—wasn't it necessary for the present that Henry should conform to Drinkwater's methods?

"Sixty thousand dollars," repeated Henry in a frightened voice that made her want to cry. "I don't know where I am going to get enough to buy it on mortgage." He sank into a chair. "I might go and see the people you dealt with tomorrow and make a compromise—let some of your nine thousand go."

"I don't think they would," she said, her face set. "They were awfully anxious to sell—the owner's going away."

She had acted on impulse, she said, thinking that in their increasing prosperity the money would be available. He had been so generous about the new car—she supposed that now at last they could afford what they wanted.

It was typical of McComas that after the first moment of surprise he wasted no energy in reproaches. But two days later he came home from work with such a heavy and dispirited look on his face that she could not help but guess that he and Ted Drinkwater had had it out—and that what she wanted had come true. That night in shame and pity she cried herself to sleep.

A new routine was inaugurated in Henry McComas' life. Each morning Stella woke him at eight and he lay for fifteen minutes in an unwilling trance, as if his body were surprised at this departure from the custom of a decade. He reached the office at nine-thirty as promptly as he had once reached it at eleven—on the first morning his appearance caused a flutter of astonishment among the older employees—and he limited his lunch time to a conscientious hour. No longer could he be found asleep on his office couch between two and three o'clock on summer afternoons—the couch itself vanished into that limbo which held his leisurely periods of digestion and his cherished surfeit of sleep. These were his concessions to Drinkwater in exchange for the withdrawal of sufficient money to cover his immediate needs.

Drinkwater of course could have bought him out, but for various reasons the senior partner did not consider this advisable. One of them, though he didn't admit it to himself, was his absolute reliance on McComas in all matters of initiative and decision. Another reason was the tumultuous condition of the market, for as 1916 boomed on with the tragic battle of the Somme the allied agents sailed once more to the city of plenty for the wherewithal of another year. Coincidently Drinkwater and McComas moved into a suite that was like a floor in a country club and there they sat all day while anxious and gesticulating strangers explained what they must have, helplessly pledging their peoples to thirty years of economic depression. Drinkwater and McComas farmed out a dozen contracts a week and started the movement of countless tons toward Europe. Their names were known up and down the Street now—they had forgotten what it was to be kept waiting on a telephone.

But though profits increased and Stella, settled in the Long Island house, seemed for the first time in years perfectly satisfied, Henry McComas found himself growing irritable and nervous. What he missed most was the sleep for which his body hungered and which seemed to descend upon him at its richest just as he was shocked back into the living world each morning. And in spite of all material gains he was always aware that he was walking in his own paths no longer.

Their interests broadened and Drinkwater was frequently away on trips to the industrial towns of New England or the South. In consequence the detail of the office fell upon McComas—and he took it hard. A man capable of enormous concentration, he had previously harvested his power for hours of importance. Now he was inclined to fritter it away upon things that in perspective often proved to be inessentials. Sometimes he was engaged in office routine until six, then at home working until midnight when he tumbled, worn out but often still wide-eyed, into his beleaguered bed.

The firm's policy was to slight their smaller accounts in Cuba and the West Indies and concentrate upon the tempting business of the war, and all through the summer they were hurrying to clear the scenes for the arrival of a new purchasing commission in September. When it arrived it unexpectedly found Drinkwater in Pennsylvania, temporarily out of reach. Time was short and the orders were to be placed in bulk. After much anxious parley over the telephone McComas persuaded four members of the commission to meet him for an hour at his own house that night.

Thanks to his own foresight everything was in order. If he hadn't been able to be specific over the phone the coup toward which he had been working would have ended in failure. When it was brought off he was due for a rest and he knew it acutely. He'd had sharp fierce headaches in the past few weeks—he had never known a headache before.

The commissioners had been indefinite as to what time he could expect them that night. They were engaged for dinner and would be free somewhere between nine and eleven. McComas reached home at six, rested for a half hour in a steaming bath and then stretched himself gratefully on his bed. Tomorrow he would join Stella and the children in the country. His week-ends had been too infrequent in this long summer of living alone in the Ninety-second Street house with a deaf housekeeper. Ted Drinkwater would have nothing to say now, for this deal, the most ambitious of all, was his own. He had originated and engineered it—it seemed as if fate had arranged Drinkwater's absence in order to give him the opportunity of concluding it himself.

He was hungry. He considered whether to take cold chicken and buttered toast at the hands of the housekeeper or to dress and go out to the little restaurant on the corner. Idly he reached his hand toward the bell, abandoned the attempt in the air, overcome by a pleasing languor which dispelled the headache that had bothered him all day.

That reminded him to take some aspirin and as he got up to go toward the bureau he was surprised at the weakened condition in which the hot bath had left him. After a step or two he turned about suddenly and plunged rather than fell back upon the bed. A faint feeling of worry passed over him and then an iron belt seemed to wind itself around his head and tighten, sending a spasm of pain through his body. He would ring for Mrs. Corcoran, who would call a doctor to fix him up. In a moment he would reach up his hand to the bell beside his bed. In a minute—he wondered at his indecision—then he cried out sharply as he realized the cause of it. His will had already given his brain the order and his brain had signaled it to his hand. It was his hand that would not obey.

He looked at his hand. Rather white, relaxed, motionless, it lay upon the counterpane. Again he gave it a command, felt his neck cords tighten with the effort. It did not move.

"It's asleep," he thought, but with rising alarm. "It'll pass off in a minute."

Then he tried to reach his other hand across his body to massage away the numbness but the other hand remained with a sort of crazy indifference on its own side of the bed. He tried to lift his foot—his knees. . . .

After a few seconds he gave a snort of nervous laughter. There was something ridiculous about not being able to move your own foot. It was like someone else's foot, a foot in a dream. For a moment he had the fantastic notion that he must be asleep. But no—the unmistakable sense of reality was in the room.

"This is the end," he thought, without fear, almost without emotion. "This thing, whatever it is, is creeping over me. In a minute I shall be dead."

But the minute passed and another minute, and nothing happened, nothing moved except the hand of the little leather clock on his dresser which crept slowly over the point of seven minutes to seven. He turned his head quickly from side to side, shaking it as a runner kicks his legs to warm up. But there was no answering response from the rest of his body, only a slight rise and fall between belly and chest as he breathed out and in and a faint tremble of his helpless limbs from the faint tremble of the bed.

"Help!" he called out, "Mrs. Corcoran. Mrs. Cor-cor-an, help! Mrs. Corcor—"

There was no answer. She was in the kitchen probably. No way of calling her except by the bell, two feet over his head. Nothing to do but lie there until this passed off, or until he died, or until someone inquired for him at the front door.

The clock ticked past nine o'clock. In a house two blocks away the four members of the commission finished dinner, looked at their watches and issued forth into the September night with brief-cases in their hands. Outside a private detective nodded and took his place beside the chauffeur in the waiting limousine. One of the men gave an address on Ninety-second Street.

Ten minutes later Henry McComas heard the doorbell ring through the house. If Mrs. Corcoran was in the kitchen she would hear it too. On the contrary if she was in her room with the door shut she would hear nothing.

He waited, listening intently for the sound of footsteps. A minute passed. Two minutes. The doorbell rang again.

"Mrs. Corcoran!" he cried desperately.

Sweat began to roll from his forehead and down the folds of his neck. Again he shook his head desperately from side to side, and his will made a last mighty effort to kick his limbs into life. Not a movement, not a sound, except a third peal of the bell, impatient and sustained this time and singing like a trumpet of doom in his ear.

Suddenly he began to swear at the top of his voice calling in turn upon Mrs. Corcoran, upon the men in the street, asking them to break down the door, reassuring, imprecating, explaining. When he finished, the bell had stopped ringing; there was silence once more within the house.

A few minutes later the four men outside reentered their limousine and drove south and west toward the docks. They were to sleep on board ship that night. They worked late for there were papers to go ashore but long after the last of them was asleep Henry McComas lay awake and felt the sweat rolling from his neck and forehead. Perhaps all his body was sweating. He couldn't tell.

For a year and a half Henry McComas lay silent in hushed and darkened rooms and fought his way back to life. Stella listened while a famous specialist explained that certain nervous systems were so constituted that only the individual could judge what was, or wasn't, a strain. The specialist realized that a host of hypochondriacs imposed upon this fact to nurse and pamper themselves through life when in reality they were as hardy and phlegmatic as the policeman on the corner, but it was nevertheless a fact. Henry McComas' large, lazy body had been the protection and insulation of a nervous intensity as fine and taut as a hair wire. With proper rest it functioned brilliantly for three or four hours a day—fatigued ever so slightly over the danger line it snapped like a straw.

Stella listened, her face wan and white. Then a few weeks later she went to Ted Drinkwater's office and told him what the specialist had said. Drinkwater frowned uncomfortably—he remarked that specialists were paid to invent consoling nonsense. He was sorry but business must go on, and he thought it best for everyone, including Henry, that the partnership be dissolved. He didn't blame Henry but he couldn't forget that just because his partner didn't see fit to keep in good condition they had missed the opportunity of a lifetime.

After a year Henry McComas found one day that he could move his arms down to the wrists; from that hour onward he grew rapidly well. In 1919 he went into business for himself with very little except his abilities and his good name and by the time this story ends, in 1926, his name alone was good for several million dollars.

What follows is another story. There are different people in it and it takes place when Henry McComas' personal problems are more or less satisfactorily solved; yet it belongs to what has gone before. It concerns Henry McComas' daughter.

Honoria was nineteen, with her father's yellow hair (and, in the current fashion, not much more of it), her mother's small pointed chin and eyes that she might have invented herself, deep-set yellow eyes with short stiff eyelashes that sprang from them like the emanations from a star in a picture. Her figure was slight and childish and when she smiled you were afraid that she might expose the loss of some baby teeth, but the teeth were there, a complete set, little and white. Many men had looked upon Honoria in flower. She expected to be married in the fall.

Whom to marry was another matter. There was a young man who traveled incessantly back and forth between London and Chicago playing in golf tournaments. If she married him she would at least be sure of seeing her husband every time he passed through New York. There was Max Van Camp who was unreliable, she thought, but good-looking in a brisk sketchy way. There was a dark man named Strangler who played polo and would probably beat her with a riding crop like the heroes of Ethel M. Dell. And there was Russel Codman, her father's right-hand man, who had a future and whom she liked best of all.

He was not unlike her father in many ways—slow in thought, leisurely and inclined to stoutness—and perhaps these qualities had first brought him to Henry McComas' favor. He had a genial manner and a hearty confident smile, and he had made up his mind about Honoria when he first saw her stroll into her father's office one day three years before. But so far he hadn't asked her to marry him, and though this annoyed Honoria she liked him for it too—he wanted to be secure and successful before he asked her to share his life. Max Van Camp, on the other hand, had asked her a dozen times. He was a quick-witted "alive" young man of the new school, continually bubbling over with schemes that never got beyond McComas' waste-paper basket—one of those curious vagabonds of business who drift from position to position like strolling minstrels and yet manage to keep moving in an upward direction all their lives. He had appeared in McComas' office the year before bearing an introductory letter from a friend.

He got the position. For a long while neither he nor his employer, nor anyone in the office, was quite sure what the position was. McComas at that time was interested in exporting, in real estate developments and, as a venture, in the possibilities of carrying the chain store idea into new fields.

Van Camp wrote advertising, investigated properties and accomplished such vague duties as might come under the phrase, "We'll get Van Camp to do that." He gave the effect always of putting much more clamor and energy into a thing than it required and there were those who, because he was somewhat flashy and often wasted himself like an unemployed dynamo, called him a bluff and pronounced that he was usually wrong.

"What's the matter with you young fellows?" Henry McComas said to him one day. "You seem to think business is some sort of trick game, discovered about 1910, that nobody ever heard of before. You can't even look at a proposition unless you put it into this new language of your own. What do you mean you want to 'sell' me this proposition? Do you want to suggest it—or are you asking money for it?"

"Just a figure of speech, Mr. McComas."

"Well, don't fool yourself that it's anything else. Business sense is just common sense with your personal resources behind it—nothing more."

"I've heard Mr. Codman say that," agreed Max Van Camp meekly.

"He's probably right. See here—" he looked keenly at Van Camp; "how would you like a little competition with that same gentleman? I'll put up a bonus of five hundred dollars on who comes in ahead."

"I'd like nothing better, Mr. McComas."

"All right. Now listen. We've got retail hardware stores in every city of over a thousand population in Ohio and Indiana. Some fellow named McTeague is horning in on the idea—he's taken the towns of twenty thousand and now he's got a chain as long as mine. I want to fight him in the towns of that size. Codman's gone to Ohio. Suppose you take Indiana. Stay six weeks. Go to every town of over twenty thousand in the state and buy up the best hardware stores in sight."

"Suppose I can only get the second-best?"

"Do what you can. There isn't any time to waste because McTeague's got a good start on us. Think you can leave tonight?"

He gave some further instructions while Van Camp fidgeted impatiently. His mind had grasped what was required of him and he wanted to get away. He wanted to ask Honoria McComas one more question, the same one, before it was time to go.

He received the same answer because Honoria knew she was going to marry Russel Codman, just as soon as he asked her to. Sometimes when she was alone with Codman she would shiver with excitement, feeling that now surely the time had come at last—in a moment the words would flow romantically from his lips. What the words would be she didn't know, couldn't imagine, but they would be thrilling and extraordinary, not like the spontaneous appeals of Max Van Camp which she knew by heart.

She waited excitedly for Russel Codman's return from the West. This time, unless he spoke, she would speak herself. Perhaps he didn't want her after all, perhaps there was someone else. In that case she would marry Max Van Camp and make him miserable by letting him see that he was getting only the remnants of a blighted life.

Then before she knew it the six weeks were up and Russel Codman came back to New York. He reported to her father that he was going to see her that night. In her excitement Honoria found excuses for being near the front door. The bell rang finally and a maid stepped past her and admitted a visitor into the hall.

"Max," she cried.

He came toward her and she saw that his face was tired and white.

"Will you marry me?" he demanded without preliminaries.

She sighed.

"How many times, Max?"

"I've lost count," he said cheerfully. "But I haven't even begun. Do I understand that you refuse?"

"Yes, I'm sorry."

"Waiting for Codman?"

She grew annoyed.

"That's not your affair."

"Where's your father?"

She pointed, not deigning to reply.

Max entered the library where McComas rose to meet him.

"Well?" inquired the older man. "How did you make out?"

"How did Codman make out?" demanded Van Camp.

"Codman did well. He bought about eighteen stores—in several cases the very stores McTeague was after."

"I knew he would," said Van Camp.

"I hope you did the same."

"No," said Van Camp unhappily. "I failed."

"What happened?" McComas slouched his big body reflectively back in his chair and waited.

"I saw it was no use," said Van Camp after a moment. "I don't know what sort of places Codman picked up in Ohio but if it was anything like Indiana they weren't worth buying. These towns of twenty thousand haven't got three good hardware stores. They've got one man who won't sell out on account of the local wholesaler; then there's one man that McTeague's got, and after that only little places on the corner. Anything else you'll have to build up yourself. I saw right away that it wasn't worth while." He broke off. "How many places did Codman buy?"

"Eighteen or nineteen."

"I bought three."

McComas looked at him impatiently.

"How did you spend your time?" he asked. "Take you two weeks apiece to get them?"

"Took me two days," said Van Camp gloomily. "Then I had an idea."

"What was that?" McComas' voice was ironical.

"Well—McTeague had all the good stores."

"Yes."

"So I thought the best thing was to buy McTeague's company over his head."

"What?"

"Buy his company over his head," and Van Camp added with seeming irrelevance, "you see, I heard that he'd had a big quarrel with his uncle who owned fifteen per cent of the stock."

"Yes," McComas was leaning forward now—the sarcasm gone from his face.

"McTeague only owned twenty-five per cent and the storekeepers themselves owned forty. So if I could bring round the uncle we'd have a majority. First I convinced the uncle that his money would be safer with McTeague as a branch manager in our organization—"

"Wait a minute—wait a minute," said McComas. "You go too fast for me. You say the uncle had fifteen per cent—how'd you get the other forty?"

"From the owners. I told them the uncle had lost faith in McTeague and I offered them better terms. I had all their proxies on condition that they would be voted in a majority only."

"Yes," said McComas eagerly. Then he hesitated. "But it didn't work, you say. What was the matter with it? Not sound?"

"Oh, it was a sound scheme all right."

"Sound schemes always work."

"This one didn't."

"Why not?"

"The uncle died."

McComas laughed. Then he stopped suddenly and considered. "So you tried to buy McTeague's company over his head?"

"Yes," said Max with a shamed look. "And I failed."

The door flew open suddenly and Honoria rushed into the room.

"Father," she cried. At the sight of Max she stopped, hesitated, and then carried away by her excitement continued:

"Father—did you ever tell Russel how you proposed to Mother?"

"Why, let me see—yes, I think I did."

Honoria groaned.

"Well, he tried to use it again on me."

"What do you mean?"

"All these months I've been waiting—" she was almost in tears, "waiting to hear what he'd say. And then—when it came—it sounded *familiar*—as if I'd heard it before."

"It's probably one of my proposals," suggested Van Camp. "I've used so many."

She turned on him quickly.

"Do you mean to say you've ever proposed to any other girl but me?"

"Honoria—would you mind?"

"Mind. Of course I wouldn't mind. I'd never speak to you again as long as I lived."

"You say Codman proposed to you in the words I used to your mother?" demanded McComas.

"Exactly," she wailed. "He knew them by heart."

"That's the trouble with him," said McComas thoughtfully. "He always was my man and not his own. You'd better marry Max, here."

"Why—" she looked from one to the other, "why—I never knew you liked Max, Father. You never showed it."

"Well, that's just the difference," said her father, "between your way and mine."

The Love Boat

(*The Saturday Evening Post*, 8 October 1927)

"The Love Boat" was written in August 1927 at "Ellerslie," a rented mansion near Wilmington, Delaware. Fitzgerald had returned to America to write *Tender Is the Night*, but the work on the novel was interrupted and postponed while he wrote money-making stories. The *Post* paid $3500 for it, a raise of $500 over Fitzgerald's previous story price.

Written at a time when Fitzgerald's life was increasingly undisciplined, "The Love Boat" treats a search for the lost hopes or ideals of youth. It belongs to a group of retrospective stories he wrote at "Ellerslie," notably the Basil Duke Lee stories about a boy growing up in St. Paul and going off to boarding school in the East. Fitzgerald's attempt to reorganize his life abroad had proved a failure, and these retrospective stories represent a return to American experience by a return to youth.

The boat floated down the river through the summer night like a Fourth of July balloon footloose in the heavens. The decks were brightly lit and restless with dancers, but bow and stern were in darkness; so the boat had no more outline than an accidental cluster of stars. Between the black banks it floated, softly parting the mild dark tide from the sea and leaving in its wake small excited gusts of music—"Babes in the Woods" over and over, and "Moonlight Bay." Past the scattered lights of Pokus Landing, where a poet in an attic window saw yellow hair gleam in the turn of a dance. Past Ulm, where the moon came up out of a boiler works, and West Esther, where it slid, unregretted, behind a cloud.

The radiance of the boat itself was enough for, among others, the three young Harvard graduates; they were weary and a little depressed and they gave themselves up promptly to its enchantment. Their own boat was casually drifting and a collision was highly possible, but no one made a movement to start the engine and get out of the way.

"It makes me very sad," one of them said. "It is so beautiful that it makes me want to cry."

"Go on and cry, Bill."

"Will you cry too?"

"We'll all cry."

His loud, facetious "Boo-hoo!" echoed across the night, reached the steamer and brought a small lively crowd to the rail.

"Look! It's a launch."

"Some guys in a launch."

Bill got to his feet. The two crafts were scarcely ten feet apart.

"Throw us a hempen rope," he pleaded eloquently. "Come on—be impulsive. Please do."

Once in a hundred years there would have been a rope at hand. It was there that night. With a thud the coil struck the wooden bottom and in an instant the motorboat was darting along behind the steamer, as if in the wake of a harpooned whale.

Fifty high-school couples left the dance and scrambled for a place around the suddenly interesting stern rail. Fifty girls gave forth immemorial small cries of excitement and sham fright. Fifty young men forgot the mild exhibitionism which had characterized their manner of the evening and looked grudgingly at the more effectual show-off of three others. Mae Purley, without the involuntary quiver of an eyelash, fitted the young man standing in the boat into her current dream, where he displaced Al Fitzpatrick with laughable ease. She put her hand on Al Fitzpatrick's arm and squeezed it a little because she had stopped thinking about him entirely and felt that he must be aware of it. Al, who had been standing with his eyes squinted up, watching the towed boat, looked tenderly at Mae and tried to put his arm about her shoulder. But Mae Purley and Bill Frothington, handsome and full of all the passionate promise in the world, had locked eyes across the intervening space.

They made love. For a moment they made love as no one ever dares to do after. Their glance was closer than an embrace, more urgent than a call. There were no words for it. Had there been, and had Mae heard them, she would have fled to the darkest corner of the ladies' washroom and hid her face in a paper towel.

"We want to come on board!" Bill called. "We're life-preserver salesmen! How about pulling us around to the side?"

Mr. McVitty, the principal, arrived on the scene too late to interfere. The three young Harvard graduates—Ellsworth Ames soaking wet, unconsciously Byronic with his dark curls plastered damply to his forehead, Hamilton Abbot and Bill Frothington surer-footed and dry—climbed and were hoisted over the side. The motorboat bobbed on behind.

With a sort of instinctive reverence for the moment, Mae Purley hung back in the shadow, not through lack of confidence but through excess of it. She knew that he would come straight to her. That was never the trouble and never had been—the trouble was in keeping up her own interest after she had satisfied the deep but casual curiosity of her lips. But tonight was going to be different. She knew this when she saw that he was in no hurry; he was leaning against the rail making a couple of high-school seniors—who suddenly seemed very embryonic to themselves—feel at ease.

He looked at her once.

"It's all right," his eyes said, without a movement of his face, "I understand as well as you. I'll be there in just a minute."

Life burned high in them both; the steamer and its people were at a distance and in darkness. It was one of those times.

"I'm a Harvard man," Mr. McVitty was saying, "class of 1907." The three young men nodded with polite indifference. "I'm glad to know we won the race," continued the principal, simulating a reborn enthusiasm which had never existed. "I haven't been to New London in fifteen years."

"Bill here rowed Number Two," said Ames. "That's a coaching launch we've got."

"Oh. You were on the crew?"

"Crew's over now," said Bill impatiently. "Everything's over."

"Well, let me congratulate you."

Shortly they froze him into silence. They were not his sort of Harvard man; they wouldn't have known his name in four years there together. But they would have been much more gracious and polite about it had it not been this particular night. They hadn't broken away from the hilarious mobs of classmates and relatives at New London to exchange discomfort with the master of a mill-town high school.

"Can we dance?" they demanded.

A few minutes later Bill and Mae Purley were walking down the deck side by side. Life had met over the body of Al Fitzpatrick, engulfing him. The two clear voices:

"Perhaps you'll dance with me," with the soft assurance of the moonlight itself, and: "I'd love to," were nothing that could be argued about, not by twice what Al Fitzpatrick pretended to be. The most consoling thought in Al's head was that they might be fought over.

What was it they said? Did you hear it? Can you remember? Later that night she remembered only his pale wavy hair and the long limbs that she followed around the dancing floor.

She was thin, a thin burning flame, colorless yet fresh. Her smile came first slowly, then with a rush, pouring out of her heart, shy and bold, as if all the life of that little body had gathered for a moment around her mouth and the rest of her was a wisp that the least wind would blow away. She was a changeling whose lips alone had escaped metamorphosis, whose lips were the only point of contact with reality.

"Then you live near?"

"Only about twenty-five miles from you," Bill said. "Isn't it funny?"

"Isn't it funny?"

They looked at each other, a trifle awed in the face of such manifest destiny. They stood between two lifeboats on the top deck. Mae's hand lay on his arm, playing with a loose ravel of his tweed coat. They had not kissed yet—that was coming in a minute. That was coming any time now, as soon as every cup of emotional moonlight had been drained of its possibilities and cast aside. She was seventeen.

"Are you glad I live near?"

She might have said "I'm delighted" or "Of course I am." But she whispered, "Yes; are you?"

"Mae—with an *e*," he said and laughed in a husky whisper. Already they had a joke together. "You look so darn beautiful."

She accepted the compliment in silence, meeting his eyes. He pressed her to him by her merest elbow in a way that would have been impossible had she not been eager too. He never expected to see her after tonight.

"Mae." His whisper was urgent. Mae's eyes came nearer, grew larger, dissolved against his face, like eyes on a screen. Her frail body breathed imperceptibly in his arms.

A dance stopped. There was clapping for an encore. Then clapping for another encore with what had seemed only a poor bar of music in between. There was another dance, scarcely longer than a kiss. They were heavily endowed for love, these two, and both of them had played with it before.

Down below, Al Fitzpatrick's awareness of time and space had reached a pitch that would have been invaluable to an investigator of the new mathematics. Bit by bit the boat presented itself to him as it really was, a wooden hulk garish with forty-watt bulbs, peopled by the commonplace young people of a commonplace town. The river was water, the moon was a flat meaningless symbol in the sky. He was in agony—which is to speak tritely. Rather, he was in deadly fear; his throat was dry, his mouth drooped into a hurt half moon as he tried to talk to some of the other boys—shy unhappy boys, who loitered around the stern.

Al was older than the rest—he was twenty-two, and out in the world for seven years. He worked in the Hammacker Mills and attended special high-school classes at night. Another year might see him assistant manager of the shops, and Mae Purley, with about as much eagerness as was to be expected in a girl who was having everything her own way, had half promised to marry him when she was eighteen. His wasn't a temperament to go to pieces. When he had brooded up to the limit of his nature he felt a necessity for action. Miserably and desperately he climbed up to the top deck to make trouble.

Bill and Mae were standing close together by the lifeboat, quiet, absorbed and happy. They moved a little apart as he came near. "Is that you, Mae?" called Al in a hard voice. "Aren't you going to come down and dance?"

"We were just coming."

They walked toward him in a trance.

"What's the idea?" Al said hoarsely. "You've been up here over two hours."

At their indifference he felt pain swelling and spreading inside him, constricting his breath.

"Have you met Mr. Frothington?" She laughed shyly at the unfamiliar name.

"Yeah," said Al rudely. "I don't see the idea of his keeping you up here."

"I'm sorry," said Bill. "We didn't realize."

"Oh, you didn't? Well, I did." His jealousy cut through their absorption. They acknowledged it by an effort to hurry, to be impersonal, to defer to his wishes. Ungraciously he followed and the three of them came in a twinkling upon a scene that had suddenly materialized on the deck below.

Ellsworth Ames, smiling, but a little flushed, was leaning against the rail while Ham Abbot attempted to argue with a distraught young husky who kept trying to brush past him and get at Ames. Near them stood an indignant girl with another girl's soothing arm around her waist.

"What is it?" demanded Bill quickly.

The distraught young man glared at him. "Just a couple of snobs that come here and try to spoil everybody else's good time!" he cried wildly.

"He doesn't like me," said Ellsworth lightly. "I invited his girl to dance."

"She didn't want to dance with you!" shouted the other. "You think you're so damn smart—ask her if she wanted to dance with you."

The girl murmured indistinguishable words and disclaimed all responsibility by beginning to cry.

"You're too fresh, that's the trouble!" continued her defender. "I know what you said to her when you danced with her before. What do you think these girls are? They're just as good as anybody, see?"

Al Fitzpatrick moved in closer.

"Let's put 'em all off the boat," he suggested, stubborn and ashamed. "They haven't got any business butting in here."

A mild protest went up from the crowd, especially from the girls, and Abbot put his hand conciliatingly on the husky's shoulder. But it was too late.

"You'll put me off?" Ellsworth was saying coldly. "If you try to lay your hands on me I'll rearrange your whole face."

"Shut up, Ellie!" snapped Bill. "No use getting disagreeable. They don't want us; we'd better go." He stepped close to Mae, and whispered, "Good night. Don't forget what I said. I'll drive over and see you Sunday afternoon."

As he pressed her hand quickly and turned away he saw the argumentative boy swing suddenly at Ames, who caught the blow with his left arm. In a moment they were slugging and panting, knee to knee in the small space left by the gathering crowd. Simultaneously Bill felt a hand pluck at his sleeve and he turned to face Al Fitzpatrick. Then the deck was in an uproar. Abbot's attempt to separate Ames and his antagonist was misinterpreted; instantly he was involved in a battle of his own, cannonading against the other pairs, slipping on the smooth deck, bumping against noncombatants and scurrying girls who sent up shrill cries. He saw Al Fitzpatrick slap the deck suddenly with his whole body, not to rise again. He heard calls of "Get Mr. McVitty!" and then his own opponent was dropped by a blow he did not strike, and Bill's voice said: "Come on to the boat!"

The next few minutes streaked by in wild confusion. Avoiding Bill, whose hammerlike arms had felled their two champions, the high-school boys tried to pull down Ham and Ellie, and the harassed group edged and revolved toward the stern rail.

"Hidden-ball stuff!" Bill panted. "Save it for Haughton. I'm G-Gardner, you're Bradlee and Mahan—hip!"

Mr. McVitty's alarmed face appeared above the combat, and his high voice, ineffectual at first, finally pierced the heat of battle.

"Aren't you ashamed of yourselves! Bob—Cecil—George Roberg! Let go, I say!"

Abruptly the battle was over and the combatants, breathing hard, eyed one another impassively in the moonlight.

Ellie laughed and held out a pack of cigarettes. Bill untied the motor boat and walked forward with the painter to bring it alongside.

"They claim you insulted one of the girls," said Mr. McVitty uncertainly. "Now that's no way to behave after we took you aboard."

"That's nonsense," snapped Ellie, between gasps. "I only told her I'd like to bite her neck."

"Do you think that was a very gentlemanly thing to say?" demanded Mr. McVitty heatedly.

"Come on, Ellie!" Bill cried. "Good-by, everybody! Sorry there was such a row!"

They were already shadows of the past as they slipped one by one over the rail. The girls were turning cautiously back to their own men, and not one of them answered, and not one of them waved farewell.

"A bunch of meanies," remarked Ellie ironically. "I wish all you ladies had one neck so I could bite it all at once. I'm a glutton for ladies' necks."

Feeble retorts went up here and there like muffled pistol shots.

"*Good night, ladies,*" Ham sang, as Bill shoved away from the side:

Good night, ladies,
Good night, ladies,
We're going to leave you now-ow-ow.

The boat moved up the river through the summer night, while the launch, touched by its swell, rocked to and fro gently in the wide path of the moon.

II

On the following Sunday afternoon Bill Frothington drove over from Truro to the isolated rural slum known as Wheatly Village. He had stolen away from a house full of guests, assembled for his sister's wedding, to pursue what his mother would have called an "unworthy affair." But behind him lay an extremely successful career at Harvard and a youth somewhat more austere than the average, and this fall he would disappear for life into the banking house of Read, Hoppe and Company in Boston. He felt that the summer was his own. And had the purity of his intentions toward Mae Purley been questioned he would have defended himself with righteous anger. He had been thinking of her for five days. She attracted him violently, and he was following the attraction with eyes that did not ask to see.

Mae lived in the less offensive quarter of town on the third floor of its only apartment house, an unsuccessful relic of those more prosperous days of New England textile weaving that ended twenty years ago. Her father was a timekeeper who had fallen out of the white-collar class; Mae's two older brothers were working at the loom, and Bill's only impression as he entered the dingy flat was one of hopeless decay. The mountainous, soiled mother, at once suspicious and deferential, and the anaemic, beaten Anglo-Saxon asleep on the couch after his Sunday dinner were no more than shadows against the poor walls. But Mae was clean and fresh. No breath of squalor touched her. The pale pure youth of her cheeks, and her thin childish body shining through a new organdie dress, measured up full to the summer day.

"Where you going to take my little girl?" Mrs. Purley asked anxiously.

"I'm going to run away with her," he said, laughing.

"Not with my little girl."

"Oh, yes, I am. I don't see why she hasn't been run away with before."

"Not my little girl."

They held hands going downstairs, but not for an hour did the feeling of being intimate strangers pass. When the first promise of evening blew into the air at five o'clock and the light changed from white to yellow, their eyes met once in a certain way and Bill knew that it was time. They turned up a side road and down a wagon track, and in a moment the spell was around them again—the equal and opposite urge that drew them together. They talked about each other and then their voices grew quiet and they kissed, while chestnut blossoms slid in white diagonals through the air and fell across the car. After a long while an instinct told her that they had stayed long enough. He drove her home.

It went on like that for two months. He would come for her in the late afternoon and they would go for dinner to the shore. Afterward they would drive around until they found the center of the summer night and park there while the enchanted silence spread over them like leaves over the babes in the wood. Some day, naturally, they were going to marry. For the present it was impossible; he must go to work in the fall. Vaguely and with more than a touch of sadness both of them realized that this wasn't true; that if Mae had been of another class an engagement would have been arranged at once. She knew that he lived in a great country house with a park and a caretaker's lodge, that there were stables full of cars and horses, and that house parties and dances took place there all summer. Once they had driven past the gate and Mae's heart was leaden in her breast as she saw that those wide acres would lie between them all her life.

On his part Bill knew that it was impossible to marry Mae Purley. He was an only son and he wore one of those New England names that are carried with one always. Eventually he broached the subject to his mother.

"It isn't her poverty and ignorance," his mother said, among other things. "It's her lack of any standards—common women are common for life. You'd see her impressed by cheap and shallow people, by cheap and shallow things."

"But, mother, this isn't 1850. It isn't as if she were marrying into the royal family."

"If it were, it wouldn't matter. But you have a name that for many generations has stood for leadership and self-control. People who have given up less and taken fewer responsibilities have had nothing to say aloud when men like your father and your Uncle George and your Great-grandfather Frothington held their heads high. Toss your pride away and see what you've left at thirty-five to take you through the rest of your life."

"But you can only live once," he protested—knowing, nevertheless, that what she said was, for him, right. His youth had been pointed to make him understand that exposition of superiority. He knew what it was to be the best, at home, at school, at Harvard. In his senior year he had known men to dodge behind a building and wait in order to walk with him across the Harvard Yard, not to be seen with him out of mere poor snobbishness, but to get something intangible, something he carried within him of the less obvious, less articulate experience of the race.

Several days later he went to see Mae and met her coming out of the flat. They sat on the stairs in the half darkness.

"Just think of these stairs," he said huskily. "Think how many times you've kissed me on these stairs. At night when I've brought you home. On every landing. Last month when we walked up and down together five times before we could say good night."

"I hate these stairs. I wish I never had to go up them any more."

"Oh, Mae, what are we going to do?"

She didn't answer for a moment. "I've been thinking a lot these last three days," she said. "I don't think it's fair to myself to go on like this—or to Al."

"To Al," he said startled. "Have you been seeing Al?"

"We had a long talk last night."

"Al!" he repeated incredulously.

"He wants to get married. He isn't mad any more."

Bill tried suddenly to face the situation he had been dodging for two months, but the situation, with practiced facility, slid around the corner. He moved up a step till he was beside Mae, and put his arm around her.

"Oh, let's get married!" she cried desperately. "You can. If you want to, you can."

"I do want to."

"Then why can't we?"

"We can, but not yet."

"Oh, God, you've said that before."

For a tragic week they quarreled and came together over the bodies of unresolved arguments and irreconcilable facts. They parted finally on a trivial question as to whether he had once kept her waiting half an hour.

Bill went to Europe on the first possible boat and enlisted in an ambulance unit. When America went into the war he transferred to the aviation and Mae's pale face and burning lips faded off, faded out, against the wild dark background of the war.

III

In 1919 Bill fell romantically in love with a girl of his own set. He met her on the Lido and wooed her on golf courses and in fashionable speak-easies and in cars parked at night, loving her much more from the first than he had ever loved Mae. She was a better person, prettier and more intelligent and with a kindlier heart. She loved him; they had much the same tastes and more than ample money.

There was a child, after a while there were four children, then only three again. Bill grew a little stout after thirty, as athletes will. He was always going to take up something strenuous and get into real condition. He worked hard and drank a little too freely every week-end. Later he inherited the country house and lived there in the summer.

When he and Stella had been married eight years they felt safe for each other, safe from the catastrophes that had overtaken the majority of their friends. To Stella this brought relief; Bill, once he had accepted the idea of their safety, was conscious of a certain discontent, a sort of chemical restlessness. With a feeling of disloyalty to Stella, he shyly sounded his friends on the subject and found that in men of his age the symptoms were almost universal. Some blamed it on the war: "There'll never be anything like the war."

It was not variety of woman that he wanted. The mere idea appalled him. There were always women around. If he took a fancy to someone Stella invited her for a week-end, and men who liked Stella fraternally, or even somewhat sentimentally, were as often in the house. But the feeling persisted and grew stronger. Sometimes it would steal over him at dinner—a vast nostalgia—and the people at table would fade out and odd memories of his youth would come back to him. Sometimes a familiar taste or a smell would give him this sensation. Chiefly it had to do with the summer night.

One evening, walking down the lawn with Stella after dinner, the feeling seemed so close that he could almost grasp it. It was in the rustle of the pines, in the wind, in the gardener's radio down behind the tennis court.

"Tomorrow," Stella said, "there'll be a full moon."

She had stopped in a broad path of moonlight and was looking at him. Her hair was pale and lovely in the gentle light. She regarded him for a moment oddly, and he took a step forward as if to put his arms around her; then he stopped, unresponsive and dissatisfied. Stella's expression changed slightly and they walked on.

"That's too bad," he said suddenly. "Because tomorrow I've got to go away."

"Where?"

"To New York. Meeting of the trustees of school. Now that the kids are entered I feel I should."

"You'll be back Sunday?"

"Unless something comes up and I telephone."

"Ad Haughton's coming Sunday, and maybe the Ameses."

"I'm glad you won't be alone."

Suddenly Bill had remembered the boat floating down the river and Mae Purley on the deck under the summer moon. The image became a symbol of his youth, his introduction to life. Not only did he remember the deep excitement of that night but felt it again, her face against his, the rush of air about them as they stood by the lifeboat and the feel of its canvas cover to his hand.

When his car dropped him at Wheatly Village next afternoon he experienced a sensation of fright. Eleven years—she might be dead; quite possibly she had moved away. Any moment he might pass her on the street, a tired, already faded woman pushing a baby carriage and leading an extra child.

"I'm looking for a Miss Mae Purley," he said to a taxi driver. "It might be Fitzpatrick now."

"Fitzpatrick up at the works?"

Inquiries within the station established the fact that Mae Purley was indeed Mrs. Fitzpatrick. They lived just outside of town.

Ten minutes later the taxi stopped before a white Colonial house.

"They made it over from a barn," volunteered the taxi man. "There was a picture of it in one of them magazines."

Bill saw that someone was regarding him from behind the screen door. It was Mae. The door opened slowly and she stood in the hall, unchanged, slender as of old. Instinctively he raised his arms and then, as he took another step forward, instinctively he lowered them.

"Mae."

"Bill."

She was there. For a moment he possessed her, her frailty, her thin smoldering beauty; then he had lost her again. He could no more have embraced her than he could have embraced a stranger.

On the sun porch they stared at each other. "You haven't changed," they said together.

It was gone from her. Words, casual, trivial, and insincere, poured from her mouth as if to fill the sudden vacancy in his heart:

"Imagine seeing you—know you anywhere—thought you'd forgotten me—talking about you only the other night."

Suddenly he was without any inspiration. His mind became an utter blank, and try as he might, he could summon up no attitude to fill it.

"It's a nice place you have here," he said stupidly.

"We like it. You'd never guess it, but we made it out of an old barn."

"The taxi driver told me."

"——stood here for a hundred years empty—got it for almost nothing—pictures of it before and after in *Home and Country Side*."

Without warning his mind went blank again. What was the matter? Was he sick? He had even forgotten why he was here.

He knew only that he was smiling benevolently and that he must hang on to that smile, for if it passed he could never re-create it. What did it mean when one's mind went blank? He must see a doctor tomorrow.

"——since Al's done so well. Of course Mr. Kohlsatt leans on him, so he don't get away much. I get away to New York sometimes. Sometimes we both get away together."

"Well, you certainly have a nice place here," he said desperately. He must see a doctor in the morning. Doctor Flynn or Doctor Keyes or Doctor Given who was at Harvard with him. Or perhaps that specialist who was recommended to him by that woman at the Ameses'; or Doctor Gross or Doctor Studeford or Doctor de Martel——

"——I never touch it, but Al always keeps something in the house. Al's gone to Boston, but I think I can find the key."

——or Doctor Ramsay or old Doctor Ogden, who had brought

him into the world. He hadn't realized that he knew so many doctors. He must make a list.

"——you're just exactly the same."

Suddenly Bill put both hands on his stomach, gave a short coarse laugh and said "Not here." His own act startled and surprised him, but it dissipated the blankness for a moment and he began to gather up the pieces of his afternoon. From her chatter he discovered her to be under the impression that in some vague and sentimental past she had thrown him over. Perhaps she was right. Who was she anyhow— this hard, commonplace article wearing Mae's body for a mask of life? Defiance rose in him.

"Mae, I've been thinking about that boat," he said desperately.

"What boat?"

"The steamboat on the Thames, Mae. I don't think we should let ourselves get old. Get your hat, Mae. Let's go for a boat ride tonight."

"But I don't see the point," she protested. "Do you think just riding on a boat keeps people young? Maybe if it was salt water——"

"Don't you remember that night on the boat?" he said, as if he were talking to a child. "That's how we met. Two months later you threw me over and married Al Fitzpatrick."

"But I didn't marry Al then," she said. "It wasn't till two years later when he got a job as superintendent. There was a Harvard man I used to go around with that I almost married. He knew you. His name was Abbot—Ham Abbot."

"Ham Abbot—you saw him again?"

"We went around for almost a year. I remember Al was wild. He said if I had any more Harvard men around he'd shoot them. But there wasn't anything wrong with it. Ham was just cuckoo about me and I used to let him rave."

Bill had read somewhere that every seven years a change is completed in the individual that makes him different from his self of seven years ago. He clung to the idea desperately. Dimly he saw this person pouring him an enormous glass of applejack, dimly he gulped it down and, through a description of the house, fought his way to the front door.

"Notice the original beams. The beams were what we liked best——" She broke off suddenly. "I remember now about the boat. You were in a launch and you got on board with Ham Abbot that night."

The applejack was strong. Evidently it was fragrant also, for as they started off, the taxi driver volunteered to show him where the gentleman could get some more. He would give him a personal introduction in a place down by the wharf.

Bill sat at a dingy table behind swinging doors and, while the sun went down behind the Thames, disposed of four more applejacks. Then he remembered that he was keeping the taxi waiting. Outside a boy told him that the driver had gone home to supper and would be back in half an hour.

He sauntered over to a bale of goods and sat down, watching the mild activity of the docks. It was dusk presently. Stevedores appeared momentarily against the lighted hold of a barge and jerked quickly out of sight down an invisible incline. Next to the barge lay a steamer and people were going aboard; first a few people and then an increasing crowd. There was a breeze in the air and the moon came up rosy gold with a haze around.

Someone ran into him precipitately in the darkness, tripped, swore and staggered to his feet.

"I'm sorry," said Bill cheerfully. "Hurt yourself?"

"Pardon me," stuttered the young man. "Did I hurt you?"

"Not at all. Here, have a light."

They touched cigarettes.

"Where's the boat going?"

"Just down the river. It's the high-school picnic tonight."

"What?"

"The Wheatly High School picnic. The boat goes down to Groton, then it turns around and comes back."

Bill thought quickly. "Who's the principal of the high school?"

"Mr. McVitty." The young man fidgeted impatiently. "So long, bud. I got to go aboard."

"Me too," whispered Bill to himself. "Me too."

Still he sat there lazily for a moment, listening to the sounds clear and distinct now from the open deck: the high echolalia of the girls, the boys calling significant but obscure jokes to one another across the night. He was feeling fine. The air seemed to have distributed the applejack to all the rusty and unused corners of his body. He bought another pint, stowed it in his hip pocket and walked on board with all the satisfaction, the insouciance of a trans-atlantic traveler.

A girl standing in a group near the gangplank raised her eyes to him as he went past. She was slight and fair. Her mouth curved down and then broke upward as she smiled, half at him, half at the man beside her. Someone made a remark and the group laughed. Once again her glance slipped sideways and met his for an instant as he passed by.

Mr. McVitty was on the top deck with half a dozen other teachers, who moved aside at Bill's breezy approach.

"Good evening, Mr. McVitty. You don't remember me."

"I'm afraid I don't, sir." The principal regarded him with tentative noncommittal eyes.

"Yet I took a trip with you on this same boat, exactly eleven years ago tonight."

"This boat, sir, was only built last year."

"Well, a boat like it," said Bill. "I wouldn't have known the difference myself."

Mr. McVitty made no reply. After a moment Bill continued confidently, "We found that night that we were both sons of John Harvard."

"Yes?"

"In fact on that very day I had been pulling an oar against what I might refer to as dear old Yale."

Mr. McVitty's eyes narrowed. He came closer to Bill and his nose wrinkled slightly.

"Old Eli," said Bill; "in fact, Eli Yale."

"I see," said Mr. McVitty dryly. "And what can I do for you tonight?"

Someone came up with a question and in the enforced silence it occurred to Bill that he was present on the slightest of all pretexts—a previous and unacknowledged acquaintance. He was relieved when a dull rumble and a quiver of the deck indicated that they had left the shore.

Mr. McVitty, disengaged, turned toward him with a slight frown. "I seem to remember you now," he said. "We took three of you aboard from a motor boat and we let you dance. Unfortunately the evening ended in a fight."

Bill hesitated. In eleven years his relation to Mr. McVitty had somehow changed. He recalled Mr. McVitty as a more negligible, more easily dealt with person. There had been no such painful difficulties before.

"Perhaps you wonder how I happen to be here?" he suggested mildly.

"To be frank, I do, Mr——"

"Frothington," supplied Bill, and he added brazenly, "It's rather a sentimental excursion for me. My greatest romance began on the evening you speak of. That was when I first met—my wife."

Mr. McVitty's attention was caught at last. "You married one of our girls?"

Bill nodded. "That's why I wanted to take this trip tonight."

"Your wife's with you?"

"No."

"I don't understand——" He broke off, and suggested gently, "Or maybe I do. Your wife is dead?"

After a moment Bill nodded. Somewhat to his surprise two great tears rolled suddenly down his face.

Mr. McVitty put his hand on Bill's shoulder. "I'm sorry," he said. "I understand your feeling, Mr. Frothington, and I respect it. Please make yourself at home."

After a nibble at his bottle Bill stood in the door of the salon watching the dance. It might have been eleven years ago. There were the high-school characters that he and Ham and Ellie had laughed at afterward—the fat boy who surely played center on the football team and the adolescent hero with the pompadour and the blatant good manners, president of his class. The pretty girl who had looked at him by the gangplank danced past him, and with a quick lift of his heart he placed her, too; her confidence and the wide but careful distribution of her favors—she was the popular girl, as Mae had been eleven years before.

Next time she went past he touched the shoulder of the boy she was dancing with. "May I have some of this?" he said.

"What?" her partner gasped.

"May I have some of this dance?"

The boy stared at him without relinquishing his hold.

"Oh, it's all right, Red," she said impatiently. "That's the way they do now."

Red stepped sulkily aside. Bill bent his arm as nearly as he could into the tortuous clasp that they were all using, and started.

"I saw you talking to Mr. McVitty," said the girl, looking up into his face with a bright smile. "I don't know you, but I guess it's all right."

"I saw you before that."

"When?"

"Getting on the boat."

"I don't remember."

"What's your name?" he asked.

"May Schaffer. What's the matter?"

"Do you spell it with an *e*?"

"No; why?"

A quartet of boys had edged toward them. One of its members suddenly shot out as if propelled from inside the group and bumped awkwardly against Bill.

"Can I have part of this dance?" asked the boy with a sort of giggle.

Without enthusiasm Bill let go. When the next dance began he cut in again. She was lovely. Her happiness in herself, in the evening would have transfigured a less pretty girl. He wanted to talk to her alone and was about to suggest that they go outside when there was a repetition of what had happened before—a young man was apparently shot by force from a group to Bill's side.

"Can I have part of this dance?"

Bill joined Mr. McVitty by the rail. "Pleasant evening," he remarked. "Don't you dance?"

"I enjoy dancing," said Mr. McVitty; and he added pointedly, "In my position it doesn't seem quite the thing to dance with young girls."

"That's nonsense," said Bill pleasantly. "Have a drink?"

Mr. McVitty walked suddenly away.

When he danced with May again he was cut in on almost immediately. People were cutting in all over the floor now—evidently he had started something. He cut back, and again he started to suggest that they go outside, but he saw that her attention was held by some horseplay going on across the room.

"I got a swell love nest up in the Bronx," somebody was saying.

"Won't you come outside?" said Bill. "There's the most wonderful moon."

"I'd rather dance."

"We could dance out there."

She leaned away from him and looked up with innocent scorn into his eyes.

"Where'd you get it?" she said.

"Get what?"

"All the happiness."

Before he could answer, someone cut in. For a moment he imagined that the boy had said, "Part of this dance, daddy?" but his annoyance at May's indifference drove the idea from his mind. Next time he went to the point at once.

"I live near here," he said. "I'd be awfully pleased if I could call and drive you over for a week-end sometime."

"What?" she asked vaguely. Again she was listening to a miniature farce being staged in the corner.

"My wife would like so much to have you," went on Bill. Great dreams of what he could do for this girl for old times' sake rose in his mind.

Her head swung toward him curiously. "Why, Mr. McVitty told somebody your wife was dead."

"She isn't," said Bill.

Out of the corner of his eye he saw the inevitable catapult coming and danced quickly away from it.

A voice rang out: "Just look at old daddy step."

"Ask him if I can have some of this dance."

Afterward Bill only remembered the evening up to that point. A crowd swirled around him and someone kept demanding persistently who was a young boiler maker.

He decided, naturally enough, to teach them a lesson, as he had done before, and he told them so. Then there was a long discussion as to whether he could swim. After that the confusion deepened; there were blows and a short sharp struggle. He picked up the story himself in what must have been several minutes later, when his head emerged from the cool waters of the Thames River.

The river was white with the moon, which had changed from rosy gold to a wafer of shining cheese on high. It was some time before he could locate the direction of the shore, but he moved around unworried in the water. The boat was a mere speck now, far down the river, and he laughed to think how little it all mattered, how little anything mattered. Then, feeling sure that he had his wind and wondering if the taxi was still waiting at Wheatly Village, he struck out for the dark shore.

IV

He was worried as he drew near home next afternoon, possessed of a dark, unfounded fear. It was based, of course, on his own silly transgression. Stella would somehow hear of it. In his reaction from the debonair confidence of last night, it seemed inevitable that Stella would hear of it.

"Who's here?" he asked the butler immediately.

"No one, sir. The Ameses came about an hour ago, but there was no word, so they went on. They said——"

"Isn't my wife here?"

"Mrs. Frothington left yesterday just after you."

The whips of panic descended upon him.

"How long after me?"

"Almost immediately, sir. The telephone rang and she answered it, and almost immediately she had her bag packed and left the house."

"Mr. Ad Haughton didn't come?"

"I haven't seen Mr. Haughton."

It had happened. The spirit of adventure had seized Stella too. He knew that her life had been not without a certain pressure from sentimental men, but that she would ever go anywhere without telling him——

He threw himself face downward on a couch. What had happened? He had never meant things to happen. Was that what she had meant when she had looked at him in that peculiar way the other night?

He went upstairs. Almost as soon as he entered the big bedroom he saw the note, written on blue stationery lest he miss it against the white pillow. In his misery an old counsel of his mother's came back to him: "The more terrible things seem the more you've got to keep yourself in shape."

Trembling, he divested himself of his clothes, turned on a bath and lathered his face. Then he poured himself a drink and shaved. It was like a dream, this change in his life. She was no longer his; even if she came back she was no longer his. Everything was different—this room, himself, everything that had existed yesterday. Suddenly he wanted it back. He got out of the bathtub and knelt down on the bath mat beside it and prayed. He prayed for Stella and himself and Ad Haughton; he prayed crazily for the restoration of his life—the life that he had just as crazily cut in two. When he came out of the bathroom with a towel around him, Ad Haughton was sitting on the bed.

"Hello, Bill. Where's your wife?"

"Just a minute," Bill answered. He went back into the bathroom and swallowed a draught of rubbing alcohol guaranteed to produce violent gastric disturbances. Then he stuck his head out the door casually.

"Mouthful of gargle," he explained. "How are you, Ad? Open that envelope on the pillow and we'll see where she is."

"She's gone to Europe with a dentist. Or rather her dentist is going to Europe, so she had to dash to New York——"

He hardly heard. His mind, released from worry, had drifted off again. There would be a full moon tonight, or almost a full moon. Something had happened under a full moon once. What it was he was unable for the moment to remember.

His long, lanky body, his little lost soul in the universe, sat there on the bathroom window seat.

"I'm probably the world's worst guy," he said, shaking his head at himself in the mirror—"probably the world's worst guy. But I can't help it. At my age you can't fight against what you know you are."

Trying his best to be better, he sat there faithfully for an hour. Then it was twilight and there were voices downstairs, and suddenly there it was, in the sky over his lawn, all the restless longing after fleeing youth in all the world—the bright uncapturable moon.

The Bowl

(*The Saturday Evening Post*, 21 January 1928)*

"The Bowl" was written in September-November 1927 at "Ellerslie." It began as what Fitzgerald described as a "two part sophisticated football story" and gave him considerable trouble as he tried to rush it for publication during the football season. After Fitzgerald cut it, Thomas Costain, fiction editor of the *Post*, was happy to buy it for $3500, informing Harold Ober that Fitzgerald had "got the real spirit of the game as it has perhaps never been done before."

Given Fitzgerald's dreams of gridiron glory ("the shoulder pads worn for one day on the Princeton freshman football field") and his admiration for the Ivy League football gods of his youth (Hobey Baker and Buz Law of Princeton and Ted Coy of Yale), it is surprising that he did not write more football fiction. The game as it was played before World War I appealed to his romantic instincts—a gentleman's sport dominated by Ivy League aristocrats. Fitzgerald's second story, "Reade, Substitute Right Half" (*St. Paul Academy Now and Then*, February 1910) expressed Fitzgerald's hopes for football recognition; but except for two Basil stories with football scenes, "The Bowl" is Fitzgerald's only professionally published football story. This story is also about something else: Fitzgerald's respect for disciplined young women. Daisy Cary, the actress, is a proper mate for Dolly Harlan because she understands the responsibilities of being a public figure. Daisy is obviously a trial sketch for Rosemary Hoyt of *Tender Is the Night*, for both were based on Lois Moran, the actress Fitzgerald met in Hollywood in 1927.

There was a man in my class at Princeton who never went to football games. He spent his Saturday afternoons delving for minutiae about Greek athletics and the somewhat fixed battles between Christians and wild beasts under the Antonines. Lately—several years out of college—he has discovered football players and is making etchings of them in the manner of the late George Bellows. But he was once unresponsive to the very spectacle at his door, and I suspect the originality of his judgments on what is beautiful, what is remarkable and what is fun.

I reveled in football, as audience, amateur statistician and foiled participant—for I had played in prep school, and once there was a

*"The Bowl" is in *The Bodley Head Scott Fitzgerald*, Vol. V (London: Bodley Head, 1963) but has not been collected in an American edition.

headline in the school newspaper: "Deering and Mullins Star Against Taft in Stiff Game Saturday." When I came in to lunch after the battle the school stood up and clapped and the visiting coach shook hands with me and prophesied—incorrectly—that I was going to be heard from. The episode is laid away in the most pleasant lavender of my past. That year I grew very tall and thin, and when at Princeton the following fall I looked anxiously over the freshman candidates and saw the polite disregard with which they looked back at me, I realized that that particular dream was over. Keene said he might make me into a very fair pole vaulter—and he did—but it was a poor substitute; and my terrible disappointment that I wasn't going to be a great football player was probably the foundation of my friendship with Dolly Harlan. I want to begin this story about Dolly with a little rehashing of the Yale game up at New Haven, sophomore year.

Dolly was started at halfback; this was his first big game. I roomed with him and I had scented something peculiar about his state of mind, so I didn't let him out of the corner of my eye during the whole first half. With field glasses I could see the expression on his face; it was strained and incredulous, as it had been the day of his father's death, and it remained so, long after any nervousness had had time to wear off. I thought he was sick and wondered why Keene didn't see and take him out; it wasn't until later that I learned what was the matter.

It was the Yale Bowl. The size of it or the inclosed shape of it or the height of the sides had begun to get on Dolly's nerves when the team practiced there the day before. In that practice he dropped one or two punts, for almost the first time in his life, and he began thinking it was because of the Bowl.

There is a new disease called agoraphobia—afraid of crowds— and another called siderodromophobia—afraid of railroad travel-ing—and my friend Doctor Glock, the psychoanalyst, would probably account easily for Dolly's state of mind. But here's what Dolly told me afterward:

"Yale would punt and I'd look up. The minute I looked up, the sides of that damn pan would seem to go shooting up too. Then when the ball started to come down, the sides began leaning forward and bending over me until I could see all the people on the top seats screaming at me and shaking their fists. At the last minute I couldn't see the ball at all, but only the Bowl; every time it was just luck that I was under it and every time I juggled it in my hands."

To go back to the game. I was in the cheering section with a good seat on the forty-yard line—good, that is, except when a very vague graduate, who had lost his friends and his hat, stood up in front of me at intervals and faltered, "Stob Ted Coy!" under the impression that we were watching a game played a dozen years before. When he realized finally that he was funny he began performing for the gallery and aroused a chorus of whistles and boos until he was dragged unwillingly under the stand.

It was a good game—what is known in college publications as a historic game. A picture of the team that played it now hangs in every barber shop in Princeton, with Captain Gottlieb in the middle wearing a white sweater, to show that they won a championship. Yale had had a poor season, but they had the breaks in the first quarter, which ended 3 to 0 in their favor.

Between quarters I watched Dolly. He walked around panting and sucking a water bottle and still wearing that strained stunned expression. Afterward he told me he was saying over and over to himself: "I'll speak to Roper. I'll tell him between halves. I'll tell him I can't go through this any more." Several times already he had felt an almost irresistible impulse to shrug his shoulders and trot off the field, for it was not only this unexpected complex about the Bowl; the truth was that Dolly fiercely and bitterly hated the game.

He hated the long, dull period of training, the element of personal conflict, the demand on his time, the monotony of the routine and the nervous apprehension of disaster just before the end. Sometimes he imagined that all the others detested it as much as he did, and fought down their aversion as he did and carried it around inside them like a cancer that they were afraid to recognize. Sometimes he imagined that a man here and there was about to tear off the mask and say, "Dolly, do you hate this lousy business as much as I do?"

His feeling had begun back at St. Regis' School and he had come up to Princeton with the idea that he was through with football forever. But upper classmen from St. Regis kept stopping him on the campus and asking him how much he weighed, and he was nominated for vice president of our class on the strength of his athletic reputation—and it was autumn, with achievement in the air. He wandered down to freshman practice one afternoon, feeling oddly lost and dissatisfied, and smelled the turf and smelled the thrilling season. In half an hour he was lacing on a pair of borrowed shoes and two weeks later he was captain of the freshman team.

Once committed, he saw that he had made a mistake; he even considered leaving college. For, with his decision to play, Dolly assumed a moral responsibility, personal to him, besides. To lose or to let down, or to be let down, was simply intolerable to him. It offended his Scotch sense of waste. Why sweat blood for an hour with only defeat at the end?

Perhaps the worst of it was that he wasn't really a star player. No team in the country could have spared using him, but he could do no spectacular thing superlatively well, neither run, pass nor kick. He was five-feet-eleven and weighed a little more than a hundred and sixty; he was a first-rate defensive man, sure in interference, a fair line plunger and a fair punter. He never fumbled and he was never inadequate; his presence, his constant cold sure aggression, had a strong effect on other men. Morally, he captained any team he played on and that was why Roper had spent so much time trying to get length in his kicks all season—he wanted him in the game.

In the second quarter Yale began to crack. It was a mediocre team composed of flashy material, but uncoordinated because of injuries and impending changes in the Yale coaching system. The quarterback, Josh Logan, had been a wonder at Exeter—I could testify to that—where games can be won by the sheer confidence and spirit of a single man. But college teams are too highly organized to respond so simply and boyishly, and they recover less easily from fumbles and errors of judgment behind the line.

So, with nothing to spare, with much grunting and straining, Princeton moved steadily down the field. On the Yale twenty-yard line things suddenly happened. A Princeton pass was intercepted; the Yale man, excited by his own opportunity, dropped the ball and it bobbed leisurely in the general direction of the Yale goal. Jack Devlin and Dolly Harlan of Princeton and somebody—I forget who—from Yale were all about the same distance from it. What Dolly did in that split second was all instinct; it presented no problem to him. He was a natural athlete and in a crisis his nervous system thought for him. He might have raced the two others for the ball; instead, he took out the Yale man with savage precision while Devlin scooped up the ball and ran ten yards for a touchdown.

This was when the sports writers still saw games through the eyes of Ralph Henry Barbour. The press box was right behind me, and as Princeton lined up to kick goal I heard the radio man ask:

"Who's Number 22?"

"Harlan."

"Harlan is going to kick goal. Devlin, who made the touchdown, comes from Lawrenceville School. He is twenty years old. The ball went true between the bars."

Between the halves, as Dolly sat shaking with fatigue in the locker room, Little, the back-field coach, came and sat beside him.

"When the ends are right on you, don't be afraid to make a fair catch," Little said. "That big Havemeyer is liable to jar the ball right out of your hands."

Now was the time to say it: "I wish you'd tell Bill——" But the words twisted themselves into a trivial question about the wind. His feeling would have to be explained, gone into, and there wasn't time. His own self seemed less important in this room, redolent with the tired breath, the ultimate effort, the exhaustion of ten other men. He was shamed by a harsh sudden quarrel that broke out between an end and tackle; he resented the former players in the room—especially the graduate captain of two years before, who was a little tight and over-vehement about the referee's favoritism. It seemed terrible to add one more jot to all this strain and annoyance. But he might have come out with it all the same if Little hadn't kept saying in a low voice: "What a take-out, Dolly! What a beautiful take-out!" and if Little's hand hadn't rested there, patting his shoulder.

II

In the third quarter Joe Dougherty kicked an easy field goal from the twenty-yard line and we felt safe, until toward twilight a series of desperate forward passes brought Yale close to a score. But Josh Logan had exhausted his personality in sheer bravado and he was outguessed by the defense at the last. As the substitutes came running in, Princeton began a last march down the field. Then abruptly it was over and the crowd poured from the stands, and Gottlieb, grabbing the ball, leaped up in the air. For a while everything was confused and crazy and happy; I saw some freshmen try to carry Dolly, but they were shy and he got away.

We all felt a great personal elation. We hadn't beaten Yale for three years and now everything was going to be all right. It meant a good winter at college, something pleasant and slick to think back upon in the damp cold days after Christmas, when a bleak futility settles over a university town. Down on the field, an improvised and uproarious team ran through plays with a derby, until the snake dance rolled over them and blotted them out. Outside the Bowl, I saw two abysmally gloomy and disgusted Yale men get into a waiting taxi and in a tone of final abnegation tell the driver "New York." You couldn't find Yale men; in the manner of the vanquished, they had absolutely melted away.

I begin Dolly's story with my memories of this game because that evening the girl walked into it. She was a friend of Josephine Pickman's and the four of us were going to drive up to the Midnight Frolic in New York. When I suggested to him that he'd be too tired he laughed dryly—he'd have gone anywhere that night to get the feel and rhythm of football out of his head. He walked into the hall of

Josephine's house at half-past six, looking as if he'd spent the day in the barber shop save for a small and fetching strip of court plaster over one eye. He was one of the handsomest men I ever knew, anyhow; he appeared tall and slender in street clothes, his hair was dark, his eyes big and sensitive and dark, his nose aquiline and, like all his features, somehow romantic. It didn't occur to me then, but I suppose he was pretty vain—not conceited, but vain—for he always dressed in brown or soft light gray, with black ties, and people don't match themselves so successfully by accident.

He was smiling a little to himself as he came in. He shook my hand buoyantly and said, "Why, what a surprise to meet you here, Mr. Deering," in a kidding way. Then he saw the two girls through the long hall, one dark and shining, like himself, and one with gold hair that was foaming and frothing in the firelight, and said in the happiest voice I've ever heard, "Which one is mine?"

"Either you want, I guess."

"Seriously, which is Pickman?"

"She's light."

"Then the other one belongs to me. Isn't that the idea?"

"I think I'd better warn them about the state you're in."

Miss Thorne, small, flushed and lovely, stood beside the fire. Dolly went right up to her.

"You're mine," he said; "you belong to me."

She looked at him coolly, making up her mind; suddenly she liked him and smiled. But Dolly wasn't satisfied. He wanted to do something incredibly silly or startling to express his untold jubilation that he was free.

"I love you," he said. He took her hand, his brown velvet eyes regarding her tenderly, unseeingly, convincingly. "I love you."

For a moment the corners of her lips fell as if in dismay that she had met someone stronger, more confident, more challenging than herself. Then, as she drew herself together visibly, he dropped her hand and the little scene in which he had expended the tension of the afternoon was over.

It was a bright cold November night and the rush of air past the open car brought a vague excitement, a sense that we were hurrying at top speed toward a brilliant destiny. The roads were packed with cars that came to long inexplicable halts while police, blinded by the lights, walked up and down the line giving obscure commands. Before we had been gone an hour New York began to be a distant hazy glow against the sky.

Miss Thorne, Josephine told me, was from Washington, and had just come down from a visit in Boston.

"For the game?" I said.

"No; she didn't go to the game."

"That's too bad. If you'd let me know I could have picked up a seat——"

"She wouldn't have gone. Vienna never goes to games."

I remembered now that she hadn't even murmured the conventional congratulations to Dolly.

"She hates football. Her brother was killed in a prep-school game last year. I wouldn't have brought her tonight, but when we got home from the game I saw she'd been sitting there holding a book open at the same page all afternoon. You see, he was this wonderful kid and her family saw it happen and naturally never got over it."

"But does she mind being with Dolly?"

"Of course not. She just ignores football. If anyone mentions it she simply changes the subject."

I was glad that it was Dolly and not, say, Jack Devlin who was sitting back there with her. And I felt rather sorry for Dolly. However strongly he felt about the game, he must have waited for some acknowledgment that his effort had existed.

He was probably giving her credit for a subtle consideration, yet, as the images of the afternoon flashed into his mind he might have welcomed a compliment to which he could respond "What nonsense!" Neglected entirely, the images would become insistent and obtrusive.

I turned around and was somewhat startled to find that Miss Thorne was in Dolly's arms; I turned quickly back and decided to let them take care of themselves.

As we waited for a traffic light on upper Broadway, I saw a sporting extra headlined with the score of the game. The green sheet was more real than the afternoon itself—succinct, condensed and clear:

PRINCETON CONQUERS YALE 10-3

SEVENTY THOUSAND WATCH TIGER TRIM
BULLDOG

DEVLIN SCORES ON YALE FUMBLE

There it was—not like the afternoon, muddled, uncertain, patchy and scrappy to the end, but nicely mounted now in the setting of the past:

PRINCETON, 10; YALE, 3

Achievement was a curious thing, I thought. Dolly was largely responsible for that. I wondered if all things that screamed in the headlines were simply arbitrary accents. As if people should ask, "What does it look like?"

"It looks most like a cat."

"Well, then, let's call it a cat."

My mind, brightened by the lights and the cheerful tumult, suddenly grasped the fact that all achievement was a placing of emphasis—a molding of the confusion of life into form.

Josephine stopped in front of the New Amsterdam Theater, where her chauffeur met us and took the car. We were early, but a small buzz of excitement went up from the undergraduates waiting in the lobby—"There's Dolly Harlan"—and as we moved toward the elevator several acquaintances came up to shake his hand. Apparently oblivious to these ceremonies, Miss Thorne caught my eye and smiled. I looked at her with curiosity; Josephine had imparted the rather surprising information that she was just sixteen years old. I suppose my return smile was rather patronizing, but instantly I realized that the fact could not be imposed on. In spite of all the warmth and delicacy of her face, the figure that somehow reminded me of an exquisite, romanticized little ballerina, there was a quality in her that was as hard as steel. She had been brought up in Rome, Vienna and Madrid, with flashes of Washington; her father was one of those charming American diplomats who, with fine obstinacy, try to re-create the Old World in their children by making their education rather more royal than that of princes. Miss Thorne was sophisticated. In spite of all the abandon of American young people, sophistication is still a Continental monopoly.

We walked in upon a number in which a dozen chorus girls in orange and black were racing wooden horses against another dozen dressed in Yale blue. When the lights went on, Dolly was recognized and some Princeton students set up a clatter of approval with the little wooden hammers given out for applause; he moved his chair unostentatiously into a shadow.

Almost immediately a flushed and very miserable young man appeared beside our table. In better form he would have been extremely prepossessing; indeed, he flashed a charming and dazzling smile at Dolly, as if requesting his permission to speak to Miss Thorne.

Then he said, "I thought you weren't coming to New York tonight."

"Hello, Carl." She looked up at him coolly.

"Hello, Vienna. That's just it; 'Hello Vienna—Hello Carl.' But why? I thought you weren't coming to New York tonight."

Miss Thorne made no move to introduce the man, but we were conscious of his somewhat raised voice.

"I thought you promised me you weren't coming."

"I didn't expect to, child. I just left Boston this morning."

"And who did you meet in Boston—the fascinating Tunti?" he demanded.

"I didn't meet anyone, child."

"Oh, yes, you did! You met the fascinating Tunti and you discussed living on the Riviera." She didn't answer. "Why are you so dishonest, Vienna?" he went on. "Why did you tell me on the phone——"

"I am not going to be lectured," she said, her tone changing suddenly. "I told you if you took another drink I was through with you. I'm a person of my word and I'd be enormously happy if you went away."

"Vienna!" he cried in a sinking, trembling voice.

At this point I got up and danced with Josephine. When we came back there were people at the table—the men to whom we were to hand over Josephine and Miss Thorne, for I had allowed for Dolly being tired, and several others. One of them was Al Ratoni, the composer, who, it appeared, had been entertained at the embassy in Madrid. Dolly Harlan had drawn his chair aside and was watching the dancers. Just as the lights went down for a new number a man came up out of the darkness and leaning over Miss Thorne whispered in her ear. She started and made a motion to rise, but he put his hand on her shoulder and forced her down. They began to talk together in low excited voices.

The tables were packed close at the old Frolic. There was a man rejoining the party next to us and I couldn't help hearing what he said:

"A young fellow just tried to kill himself down in the wash room. He shot himself through the shoulder, but they got the pistol away before——" A minute later his voice again: "Carl Sanderson, they said."

When the number was over I looked around. Vienna Thorne was staring very rigidly at Miss Lillian Lorraine, who was rising toward the ceiling as an enormous telephone doll. The man who had leaned over Vienna was gone and the others were obliviously unaware that anything had happened. I turned to Dolly and suggested that he and I had better go, and after a glance at Vienna in which reluctance, weariness and then resignation were mingled, he consented. On the way to the hotel I told Dolly what had happened.

"Just some souse," he remarked after a moment's fatigued

consideration. "He probably tried to miss himself and get a little sympathy. I suppose those are the sort of things a really attractive girl is up against all the time."

This wasn't my attitude. I could see that mussed white shirt front with very young blood pumping over it, but I didn't argue, and after a while Dolly said, "I suppose that sounds brutal, but it seems a little soft and weak, doesn't it? Perhaps that's just the way I feel tonight."

When Dolly undressed I saw that he was a mass of bruises, but he assured me that none of them would keep him awake. Then I told him why Miss Thorne hadn't mentioned the game and he woke up suddenly; the familiar glitter came back into his eyes.

"So that was it! I wondered. I thought maybe you'd told her not to say anything about it."

Later, when the lights had been out half an hour, he suddenly said "I see" in a loud clear voice. I don't know whether he was awake or asleep.

III

I've put down as well as I can everything I can remember about the first meeting between Dolly and Miss Vienna Thorne. Reading it over, it sounds casual and insignificant, but the evening lay in the shadow of the game and all that happened seemed like that. Vienna went back to Europe almost immediately and for fifteen months passed out of Dolly's life.

It was a good year—it still rings true in my memory as a good year. Sophomore year is the most dramatic at Princeton, just as junior year is at Yale. It's not only the elections to the upperclass clubs but also everyone's destiny begins to work itself out. You can tell pretty well who's going to come through, not only by their immediate success but by the way they survive failure. Life was very full for me. I made the board of the Princetonian, and our house burned down out in Dayton, and I had a silly half-hour fist fight in the gymnasium with a man who later became one of my closest friends, and in March Dolly and I joined the upperclass club we'd always wanted to be in. I fell in love, too, but it would be an irrelevancy to tell about that here.

April came and the first real Princeton weather, the lazy green-and-gold afternoons and the bright thrilling nights haunted with the hour of senior singing. I was happy, and Dolly would have been happy except for the approach of another football season. He was playing baseball, which excused him from spring practice, but the bands were beginning to play faintly in the distance. They rose to concert pitch during the summer, when he had to answer the question, "Are you going back early for football?" a dozen times a day. On the fifteenth of September he was down in the dust and heat of late-summer Princeton, crawling over the ground on all fours, trotting through the old routine and turning himself into just the sort of specimen that I'd have given ten years of my life to be.

From first to last, he hated it, and never let down for a minute. He went into the Yale game that fall weighing a hundred and fifty-three pounds, though that wasn't the weight printed in the paper, and he and Joe McDonald were the only men who played all through that disastrous game. He could have been captain by lifting his finger— but that involves some stuff that I know confidentially and can't tell. His only horror was that by some chance he'd have to accept it. Two seasons! He didn't even talk about it now. He left the room or the club when the conversation veered around to football. He stopped announcing to me that he "wasn't going through that business any more." This time it took the Christmas holidays to drive that unhappy look from his eyes.

Then at the New Year Miss Vienna Thorne came home from Madrid and in February a man named Case brought her down to the Senior Prom.

IV

She was even prettier than she had been before, softer, externally at least, and a tremendous success. People passing her on the street jerked their heads quickly to look at her—a frightened look, as if they realized that they had almost missed something. She was temporarily tired of European men, she told me, letting me gather that there had been some sort of unfortunate love affair. She was coming out in Washington next fall.

Vienna and Dolly. She disappeared with him for two hours the night of the club dances, and Harold Case was in despair. When they walked in again at midnight I thought they were the handsomest pair I saw. They were both shining with that peculiar luminosity that dark people sometimes have. Harold Case took one look at them and went proudly home.

Vienna came back a week later, solely to see Dolly. Late that evening I had occasion to go up to the deserted club for a book and they called me from the rear terrace, which opens out to the ghostly stadium and to an unpeopled sweep of night. It was an hour of thaw, with spring voices in the warm wind, and wherever there was light

enough you could see drops glistening and falling. You could feel the
cold melting out of the stars and the bare trees and shrubbery toward
Stony Brook turning lush in the darkness.

They were sitting together on a wicker bench, full of themselves
and romantic and happy.

"We had to tell someone about it," they said.

"Now can I go?"

"No, Jeff," they insisted; "stay here and envy us. We're in the
stage where we want someone to envy us. Do you think we're a good
match?"

What could I say?

"Dolly's going to finish at Princeton next year," Vienna went on,
"but we're going to announce it after the season in Washington in the
autumn."

I was vaguely relieved to find that it was going to be a long
engagement.

"I approve of you, Jeff," Vienna said.

"I want Dolly to have more friends like you. You're stimulating
for him—you have ideas. I told Dolly he could probably find others
like you if he looked around his class."

Dolly and I both felt a little uncomfortable.

"She doesn't want me to be a Babbitt," he said lightly.

"Dolly's perfect," asserted Vienna. "He's the most beautiful
thing that ever lived, and you'll find I'm very good for him, Jeff.
Already I've helped him make up his mind about one important
thing." I guessed what was coming. "He's going to speak a little piece
if they bother him about playing football next autumn, aren't you,
child?"

"Oh, they won't bother me," said Dolly uncomfortably. "It isn't
like that——"

"Well, they'll try to bully you into it, morally."

"Oh, no," he objected. "It isn't like that. Don't let's talk about it
now, Vienna. It's such a swell night."

Such a swell night! When I think of my own love passages at
Princeton, I always summon up that night of Dolly's, as if it had been
I and not he who sat there with youth and hope and beauty in his
arms.

Dolly's mother took a place on Ram's Point, Long Island, for the
summer, and late in August I went East to visit him. Vienna had been
there a week when I arrived, and my impressions were: first, that he
was very much in love; and, second, that it was Vienna's party. All
sorts of curious people used to drop in to see Vienna. I wouldn't mind
them now—I'm more sophisticated—but then they seemed rather a

blot on the summer. They were all slightly famous in one way or another, and it was up to you to find out how. There was a lot of talk, and especially there was much discussion of Vienna's personality. Whenever I was alone with any of the other guests we discussed Vienna's sparkling personality. They thought I was dull, and most of them thought Dolly was dull. He was better in his line than any of them were in theirs, but his was the only specialty that wasn't mentioned. Still, I felt vaguely that I was being improved and I boasted about knowing most of those people in the ensuing year, and was annoyed when people failed to recognize their names.

The day before I left, Dolly turned his ankle playing tennis, and afterward he joked about it to me rather somberly.

"If I'd only broken it things would be so much easier. Just a quarter of an inch more bend and one of the bones would have snapped. By the way, look here."

He tossed me a letter. It was a request that he report at Princeton for practice on September fifteenth and that meanwhile he begin getting himself in good condition.

"You're not going to play this fall?"

He shook his head.

"No. I'm not a child any more. I've played for two years and I want this year free. If I went through it again it'd be a piece of moral cowardice."

"I'm not arguing, but—would you have taken this stand if it hadn't been for Vienna?"

"Of course I would. If I let myself be bullied into it I'd never be able to look myself in the face again."

Two weeks later I got the following letter:

Dear Jeff: When you read this you'll be somewhat surprised. I have, actually, this time, broken my ankle playing tennis. I can't even walk with crutches at present; it's on a chair in front of me swollen up and wrapped up as big as a house as I write. No one, not even Vienna, knows about our conversation on the same subject last summer and so let us both absolutely forget it. One thing, though—an ankle is a darn hard thing to break, though I never knew it before.

I feel happier than I have for years—no early-season practice, no sweat and suffer, a little discomfort and inconvenience, but free. I feel as if I've outwitted a whole lot of people, and it's nobody's business but that of your

Machiavellian (sic) friend,

DOLLY.

P.S. You might as well tear up this letter.

It didn't sound like Dolly at all.

V

Once down at Princeton I asked Frank Kane—who sells sporting goods on Nassau Street and can tell you offhand the name of the scrub quarterback in 1901—what was the matter with Bob Tatnall's team senior year.

"Injuries and tough luck," he said. "They wouldn't sweat after the hard games. Take Joe McDonald, for instance, All-American tackle the year before; he was slow and stale, and he knew it and didn't care. It's a wonder Bill got that outfit through the season at all."

I sat in the stands with Dolly and watched them beat Lehigh 3-0 and tie Bucknell by a fluke. The next week we were trimmed 14-0 by Notre Dame. On the day of the Notre Dame game Dolly was in Washington with Vienna, but he was awfully curious about it when he came back next day. He had all the sporting pages of all the papers and he sat reading them and shaking his head. Then he stuffed them suddenly into the waste-paper basket.

"This college is football crazy," he announced. "Do you know that English teams don't even train for sports?"

I didn't enjoy Dolly so much in those days. It was curious to see him with nothing to do. For the first time in his life he hung around—around the room, around the club, around casual groups— he who had always been going somewhere with dynamic indolence. His passage along a walk had once created groups—groups of classmates who wanted to walk with him, of underclassmen who followed with their eyes a moving shrine. He became democratic, he mixed around, and it was somehow not appropriate. He explained that he wanted to know more men in his class.

But people want their idols a little above them, and Dolly had been a sort of private and special idol. He began to hate to be alone, and that, of course, was most apparent to me. If I got up to go out and he didn't happen to be writing a letter to Vienna, he'd ask "Where are you going?" in a rather alarmed way and make an excuse to limp along with me.

"Are you glad you did it, Dolly?" I asked him suddenly one day. He looked at me with reproach behind the defiance in his eyes. "Of course I'm glad."

"I wish you were in that back field, all the same."

"It wouldn't matter a bit. This year's game's in the Bowl. I'd probably be dropping kicks for them."

The week of the Navy game he suddenly began going to all the practices. He worried; that terrible sense of responsibility was at work. Once he had hated the mention of football; now he thought and talked of nothing else. The night before the Navy game I woke up several times to find the lights burning brightly in his room.

We lost 7 to 3 on Navy's last-minute forward pass over Devlin's head. After the first half Dolly left the stands and sat down with the players on the field. When he joined me afterward his face was smudgy and dirty as if he had been crying.

The game was in Baltimore that year. Dolly and I were going to spend the night in Washington with Vienna, who was giving a dance. We rode over there in an atmosphere of sullen gloom and it was all I could do to keep him from snapping out at two naval officers who were holding an exultant post mortem in the seat behind.

The dance was what Vienna called her second coming-out party. She was having only the people she liked this time, and these turned out to be chiefly importations from New York. The musicians, the playwrights, the vague supernumeraries of the arts, who had dropped in at Dolly's house on Ram's Point, were here in force. But Dolly, relieved of his obligations as host, made no clumsy attempt to talk their language that night. He stood moodily against the wall with some of that old air of superiority that had first made me want to know him. Afterward, on my way to bed, I passed Vienna's sitting room and she called me to come in. She and Dolly, both a little white, were sitting across the room from each other and there was tensity in the air.

"Sit down, Jeff," said Vienna wearily. "I want you to witness the collapse of a man into a schoolboy." I sat down reluctantly. "Dolly's changed his mind," she said. "He prefers football to me."

"That's not it," said Dolly stubbornly.

"I don't see the point," I objected. "Dolly can't possibly play."

"But he thinks he can. Jeff, just in case you imagine I'm being pig-headed about it, I want to tell you a story. Three years ago, when we first came back to the United States, father put my young brother in school. One afternoon we all went out to see him play football. Just after the game started he was hurt, but father said, 'It's all right. He'll be up in a minute. It happens all the time.' But, Jeff, he never got up. He lay there, and finally they carried him off the field and put a blanket over him. Just as we got to him he died."

She looked from one to the other of us and began to sob convulsively. Dolly went over, frowning, and put his arm around her shoulder.

"Oh, Dolly," she cried, "won't you do this for me—just this one little thing for me?"

He shook his head miserably. "I tried, but I can't," he said.

"It's my stuff, don't you understand, Vienna? People have got to do their stuff."

Vienna had risen and was powdering her tears at a mirror; now she flashed around angrily.

"Then I've been laboring under a misapprehension when I supposed you felt about it much as I did."

"Let's not go over all that. I'm tired of talking, Vienna; I'm tired of my own voice. It seems to me that no one I know does anything but talk any more."

"Thanks. I suppose that's meant for me."

"It seems to me your friends talk a great deal. I've never heard so much jabber as I've listened to tonight. Is the idea of actually doing anything repulsive to you, Vienna?"

"It depends upon whether it's worth doing."

"Well, this is worth doing—to me."

"I know your trouble, Dolly," she said bitterly. "You're weak and you want to be admired. This year you haven't had a lot of little boys following you around as if you were Jack Dempsey, and it almost breaks your heart. You want to get out in front of them all and make a show of yourself and hear the applause."

He laughed shortly. "If that's your idea of how a football player feels——"

"Have you made up your mind to play?" she interrupted.

"If I'm any use to them—yes."

"Then I think we're both wasting our time."

Her expression was ruthless, but Dolly refused to see that she was in earnest. When I got away he was still trying to make her "be rational," and next day on the train he said that Vienna had been "a little nervous." He was deeply in love with her, and he didn't dare think of losing her; but he was still in the grip of the sudden emotion that had decided him to play, and his confusion and exhaustion of mind made him believe vainly that everything was going to be all right. But I had seen that look on Vienna's face the night she talked with Mr. Carl Sanderson at the Frolic two years before.

Dolly didn't get off the train at Princeton Junction, but continued on to New York. He went to two orthopedic specialists and one of them arranged a bandage braced with a whole little fence of whalebones that he was to wear day and night. The probabilities were that it would snap at the first brisk encounter, but he could run on it and stand on it when he kicked. He was out on University Field in uniform the following afternoon.

His appearance was a small sensation. I was sitting in the stands watching practice with Harold Case and young Daisy Cary. She was just beginning to be famous then, and I don't know whether she or Dolly attracted the most attention. In those times it was still rather daring to bring down a moving-picture actress; if that same young lady went to Princeton today she would probably be met at the station with a band.

Dolly limped around and everyone said, "He's limping!" He got under a punt and everyone said, "He did that pretty well!" The first team were laid off after the hard Navy game and everyone watched Dolly all afternoon. After practice I caught his eye and he came over and shook hands. Daisy asked him if he'd like to be in a football picture she was going to make. It was only conversation, but he looked at me with a dry smile.

When he came back to the room his ankle was swollen up as big as a stove pipe, and next day he and Keene fixed up an arrangement by which the bandage would be loosened and tightened to fit its varying size. We called it the balloon. The bone was nearly healed, but the little bruised sinews were stretched out of place again every day. He watched the Swarthmore game from the sidelines and the following Monday he was in scrimmage with the second team against the scrubs.

In the afternoons sometimes he wrote to Vienna. His theory was that they were still engaged, but he tried not to worry about it, and I think the very pain that kept him awake at night was good for that. When the season was over he would go and see.

We played Harvard and lost 7 to 3. Jack Devlin's collar bone was broken and he was out for the season, which made it almost sure that Dolly would play. Amid the rumors and fears of mid-November the news aroused a spark of hope in an otherwise morbid undergraduate body—hope all out of proportion to Dolly's condition. He came back to the room the Thursday before the game with his face drawn and tired.

"They're going to start me," he said, "and I'm going to be back for punts. If they only knew——"

"Couldn't you tell Bill how you feel about that?"

He shook his head and I had a sudden suspicion that he was punishing himself for his "accident" last August. He lay silently on the couch while I packed his suitcase for the team train.

The actual day of the game was, as usual, like a dream—unreal with its crowds of friends and relatives and the inessential trappings of a gigantic show. The eleven little men who ran out on the field at last were like bewitched figures in another world, strange and infinitely romantic, blurred by a throbbing mist of people and sound. One aches with them intolerably, trembles with their excitement, but they have no traffic with us now, they are beyond help, consecrated and unreachable—vaguely holy.

The field is rich and green, the preliminaries are over and the teams trickle out into position. Head guards are put on; each man claps his hands and breaks into a lonely little dance. People are still talking around you, arranging themselves, but you have fallen silent and your eye wanders from man to man. There's Jack Whitehead, a senior, at end; Joe McDonald, large and reassuring, at tackle; Toole, a sophomore, at guard; Red Hopman, center; someone you can't identify at the other guard—Bunker probably—he turns and you see his number—Bunker; Bean Gile, looking unnaturally dignified and significant at the other tackle; Poore, another sophomore at end. Back of them is Wash Sampson at quarter—imagine how he feels! But he runs here and there on light feet, speaking to this man and that, trying to communicate his alertness and his confidence of success. Dolly Harlan stands motionless, his hands on his hips, watching the Yale kicker tee up the ball; near him is Captain Bob Tatnall——

There's the whistle! The line of the Yale team sways ponderously forward from its balance and a split second afterward comes the sound of the ball. The field streams with running figures and the whole Bowl strains forward as if thrown by the current of an electric chair.

Suppose we fumbled right away.

Tatnall catches it, goes back ten yards, is surrounded and blotted out of sight. Spears goes through center for three. A short pass, Sampson to Tatnall, is completed, but for no gain. Harlan punts to Devereaux, who is downed in his tracks on the Yale forty-yard line.

Now we'll see what they've got.

It developed immediately that they had a great deal. Using an effective crisscross and a short pass over center, they carried the ball fifty-four yards to the Princeton six-yard line, where they lost it on a fumble, recovered by Red Hopman. After a trade of punts, they began another push, this time to the fifteen-yard line, where, after four hair-raising forward passes, two of them batted down by Dolly, we got the ball on downs. But Yale was still fresh and strong, and with a third onslaught the weaker Princeton line began to give way. Just after the second quarter began Devereaux took the ball over for a touchdown and the half ended with Yale in possession of the ball on our ten-yard line. Score, Yale, 7; Princeton, 0.

We hadn't a chance. The team was playing above itself, better than it had played all year, but it wasn't enough. Save that it was the Yale game, when anything could happen, anything *had* happened, the atmosphere of gloom would have been deeper than it was, and in the cheering section you could cut it with a knife.

Early in the game Dolly Harlan had fumbled Devereaux's high punt, but recovered without gain; toward the end of the half another kick slipped through his fingers, but he scooped it up, and slipping past the end, went back twelve yards. Between halves he told Roper he couldn't seem to get under the ball, but they kept him there. His own kicks were carrying well and he was essential in the only back-field combination that could hope to score.

After the first play of the game he limped slightly, moving around as little as possible to conceal the fact. But I knew enough about football to see that he was in every play, starting at that rather slow pace of his and finishing with a quick side lunge that almost always took out his man. Not a single Yale forward pass was finished in his territory, but toward the end of the third quarter he dropped another kick—backed around in a confused little circle under it, lost it and recovered on the five-yard line just in time to avert a certain score. That made the third time, and I saw Ed Kimball throw off his blanket and begin to warm up on the sidelines.

Just at that point our luck began to change. From a kick formation, with Dolly set to punt from behind our goal, Howard Bement, who had gone in for Wash Sampson at quarter, took the ball through the center of the line, got by the secondary defense and ran twenty-six yards before he was pulled down. Captain Tasker, of Yale, had gone out with a twisted knee, and Princeton began to pile plays through his substitute, between Bean Gile and Hopman, with George Spears and sometimes Bob Tatnall carrying the ball. We went up to the Yale forty-yard line, lost the ball on a fumble and recovered it on another as the third quarter ended. A wild ripple of enthusiasm ran through the Princeton stands. For the first time we had the ball in their territory with first down and the possibility of tying the score. You could hear the tenseness growing all around you in the intermission; it was reflected in the excited movements of the cheer leaders and the uncontrollable patches of sound that leaped out of the crowd, catching up voices here and there and swelling to an undisciplined roar.

I saw Kimball dash out on the field and report to the referee and I thought Dolly was through at last, and was glad, but it was Bob Tatnall who came out, sobbing, and brought the Princeton side cheering to its feet.

With the first play pandemonium broke loose and continued to the end of the game. At intervals it would swoon away to a plaintive humming; then it would rise to the intensity of wind and rain and thunder, and beat across the twilight from one side of the Bowl to the other like the agony of lost souls swinging across a gap in space.

The teams lined up on Yale's forty-one yard line and Spears immediately dashed off tackle for six yards. Again he carried the ball—he was a wild unpopular Southerner with inspired moments—going through the same hole for five more and a first down. Dolly made two on a cross buck and Spears was held at center. It was third down, with the ball on Yale's twenty-nine-yard line and eight to go.

There was some confusion immediately behind me, some pushing and some voices; a man was sick or had fainted—I never discovered which. Then my view was blocked out for a minute by rising bodies and then everything went definitely crazy. Substitutes were jumping around down on the field, waving their blankets, the air was full of hats, cushions, coats and a deafening roar. Dolly Harlan, who had scarcely carried the ball a dozen times in his Princeton career, had picked a long pass from Kimball out of the air and, dragging a tackler, struggled five yards to the Yale goal.

VI

Some time later the game was over. There was a bad moment when Yale began another attack, but there was no scoring and Bob Tatnall's eleven had redeemed a mediocre season by tying a better Yale team. For us there was the feel of victory about it, the exaltation if not the jubilance, and the Yale faces issuing from out the Bowl wore the look of defeat. It would be a good year, after all—a good fight at the last, a tradition for next year's team. Our class—those of us who cared—would go out from Princeton without the taste of final defeat. The symbol stood—such as it was; the banners blew proudly in the wind. All that is childish? Find us something to fill the niche of victory.

I waited for Dolly outside the dressing rooms until almost everyone had come out; then, as he still lingered, I went in. Someone had given him a little brandy, and since he never drank much, it was swimming in his head.

"Have a chair, Jeff." He smiled, broadly and happily. "Rubber! Tony! Get the distinguished guest a chair. He's an intellectual and he wants to interview one of the bone-headed athletes. Tony, this is Mr. Deering. They've got everything in this funny Bowl but armchairs. I love this Bowl. I'm going to build here."

He fell silent, thinking about all things happily. He was content. I persuaded him to dress—there were people waiting for us. Then he insisted on walking out upon the field, dark now, and feeling the crumbled turf with his shoe.

He picked up a divot from a cleat and let it drop, laughed, looked distracted for a minute, and turned away.

With Tad Davis, Daisy Cary and another girl, we drove to New York. He sat beside Daisy and was silly, charming and attractive. For the first time since I'd known him he talked about the game naturally, even with a touch of vanity.

"For two years I was pretty good and I was always mentioned at the bottom of the column as being among those who played. This year I dropped three punts and slowed up every play till Bob Tatnall kept yelling at me, 'I don't see why they won't take you out!' But a pass not even aimed at me fell in my arms and I'll be in the headlines tomorrow."

He laughed. Somebody touched his foot; he winced and turned white.

"How did you hurt it?" Daisy asked. "In football?"

"I hurt it last summer," he said shortly.

"It must have been terrible to play on it."

"It was."

"I suppose you had to."

"That's the way sometimes."

They understood each other. They were both workers; sick or well, there were things that Daisy also had to do. She spoke of how, with a vile cold, she had had to fall into an open-air lagoon out in Hollywood the winter before.

"Six times—with a fever of a hundred and two. But the production was costing ten thousand dollars a day."

"Couldn't they use a double?"

"They did whenever they could—I only fell in when it had to be done."

She was eighteen and I compared her background of courage and independence and achievement, of politeness based upon the realities of cooperation, with that of most society girls I had known. There was no way in which she wasn't inestimably their superior—if she had looked for a moment my way—but it was Dolly's shining velvet eyes that signaled to her own.

"Can't you go out with me tonight?" I heard her ask him.

He was sorry, but he had to refuse. Vienna was in New York; she was going to see him. I didn't know, and Dolly didn't know, whether there was to be a reconciliation or a good-by.

When she dropped Dolly and me at the Ritz there was real regret, that lingering form of it, in both their eyes.

"There's a marvelous girl," Dolly said. I agreed. "I'm going up to see Vienna. Will you get a room for us at the Madison?"

So I left him. What happened between him and Vienna I don't know; he has never spoken about it to this day. But what happened later in the evening was brought to my attention by several surprised and even indignant witnesses to the event.

Dolly walked into the Ambassador Hotel about ten o'clock and went to the desk to ask for Miss Cary's room. There was a crowd around the desk, among them some Yale or Princeton undergraduates from the game. Several of them had been celebrating and evidently one of them knew Daisy and had tried to get her room by phone. Dolly was abstracted and he must have made his way through them in a somewhat brusque way and asked to be connected with Miss Cary.

One young man stepped back, looked at him unpleasantly and said, "You seem to be in an awful hurry. Just who are you?"

There was one of those slight silent pauses and the people near the desk all turned to look. Something happened inside Dolly; he felt as if life had arranged his role to make possible this particular question—a question that now he had no choice but to answer. Still, there was silence. The small crowd waited.

"Why, I'm Dolly Harlan," he said deliberately. "What do you think of that?"

It was quite outrageous. There was a pause and then a sudden little flurry and chorus: "Dolly Harlan! What? What did he say?"

The clerk had heard the name; he gave it as the phone was answered from Miss Cary's room.

"Mr. Harlan's to go right up, please."

Dolly turned away, alone with his achievement, taking it for once to his breast. He found suddenly that he would not have it long so intimately; the memory would outlive the triumph and even the triumph would outlive the glow in his heart that was best of all. Tall and straight, an image of victory and pride, he moved across the lobby, oblivious alike to the fate ahead of him or the small chatter behind.

At Your Age

(*The Saturday Evening Post*, 17 August 1929)

"At Your Age" was written in Paris in June 1929. Tranquility had eluded the Fitzgeralds at "Ellerslie," and he returned to France in the spring of 1929 with *Tender Is the Night* still unfinished. The departure from America was motivated by Zelda's desire to study ballet in Paris as well as by Fitzgerald's feeling that he would be able to work on his novel more effectively in its setting.

Harold Ober's response to "At Your Age" was: "At this minute it seems to me the finest story you have ever written—and the finest I have ever read." His enthusiasm brought a raise to $4000 from the *Post*, Fitzgerald's peak story price. Ober was probably responsible for its selection for the Modern Library *Great Modern Short Stories* (1930) because "At Your Age" was not among the five stories Fitzgerald nominated.

Tom Squires came into the drug store to buy a toothbrush, a can of talcum, a gargle, Castile soap, Epsom salts and a box of cigars. Having lived alone for many years, he was methodical, and while waiting to be served he held the list in his hand. It was Christmas week and Minneapolis was under two feet of exhilarating, constantly refreshed snow; with his cane Tom knocked two clean crusts of it from his overshoes. Then, looking up, he saw the blonde girl.

She was a rare blonde, even in that Promised Land of Scandinavians, where pretty blondes are not rare. There was warm color in her cheeks, lips and pink little hands that folded powders into papers; her hair, in long braids twisted about her head, was shining and alive. She seemed to Tom suddenly the cleanest person he knew of, and he caught his breath as he stepped forward and looked into her gray eyes.

"A can of talcum."

"What kind?"

"Any kind. . . . That's fine."

She looked back at him apparently without self-consciousness, and, as the list melted away, his heart raced with it wildly.

"I am not old," he wanted to say. "At fifty I'm younger than most men of forty. Don't I interest you at all?"

But she only said "What kind of gargle?"

And he answered, "What can you recommend? . . . That's fine."

Almost painfully he took his eyes from her, went out and got into his coupe.

"If that young idiot only knew what an old imbecile like me could do for her," he thought humorously—"what worlds I could open out to her!"

As he drove away into the winter twilight he followed this train of thought to a totally unprecedented conclusion. Perhaps the time of day was the responsible stimulant, for the shop windows glowing into the cold, the tinkling bells of a delivery sleigh, the white gloss left by shovels on the sidewalks, the enormous distance of the stars, brought back the feel of other nights thirty years ago. For an instant the girls he had known then slipped like phantoms out of their dull matronly selves of today and fluttered past him with frosty, seductive laughter, until a pleasant shiver crawled up his spine.

"Youth! Youth! Youth!" he apostrophized with conscious lack of originality, and, as a somewhat ruthless and domineering man of no morals whatsoever, he considered going back to the drug store to seek the blonde girl's address. It was not his sort of thing, so the half-formed intention passed; the idea remained.

"Youth, by heaven—youth!" he repeated under his breath. "I want it near me, all around me, just once more before I'm too old to care."

He was tall, lean and handsome, with the ruddy, bronzed face of a sportsman and a just faintly graying mustache. Once he had been among the city's best beaus, organizer of cotillions and charity balls, popular with men and women, and with several generations of them. After the war he had suddenly felt poor, gone into business, and in ten years accumulated nearly a million dollars. Tom Squires was not introspective, but he perceived now that the wheel of his life had revolved again, bringing up forgotten, yet familiar, dreams and yearnings. Entering his house, he turned suddenly to a pile of disregarded invitations to see whether or not he had been bidden to a dance tonight.

Throughout his dinner, which he ate alone at the Downtown Club, his eyes were half closed and on his face was a faint smile. He was practicing so that he would be able to laugh at himself painlessly, if necessary.

"I don't even know what they talk about," he admitted. "They pet—prominent broker goes to petting party with debutante. What is a petting party? Do they serve refreshments? Will I have to learn to play a saxophone?"

These matters, lately as remote as China in a news reel, came alive to him. They were serious questions. At ten o'clock he walked up the steps of the College Club to a private dance with the same sense of entering a new world as when he had gone into a training camp back in '17. He spoke to a hostess of his generation and to her daughter, overwhelmingly of another, and sat down in a corner to acclimate himself.

He was not alone long. A silly young man named Leland Jaques, who lived across the street from Tom, remarked him kindly and came over to brighten his life. He was such an exceedingly fatuous young man that, for a moment, Tom was annoyed, but he perceived craftily that he might be of service.

"Hello, Mr. Squires. How are you, sir?"

"Fine, thanks, Leland. Quite a dance."

As one man of the world with another, Mr. Jaques sat, or lay, down on the couch and lit—or so it seemed to Tom—three or four cigarettes at once.

"You should of been here last night, Mr. Squires. Oh, boy, that was a party and a half! The Caulkins. Hap-past five!"

"Who's that girl who changes partners every minute?" Tom asked. . . . "No, the one in white passing the door."

"That's Annie Lorry."

"Arthur Lorry's daughter?"

"Yes."

"She seems popular."

"About the most popular girl in town—anyway, at a dance."

"Not popular except at dances?"

"Oh, sure, but she hangs around with Randy Cambell all the time."

"What Cambell?"

"D. B."

There were new names in town in the last decade.

"It's a boy-and-girl affair." Pleased with this phrase, Jaques tried to repeat it: "One of those boy-and-girls affair—boys-and-girl affairs——" He gave it up and lit several more cigarettes, crushing out the first series on Tom's lap.

"Does she drink?"

"Not especially. At least I never saw her passed out. . . . That's Randy Cambell just cut in on her now."

They were a nice couple. Her beauty sparkled bright against his strong, tall form, and they floated hoveringly, delicately, like two people in a nice, amusing dream. They came near and Tom admired the faint dust of powder over her freshness, the guarded sweetness of her smile, the fragility of her body calculated by Nature to a millimeter to suggest a bud, yet guarantee a flower. Her innocent, passionate eyes were brown, perhaps; but almost violet in the silver light.

"Is she out this year?"

"Who?"

"Miss Lorry."

"Yes."

Although the girl's loveliness interested Tom, he was unable to picture himself as one of the attentive, grateful queue that pursued her around the room. Better meet her when the holidays were over and most of these young men were back in college "where they belonged." Tom Squires was old enough to wait.

He waited a fortnight while the city sank into the endless northern midwinter, where gray skies were friendlier than metallic blue skies, and dusk, whose lights were a reassuring glimpse into the continuity of human cheer, was warmer than the afternoons of bloodless sunshine. The coat of snow lost its press and became soiled and shabby, and ruts froze in the street; some of the big houses on Crest Avenue began to close as their occupants went South. In those cold days Tom asked Annie and her parents to go as his guests to the last Bachelors' Ball.

The Lorrys were an old family in Minneapolis, grown a little harassed and poor since the war. Mrs. Lorry, a contemporary of Tom's, was not surprised that he should send mother and daughter orchids and dine them luxuriously in his apartment on fresh caviar, quail and champagne. Annie saw him only dimly—he lacked vividness, as the old do for the young—but she perceived his interest in her and performed for him the traditional ritual of young beauty—smiles, polite, wide-eyed attention, a profile held obligingly in this light or in that. At the ball he danced with her twice, and, though she was teased about it, she was flattered that such a man of the world—he had become that instead of a mere old man—had singled her out. She accepted his invitation to the symphony the following week, with the idea that it would be uncouth to refuse.

There were several "nice invitations" like that. Sitting beside him, she dozed in the warm shadow of Brahms and thought of Randy Cambell and other romantic nebulosities who might appear tomorrow. Feeling casually mellow one afternoon, she deliberately provoked Tom to kiss her on the way home, but she wanted to laugh when he took her hands and told her fervently he was falling in love.

"But how could you?" she protested. "Really, you musn't say such crazy things. I won't go out with you any more, and then you'll be sorry."

A few days later her mother spoke to her as Tom waited outside in his car:

"Who's that, Annie?"

"Mr. Squires."

"Shut the door a minute. You're seeing him quite a bit."

"Why not?"

"Well, dear, he's fifty years old."

"But, mother, there's hardly anybody else in town."

"But you musn't get any silly ideas about him."

"Don't worry. Actually, he bores me to extinction most of the time." She came to a sudden decision: "I'm not going to see him any more. I just couldn't get out of going with him this afternoon."

And that night, as she stood by her door in the circle of Randy Cambell's arm, Tom and his single kiss had no existence for her.

"Oh, I do love you so," Randy whispered. "Kiss me once more."

Their cool cheeks and warm lips met in the crisp darkness, and, watching the icy moon over his shoulder, Annie knew that she was his surely and, pulling his face down, kissed him again, trembling with emotion.

"When'll you marry me then?" he whispered.

"When can you—we afford it?"

"Couldn't you announce our engagement? If you knew the misery of having you out with somebody else and then making love to you."

"Oh, Randy, you ask so much."

"It's so awful to say good night. Can't I come in for a minute?"

"Yes."

Sitting close together in a trance before the flickering, lessening fire, they were oblivious that their common fate was being coolly weighed by a man of fifty who lay in a hot bath some blocks away.

II

Tom Squires had guessed from Annie's extremely kind and detached manner of the afternoon that he had failed to interest her. He had promised himself that in such an eventuality he would drop the matter, but now he found himself in no such humor. He did not want to marry her; he simply wanted to see her and be with her a little; and up to the moment of her sweetly casual, half passionate, yet wholly unemotional kiss, giving her up would have been easy, for he was past the romantic age; but since that kiss the thought of her made his heart move up a few inches in his chest and beat there steady and fast.

"But this is the time to get out," he said to himself. "My age; no possible right to force myself into her life."

He rubbed himself dry, brushed his hair before the mirror, and, as he laid down the comb, said decisively: "That is that." And after reading for an hour he turned out the lamp with a snap and repeated aloud: "That is that."

In other words, that was not that at all, and the click of material things did not finish off Annie Lorry as a business decision might be settled by the tap of a pencil on the table.

"I'm going to carry this matter a little further," he said to himself about half-past four; on that acknowledgment he turned over and found sleep.

In the morning she had receded somewhat, but by four o'clock in the afternoon she was all around him—the phone was for calling her, a woman's footfalls passing his office were her footfalls, the snow outside the window was blowing, perhaps, against her rosy face.

"There is always the little plan I thought of last night," he said to himself. "In ten years I'll be sixty, and then no youth, no beauty for me ever any more."

In a sort of panic he took a sheet of note paper and composed a carefully phrased letter to Annie's mother, asking permission to pay court to her daughter. He took it himself into the hall, but before the letter slide he tore it up and dropped the pieces in a cuspidor.

"I couldn't do such an underhand trick," he told himself, "at my age." But this self-congratulation was premature, for he rewrote the letter and mailed it before he left his office that night.

Next day the reply he had counted on arrived—he could have guessed its very words in advance. It was a curt and indignant refusal. It ended:

I think it best that you and my daughter meet no more.
Very Sincerely Yours,
MABEL TOLLMAN LORRY.

"And now," Tom thought coolly, "we'll see what the girl says to that."

He wrote a note to Annie. Her mother's letter had surprised him, it said, but perhaps it was best that they should meet no more, in view of her mother's attitude.

By return post came Annie's defiant answer to her mother's fiat: "This isn't the Dark Ages. I'll see you whenever I like." She named a rendezvous for the following afternoon. Her mother's short-sightedness brought about what he had failed to achieve directly; for where Annie had been on the point of dropping him, she was now determined to do nothing of the sort. And the secrecy engendered by disapproval at home simply contributed the missing excitement. As February hardened into deep, solemn, interminable winter, she met him frequently and on a new basis. Sometimes they drove over to St. Paul to see a picture or to have dinner; sometimes they parked far out on a boulevard in his coupe, while the bitter sleet glazed the windshield to opacity and furred his lamps with ermine. Often he brought along something special to drink—enough to make her gay, but, carefully, never more; for mingled with his other emotions about her was something paternally concerned.

Laying his cards on the table, he told her that it was her mother who had unwittingly pushed her toward him, but Annie only laughed at his duplicity.

She was having a better time with him than with anyone else she had ever known. In place of the selfish exigency of a younger man, he showed her a never-failing consideration. What if his eyes were tired, his cheeks a little leathery and veined, if his will was masculine and strong. Moreover, his experience was a window looking out upon a wider, richer world; and with Randy Cambell next day she would feel less taken care of, less valued, less rare.

It was Tom now who was vaguely discontented. He had what he wanted—her youth at his side—and he felt that anything further would be a mistake. His liberty was precious to him and he could offer her only a dozen years before he would be old, but she had become something precious to him and he perceived that drifting wasn't fair. Then one day late in February the matter was decided out of hand.

They had ridden home from St. Paul and dropped into the College Club for tea, breaking together through the drifts that masked the walk and rimmed the door. It was a revolving door; a young man came around in it, and stepping into his space, they smelt onions and whisky. The door revolved again after them, and he was back within, facing them. It was Randy Cambell; his face was flushed, his eyes dull and hard.

"Hello, beautiful," he said, approaching Annie.

"Don't come so close," she protested lightly. "You smell of onions."

"You're particular all of a sudden."

"Always. I'm always particular." Annie made a slight movement back toward Tom.

"Not always," said Randy unpleasantly. Then, with increased emphasis and a fractional glance at Tom: "Not always." With his remark he seemed to join the hostile world outside. "And I'll just give you a tip," he continued: "Your mother's inside."

The jealous ill-temper of another generation reached Tom only faintly, like the protest of a child, but at this impertinent warning he bristled with annoyance.

"Come on, Annie," he said brusquely. "We'll go in."

With her glance uneasily averted from Randy, Annie followed Tom into the big room.

It was sparsely populated; three middle-aged women sat near the fire. Momentarily Annie drew back, then she walked toward them.

"Hello, mother . . . Mrs. Trumble . . . Aunt Caroline."

The two latter responded; Mrs. Trumble even nodded faintly at Tom. But Annie's mother got to her feet without a word, her eyes frozen, her mouth drawn. For a moment she stood staring at her daughter; then she turned abruptly and left the room.

Tom and Annie found a table across the room.

"Wasn't she terrible?" said Annie, breathing aloud. He didn't answer.

"For three days she hasn't spoken to me." Suddenly she broke out: "Oh, people can be so small! I was going to sing the leading part in the Junior League show, and yesterday Cousin Mary Betts, the president, came to me and said I couldn't."

"Why not?"

"Because a representative Junior League girl musn't defy her mother. As if I were a naughty child!"

Tom stared on at a row of cups on the mantelpiece—two or three of them bore his name. "Perhaps she was right," he said suddenly. "When I begin to do harm to you it's time to stop."

"What do you mean?"

At her shocked voice his heart poured a warm liquid forth into his body, but he answered quietly: "You remember I told you I was going South? Well, I'm going tomorrow."

There was an argument, but he had made up his mind. At the station next evening she wept and clung to him.

"Thank you for the happiest month I've had in years," he said.

"But you'll come back, Tom."

"I'll be two months in Mexico; then I'm going East for a few weeks."

He tried to sound fortunate, but the frozen city he was leaving seemed to be in blossom. Her frozen breath was a flower on the air, and his heart sank as he realized that some young man was waiting outside to take her home in a car hung with blooms.

"Good-by, Annie. Good-by, sweet!"

Two days later he spent the morning in Houston with Hal Meigs, a classmate at Yale.

"You're in luck for such an old fella," said Meigs at luncheon, "because I'm going to introduce you to the cutest little traveling companion you ever saw, who's going all the way to Mexico City."

The lady in question was frankly pleased to learn at the station that she was not returning alone. She and Tom dined together on the train and later played rummy for an hour; but when, at ten o'clock, standing in the door of the stateroom, she turned back to him suddenly with a certain look, frank and unmistakable, and stood there holding that look for a long moment, Tom Squires was suddenly in the grip of an emotion that was not the one in question. He wanted desperately to see Annie, cail her for a second on the phone, and then fall asleep, knowing she was young and pure as a star, and safe in bed.

"Good night," he said, trying to keep any repulsion out of his voice.

"Oh! Good night."

Arriving in El Paso next day, he drove over the border to Juarez. It was bright and hot, and after leaving his bags at the station he went into a bar for an iced drink; as he sipped it a girl's voice addressed him thickly from the table behind:

"You'n American?"

He had noticed her slumped forward on her elbows as he came in; now, turning, he faced a young girl of about seventeen, obviously drunk, yet with gentility in her unsteady, sprawling voice. The American bartender leaned confidentially forward.

"I don't know what to do about her," he said. "She come in about three o'clock with two young fellows—one of them her sweetie. They had a fight and the men went off, and this one's been here ever since."

A spasm of distaste passed over Tom—the rules of his generation were outraged and defied. That an American girl should be drunk and deserted in a tough foreign town—that such things happened, might happen to Annie. He looked at his watch, hesitated.

"Has she got a bill?" he asked.

"She owes for five gins. But suppose her boy friends come back?"

"Tell them she's at the Roosevelt Hotel in El Paso."

Approaching, he put his hand on her shoulder. She looked up.

"You look like Santa Claus," she said vaguely. "You couldn't possibly be Santa Claus, could you?"

"I'm going to take you to El Paso."

"Well," she considered, "you look perfectly safe to me."

She was so young—a drenched little rose. He could have wept for her wretched unconsciousness of the old facts, the old penalties of life.

Jousting at nothing in an empty tilt yard with a shaking spear. The taxi moved too slowly through the suddenly poisonous night.

Having explained things to a reluctant night clerk, he went out and found a telegraph office.

"Have given up Mexican trip," he wired. "Leaving here tonight. Please meet train in the St. Paul station at three o'clock and ride with me to Minneapolis, as I can't spare you for another minute. All my love."

He could at least keep an eye on her, advise her, see what she did with her life. That silly mother of hers!

On the train, as the baked tropical lands and green fields fell away and the North swept near again with patches of snow, then fields of it, fierce winds in the vestibule and bleak, hibernating farms, he paced the corridors with intolerable restlessness. When they drew into the St. Paul station he swung himself off like a young man and searched the platform eagerly, but his eyes failed to find her. He had counted on those few minutes between the cities; they had become a symbol of her fidelity to their friendship, and as the train started again he searched it desperately from smoker to observation car. But he could not find her, and now he knew that he was mad for her; at the thought that she had taken his advice and plunged into affairs with other men, he grew weak with fear.

Drawing into Minneapolis, his hands fumbled so that he must call the porter to fasten his baggage. Then there was an interminable wait in the corridor while the baggage was taken off and he was pressed up against a girl in a squirrel-trimmed coat.

"Tom!"

"Well, I'll be——"

Her arms went up around his neck. "But, Tom," she cried, "I've been right here in this car since St. Paul!"

His cane fell in the corridor, he drew her very tenderly close and their lips met like starved hearts.

III

The new intimacy of their definite engagement brought Tom a feeling of young happiness. He awoke on winter mornings with the sense of undeserved joy hovering in the room; meeting young men, he found himself matching the vigor of his mind and body against theirs. Suddenly his life had a purpose and a background; he felt rounded and complete. On gray March afternoons when she wandered familiarly in his apartment the warm sureties of his youth flooded back—ecstasy and poignancy, the mortal and the eternal posed in their immemorially tragic juxtaposition and, a little astounded, he found himself relishing the very terminology of young romance. But he was more thoughtful than a younger lover; and to Annie he seemed to "know everything," to stand holding open the gates for her passage into the truly golden world.

"We'll go to Europe first," he said.

"Oh, we'll go there a lot, won't we? Let's spend our winters in Italy and the spring in Paris."

"But, little Annie, there's business."

"Well, we'll stay away as much as we can anyhow. I hate Minneapolis."

"Oh, no." He was a little shocked. "Minneapolis is all right."

"When you're here it's all right."

Mrs. Lorry yielded at length to the inevitable. With ill grace she acknowledged the engagement, asking only that the marriage should not take place until fall.

"Such a long time," Annie sighed.

"After all, I'm your mother. It's so little to ask."

It was a long winter, even in a land of long winters. March was full of billowy drifts, and when it seemed at last as though the cold must be defeated, there was a series of blizzards, desperate as last stands. The people waited; their first energy to resist was spent, and man, like weather, simply hung on. There was less to do now and the general restlessness was expressed by surliness in daily contacts. Then, early in April, with a long sigh the ice cracked, the snow ran into the ground and the green, eager spring broke up through.

One day, riding along a slushy road in a fresh, damp breeze with a little starved, smothered grass in it, Annie began to cry. Sometimes she cried for nothing, but this time Tom suddenly stopped the car and put his arm round her.

"Why do you cry like that? Are you unhappy?"

"Oh, no, no!" she protested.

"But you cried yesterday the same way. And you wouldn't tell me why. You must always tell me."

"Nothing, except the spring. It smells so good, and it always has so many sad thoughts and memories in it."

"It's our spring, my sweetheart," he said. "Annie, don't let's wait. Let's be married in June."

"I promised mother, but if you like we can announce our engagement in June."

The spring came fast now. The sidewalks were damp, then dry, and the children roller-skated on them and boys played baseball in the soft, vacant lots. Tom got up elaborate picnics of Annie's contemporaries and encouraged her to play golf and tennis with them. Abruptly, with a final, triumphant lurch of Nature, it was full summer.

On a lovely May evening Tom came up the Lorrys' walk and sat down beside Annie's mother on the porch.

"It's so pleasant," he said, "I thought Annie and I would walk instead of driving this evening. I want to show her the funny old house I was born in."

"On Chambers Street, wasn't it? Annie'll be home in a few minutes. She went riding with some young people after dinner."

"Yes, on Chambers Street."

He looked at his watch presently, hoping Annie would come while it was still light enough to see. Quarter of nine. He frowned. She had kept him waiting the night before, kept him waiting an hour yesterday afternoon.

"If I was twenty-one," he said to himself, "I'd make scenes and we'd both be miserable."

He and Mrs. Lorry talked; the warmth of the night precipitated the vague evening lassitude of the fifties and softened them both, and for the first time since his attentions to Annie began, there was no unfriendliness between them. By and by long silences fell, broken only by the scratch of a match or the creak of her swinging settee. When Mr. Lorry came home Tom threw away his second cigar in surprise and looked at his watch; it was after ten.

"Annie's late," Mrs. Lorry said.

"I hope there's nothing wrong," said Tom anxiously. "Who is she with?"

"There were four when they started out. Randy Cambell and another couple—I didn't notice who. They were only going for a soda."

"I hope there hasn't been any trouble. Perhaps——Do you think I ought to go and see?"

"Ten isn't late nowadays. You'll find——" Remembering that Tom Squires was marrying Annie, not adopting her, she kept herself from adding: "You'll get used to it."

Her husband excused himself and went up to bed, and the conversation became more forced and desultory. When the church clock over the way struck eleven they both broke off and listened to the beats. Twenty minutes later just as Tom impatiently crushed out his last cigar, an automobile drifted down the street and came to rest in front of the door.

For a minute no one moved on the porch or in the auto. Then Annie, with a hat in her hand, got out and came quickly up the walk.

Defying the tranquil night, the car snorted away.

"Oh, hello!" she cried. "I'm so sorry! What time is it? Am I terribly late?"

Tom didn't answer. The street lamp threw wine color upon her face and expressed with a shadow the heightened flush of her cheek. Her dress was crushed, her hair was in brief, expressive disarray. But it was the strange little break in her voice that made him afraid to speak, made him turn his eyes aside.

"What happened?" Mrs. Lorry asked casually.

"Oh, a blow-out and something wrong with the engine—and we lost our way. Is it terribly late?"

And then, as she stood before them, her hat still in her hand, her breast rising and falling a little, her eyes wide and bright, Tom realized with a shock that he and her mother were people of the same age looking at a person of another. Try as he might, he could not separate himself from Mrs. Lorry. When she excused herself he suppressed a frantic tendency to say, "But why should you go now? After sitting here all evening?"

They were alone. Annie came up to him and pressed his hand. He had never been so conscious of her beauty; her damp hands were touched with dew.

"You were out with young Cambell," he said.

"Yes. Oh, don't be mad. I feel—I feel so upset tonight."

"Upset?"

She sat down, whimpering a little.

"I couldn't help it. Please don't be mad. He wanted so for me to take a ride with him and it was such a wonderful night, so I went just for an hour. And we began talking and I didn't realize the time. I felt so sorry for him."

"How do you think I felt?" He scorned himself, but it was said now.

"Don't, Tom. I told you I was terribly upset. I want to go to bed."

"I understand. Good night, Annie."

"Oh, please don't act that way, Tom. Can't you understand?"

But he could, and that was just the trouble. With the courteous bow of another generation, he walked down the steps and off into the obliterating moonlight. In a moment he was just a shadow passing the street lamps and then a faint footfall up the street.

IV

All through that summer he often walked abroad in the evenings. He liked to stand for a minute in front of the house where he was born, and then in front of another house where he had been a little boy. On his customary routes there were other sharp landmarks of the 90's, converted habitats of gayeties that no longer existed—the shell of Jansen's Livery Stables and the old Nushka Rink, where every winter his father had curled on the well-kept ice.

"And it's a darn pity," he would mutter. "A darn pity."

He had a tendency, too, to walk past the lights of a certain drug store, because it seemed to him that it had contained the seed of another and nearer branch of the past. Once he went in, and inquiring casually about the blonde clerk, found that she had married and departed several months before. He obtained her name and on an impulse sent her a wedding present "from a dumb admirer," for he felt he owed something to her for his happiness and pain. He had lost the battle against youth and spring, and with his grief paid the penalty for age's unforgivable sin—refusing to die. But he could not have walked down wasted into the darkness without being used up a little; what he had wanted, after all, was only to break his strong old heart. Conflict itself has a value beyond victory and defeat, and those three months—he had them forever.

Indecision

(*The Saturday Evening Post*, 16 May 1931)

"Indecision" was written in January-February 1931—probably in Lausanne, Switzerland, where Fitzgerald was staying at the Hotel de la Paix while Zelda Fitzgerald was under treatment at the Prangins clinic.* The *Post* paid $4000 for it. After Zelda's breakdown in April 1930 Fitzgerald concentrated on short stories—instead of his novel—for two years, writing sixteen stories to earn the money for hospital bills. In 1931—his most lucrative year before Hollywood—his income from nine stories was $36,000 (less 10% commission), whereas his total royalties from seven books was $100. Although the 1930-1931 stories include two intensely personal masterpieces, "One Trip Abroad" and "Babylon Revisited," most of them are clearly contrived.

The Switzerland of "Indecision" and "Hotel Child" is largely populated with unattractive people. Fitzgerald had little reason to write pleasant stories about Switzerland because for him it was a land of illness and despair. "A country where few things begin, but many things end"—as he noted in "One Trip Abroad."

In May 1931 Harold Ober relayed the *Post*'s reservations about Fitzgerald's recent stories, adding: "These last three stories of yours, FLIGHT AND PURSUIT, A NEW LEAF, and INDECISION, have been interesting to me because they were very vivid bits of life but I do feel that in these three stories you have failed to make the reader care about any one of the characters."

This one was dressed in a horizon-blue Swiss skiing suit with, however, the unmistakable touch of a Paris shears about it. Above it shone her snow-warm cheeks and her eyes that were less confident than brave. With his hat, Tommy McLane slapped snow from his dark, convictlike costume. He was already reflecting that he might have been out with Rosemary, dancing around Rosemary and the two "ickle durls" down at the other hotel, amid the gleam of patent Argentine hair, to the soothing whispers of "I'm Getting Myself Ready for You." When he was with Emily he felt always a faint nostalgia for young Rosemary and for the sort of dance that seemed to

---

*It is difficult to be exact about Fitzgerald's residences in 1931. While Zelda Fitzgerald was at Prangins clinic, he stayed at hotels in Switzerland and visited his daughter Scottie in Paris.

go on inside and all around Rosemary and the two "ickle durls." He knew just how much happened there—not much; just a limited amount of things, just a pleasant lot of little things strung into hours, moving to little melodies hither and thither. But he missed it; it was new to him again after four years, and he missed it. Likewise when he was with Rosemary, making life fun with jokes for her, he thought of Emily, who was twenty-five and carried space around with her into which he could step and be alone with their two selves, mature and complicated and trusting, and almost in love.

Out the window, the snow on the pine trees was turning lilac in the first dusk; and because the world was round, or for some such reason, there was rosy light still on that big mountain, the Dent de Something. Bundled-up children were splattering back to their hotels for tea as if the outdoors were tired of them and wanted to change its dress in quiet dignity. Down in the valley there were already bright windows and misty glows from the houses and hotels of the town.

He left Emily at her hotel door. She had never seemed so attractive, so good, so tranquil a person, given a half-decent chance. He was annoyed that he was already thinking of Rosemary.

"We'll meet in the bar down there at 7:30," he said, "and don't dress."

Putting on his jacket and flat cap, Tommy stepped out into the storm. It was a welcome blizzard and he inhaled damp snowflakes that he could no longer see against the darkening sky. Three flying kids on a sled startled him with a warning in some strange language and he just managed to jump out of their path. He heard them yell at the next bend, and then, a little farther on, he heard sleigh bells coming up the hill in the dark. It was all very pleasant and familiar, yet it did not remind him of Minneapolis, where he was born, because the automobile had spoiled all that side of Northwestern life while he was still a baby. It was pleasant and familiar because these last five days here among alien mountains held some of the happiest moments of his life.

He was twenty-seven; he was assistant manager and slated for manager of a New York bank in Paris, or else he would be offered the option of Chicago next spring at a larger salary. He had come up here to one of the gayest places in Switzerland with the idea that if he had nothing else to think of for ten days he might fall in love. He could afford to fall in love, but in Paris the people he saw all knew it, and he had instinctively become analytical and cagy. Here he felt free; the first night he had seen at least a dozen girls and women, "any one of whom"; on the second night, there had still been half a dozen; the third night there were three, with one new addition—Emily Elliot from the other hotel. Now, on the day after Christmas, it had narrowed down to two—Emily, and Rosemary Merriweather. He had actually written all this down on a blotter as if he were in his office in the Place Vendome, added and subtracted them, listed points.

"Two really remarkable girls," he said to himself in a tone not unlike the clumping squeak of his big shoes on the snow. "Two absolutely good ones."

Emily Elliot was divorced and twenty-five. Rosemary was eighteen.

He saw her immediately as he went into his hotel—a blonde, ravishing, Southern beauty like so many that had come before her and so many yet to be born. She was from "N'Awlins 'rigin'ly," but now from "Athens, Joja." He had first spoken to her on Christmas Eve, after an unavailing search for someone to introduce him, some means to pierce the wall of vacationing boys within which she seemed hermetically sealed. Sitting with another man, he stared at her across the room, admiring her with his eyes, frankly and tauntingly. Presently she spoke to her escort; they crossed the room and sat down at the table next to him, with Rosemary's back just one inch from him. She sent her young man for something; Tommy spoke. The next day, at the risk of both their lives, he took her down the big bob run.

Rosemary saw him now as he came in. She was revolving slowly through the last of the tea hour with a young Levantine whom he disliked. She wore white and her face lighted up white, like an angel under an arc lamp. "Where you been?" her big eyes said.

But Tommy was shrewd, and he merely nodded to her and to the two "ickle durls" who danced by, and found a seat in a far corner. He knew that a surfeit of admiration such as Rosemary's breeds an appreciation of indifference. And presently she came over to him, dragging her bridling partner by an interlaced little finger.

"Where you been?" she demanded.

"Tell that Spic to go count his piasters and I'll talk turkey with you."

She bestowed upon the puzzled darkling a healing smile.

"You don't mind, honey, if I sit this out? See you later."

When he had departed, Tommy protested, " 'Honey'! Do you call him 'honey'? Why don't you call him 'greasy'?"

She laughed sweetly.

"Where you been?"

"Skiing. But every time I go away, that doesn't mean you can go dance with a whole lot of gigolo numbers from Cairo. Why does he hold his hand parallel to the floor when he dances? Does he think he's stilling the waves? Does he think the floor's going to swing up and crack him?"

"He's a Greek, honey."

"That's no reason. And you better get that word 'honey' cleaned and pressed before you use it on me again." He felt very witty. "Let's go to my boudoir," he suggested.

He had a bedroom and bath and a tiny salon. Once inside the door of the latter, he shot the bolt and took her in his arms, but she drew away from him.

"You been up at that other hotel," she said.

"I had to invite a girl to dinner. Did you know you're having dinner with me tonight? . . . You're beautiful."

It was true. Her face, flushed with cold and then warmed again with the dance, was a riot of lovely, delicate pinks, like many carnations, rising in many shades from the white of her nose to the high spot of her cheeks. Her breathing was very young as she came close to him—young and eager and exciting. Her lips were faintly chapped, but soft in the corners.

After a moment she sat with him in a single chair. And just for a second words formed on his lips that it was hard not to utter. He knew she was in love with him and would probably marry him, but the old terror of being held rose in him. He would have to tell this girl so many things. He looked closely at her, holding her face under his, and if she had said one wise or witty thing he might have spoken, but she only looked up with a glaze of childish passion in her eyes and said: "What are you thinking, honey?"

The moment passed. She fell back smoothly into being only a part of the day's pleasure, the day's excitement. She was desirable here, but she was desirable downstairs too. The mountains were bewitching his determinations out of him.

Drawing her close to him, lightly he said: "So you like the Spics, eh? I suppose the boys are all Spics down in New Orleans?"

As she squeezed his face furiously between thumb and finger, his mind was already back with Emily at the other hotel a quarter of a mile away.

II

Tommy's dinner was not to be at his hotel. After meeting in the bar they sledded down into the village to a large old-fashioned Swiss taproom, a thing of woodwork, clocks, steins, kegs and antlers. There were other parties like their own, bound together by the common plan of eating *fondue*—a peculiarly indigestible form of Welsh rabbit—and drinking spiced wine, and then hitching on the backs of sleighs to Doldorp several miles away, where there was a townspeople's ball.

His own party included Emily; her cousin, young Frank Forrester; young Count de Caros Moros, a friend of Rosemary's—she played ping-pong with him and harked to his guitar and to his tales of machine-gunning his discontented fellow countrymen in Andalusia—a Cambridge University hockey hero named Harry Whitby, and lastly the two "ickle durls"—Californians who were up from a Montreux school for the holidays and very anxious to be swept off their feet. Six Americans, two Europeans.

It was a good party. Some gray-haired men of the golden 90's sang ancient glees at the piano, the *fondue* was fun, the wine was pert and heady, and smoke swirled out of the brown walls and toned the bright costumes into the room. They were all on a ship going somewhere, with the port just ahead; the faces of girls and young men bore the same innocent and unlined expectations of the great possibilities inherent in the situation and the night. The Latins became Americans easily, the English with more effort. Then it was over and one hundred five-pound boots stamped toward the sleighs that waited at the door.

For a moment Tommy lingered, engrossed in conversation with Emily, yet with sudden twinges of conscience about Rosemary. She had been on his left; he had last seen her listening to young Caros Moros perform upon his extremely portable guitar. Outside in the crisp moonlight he saw her tying her sled to one of the sleighs ahead. The sleighs were moving off; he and Emily caught one, and at the crisp-cracking whips the horses pulled, breasting the dark air. Past them figures ran and scrambled, the younger people pushing one another off, landing in a cloud of soft snow, then panting after the horses, to fling themselves exhausted on a sled, or else wail that they were being left behind. On either side the fields were tranquil; the space through which the cavalcade moved was high and limitless. After they were in the country there was less noise; perhaps ears were listening atavistically for wolves howling in the clumps of trees far across the snow.

At Doldorp he stood with Emily in the doorway, watching the others go in.

"Everybody's first husband with everybody's first wife," she remarked. "Who believes in marriage? I do. A plucky girl—takes the count of nine and comes up for more. But not for two years; I'm over here to do some straight thinking."

It occurred to Tommy that two years was a long time, but he knew that girls so frequently didn't mean what they said. He and Emily watched the entrance of Mr. Cola, nicknamed Capone, with his harem, consisting of wife, daughters, wife's friend, and three Siamese. Then they went inside.

The crowd was enormous—peasants, servants from the hotels, shopkeepers, guides, outlanders, cow herders, ski teachers and tourists. They all got seats where they could, and Tommy saw Rosemary with a crowd of young people across the room; she seemed a little tired and pale, sitting back with her lips apart and her eyes fixed and sleepy. When someone waltzed off with Emily, he went over and asked her to dance.

"I don't want to dance. I'm tired."

"Let's go sit where we can hear the yodeling."

"I can hear it here."

"What am I accused of?" he demanded.

"Nothing. I haven't even seen you."

Her current partner smiled at him ingratiatingly, but Tommy was growing annoyed:

"Didn't I explain that this dinner was for a girl who'd been particularly nice to me? I told you I'd have to devote a lot of the evening to her."

"Go on devote it, then. I'm leaving soon."

"Who with?"

"Capone has a sleigh."

"Yes, you're leaving with him. He'll take you for a ride; you'll be on the spot if you don't look out."

He felt a touch of uneasiness. The mystery she had lacked this afternoon was strong in her now. Before he should be so weak as to grant her another advantage, he turned and asked one of the "ickle durls" to dance.

The "ickle durl" bored him. She admired him; she was used to clasping her hands together in his wake and heaving audible sighs. When the music stopped he gave her an outrageous compliment to atone for his preoccupation and left her at her table. The night was ruined. He realized that it was Rosemary who moved him most deeply, and his eyes wandered to her across the room. He told himself that she was playing him jealously, but he hated the way she was fooling with young Caros Moros; and he liked it still less when he glanced over a little later and found that the two of them were gone.

He sprang up and dashed out of the door; there was the snow, lightly falling, there were the waiting sleighs, the horses patient in their frozen harness, and there was a small, excited crowd of Swiss gathered around Mr. Cola's sleigh.

"*Salaud!*" he heard. "*Salaud Français!*"

It appeared that the French courier, long accepted as a member of the Cola menage, had spent the afternoon tippling with his master; the courier had not survived. Cola had been compelled to assist him outdoors, where he promptly gave tongue to a series of insults directed at the Swiss. They were all boches. Why hadn't they come in the war? A crowd gathered, and as it included several Swiss who were in the same state as the Frenchman, the matter was growing complicated; the women were uncomfortable, the Siamese were smiling diplomatically among themselves. One of the Swiss was on the runner of the sleigh, leaning over Mrs. Cola and shaking his fist in the courier's face. Mr. Cola stood up in the sleigh and addressed them in hoarse American as to "the big idea?"

"Dirty Frenchmen!" cried the Swiss. "Yes, and during your Revolution did you not cut the Swiss Guards down to the last man?"

"Get out of here!" shouted Cola. "Hey, coachman, drive right over 'em! You guys go easy there! Take your hands off the sleigh. . . . Shut up, you!"—this to the courier, who was still muttering wildly. Cola looked at him as if he contemplated throwing him to the crowd. In a moment Tommy edged himself between the outraged Swiss patriot and the sleigh.

"Ne'mine what they say! Drive on!" cried Cola again. "We got to get these girls out of here!"

Conscious of Rosemary's eyes staring at him out of a bearskin robe, and of Caros Moros next to her, Tommy raised his voice:

"*Ce sont des dames Americaines; il n'y a qu'un Français. Voyons! Qu'est-ce que vous voulez?*"

But the massacre of the Swiss Guards was not to be disposed of so lightly.

Tommy had an inspiration. "But who tried to save the Swiss Guards? Answer me that!" he shouted. "An American—Benjamin Franklin! He almost saved them!"

His preposterous statement rang out strong and true upon the electric air. The protagonist of the martyrs was momentarily baffled.

"An American saved them!" Tommy cried. "Hurray for America and Switzerland!" And he added quickly, to the coachman, "Drive on now—and fast!"

The sleigh started with a lurch. Two men clung to it for a moment and then let go, and the conveyance slid free behind the swiftly trotting horses.

"*Vive l'Amerique! Vive la Suisse!*" Tommy shouted.

"*Vive la Fra——*" began the courier, but Cola put his fur glove in the man's mouth. They drove rapidly for a few minutes.

"Drop me here," Tommy said. "I have to go back to the dance."
He looked at Rosemary, but she would not meet his eye. She was a
bundle of fur next to Caros Moros, and he saw the latter drop his arm
around her till they were one mass of fur together. The sight was
horrible; of all the people in the world she had become the most
desirable, and he wanted every bit of her youth and freshness. He
wanted to jerk Caros Moros to his feet and pull him from the sleigh.
He saw how stupid it had been to play so long with her innocence and
sincerity, until now she scarcely saw him any more, scarcely knew he
was there.

As he swung himself off the sleigh, Rosemary and Caros Moros
were singing softly:

> . . . *I wouldn't stoop*
> *To onion soup;*
> *With corn-beef hash I'm all*
> *through——*

and the Spaniard winked at Tommy as if to say, "We know how to
handle this little girl, don't we?"

The courier struggled and then cried in a blurred voice: "Beeb wa
Fwance."

"Keep your glove in his mouth," said Tommy savagely. "Choke
him to death."

He walked off down the road, utterly miserable.

III

His first instinct next morning was to phone her immediately;
his second was to sulk proudly in his room, hoping against hope that
his own phone would ring. After luncheon he went downstairs,
where he was addressed by the objectionable Greek who had danced
with her at tea yesterday afternoon—ages ago.

"Tell me; you like to play the ping-pong?"

"It depends who with," Tommy answered rudely. Immediately
he was so sorry that he went downstairs with the man and batted the
white puff-balls for half an hour.

At four he skied over to Emily's hotel, resolving to drive the other
and more vivid image from his mind. The lobby was filled with
children in fancy dress, who had gathered there from many hotels for
the children's Christmas ball.

Emily was a long time coming down, and when she did she was
hurried and distracted.

"I'm so sorry. I've been costuming my children, and now I've got to get them launched into this orgy, because they're both very shy."

"Sit and get your breath a minute. We'll talk about love."

"Honestly, I can't, Tommy. I'll see you later." And she added quickly, "Can't you get your little Southern girl? She seemed to worry you a lot last night."

After half an hour of diffident grand marches, Emily came back to him, but Tommy's patience was exhausted and he was on his feet to go. Even now she showed him that he was asking for time and attention out of turn, and, being unavailable, she had again grown as mysterious as Rosemary.

"It's been a hard day in lots of ways," she explained as she walked with him to the door. "Things I can't tell you about."

"Oh, yes?" People had so many affairs. You never knew how much space you actually occupied in their lives.

Outdoors he came across her young cousin, Frank Forrester, buckling on his skis. Pushing off together, they drifted slowly down a slushy hill.

"Let me tell you something," Frank burst out. "I'm never going to get married. I've seen too much of it. And if any girl asked my advice, I'd tell her to stay out." He was full of the idea: "There's my mother, for instance. She married a second husband, and what does he do but have her spied on and bribe her maids to open her mail? Then there's Emily. You know what happened to her; one night her husband came home and told her she was acting cold to him, but that he'd fix that up. So he built a bonfire under her bed, made up of shoes and things, and set fire to it. And if the leather hadn't smelled so terrible she'd have been burned to death."

"That's just two marriages."

"Two!" said Frank resentfully. "Isn't that enough? Now we think Emily's husband is having her spied on. There's a man keeps watching us in the dining room."

As Tommy stemmed into the driveway of his hotel, he wondered if he was really attractive to women at all. Yesterday he had been sure of these two, holding them in the hollow of his hand. As he dressed for dinner he realized that he wanted them both. It was an outrage that he couldn't have them both. Wouldn't a girl rather have half of him than all of Harry Whitby, or a whole Spic with a jar of pomade thrown in? Life was so badly arranged—better no women at all than only one woman.

He shouted "Come in!" to a knock at his salon door, and leaning around the corner, his hand on his dress tie, found the two "ickle durls."

He started. Had they inherited him from Rosemary? Had he been theirs since the superior pair seemed to have relinquished their claims? Were they really presuming that he might escort them to the fancy-dress ball tonight?

Slipping on his coat, he went into his parlor. They were got up as Arlésienne peasant girls, with high black bonnets and starched aprons.

"We've come about Rosemary," they said directly. "We wanted to see if you won't do something about it. She's been in bed all day and she says she isn't coming to the party tonight. Couldn't you at least call her up?"

"Why should I call her up?"

"You know she's perfectly crazy about you, and last night was the most miserable she ever spent in her life. After she broke Caros Moros' guitar, we couldn't stop her crying."

A contented glow spread over Tommy. His instinct was to telephone at once, but, curiously enough, to telephone Emily, so that he could talk to her with his newborn confidence.

The "ickle durls" moved toward the door. "You will call her up," they urged him respectfully.

"Right now." He took them each in one arm, like a man in a musical comedy, and kissed the rouge on their cheeks. When they were gone, he telephoned Rosemary. Her "hello" was faint and frightened.

"Are you sorry you were so terrible to me last night, baby?" he demanded. "No real pickaninny would——"

"You were the terrible one."

"Are you coming to the party tonight?"

"Oh, I will if you'll act differently. But I'll be hours; I'm still in bed. I can't get down till after dinner."

With Rosemary safely locked up again in the tranquil cells of his mind, he rang up Emily.

"I'm sorry I was so short with you this afternoon," she said immediately.

"Are you in love with me?"

"Why, no; I don't think so."

"Aren't you a little bit in love with me?"

"I like you a lot."

"Dear Emily. What's this about being spied on?"

"Oh, there's a man here who walked into my room—maybe by accident. But he always watches us."

"I can't stand having you annoyed," he said. "Please call on me if anything definite happens. I'd be glad to come up and rub his face in the snow."

There was a pregnant telephone silence.

"I wish I was with you now," he said gently.

After a moment she whispered, "I do too."

He had nothing to complain of; the situation was readjusted; things were back where they had been twenty-four hours ago. Eating dinner alone, he felt that in reality both girls were beside him, one on either hand. The dining room was shimmering with unreality for the fancy-dress party, for tonight was the last big event of the Christmas season. Most of the younger people who gave it its real color would start back to school tomorrow.

And Tommy felt that in the evening somewhere—but in whose company he couldn't say—there would come a moment; perhaps the moment. Probably very late, when the orchestra and what remained of the party—the youth and cream of it—would move into the bar, and Abdul, with Oriental delight in obscurity, would manipulate the illumination in a sort of counterpoint whose other tone was the flashing moon from the ice rink, bouncing in the big windows. Tommy had danced with Rosemary in that light a few hours after their first meeting; he remembered the mysterious darkness, with the cigarette points turning green or silver when the lights shone red, the sense of snow outside and the occasional band of white falling across the dancers as a door was opened and shut. He remembered her in his arms and the plaint of the orchestra playing:

> *That's why mother made me*
> *Promise to be true*

and the other vague faces passing in the darkness.

> *She knew I'd meet someone*
> *Exactly like you.*

He thought now of Emily. They would have a very long, serious conversation, sitting in the hall. Then they would slip away and talk even more seriously, but this time with her very close to him. Anything might happen—anything.

But he was thinking of the two apart; and tonight they would both be here in full view of each other. There must be no more complications like last evening; he must dovetail the affairs with skill and thought.

Emerging from dinner, he strolled down the corridor, already filled with graces and grotesques, conventional clouds of columbines, clowns, peasants, pirates and ladies of Spain. He never wore costume himself and the sight of a man in motley made him sad, but some of the girls were lovelier than in life, and his heart jumped as he caught sight of a snow-white ballet dancer at the end of the corridor, and recognized Rosemary. But almost as he started toward her, another party emerged from the cloakroom, and in it was Emily.

He thought quickly. Neither one had seen him, and to greet one with the other a few yards away was to get off on the wrong foot, for he had invented opening remarks for each one—remarks which must be made alone. With great presence of mind, he dove for the men's wash room and stood there tensely.

Emerging in a few minutes, he hovered cautiously along the hall. Passing the lounge, he saw, in a side glance, that Caros Moros was with Rosemary and that she was glancing about impatiently. Emily looked up from her table, saw him and beckoned. Without moving a muscle of his face, Tommy stared above her and passed on. He decided to wait in the bar until the dancing actually started; it would be easier when the two were separated in the crowd. In the bar he was hailed gratefully by Mr. Cola; Mr. Cola was killing time there desperately, with his harem waiting outside.

"I'm having them all psychoanalyzed," he said. "I got a guy down from Zurich, and he's doing one a day. I never saw such a gloomy bunch of women; always bellyaching wherever I take 'em. A man I knew told me he had his wife psychonanalyzed and she was easier to be with afterward."

Tommy heard only vaguely. He had become aware that, as if they had planned it in collusion, Emily and Rosemary had sauntered simultaneously into the bar. Blind-eyed and breathless, he strode out and into the ballroom. One of the "ickle durls" danced by him and he seized her gratefully.

"Rosemary was looking for you," she told him, turning up the flattered face of seventeen.

Presently he felt silly dancing with her, but, perhaps because of her admirers' deference to his maturer years, three encores passed and no one cut in. He began to feel like a man pushing a baby carriage. He took a dislike to her colonial costume, the wig of which sent gusts of powder up his nose. She even smelled young—of very pure baby soap and peppermint candy. Like almost every act he had performed in the last two days, he was unable to realize why he had cut in on her at all.

He saw Rosemary dancing with Caros Moros, then with other partners, and then again with Caros Moros. He had now been a half hour with the "ickle durl"; his gayety was worn thin and his smile was becoming strained when at last he was cut in on. Feeling ruffled and wilted, he looked around, to find that Rosemary and Caros Moros had disappeared. With the discovery, he came to the abrupt decision that he would ask her to marry him.

He went searching; plowing brusquely through crowds like a swimmer in surf. Just as, finally, he caught sight of the white-pointed cap and escaping yellow curls, he was accosted by Frank Forrester:

"Emily sent me to look for you. Her maid telephoned that somebody tried to get into her room, and we think it's the man who keeps watching her in the dining room."

Tommy stared at him vaguely, and Frank continued:

"Don't you think you and I ought to go up there now and rub his face in the snow?"

"Where?"

"To our hotel."

Tommy's eyes begged around him. There was nothing he wanted less.

"We'd like to find out one way or another." And then, as Tommy still hesitated: "You haven't lost your nerve, have you? About rubbing his face in the snow?"

Evasion was impossible. Tommy threw a last quick glance at Rosemary, who was moving with Caros Moros back toward the dancing floor.

At Emily's hotel the maid waited in the lower hall. It seemed that the bedroom door had opened slowly a little way; then closed again quickly. She had fled downstairs. Silently Tommy and Frank mounted the stairs and approached the room; they breathed quietly at the threshold and flung open the door. The room was empty.

"I think this was a great flight of the imagination," Tommy scolded. "We might as well go back——"

He broke off, as there were light footsteps in the corridor and a man walked coolly into the room.

"*Ach je!*" he exclaimed sharply.

"Aha!" Frank stepped behind him and shut the door. "We got you."

The man looked from one to the other in alarm.

"I must be in the wrong room!" he exclaimed, and then, with an uncomfortable laugh: "I see! My room is just above this and I got the wrong floor again. In my last hotel I was on the third floor, so I got the habit——"

"Why do you always listen to every word we say at table?" demanded Frank.

"I like to look at you because you are such nice, handsome, wealthy American people. I've come to this hotel for years."

"We're wasting time," said Tommy impatiently. "Let's go to the manager."

The intruder was more than willing. He proved to be a coal

dealer from Berlin, an old and valued client of the house. They apologized; there was no hard feeling; they must join him in a drink. It was ten minutes before they got away, and Tommy led a furious pace back toward the dance. He was chiefly furious at Emily. Why should people be spied upon? What sort of women were spied upon? He felt as if this were a plan of Emily's to keep him away from Rosemary, who with every instant was dancing farther and farther off with Caros Moros into a youthful Spanish dream. At the drive of the hotel Frank said good night.

"You're not going back to the dance?"

"It's finished; the ballroom's dark. Everybody's probably gone to Doldorp, because here it always closes early on Sunday night."

Tommy dashed up the drive to the hotel. In the gloomy half light of the office a last couple were struggling into overshoes; the dance was over.

"For you, Mr. McLane." The night concierge handed him a telegram. Tommy stared at it for a moment before he tore it open.

> GENEVA SWITZERLAND 2/1/31
>
> H.P. EASTBY ARRIVED TONIGHT FROM PARIS STOP ABSOLUTELY ESSENTIAL YOU BE HERE FOR EARLY LUNCH MONDAY STOP AFTERWARD ACCOMPANYING HIM TO DIJON   SAGE

For a moment he couldn't understand. When he had grasped the utterly inarguable dictum, he took the concierge by both arms.

"You know Miss Merriweather. Did she go to Doldorp?"

"I think she did."

"Get me a sleigh."

"Every sleigh in town has gone over there; some with ten people in them. These last people here couldn't get sleighs."

"Any price!" cried Tommy fiercely. "Think!"

He threw down five large silver wheels on the desk.

"There's the station sleigh, but the horses have got to be out at seven in the morning. If you went to the stables and asked Eric——"

Half an hour later the big, glassed-in carryall jingled out on the Doldorp road with a solitary passenger. After a mile a first open sleigh dashed past them on its way home, and Tommy leaned out and glared into the anonymous bundles of fur and called "Rosemary!" in a firm but unavailing voice. When they had gone another mile, sleighs began to pass in increasing numbers. Sometimes a taunting shout drifted back to him; sometimes his voice was drowned in a chorus of "Jingle Bells" or "Merrily We Roll Along." It was hopeless; the sleighs were coming so fast now that he couldn't examine the occupants; and then there were no more sleighs and he sat upright in the great, hearselike vehicle, rocking on toward a town that he knew no longer held what he was after. A last chorus rang in his ears:

> *Good night, ladies,*
> *Good night, ladies,*
> *Good night, lay-de-es,*
> *I'm going to leave you now.*

IV

He was awake at seven with the *valet de chambre* shaking his shoulders. The sun was waving gold, green and white flags on the Wildstrubel as he fumbled clumsily for his razor. The great fiasco of the night before drifted over him, and he could hear even the great blackbirds cawing, "You went away too far," on the white balcony outside.

Desperately he considered telephoning her, wondering if he could explain to a girl still plunged in drowsiness what he would have had trouble in explaining in person. But it was already time to go; he drove off in a crowded sleigh with other faces wan in the white morning.

They were passing the crisp pale green rink where Wiener waltzes blared all day and the blazing colors of many schools flashed against pale blue skies. Then there was the station full of frozen breath; he was in the first-class carriage of the train drawing away from the little valley, past pink pines and fresh, diamond-strewn snow.

Across from him women were weeping softly for temporarily lost children whom they had left up there for another term at school. And in a compartment farther up he suddenly glimpsed the two "ickle durls." He drew back; he couldn't stand that this morning. But he was not to escape so readily. As the train passed Caux, high on its solitary precipice, the "ickle durls" came along the corridor and spied him.

"Hey, there!" They exchanged glances. "We didn't think you were on the train."

"Do you know," began the older one—the one he had danced with last night—"what we'd like?"

It was something daring evidently, for they went off into spasms of suppressed giggles.

"What we'd like," the "ickle durl" continued, "is to ask you if—we wondered if you would send us a photo."

"Of what?" asked Tommy.

"Of yourself."

"She's asking for herself," declared the other "ickle durl" indignantly. "I wouldn't be so darn fresh."

"I haven't had a photo taken for years."

"Even an old one," pursued the "ickle durl" timidly.

"And listen," said the other one: "Won't you come up for just a minute and say good-by to Rosemary? She's still crying her eyes out, and I think she'd like it if you even came up to say good-by."

He jerked forward as if thrown by the train.

"Rosemary!"

"She cried all the way to Doldorp and all the way back, and then she broke Caros Moros' other guitar that he keeps in reserve; so he feels awful, being up there another month without any guitar."

But Tommy was gone. As the train began traversing back and forth toward Lake Geneva, the two "ickle durls" sat down resignedly in his compartment.

"So then——" he was saying at the moment. "No, don't move; I don't mind a bit. I like you like that. Use my handkerchief. . . . Listen. If you've got to go to Paris, can't you possibly come by way of Geneva and Dijon?"

"Oh, I'd love to. I don't want to let you out of my sight—not now, anyhow."

At that moment—perhaps out of habit, perhaps because the two girls had become almost indissolubly wedded in his mind—he had a sharp, vivid impression of Emily. Wouldn't it be better for him to see them both together before coming to such an important decision?

"Will you marry me?" he cried desperately. "Are we engaged? Can't we put it in writing?"

With the sound of his own voice the other image faded from his mind forever.

Flight and Pursuit

(*The Saturday Evening Post*, 14 May 1932)

"Flight and Pursuit" was probably written in Switzerland in April 1931. The *Post* bought the story with some reluctance for $4000, and Harold Ober reported to Fitzgerald: "The Post are taking FLIGHT AND PURSUIT but they want me to tell you that they do not feel that your last three stories have been up to the best you can do. They think it might be a good idea for you to write some American stories—that is stories laid on this side of the Atlantic and they feel that the last stories have been lacking in plot." The *Post* indicated its reservations about this story by holding it for a year before publishing it in fourth position and leaving Fitzgerald's name off the cover. (His name appeared on the cover only once again, for the 4 June 1932 issue.)

"Flight and Pursuit" again drew on Fitzgerald's unhappy impressions of Switzerland. As he commented in "The Hotel Child," "this corner of Europe does not draw people; rather, it accepts them without too many inconvenient questions."

In 1918, a few days before the Armistice, Caroline Martin, of Derby, in Virginia, eloped with a trivial young lieutenant from Ohio. They were married in a town over the Maryland border and she stayed there until George Corcoran got his discharge—then they went to his home in the North.

It was a desperate, reckless marriage. After she had left her aunt's house with Corcoran, the man who had broken her heart realized that he had broken his own too; he telephoned, but Caroline had gone, and all that he could do that night was to lie awake and remember her waiting in the front yard, with the sweetness draining down into her out of the magnolia trees, out of the dark world, and remember himself arriving in his best uniform, with boots shining and with his heart full of selfishness that, from shame, turned into cruelty. Next day he learned that she had eloped with Corcoran and, as he had deserved, he had lost her.

In Sidney Lahaye's overwhelming grief, the petty reasons for his act disgusted him—the alternative of a long trip around the world or of a bachelor apartment in New York with four Harvard friends; more positively the fear of being held, of being bound. The trip—they could have taken it together. The bachelor apartment—it had resolved into its bare, cold constituent parts in a single night. Being held? Why, that was all he wanted—to be close to that freshness, to be held in those young arms forever.

He had been an egoist, brought up selfishly by a selfish mother; this was his first suffering. But like his small, wiry, handsome person, he was all knit of one piece and his reactions were not trivial. What he did he carried with him always, and he knew he had done a contemptible and stupid thing. He carried his grief around, and eventually it was good for him. But inside of him, utterly unassimilable, indigestible, remained the memory of the girl.

Meanwhile, Caroline Corcoran, lately the belle of a Virginia town, was paying for the luxury of her desperation in a semi-slum of Dayton, Ohio.

II

She had been three years in Dayton and the situation had become intolerable. Brought up in a district where everyone was comparatively poor, where not two gowns out of fifty at country-club dances cost more than thirty dollars, lack of money had not been formidable in itself. This was very different. She came into a world not only of straining poverty but of a commonness and vulgarity that she had never touched before. It was in this regard that George Corcoran had deceived her. Somewhere he had acquired a faint patina of good breeding and he had said or done nothing to prepare her for his mother, into whose two-room flat he introduced her. Aghast, Caroline realized that she had stepped down several floors. These people had no position of any kind; George knew no one; she was literally alone in a strange city. Mrs. Corcoran disliked Caroline— disliked her good manners, her Southern ways, the added burden of her presence. For all her airs, she had brought them nothing save, eventually, a baby. Meanwhile George got a job and they moved to more spacious quarters, but mother came, too, for she owned her son, and Caroline's months went by in unimaginable dreariness. At first she was too ashamed and too poor to go home, but at the end of a year her aunt sent her money for a visit and she spent a month in Derby with her little son, proudly reticent, but unable to keep some of the truth from leaking out to her friends. Her friends had done well, or less well, but none of them had fared quite so ill as she.

But after three years, when Caroline's child became less dependent, and when the last of her affection for George had been frittered away, as his pleasant manners became debased with his own inadequacies, and when her bright, unused beauty still plagued her in the mirror, she knew that the break was coming. Not that she had specific hopes of happiness—for she accepted the idea that she had wrecked her life, and her capacity for dreaming had left her that November night three years before—but simply because conditions were intolerable. The break was heralded by a voice over the phone— a voice she remembered only as something that had done her terrible injury long ago.

"Hello," said the voice—a strong voice with strain in it. "Mrs. George Corcoran?"

"Yes."

"Who was Caroline Martin?"

"Who is this?"

"This is someone you haven't seen for years. Sidney Lahaye."

After a moment she answered in a different tone: "Yes?"

"I've wanted to see you for a long time," the voice went on.

"I don't see why," said Caroline simply.

"I want to see you. I can't talk over the phone."

Mrs. Corcoran, who was in the room, asked "Who is it?" forming the words with her mouth. Caroline shook her head slightly.

"I don't see why you want to see me," she said, "and I don't think I want to see you." Her breath came quicker; the old wound opened up again, the injury that had changed her from a happy young girl in love into whatever vague entity in the scheme of things she was now.

"Please don't ring off," Sidney said. "I didn't call you without thinking it over carefully. I heard things weren't going well with you."

"That's not true." Caroline was very conscious now of Mrs. Corcoran's craning neck. "Things are going well. And I can't see what possible right you have to intrude in my affairs."

"Wait, Caroline! You don't know what happened back in Derby after you left. I was frantic——"

"Oh, I don't care——" she cried. "Let me alone; do you hear?"

She hung up the receiver. She was outraged that this man, almost forgotten now save as an instrument of her disaster, should come back into her life!

"Who was it?" demanded Mrs. Corcoran.

"Just a man—a man I loathe."

"Who?"

"Just an old friend."

Mrs. Corcoran looked at her sharply. "It wasn't that man, was it?" she asked.

"What man?"

"The one you told Georgie about three years ago, when you were first married—it hurt his feelings. The man you were in love with that threw you over."

"Oh, no," said Caroline. "That is my affair."

She went to the bedroom that she shared with George. If Sidney should persist and come here, how terrible—to find her sordid in a mean street.

When George came in, Caroline heard the mumble of his mother's conversation behind the closed door; she was not surprised when he asked at dinner:

"I hear that an old friend called you up."

"Yes. Nobody you know."

"Who was it?"

"It was an old acquaintance, but he won't call again," she said.

"I'll bet he will," guessed Mrs. Corcoran. "What was it you told him wasn't true?"

"That's my affair."

Mrs. Corcoran glanced significantly at George, who said:

"It seems to me if a man calls up my wife and annoys her, I have a right to know about it."

"You won't, and that's that." She turned to his mother: "Why did you have to listen, anyhow?"

"I was there. You're my son's wife."

"You make trouble," said Caroline quietly; "you listen and watch me and make trouble. How about the woman who keeps calling up George—you do your best to hush that up."

"That's a lie!" George cried. "And you can't talk to my mother like that! If you don't think I'm sick of your putting on a lot of dog when I work all day and come home to find——"

As he went off into a weak, raging tirade, pouring out his own self-contempt upon her, Caroline's thoughts escaped to the fifty-dollar bill, a present from her grandmother hidden under the paper in a bureau drawer. Life had taken much out of her in three years; she did not know whether she had the audacity to run away—it was nice, though, to know the money was there.

Next day, in the spring sunlight, things seemed better—and she and George had a reconciliation. She was desperately adaptable, desperately sweet-natured, and for an hour she had forgotten all the trouble and felt the old emotion of mingled passion and pity for him. Eventually his mother would go; eventually he would change and improve; and meanwhile there was her son with her own kind, wise smile, turning over the pages of a linen book on the sunny carpet. As her soul sank into a helpless, feminine apathy, compounded of the next hour's duty, of a fear of further hurt or incalculable change, the phone rang sharply through the flat.

Again and again it rang, and she stood rigid with terror. Mrs. Corcoran was gone to market, but it was not the old woman she feared. She feared the black cone hanging from the metal arm, shrilling and shrilling across the sunny room. It stopped for a minute, replaced by her heartbeats; then began again. In a panic she rushed into her room, threw little Dexter's best clothes and her only presentable dress and shoes into a suitcase and put the fifty-dollar bill in her purse. Then taking her son's hand, she hurried out of the door, pursued down the apartment stairs by the persistent cry of the telephone. The windows were open, and as she hailed a taxi and directed it to the station, she could still hear it clamoring out into the sunny morning.

III

Two years later, looking a full two years younger, Caroline regarded herself in the mirror, in a dress that she had paid for. She was a stenographer, employed by an importing firm in New York; she and young Dexter lived on her salary and on the income of ten thousand dollars in bonds, a legacy from her aunt. If life had fallen short of what it had once promised, it was at least livable again, less than misery. Rising to a sense of her big initial lie, George had given her freedom and the custody of her child. He was in kindergarten now, and safe until 5:30, when she would call for him and take him to the small flat that was at least her own. She had nothing warm near her, but she had New York, with its diversion for all purses, its curious yielding up of friends for the lonely, its quick metropolitan rhythm of love and birth and death that supplied dreams to the unimaginative, pageantry and drama to the drab.

But though life was possible it was less than satisfactory. Her work was hard, she was physically fragile; she was much more tired at the day's end than the girls with whom she worked. She must consider a precarious future when her capital should be depleted by her son's education. Thinking of the Corcoran family, she had a horror of being dependent on her son; and she dreaded the day when she must push him from her. She found that her interest in men had gone. Her two experiences had done something to her; she saw them clearly and she saw them darkly, and that part of her life was sealed up, and it grew more and more faint, like a book she had read long ago. No more love.

Caroline saw this with detachment, and not without a certain, almost impersonal, regret. In spite of the fact that sentiment was the legacy of a pretty girl, it was just one thing that was not for her. She surprised herself by saying in front of some other girls that she disliked men, but she knew it was the truth. It was an ugly phrase, but now, moving in an approximately foursquare world, she detested the compromises and evasions of her marriage. "I hate men—I, Caroline, hate men. I want from them no more than courtesy and to be left alone. My life is incomplete, then, but so be it. For others it is complete, for me it is incomplete."

The day that she looked at her evening dress in the mirror, she was in a country house on Long Island—the home of Evelyn Murdock, the most spectacularly married of all her old Virginia friends. They had met in the street, and Caroline was there for the week-end, moving unfamiliarly through a luxury she had never imagined, intoxicated at finding that in her new evening dress she was as young and attractive as these other women, whose lives had followed more glamorous paths. Like New York the rhythm of the week-end, with its birth, its planned gayeties and its announced end, followed the rhythm of life and was a substitute for it. The sentiment had gone from Caroline, but the patterns remained. The guests, dimly glimpsed on the veranda, were prospective admirers. The visit to the nursery was a promise of future children of her own; the descent to dinner was a promenade down a marriage aisle, and her gown was a wedding dress with an invisible train.

"The man you're sitting next to," Evelyn said, "is an old friend of yours. Sidney Lahaye—he was at Camp Rosecrans."

After a confused moment she found that it wasn't going to be difficult at all. In the moment she had met him—such a quick moment that she had no time to grow excited—she realized that he was gone for her. He was only a smallish, handsome man, with a flushed, dark skin, a smart little black mustache and very fine eyes. It was just as gone as gone. She tried to remember why he had once seemed the most desirable person in the world, but she could only remember that he had made love to her, that he had made her think of them as engaged, and then that he had acted badly and thrown her over—into George Corcoran's arms. Years later he had telephoned like a traveling salesman remembering a dalliance in a casual city. Caroline was entirely unmoved and at her ease as they sat down at table.

But Sidney Lahaye was not relinquishing her so easily.

"So I called you up that night in Derby," he said; "I called you for half an hour. Everything had changed for me in that ride out to camp."

"You had a beautiful remorse."

"It wasn't remorse; it was self-interest. I realized I was terribly in love with you. I stayed awake all night——"

Caroline listened indifferently. It didn't even explain things; nor did it tempt her to cry out on fate—it was just a fact.

He stayed near her, persistently. She knew no one else at the party; there was no niche in any special group for her. They talked on the veranda after dinner, and once she said coolly:

"Women are fragile that way. You do something to them at certain times and literally nothing can ever change what you've done."

"You mean that you definitely hate me."

She nodded. "As far as I feel actively about you at all."

"I suppose so. It's awful, isn't it?"

"No. I even have to think before I can really remember how I stood waiting for you in the garden that night, holding all my dreams and hopes in my arms like a lot of flowers—they were that to me, anyhow. I thought J was pretty sweet. I'd saved myself up for that—all ready to hand it all to you. And then you came up to me and kicked me." She laughed incredulously. "You behaved like an awful person. Even though I don't care any more, you'll always be an awful person to me. Even if you'd found me that night, I'm not at all sure that anything could have been done about it. Forgiveness is just a silly word in a matter like that."

Feeling her own voice growing excited and annoyed, she drew her cape around her and said in an ordinary voice:

"It's getting too cold to sit here."

"One more thing before you go," he said. "It wasn't typical of me. It was so little typical that in the last five years I've never spent an unoccupied moment without remembering it. Not only I haven't married, I've never even been faintly in love. I've measured up every girl I've met to you, Caroline—their faces, their voices, the tips of their elbows."

"I'm sorry I had such a devastating effect on you. It must have been a nuisance."

"I've kept track of you since I called you in Dayton; I knew that, sooner or later, we'd meet."

"I'm going to say good night."

But saying good night was easier than sleeping, and Caroline had only an hour's haunted doze behind her when she awoke at seven. Packing her bag, she made up a polite, abject letter to Evelyn Murdock, explaining why she was unexpectedly leaving on Sunday morning. It was difficult and she disliked Sidney Lahaye a little bit more intensely for that.

IV

Months later Caroline came upon a streak of luck. A Mrs. O'Connor, whom she met through Evelyn Murdock, offered her a post as private secretary and traveling companion. The duties were light, the traveling included an immediate trip abroad, and Caroline, who was thin and run down from work, jumped at the chance. With astonishing generosity the offer included her boy.

From the beginning Caroline was puzzled as to what had attracted Helen O'Connor to her. Her employer was a woman of thirty, dissipated in a discreet way, extremely worldly and, save for her curious kindness to Caroline, extremely selfish. But the salary was good and Caroline shared in every luxury and was invariably treated as an equal.

The next three years were so different from anything in her past that they seemed years borrowed from the life of someone else. The Europe in which Helen O'Connor moved was not one of tourists but of seasons. Its most enduring impression was a phantasmagoria of the names of places and people—of Biarritz, of Mme de Colmar, of Deauville, of the Comte de Berme, of Cannes, of the Derehiemers, of Paris and the Chateau de Madrid. They lived the life of casinos and hotels so assiduously reported in the Paris American papers—Helen O'Connor drank and sat up late, and after a while Caroline drank and sat up late. To be slim and pale was fashionable during those years, and deep in Caroline was something that had become directionless and purposeless, that no longer cared. There was no love; she sat next to many men at table, appreciated compliments, courtesies and small gallantries, but the moment something more was hinted, she froze very definitely. Even when she was stimulated with excitement and wine, she felt the growing hardness of her sheath like a breastplate. But in other ways she was increasingly restless.

At first it had been Helen O'Connor who urged her to go out; now it became Caroline herself for whom no potion was too strong or any evening too late. There began to be mild lectures from Helen.

"This is absurd. After all, there's such a thing as moderation."

"I suppose so, if you really want to live."

"But you want to live; you've got a lot to live for. If my skin was like yours, and my hair——Why don't you look at some of the men that look at you?"

"Life isn't good enough, that's all," said Caroline. "For a while I made the best of it, but I'm surer every day that it isn't good enough. People get through by keeping busy; the lucky ones are those with interesting work. I've been a good mother, but I'd certainly be an idiot putting in a sixteen-hour day mothering Dexter into being a sissy."

"Why don't you marry Lahaye? He has money and position and everything you could want."

There was a pause. "I've tried men. To hell with men."

Afterward she wondered at Helen's solicitude, having long realized that the other woman cared nothing for her. They had not even mutual tastes; often they were openly antipathetic and didn't meet for days at a time. Caroline wondered why she was kept on, but she had grown more self-indulgent in these years and she was not inclined to quibble over the feathers that made soft her nest.

One night on Lake Maggiore things changed in a flash. The blurred world seen from a merry-go-round settled into place; the merry-go-round suddenly stopped.

They had gone to the hotel in Locarno because of Caroline. For months she had had a mild but persistent asthma and they had come there for rest before the gayeties of the fall season at Biarritz. They met friends, and with them Caroline wandered to the Kursaal to play mild *boule* at a maximum of two Swiss francs. Helen remained at the hotel.

Caroline was sitting in the bar. The orchestra was playing a Wiener Walzer, and suddenly she had the sensation that the chords were extending themselves, that each bar of three-four time was bending in the middle, dropping a little and thus drawing itself out, until the waltz itself, like a phonograph running down, became a torture. She put her fingers in her ears; then suddenly she coughed into her handkerchief.

She gasped.

The man with her asked: "What is it? Are you sick?"

She leaned back against the bar, her handkerchief with the trickle of blood clasped concealingly in her hand. It seemed to her half an hour before she answered, "No, I'm all right," but evidently it was only a few seconds, for the man did not continue his solicitude.

"I must get out," Caroline thought. "What is it?" Once or twice before she had noticed tiny flecks of blood, but never anything like this. She felt another cough coming and, cold with fear and weakness, wondered if she could get to the wash room.

After a long while the trickle stopped and someone wound the orchestra up to normal time. Without a word she walked slowly from the room, holding herself delicately as glass. The hotel was not a block away; she set out along the lamplit street. After a minute she wanted to cough again, so she stopped and held her breath and leaned against the wall. But this time it was no use; she raised her handkerchief to her mouth and lowered it after a minute, this time concealing it from her eyes. Then she walked on.

In the elevator another spell of weakness overcame her, but she managed to reach the door of her suite, where she collapsed on a little sofa in the antechamber. Had there been room in her heart for any emotion except terror, she would have been surprised at the sound of an excited dialogue in the salon, but at the moment the voices were part of a nightmare and only the shell of her ear registered what they said.

"I've been six months in Central Asia, or I'd have caught up with this before," a man's voice said, and Helen answered, "I've no sense of guilt whatsoever."

"I don't suppose you have. I'm just panning myself for having picked you out."

"May I ask who told you this tale, Sidney?"

"Two people. A man in New York had seen you in Monte Carlo and said for a year you'd been doing nothing but buying drinks for a bunch of cadgers and spongers. He wondered who was backing you. Then I saw Evelyn Murdock in Paris, and she said Caroline was dissipating night after night; she was thin as a rail and her face looked like death. That's what brought me down here."

"Now listen, Sidney. I'm not going to be bullied about this. Our arrangement was that I was to take Caroline abroad and give her a good time, because you were in love with her or felt guilty about her, or something. You employed me for that and you backed me. Well, I've done just what you wanted. You said you wanted her to meet lots of men."

"I said men."

"I've rounded up what I could. In the first place, she's absolutely indifferent, and when men find that out, they're liable to go away."

He sat down. "Can't you understand that I wanted to do her good, not harm? She's had a rotten time; she's spent most of her youth paying for something that was my fault, so I wanted to make it up the best way I could. I wanted her to have two years of pleasure; I wanted her to learn not to be afraid of men and to have some of the gayety that I cheated her out of. With the result that you led her into two years of dissipation——" He broke off: "What was that?" he demanded.

Caroline had coughed again, irrepressibly. Her eyes were closed and she was breathing in little gasps as they came into the hall. Her hand opened and her handkerchief dropped to the floor.

In a moment she was lying on her own bed and Sidney was talking rapidly into the phone. In her dazed state the passion in his voice shook her like a vibration, and she whispered "Please! Please!"

in a thin voice. Helen loosened her dress and took off her slippers and stockings.

The doctor made a preliminary examination and then nodded formidably at Sidney. He said that by good fortune a famous Swiss specialist on tuberculosis was staying at the hotel; he would ask for an immediate consultation.

The specialist arrived in bedroom slippers. His examination was as thorough as possible with the instruments at hand. Then he talked to Sidney in the salon.

"So far as I can tell without an X ray, there is a sudden and widespread destruction of tissue on one side—sometimes happens when the patient is run down in other ways. If the X ray bears me out, I would recommend an immediate artificial pneumothorax. The only chance is to completely isolate the left lung."

"When could it be done?"

The doctor considered. "The nearest center for this trouble is Montana Vermala, about three hours from here by automobile. If you start immediately and I telephone to a colleague there, the operation might be performed tomorrow morning."

In the big, springy car Sidney held her across his lap, surrounding with his arms the mass of pillows. Caroline hardly knew who held her, nor did her mind grasp what she had overheard. Life jostled you around so—really very tiring. She was so sick, and probably going to die, and that didn't matter, except that there was something she wanted to tell Dexter.

Sidney was conscious of a desperate joy in holding her, even though she hated him, even though he had brought her nothing but harm. She was his in these night hours, so fair and pale, dependent on his arms for protection from the jolts of the rough road, leaning on his strength at last, even though she was unaware of it; yielding him the responsibility he had once feared and ever since desired. He stood between her and disaster.

Past Dome d'Ossola, a dim, murkily lighted Italian town; past Brig, where a kindly Swiss official saw his burden and waved him by without demanding his passport; down the valley of the Rhone, where the growing stream was young and turbulent in the moonlight. Then Sierre, and the haven, the sanctuary in the mountains, two miles above, where the snow gleamed. The funicular waited: Caroline sighed a little as he lifted her from the car.

"It's very good of you to take all this trouble," she whispered formally.

V

For three weeks she lay perfectly still on her back. She breathed and she saw flowers in her room. Eternally her temperature was taken. She was delirious after the operation and in her dreams she was again a girl in Virginia, waiting in the yard for her lover. Dress stay crisp for him—button stay put—bloom magnolia—air stay still and sweet. But the lover was neither Sidney Lahaye nor an abstraction of many men—it was herself, her vanished youth lingering in that garden, unsatisfied and unfulfilled; in her dream she waited there under the spell of eternal hope for the lover that would never come, and who now no longer mattered.

The operation was a success. After three weeks she sat up, in a month her fever had decreased and she took short walks for an hour every day. When this began, the Swiss doctor who had performed the operation talked to her seriously.

"There's something you ought to know about Montana Vermala; it applies to all such places. It's a well-known characteristic of tuberculosis that it tends to hurt the morale. Some of these people you'll see on the streets are back here for the third time, which is usually the last time. They've grown fond of the feverish stimulation of being sick; they come up here and live a life almost as gay as life in Paris—some of the champagne bills in this sanatorium are amazing. Of course, the air helps them, and we manage to exercise a certain salutary control over them, but that kind are never really cured, because in spite of their cheerfulness they don't want the normal world of responsibility. Given the choice, something in them would prefer to die. On the other hand, we know a lot more than we did twenty years ago, and every month we send away people of character completely cured. You've got that chance because your case is fundamentally easy; your right lung is utterly untouched. You can choose; you can run with the crowd and perhaps linger along three years, or you can leave in one year as well as ever."

Caroline's observation confirmed his remarks about the environment. The village itself was like a mining town—hasty, flimsy buildings dominated by the sinister bulk of four or five sanatoriums; chastely cheerful when the sun glittered on the snow, gloomy when the cold seeped through the gloomy pines. In contrast were the flushed, pretty girls in Paris clothes whom she passed on the street, and the well-turned-out men. It was hard to believe they were fighting such a desperate battle, and as the doctor had said, many of them were not. There was an air of secret ribaldry—it was considered funny to send miniature coffins to new arrivals, and there was a continual undercurrent of scandal. Weight, weight, weight; everyone talked of weight—how many pounds one had put on last month or lost the week before.

She was conscious of death around her, too, but she felt her own strength returning day by day in the high, vibrant air, and she knew she was not going to die.

After a month came a stilted letter from Sidney. It said:

I stayed only until the immediate danger was past. I knew that, feeling as you do, you wouldn't want my face to be the first thing you saw. So I've been down here in Sierre at the foot of the mountain, polishing up my Cambodge diary. If it's any consolation for you to have someone who cares about you within call, I'd like nothing better than to stay on here. I hold myself utterly responsible for what happened to you, and many times I've wished I had died before I came into your life. Now there's only the present—to get you well.

About your son—once a month I plan to run up to his school in Fontainebleau and see him for a few days—I've seen him once now and we like each other. This summer I'll either arrange for him to go to a camp or take him through the Norwegian fjords with me, whichever plan seems advisable.

The letter depressed Caroline. She saw herself sinking into a bondage of gratitude to this man—as though she must thank an attacker for binding up her wounds. Her first act would be to earn the money to pay him back. It made her tired even to think of such things now, but it was always present in her subconscious, and when she forgot it she dreamed of it. She wrote:

Dear Sidney: It's absurd your staying there and I'd much rather you didn't. In fact, it makes me uncomfortable. I am, of course, enormously grateful for all you've done for me and for Dexter. If it isn't too much trouble, will you come up here before you go to Paris, as I have some things to send him? Sincerely,
CAROLINE M. CORCORAN.

He came a fortnight later, full of a health and vitality that she found as annoying as the look of sadness that was sometimes in his eyes. He adored her and she had no use for his adoration. But her strongest sensation was one of fear—fear that since he had made her suffer so much, he might be able to make her suffer again.

"I'm doing you no good, so I'm going away," he said. "The doctors seem to think you'll be well by September. I'll come back and see for myself. After that I'll never bother you again."

If he expected to move her, he was disappointed.

"It may be some time before I can pay you back," she said.

"I got you into this."

"No, I got myself into it. . . . Good-by, and thank you for everything you've done."

Her voice might have been thanking him for bringing a box of candy. She was relieved at his departure. She wanted only to rest and be alone.

The winter passed. Toward the end she skied a little, and then spring came sliding up the mountain in wedges and spear points of green. Summer was sad, for two friends she had made there died within a week and she followed their coffins to the foreigners' graveyard in Sierre. She was safe now. Her affected lung had again expanded; it was scarred, but healed; she had no fever, her weight was normal and there was a bright mountain color in her cheeks.

October was set as the month of her departure, and as autumn approached, her desire to see Dexter again was overwhelming. One day a wire came from Sidney in Tibet stating that he was starting for Switzerland.

Several mornings later the floor nurse looked in to toss her a copy of the *Paris Herald* and she ran her eyes listlessly down the columns. Then she sat up suddenly in bed.

AMERICAN FEARED LOST IN BLACK SEA
Sidney Lahaye, Millionaire Aviator, and Pilot Missing Four Days.
Teheran, Persia, October 5——

Caroline sprang out of bed, ran with the paper to the window, looked away from it, then looked at it again.

AMERICAN FEARED LOST IN BLACK SEA
Sidney Lahaye, Millionaire Aviator——

"The Black Sea," she repeated, as if that was the important part of the affair—"in the Black Sea."

She stood there in the middle of an enormous quiet. The pursuing feet that had thundered in her dream had stopped. There was a steady, singing silence.

"Oh-h-h!" she said.

AMERICAN FEARED LOST IN BLACK SEA
Sidney Lahaye, Millionaire Aviator, and Pilot Missing Four Days.
Teheran, Persia, October 5——

Caroline began to talk to herself in an excited voice.

"I must get dressed," she said; "I must get to the telegraph and see whether everything possible has been done. I must start for there." She moved around the room, getting into her clothes. "Oh-h-h!" she whispered. "Oh-h-h!" With one shoe on, she fell face downward across the bed. "Oh, Sidney—Sidney!" she cried, and then again, in terrible protest: "Oh-h-h!" She rang for the nurse. "First, I must eat and get some strength; then I must find out about trains."

She was so alive now that she could feel parts of herself uncurl, unroll. Her heart picked up steady and strong, as if to say, "I'll stick by you," and her nerves gave a sort of jerk as all the old fear melted out of her. Suddenly she was grown, her broken girlhood dropped away from her, and the startled nurse answering her ring was talking to someone she had never seen before.

"It's all so simple. He loved me and I loved him. That's all there is. I must get to the telephone. We must have a consul there somewhere."

For a fraction of a second she tried to hate Dexter because he was not Sidney's son, but she had no further reserve of hate. Living or dead, she was with her love now, held close in his arms. The moment that his footsteps stopped, that there was no more menace, he had overtaken her. Caroline saw that what she had been shielding was valueless—only the little girl in the garden, only the dead, burdensome past.

"Why, I can stand anything," she said aloud—"anything—even losing him."

The doctor, alarmed by the nurse, came hurrying in.

"Now, Mrs. Corcoran, you're to be quiet. No matter what news you've had, you——Look here, this may have some bearing on it, good or bad."

He handed her a telegram, but she could not open it, and she handed it back to him mutely. He tore the envelope and held the message before her:

PICKED UP BY COALER CITY OF CLYDE STOP ALL WELL——

The telegram blurred; the doctor too. A wave of panic swept over her as she felt the old armor clasp her metallically again. She waited a minute, another minute; the doctor sat down.

"Do you mind if I sit in your lap a minute?" she said. "I'm not contagious any more, am I?"

With her head against his shoulder, she drafted a telegram with his fountain pen on the back of the one she had just received. She wrote:

PLEASE DON'T TAKE ANOTHER AEROPLANE BACK HERE. WE'VE GOT EIGHT YEARS TO MAKE UP, SO WHAT DOES A DAY OR TWO MATTER? I LOVE YOU WITH ALL MY HEART AND SOUL.

On Your Own

(unpublished)

"On Your Own" was written as "Home to Maryland" in the spring of
1931 after Fitzgerald's return to Europe from his father's funeral, a strongly
emotional event for him. Edward Fitzgerald was buried in the little cemetery
of St. Mary's Catholic Church in Rockville, Maryland—changed to
"Rocktown" in the story—now a suburb of Washington, but then the sleepy
county seat where he had been raised during and after the Civil War. "Then it
was over," the story says, "and the country doctor lay among a hundred
Lovejoys and Dorseys and Crawshaws."

This story shows the way Fitzgerald took an emotion and wove his
hyperbolic magic around it. Though he had no ancestors named Lovejoy or
Crawshaw, he was indeed descended from a long line of imposing Dorseys
going back to the original Edward, who moved to Maryland from Virginia in
1650. Not a Dorsey is buried at St. Mary's but a few Scotts, with whom they
intermarried, are, inspiring the line repeated in *Tender Is the Night*, "It was
very friendly leaving him there with all his relations around him." Later in
the story, the heroine is asked why she doesn't buy and restore "a fine old
house called Lovejoy Hall" in "St. Charles County," which had belonged to
one of her Lovejoy forebears. This is a reference to "Tudor Hall," home of
Fitzgerald's great-great-grandfather Philip Key, a member of the Continental
Congress, in the southern Maryland county of St. Mary's. It was for sale at
that time, as he must have heard from relatives at the funeral.

Over the five years after it was written, "On Your Own" was declined by
seven magazines, the first time this had happened to a Fitzgerald story since
his apprentice days. It is one of the stories he "stripped" for his *Notebooks*,
salvaging favorite passages for later use. "On Your Own" is included here
because it is the only remaining unpublished story bearing, in his
words, that "one little drop of something . . . the extra I had."

The third time he walked around the deck Evelyn stared at him. She
stood leaning against the bulwark and when she heard his footsteps
again she turned frankly and held his eyes for a moment until his
turned away, as a woman can when she has the protection of other
men's company. Barlotto, playing ping-pong with Eddie O'Sullivan,
noticed the encounter. "Aha!" he said, before the stroller was out of
hearing, and when the rally was finished: "Then you're still
interested even if it's not the German Prince."

"How do you know it's not the German Prince?" Evelyn
demanded.

"Because the German Prince is the horse-faced man with white eyes. This one——" He took a passenger list from his pocket, "——is either Mr. George Ives, Mr. Jubal Early Robbins and valet, or Mr. Joseph Widdle with Mrs. Widdle and six children."

It was a medium-sized German boat, five days westbound from Cherbourg. The month was February and the sea was dingy grey and swept with rain. Canvas sheltered all the open portions of the promenade deck, even the ping-pong table was wet.

K'*tap* K'*tap* K'*tap* K'*tap*. Barlotto looked like Valentino—— since he got fresh in the rumba number she had disliked playing opposite him. But Eddie O'Sullivan had been one of her best friends in the company.

Subconsciously she was waiting for the solitary promenader to round the deck again but he didn't. She faced about and looked at the sea through the glass windows; instantly her throat closed and she held herself close to the wooden rail to keep her shoulders from shaking. Her thoughts rang aloud in her ears: My father is dead— when I was little we would walk to town on Sunday morning, I in my starched dress, and he would buy the Washington paper and a cigar and he was so proud of his pretty little girl. He was always so proud of me—he came to New York to see me when I opened with the Marx Brothers and he told everybody in the hotel he was my father, even the elevator boys. I'm glad he did, it was so much pleasure for him, perhaps the best time he ever had since he was young. He would like it if he knew I was coming all the way from London.

"Game and set," said Eddie.

She turned around.

"We'll go down and wake up the Barneys and have some bridge, eh?" suggested Barlotto.

Evelyn led the way, pirouetting once and again on the moist deck, then breaking into an "Off to Buffalo" against a sudden breath of wet wind. At the door she slipped and fell inward down the stair, saved herself by a perilous one-arm swing—and was brought up against the solitary promenader. Her mouth fell open comically—she balanced for a moment. Then the man said "I beg your pardon," in an unmistakably southern voice. She met his eyes again as the three of them passed on.

The man picked up Eddie O'Sullivan in the smoking room the next afternoon.

"Aren't you the London cast of *Chronic Affection?*"

"We were until three days ago. We were going to run another two weeks but Miss Lovejoy was called to America so we closed."

"The whole cast on board?" The man's curiosity was inoffensive, it was a really friendly interest combined with a polite deference to the romance of the theater. Eddie O'Sullivan liked him.

"Sure, sit down. No, there's only Barlotto, the juvenile, and Miss Lovejoy and Charles Barney, the producer, and his wife. We left in twenty-four hours—the others are coming on the *Homeric*."

"I certainly did enjoy seeing your show. I've been on a trip around the world and I turned up in London two weeks ago just ready for something American—and you had it."

An hour later Evelyn poked her head around the corner of the smoking room door and found them there.

"Why are you hiding out on us?" she demanded. "Who's going to laugh at my stuff? That bunch of card sharps down there?"

Eddie introduced Mr. George Ives. Evelyn saw a handsome, well-built man of thirty with a firm and restless face. At the corners of his eyes two pairs of fine wrinkles indicated an effort to meet the world on some other basis than its own. On his part George Ives saw a rather small dark-haired girl of twenty-six, burning with a vitality that could only be described as "professional." Which is to say it was not amateur—it could never use itself up upon any one person or group. At moments it possessed her so entirely, turning every shade of expression, every casual gesture, into a thing of such moment that she seemed to have no real self of her own. Her mouth was made of two small intersecting cherries pointing off into a bright smile; she had enormous, dark brown eyes. She was not beautiful but it took her only about ten seconds to persuade people that she was. Her body was lovely with little concealed muscles of iron. She was in black now and overdressed—she was always very *chic* and a little overdressed.

"I've been admiring you ever since you hurled yourself at me yesterday afternoon," he said.

"I had to make you some way or other, didn't I? What's a girl going to do with herself on a boat—fish?"

They sat down.

"Have you been in England long?" George asked.

"About five years—I go bigger over there." In its serious moments her voice had the ghost of a British accent. "I'm not really very good at anything—I sing a little, dance a little, clown a little, so the English think they're getting a bargain. In New York they want specialists."

It was apparent that she would have preferred an equivalent popularity in New York.

Barney, Mrs. Barney and Barlotto came into the bar.

"Aha!" Barlotto cried when George Ives was introduced. "She won't believe he's not the Prince." He put his hand on George's knee. "Miss Lovejoy was looking for the Prince the first day when she heard he was on board. We told her it was you."

Evelyn was weary of Barlotto, weary of all of them, except Eddie O'Sullivan, though she was too tactful to have shown it when they were working together. She looked around. Save for two Russian priests playing chess their party was alone in the smoking room—there were only thirty first-class passengers, with accommodations for two hundred. Again she wondered what sort of an America she was going back to. Suddenly the room depressed her—it was too big, too empty to fill and she felt the necessity of creating some responsive joy and gaiety around her.

"Let's go down to my salon," she suggested, pouring all her enthusiasm into her voice, making them a free and thrilling promise. "We'll play the phonograph and send for the handsome doctor and the chief engineer and get them in a game of stud. I'll be the decoy."

As they went downstairs she knew she was doing this for the new man. She wanted to play to him, show him what a good time she could give people. With the phonograph wailing "You're driving me crazy" she began building up a legend. She was a "gun moll" and the whole trip had been a frame to get Mr. Ives into the hands of the mob. Her throaty mimicry flicked here and there from one to the other; two ship's officers coming in were caught up in it and without knowing much English still understood the verve and magic of the impromptu performance. She was Anne Pennington, Helen Morgan, the effeminate waiter who came in for an order, she was everyone there in turn, and all in pace with the ceaseless music.

Later George Ives invited them all to dine with him in the upstairs restaurant that night. And as the party broke up and Evelyn's eyes sought his approval he asked her to walk with him before dinner.

The deck was still damp, still canvassed in against the persistent spray of rain. The lights were a dim and murky yellow and blankets tumbled awry on empty deck chairs.

"You were a treat," he said. "You're like—Mickey Mouse."

She took his arm and bent double over it with laughter.

"I like being Mickey Mouse. Look—there's where I stood and stared at you every time you walked around. Why didn't you come around the fourth time?"

"I was embarrassed so I went up to the boat deck."

As they turned at the bow there was a great opening of doors and a flooding out of people who rushed to the rail.

"They must have had a poor supper," Evelyn said. "No—look!"

It was the *Europa*—a moving island of light. It grew larger minute by minute, swelled into a harmonious fairyland with music from its deck and searchlights playing on its own length. Through field-glasses they could discern figures lining the rail and Evelyn spun out the personal history of a man who was pressing his own pants in a cabin. Charmed they watched its sure matchless speed.

"Oh, Daddy, buy me that!" Evelyn cried, and then something suddenly broke inside her—the sight of beauty, the reaction to her late excitement choked her up and she thought vividly of her father. Without a word she went inside.

Two days later she stood with George Ives on the deck while the gaunt scaffolding of Coney Island slid by.

"What was Barlotto saying to you just now?" she demanded.

George laughed.

"He was saying just about what Barney said this afternoon, only he was more excited about it."

She groaned.

"He said that you played with everybody—and that I was foolish if I thought this little boat flirtation meant anything—everybody had been through being in love with you and nothing ever came of it."

"He wasn't in love with me," she protested. "He got fresh in a dance we had together and I called him for it."

"Barney was wrought up too—said he felt like a father to you."

"They make me tired," she exclaimed. "Now they think they're in love with me just because—"

"Because they see I am."

"Because they think I'm interested in you. None of them were so eager until two days ago. So long as I make them laugh it's all right but the minute I have any impulse of my own they all bustle up and think they're being so protective. I suppose Eddie O'Sullivan will be next."

"It was my fault telling them we found we lived only a few miles from each other in Maryland."

"No, it's just that I'm the only decent-looking girl on an eight-day boat, and the boys are beginning to squabble among themselves. Once they're in New York they'll forget I'm alive."

Still later they were together when the city burst thunderously upon them in the early dusk—the high white range of lower New York swooping down like a strand of a bridge, rising again into uptown New York, hallowed with diadems of foamy light, suspended from the stars.

"I don't know what's the matter with me," Evelyn sobbed. "I cry so much lately. Maybe I've been handling a parrot."

The German band started to play on deck but the sweeping majesty of the city made the march trivial and tinkling; after a moment it died away.

"Oh, God! It's so beautiful," she whispered brokenly.

If he had not been going south with her the affair would probably have ended an hour later in the customs shed. And as they rode south to Washington next day he receded for the moment and her father came nearer. He was just a nice American who attracted her physically—a little necking behind a life-boat in the darkness. At the iron grating in the Washington station where their ways divided she kissed him goodbye and for the time forgot him altogether as her train shambled down into the low-forested clayland of southern Maryland. Screening her eyes with her hands Evelyn looked out upon the dark infrequent villages and the scattered farm lights. Rocktown was a shrunken little station and there was her brother with a neighbor's Ford—she was ashamed that her luggage was so good against the exploded upholstery. She saw a star she knew and heard Negro laughter from out of the night; the breeze was cool but in it there was some smell she recognized—she was home.

At the service next day in the Rocktown churchyard, the sense that she was on a stage, that she was being watched, froze Evelyn's grief—then it was over and the country doctor lay among a hundred Lovejoys and Dorseys and Crawshaws. It was very friendly leaving him there with all his relations around him. Then as they turned from the grave-side her eyes fell on George Ives who stood a little apart with his hat in his hand. Outside the gate he spoke to her.

"You'll excuse my coming. I had to see that you were all right."

"Can't you take me away somewhere now?" she asked impulsively. "I can't stand much of this. I want to go to New York tonight."

His face fell. "So soon?"

"I've got to be learning a lot of new dance routines and freshening up my stuff. You get sort of stale abroad."

He called for her that afternoon, crisp and shining as his coupe. As they started off she noticed that the men in the gasoline stations seemed to know him with liking and respect. He fitted into the quickening spring landscape, into a legendary Maryland of graciousness and gallantry. He had not the range of a European; he gave her little of that constant reassurance as to her attractiveness—there were whole half hours when he seemed scarcely aware of her at all.

They stopped once more at the churchyard—she brought a great armful of flowers to leave as a last offering on her father's grave. Leaving him at the gate she went in.

The flowers scattered on the brown unsettled earth. She had no more ties here now and she did not know whether she would come back any more. She knelt down. All these dead, she knew them all, their weather-beaten faces with hard blue flashing eyes, their spare violent bodies, their souls made of new earth in the long forest-heavy darkness of the seventeenth century. Minute by minute the spell grew on her until it was hard to struggle back to the old world where she had dined with kings and princes, where her name in letters two feet high challenged the curiosity of the night. A line of William McFee's surged through her:

> *O staunch old heart that toiled so long for me*
> *I waste my years sailing along the sea.*

The words released her—she broke suddenly and sat back on her heels, crying.

How long she was staying she didn't know; the flowers had grown invisible when a voice called her name from the churchyard and she got up and wiped her eyes.

"I'm coming." And then, "Goodbye then Father, all my fathers."

George helped her into the car and wrapped a robe around her. Then he took a long drink of country rye from his flask.

"Kiss me before we start," he said suddenly.

She put up her face toward him.

"No, really kiss me."

"Not now."

"Don't you like me?"

"I don't feel like it, and my face is dirty."

"As if that mattered."

His persistence annoyed her.

"Let's go on," she said.

He put the car into gear.

"Sing me a song."

"Not now, I don't feel like it."

He drove fast for half an hour—then he stopped under thick sheltering trees.

"Time for another drink. Don't you think you better have one—it's getting cold."

"You know I don't drink. You have one."

"If you don't mind."

When he had swallowed he turned toward her again.

"I think you might kiss me now."

Again she kissed him obediently but he was not satisfied.

"I mean really," he repeated. "Don't hold away like that. You know I'm in love with you and you say you like me."

"Of course I do," she said impatiently, "but there are times and times. This isn't one of them. Let's go on."

"But I thought you liked me."

"I won't if you act this way."

"You don't like me then."

"Oh don't be absurd," she broke out, "of course I like you, but I want to get to Washington."

"We've got lots of time." And then as she didn't answer, "Kiss me once before we start."

She grew angry. If she had liked him less she could have laughed him out of this mood. But there was no laughter in her—only an increasing distaste for the situation.

"Well," he said with a sigh, "this car is very stubborn. It refuses to start until you kiss me." He put his hand on hers but she drew hers away.

"Now look here." Her temper mounted into her cheeks, her forehead. "If there was anything you could do to spoil everything it was just this. I thought people only acted like this in cartoons. It's so utterly crude and—" she searched for a word, "—and *American*. You only forgot to call me 'baby.' "

"Oh." After a minute he started the engine and then the car. The lights of Washington were a red blur against the sky.

"Evelyn," he said presently. "I can't think of anything more natural than wanting to kiss you, I—"

"Oh, it was so clumsy," she interrupted. "Half a pint of corn whiskey and then telling me you wouldn't start the car unless I kissed you. I'm not used to that sort of thing. I've always had men treat me with the greatest delicacy. Men have been challenged to duels for staring at me in a casino—and then you, that I liked so much, try a thing like that. I can't stand it—" And again she repeated, bitterly, "It's so American."

"Well, I haven't any sense of guilt about it but I'm sorry I upset you."

"Don't you *see*?" she demanded. "If I'd wanted to kiss you I'd have managed to let you know."

"I'm terribly sorry," he repeated.

They had dinner in the station buffet. He left her at the door of her pullman car.

"Goodbye," she said, but coolly now, "Thank you for an awfully interesting trip. And call me up when you come to New York."

"Isn't this silly," he protested. "You're not even going to kiss me goodbye."

She didn't want to at all now and she hesitated before leaning forward lightly from the step. But this time he drew back.

"Never mind," he said. "I understand how you feel. I'll see you when I come to New York."

He took off his hat, bowed politely and walked away. Feeling very alone and lost Evelyn went on into the car. That was for meeting people on boats, she thought, but she kept on feeling strangely alone.

II

She climbed a network of steel, concrete and glass, walked under a high echoing dome and came out into New York. She was part of it even before she reached her hotel. When she saw mail waiting for her and flowers around her suite, she was sure she wanted to live and work here with this great current of excitement flowing through her from dawn to dusk.

Within two days she was putting in several hours a morning limbering up neglected muscles, an hour of new soft-shoe stuff with Joe Crusoe, and making a tour of the city to look at every entertainer who had something new.

Also she was weighing the prospects for her next engagement. In the background was the chance of going to London as a co-featured player in a Gershwin show then playing New York. Yet there was an air of repetition about it. New York excited her and she wanted to get something here. This was difficult—she had little following in America, show business was in a bad way—after a while her agent brought her several offers for shows that were going into rehearsal this fall. Meanwhile she was getting a little in debt and it was convenient that there were almost always men to take her to dinner and the theater.

March blew past. Evelyn learned new steps and performed in half a dozen benefits; the season was waning. She dickered with the usual young impressarios who wanted to "build something around her," but who seemed never to have the money, the theater and the material at one and the same time. A week before she must decide about the English offer she heard from George Ives.

She heard directly, in the form of a telegram announcing his arrival, and indirectly in the form of a comment from her lawyer when she mentioned the fact. He whistled.

"Woman, have you snared George Ives? You don't need any more jobs. A lot of girls have worn out their shoes chasing him."

"Why, what's his claim to fame?"

"He's rich as Croesus—he's the smartest young lawyer in the south, and they're trying to run him now for governor of his state. In his spare time he's one of the best polo players in America."

Evelyn whistled.

"This is news," she said.

She was startled. Her feelings about him suddenly changed—everything he had done began to assume significance. It impressed her that while she had told him all about her public self he had hinted nothing of this. Now she remembered him talking aside with some ship reporters at the dock.

He came on a soft poignant day, gentle and spirited. She was engaged for lunch but he picked her up at the Ritz afterwards and they drove in Central Park. When she saw in a new revelation his pleasant eyes and his mouth that told how hard he was on himself, her heart swung toward him—she told him she was sorry about that night.

"I didn't object to what you did but to the way you did it," she said. "It's all forgotten. Let's be happy."

"It all happened so suddenly," he said. "It was disconcerting to look up suddenly on a boat and see the girl you've always wanted."

"It was nice, wasn't it?"

"I thought that anything so like a casual flower needn't be respected. But that was all the more reason for treating it gently."

"What nice words," she teased him. "If you keep on I'm going to throw myself under the wheels of the cab."

Oh, she liked him. They dined together and went to a play and in the taxi going back to her hotel she looked up at him and waited.

"Would you consider marrying me?"

"Yes, I'd consider marrying you."

"Of course if you married me we'd live in New York."

"Call me Mickey Mouse," she said suddenly.

"Why?"

"I don't know—it was fun when you called me Mickey Mouse." The taxi stopped at her hotel.

"Won't you come in and talk for a while?" she asked. Her bodice was stretched tight across her heart.

"Mother's here in New York with me and I promised I'd go and see her for a while."

"Oh."

"Will you dine with us tomorrow night?"

"All right."

She hurried in and up to her room and put on the phonograph.

"Oh, gosh, he's going to respect me," she thought. "He doesn't know anything about me, he doesn't know anything about women.

He wants to make a goddess out of me and I want to be Mickey Mouse." She went to the mirror swaying softly before it.

Lady play your mandolin
Lady let that tune begin.

At her agent's next morning she ran into Eddie O'Sullivan.

"Are you married yet?" he demanded. "Or did you ever see him again?"

"Eddie, I don't know what to do. I think I'm in love with him but we're always out of step with each other."

"Take him in hand."

"That's just what I don't want to do. I want to be taken in hand myself."

"Well, you're twenty-six—you're in love with him. Why don't you marry him? It's a bad season."

"He's so American," she answered.

"You've lived abroad so long that you don't know what you want."

"It's a man's place to make me certain."

It was in a mood of revolt against what she felt was to be an inspection that she made a midnight rendezvous for afterwards to go to Chaplin's film with two other men, "—because I frightened him in Maryland and he'll only leave me politely at my door." She pulled all her dresses out of her wardrobe and defiantly chose a startling gown from Vionnet; when George called for her at seven she summoned him up to her suite and displayed it, half hoping he would protest.

"Wouldn't you rather I'd go as a convent girl?"

"Don't change anything. I worship you."

But she didn't want to be worshipped.

It was still light outside and she liked being next to him in the car. She felt fresh and young under the fresh young silk—she would be glad to ride with him forever, if only she were sure they were going somewhere.

. . . The suite at the Plaza closed around them; lamps were lighted in the salon.

"We're really almost neighbors in Maryland," said Mrs. Ives. "Your name's familiar in St. Charles county and there's a fine old house called Lovejoy Hall. Why don't you buy it and restore it?".

"There's no money in the family," said Evelyn bluntly. "I'm the only hope, and actresses never save."

When the other guest arrived Evelyn started. Of all shades of her past—Colonel Cary. She wanted to laugh, or else hide—for an instant she wondered if this had been calculated. But she saw in his surprise that it was impossible.

"Delighted to see you again," he said simply.

As they sat down at table Mrs. Ives remarked:

"Miss Lovejoy is from our part of Maryland."

"I see," Colonel Cary looked at Evelyn with the equivalent of a wink. His expression annoyed her and she flushed. Evidently he knew nothing about her success on the stage, remembered only an episode of six years ago. When champagne was served she let a waiter fill her glass lest Colonel Cary think that she was playing an unsophisticated role.

"I thought you were a teetotaller," George observed.

"I am. This is about the third drink I ever had in my life."

The wine seemed to clarify matters; it made her see the necessity of anticipating whatever the Colonel might afterwards tell the Ives. Her glass was filled again. A little later Colonel Cary gave an opportunity when he asked:

"What have you been doing all these years?"

"I'm on the stage." She turned to Mrs. Ives. "Colonel Cary and I met in my most difficult days."

"Yes?"

The Colonel's face reddened but Evelyn continued steadily.

"For two months I was what used to be called a 'party girl.' "

"A party girl?" repeated Mrs. Ives puzzled.

"It's a New York phenomenon," said George.

Evelyn smiled at the Colonel. "It used to amuse me."

"Yes, very amusing," he said.

"Another girl and I had just left school and decided to go on the stage. We waited around agencies and offices for months and there were literally days when we didn't have enough to eat."

"How terrible," said Mrs. Ives.

"Then somebody told us about 'party girls.' Business men with clients from out of town sometimes wanted to give them a big time—singing and dancing and champagne, all that sort of thing, make them feel like regular fellows seeing New York. So they'd hire a room in a restaurant and invite a dozen party girls. All it required was to have a good evening dress and to sit next to some middle-aged man for two hours and laugh at his jokes and maybe kiss him good night. Sometimes you'd find a fifty-dollar bill in your napkin when you sat down at table. It sounds terrible, doesn't it—but it was salvation to us in that awful three months."

A silence had fallen, short as far as seconds go but so heavy that Evelyn felt it on her shoulders. She knew that the silence was coming from some deep place in Mrs. Ives's heart, that Mrs. Ives was ashamed for her and felt that what she had done in the struggle for survival was unworthy of the dignity of woman. In those same seconds she sensed the Colonel chuckling maliciously behind his bland moustache, felt the wrinkles beside George's eyes straining.

"It must be terribly hard to get started on the stage," said Mrs. Ives. "Tell me—have you acted mostly in England?"

"Yes."

What had she said? Only the truth and the whole truth in spite of the old man leering there. She drank off her glass of champagne.

George spoke quickly, under the Colonel's roar of conversation: "Isn't that a lot of champagne if you're not used to it?"

She saw him suddenly as a man dominated by his mother; her frank little reminiscence had shocked him. Things were different for a girl on her own and at least he should see that it was wiser than that Colonel Cary might launch dark implications thereafter. But she refused further champagne.

After dinner she sat with George at the piano.

"I suppose I shouldn't have said that at dinner," she whispered.

"Nonsense! Mother knows everything's changed nowadays."

"She didn't like it," Evelyn insisted. "And as for that old boy that looks like a Peter Arno cartoon!"

Try as she might Evelyn couldn't shake off the impression that some slight had been put upon her. She was accustomed only to having approval and admiration around her.

"If you had to choose again would you choose the stage?" Mrs. Ives asked.

"It's a nice life," Evelyn said emphatically. "If I had daughters with talent I'd choose it for them. I certainly wouldn't want them to be society girls."

"But we can't all have talent," said Colonel Cary.

"Of course most people have the craziest prejudices about the stage," pursued Evelyn.

"Not so much nowadays," said Mrs. Ives. "So many nice girls go on the stage."

"Girls of position," added Colonel Cary.

"They don't usually last very long," said Evelyn. "Every time some debutante decides to dazzle the world there's another flop due on Broadway. But the thing that makes me maddest is the way people condescend. I remember one season on the road—all the small-town social leaders inviting you to parties and then whispering and snickering in the corner. Snickering at Gladys Knowles!" Evelyn's voice rang with indignation: "When Gladys goes to Europe she dines with the most prominent people in every country, the people who don't know these back-woods social leaders exist—"

"Does she dine with their wives too?" asked Colonel Cary.

"With their wives too." She glanced sharply at Mrs. Ives. "Let me tell you that girls on the stage don't feel a bit inferior, and the really fashionable people don't think of patronizing them."

The silence was there again heavier and deeper, but this time excited by her own words Evelyn was unconscious of it.

"Oh, it's American women," she said. "The less they have to offer the more they pick on the ones that have."

She drew a deep breath, she felt that the room was stifling.

"I'm afraid I must go now," she said.

"I'll take you," said George.

They were all standing. She shook hands. She liked George's mother, who after all had made no attempt to patronize her.

"It's been very nice," said Mrs. Ives.

"I hope we'll meet soon. Good night."

With George in a taxi she gave the address of a theater on Broadway.

"I have a date," she confessed.

"I see."

"Nothing very important." She glanced at him, and put her hand on his. Why didn't he ask her to break the date? But he only said:

"He better go over Forty-fifth Street."

Ah, well, maybe she'd better go back to England—and be Mickey Mouse. He didn't know anything about women, anything about love, and to her that was the unforgivable sin. But why in a certain set of his face under the street lamps did he remind her of her father?

"Won't you come to the picture?" she suggested.

"I'm feeling a little tired—I'm turning in."

"Will you phone me tomorrow?"

"Certainly."

She hesitated. Something was wrong and she hated to leave him. He helped her out of the taxi and paid it.

"Come with us?" she asked almost anxiously. "Listen, if you like—"

"I'm going to walk for a while!"

She caught sight of the men waiting for her and waved to them.

"George, is anything the matter?" she said.

"Of course not."

He had never seemed so attractive, so desirable to her. As her friends came up, two actors, looking like very little fish beside him, he took off his hat and said:

"Good night, I hope you enjoy the picture."

"George—"

—and a curious thing happened. Now for the first time she realized that her father was dead, that she was alone. She had thought of herself as being self-reliant, making more in some seasons than his practice brought him in five years. But he had always been behind her somewhere, his love had always been behind her——She had never been a waif, she had always had a place to go.

And now she was alone, alone in the swirling indifferent crowd. Did she expect to love this man, who offered her so much, with the naive romantics of eighteen. He loved her—he loved her more than any one in the world loved her. She wasn't ever going to be a great star, she knew that, and she had reached the time when a girl had to look out for herself.

"Why, look," she said, "I've got to go. Wait—or don't wait."

Catching up her long gown she sped up Broadway. The crowd was enormous as theater after theater eddied out to the sidewalks. She sought for his silk hat as for a standard, but now there were many silk hats. She peered frantically into groups and crowds as she ran. An insolent voice called after her and again she shuddered with a sense of being unprotected.

Reaching the corner she peered hopelessly into the tangled mass of the block ahead. But he had probably turned off Broadway so she darted left down the dimmer alley of Forty-eighth Street. Then she saw him, walking briskly, like a man leaving something behind— and overtook him at Sixth Avenue.

"George," she cried.

He turned; his face looking at her was hard and miserable.

"George, I didn't want to go to that picture, I wanted you to make me not go. Why didn't you ask me not to go?"

"I didn't care whether you went or not."

"Didn't you?" she cried. "Don't you care for me any more?"

"Do you want me to call you a cab?"

"No, I want to be with you."

"I'm going home."

"I'll walk with you. What is it, George? What have I done?"

They crossed Sixth Avenue and the street became darker.

"What is it, George? Please tell me. If I did something wrong at your mother's why didn't you stop me?"

He stopped suddenly.

"You were our guest," he said.

"What did I do?"

"There's no use going into it." He signalled a passing taxi. "It's quite obvious that we look at things differently. I was going to write you tomorrow but since you ask me it's just as well to end it to-day."

"But why, George?" She wailed, "What did I do?"

"You went out of your way to make a preposterous attack on an old gentlewoman who had given you nothing but courtesy and consideration."

"Oh, George, I didn't, I didn't. I'll go to her and apologize. I'll go tonight."

"She wouldn't understand. We simply look at things in different ways."

"Oh—h-h." She stood aghast.

He started to say something further, but after a glance at her he opened the taxi door.

"It's only two blocks. You'll excuse me if I don't go with you."

She had turned and was clinging to the iron railing of a stair.

"I'll go in a minute," she said. "Don't wait."

She wasn't acting now. She wanted to be dead. She was crying for her father, she told herself—not for him but for her father.

His footsteps moved off, stopped, hesitated—came back.

"Evelyn."

His voice was close beside her.

"Oh, poor baby," it said. He turned her about gently in his arms and she clung to him.

"Oh yes," she cried in wild relief. "Poor baby—just your poor baby."

She didn't know whether this was love or not but she knew with all her heart and soul that she wanted to crawl into his pocket and be safe for ever.

Between Three and Four

(*The Saturday Evening Post*, 5 September 1931)

"Between Three and Four" was written in June 1931, probably in Switzerland. The *Post* paid $4000 for it. This story was the first in which Fitzgerald treated the Depression scene in response to the *Post*'s request for stories with American settings. Other stories in this collection which deal with the Depression are "A Change of Class," "Diagnosis," "The Rubber Check," "The Family Bus," "No Flowers," and "New Types." Although Fitzgerald began writing these stories in Europe, he had observed the effects of the Depression when he went to America for his father's funeral in January. He included none of these stories in *Taps at Reveille* (1935), indicating his recognition that he had not succeeded with this new material. Because of the requirements of the mass-circulation magazines, all of these Depression stories have happy endings—which did not accord with the experiences of readers who did not always have a nickel to buy the *Post*.

This happened nowadays, with everyone somewhat discouraged. A lot of less fortunate spirits cracked when money troubles came to be added to all the nervous troubles accumulated in the prosperity—neurosis being a privilege of people with a lot of extra money. And some cracked merely because it was in the air, or because they were used to the great, golden figure of plenty standing behind them, as the idea of prudence and glory stands behind the French, and the idea of "the thing to do" used to stand behind the English. Almost everyone cracked a little.

Howard Butler had never believed in anything, including himself, except the system, and had not believed in that with the intensity of men who were its products or its prophets. He was a quiet, introverted man, not at all brave or resilient and, except in one regard, with no particular harm in him. He thought a lot without much apparatus for thinking, and in normal circumstances one would not expect him to fly very high or sink very low. Nevertheless, he had a vision, which is the matter of this story.

Howard Butler stood in his office on the ninth floor of a building in New York, deciding something. It was a branch and a showroom of B. B. Eddington's Sons, office furniture and supplies, of which he was a branch manager—a perfect office ceremoniously equipped throughout, though now a little empty because of the decreased personnel due to hard times. Miss Wiess had just telephoned the name of an unwelcome caller, and he was deciding whether he hadn't just as well see the person now; it was a question of sooner or later. Mrs. Summer was to be shown in.

Mrs. Summer did not need to be shown in, since she had worked there for eight years, up until six months ago. She was a handsome and vital lady in her late forties, with golden-grayish hair, a stylish-stout figure with a reminiscent touch of the Gibson Girl bend to it, and fine young eyes of bright blue. To Howard Butler she was still as vivid a figure as when, as Sarah Belknap, she had declined to marry him nearly thirty years ago—with the essential difference that he hated her.

She came into his private office with an alert way she had and, in a clear, compelling voice that always affected him, said, "Hello, Howard," as if, without especially liking him, she didn't object to him at all. This time there was just a touch of strain in her manner.

"Hello, Sarah."

"Well," she breathed, "it's very strange to be back here. Tell me you've got a place for me."

He pursed his lips and shook his head. "Things don't pick up."

"H'm." She nodded and blinked several times.

"Cancellations, bad debts—we've closed two branches and there've been more pay cuts since you left. I've had to take one."

"Oh, I wouldn't expect the salary I used to get. I realize how things are. But, literally, I can't find anything. I thought, perhaps, there might be an opening, say as office manager or head stenographer, with full responsibility. I'd be very glad of fifty dollars a week."

"We're not paying anything like that."

"Or forty-five. Or even forty. I had a chance at twenty-five when I first left here and, like an idiot, I let it go. It seemed absurd after what I'd been getting; I couldn't keep Jack at Princeton on that. Of course, he's partly earning his way, but even in the colleges the competition is pretty fierce now—so many boys need money. Anyhow, last week I went back and tried to get the job at twenty-five, and they just laughed at me." Mrs. Summer smiled grimly, but with full control over herself; yet she could only hold the smile a minute and she talked on to conceal its disappearance: "I've been eating at the soup kitchens to save what little I've got left. When I think that a woman of my capacity——That's not conceit, Howard; you know I've got capacity. Mr. Eddington always thought so. I never quite understood——"

"It's tough, Sarah," he said quickly. He looked at her shoes—they were still good shoes—on top anyhow. She had always been well turned out.

"If I had left earlier, if I'd been let out before the worst times came, I could have placed myself; but when I started hunting, everyone had got panicky."

"We had to let Muller go too."

"Oh, you did," she said, with interest; the news restored her a measure of self-respect.

"A week ago."

Six months before, the choice had been between Mr. Muller and Mrs. Summer, and Sarah Summer knew, and Howard Butler knew that she knew, that he had made a ticklish decision. He had satisfied an old personal grudge by keeping Muller, who was a young man, clearly less competent and less useful to the firm than Mrs. Summer, and who received the same salary.

Now they stared at each other; she trying to fix on him, to pin him down, to budge him; he trying to avoid her, and succeeding, but only by retreating into recently hollowed out cavities in his soul, but safe cavities, from which he could even regard her plight with a certain satisfaction. Yet he was afraid of what he had done; he was trying to be hard, but in her actual presence the sophistries he had evolved did not help him.

"Howard, you've got to give me a job," she broke out. "Anything—thirty dollars, twenty-five dollars. I'm desperate. I haven't thirty dollars left. I've got to get Jack through this year—his junior year. He wants to be a doctor. He thinks he can hold out till June on his own, but someone drove him down to New York on Washington's Birthday, and he saw the way I was living. I tried to lie to him, but he guessed, and now he says he's going to quit and get a job. Howard, I'd rather be dead than stand in his way. I've been thinking of nothing else for a week. I'd be better dead. After all, I've had my life—and a lot of happiness."

For an instant Butler wavered. It could be done, but the phrase "a lot of happiness" hardened him, and he told himself how her presence in the office now would be a continual reproach.

Thirty years ago, on the porch of a gabled house in Rochester, he had sat in misery while John Summer and Sarah Belknap had told him moonily about their happiness. "I wanted you to be the first to know, Howard," Sarah had said. Butler had blundered into it that evening, bringing flowers and a new offer of his heart; then he was suddenly made aware that things were changed, that he wasn't very alive for either of them. Later, something she had said was quoted or misquoted to him—that if John Summer had not come along, she'd have been condemned to marry Howard Butler.

Years later he had walked into the office one morning to find her his subordinate. This time there was something menacing and repellent in his wooing, and she had put a stop to it immediately, definitely and finally. Then, for eight years, Butler had suffered her presence in the office, drying out in the sunshine of her vitality, growing bitter in the shadow of her indifference; aware that, despite her widowhood, her life was more complete than his.

"I can't do it," he said, as if regretfully. "Things are stripped to the bone here. There's no one you could displace. Miss Wiess has been here twelve years."

"I wonder if it would do any good to talk to Mr. Eddington."

"He's not in New York, and it wouldn't do any good."

She was beaten, but she went on evenly, "Is there any likelihood of a change, in the next month, say?"

Butler shrugged his shoulders. "How does anybody know when business will pick up? I'll keep you in mind if anything turns up." Then he added, in a surge of weakness: "Come back in a week or so, some afternoon between three and four."

Mrs. Summer got up; she looked older than when she had come into the office.

"I'll come back then." She stood twisting her gloves, and her eyes seemed to stare out into more space than the office inclosed. "If you haven't anything for me then, I'll probably just—quit permanently."

She walked quickly to the window, and he half rose from his chair.

"Nine floors is a nice height," she remarked. "You could think things out one more time on the way down."

"Oh, don't talk that way. You'll get a break any day now."

"Business Woman Leaps Nine Floors to Death," said Mrs. Summer, her eyes still fixed out the window. She sighed in a long, frightened breath, and turned toward the door. "Good-by, Howard. If you think things over, you'll see I was right in not even trying to love you. I'll be back some day next week, between three and four."

He thought of offering her five dollars, but that would break down something inside him, so he let her go like that.

II

He saw her through the transparent place where the frosting was rubbed from the glass of his door. She was thinner than she had been last week, and obviously nervous, starting at anyone coming in or going out. Her foot was turned sideways under the chair and he saw where an oval hole was stopped with a piece of white cardboard.

When her name was telephoned, he said, "Wait," letting himself be annoyed that she had come slightly before three; but the real cause of his anger lay in the fact that he wasn't up to seeing her again. To postpone his realization of the decision made in his subconscious, he dictated several letters and held a telephone conversation with the head office. When he had finished, he found it was five minutes to four; he hadn't meant to detain her an hour. He phoned Miss Wiess that he had no news for Mrs. Summer and couldn't see her.

Through the glass he watched her take the news. It seemed to him that she swayed as she got up and stood blinking at Miss Wiess.

"I hope she's gone for good," Butler said to himself. "I can't be responsible for everybody out of work in this city. I'd go crazy."

Later he came downstairs into a belt of low, stifling city heat; twice on his way home he stopped at soda fountains for cold drinks. In his apartment he locked the door, as he so often did lately, as if he were raising a barrier against all the anxiety outside. He moved about, putting away some laundry, opening bills, brushing his coat and hanging it up—for he was very neat—and singing to himself:

I can't give you anything but love, baby,
That's the only thing I've plenty of, baby——

He was tired of the song, but he continually caught himself humming it. Or else he talked to himself, like many men who live alone.

"Now, that's two colored shirts and two white ones. I'll wear this one out first, because it's almost done. Almost done. . . . Seven, eight, and two in the wash—ten——"

Six o'clock. All the offices were out now; people hurrying out of elevators, swarming down the stairs. But the picture came to Butler tonight with a curious addition; he seemed to see someone climbing up the stairs, too, passing the throng, climbing very slowly and resting momentarily on the landings.

"Oh, what nonsense!" he thought impatiently. "She'd never do it. She was just trying to get my goat."

But he kept on climbing up flights of stairs with her, the rhythm of the climbing as regular and persistent as the beat of fever. He grabbed his hat suddenly and went out to get dinner.

There was a storm coming; the sultry dust rose in swirls along the street. The people on the street seemed a long way removed from him in time and space. It seemed to him that they were all sad, all walking with their eyes fixed on the ground, save for a few who were walking and talking in pairs. These latter seemed absurd, with their obliviousness of the fact that they were making a show of themselves with those who were walking as it was fitting—silent and alone.

But he was glad that the restaurant where he went was full. Sometimes, when he read the newspapers a lot, he felt that he was almost the only man left with enough money to get along with; and it frightened him, because he knew pretty well that he was not much of a man and they might find it out and take his position away from him. Since he was not all right with himself in his private life, he had fallen helplessly into the clutches of the neurosis that gripped the nation, trying to lose sight of his own insufficiencies in the universal depression.

"Don't you like your dinner?" the waitress asked.

"Yes, sure." He began to eat self-consciously.

"It's the heat. I just seen by the papers another woman threw herself out of a ninth-story window this afternoon."

Butler's fork dropped to the floor.

"Imagine a woman doing that," she went on, as she stooped for the fork. "If I ever wanted to do that, I'd go drown myself."

"What did you say?"

"I say I'd go drown myself. I can't swim anyhow. But I said if——"

"No, before that—about a woman."

"About a woman that threw herself out of a ninth-story window. I'll get the paper."

He tried to stop her; he couldn't look at the paper. With trembling fingers he laid a dollar on the table and hurried out of the restaurant.

It couldn't possibly be her, because he had seen her at four, and it was now only twenty after seven. Three hours. A news stand drifted up to him, piled with late editions. Forming the sound of "agh" in his throat, he hurried past, hurried on, into exile.

He had better look. It couldn't be Sarah.

But he knew it was Sarah. BUSINESS WOMAN, DISPIRITED, LEAPS NINE FLOORS TO DEATH. He passed another news stand and, turning into Fifth Avenue, walked north. The rain began in large drops that sent up whiffs of dust, and Butler, looking at the crawling sidewalk, suddenly stopped, unable to go forward or to retrace his steps.

"I'll have to get a paper," he muttered. "Otherwise I won't sleep."

He walked to Madison Avenue and found a news stand; his hand felt over the stacked papers and picked up one of each; he did not look at them, but folded them under his arm. He heard the rain falling on them in crisp pats, and then more softly, as if it was shredding them away. When he reached his door, he suddenly flung the soggy bundle down a basement entrance and hurried inside. Better wait till morning.

He undressed excitedly, as if he hadn't a minute to lose. "It's probably not her," he kept repeating aloud. "And if it is, what did I have to do with it? I can't be responsible for everybody out of work in this city." With the help of this phrase and a hot double gin, he fell into a broken sleep.

He awoke at five, after a dream which left him shaken with its reality. In the dream he was talking to Sarah Belknap again. She lay in a hammock on a porch, young once more, and with a childish wistfulness. But she knew what was going to happen to her presently—she was going to be thrown from a high place and be broken and dead. Butler wanted to help her—tears were running out of his eyes and he was wringing his hands—but there was nothing he could do now; it was too late. She did not say that it was all his fault, but her eyes, grieving silently and helplessly about what was going to happen, reproached him for not having prevented it.

The sound that had awakened him was the plop of his morning paper against the door. The resurgent dream, heartbreaking and ominous, sank back into the depths from which it came, leaving him empty; and now his consciousness began to fill up with all the miserable things that made their home there. Torn between the lost world of pity and the world of meanness where he lived, Butler sprang out of bed, opened the door and took up the paper. His eyes, blurred with sleep, ran across the columns:

BUSINESS WOMAN, DISPIRITED,
LEAPS NINE FLOORS TO DEATH

For a moment he thought it was an illusion. The print massed solidly below the headline; the headline itself disappeared. He rubbed his eyes with one fist; then he counted the columns over, and found that two columns were touching that should have flanked the story— but, no; there it was:

BUSINESS WOMAN, DISPIRITED,
LEAPS NINE FLOORS TO DEATH

He heard the cleaning woman moving about in the hall, and going to the door, he flung it open.

"Mrs. Thomas!"

A pale Negress with corded glasses looked up at him from her pail.

"Look at this, Mrs. Thomas!" he cried. "My eyes are bad! I'm sick! I've got to know! Look!"

He held the paper before her; he felt his voice quivering like a muscle: "Now, you tell me. Does it say, 'Business Woman Leaps to Death'? Right there! Look, can't you?"

The Negress glanced at him curiously, bent her head obediently to the page.

"Indeed it does, Mr. Butler."

"Yes?" He passed his hand across his eyes. "Now, below that. Does it say, 'Mrs. John Summer'? Does it say, 'Mrs. John Summer'? Look carefully now."

Again she glanced sharply at him before looking at the paper. "Indeed it does, Mr. Butler. 'Mrs. John Summer.' " After a minute she added, "Man, you're sick."

Butler closed his door, got back into bed and lay staring at the ceiling. After a while he began repeating his formulas aloud:

"I musn't get to thinking that I had anything to do with it, because I didn't. She'd been offered another job, but she thought she was too good for it. What would she have done for me if she'd been in my place?"

He considered telephoning the office that he was ill, but young George Eddington was expected back any day, and he did not dare. Miss Wiess had gone on her vacation yesterday, and there was a substitute to be broken in. The substitute had not known Mrs. Summer, so there would be no discussion of what had happened.

It was a day of continuing heat, wasted unprolific heat that cradled the groans of the derrick and the roar of the electric riveters in the building going up across the street. In the heat every sound was given its full discordant value, and by early afternoon Butler was sick and dizzy. He had made up his mind to go home, and was walking restlessly about his office when the thing began to happen. He heard the clock outside his office ticking loud in the hot silence, heard the little, buzzing noise it made, passing the hour; and at the same moment he heard the sigh of pneumatic hinges, as the corridor door swung open and someone came into the outer office. Then there wasn't a sound.

For a moment he hoped that it was someone he would have to see; then he shivered and realized that he was afraid—though he did not know why—and walked toward his own door. Before reaching it, he stopped. The noise of the riveting machine started again, but it seemed farther away now. For an instant he had the impression that the clock in the next room had stopped, too, but there it was again, marking rather long seconds against the silence.

Suddenly he did not want to know who had come into the next room; yet he was irresistibly impelled to find out. In one corner of his door was the transparent spot through which almost the whole outer office was visible, but now Butler discovered a minute scrape in the painted letter B of his name. Through it he could see the floor, and the dark little hall giving on the corridor where chairs for visitors were placed. Clamping his teeth together, he put his eye to this crack.

Tucked beneath the chair and criss-crossing the chair legs were a pair of woman's tan shoes. The sole of one shoe turned toward him, and he made out a gray oval in the center. Breathlessly he moved until his eye was at the other hole. There was something sitting in the chair—rather, slumped in it, as if it had been put down there and had immediately crumpled. A dangling hand and what he could see of the face were of a diaphanous pallor, and the whole attitude was one of awful stillness. With a little, choking noise, Butler sprang back from the door.

III

It was several minutes before he was able to move from the wall against which he had backed himself. It was as if there was a sort of bargain between himself and the thing outside that, by staying perfectly still, playing dead, he was safe. But there was not a sound, not a movement, in the outer office and, after a while, a surface rationality asserted itself. He told himself that this was all the result of strain; that the frightening part of it was not the actual phantom, but that his nerves should be in a state to conjure it up. But he drew little consolation from this; if the terror existed, it was immaterial whether it originated in another world or in the dark places of his own mind.

He began making a systematic effort to pull himself together. In the first place, the noises outside were continuing as before; his office, his own body, were tangible as ever, and people were passing in the street; Miss Rousseau would answer the pressure of a bell which was within reach of his hand. Secondly, there could, conceivably, be some natural explanation of the thing outside; he had not been able to see the whole face and he could not be absolutely sure that it was what he thought it was; any number of people had cardboard in their shoes these days. In the third place—and he astonished himself at the coolness with which he deliberated this—if the matter reached an intolerable point, one could always take one's own life, thus automatically destroying whatever horror had come into it.

It was this last thought that caused him to go to the window and look down at the people passing below. He stood there for a minute, never quite turning his back on the door, and watched the people passing and the workmen on the steel scaffolding over the way. His heart tried to go out to them, and he struggled desperately to assert the common humanity he shared with them, the joys and griefs they had together, but it was impossible. Fundamentally, he despised them and—that is to say, he could make no connection with them, while his connection with the thing in the next room was manifest and profound.

Suddenly Butler wrenched himself around, walked to the door and put his eye to the aperture. The figure had moved, had slumped farther sideways, and the blood rushed up, tingling, into his head as he saw that the face, now turned sightlessly toward him, was the face of Sarah Summer.

He found himself sitting at his desk, bent over it in a fit of uncontrollable laughter.

How long he had sat there he did not know, when suddenly he heard a noise, and recognized it, after a moment, as the swishing sigh of the hinges on the outer door. Looking at his watch, he saw that it was four o'clock.

He rang for Miss Rousseau, and when she came, asked: "Is anyone waiting to see me?"

"No, Mr. Butler."

"Was there someone earlier?"

"No, sir."

"Are you sure?"

"I've been in the filing room, but the door was open; if anyone had come in I'd surely have heard them."

"All right. Thanks."

As she went out, he looked after her through the open door. The chair was now empty.

IV

He took a strong bromide that night and got himself some sleep, and his reasoning reassumed, with dawn, a certain supremacy. He went to the office, not because he felt up to it but because he knew he would never be able to go again. He was glad he had gone, when Mr. George Eddington came in late in the morning.

"Man, you look sick," Eddington said.

"It's only the heat."

"Better see a doctor."

"I will," said Butler, "but it's nothing."

"What's happened here the last two weeks?"

BUSINESS WOMAN, DISPIRITED,
LEAPS NINE FLOORS TO DEATH

"Very little," he said aloud. "We've moved out of the Two Hundredth Street warehouse."

"Whose idea was that?"

"Your brother's."

"I'd rather you'd refer all such things to me for confirmation. We may have to move in again."

"I'm sorry."

"Where's Miss Wiess?"

"Her mother's sick; I gave her three days' vacation."

"And Mrs. Summer's left. . . . Oh, by the way, I want to speak to you about that later."

Butler's heart constricted suddenly. What did he mean? Had he seen the papers?

"I'm sorry Miss Wiess is gone," said Eddington. "I wanted to go over all this last month's business."

"I'll take the books home tonight," Butler offered conciliatingly. "I can be ready to go over them with you tomorrow."

"Please do."

Eddington left shortly. Butler found something in his tone disquieting—the shortness of a man trying to prepare one for even harsher eventualities. There was so much to worry about now, Butler thought; it hardly seemed worth while worrying about so many things. He sat at his desk in a sort of despairing apathy, realizing at lunchtime that he had done nothing all morning.

At 1:30, on his way back to the office, a chill wave of terror washed suddenly over him. He walked blindly as the remorseless sun led him along a path of flat black and hostile gray. The clamor of a fire engine plunging through the quivering air had the ominous portent of things in a nightmare. He found that someone had closed his windows, and he flung them open to the sweltering machines across the street. Then, with an open ledger before him, he sat down to wait.

Half an hour passed. Butler heard Miss Rousseau's muffled typewriter in the outer office, and her voice making a connection on the phone. He heard the clock move over two o'clock with a rasping sound; almost immediately he looked at his watch and found it was 2:30. He wiped his forehead, finding how cold sweat can be. Minutes passed. Then he started bolt upright as he heard the outer door open and close slowly, with a sigh.

Simultaneously he felt something change in the day outside—as if it had turned away from him, foreshortening and receding like a view from a train. He got up with difficulty, walked to the door and peered through the transparent place into the outer office.

She was there; her form cut the shadow of the corner; he knew the line of her body under her dress. She was waiting to see if he could give her a job, so that she could keep herself, and her son might not have to give up his ambitions.

"I'm afraid there's nothing. Come back next week. Between three and four."

"I'll come back."

With a struggle that seemed to draw his last reserve of strength up from his shoes, Butler got himself under control and picked up the phone. Now he would see—he would see.

"Miss Rousseau."

"Yes, Mr. Butler."

"If there's anyone waiting to see me, please send them in."

"There's no one waiting to see you, Mr. Butler. There's——"

Uttering a choked sound, he hung up the phone and walked to the door and flung it open.

It was no use; she was there, clearly discernible, distinct and vivid as in life. And as he looked, she rose slowly, her dark garments falling about her like cerements—arose and regarded him with a wan smile, as if, at last and too late, he was going to help her. He took a step backward.

Now she came toward him slowly, until he could see the lines in her face, the wisps of gray-gold hair under her hat.

With a broken cry, he sprang backward so that the door slammed. Simultaneously he knew, with a last fragment of himself, that there was something wrong in the very nature of the logic that had brought him to this point, but it was too late now. He ran across the office like a frightened cat, and with a sort of welcome apprehension of nothingness, stepped out into the dark air beyond his window. Even had he grasped the lost fact that he sought for—the fact that the cleaning woman who had read him the newspaper could neither read nor write—it was too late for it to affect him. He was already too much engrossed in death to connect it with anything or to think what bearing it might have on the situation.

V

Mrs. Summer did not go on into Butler's office. She had not been waiting to see him, but was here in answer to a summons from Mr. Eddington, and she was intercepted by Eddington himself, who took her aside, talking:

"I'm sorry about all this." He indicated Butler's office. "We're letting him go. We've only recently discovered that he fired you practically on his own whim. Why, the number of your ideas we're using——We never considered letting you go. Things have been so mixed up."

"I came to see you yesterday," Mrs. Summer said. "I was all in and there was no one in the office at the moment. I must have fainted in the chair, because it was an hour later when I remembered anything, and then I was too tired to do anything except go home."

"We'll see about all this," Eddington said grimly. "We'll——It's one of those things——" He broke off. The office was suddenly full of confusion; there was a policeman and, behind him, many curious peering faces. "What's the matter? . . . Hello, there seems to be something wrong here. What is it, officer?"

A Change of Class

(*The Saturday Evening Post*, 26 September 1931)

"A Change of Class" was written in July 1931—probably in Switzerland. The *Post* paid $4000. During the Depression the magazine required hopeful or encouraging stories conveying the message that, even if prosperity wasn't just around the corner, the crash could be regarded as a correction of the excesses of the Twenties. The plot is not farfetched: fortunes were made during the boom on stock-market tips, and reports about rich bartenders or wealthy bootblacks were commonplace. As Fitzgerald noted in "My Lost City," "My barber retired on a half million bet in the market and I was conscious that the head waiters who bowed me, or failed to bow me, to my table were far, far wealthier than I." The setting of "A Change of Class" is Wilmington, Delaware, where the Fitzgeralds had lived at "Ellerslie" between 1927 and 1929.

Not to identify the city too closely, it is in the East and not far from New York, and its importance as a financial center is out of proportion to its small population. Three families, with their many ramifications and the two industries they all but control, are responsible for this; there is a Jadwin Street and a Jadwin Hotel, a Dunois Park and a Dunois Fountain, a Hertzog Hospital and a Hertzog Boulevard.

The Jadwins are the wealthiest; within miles of the city one cannot move out of their shadow. Only one of the many brothers and cousins is concerned with this story.

He wanted a haircut and, of course, went to Earl, in the barber shop of the Jadwin Hotel. A black porter sprang out of his lethargy, the barbers at work paid him the tribute of a secret stare, the proprietor's eyes made a quick pop at the sight of him. Only Earl, cutting a little boy's hair, kept his dignity. He tapped his shears against his comb and went over to Philip Jadwin.

"It'll be five minutes, Mr. Jadwin," he said without obsequiousness. "If you don't want to wait here, I can telephone up to your office."

"That's all right, Earl; I'll wait."

Philip Jadwin sat with glazed eyes. He was thirty-one, stiffly handsome, industrious and somewhat shy. He was in love with a typist in his office, but afraid to do anything about it, and sometimes it made him miserable. Lately it was a little better; he had himself in hand, but as he receded from the girl her face reproached him. At twenty-one or forty he might have dashed away with her to Elkton, Maryland, but he was at a conventional age, very much surrounded by the most conservative branch of his family. It wouldn't do.

As he seated himself in Earl's chair a swarthy man with long prehensile arms entered the barber shop, said "Hello, Earl," flicked his eyes over Jadwin and went on toward the manicurist. When he had passed, Earl threw after him the smile that functions in the wake of notoriety.

"He gave me a half bottle of rye today," said Earl. "It was open and he didn't like to carry it with him."

"Well, don't cut my ear off," said Jadwin.

"Don't you worry about that," Earl glanced toward the rear of the shop and frowned. "He gets a lot of manicures."

"That's a pretty manicurist."

Earl hesitated. "I'll tell you confidentially, Mr. Jadwin, she's my wife—has been for a month—but being both in the same shop, we thought we wouldn't say anything as long as we're here. The boss might not like it."

Jadwin congratulated him: "You've got a mighty pretty wife."

"I don't like her manicuring bootleggers. This Berry, now, he's all right—he just gave me a half bottle of rye, if that coon ain't drunk it up—but I tell you, I like nice people."

As Jadwin didn't answer, Earl realized he had gone beyond the volubility he permitted himself. He worked silently and well, with deft, tranquilizing hands. He was a dark-haired, good-looking young man of twenty-six, a fine barber, steady and with no bad habits save the horses, which he had given up when he married. But after the hot towel an idea which had been with him since Jadwin came in came to the surface with the final, stimulating flicker of the drink in his veins. He might be snubbed, he might even lose a customer, but this was the year 1926 and the market had already grasped the imagination of many classes. Also he had been prompted to this by many people, among them his wife.

"Hert-win preferred seems to be going up, Mr. Jadwin," he ventured.

"Yes." Jadwin was thinking again of the girl in his office or he wouldn't have broken a principle of his family by saying: "But watch it next week when——" He broke off.

"Going up more?" Earl's eyes lit excitedly, but his hands applying the bay rum were strong and steady.

"Naturally, I believe in it," said Jadwin with caution, "but only as an out-and-out buy."

"Of course," agreed Earl piously. "No face powder, that's right."

Going home in the street car that night, he told Violet about it: "We got two thousand dollars. With that I think I can get the new shop in the Cornwall Building, with three chairs. There's about twenty regular customers I'd be taking with me. What I could do, see, is buy this stock and then borrow money on it to buy the shop with. Or else I could take a chance on what he told me and buy it on margin. Let me tell you he ain't putting out much; he's vice president of Hert-win. His old man is Cecil Jadwin, you know. . . . What would you do?"

"It would be nice to make a lot," said Violet, "but we don't want to lose the money."

"That helps."

"Well, it would be nice to have a lot of money. But you decide."

He decided conservatively, content with his prospects, liking his work in the cheerful, gossipy shop, loving his wife and his new existence with her in a new little apartment. He decided conservatively, and then Hert-win moved up twenty points in as many hours. If he had played on margin, as had one of the barbers in whom he had confided the tip, he would have more than doubled his two thousand.

"Why don't you ask him for another tip?" suggested Violet.

"He wouldn't like it."

"It don't hurt him. I think you're crazy if you don't ask him again."

"I don't dare."

Nevertheless, he delayed the negotiations about the shop in the Cornwall Building.

One day about a week later, Philip Jadwin came into the shop in a wretched humor. The girl in his office had announced that she was quitting, and he knew it was the end of something, and how much he cared.

Earl, cutting his hair and shaving him, was conscious of a sinking sensation; he felt exactly as if he were going to ask Mr. Jadwin for money. The shave was over, the hot towel—in a moment it would be too late.

"I wonder if Hert-win is going to make another quick rise," Earl said in a funny voice.

Then Jadwin flared out at him. Sitting up in the chair, he said, in a low, angry voice: "What do you take me for—a race-track tipster? I don't come here to be annoyed. If you want to keep your customers——"

He got out of the chair and began putting on his collar. For Earl that was plenty. Against his own better tact and judgment, he had blundered, and now he grew red and his mouth quivered as he stood there with the apron in his hand.

Jadwin, tying his tie at the mirror, was suddenly sorry; he had snapped at three persons this morning, and now he realized that it must be his own fault. He liked Earl; for three years he had been his customer, and there was a sort of feeling between them; a physical sympathy in the moments when Earl's hands were passing over his face, in the fine razor respecting its sensibility, or the comb, which seemed proud in the last fillip with which it finished him. Earl's chair was a place to rest, a sanctuary, once he was hidden under an apron and a lather of soap, his eyes trustfully closed, his senses awake to the pleasant smells of lotions and soap. He always remembered Earl handsomely at Christmas. And he knew that Earl liked him and respected him.

"Look here," he said gruffly. "I'll tell you one thing, but don't go lose your shirt on it, because nothing's certain in this world. Look at the paper tomorrow; if the appellate-court decision in the Chester case is against the railroads, you can expect a lot of activity in all Hertwin interests." And he added carefully, "I think. Now don't ever ask me anything again."

And so Earl blundered into the Golden Age.

II

"See that fellow going out?" the barbers said to their customers three years later. "Used to work here, but quit last year to take care of all his money. Philip Jadwin gave him some tips. . . . G'by, Earl. Come in more often."

He came often. He liked the familiar cosmetic smell from the manicure corner, where the girls sat in white uniforms, freshly clean and faintly sweating lip rouge and cologne; he liked the gleaming nickel of the chairs, the sight of a case of keen razors, the joking abuse of the colored porter that made the hours pass. Sometimes he just sat around and read a paper. But he was hurried tonight, going to a party, so he got into his car and drove home.

It was a nice house in a new development, not large or lavish, for Earl wasn't throwing away his money. In fact, he had worked in the barber shop two years after he needed to, taking ten-cent tips from men he could have bought out a dozen times over. He quit because Violet insisted on it. His trade didn't go with the colored servant and the police dog, the big machine for outdoors and the many small noisy machines for the house. The Johnsons knew how to play bridge and they went quite often to New York. He was worth more than a hundred thousand dollars.

In his front yard he paused, thinking to himself that it was like a dream. That was as near as he could analyze his feelings; he was not even sure whether the dream was happy or unhappy—Violet was sure for both of them that it was happy.

She was dressing. She took very good care of herself; her nails were fever-colored and she had a water wave or a marcel every day. She had been sedate as a manicurist, but she was very lively as a young wife; she had forgotten that their circumstances had ever been otherwise and regarded each step up as a return to the world in which she belonged, just as we often deceive ourselves into thinking that we appertain to the milieu of our most distinguished friend.

"I heard something funny today——" Earl said.

But Violet interrupted sharply: "You better start putting on your tuxedo. It's half-past six."

They were short and inattentive with each other, because the world in which they moved was new and distracting. They were always rather pathetically ashamed of each other in public, though Earl still boasted of his wife's chic and she of his ability to make money. From the day when they moved into the new house, Violet adopted the manner of one following a code, a social rite, plain to herself but impossible for Earl to understand. She herself failed to understand that from their position in mid-air they were constrained merely to observe myopically and from a distance, and then try to imitate. Their friends were in the same position. They all tried to bolster up one another's lack of individuality by saying that So-and-So had a great sense of humor, or that So-and-So had a real knack of wearing clothes, but they were all made sterile and devitalized by their new environments, paying the price exacted for a passage into the middle class.

"But I heard something funny," insisted Earl, undressing, "about Howard Shalder. I heard downtown that he was a bootlegger; that he was Berry's boss."

"Did you?" she said indifferently.

"Well, what do you think about it?"

"I knew about it. Lots of nice people are bootleggers now—society people even."

"Well, I don't see why we should be friends with a bootlegger."

"But he isn't like a bootlegger," she said. "They have a beautiful home, and they're more refined than most of the people we know."

"Well, look here, Violet. Would you go to the home of that Ed that used to sell us corn when we lived on——"

Indignantly she turned around from the mirror: "You don't think Mr. Shalder peddles bottles at back doors, do you?"

"If he's a bootlegger we oughtn't to go round with them," Earl continued stubbornly. "Nice people won't have anything to do with us."

"You said your own self what a lovely girl she was. She never even takes a drink. You were the one that made friends with them."

"Well, anyhow, I'm not going to the home of a bootlegger."

"You certainly are tonight."

"I suppose we got to tonight," he said unwillingly, "but I don't like to see you sitting next to him and holding hands—even in kidding. His wife didn't like it either."

"Oh, sign off!" cried Violet impatiently. "Can't we ever go out without your trying to spoil it? If you don't like the ones we know, why don't you get to know some others? Why don't you invite some of the Jadwins and the Hertzogs to dinner, if you're so particular?"

"We ought to be able to have friends without their being boot——"

"If you say that again, I'll scream."

As they went down their walk half an hour later, they could hear the radio playing "The Breakaway" in Shalder's house. It was a fine machine, but to Earl it did not sound like the promise of a particularly good time, since if he turned on his radio he could have the same music. There were three fine cars in front of the house; one had just driven up, and they recognized a couple they had met there before—an Italian-American, Lieutenant Spirelli, and his wife. Lieutenant Spirelli wore an officer's uniform. Howard Shalder, a big, tough young man with a twice-a-day beard and a hearty voice, stood hospitably on his front steps. Like all people who have lived by rendering personal service, Earl had a sharp sense of the relative importance of people; because he was a really kind man, this didn't show itself in snobbishness. Nevertheless, as they crossed the street the sight of the broken-English Italian in his inappropriate uniform depressed him, and he felt a renewed doubt as to whether he had risen in the world. In the barber shop both Shalder and Spirelli would have been part of the day's work; meeting them this way seemed to imply that they were on the same level, that this was the way he was. He didn't like it. He felt he was in Mr. Jadwin's class—not Mr. Jadwin's equal but a part of the structure to which Mr. Jadwin belonged.

He crossed the street a little behind Violet. The sun was still yellow, but the tranquillity of evening was already in the air, with the cries of birds and children softened and individualized. Not the most bored captive of society had any more sense of being in a cage than had Earl as he walked into that house to have fun.

That was, a little later in the evening, the exact mood of Mr. Philip Jadwin, but he was escaping instead of entering. The dinner dance at the country club had affected him as singularly banal; it was an exceptionally wet, prenuptial affair, and he was on the wagon, so a moment arrived when he could stand it no longer. His very leaving was fraught with nuisances—he was lapeled by a bore who told him of a maudlin personal grief; he was cornered by a woman who insisted on walking down the drive with him to talk about investments, in spite of the cloying fact that couples in every second parked car were in various stages of intimacy. Alone at last, he drove into the main white road and breathed in the fine June night.

He was rather bored with life, interested in business, but feeling somewhat pointless lately in making more money for himself, already so rich. Apparently the boom was going on forever and things could take care of themselves; he wished he had devoted more attention to his personal desires. Three years ago he should have married that girl in his office who had made him tremble whenever she came near. He had been afraid. Now three of the relatives of whom he had been afraid were dead and a cousin of his had since married his stenographer and had not been very strongly persecuted, and she was making him a fine wife too.

This very morning Jadwin had discovered that the girl he had wanted and had been too cautious to take was now married and had a baby. He encountered her on the street; she was shy, she seemed disinclined to give him either her new name or her address. He did not know if he still loved her, but she seemed real to him, or at least someone from a time when everything seemed more real. The carefully brought-up children of wealthy Easterners grow old early; at thirty-four Philip Jadwin wasn't sure he had any emotions at all.

But he had enough sentiment to make him presently stop under the bright moonlight, look at an address in a notebook and turn his car in a new direction. He wanted to see where she lived, he wanted to eavesdrop on her; perhaps, if the lights were on, stare in on some happy domestic scene. Again, if her surroundings were squalid, he might give her husband a lift. A great girl; there was something about her that always moved him—only once in a lifetime perhaps——

He drove into a new street laid out with pleasant red brick houses; it seemed to Jadwin that he had owned this land or the adjoining parcel himself a few years back. He drove slowly along between the lighted houses, peering for the number. It was a little after ten.

No. 42, 44, 46—there. He slowed down further, looking at a brightly lit house which poured radio music out into the night. He drove a little past it and cut off his motor; then he could hear festive voices inside, and in a window he saw a man's black back against a yellow mushroom lamp. No poverty there; the house looked comfortable, the lawn well kept, and it was a pleasant neighborhood. Jadwin was glad.

He got out of his car and sauntered cautiously along the sidewalk toward the house, stopping in the shadow of the hedge as the front door opened, gleamed, slammed, and left a man standing on the steps. He was in a dinner coat and hatless. He came down the walk, and as Jadwin resumed his saunter they came face to face. At once they recognized each other.

"Why, hello, Mr. Jadwin."

"Hello, there, Earl."

"Well, well, well," Earl was a little tight and he took a long breath as if it was medicine. "They're having a party in there, but I quit."

"Isn't that where the Shalders live?"

"Sure. Big bootlegger."

Jadwin started. "Bootlegger?"

"Sure, but if he thinks he can——" He broke off and resumed with dignity: "I live over the way. The house with the col—columnade." Then he remembered that Mr. Jadwin had started him toward the acquisition of that house, and the fact sobered him further: "Maybe you remember——" he began, but Jadwin interrupted:

"Are you sure Shalder's a bootlegger?"

"Dead sure. Admits it himself."

"What does—how does his wife like it?"

"She didn't know till they were married. She told me that tonight after she had a cocktail—I made her take a cocktail because she was upset, because Shalder and my——" Again he changed the subject suddenly: "Would you care to come over to my house and smoke a cigar and have a drink?"

"Why, not tonight, thanks. I must get along."

"I don't know whether you remember the tip on the market you gave me three years ago, Mr. Jadwin. That was the start of all this." He waved his hand toward the house and brought it around as if to include the other house and his wife too.

A wave of distaste passed over Jadwin. He remembered the incident, and if this was the result, he regretted it. He was a simple man with simple tastes; his love for Irene had been founded upon them, in reaction against the complicated surfaces of the girls he knew. It shocked him to find her in this atmosphere which, at best, was only a shoddy imitation of the other. He winced as bursts of shrill laughter volleyed out into the night.

"And believe me, I'm very grateful to you, Mr. Jadwin," continued Earl. "I always said that if we ever had a son——"

"How are things going with you?" Jadwin asked hastily.

"Oh, going great. I've been making a lot of money."

"What are you doing?"

"Just watching the board," said Earl apologetically. "As a matter of fact, I'd like to get a nice position. I had to quit the barber business; it didn't seem to go with all the jack I made. But I've always been sort of sorry. There's Doctor Jordan, for instance. He tells me he's got over three hundred thousand dollars on paper and he still keeps on making five-dollar visits. Then there's a porter in the First National——"

They both turned around suddenly; a woman carrying a small bag was coming down the gravel path from the rear of the house. Where it met the sidewalk she stood for a moment in the moonlight, looking at the house; then, with a curious, despairing gesture of her shoulders, she set off quickly along the sidewalk. Before either Jadwin or Earl could move, the front door opened and a large man in a dinner coat dashed out and after her. When he caught up to her they heard fragments of conversation; excited and persuasive on his part, quiet and scornful on hers:

"You're acting crazy, I tell you!"

"I'm only going to my sister's. I'm glad I took the baby there."

"I tell you I didn't——"

"You can't kiss a woman before my eyes in my own house and have your friends go to sleep on my bed."

"Now, look here, Irene!"

After a moment she gave up, shrugged her shoulders contemptuously and dropped her bag. He picked it up, and together they went up the gravel path by which she had come out.

"That was her. That was Mrs. Shalder," said Earl.

"I recognized her."

"She's a fine young woman too. That Shalder—somebody ought to do something to him. I'd like to go in there now and get my wife."

"Why don't you?" asked Jadwin.

Earl sighed. "What's the use? There'd just be a quarrel and they'd all make it up tomorrow. I've been to a lot of parties like this since I moved out here, Mr. Jadwin. They all make it up tomorrow."

And now the house gave forth another guest. It was Violet, who marked her exit by some shrill statement to people inside before she slammed the door. It was as if the others, entering through the kitchen, had forced her out in front. Coming down the walk, she saw Earl.

"Well, I never want to see that bunch again," she began angrily.

"Sh!" Earl warned her. "Look, Vi; I want you to meet Mr. Jadwin. You've heard me speak of him. This is my wife, Violet, Mr. Jadwin."

Violet's manner changed. Her hand leaped at her hair, her lips parted in an accommodating smile.

"Why, how do you do, Mr. Jadwin; it's a pleasure indeed. I hope you'll excuse my looks; I've been——" She broke off discreetly. "Earl, why can't you ask Mr. Jadwin over to our home for a drink?"

"Oh, you're very kind, but——"

"That's our home across the way. I don't suppose it looks so very much to you."

"It looks very nice."

"Yes," said Violet, combing her mind for topics.... "I saw in the papers that your sister is getting married. I know a woman who knows her very well—a Mrs. Lemmon. Do you know her?"

"I'm afraid I——"

"She's very nice. She has a nice home on Penn Street." Again she smoothed her hair. "My, I must look a sight—and I had a wave this afternoon."

"I've got to be going along," said Jadwin.

"You sure you don't want a drink?" asked Earl.

"No, another time."

"Well, good night then," said Violet. "Any time you're passing by and want a drink, we'd be very happy if you just dropped in informally."

They went across the street together, and he saw that the encounter with him had temporarily driven the unpleasant evening from their minds. Earl walked alertly and Violet kept patting at various parts of her person. Neither of them looked around, as if that wasn't fair. The party in the Shalders' house was still going on, but there was a light now in a bedroom upstairs, and as Jadwin started his car he stared at it for a moment.

"It's all awfully mixed up," he said.

III

Nowhere in America was the drop in the market felt more acutely than in that city. Since it was the headquarters of the Hert-win industries, and since everyone had the sense of being somehow on the inside, the plunging had been enormous. In the dark autumn it seemed that every person in town was more or less involved.

Earl Johnson took the blow on his chin. Two-thirds of his money melted away in the first slumps while he looked on helplessly, grasping at every counsel in the newspapers, every wild rumor in the crowd. He felt that there was one man who might have been able to help him; if he had been still a barber and shaving Mr. Philip Jadwin, he might have asked, "What had I better do now?" and got the right answer. Once he even called at his office, but Mr. Jadwin was busy. He didn't go back.

When he met a barber from the Jadwin Hotel shop, he could not help noticing the grin back of the sympathetic words; it was human to regard his short-lived soar as comic. But he didn't really understand what had happened until several months later, when his possessions began to peel away. The automobile went, the mortgaged house went, though they continued to live there on a rental, pending its resale. Violet suggested selling her pearl necklace, but when he consented, she became so bitter that he told her not to.

These few things were literally all they had—old washing machines, radios, electric refrigerators were a drug on the market. As 1930 wabbled its way downhill Earl saw that they had salvaged nothing—not the love with which, under happy auspices, they had started life, no happy memories, only a few transient exhilarations; no new knowledge or capability—not a thing—simply a space where three years had been. In the spring of 1930 he went back to work. He had his old chair, and it was exciting when his old customers came in one by one.

"What? Earl! Well, this is like old times."

Some of them didn't know of his prosperity, and of those who did, some were delicately silent, others made only a humorously sympathetic reference to it, no one was unpleasant. Within a month personal appointments took up half his time, as in the old days—people popping in the door and saying, "In half an hour, Earl?" He was again the most popular barber, the best workman in the city. His fingers grew supple and soft, the rhythm of the shop entered into him, and something told him that he was now a barber for life. He didn't mind; the least pleasant parts of his life were hang-overs from his prosperity.

For one thing, there was Mr. Jadwin. Once his most faithful customer, he had come into the shop the first day of Earl's return, startled at the sight of him and gone to another barber. Earl's chair had been empty. The other barber was almost apologetic about it afterward. "He's your customer," he told Earl. "He's just got used to coming to the rest of us while you were gone, and he don't want to let us down right away." But Jadwin never came to Earl; in fact, he obviously avoided him, and Earl felt it deeply and didn't understand.

But his worst trouble was at home; home had become a nightmare. Violet was unable to forgive him for having caused the collapse in Wall Street, after having fooled her with the boom. She even made herself believe that she had married him when he was rich and that he had dragged her down from a higher station. She saw that life would never bounce him very high again and she was ready to get out.

Earl woke up one April morning, aware, with the consciousness that floats the last edge of sleep, that she had been up and at the window for perhaps ten minutes, perhaps a half hour.

"What is it, Vi?" he asked. "What are you looking for?"

She started and turned around. "Nothing. I was just standing here."

He went downstairs for the newspaper. When he returned she was again at the window in the attitude of watching, and she threw a last glance toward it before she went down to get breakfast. He joined her ten minutes later.

"One thing's settled," he said. "I was going to sell the Warren Files common for what I could get, but this morning it ain't even in the list of stocks at all. What do you know about that?"

"I suppose it's just as good as the rest of your investments?"

"I haven't got any more investments. Here's what I'm going to do: I'm going to take what cash I got left, which is just about enough, and buy the concession for the new barber shop in the Hertzog Building. And I'm going to do it now."

"You've got some cash?" Violet demanded. "How much?"

"There's two thousand in the savings bank. I didn't tell you because I thought we ought to have something to fall back on."

"And yet you sell the car!" Violet said. "You let me do the housework and talk about selling my jewelry!"

"Keep your shirt on, Vi. How long do you think two thousand would last, living the way we were? You better be glad we got it now, because if I have this barber shop, then it's mine, and nobody can lose me my job, no matter what happens."

He broke off. She had left the breakfast table and gone to the front window.

"What's the matter out there? You'd think there was a street parade."

"I was just wondering about the postman."

"He'll be another hour," said Earl. "Anyhow, about a month ago I took an option on this shop for two hundred dollars. I've been waiting to see if the market was ever going to change."

"How much did you say was in the bank?" she asked suddenly.

"About two thousand dollars."

When he had gone, Violet left the dishes on the table and went out on the porch, where she sat down and fixed her eyes on the Shalder house across the way. The postman passed, but, she scarcely saw him. After half an hour Irene Shalder emerged and hurried toward the street car. Still Violet waited.

At half-past ten a taxi drew up in front of the Shalder house and a few minutes later Shalder came out carrying a pair of suitcases. This was her signal. She hurried across the street and caught him as he was getting into the cab.

"I got a new idea," she said.

"Yes, but I got to go, Violet. I got to catch a train."

"Never mind. I got a new idea. Something for both of us."

"I told you we could settle that later—when I get things straightened out. I'll write you next week; I swear I will."

"But this is something for right now. It's real cash; we could get it today."

Shalder hesitated. "If you mean that necklace of yours, it wouldn't much more than get us to the Coast."

"This is two thousand dollars cash I'm talking about."

Shalder spoke to the taxi man and went across the street with her. They sat down in the parlor.

"If I get this two thousand," said Violet, "will you take me with you?"

"Where'll you get it?"

"I can get it. But you answer me first."

"I don't know," he said hesitantly. "Like I told you, that Philadelphia mob gave me twenty-four hours to get out of town. Do you think I'd go otherwise just when I'm short of money? Irene went out looking for her old job this morning."

"Does she know you're going?"

"She thinks I'm going to Chicago. I told her I'd send for her and the kid when I get started."

"I'm beginning to think that you're spoiling your life with this man"

"Not in the Guidebook," *Woman's Home Companion* (November 1925).

"Six of One—" *Redbook* (February 1932).

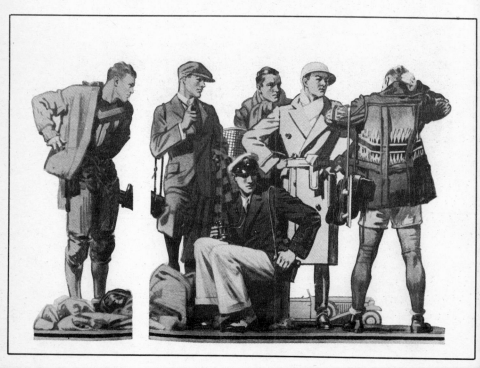

Lobby poster for 1920 movie version of "Myra Meets His Family."

Another Party Emerged From the Cloakroom. He Thought Quickly. Neither One Had Seen Him

"Indecision," *The Saturday Evening Post* (16 May 1931).

"The Unspeakable Egg," *The Saturday Evening Post* (12 July 1924).

"No Flowers," *The Saturday Evening Post* (21 July 1934).

The Fog Had Blown Back to Sea, and as They Came in Sight of the House the Lamps Were Glowing Out Into the Darkness. On the Porch Waited an Immaculate Girl in a Gleaming White Dress

"He Took Something Much More Valuable to Me Than That"

"The Love Boat," *The Saturday Evening Post* (8 October 1927).

"The Adolescent Marriage," *The Saturday Evening Post* (6 March 1926).

"*It Lasted Three Weeks. She Came Home With a Big Bruise on Her Shoulder Where He'd Hit Her*"

"The Third Casket," *The Saturday Evening Post* (31 May 1924).

" 'Trouble,' " *The Saturday Evening Post* (6 March 1937).

"Inside the House," *The Saturday Evening Post* (13 June 1936).

"I'm going to tell you something that you ought to know," Marion said; "I think you ought to hear the whole story"

"One of My Oldest Friends," *Woman's Home Companion* (September 1925).

"Her Last Case," *The Saturday Evening Post* (3 November 1934).

"Can't You See it Now? These Were My People, Bred to the Sword, Perished by the Sword! Can't You Hear?"

"Myra, I've Done a Ghastly Thing—to You, to Me, to Us. I Haven't a Word to Say in Favor of Myself"

"Myra Meets His Family," *The Saturday Evening Post* (20 March 1920).

"Too Cute for Words," *The Saturday Evening Post* (18 April 1936).

When the Sunset Fell Together in a Jumbled Heap of Color in the Bottom of the Sky, They Strolled Back Along the Quiet Road.

"John Jackson's Arcady," *The Saturday Evening Post* (26 July 1924).

Violet wet her lips. "Well, how about it? Two thousand dollars would give you a chance to look around—something to get started with."

"Where can you get it?"

"It's in a bank, and it's as much mine as it is Earl's, because it's in a joint account. But you better think quick, because he wants to put it into a barber shop. Next he'd want me to go back to manicuring. I tell you I can't stand this life much longer."

Shalder walked up and down, considering. "All right. Make me out a check," he said. "And go pack your grips."

At that moment Irene Shalder was talking to Philip Jadwin in his office in the Hertzog Building.

"Of course you can have your position back," he said. "We've missed you. Sit down a minute and tell me what you've been doing."

She sat down, and as she talked he watched her. There was a faint mask of unhappiness and fright on her face, but underneath it he felt the quiet charm that had always moved him. She spoke frankly of all that she had hoarded up inside her in two years.

"And when he sends for you?" he asked when she had finished.

"He won't send for me."

"How do you know?"

"I just know. He—well, I don't think he's going alone. There's a woman he likes. He doesn't think I know, but I couldn't help knowing. Oh, it's all just terrible. Anyhow, if he sends for anybody, it'll be for this woman. I think he'd take her with him now if he had the money."

Philip Jadwin wanted to put his arm around her and whisper, "Now you've got a friend. All this trouble is over." But he only said: "Maybe it's better for him to go. Where's your baby?"

"She's been at my sister's since Monday; I was afraid to keep her in the house. You see, Howard has been threatened by some people he used to do business with and I didn't know what they might do. That's why he's leaving town."

"I see."

Several hours later Jadwin's secretary brought in a note:

Dear Mr. Jadwin: As you probably know, I took an option on the new barber shop, depositing two hundred with Mr. Edsall. Well, I have decided to take it up, and I understand Mr. Edsall is out of town, and I would like to close the deal now, if you could see me.

Respectfully,

EARL JOHNSON.

Jadwin had not known that Earl held the option, and the news was unwelcome. He felt guilty about Earl, and from feeling guilty about him, it was only a step to disliking him. He had grown to think of him as the type of all the speculation for which big business was blamed, and having had a glimpse afterward at the questionable paradise that Earl had bought with his money, he looked at the story and at its victim himself with distaste. Having avoided Earl in the other barber shop, he was now faced with having him in the building where he had his own offices.

"I'll see if I can talk him out of it," he thought.

When Earl came in he kept him standing. "Your note was rather a surprise to me," he began.

"I only just decided," said Earl humbly.

"I mean I'm surprised that you're going on your own again so quickly. I shouldn't think you'd plunge into another speculation just at this time."

"This isn't a speculation, Mr. Jadwin. I understand the barber business. Always when the boss was gone I took charge; he'll tell you that himself."

"But any business requires a certain amount of financial experience, a certain ability to figure costs and profits. There've been a lot of failures in this town because of people starting something they couldn't handle. You'd better think it over carefully before you rush into this."

"I have thought it over carefully, Mr. Jadwin. I was going to buy a shop three years ago, but I put the money into Hert-win when I got that tip from you."

"You remember I didn't want to give you the tip and I told you you'd probably lose your shirt."

"I never blamed you, Mr. Jadwin—never. It was something I oughtn't to have meddled with. But the barber business is something I know."

"Why should you blame me?"

"I shouldn't. But when you avoided my chair I thought maybe you thought I did."

This was too close to home to be pleasant.

"Look here, Earl," said Jadwin hurriedly. "We've almost closed with another party about this barber shop. Would you consider giving up your option if we forfeit, say, two hundred dollars?"

Earl rubbed his chin. "I tell you, Mr. Jadwin, I got just two thousand dollars and I don't know what to do with it. If I knew any other way of making it work for me—but nowadays it's dangerous for a man to speculate unless he's got inside information."

"It's dangerous for everybody always," remarked Jadwin impatiently. "Then, do I understand that you insist on going into this?"

"Unless you could suggest something else," said Earl hesitantly.

"Unless I give you another tip, eh?" Jadwin smiled in spite of himself. "Well, if that's the way it is——Have you got the money here?"

"It's in the savings bank. I can write you a check."

Jadwin rang for his secretary and gave her a scribbled note to telephone the bank and see if the money was actually on deposit. In a few minutes she sent word that it was.

"All right, Earl," said Jadwin. "It's your barber shop. I suppose in a few months you'll be sold out for laundry bills, but that's your affair."

The phone on his desk rang and his secretary switched him on to the teller at the savings bank:

"Mr. Jadwin, just a few minutes after your secretary called, a party presented a check drawn on Earl Johnson's account."

"Well?"

"If we honor it, it leaves him a balance of only sixty-six dollars instead of two thousand and sixty-six. It's a joint account and this check is signed by Violet Johnson. The party wishing to cash it is Howard Shalder. It's made out to his order."

"Wait a minute," said Jadwin quickly, and he leaned back in his chair to think. What Irene Shalder had said came back to him: "There's a woman he likes . . . he'd take her with him now if he had the money." Now evidently the woman had found the money.

"This is a damn serious thing," he thought. "If I tell them to cash that check, Earl probably loses his wife, and with my connivance." But in the back of his mind he knew that it would set Irene Shalder free.

Philip Jadwin came to a decision and leaned forward to the receiver:

"All right, cash it." He rang off and turned to Earl. "Well, make out your check. For two thousand dollars."

He stood up, terribly aware of what he had done. He watched Earl bent over his check book, not knowing that the check would come back unhonored and that the whole transaction was meaningless. And watching the fingers twisted clumsily about the fountain pen, he thought how deft those same fingers were with a razor, handling it so adroitly that there was no pull or scrape; of those fingers manipulating a hot towel that never scalded, spreading a final, smooth lotion——

"Earl," he said suddenly, "if somebody told you that your wife was running away with another man—that she was on her way to the station—what would you do?"

Earl looked at him steadily. "Mr. Jadwin, I'd thank God," he said.

A minute later he handed the check to Jadwin and received a signed paper; the transaction was complete.

"I hope you'll patronize us sometime, Mr. Jadwin."

"What? Oh, yes, Earl. Certainly I will."

"Thank you, Mr. Jadwin. I'm going to do my best."

When he had gone, Jadwin looked at the check and tore it into small pieces. By this time Shalder and Earl's wife were probably at the station.

"I wonder what the devil I've done," he brooded.

IV

So that is how Earl Johnson happens to have the barber shop in the Hertzog Building. It is a cheerful shop, bright and modern; probably the most prosperous shop in town, although a large number of the clients insist on Earl's personal attentions. Earl is constitutionally a happy and a sociable man; eventually he will marry again. He knows his staff and sticks to it, and that is not the least important or least creditable thing that can be said about him.

Once in a while he plays the horses on tips that he gets from the paper the shop subscribes to.

"All right, sir," he says, "in twenty minutes then. I'll wait for you, Mr. Jadwin."

And, then, back at his chair: "That's Philip Jadwin. He's a nice fellow. I got to admit I like nice people."

The soul of a slave, says the Marxian. Anyhow that's the sort of soul that Earl has, and he's pretty happy with it. I like Earl.

Six of One—

(*Redbook*, February 1932)

"Six of One—" was written as "Half a Dozen of the Other," probably in Switzerland in July 1931. It is not known why the *Post* declined this story, but *Redbook* paid $3000 for it.

"Six of One—" is an indirect response to the Depression in that it excoriates "all that waste at the top" and expresses confidence in the Alger types. This story is one of Fitzgerald's rare expressions of open hostility toward the rich, mixed with a sense of regret that seriousness and privilege or ambition and glamor do not often inhabit the same skin. "Six of One—" is significant in terms of Fitzgerald's personal politics. Despite his image as the chronicler of the very rich, he regarded himself as a liberal and developed an interest in Marxism at this time. (He had listed himself as a socialist in his first *Who's Who* entry.) Nonetheless, the story is obviously not a call to class warfare, for Fitzgerald was keenly sensitive to the attractions of the aristocracy: "The young princes in velvet gathered in lovely domesticity around the queen amid the hush of rich draperies may presently grow up to be Pedro the Cruel or Charles the Mad, but the moment of beauty was there."

Barnes stood on the wide stairs looking down through a wide hall into the living-room of the country place and at the group of youths. His friend Schofield was addressing some benevolent remarks to them, and Barnes did not want to interrupt; as he stood there, immobile, he seemed to be drawn suddenly into rhythm with the group below; he perceived them as statuesque beings, set apart, chiseled out of the Minnesota twilight that was setting on the big room.

In the first place all five, the two young Schofields and their friends, were fine-looking boys, very American, dressed in a careless but not casual way over well-set-up bodies, and with responsive faces open to all four winds. Then he saw that they made a design, the faces profile upon profile, the heads blond and dark, turning toward Mr. Schofield, the erect yet vaguely lounging bodies, never tense but ever ready under the flannels and the soft angora wool sweaters, the hands placed on other shoulders, as if to bring each one into the solid freemasonry of the group. Then suddenly, as though a group of models posing for a sculptor were being dismissed, the composition broke and they all moved toward the door. They left Barnes with a sense of having seen something more than five young men between sixteen and eighteen going out to sail or play tennis or golf, but having gained a sharp impression of a whole style, a whole mode of youth, something different from his own less assured, less graceful generation, something unified by standards that he didn't know. He wondered vaguely what the standards of 1920 were, and whether they were worth anything—had a sense of waste, of much effort for a purely esthetic achievement. Then Schofield saw him and called him down into the living-room.

"Aren't they a fine bunch of boys?" Schofield demanded. "Tell me, did you ever see a finer bunch?"

"A fine lot," agreed Barnes, with a certain lack of enthusiasm. He felt a sudden premonition that his generation in its years of effort had made possible a Periclean age, but had evolved no prospective Pericles. They had set the scene: was the cast adequate?

"It isn't just because two of them happen to be mine," went on Schofield. "It's self-evident. You couldn't match that crowd in any city in the country. First place, they're such a husky lot. Those two little Kavenaughs aren't going to be big men—more like their father; but the oldest one could make any college hockey-team in the country right now."

"How old are they?" asked Barnes.

"Well, Howard Kavenaugh, the oldest, is nineteen—going to Yale next year. Then comes my Wister—he's eighteen, also going to Yale next year. You liked Wister, didn't you? I don't know anybody who doesn't. He'd make a great politician, that kid. Then there's a boy named Larry Patt who wasn't here today—he's eighteen too, and he's State golf champion. Fine voice too; he's trying to get in Princeton."

"Who's the blond-haired one who looks like a Greek god?"

"That's Beau Lebaume. He's going to Yale, too, if the girls will let him leave town. Then there's the other Kavenaugh, the stocky one—he's going to be an even better athlete than his brother. And finally there's my youngest, Charley; he's sixteen," Schofield sighed reluctantly. "But I guess you've heard all the boasting you can stand."

"No, tell me more about them—I'm interested. Are they anything more than athletes?"

"Why, there's not a dumb one in the lot, except maybe Beau Lebaume; but you can't help liking him anyhow. And every one of them's a natural leader. I remember a few years ago a tough gang tried to start something with them, calling them 'candies'—well, that gang must be running yet. They sort of remind me of young knights. And what's the matter with their being athletes? I seem to remember you stroking the boat at New London, and that didn't keep you from consolidating railroad systems and—"

"I took up rowing because I had a sick stomach," said Barnes. "By the way, are these boys all rich?"

"Well, the Kavenaughs are, of course; and my boys will have something."

Barnes' eyes twinkled.

"So I suppose since they won't have to worry about money, they're brought up to serve the State," he suggested. "You spoke of one of your sons having a political talent and their all being like young knights, so I suppose they'll go out for public life and the army and navy."

"I don't know about that," Schofield's voice sounded somewhat alarmed. "I think their fathers would be pretty disappointed if they didn't go into business. That's natural, isn't it?"

"It's natural, but it isn't very romantic," said Barnes good-humoredly.

"You're trying to get my goat," said Schofield. "Well, if you can match that—"

"They're certainly an ornamental bunch," admitted Barnes. "They've got what you call glamour. They certainly look like the cigarette ads in the magazines; but—"

"But you're an old sour-belly," interrupted Schofield. "I've explained that these boys are all well-rounded. My son Wister led his class at school this year, but I was a darn' sight prouder that he got the medal for best all-around boy."

The two men faced each other with the uncut cards of the future on the table before them. They had been in college together, and were friends of many years' standing. Barnes was childless, and Schofield was inclined to attribute his lack of enthusiasm to that.

"I somehow can't see them setting the world on fire, doing better than their fathers," broke out Barnes suddenly. "The more charming they are, the harder it's going to be for them. In the East people are beginning to realize what wealthy boys are up against. Match them? Maybe not now." He leaned forward, his eyes lighting up. "But I could pick six boys from any high-school in Cleveland, give them an education, and I believe that ten years from this time your young fellows here would be utterly outclassed. There's so little demanded of them, so little expected of them—what could be softer than just to have to go on being charming and athletic?"

"I know your idea," objected Schofield scoffingly. "You'd go to a big municipal high-school and pick out the six most brilliant scholars—"

"I'll tell you what I'll do—" Barnes noticed that he had unconsciously substituted "I will" for "I would," but he didn't correct himself. "I'll go to the little town in Ohio, where I was born—there probably aren't fifty or sixty boys in the high-school there, and I wouldn't be likely to find six geniuses out of that number."

"And what?"

"I'll give them a chance. If they fail, the chance is lost. That is a serious responsibility, and they've got to take it seriously. That's what these boys haven't got—they're only asked to be serious about trivial things." He thought for a moment. "I'm going to do it."

"Do what?"

"I'm going to see."

A fortnight later he was back in the small town in Ohio where he had been born, where, he felt, the driving emotions of his own youth still haunted the quiet streets. He interviewed the principal of the high-school, who made suggestions; then by the, for Barnes, difficult means of making an address and afterward attending a reception, he got in touch with teachers and pupils. He made a donation to the school, and under cover of this found opportunities of watching the boys at work and at play.

It was fun—he felt his youth again. There were some boys that he liked immediately, and he began a weeding-out process, inviting them in groups of five or six to his mother's house, rather like a fraternity rushing freshmen. When a boy interested him, he looked up his record and that of his family—and at the end of a fortnight he had chosen five boys.

In the order in which he chose them, there was first Otto Schlach, a farmer's son who had already displayed extraordinary mechanical aptitude and a gift for mathematics. Schlach was highly recommended by his teachers, and he welcomed the opportunity offered him of entering the Massachusetts Institute of Technology.

A drunken father left James Matsko as his only legacy to the town of Barnes' youth. From the age of twelve, James had supported himself by keeping a newspaper-and-candy store with a three-foot frontage; and now at seventeen he was reputed to have saved five hundred dollars. Barnes found it difficult to persuade him to study money and banking at Columbia, for Matsko was already assured of his ability to make money. But Barnes had prestige as the town's most successful son, and he convinced Matsko that otherwise he would lack frontage, like his own place of business.

Then there was Jack Stubbs, who had lost an arm hunting, but in spite of this handicap played on the high-school football team. He was not among the leaders in studies; he had developed no particular bent; but the fact that he had overcome that enormous handicap enough to play football—to tackle and to catch punts—convinced Barnes that no obstacles would stand in Jack Stubbs' way.

The fourth selection was George Winfield, who was almost twenty. Because of the death of his father, he had left school at fourteen, helped to support his family for four years, and then, things being better, he had come back to finish high-school. Barnes felt, therefore, that Winfield would place a serious value on an education.

Next came a boy whom Barnes found personally antipathetic. Louis Ireland was at once the most brilliant scholar and most difficult boy at school. Untidy, insubordinate and eccentric, Louis drew scurrilous caricatures behind his Latin book, but when called upon inevitably produced a perfect recitation. There was a big talent nascent somewhere in him—it was impossible to leave him out.

The last choice was the most difficult. The remaining boys were mediocrities, or at any rate they had so far displayed no qualities that set them apart. For a time Barnes, thinking patriotically of his old university, considered the football captain, a virtuostic halfback who would have been welcome on any Eastern squad; but that would have destroyed the integrity of the idea.

He finally chose a younger boy, Gordon Vandervere, of a rather higher standing than the others. Vandervere was the handsomest and one of the most popular boys in school. He had been intended for college, but his father, a harassed minister, was glad to see the way made easy.

Barnes was content with himself; he felt godlike in being able to step in to mold these various destinies. He felt as if they were his own sons, and he telegraphed Schofield in Minneapolis:

HAVE CHOSEN HALF A DOZEN OF THE OTHER, AND AM BACKING THEM AGAINST THE WORLD.

And now, after all this biography, the story begins. . . .

The continuity of the frieze is broken. Young Charley Schofield had been expelled from Hotchkiss. It was a small but painful tragedy—he and four other boys, nice boys, popular boys, broke the honor system as to smoking. Charley's father felt the matter deeply, varying between disappointment about Charley and anger at the school. Charley came home to Minneapolis in a desperate humor and went to the country day-school while it was decided what he was to do.

It was still undecided in midsummer. When school was over, he spent his time playing golf, or dancing at the Minnekada Club—he was a handsome boy of eighteen, older than his age, with charming manners, with no serious vices, but with a tendency to be easily influenced by his admirations. His principal admiration at the time was Gladys Irving, a young married woman scarcely two years older than himself. He rushed her at the club dances, and felt sentimentally about her, though Gladys on her part was in love with her husband and asked from Charley only the confirmation of her own youth and charm that a belle often needs after her first baby.

Sitting out with her one night on the veranda of the Lafayette Club, Charley felt a necessity to boast to her, to pretend to be more experienced, and so more potentially protective.

"I've seen a lot of life for my age," he said. "I've done things I couldn't even tell you about."

Gladys didn't answer.

"In fact last week—" he began, and thought better of it. "In any case I don't think I'll go to Yale next year—I'd have to go East right away, and tutor all summer. If I don't go, there's a job open in Father's office; and after Wister goes back to college in the fall, I'll have the roadster to myself."

"I thought you were going to college," Gladys said coldly.

"I was. But I've thought things over, and now I don't know. I've usually gone with older boys, and I feel older than boys my age. I like older girls, for instance." When Charley looked at her then suddenly, he seemed unusually attractive to her—it would be very pleasant to have him here, to cut in on her at dances all summer. But Gladys said:

"You'd be a fool to stay here."

"Why?"

"You started something—you ought to go through with it. A few years running around town, and you won't be good for anything."

"You think so," he said indulgently.

Gladys didn't want to hurt him or to drive him away from her; yet she wanted to say something stronger.

"Do you think I'm thrilled when you tell me you've had a lot of dissipated experience? I don't see how anybody could claim to be your friend and encourage you in that. If I were you, I'd at least pass your examinations for college. Then they can't say you just lay down after you were expelled from school."

"You think so?" Charley said, unruffled, and in his grave, precocious manner, as though he were talking to a child. But she had convinced him, because he was in love with her and the moon was around her. *"Oh me, oh my, oh you,"* was the last music they had danced to on the Wednesday before, and so it was one of those times.

Had Gladys let him brag to her, concealing her curiosity under a mask of companionship, if she had accepted his own estimate of himself as a man formed, no urging of his father's would have mattered. As it was, Charley passed into college that fall, thanks to a girl's tender reminiscences and her own memories of the sweetness of youth's success in young fields.

And it was well for his father that he did. If he had not, the catastrophe of his older brother Wister that autumn would have broken Schofield's heart. The morning after the Harvard game the New York papers carried a headline:

> YALE BOYS AND FOLLIES GIRLS IN
> MOTOR CRASH NEAR RYE
> IRENE DALEY IN GREENWICH HOS-
> PITAL THREATENS BEAUTY SUIT
> MILLIONAIRE'S SON INVOLVED

The four boys came up before the dean a fortnight later. Wister Schofield, who had driven the car, was called first.

"It was not your car, Mr. Schofield," the dean said. "It was Mr. Kavenaugh's car, wasn't it?"

"Yes sir."

"How did you happen to be driving?"

"The girls wanted me to. They didn't feel safe."

"But you'd been drinking too, hadn't you?"

"Yes, but not so much."

"Tell me this," asked the dean: "Haven't you ever driven a car when you'd been drinking—perhaps drinking even more than you were that night?"

"Why—perhaps once or twice, but I never had any accidents. And this was so clearly unavoidable—"

"Possibly," the dean agreed; "but we'll have to look at it this way: Up to this time you had no accidents even when you deserved to have them. Now you've had one when you didn't deserve it. I don't want you to go out of here feeling that life or the University or I myself haven't given you a square deal, Mr. Schofield. But the newspapers have given this a great deal of prominence, and I'm afraid that the University will have to dispense with your presence."

Moving along the frieze to Howard Kavenaugh, the dean's remarks to him were substantially the same.

"I am particularly sorry in your case, Mr. Kavenaugh. Your father has made substantial gifts to the University, and I took pleasure in watching you play hockey with your usual brilliance last winter."

Howard Kavenaugh left the office with uncontrollable tears running down his cheeks.

Since Irene Daley's suit for her ruined livelihood, her ruined beauty, was directed against the owner and the driver of the automobile, there were lighter sentences for the other two occupants of the car. Beau Lebaume came into the dean's office with his arm in a sling and his handsome head swathed in bandages and was suspended for the remainder of the current year. He took it jauntily and said good-by to the dean with as cheerful a smile as could show through the bandages. The last case, however, was the most difficult. George Winfield, who had entered high-school late because work in the world had taught him the value of an education, came in looking at the floor.

"I can't understand your participation in this affair," said the dean. "I know your benefactor, Mr. Barnes, personally. He told me how you left school to go to work, and how you came back to it four years later to continue your education, and he felt that your attitude toward life was essentially serious. Up to this point you have a good record here at New Haven, but it struck me several months ago that you were running with a rather gay crowd, boys with a great deal of money to spend. You are old enough to realize that they couldn't possibly give you as much in material ways as they took away from you in others. I've got to give you a year's suspension. If you come back, I have every hope you'll justify the confidence that Mr. Barnes reposed in you."

"I won't come back," said Winfield. "I couldn't face Mr. Barnes after this. I'm not going home."

At the suit brought by Irene Daley, all four of them lied loyally for Wister Schofield. They said that before they hit the gasoline pump they had seen Miss Daley grab the wheel. But Miss Daley was in court, with her face, familiar to the tabloids, permanently scarred; and her counsel exhibited a letter canceling her recent moving-picture contract. The students' case looked bad; so in the intermission, on their lawyer's advice, they settled for forty thousand dollars. Wister Schofield and Howard Kavenaugh were snapped by a dozen photographers leaving the courtroom, and served up in flaming notoriety next day.

That night, Wister, the three Minneapolis boys, Howard and Beau Lebaume started for home. George Winfield said good-by to them in the Pennsylvania station; and having no home to go to, walked out into New York to start life over.

Of all Barnes' protégés, Jack Stubbs with his one arm was the favorite. He was the first to achieve fame—when he played on the tennis team at Princeton, the rotogravure section carried pictures showing how he threw the ball from his racket in serving. When he was graduated, Barnes took him into his own office—he was often spoken of as an adopted son. Stubbs, together with Schlach, now a prominent consulting engineer, were the most satisfactory of his experiments, although James Matsko at twenty-seven had just been made a partner in a Wall Street brokerage house. Financially he was the most successful of the six, yet Barnes found himself somewhat repelled by his hard egoism. He wondered, too, if he, Barnes, had really played any part in Matsko's career—did it after all matter whether Matsko was a figure in metropolitan finance or a big merchant in the Middle West, as he would have undoubtedly become without any assistance at all.

One morning in 1930 he handed Jack Stubbs a letter that led to a balancing up of the book of boys.

"What do you think of this?"

The letter was from Louis Ireland in Paris. About Louis they did not agree, and as Jack read, he prepared once more to intercede in his behalf.

My dear Sir:

After your last communication, made through your bank here and enclosing a check which I hereby acknowledge, I do not feel that I am under any obligation to write you at all. But because the concrete fact of an object's commercial worth may be able to move you, while you remain utterly insensitive to the value of an abstract idea—because of this I write to tell you that my exhibition was an unqualified success. To bring the matter even nearer to your intellectual level, I may tell you that I sold two pieces—a head of Lallette, the actress, and a bronze animal group—for a total of seven thousand francs ($280.00). Moreover I have commissions which will take me all summer—I enclose a piece about me cut from CAHIERS D'ART, which will show you that whatever your estimate of my abilities and my career, it is by no means unanimous.

This is not to say that I am ungrateful for your well-intentioned attempt to "educate" me. I suppose that Harvard was no worse than any other polite finishing school—the years that I wasted there gave me a sharp and well-documented attitude on American life and institutions. But your suggestions that I come to America and make standardized nymphs for profiteers' fountains was a little too much—

Stubbs looked up with a smile.

"Well," Barnes said, "what do you think? Is he crazy—or now that he has sold some statues, does it prove that I'm crazy?"

"Neither one," laughed Stubbs. "What you objected to in Louis wasn't his talent. But you never got over that year he tried to enter a monastery and then got arrested in the Sacco-Vanzetti demonstrations, and then ran away with the professor's wife."

"He was just forming himself," said Barnes dryly, "just trying his little wings. God knows what he's been up to abroad."

"Well, perhaps he's formed now," Stubbs said lightly. He had always liked Louis Ireland—privately he resolved to write and see if he needed money.

"Anyhow, he's graduated from me," announced Barnes. "I can't do any more to help him or hurt him. Suppose we call him a success, though that's pretty doubtful—let's see how we stand. I'm going to see Schofield out in Minneapolis next week, and I'd like to balance accounts. To my mind, the successes are you, Otto Schlach, James Matsko,—whatever you and I may think of him as a man,—and let's assume that Louis Ireland is going to be a great sculptor. That's four. Winfield's disappeared. I've never had a line from him."

"Perhaps he's doing well somewhere."

"If he were doing well, I think he'd let me know. We'll have to count him as a failure so far as my experiment goes. Then there's Gordon Vandervere."

Both were silent for a moment.

"I can't make it out about Gordon," Barnes said. "He's such a nice fellow, but since he left college, he doesn't seem to come through. He was younger than the rest of you, and he had the advantage of two years at Andover before he went to college, and at Princeton he knocked them cold, as you say. But he seems to have worn his wings out—for four years now he's done nothing at all; he can't hold a job; he can't get his mind on his work, and he doesn't seem to care. I'm about through with Gordon."

At this moment Gordon was announced over the phone.

"He asked for an appointment," explained Barnes. "I suppose he wants to try something new."

A personable young man with an easy and attractive manner strolled in to the office.

"Good afternoon, Uncle Ed. Hi there, Jack!" Gordon sat down. "I'm full of news."

"About what?" asked Barnes.

"About myself."

"I know. You've just been appointed to arrange a merger between J. P. Morgan and the Queensborough Bridge."

"It's a merger," agreed Vandervere, "but those are not the parties to it. I'm engaged to be married."

Barnes glowered.

"Her name," continued Vandervere, "is Esther Crosby."

"Let me congratulate you," said Barnes ironically. "A relation of H. B. Crosby, I presume."

"Exactly," said Vandervere unruffled. "In fact, his only daughter."

For a moment there was silence in the office. Then Barnes exploded.

"*You're* going to marry H. B. Crosby's daughter? Does he know that last month you retired by request from one of his banks?"

"I'm afraid he knows everything about me. He's been looking me over for four years. You see, Uncle Ed," he continued cheerfully, "Esther and I got engaged during my last year at Princeton—my roommate brought her down to a house-party, but she switched over to me. Well, quite naturally Mr. Crosby wouldn't hear of it until I'd proved myself."

"Proved yourself!" repeated Barnes. "Do you consider that you've proved yourself?"

"Well—yes."

"How?"

"By waiting four years. You see, either Esther or I might have married anybody else in that time, but we didn't. Instead we sort of wore him away. That's really why I haven't been able to get down to anything. Mr. Crosby is a strong personality, and it took a lot of time and energy wearing him away. Sometimes Esther and I didn't see each other for months, so she couldn't eat; so then thinking of that I couldn't eat, so then I couldn't work—"

"And you mean he's really given his consent?"

"He gave it last night."

"Is he going to let you loaf?"

"No. Esther and I are going into the diplomatic service. She feels that the family has passed through the banking phase." He winked at Stubbs. "I'll look up Louis Ireland when I get to Paris, and send Uncle Ed a report."

Suddenly Barnes roared with laughter.

"Well, it's all in the lottery-box," he said. "When I picked out you six, I was a long way from guessing—" He turned to Stubbs and demanded: "Shall we put him under *failure* or under *success*?"

"A howling success," said Stubbs. "Top of the list."

A fortnight later Barnes was with his old friend Schofield in Minneapolis. He thought of the house with the six boys as he had last seen it—now it seemed to bear scars of them, like the traces that pictures leave on a wall that they have long protected from the mark of time. Since he did not know what had become of Schofield's sons, he refrained from referring to their conversation of ten years before until he knew whether it was dangerous ground. He was glad of his reticence later in the evening when Schofield spoke of his elder son, Wister.

"Wister never seems to have found himself—and he was such a high-spirited kid! He was the leader of every group he went into; he could always make things go. When he was young, our houses in town and at the lake were always packed with young people. But after he left Yale, he lost interest in things—got sort of scornful about everything. I thought for a while that it was because he drank too much, but he married a nice girl and she took that in hand. Still, he hasn't any ambition—he talked about country life, so I bought him a silver-fox farm, but that didn't go; and I sent him to Florida during the boom, but that wasn't any better. Now he has an interest in a dude-ranch in Montana; but since the depression—"

Barnes saw his opportunity and asked:

"What became of those friends of your sons' that I met one day?"

"Let's see—I wonder who you mean. There was Kavenaugh—you know, the flour people—he was here a lot. Let's see—he eloped with an Eastern girl, and for a few years he and his wife were the leaders of the gay crowd here—they did a lot of drinking and not much else. It seems to me I heard the other day that Howard's getting a divorce. Then there was the younger brother—he never could get into college. Finally he married a manicurist, and they live here rather quietly. We don't hear much about them."

They had had a glamour about them, Barnes remembered; they had been so sure of themselves, individually, as a group; so high-spirited, a frieze of Greek youths, graceful of body, ready for life.

"Then Larry Patt, you might have met him here. A great golfer. He couldn't stay in college—there didn't seem to be enough fresh air there for Larry." And he added defensively: "But he capitalized what he could do—he opened a sporting-goods store and made a good thing of it, I understand. He has a string of three or four."

"I seem to remember an exceptionally handsome one."

"Oh—Beau Lebaume. He was in that mess at New Haven too. After that he went to pieces—drink and what-not. His father's tried everything, and now he won't have anything more to do with him." Schofield's face warmed suddenly; his eyes glowed. "But let me tell you, I've got a boy—my Charley! I wouldn't trade him for the lot of them—he's coming over presently, and you'll see. He had a bad start, got into trouble at Hotchkiss—but did he quit? Never. He went back and made a fine record at New Haven, senior society and all that. Then he and some other boys took a trip around the world, and then he came back here and said: 'All right, Father, I'm ready—when do I start?' I don't know what I'd do without Charley. He got married a few months back, a young widow he'd always been in love with; and

his mother and I are still missing him, though they come over
often—"

Barnes was glad about this, and suddenly he was reconciled at
not having any sons in the flesh—one out of two made good, and
sometimes better, and sometimes nothing; but just going along
getting old by yourself when you'd counted on so much from sons—

"Charley runs the business," continued Schofield. "That is, he
and a young man named Winfield that Wister got me to take on five or
six years ago. Wister felt responsible about him, felt he'd got him into
this trouble at New Haven—and this boy had no family. He's done
well here."

Another one of Barnes' six accounted for! He felt a surge of
triumph, but he saw he must keep it to himself; a little later when
Schofield asked him if he'd carried out his intention of putting some
boys through college, he avoided answering. After all, any given
moment has its value; it can be questioned in the light of after-events,
but the moment remains. The young princes in velvet gathered in
lovely domesticity around the queen amid the hush of rich draperies
may presently grow up to be Pedro the Cruel or Charles the Mad, but
the moment of beauty was there. Back there ten years, Schofield had
seen his sons and their friends as samurai, as something shining and
glorious and young, perhaps as something he had missed from his
own youth. There was later a price to be paid by those boys, all too
fulfilled, with the whole balance of their life pulled forward into their
youth so that everything afterward would inevitably be anticlimax;
these boys brought up as princes with none of the responsibilities of
princes! Barnes didn't know how much their mothers might have had
to do with it, what their mothers may have lacked.

But he was glad that his friend Schofield had one true son.

His own experiment—he didn't regret it, but he wouldn't have
done it again. Probably it proved something, but he wasn't quite sure
what. Perhaps that life is constantly renewed, and glamour and
beauty make way for it; and he was glad that he was able to feel that
the republic could survive the mistakes of a whole generation,
pushing the waste aside, sending ahead the vital and the strong. Only
it was too bad and very American that there should be all that waste at
the top; and he felt that he would not live long enough to see it end, to
see great seriousness in the same skin with great opportunity—to see
the race achieve itself at last.

A Freeze-Out

(*The Saturday Evening Post*, 19 December 1931)

"A Freeze-Out" was probably the last story Fitzgerald wrote in Switzerland before sailing home with his family in September 1931. The *Post* paid $4000.

In this story Fitzgerald found an American subject and avoided the Depression, returning to St. Paul for his setting. "A Freeze-Out" is a reversion to the confident spirit of his earlier stories, showing none of the troubles or troublesome people who appear in some of the other stories written in this period. In "A Freeze-Out" the problems are solved by good sense and right instincts. The depiction of old Mrs. Winslow is noteworthy, showing Fitzgerald's lifelong respect for solid characters—representatives of old American standards—who do their duty.

Here and there in a sunless corner skulked a little snow under a veil of coal specks, but the men taking down storm windows were laboring in shirt sleeves and the turf was becoming firm underfoot.

In the streets, dresses dyed after fruit, leaf and flower emerged from beneath the shed somber skins of animals; now only a few old men wore mousy caps pulled down over their ears. That was the day Forrest Winslow forgot the long fret of the past winter as one forgets inevitable afflictions, sickness, and war, and turned with blind confidence toward the summer, thinking he already recognized in it all the summers of the past—the golfing, sailing, swimming summers.

For eight years Forrest had gone East to school and then to college; now he worked for his father in a large Minnesota city. He was handsome, popular and rather spoiled in a conservative way, and so the past year had been a comedown. The discrimination that had picked Scroll and Key at New Haven was applied to sorting furs; the hand that had signed the Junior Prom expense checks had since rocked in a sling for two months with mild *dermatitis venenata*. After work, Forrest found no surcease in the girls with whom he had grown up. On the contrary, the news of a stranger within the tribe stimulated him and during the transit of a popular visitor he displayed a convulsive activity. So far, nothing had happened; but here was summer.

On the day spring broke through and summer broke through—it is much the same thing in Minnesota—Forrest stopped his coupe in front of a music store and took his pleasant vanity inside. As he said to the clerk, "I want some records," a little bomb of excitement exploded in his larynx, causing an unfamiliar and almost painful vacuum in his upper diaphragm. The unexpected detonation was caused by the sight of a corn-colored girl who was being waited on across the counter.

She was a stalk of ripe corn, but bound not as cereals are but as a rare first edition, with all the binder's art. She was lovely and expensive, and about nineteen, and he had never seen her before. She looked at him for just an unnecessary moment too long, with so much self-confidence that he felt his own rush out and away to join hers—". . . from him that hath not shall be taken away even that which he hath." Then her head swayed forward and she resumed her inspection of a catalogue.

Forrest looked at the list a friend had sent him from New York. Unfortunately, the first title was: "When Voo-do-o-do Meets Boop-boop-a-doop, There'll Soon be a Hot-Cha-Cha." Forrest read it with horror. He could scarcely believe a title could be so repulsive.

Meanwhile the girl was asking: "Isn't there a record of Prokofiev's 'Fils Prodigue?' "

"I'll see, madam." The saleswoman turned to Forrest.

" 'When Voo——' " Forrest began, and then repeated, " 'When Voo——' "

There was no use; he couldn't say it in front of that nymph of the harvest across the table.

"Never mind that one," he said quickly. "Give me 'Hugga-ble——' " Again he broke off.

" 'Huggable, Kissable You?' " suggested the clerk helpfully, and her assurance that it was very nice suggested a humiliating community of taste.

"I want Stravinsky's 'Fire Bird,' " said the other customer, "and this album of Chopin waltzes."

Forrest ran his eye hastily down the rest of his list: "Digga Diggity," "Ever So Goosy," "Bunkey Doodle I Do."

"Anybody would take me for a moron," he thought. He crumpled up the list and fought for air—his own kind of air, the air of casual superiority.

"I'd like," he said coldly, "Beethoven's 'Moonlight Sonata.' "

There was a record of it at home, but it didn't matter. It gave him the right to glance at the girl again and again. Life became interesting; she was the loveliest concoction; it would be easy to trace her. With the "Moonlight Sonata" wrapped face to face with "Huggable, Kissable You," Forrest quitted the shop.

There was a new book store down the street, and here also he entered, as if books and records could fill the vacuum that spring was making in his heart. As he looked among the lifeless words of many titles together, he was wondering how soon he could find her, and what then.

"I'd like a hard-boiled detective story," he said.

A weary young man shook his head with patient reproof; simultaneously, a spring draft from the door blew in with it the familiar glow of cereal hair.

"We don't carry detective stories or stuff like that," said the young man in an unnecessarily loud voice. "I imagine you'll find it at a department store."

"I thought you carried books," said Forrest feebly.

"Books, yes, but not that kind." The young man turned to wait on his other customer.

As Forrest stalked out, passing within the radius of the girl's perfume, he heard her ask:

"Have you got anything of Louis Arragon's, either in French or in translation?"

"She's just showing off," he thought angrily. "They skip right from Peter Rabbit to Marcel Proust these days."

Outside, parked just behind his own adequate coupe, he found an enormous silver-colored roadster of English make and custom design. Disturbed, even upset, he drove homeward through the moist, golden afternoon.

The Winslows lived in an old, wide-verandaed house on Crest Avenue—Forrest's father and mother, his great-grandmother and his sister Eleanor. They were solid people as that phrase goes since the war. Old Mrs. Forrest was entirely solid; with convictions based on a way of life that had worked for eighty-four years. She was a character in the city; she remembered the Sioux war and she had been in Stillwater the day the James brothers shot up the main street.

Her own children were dead and she looked on these remoter descendants from a distance, oblivious of the forces that had formed them. She understood that the Civil War and the opening up of the West were forces, while the free-silver movement and the World War had reached her only as news. But she knew that her father, killed at Cold Harbor, and her husband, the merchant, were larger in scale than her son or her grandson. People who tried to explain contemporary phenomena to her seemed, to her, to be talking against the evidence of their own senses. Yet she was not atrophied; last summer she had traveled over half of Europe with only a maid.

Forrest's father and mother were something else again. They had been in the susceptible middle thirties when the cocktail party and its concomitants arrived in 1921. They were divided people, leaning forward and backward. Issues that presented no difficulty to Mrs. Forrest caused them painful heat and agitation. Such an issue arose before they had been five minutes at table that night.

"Do you know the Rikkers are coming back?" said Mrs. Winslow. "They've taken the Warner house." She was a woman with many uncertainties, which she concealed from herself by expressing her opinions very slowly and thoughtfully, to convince her own ears. "It's a wonder Dan Warner would rent them his house. I suppose Cathy thinks everybody will fall all over themselves."

"What Cathy?" asked old Mrs. Forrest.

"She was Cathy Chase. Her father was Reynold Chase. She and her husband are coming back here."

"Oh, yes."

"I scarcely knew her," continued Mrs. Winslow, "but I know that when they were in Washington they were pointedly rude to everyone from Minnesota—went out of their way. Mary Cowan was spending a winter there, and she invited Cathy to lunch or tea at least half a dozen times. Cathy never appeared."

"I could beat that record," said Pierce Winslow. "Mary Cowan could invite me a hundred times and I wouldn't go."

"Anyhow," pursued his wife slowly, "in view of all the scandal, it's just asking for the cold shoulder to come out here."

"They're asking for it, all right," said Winslow. He was a Southerner, well liked in the city, where he had lived for thirty years. "Walter Hannan came in my office this morning and wanted me to second Rikker for the Kennemore Club. I said: 'Walter, I'd rather second Al Capone.' What's more, Rikker'll get into the Kennemore Club over my dead body."

"Walter had his nerve. What's Chauncey Rikker to you? It'll be hard to get anyone to second him."

"Who are they?" Eleanor asked. "Somebody awful?"

She was eighteen and a debutante. Her current appearances at home were so rare and brief that she viewed such table topics with as much detachment as her great-grandmother.

"Cathy was a girl here; she was younger then I was, but I remember that she was always considered fast. Her husband, Chauncey Rikker, came from some little town upstate."

"What did they do that was so awful?"

"Rikker went bankrupt and left town," said her father. "There were a lot of ugly stories. Then he went to Washington and got mixed up in the alien-property scandal; and then he got in trouble in New York—he was in the bucket-shop business—but he skipped out to Europe. After a few years the chief Government witness died and he came back to America. They got him for a few months for contempt of court." He expanded into eloquent irony: "And now, with true patriotism, he comes back to his beautiful Minnesota, a product of its lovely woods, its rolling wheat fields——"

Forrest called him impatiently: "Where do you get that, father? When did two Kentuckians ever win Nobel prizes in the same year? And how about an upstate boy named Lind——"

"Have the Rikkers any children?" Eleanor asked.

"I think Cathy has a daughter about your age, and a boy about sixteen."

Forrest uttered a small, unnoticed exclamation. Was it possible? French books and Russian music—that girl this afternoon had lived abroad. And with the probability his resentment deepened—the daughter of a crook putting on all that dog! He sympathized passionately with his father's refusal to second Rikker for the Kennemore Club.

"Are they rich?" old Mrs. Forrest suddenly demanded.

"They must be well off if they took Dan Warner's house."

"Then they'll get in all right."

"They won't get into the Kennemore Club," said Pierce Winslow. "I happen to come from a state with certain traditions."

"I've seen the bottom rail get to be the top rail many times in this town," said the old lady blandly.

"But this man's a criminal, grandma," explained Forrest. "Can't you see the difference? It isn't a social question. We used to argue at New Haven whether we'd shake hands with Al Capone if we met him——"

"Who is Al Capone?" asked Mrs. Forrest.

"He's another criminal, in Chicago."

"Does he want to join the Kennemore Club too?"

They laughed, but Forrest had decided that if Rikker came up for the Kennemore Club, his father's would not be the only black ball in the box.

Abruptly it became full summer. After the last April storm someone came along the street one night, blew up the trees like balloons, scattered bulbs and shrubs like confetti, opened a cage full of robins and, after a quick look around, signaled up the curtain upon a new backdrop of summer sky.

Tossing back a strayed baseball to some kids in a vacant lot, Forrest's fingers, on the stitched seams of the stained leather cover, sent a wave of ecstatic memories to his brain. One must hurry and get there—"there" was now the fairway of the golf course, but his feeling was the same. Only when he teed off at the eighteenth that afternoon did he realize that it wasn't the same, that it would never be enough any more. The evening stretched large and empty before him, save for the set pieces of a dinner party and bed.

While he waited with his partner for a match to play off, Forrest glanced at the tenth tee, exactly opposite and two hundred yards away.

One of the two figures on the ladies' tee was addressing her ball; as he watched, she swung up confidently and cracked a long drive down the fairway.

"Must be Mrs. Horrick," said his friend. "No other woman can drive like that."

At that moment the sun glittered on the girl's hair and Forrest knew who it was; simultaneously, he remembered what he must do this afternoon. That night Chauncey Rikker's name was to come up before the membership committee on which his father sat, and before going home, Forrest was going to pass the clubhouse and leave a certain black slip in a little box. He had carefully considered all that; he loved the city where his people had lived honorable lives for five generations. His grandfather had been a founder of this club in the 90's when it went in for sailboat racing instead of golf, and when it took a fast horse three hours to trot out here from town. He agreed with his father that certain people were without the pale. Tightening his face, he drove his ball two hundred yards down the fairway, where it curved gently into the rough.

The eighteenth and tenth holes were parallel and faced in opposite directions. Between tees they were separated by a belt of trees forty feet wide. Though Forrest did not know it, Miss Rikker's hostess, Helen Hannan, had dubbed into this same obscurity, and as he went in search of his ball he heard female voices twenty feet away.

"You'll be a member after tonight," he heard Helen Hannan say, "and then you can get some real competition from Stella Horrick."

"Maybe I won't be a member," said a quick, clear voice. "Then you'll have to come and play with me on the public links."

"Alida, don't be absurd."

"Why? I played on the public links in Buffalo all last spring. For the moment there wasn't anywhere else. It's like playing on some courses in Scotland."

"But I'd feel so silly. . . . Oh, gosh, let's let the ball go."

"There's nobody behind us. As to feeling silly—if I cared about public opinion any more, I'd spend my time in my bedroom." She laughed scornfully. "A tabloid published a picture of me going to see father in prison. And I've seen people change their tables away from us on steamers, and once I was cut by all the American girls in a French school. . . . Here's your ball."

"Thanks. . . . Oh, Alida, it seems terrible."

"All the terrible part is over. I just said that so you wouldn't be too sorry for us if people didn't want us in this club. I wouldn't care; I've got a life of my own and my own standard of what trouble is. It wouldn't touch me at all."

They passed out of the clearing and their voices disappeared into the open sky on the other side. Forrest abandoned the search for his lost ball and walked toward the caddie house.

"What a hell of a note," he thought. "To take it out on a girl that had nothing to do with it"—which was what he was doing this minute as he went up toward the club. "No," he said to himself abruptly, "I can't do it. Whatever her father may have done, she happens to be a lady. Father can do what he feels he has to do, but I'm out."

After lunch the next day, his father said rather diffidently: "I see you didn't do anything about the Rikkers and the Kennemore Club."

"No."

"It's just as well," said his father. "As a matter of fact, they got by. The club has got rather mixed anyhow in the last five years—a good many queer people in it. And, after all, in a club you don't have to know anybody you don't want to. The other people on the committee felt the same way."

"I see," said Forrest dryly. "Then you didn't argue against the Rikkers?"

"Well, no. The thing is I do a lot of business with Walter Hannan, and it happened yesterday I was obliged to ask him rather a difficult favor."

"So you traded with him." To both father and son, the word "traded" sounded like traitor.

"Not exactly. The matter wasn't mentioned."

"I understand," Forrest said. But he did not understand, and some old childhood faith in his father died at that moment.

II

To snub anyone effectively one must have him within range. The admission of Chauncey Rikker to the Kennemore Club and, later, to the Downtown Club was followed by angry talk and threats of resignation that simulated the sound of conflict, but there was no indication of a will underneath. On the other hand, unpleasantness in crowds is easy, and Chauncey Rikker was a facile object for personal dislike; moreover, a recurrent echo of the bucket-shop scandal sounded from New York, and the matter was reviewed in the local newspapers, in case anyone had missed it. Only the liberal Hannan family stood by the Rikkers, and their attitude aroused considerable resentment, and their attempt to launch them with a series of small parties proved a failure. Had the Rikkers attempted to "bring Alida out," it would have been for the inspection of a motley crowd indeed, but they didn't.

When, occasionally during the summer, Forrest encountered Alida Rikker, they crossed eyes in the curious way of children who don't know each other. For a while he was haunted by her curly yellow head, by the golden-brown defiance of her eyes; then he became interested in another girl. He wasn't in love with Jane Drake, though he thought he might marry her. She was "the girl across the street"; he knew her qualities, good and bad, so that they didn't matter. She had an essential reality underneath, like a relative. It would please their families. Once, after several highballs and some casual necking, he almost answered seriously when she provoked him with "But you don't really care about me"; but he sat tight and next morning was relieved that he had. Perhaps in the dull days after Christmas——Meanwhile, at the Christmas dances among the Christmas girls he might find the ecstasy and misery, the infatuation that he wanted. By autumn he felt that his predestined girl was already packing her trunk in some Eastern or Southern city.

It was in his more restless mood that one November Sunday he went to a small tea. Even as he spoke to his hostess he felt Alida Rikker across the firelit room; her glowing beauty and her unexplored novelty pressed up against him, and there was a relief in being presented to her at last. He bowed and passed on, but there had been some sort of communication. Her look said that she knew the stand that his family had taken, that she didn't mind, and was even sorry to see him in such a silly position, for she knew that he admired her. His look said: "Naturally, I'm sensitive to your beauty, but you see how it is; we've had to draw the line at the fact that your father is a dirty dog, and I can't withdraw from my present position."

Suddenly in a silence, she was talking, and his ears swayed away from his own conversation.

". . . Helen had this odd pain for over a year and, of course, they suspected cancer. She went to have an X ray; she undressed behind a screen, and the doctor looked at her through the machine, and then he said, 'But I told you to take off all your clothes,' and Helen said, 'I have.' The doctor looked again, and said, 'Listen, my dear, I brought you into the world, so there's no use being modest with me. Take off everything.' So Helen said, 'I've got every stitch off; I swear.' But the doctor said, 'You have not. The X ray shows me a safety pin in your brassiere.' Well, they finally found out that she'd been suspected of swallowing a safety pin when she was two years old."

The story, floating in her clear, crisp voice upon the intimate air, disarmed Forrest. It had nothing to do with what had taken place in Washington or New York ten years before. Suddenly he wanted to go and sit near her, because she was the tongue of flame that made the firelight vivid. Leaving, he walked for an hour through feathery snow, wondering again why he couldn't know her, why it was his business to represent a standard.

"Well, maybe I'll have a lot of fun some day doing what I ought to do," he thought ironically—"when I'm fifty."

The first Christmas dance was the charity ball at the armory. It was a large, public affair; the rich sat in boxes. Everyone came who felt he belonged, and many out of curiosity, so the atmosphere was tense with a strange haughtiness and aloofness.

The Rikkers had a box. Forrest, coming in with Jane Drake, glanced at the man of evil reputation and at the beaten woman frozen with jewels who sat beside him. They were the city's villains, gaped at by the people of reserved and timid lives. Oblivious of the staring eyes, Alida and Helen Hannan held court for several young men from out of town. Without question, Alida was incomparably the most beautiful girl in the room.

Several people told Forrest the news—the Rikkers were giving a big dance after New Year's. There were written invitations, but these were being supplemented by oral ones. Rumor had it that one had merely to be presented to any Rikker in order to be bidden to the dance.

As Forrest passed through the hall, two friends stopped him and with a certain hilarity introduced him to a youth of seventeen, Mr. Teddy Rikker.

"We're giving a dance," said the young man immediately. "January third. Be very happy if you could come."

Forrest was afraid he had an engagement.

"Well, come if you change your mind."

"Horrible kid, but shrewd," said one of his friends later. "We were feeding him people, and when we brought up a couple of saps, he looked at them and didn't say a word. Some refuse and a few accept and most of them stall, but he goes right on; he's got his father's crust."

Into the highways and byways. Why didn't the girl stop it? He was sorry for her when he found Jane in a group of young women reveling in the story.

"I hear they asked Bodman, the undertaker, by mistake, and then took it back."

"Mrs. Carleton pretended she was deaf."

"There's going to be a carload of champagne from Canada."

"Of course, I won't go, but I'd love to, just to see what happens. There'll be a hundred men to every girl—and that'll be meat for her."

The accumulated malice repelled him, and he was angry at Jane for being part of it. Turning away, his eyes fell on Alida's proud form swaying along a wall, watched the devotion of her partners with an unpleasant resentment. He did not know that he had been a little in love with her for many months. Just as two children can fall in love during a physical struggle over a ball, so their awareness of each other had grown to surprising proportions.

"She's pretty," said Jane. "She's not exactly overdressed, but considering everything, she dresses too elaborately."

"I suppose she ought to wear sackcloth and ashes or half mourning."

"I was honored with a written invitation, but, of course, I'm not going."

"Why not?"

Jane looked at him in surprise. "You're not going."

"That's different. I would if I were you. You see, you don't care what her father did."

"Of course, I care."

"No, you don't. And all this small meanness just debases the whole thing. Why don't they let her alone? She's young and pretty and she's done nothing wrong."

Later in the week he saw Alida at the Hannans' dance and noticed that many men danced with her. He saw her lips moving, heard her laughter, caught a word or so of what she said; irresistibly he found himself guiding partners around in her wake. He envied visitors to the city who didn't know who she was.

The night of the Rikkers' dance he went to a small dinner; before they sat down at table he realized that the others were all going on to the Rikkers'. They talked of it as a sort of comic adventure; insisted that he come too.

"Even if you weren't invited, it's all right," they assured him. "We were told we could bring anyone. It's just a free-for-all; it doesn't put you under any obligations. Norma Nash is going and she didn't invite Alida Rikker to her party. Besides, she's really very nice. My brother's quite crazy about her. Mother is worried sick, because he says he wants to marry her."

Clasping his hand about a new highball, Forrest knew that if he drank it he would probably go. All his reasons for not going seemed old and tired, and, fatally, he had begun to seem absurd to himself. In vain he tried to remember the purpose he was serving, and found none. His father had weakened on the matter of the Kennemore Club. And now suddenly he found reasons for going—men could go where their women could not.

"All right," he said.

The Rikkers' dance was in the ballroom of the Minnekada Hotel. The Rikkers' gold, ill-gotten, tainted, had taken the form of a forest of palms, vines and flowers. The two orchestras moaned in pergolas lit with fireflies, and many-colored spotlights swept the floor, touching a buffet where dark bottles gleamed. The receiving line was still in action when Forrest's party came in, and Forrest grinned ironically at the prospect of taking Chauncey Rikker by the hand. But at the sight of Alida, her look that at last fell frankly on him, he forgot everything else.

"Your brother was kind enough to invite me," he said.

"Oh, yes," she was polite, but vague; not at all overwhelmed by his presence. As he waited to speak to her parents, he started, seeing his sister in a group of dancers. Then, one after another, he identified people he knew: it might have been any one of the Christmas dances; all the younger crowd were there. He discovered abruptly that he and Alida were alone; the receiving line had broken up. Alida glanced at him questioningly and with a certain amusement.

So he danced out on the floor with her, his head high, but slightly spinning. Of all things in the world, he had least expected to lead off the Chauncey Rikkers' ball.

III

Next morning his first realization was that he had kissed her; his second was a feeling of profound shame for his conduct of the evening. Lord help him, he had been the life of the party; he had helped to run the cotillion. From the moment when he danced out on the floor, coolly meeting the surprised and interested glances of his friends, a mood of desperation had come over him. He rushed Alida Rikker, until a friend asked him what Jane was going to say. "What business is it of Jane's?" he demanded impatiently. "We're not engaged." But he was impelled to approach his sister and ask her if he looked all right.

"Apparently," Eleanor answered, "but when in doubt, don't take any more."

So he hadn't. Exteriorly he remained correct, but his libido was in a state of wild extraversion. He sat with Alida Rikker and told her he had loved her for months.

"Every night I thought of you just before you went to sleep," his voice trembled with insincerity, "I was afraid to meet you or speak to you. Sometimes I'd see you in the distance moving along like a golden chariot, and the world would be good to live in."

After twenty minutes of this eloquence, Alida began to feel exceedingly attractive. She was tired and rather happy, and eventually she said:

"All right, you can kiss me if you want to, but it won't mean anything. I'm just not in that mood."

But Forrest had moods enough for both; he kissed her as if they stood together at the altar. A little later he had thanked Mrs. Rikker with deep emotion for the best time he had ever had in his life.

It was noon, and as he groped his way upright in bed, Eleanor came in in her dressing gown.

"How are you?" she asked.

"Awful."

"How about what you told me coming back in the car? Do you actually want to marry Alida Rikker?"

"Not this morning."

"That's all right then. Now, look: the family are furious."

"Why?" he asked with some redundancy.

"Both you and I being there. Father heard that you led the cotillion. My explanation was that my dinner party went, and so I had to go; but then you went too!"

Forrest dressed and went down to Sunday dinner. Over the table hovered an atmosphere of patient, puzzled, unworldly disappointment. Finally Forrest launched into it:

"Well, we went to Al Capone's party and had a fine time."

"So I've heard," said Pierce Winslow dryly. Mrs. Winslow said nothing.

"Everybody was there—the Kayes, the Schwanes, the Martins and the Blacks. From now on, the Rikkers are pillars of society. Every house is open to them."

"Not this house," said his mother. "They won't come into this house." And after a moment: "Aren't you going to eat anything, Forrest?"

"No, thanks. I mean, yes, I am eating." He looked cautiously at his plate. "The girl is very nice. There isn't a girl in town with better manners or more stuff. If things were like they were before the war, I'd say——"

He couldn't think exactly what it was he would have said; all he knew was that he was now on an entirely different road from his parents'.

"This city was scarcely more than a village before the war," said old Mrs. Forrest.

"Forrest means the World War, granny," said Eleanor.

"Some things don't change," said Pierce Winslow. Both he and Forrest thought of the Kennemore Club matter and, feeling guilty, the older man lost his temper:

"When people start going to parties given by a convicted criminal, there's something serious the matter with them."

"We won't discuss it any more at table," said Mrs. Winslow hastily.

About four, Forrest called a number on the telephone in his room. He had known for some time that he was going to call a number.

"Is Miss Rikker at home? . . . Oh, hello. This is Forrest Winslow."

"How are you?"

"Terrible. It was a good party."

"Wasn't it?"

"Too good. What are you doing?"

"Entertaining two awful hangovers."

"Will you entertain me too?"

"I certainly will. Come on over."

The two young men could only groan and play sentimental music on the phonograph, but presently they departed; the fire leaped up, day went out behind the windows, and Forrest had rum in his tea.

"So we met at last," he said.

"The delay was all yours."

"Damn prejudice," he said. "This is a conservative city, and your father being in this trouble——"

"I can't discuss my father with you."

"Excuse me. I only wanted to say that I've felt like a fool lately for not knowing you. For cheating myself out of the pleasure of knowing you for a silly prejudice," he blundered on. "So I decided to follow my own instincts."

She stood up suddenly. "Good-by, Mr. Winslow."

"What? Why?"

"Because it's absurd for you to come here as if you were doing me a favor. And after accepting our hospitality, to remind me of my father's troubles is simply bad manners."

He was on his feet, terribly upset. "That isn't what I meant. I said I had felt that way, and I despised myself for it. Please don't be sore."

"Then don't be condescending." She sat back in her chair. Her mother came in, stayed only a moment, and threw Forrest a glance of resentment and suspicion as she left. But her passage through had brought them together, and they talked frankly for a long time.

"I ought to be upstairs dressing."

"I ought to have gone an hour ago, and I can't."

"Neither can I."

With the admission they had traveled far. At the door he kissed her unreluctant lips and walked home, throwing futile buckets of reason on the wild fire.

Less than two weeks later it happened. In a car parked in a blizzard he poured out his worship, and she lay on his chest, sighing, "Oh, me too—me too."

Already Forrest's family knew where he went in the evenings; there was a frightened coolness, and one morning his mother said:

"Son, you don't want to throw yourself away on some girl that isn't up to you. I thought you were interested in Jane Drake."

"Don't bring that up. I'm not going to talk about it."

But it was only a postponement. Meanwhile the days of this February were white and magical, the nights were starry and crystalline. The town lay under a cold glory; the smell of her furs was incense, her bright cheeks were flames upon a northern altar. An ecstatic pantheism for his land and its weather welled up in him. She had brought him finally back to it; he would live here always.

"I want you so much that nothing can stand in the way of that," he said to Alida. "But I owe my parents a debt that I can't explain to you. They did more than spend money on me; they tried to give me something more intangible—something that their parents had given them and that they thought was worth handing on. Evidently it didn't take with me, but I've got to make this as easy as possible for them." He saw by her face that he had hurt her. "Darling——"

"Oh, it frightens me when you talk like that," she said. "Are you going to reproach me later? It would be awful. You'll have to get it out of your head that you're doing anything wrong. My standards are as high as yours, and I can't start out with my father's sins on my shoulders." She thought for a moment. "You'll never be able to reconcile it all like a children's story. You've got to choose. Probably you'll have to hurt either your family or hurt me."

A fortnight later the storm broke at the Winslow house. Pierce Winslow came home in a quiet rage and had a session behind closed doors with his wife. Afterward she knocked at Forrest's door.

"Your father had a very embarrassing experience today. Chauncey Rikker came up to him in the Downtown Club and began talking about you as if you were on terms of some understanding with his daughter. Your father walked away, but we've got to know. Are you serious about Miss Rikker?"

"I want to marry her," he said.

"Oh, Forrest!"

She talked for a long time, recapitulating, as if it were a matter of centuries, the eighty years that his family had been identified with the city; when she passed from this to the story of his father's health, Forrest interrupted:

"That's all so irrelevant, mother. If there was anything against Alida personally, what you say would have some weight, but there isn't."

"She's overdressed; she runs around with everybody——"

"She isn't a bit different from Eleanor. She's absolutely a lady in every sense. I feel like a fool even discussing her like this. You're just afraid it'll connect you in some way with the Rikkers."

"I'm not afraid of that," said his mother, annoyed. "Nothing would ever do that. But I'm afraid that it'll separate you from everything worth while, everybody that loves you. It isn't fair for you to upset our lives, let us in for disgraceful gossip——"

"I'm to give up the girl I love because you're afraid of a little gossip."

The controversy was resumed next day, with Pierce Winslow debating. His argument was that he was born in old Kentucky, that he had always felt uneasy at having begotten a son upon a pioneer Minnesota family, and that this was what he might have expected. Forrest felt that his parents' attitude was trivial and disingenuous. Only when he was out of the house, acting against their wishes, did he feel any compunction. But always he felt that something precious was being frayed away—his youthful companionship with his father and his love and trust for his mother. Hour by hour he saw the past being irreparably spoiled, and save when he was with Alida, he was deeply unhappy.

One spring day when the situation had become unendurable, with half the family meals taken in silence, Forrest's great-grandmother stopped him on the stair landing and put her hand on his arm.

"Has this girl really a good character?" she asked, her fine, clear, old eyes resting on his.

"Of course she has, gramma."

"Then marry her."

"Why do you say that?" Forrest asked curiously.

"It would stop all this nonsense and we could have some peace. And I've been thinking I'd like to be a great-great-grandmother before I die."

Her frank selfishness appealed to him more than the righteousness of the others. That night he and Alida decided to be married the first of June, and telephoned the announcement to the papers.

Now the storm broke in earnest. Crest Avenue rang with gossip— how Mrs. Rikker had called on Mrs. Winslow, who was not at home. How Forrest had gone to live in the University Club. How Chauncey Rikker and Pierce Winslow had had words in the Downtown Club.

It was true that Forrest had gone to the University Club. On a May night, with summer sounds already gathered on the window screens, he packed his trunk and his suitcases in the room where he had lived as a boy. His throat contracted and he smeared his face with his dusty hand as he took a row of golf cups off the mantelpiece, and he choked to himself: "If they won't take Alida, then they're not my family any more."

As he finished packing, his mother came in.

"You're not really leaving." Her voice was stricken.

"I'm moving to the University Club."

"That's so unnecessary. No one bothers you here. You do what you want."

"I can't bring Alida here."

"Father——"

"Hell with father!" he said wildly.

She sat down on the bed beside him. "Stay here, Forrest. I promise not to argue with you any more. But stay here."

"I can't."

"I can't have you go!" she wailed. "It seems as if we're driving you out, and we're not!"

"You mean it looks as though you were driving me out."

"I don't mean that."

"Yes, you do. And I want to say that I don't think you and father really care a hang about Chauncey Rikker's moral character."

"That's not true, Forrest. I hate people that behave badly and break the laws. My own father would never have let Chauncey Rikker——"

"I'm not talking about your father. But neither you nor my father care a bit what Chauncey Rikker did. I bet you don't even know what it was."

"Of course I know. He stole some money and went abroad, and when he came back they put him in prison."

"They put him in prison for contempt of court."

"Now you're defending him, Forrest."

"I'm not! I hate his guts; undoubtedly he's a crook. But I tell you it was a shock to me to find that father didn't have any principles. He and his friends sit around the Downtown Club and pan Chauncey Rikker, but when it comes to keeping him out of a club, they develop weak spines."

"That was a small thing."

"No, it wasn't. None of the men of father's age have any principles. I don't know why. I'm willing to make an allowance for an honest conviction, but I'm not going to be booed by somebody that hasn't got any principles and simply pretends to have."

His mother sat helplessly, knowing that what he said was true. She and her husband and all their friends had no principles. They were good or bad according to their natures; often they struck attitudes remembered from the past, but they were never sure as her father or her grandfather had been sure. Confusedly she supposed it was something about religion. But how could you get principles just by wishing for them?

The maid announced the arrival of a taxi.

"Send up Olsen for my baggage," said Forrest; then to his mother, "I'm not taking the coupe; I left the keys. I'm just taking my clothes. I suppose father will let me keep my job down town."

"Forrest, don't talk that way. Do you think your father would take your living away from you, no matter what you did?"

"Such things have happened."

"You're hard and difficult," she wept. "Please stay here a little longer, and perhaps things will be better and father will get a little more reconciled. Oh, stay, stay! I'll talk to father again. I'll do my best to fix things."

"Will you let me bring Alida here?"

"Not now. Don't ask me that. I couldn't bear——"

"All right," he said grimly.

Olsen came in for the bags. Crying and holding on to his coat sleeve, his mother went with him to the front door.

"Won't you say good-by to father?"

"Why? I'll see him tomorrow in the office."

"Forrest, I was thinking, why don't you go to a hotel instead of the University Club?"

"Why, I thought I'd be more comfortable——" Suddenly he realized that his presence would be less conspicuous at a hotel. Shutting up his bitterness inside him, he kissed his mother roughly and went to the cab.

Unexpectedly, it stopped by the corner lamp-post at a hail from the sidewalk, and the May twilight yielded up Alida, miserable and pale.

"What is it?" he demanded.

"I had to come," she said. "Stop the car. I've been thinking of you leaving your house on account of me, and how you loved your family—the way I'd like to love mine—and I thought how terrible it was to spoil all that. Listen, Forrest! Wait! I want you to go back. Yes, I do. We can wait. We haven't any right to cause all this pain. We're young. I'll go away for a while, and then we'll see."

He pulled her toward him by her shoulders.

"You've got more principles than the whole bunch of them," he said. "Oh, my girl, you love me and, gosh, it's good that you do!"

IV

It was to be a house wedding, Forrest and Alida having vetoed the Rikkers' idea that it was to be a sort of public revenge. Only a few intimate friends were invited.

During the week before the wedding, Forrest deduced from a series of irresolute and ambiguous telephone calls that his mother wanted to attend the ceremony, if possible. Sometimes he hoped passionately she would; at others it seemed unimportant.

The wedding was to be at seven. At five o'clock Pierce Winslow was walking up and down the two interconnecting sitting rooms of his house.

"This evening," he murmured, "my only son is being married to the daughter of a swindler."

He spoke aloud so that he could listen to the words, but they had been evoked so often in the past few months that their strength was gone and they died thinly upon the air.

He went to the foot of the stairs and called: "Charlotte!" No answer. He called again, and then went into the dining room, where the maid was setting the table.

"Is Mrs. Winslow out?"

"I haven't seen her come in, Mr. Winslow."

Back in the sitting room he resumed his walking; unconsciously he was walking like his father, the judge, dead thirty years ago; he was parading his dead father up and down the room.

"You can't bring that woman into this house to meet your mother. Bad blood is bad blood."

The house seemed unusually quiet. He went upstairs and looked into his wife's room, but she was not there; old Mrs. Forrest was slightly indisposed; Eleanor, he knew, was at the wedding.

He felt genuinely sorry for himself as he went downstairs again. He knew his role—the usual evening routine carried out in complete obliviousness of the wedding—but he needed support, people begging him to relent, or else deferring to his wounded sensibilities. This isolation was different; it was almost the first isolation he had ever felt, and like all men who are fundamentally of the group, of the herd, he was incapable of taking a strong stand with the inevitable loneliness that it implied. He could only gravitate toward those who did.

"What have I done to deserve this?" he demanded of the standing ash tray. "What have I failed to do for my son that lay within my power?"

The maid came in. "Mrs. Winslow told Hilda she wouldn't be here for dinner, and Hilda didn't tell me."

The shameful business was complete. His wife had weakened, leaving him absolutely alone. For a moment he expected to be furiously angry with her, but he wasn't; he had used up his anger exhibiting it to others. Nor did it make him feel more obstinate, more determined; it merely made him feel silly.

"That's it. I'll be the goat. Forrest will always hold it against me, and Chauncey Rikker will be laughing up his sleeve."

He walked up and down furiously.

"So I'm left holding the bag. They'll say I'm an old grouch and drop me out of the picture entirely. They've licked me. I suppose I might as well be graceful about it." He looked down in horror at the hat he held in his hand. "I can't—I can't bring myself to do it, but I must. After all, he's my only son. I couldn't bear that he should hate me. He's determined to marry her, so I might as well put a good face on the matter."

In sudden alarm he looked at his watch, but there was still time. After all, it was a large gesture he was making, sacrificing his principles in this manner. People would never know what it cost him.

An hour later, old Mrs. Forrest woke up from her doze and rang for her maid.

"Where's Mrs. Winslow?"

"She's not in for dinner. Everybody's out."

The old lady remembered.

"Oh, yes, they've gone over to get married. Give me my glasses and the telephone book. . . . Now, I wonder how you spell Capone."

"Rikker, Mrs. Forrest."

In a few minutes she had the number. "This is Mrs. Hugh Forrest," she said firmly. "I want to speak to young Mrs. Forrest Winslow. . . . No, not to Miss Rikker; to Mrs. Forrest Winslow." As there was as yet no such person, this was impossible. "Then I will call after the ceremony," said the old lady.

When she called again, in an hour, the bride came to the phone.

"This is Forrest's great-grandmother. I called up to wish you every happiness and to ask you to come and see me when you get back from your trip if I'm still alive."

"You're very sweet to call, Mrs. Forrest."

"Take good care of Forrest, and don't let him get to be a ninny like his father and mother. God bless you."

"Thank you."

"All right. Good-by, Miss Capo——Good-by, my dear."

Having done her whole duty, Mrs. Forrest hung up the receiver.

Diagnosis

(*The Saturday Evening Post*, 20 February 1932)

"Diagnosis" was probably the first story written after the Fitzgeralds'
return to America in September 1931 following Zelda Fitzgerald's discharge
from Prangins. The *Post* paid $4000. It was written in Montgomery,
Alabama, where they considered settling—a plan that was altered by Zelda's
relapse in 1932. The Fitzgeralds did a good deal of driving around Alabama at
this time, which provided the setting of this story.

"Diagnosis" combines the hopeful Depression subject with the
pilgrimage motif. When Fitzgerald found that the material for a story was
thin—or that he was not emotionally committed to it—he padded the story
with plot complications. In the case of "Diagnosis" what might have been a
serious story is marred by the business of the suppressed will and the hidden
money.

The *Post*'s positioning of "Diagnosis" was a signal that the magazine
was unhappy with Fitzgerald's recent submissions. It was the fourth story in
the issue—the first time he had appeared that far back since 1920.

For a while the big liner, so sure and proud in the open sea, was
shoved ignominiously around by the tugs like a helpless old woman:
her funnels gave a snort of relief as she slid into her pier at last. From
the deck Sara Etherington saw Charlie standing waiting for her in
New York, and something happened to her. The New York that she
had watched with ever new pride and wonder shrank into him; he
summed up its flashing, dynamic good looks, its tall man's quick-
step, and all was as familiar as it had been four months before. Then,
as she caught his attention, she saw that something was different and
strange about him: but as she bounced into his arms at the foot of the
gangplank she forgot it in the thrilling staccato joy of the meeting.

"Darling, darling——"

"Let me look——"

They stood under "E" for the customs inspection, and Sara
noticed a funny new line between his fine eyes, and that, instead of
handling things casually, he fussed and fretted with the customs
agent as if it were a hopelessly tangled matter. "I'll have to hurry back
to the office," he said several times.

The people from the boat, passing, darted a last glance at her,
because she had been the prettiest girl on the passenger list. She was

tall, with fresh, starry eyes that did whatever her mouth did—that really were amused or anxious or sad when her mouth was. Through the summer men had told her about it in Europe, but there was Charlie, Charlie ringing in her mind, and many times in those months she had dreams that he snatched her up on his charger and raced her away. He was one of those men who had a charger; she always knew it was tethered outside, chafing at its bit. But now, for once, she didn't hear it, though she listened for the distant snort and fidgeting of hoofs.

Later they were alone together, and with his arms around her, she demanded:

"Why are you so pale? Is my boy working too hard? Isn't everything all right, now I'm home? We'll have each other permanently so soon."

He jerked his head backward in an uncharacteristic, challenging gesture, as if to say: "All right, since you brought it up!" and remarked: "Do you read the papers? Do you realize how things are here?"

"You're not in trouble, are you?"

"Not yet; at least not immediately."

"Well, let's be glad of that. Just for now let's not——"

He shook his head, looking out somewhere she couldn't follow.

"You don't understand," he shot forth. "You've only just arrived; wait a few days. Everything's collapsed and nobody knows what to do about it." With a sudden effort he got himself under control: "I know this isn't the way to meet you, Sara. I'm sorry. Maybe I exaggerate, though I don't see how; but——" Again his eyes were fixed on some dark point ahead of him, and hastily Sara changed the subject:

"Did Ben make the Triangle or whatever it was at Princeton? Oh, listen—I've got the most gorgeous Greek and Roman soldiers for Dicky—and Egyptians. I want to keep them myself. And a dressing gown from Tripler for Ben, and a secret for you."

This reminded him of something: "Those people on the pier seemed to have plenty of luxuries in their trunks. I was rather astonished."

"But aren't we supposed to buy things? Isn't that the trouble?"

"The trouble is——" he said, and again stopped himself.

He was so handsome and his face was so kind, and his voice, with Southern gentlenesses still lingering in it! Never, in the year of their engagement, had Sara seen him show a worry or care. Four months ago she had left a successful young Wall Street man, self-made, sturdy and cynical, who had happened through the first market collapses with no enormous losses and with his confidence unimpaired. Tomorrow she must find out exactly what had made the difference.

Tomorrow was Sunday, and Charlie called for her and took her to his apartment, where he was father and mother to his two younger brothers. Ben was at college; Dicky, who was eleven, spread out the soldiers with the sober eyes and eager fingers of delight.

They were Roman legionaries with short, bright swords and helmets and shields shining with gilt, a conqueror in his chariot with six horses, and an entourage of sparkling, plumed Roman knights, captured Gauls in chains, Greeks in buskins and tunics of Ionian blue, black Egyptians in flashing desert reds with images of Isis and Osiris, a catapult and, in person, Hannibal, Caesar, Rameses and Alexander.

Charlie stared at the splendid panoply.

"Things like that," he said absently—"I wonder if they'll make them much longer."

Setting up the soldiers, Sara didn't answer.

"It seems almost blasphemous," Charlie continued; and then to Dicky: "You'd better eat, drink and be merry. This is quite possibly the last nice present you'll ever have. You may be glad of an old bat and ball up some smashed alley."

With the look of alarm that sprang into Dicky's eyes, Sara realized that such remarks had been made to him before.

"That's preposterous," she said sharply. "I think it's awful to let children in on the depression. They can't do anything about it; they can only be afraid. They don't understand that grown people don't mean everything they say."

"But I do mean it. Let them know the truth. If we hadn't lived in a golden dream so long, maybe we could face things better."

That afternoon Sara tried again as they drove quietly through Central Park.

"Tell me calmly what's happened to you," she asked him. "You know I love you, and maybe I could help. I can see how all this gloomy time is on your nerves, but there's something else, and telling me about it will do you good."

Charlie tightened his arm around her. "You're a sweet, brave person," he said. "But, Sara, I'll swear to you there's nothing else. I had an insurance examination just last month and they told me I was in fine shape. I was glad, because I have a horror of falling sick just now. Financially, I've been lucky. And I love you more than anything in the world."

"Then we'll be married next month?"

He looked at her hesitantly. "If you think it's wise, just at this time."

She laughed, a little sadly. "Everybody can't stop being in love until business picks up."

"It seems sort of a big step right now."

"Are you throwing me over?"

"That's absurd. I only said——"

Her sigh interrupted him. "Charlie, what is it? Last winter you helped run a bread line, but you got it out of your head when you came away from it. When did this constant worry begin?"

"About the time you left. A friend of mine shot himself, and then a brokerage house here in New York crashed, and then all those banks out in Ohio. Everybody talked of nothing else. You'd go to a party, and as some woman was handing you a cocktail, she'd say, 'Do you know such and such a stock is off four points?' I began to realize that every specialty of ours is beginning to be made in some part of the world cheaper than we can make it in America. Do you know that the Five Year Plan——"

"Shut up, Charlie! I won't listen! Heavens, suppose it's true! You and I are young. We needn't be afraid to start over. I can't stand you going to pieces like this"—she looked at him mercilessly—"lying on your back and kicking."

"I'm thinking about you, and about Dicky. I'm getting a job for Ben this June. If he waits another year to graduate, there may be no more jobs left."

Then Sara realized she was talking to a sick man and that for the moment there was nothing more to say. She tried to gain his confidence by listening without argument. She suggested that he go away for a while, but he laughed at the suggestion.

"Why, Eddie Brune went away for three days, leaving word he wasn't to be disturbed. When he got back he found——"

Sara was sick at heart. For almost the first time in her life she didn't know what to do. She knew enough about modern psychology to guess that Charlie's mood might be an externalizing of some private trouble, but she knew also that Charlie thought that psychoanalysis was a refuge for the weak and the unstable.

As the days passed she found that her tenderness could no longer reach him. She was frightened.

Then, at the week's end, he came to see her with sleepless and despairing eyes.

"You think I'm crazy," he broke out. "You may be right. Quite possibly. There are some times—especially in the morning when I've had a good sleep, or after a cocktail or two—when the troubles of the world seem to clear away and I feel like I used to about things. But those moments are getting rarer. One thing I know—Henry Cortelyou thinks I'm not so hot anymore. He looks at me in a curious

way and several times he's spoken shortly down at the office. I doubt if
I'll be there much longer."

He talked coolly and logically. He wanted to release her from her
promise to marry him. He had thought her return might help, but it
hadn't. When he left the house their engagement was over, but her
love for him was not over and her hope was not gone, and her actions
had only begun.

II

The next morning she made an appointment to see Henry
Cortelyou, the senior partner of the firm. Through him they had first
met.

"Have you noticed anything strange about Charlie?" she asked.

"Yes. He's acting as if he's planning a nervous breakdown.
People take things hard these days."

"I don't think it's that," Sara said slowly. She told about Dicky's
soldiers, about Ben's leaving college, and about the broken
engagement. "People in actual want may be melancholy and suicidal
just on account of the depression, but that isn't Charlie's case. Just
suppose a man had some secret trouble, some maladjustment with his
surroundings. And then success picked him up and whirled him
along for a couple of years so fast that he hadn't any time for normal
anxieties. And then suddenly he was set down and told to walk—no
more joy riding. Well, he'd find himself in a great silence and his
private trouble would creep back, and perhaps he'd have forgotten
how to deal with it. Naturally, he'd confuse it with the rough road he
was traveling and blame every stone in the road rather than look at the
truth. All this whining in limousines. Anyhow, I can't believe that
Charlie is this way without a reason."

"And what's the reason?"

"He'll have to find out himself," said Sara. "But I think the first
thing you ought to do is to ask him to resign from the firm."

"That might be the last straw," objected Cortelyou. "As a matter
of fact, his work goes well enough. Only he's rather depressing
around the office lately, and we don't like the way he talks outside. It
might make people think there was something the matter here."

"Then make him take a year's vacation without pay," said Sara.
"He has plenty of money. He won't be surprised. And I think he needs
to have all the things happen to him that he's afraid of and find out
that they're not what's really the matter. I love him, Uncle Henry. I
haven't given up at all."

"I'll take till tomorrow to think it over."

The following afternoon, when Charlie returned to his apartment, he found a letter from Sara. He was still so absorbed by his talk with Henry Cortelyou that he sat for a long time without opening it. The blow of his dismissal should have numbed him; actually he felt a certain relief. Now he would look for work and find out the worst; he would be part of that great army driven by the dark storm. As he mingled with it already in his mind, sharing its scant bread, he felt a satisfaction in the promise of submerging himself in it. Everything was gone—security, hope and love. He opened Sara's letter:

> For the sake of the past, please do one last thing for me. Darling, I beg you to do this; I'm on my knees to you, trying to put into this letter the force with which I want you to do it. Do it blindly, unwillingly, because you loved me and for a little while we were happy together. I want you to see a man named Marston Raines, whose address I inclose. He is the wisest man I know, and *not* a psychoanalyst; his chief interest in life is old church music and he doesn't even like to use his gift for people. But to a whole lot of his friends he's been a sort of quiet god for years. I've told him about you and he said that maybe if you liked him he could help you. Darling, please.

Charlie dropped the letter.

"Quackery," he thought. "Sweeten the bitter pill by giving it a Greek name. Introvert, Extravert and Company. Good Lord, I'd rather be an ancient Israelite and think that a plague was the punishment of God than learn a lot of nice soft new lies to tell to myself."

But when, at luncheon, he lost control and told little Dicky he had no job, and when, afterward, he found Dicky crying in his room and talking of selling his soldiers to keep from going to the poorhouse—then he saw himself momentarily from outside. He knew he couldn't go on like this, and he went back to Sara's letter.

It was late afternoon when he went to see Marston Raines. Raines lived in a high apartment on Madison Avenue, and as Charlie was admitted into a wide-vistaed room, the evening gem play of New York was already taking place outside the window. But as Charlie gazed at it, it seemed to him tawdry and theatrical, a great keeping up of appearances after the reality was gone. Each new tower was something erected in defiance of obvious and imminent disaster; each beam of light a final despairing attempt to pretend that all was well.

"But it's not all right!" he exclaimed as Raines came into the room. "It looks all right for just a minute; after that it's simply an insult to people who see things as they are."

"But then, so is the Taj Mahal," Raines said, "and Notre Dame de Paris and the Pantheon."

"But they had their time. For a while they represented a reality. These things are scarcely built; not a single generation saw them and passed away before we ceased to believe."

"In what?"

"In the future. In our destiny. In the idea, whatever it is."

"Have a cigarette. . . . You'll stay to dinner, naturally."

"Why? Can you help me? Can you build up something that's gone? Certain organs reproduce themselves, like the liver, but what's gone out of me will never come back."

He looked closely at Raines, a man with soft gray hair and the face of a fine old lady, dressed in a rumpled white-flannel suit. His eyes were direct, but they only looked at Charlie occasionally, as if, when they did, they saw so much that it amounted to an intrusion. The background of the apartment was composed of the musical instruments of many lands and centuries, masses of musical books and folios, and priceless old sheets and scores under glass. There was a bust of Mozart and one of Haydn.

"There's no use looking at things, because you don't like things," remarked Raines, in answer to his polite interest.

"No," said Charlie frankly, "I don't."

"You like only rhythms, with things marking the beats, and now your rhythm is broken."

"Everything's broken. The future's gone, love's gone, even the past seems a joke—it's gone too."

He was looking at the backgammon board spread before him.

"Do you mind playing one game with me? I always play at this hour," said Raines. "We'll be a long time here, so just let me keep my own direction, since you admit you haven't any. By the way, do you like me all right?"

"As well as I could like any stranger in my present condition."

"Good. . . . You have some brothers, Sara says?"

"Three half brothers."

"Really."

"My father had a son by his first marriage, I was his son by his second marriage, and there were two children by the third marriage—those are the two I'm bringing up."

"You're a Southerner?"

"I came here from a small town in Alabama about ten years ago. When I'd more or less established myself I sent for my younger brothers, who had been with an aunt."

"You've done well here, haven't you?"

"I thought so, up until now."

"Your hand shakes; you rattle the piece against the board."

"Perhaps I'd better not play," said Charlie rigidly.

"I'll get you a little drink.... You believe in something," he said, after a long time. "I don't know yet what it is. You're lucky to believe in something."

"I believe in nothing."

"Yes, you do. You believe in something that's crouching in this room very near you now—something that you tried to do without and couldn't do without. And now it's gradually taking form again and you're afraid."

Charlie sprang to his feet, his mouth quivering. "No!" he cried. "I'm—I'm——"

"Sit down," said Raines quietly. He looked at his watch. "We have all night; it's only eleven."

Charlie gave a quick glance around and sat down, covering his face for a minute with his hands.

III

Two days later Charlie Clayhorne got off the train at Montgomery, feeling strange as he felt himself enveloped by the familiar, unforgotten atmosphere of many Negroes and voices pleading-calm and girls painted bright as savages to stand out against the tropical summer. The streets were busier than he remembered in those days when he considered Montgomery a metropolis. He wondered how severely they felt the depression, and he was surprised when no beggars approached him in the street. Later, on the local train that bore him an hour farther south, he felt himself merging minute by minute with the hot countryside, the lush vegetation, the clay roads, the strange, sluggish, primeval rivers flowing softly under soft Indian names. Then Tuscarora; the broken-down station with the mules and horse rigs hitched in the yard. Nothing changed—the sign still hung crooked on the Yancy Hotel across the street.

Suddenly someone spoke to him, and then someone else—he had to struggle for their names. To his annoyance—for he wanted to be alone—they both followed him to the hotel and sat at his table while he had supper. He learned that Pete, his elder brother, had a farm near here and often came to town. He learned, too, that the Clayhorne place hadn't been rented for five years. Had he come to try to sell it? They had heard it was to be torn down, and at the news Charlie's heart gave a jump.

Mr. Chevril, the Confederate veteran who had lived at the hotel for fifty years, limped over to join them.

"How are things down here?" Charlie asked. "I mean the cotton situation?"

He waited for their faces to change, as they did in New York when one asked about a man's business, but here was not that sudden dispirited expression of the mouth and eyes.

"Are there many people out of work and hungry?"

"Not so many that I see," one answered. "I heard tell of cases down country, and a lot of the niggers had a hard time last winter."

"It's terrible in New York," Charlie said defiantly, as if they were holding out on him.

"You see, we never had much of a boom down here, though they did lay the foundations of a cotton factory over at King's Hill; so I guess we don't feel the depression so much. Never was much cash money in this town."

Old Mr. Chevril spat tobacco juice. "I don't think you fellas know what hard times are," he said. "When we got back here from Appomattox Court House in '65, I had a mule from the horse artillery, and Jim Mason had one plow that Stoneman hadn't smashed, and we had a crop planted before we dared think how we'd eat next winter. And we did a sight less hollerin' than you see in these Yankee newspapers."

"You don't understand," said Charlie angrily. "When you have primitive conditions hardship is just a matter of degree, but when the whole elaborate economic structure——"

He broke off as he saw that they were not following him. He felt that he must get away and be alone. Their faces seemed insensitive, uncomprehending, not to be communicated with. He made an excuse to go to his room.

It was still daylight, the red heat had gathered for one last assault upon the town; he wanted to wait until dark. He looked from the window at a proud, white-pillared Acropolis that a hundred years ago had been the center of a plantation and now housed a row of stores, at the old courthouse with its outside staircase, and at the brash new courthouse being built in its front yard, and then at the youths with sideburns lounging outside the drug store. The curious juxta-positions made him feel the profound waves of change that had already washed this country—the desperate war that had rendered the plantation house obsolete, the industrialization that had spoiled the easy-going life centering around the old courthouse. And then the years yielding up eventually in this backwater those curious young products who were neither peasants, nor bourgeois, nor scamps, but a little of all three, gathered there in front of the store. After the next wave of change, would there be pigeon cotes in Wall Street, and then what, and then what?

He pulled himself together sharply. It was growing darker. He waited until it was quite dark before he went out and sauntered by a circuitous route to the edge of town. Then he set off down a clay road, white-bright in the moonlight, toward the house where he had been born.

The road went through a tangled wood he knew well, and that had not changed, but the house, breaking out suddenly against the sky, startled him. It seemed smaller, but its silhouette was a face that he knew and that knew him. It was a white-columned manor house dating from the time when the Cherokee War had made living safe in these parts; a first attempt to bring ease and spaciousness to a land from which the frontier had only just been pushed away. Now it was an irreparable wreck, with rotting timbers exposed like bones. Feeling in his pocket for candles and matches, Charlie pushed open the drunken pretense of a door and went inside.

Through the must and dust he smelled a familiar odor, unidentifiable but nostalgic. There was some broken furniture about, split stuffing and rusty springs, stained mattresses and a one-wheeled baby carriage—things that no one would carry away.

Charlie set his candle down and listened to the silence. Then he went over to the mantelpiece; it had settled forward, away from the wall, leaving the crack where mantel and wall had touched. He tried gently, then more determinedly, to pull it farther out, but there was only a sound of plaster splitting; it yielded no more.

"That's all right," he breathed to himself. He took from his pocket a wire and straightened it, leaving a hook at the end; then poking it down through the crack at the extreme left, he fished. There was no bite. After a moment he put his eye sideways and flashed a pocket light inside the crack; it was empty.

Cold with fear, he sat down in a broken rocker. Almost immediately he got up and looked into the corresponding crack at the other end, and the blood rushed back into his hands and feet again. In a moment he had drawn out an envelope covered with dust and mold. He brushed off the square white envelope. He did not know what was inside it, and if he should destroy it no living person would ever know or even guess that it had existed. Moreover, he would not know himself and could believe what he liked.

But would that solve anything? The element of conscience was now so deeply tangled with the element of fear that there was no certainty of any relief in merely knowing that he would never be found out. If he opened it, though, there would presumably be further commitments, shameful and difficult; while if he destroyed it there would be something done and finished. He held the evidence in his hands as he had a certain afternoon ten years before.

He was twenty, then, and the head of the family. His older brother, Pete, was serving in prison upstate; his younger brothers were children; his father was senile, but only Charlie realized it; the old man was well preserved and still made a suave, masterly appearance on his daily trip to town.

Characteristically the father turned against Charlie. He informed him he was taking him out of his will and substituting the imprisoned Pete as arbiter of the younger children's destinies. And one day Charlie saw Julia and Sam, the servants, signing some document in his father's room.

One afternoon a few weeks later he went into his father's room and found the old man dead in his chair. Charlie was alone. He took the key from the dead man's neck and opened the strong box. There was the will he had made in his sane mind, and there beside it was a new envelope, marked "To be opened after my death." With the envelope under his coat Charlie went into the living room. Julia was in the hall and, calling her sharply, he pointed to his father's room. When she had gone in he slipped the letter into the crack of the mantelpiece and heard it fall lightly a foot below.

There was no complication; no one spoke of the envelope or of a later will. The fortune was less than had been expected—sixteen thousand dollars in money and property, to be divided among the three younger children. Charlie's share gave him his start in New York.

New York was very far away now, he thought; and he himself was far away from the conscientious boy who had worried about the letter for years. Rightly or wrongly, he had defrauded his elder brother. He held the letter in his hand and opened it slowly, like a man unwinding the last bandage from a wound. Even as he bent to read it, there was a sound outside as if someone had moved on the creaky porch.

"Who's there?" he called, shoving the letter into his pocket. No answer. Maybe a night-bound Negro, seeking shelter. Charlie leaned forward and blew out the candle. Simultaneously there was a loud knocking at the front door.

Grasping the broken arm of a chair, Charlie took two steps toward the hall. As he reached it, the door opened and a figure blocked out the moonlight, paused and then took a step forward.

"Just a minute there!" Charlie cried. He threw his flash light upon a mild little man in country clothes. The man stood still and remarked in a placid voice:

"That's Charlie, isn't it? Don't you know your brother?"

One by one, Pete's features revealed themselves.

"Come in," Charlie said. "I'll light the candle."

"I wondered why you put it out."

They sat with the flickering light between them. Pete's face was trivial and sad, with something broken in it, but it was not the map of degeneracy Charlie had somehow expected to see.

"I heard this evening you were in town," said Pete. "You weren't at the hotel, and so I reckoned you'd come out here to look the old place over."

"It looks like hell, doesn't it?"

"Sure does. My wife and I tried living here a year, but she was afraid it would come down on our heads, so we moved to Lowndes County."

"How are things going with you?" asked Charlie.

"Going all right." The little man spoke up suddenly and eagerly. "I've been fixing to write you for a long while."

Charlie's heart rose in his throat.

"Yeah, I been wanting to talk to you," Pete continued. "You know, Charlie, I'm good now. You know? I mean I'm good. I want to do right. After I got out of the pen up in Birmingham I came back here for a while and tried to farm this place." He paused and lowered his voice and he leaned forward. "Charlie, did it ever strike you the old man left mighty little money for what we guessed he had?"

Charlie looked up. "Yes, it struck me at the time."

"Well, there was ten thousand dollars cash under the spring house." Pete stared at Charlie, licking his lips uncertainly. "Wait a minute. Don't say anything yet awhile. Well, after I found it I tried to figure like it was my share that I'd been done out of. I bought my farm in Lowndes County. But I got full up with corn one night and told my wife and, shucks, you know, we don't like to go to prayer meeting with that thing on our conscience. She's got religion, and thinking of it about drives her nutty, and I don't feel too good about it myself."

"I can understand," Charlie said.

"I figure you might be willing to make an arrangement. I got a couple thousand left and I could put a little mortgage on the farm. If I paid you all—you and the boys—thirty-five hundred dollars, then I'd have my fourth of what daddy left."

"You can keep it all, Pete. I'll make it up to Ben and Dicky."

"Hold on! I wasn't asking——"

"I've had the luck. You wouldn't believe how much money I've made up there, and I guess I can keep on. I'll look out for Ben and Dicky."

Was it a fortnight ago he had told Ben he must leave college?

"Keep it," he repeated. "Daddy didn't mean that money for us, or he'd have mentioned it."

Pete laughed nervously. "Well, you sound to me like a right good fellow."

"I'm a louse," admitted Charlie. "But just like you, I want to get square and start over. So listen."

He reached his hand into his pocket, drew out the paper, and unfolded it; he shut his eyes and opened them, ready for whatever he should see.

The paper he had thought was a will was not a will; it was a letter addressed to himself. He read aloud:

To my good son Charlie: You thought I did not mean it—you thought I was crazy. I am drawing my will over again, changing one little thing. Part of my money is where it's none of your business, and I am going to my Maker taking that secret with me, so I am leaving out the part that tells where to find it. I have not got any loving sons, so it will go to whoever finds it. It wasn't so smart to quarrel with your old daddy after all.

"By golly!" Pete exclaimed. "Then you knew all the time that there was more money somewhere?"

"No," said Charlie slowly. "I hadn't had time to open this letter."

IV

One morning a fortnight later, Sara telephoned to Marston Raines.

"Charlie Clayhorne is back in town," she said.

"Have you seen him?"

"He came to see me yesterday. He's been down in Alabama where he was born."

"Does he seem better?"

"I think so. That's what I telephoned you about. It's me now— something seems to have happened to me."

"Tell me about it."

"He came in yesterday afternoon and sat down and said, 'I'm all right now, Sara!' Nothing more than that, though I rather encouraged an explanation."

"That's good. It looks as if he's cleared it up."

"Then he told me he'd gone to work in a bond house—of course, after he left I called up Henry Cortelyou at once and asked Henry to give him a chance and of course Henry was glad to. I didn't tell Charlie—anyhow, Charlie said he thought he saw his future clear before him again and he asked me whether I could ever again consider marrying him. Marston, I didn't know what to tell him. When he was so sick, I'd have married him to try and help, but now I seem to have exhausted myself about him. I love him—I'll always somehow love him, but I don't feel the impetus to do anything more. Seeing a man break down like that——I wonder if he won't always depend on me for his sense of direction—and I would want to depend on him for that."

"But he was sick," Marston interrupted. "And you must keep remembering that. Any doctor or nurse will tell you the strongest men are like drowning kittens when they're sick. It may make you cynical about men in general, but it needn't discourage you about Clayhorne."

Silence on the wire for a moment.

"I'll have to think it over."

"You're in a state of reaction. When love is intact, the merest pin prick—a touch of jealousy, for instance—will start it ticking again."

"Thank you," Sara said. "I'll have to think it over."

At five that evening she went over to Charlie's apartment. Dicky was in the living room, digging into a confusion of wrapping paper and string.

"Isn't Charlie funny?" he cried presently. "Last month he was talking about how extravagant those soldiers were you brought me from Europe, and now's he's sent me up a whole lot more—with Napoleon in it! And look at this one——"

"It's Joan of Arc."

"And knights charging and bow-and-arrow shooters! Look, this is an executioner, and here are a whole lot of other people. I don't know what they are."

"Isn't that wonderful?"

"Yes," said Dicky. . . . "Ben's home, but Charlie isn't. . . . Ben!"

When Charlie came in she saw his face in the hall a minute before he saw her, and she knew then with sudden illumination that she was looking at the face she had expected to see on the pier a month before. All of him was there again.

"A nice thing has happened, Sara," he told her. "Henry Cortelyou called up. He wants me back."

"Yes, I——" Sara stopped herself. That was something he needn't ever know. It was a compensation for his solitary trip into his own buried past where she could not follow. Everything was fine now.

Marston Raines was right—his sending the soldiers to Dicky was enough to start the clock ticking again, and Sara felt a sudden shiver of emotion. Everything was all right again now; she belonged to somebody. She grew happier and happier. Suddenly she was wildly happy and she couldn't keep it to herself.

The Rubber Check

(*The Saturday Evening Post*, 6 August 1932)

"The Rubber Check" was written in May 1932—probably in Montgomery just before Fitzgerald moved to Maryland. The *Post* paid $3000 for this story, a cut of $1000 from Fitzgerald's top price—which was a result of the magazine's falling revenues as well as an indication that he was no longer regarded as a magazine-seller.

This underrated story draws upon the familiar Fitzgerald subject of a poor boy's love for a rich girl. Here the treatment is complicated by the circumstance that Val is partly a fortune-hunter; moreover, he is hardened by his exposure to the rich, and at the end of the story he has learned how to use arrogance to win a rich girl he doesn't love.

When Val was twenty-one his mother told him of her fourth venture into marriage. "I thought I might as well have someone." She looked at him reproachfully. "My son seems to have very little time for me."

"All right," said Val with indifference, "if he doesn't get what's left of your money."

"He has some of his own. We're going to Europe and I'm going to leave you an allowance of twenty-five dollars a month in case you lose your position. Another thing——" She hesitated. "I've arranged that if you should—if anything should happen to you," she smiled apologetically, "it won't, but if it should—the remains will be kept in cold storage until I return. I mean I haven't enough money to be able to rush home. . . . You understand, I've tried to think of everything."

"I understand," Val laughed. "Of course, the picture of myself on ice is not very inspiring. But I'm glad you thought of everything." He considered for a moment, "I think that this time, if you don't mind, I'll keep my name—or rather your name—or rather the name I use now."

His social career had begun with that name—three years before it had emboldened him to go through a certain stone gate. There was just a minute when if his name had been Jones he wouldn't have gone, and yet his name was Jones; he had adopted the name Schuyler from his second stepfather.

The gate opened into a heavenlike lawn with driveways curling on it and a pet bear chained in the middle—and a great fantastic, self-indulgent house with towers, wings, gables and verandas, a conservatory, tennis courts, a circus ring for ponies and an empty pool. The gardener, grooming some proud, lucky roses, swung the bowl of his pipe toward him.

"The Mortmains are coming soon?" Val asked.

Val's voice was cultivated—literally, for he had cultivated it himself. The gardener couldn't decide whether he was a friend or an intruder.

"Coming Friday afternoon," he allowed.

"For all summer?"

"I dunno. Maybe a week; maybe three months. Never can tell with them."

"It was a shame to see this beautiful place closed last season," said Val.

He sauntered on calmly, sniffing the aristocratic dust that billowed from the open windows on the ground floor. Where there were not maids cleaning, he walked close and peered in.

"This is where I belong," he thought.

The sight of dogs by the stables dissuaded him from further progress; then, departing, he said good-by so tenderly to the gardener that the man tipped his cap.

After his adopted name his next lucky break was to meet the Mortmains, riding out on the train from New York four days later. They were across the aisle, and he waited. Presently the opportunity came, and, leaning toward them, he proffered with just the right smile of amusement:

"Excuse me, but the tennis court *is* weeded, but there's no water in the pool—or wasn't Monday."

They were startled—that was inevitable; one couldn't crash right in on people without tearing a little bit of diaphanous material, but Val stepped so fast that after a few minutes he was really inside.

"——simply happened to be going by and it looked so nice in there that I wandered in. Lovely place—charming place."

He was eighteen and tall, with blue eyes and sandy hair, and he made Mrs. Mortmain wish that her own children had as good manners.

"Do you live in Beardsly?" she inquired.

"Quite near." Val gave no hint that they were "summer people" at the beach, differentiating them from the "estate people" farther back in the hills.

The face of young Ellen Mortmain regarded him with the contagious enthusiasm that later launched a famous cold cream. Her childish beauty was wistful and sad about being so rich and sixteen. Mrs. Mortmain liked him, too; so did Fräulein and the parrot and the twins. All of them liked him except Ellen's cousin, Mercia Templeton, who was shy and felt somehow cut out. By the time Mrs. Mortmain had identified him as a nobody she had accepted him, at least on the summer scale. She even called on Val's mother, finding her "a nervous, pretentious little person." Mrs. Mortmain knew that Ellen adored Val, but Val knew his place and she was grateful to him for it. So he kept the friendship of the family through the years that followed—the years of his real education.

With the Mortmains he met other young people till one autumn his name landed on the lists of young men eligible for large dances in New York. In consequence the "career" that he pursued in a brokerage office was simply an interlude between debutante parties at the Ritz and Plaza where he pulsated ecstatically in the stag lines; only occasionally reminding himself of "Percy and Ferdie, the Hallroom Boys" in the funny paper. That was all right; he more than paid his entrance fee with his cheerfulness and wit and good manners. What stamped him as an adventurer was that he just could not make any money.

He was trying as hard as he knew how to learn the brokerage business, but he was simply rotten at it. The least thing that happened around the office was more interesting than the stock board or the work on his desk. There was, for instance, Mr. Percy Wrackham, the branch manager, who spent his time making lists of the Princeton football team, and of the second team and the third team; one busy morning he made a list of all the quarterbacks at Princeton for thirty years. He was utterly unable to concentrate. His drawer was always full of such lists. So Val, almost helpless against this bad influence, gradually gave up all hopes of concentrating and made lists of girls he had kissed and clubs he would like to belong to and prominent debutantes instead.

It was nice after closing hours to meet a crowd at the movies on Fifty-ninth Street, which was quite the place to spend the afternoon. The young people sat in the balcony that was like a club, and said whatever came into their minds and kicked the backs of the seats for applause. By and by an usher came up and was tortured for a while— kept rushing into noisy corners, only to find them innocent and silent; but finally the management realized that since he had developed this dependable clientele it were well to let them have their way.

Val never made love to Ellen in the movies, but one day he told her about his mother's new marriage and the thoughtful disposal of the body. He had a very special fascination for her, though now she was a debutante with suitors who had many possessions and went about the business of courtship with dashing intensity. But Val never took advantage of the romantic contrast between his shining manners and his shiny suits.

"That's terrible!" she exclaimed. "Doesn't your mother love you?"

"In her way. But she hates me, too, because she couldn't own me. I don't want to be owned."

"How would you like to come to Philadelphia with me this week-end?" she asked impulsively. "There's a dance for my cousin, Mercia Templeton."

His heart leaped. Going to a Philadelphia function was something more than "among those present were Mssrs. Smith, Brown, Schuyler, Brown, Smith." And with Ellen Mortmain! It would be: "Yes. I came down with Ellen Mortmain," or "Ellen Mortmain asked me to bring her down."

Driving to Philadelphia in a Mortmain limousine, his role took possession of him. He became suddenly a new figure, "Val Schuyler of New York." Beside him Ellen glowed away in the morning sunshine, white and dark and fresh and new, very sure of herself, yet somehow dependent on him.

His role widened; it included being in love with her, appearing as her devoted suitor, as a favorably considered suitor. And suddenly he really was in love with her.

"No one has ever been so beautiful," he broke out. "All season there's been talk about you; they say that no girl has come out for years who has been so authentically beautiful."

"Val! Aren't you divine? You make me feel marvelous!"

The compliment excited her and she wondered if his humorous friendliness of several years concealed some deep way he felt about her underneath. When she told him that in a month she was going to London to be presented at court he cried:

"What shall I do without you?"

"You'll get along. We haven't seen so much of each other lately."

"How can I help that? You're rich and I'm poor."

"That doesn't matter if two people really——" She stopped.

"But it does matter," he said. "Don't you think I have any pride?"

Pride was not among his virtues, yet he seemed very proud and lonely to Ellen as he said this. She put her hand on his arm.

"I'll be back."

"Yes, and probably engaged to the Prince of Wales."

"I don't want to go," Ellen said. "I was never so happy as that first summer. I used to go to sleep and wake up thinking of you. Always, whenever I see you, I think of that and it does something to me."

"And to me. But it all seems so hopeless."

The intimacy of the car, its four walls whisking them along toward a new adventure, had drawn them together. They had never talked this way before—and never would have in New York. Their hands clung together for a moment, their glances mingled and blurred into one intimate glance.

"I'll see you at seven," she whispered when she left him at his hotel.

He arrived early at the Templetons'. The less formal atmosphere of Philadelphia made him feel himself even more definitely as Val Schuyler of New York and he made the circle of the room with the confidence of a grand duke. Save for his name and his fine appearance, the truth was lost back in the anonymity of a great city, and as the escort of Ellen Mortmain, he was almost a visiting celebrity. Ellen had not appeared, and he talked to a nervous girl projecting muscularly from ill-chosen clothes. With a kindliness that came natural to him, he tried to put her at her ease.

"I'm shy," he said. "I've never been in Philadelphia before."

"I'm shyer still, and I've lived here all my life."

"Why are you?"

"Nothing to hang on to. No bridle—nothing. I'd like to be able to carry a swagger stick; fans break when you get too nervous."

"Hang on to me."

"I'd just trip you. I wish this were over."

"Nonsense! You'll probably have a wonderful time."

"No, I won't, but maybe I'll be able to look as if I am."

"Well, I'm going to dance with you as often as I can find you," he promised.

"It's not that. Lots of men will dance with me, since it's my party."

Suddenly Val recognized the little girl of three years ago. "Oh, you're Mercia Templeton."

"You're that boy——"

"Of course."

Both of them tried to appear pleasantly surprised, but after a moment Mercia gave up.

"How we disliked each other," she sighed. "One of the bad memories of my youth. You always made me wriggle."

"I won't make you wriggle any more."

"Are you sure?" she said doubtfully. "You were very superficial then. You only cared about the surface. Of course I see now that you neglected me because my name wasn't Mortmain; but then I thought you'd made a personal choice between Ellen and myself."

Resentment stirred in Val; he hated the reproach of superficiality unless he made it humorously about himself. Actually he cared deeply about things, but the things he cared about were generally considered trivial. He was glad when Ellen Mortmain came into the room.

His eyes met hers, and then all through the evening he followed the shining angel in bluish white that she had become, finding her through intervening flowers at table, behind concealing black backs at the dance. Their mutual glance said: "You and I together among these strange people—we understand."

They danced together, so that other people stopped dancing to watch. Dancing was his great accomplishment and that night was a triumph. They floated together in such unity that other beaus were intimidated, muttering, "Yes, but she's crazy about this Schuyler she came down with."

Sometime in the early morning they were alone and her damp, powdery young body came up close to him in a crush of tired cloth, and he kissed her trying not to think of the gap between them. But with her presence giving him strength he whispered:

"You'll be so gone."

"Perhaps I won't go. I don't want to go away from you, ever."

Was it conceivable that they could take that enormous chance? The idea was in both their minds, and in the mind of Mercia Templeton as she passed the door of the cloak room and saw them there crushed against a background of other people's hats and wraps, clinging together. Val went to sleep with the possibility burning in his mind.

Ellen telephoned his hotel in the morning:

"Do you still feel—like we did?"

"Yes, but much more," he answered.

"I'm making Mercia have lunch down there at the hotel. I've got an idea. There may be a few others, but we can sit next to each other."

Eventually there were nine others, all from last night's party, and Val began to think about his mother when they began lunch at two o'clock. Her boat left at seven-thirty. But sitting next to Ellen, he forgot for a while.

"I asked some questions," Ellen whispered, "without letting anyone guess. There's a place called Elkton just over the Maryland border, where there's a minister——"

He was intoxicated with his haughty masquerade.

"Why not?" he said concretely.

If Mercia Templeton wouldn't stare at him so cynically from farther down the table!

The waiter laid a check at his elbow. Val started; he had had no intention of giving the party, but no one spoke up; the men at the table were as young as himself and as used to being paid for. He carried the check into his lap and looked at it. It was for eighty dollars, and he had nine dollars and sixty-five cents. Once more he glanced about the table—once more he saw Mercia Templeton's eyes fixed suspiciously upon him.

"Bring me a blank check," he said.

"Yes, sir."

In a minute the waiter returned.

"Could you come to the manager's office?"

"Certainly."

Waiting for the manager, he looked at the clock. It was quarter of four; if he was to see his mother off he would have to leave within the hour. On the other hand, this was overwhelmingly the main chance.

"I find I'm a little short," he said in his easy voice. "I came down for a dance and I miscalculated. Can you take my check on"—he named his mother's bank—"for a hundred dollars?"

He had once before done this in an emergency. He hadn't an account at the bank, but his mother made it good.

"Have you any references here, Mr. Schuyler?"

He hesitated.

"Certainly—the Charles M. Templetons."

The manager disappeared behind a partition and Val heard him take up a telephone receiver. After a moment the manager returned.

"It's all right, Mr. Schuyler. We'll be glad to take your check for a hundred dollars."

He wrote out a wire to his mother, advising her, and returned to the table.

"Well?" Ellen said.

He felt a sudden indifference toward her.

"I'd better go back to the Templetons'," she whispered. "You hire a car from the hotel and call for me in an hour. I've got plenty of money."

His guests thanked him for his hospitality.

"It's nothing," he said lightly. "I think Philadelphia is charming."

"Good-by, Mr. Schuyler." Mercia Templeton's voice was cool and accusing.

"Good-by," Ellen whispered. "In an hour."

As he went inside a telegram was handed him:

YOU HAVE NO RIGHT TO CASH SUCH A CHECK AND I AM
INSTRUCTING BANK TO RETURN IT. YOU MUST MAKE IT UP OUT OF
WHAT MONEY YOU HAVE AND IT WILL BE A LESSON TO YOU. IF YOU
CANNOT FIND TIME TO COME TO NEW YORK THIS WILL SAY GOOD-BY.
MOTHER.

Hurrying to a booth Val called the Templeton house, but the car
had not yet returned. Never had he imagined such a situation. His
only fear had been that in cashing the check he would be irritating his
mother, but she had let him down; he was alone. He thought of
reclaiming the check from the office, but would they let him leave the
hotel? There was no alternative—he must catch his mother before she
sailed.

He called Ellen again. Still she was not there and the clock ticked
toward five. In a panic he seized his grip and raced for Broad Street
Station.

Three hours later, as he ran up the interminable steps of the pier
and through the long sheds, he heard a deep siren from the river. The
boat was moving, slowly, but moving; there was no touch with shore.
He saw his mother on deck not fifty feet away from him.

"Mother! Mother!" he called.

Mrs. Schuyler repressed a look of annoyance and nudged the man
beside her as if to say—"That tall handsome boy there—my son—
how hard it is to leave him!"

"Good-by, Val. Be a good boy."

He could not bring himself to return immediately to
Philadelphia. Still stunned by his mother's desertion, it did not occur
to him that the most logical way to raise a hundred dollars was to raise
a million. He simply could not face Ellen Mortmain with the matter
of the check hanging over his head.

Raising money is a special gift; it is either easy or very difficult.
To try it in a moment of panic tends to chill the blood of the
prospective lender. The next day Val raised fifty dollars—twenty-five
on his salary, fifteen on his second father's cuff links, and ten from a
friend. Then, in despair, he waited. Early in the week came a stern
letter from the hotel, and in the same mail another letter, which
caused him even more acute pain:

Dear Sir: It appears there has been some trouble about a check which I
recommended the hotel to cash for you while you were in this city. I will be
greatly obliged if you will arrange this matter at once, as it has given us some
inconvenience.

Very truly yours,
V. TEMPLETON,
(MRS. CHARLES MARTIN TEMPLETON.)

For another day Val squirmed with despair. Then, when there seemed nothing to do but hand himself over to the authorities, came a letter from the bank saying that his mother had cabled them word to honor the check. Somewhere in midocean she had decided that he had probably learned his lesson.

Only then did he summon the courage to telephone Ellen Mortmain. She had departed for Hot Springs. He hoped she did not know about the check; he even preferred for her to believe that he had thrown her over. In his relief at being spared the more immediate agony, he hardly realized that he had lost her.

II

Val wore full evening dress to the great debutante balls and danced a stately, sweeping Wiener Walzer to the sad and hopeful minors of "So Blue." He was an impressive figure; to imported servants who recognized his lordly manners the size of his tips did not matter. Sometimes he was able to forget that he really wasn't anybody at all.

At Miss Nancy Lamb's debutante dance he stood in the stag line like a very pillar of the social structure. He was only twenty-two, but for three years he had attended such functions, and viewing this newest bevy of girls, he felt rather as if he himself were bringing them out.

Cutting in on one of the newest and prettiest, he was struck by a curious expression that passed over her face. As they moved off together her body seemed to follow him with such reluctance that he asked:

"Is something the matter?"

"Oh, Val——" She hesitated in obvious embarrassment. "Would you mind not dancing with me any more tonight?"

He stopped in surprise.

"Why, what's the matter?"

She was on the verge of tears.

"Mother told me she didn't want me to."

As Val was about to demand an explanation he was cut in on. Shocked, he retreated to the stag line and recapitulated his relations with the girl. He had danced with her twice at every party, once he had sat beside her at supper; he had never phoned her or asked if he could call.

In five minutes another girl made him the same request.

"But what's the matter?" he demanded desperately.

"Oh, I don't know, Val. It's something you're supposed to have done." Again he was cut in on before he could get definite information. His alarm grew. He could think of no basis upon which any girl's mother should resent his dancing with her daughter. He was invariably correct and dignified, he never drank too much, he had tried to make no enemies, he had been involved in no scandal. As he stood brooding and trying to conceal his wounds and his uncertainty, he saw Mercia Templeton on the floor.

Possibly she had brought up from Philadelphia the story of the check he had cashed at the hotel. He knew that she didn't like him, but it seemed incredible that she would initiate a cabal against him. With his jaw set he cut in on her.

"I'm surprised to see you in New York," he said coldly.

"I come occasionally."

"I'd like very much to speak to you. Can we sit out for a minute?"

"Why, I'm afraid not. My mother——What is it you want to say?"

His eyes lifted to the group of older women who sat on a balcony above the dancers. There, between the mothers of the two girls who had refused him, sat Mrs. Charles Martin Templeton, of Philadelphia, the crisp "V. Templeton" of the note. He looked no farther.

The next hour was horrible. Half a dozen girls with whom he usually danced asked him with varying shades of regret not to dance with them any more. One girl admitted that she had been so instructed but intended to dance with him anyhow; and from her he learned the truth—that he was a young man who foisted bad checks upon trusting Philadelphians. No doubt his pocket was full of such paper, which he intended to dispose of to guileless debutantes.

With helpless rage he glared up at the calm dowagers in the balcony. Then, abruptly and without knowing exactly what he was going to say, he mounted the stairs.

At the moment Mrs. Templeton was alone. She turned her lorgnette upon him, cautiously, as one uses a periscope. She did not recognize him, or she pretended not to.

"My name is Val Schuyler," he blurted out, his poise failing him. "About that check in Philadelphia; I don't think you understand—it was an accident. It was a bill for a luncheon for your guests. College boys do those things all the time. It doesn't seem fair to hold it against me—to tell New York people."

For another moment she stared at him.

"I don't know what you're talking about," she said coldly, and swung herself and her lorgnette back to the dancers.

"Oh, yes, you do." He stopped, his sense of form asserting itself. He turned and went downstairs and directly to the coat room.

A proud man would have attended no more dances, but new invitations seemed to promise that the matter was but an incident. In a sense this proved true; the Templetons returned to Philadelphia, and even the girls who had turned Val down retracted on the next occasion. Nevertheless, the business had an inconvenient way of cropping up. A party would pass off without any untoward happening; the very next night he would detect that embarrassed look in a new partner and prepare for "I'm very sorry but——" He invented defenses—some witty, some bitter, but he found it increasingly insupportable to go around with the threat of a rebuff imminent every time he left the stag line.

With the waning season he stopped going out; the younger generation bored him, he said. No longer did Miss Moon or Miss Whaley at the office say with a certain concealed respect, "Well, I see in the papers you were in society last night." No longer did he leave the office with the sense that in the next few hours he would be gliding through a rich and scintillant world. No longer did the preview of himself in the mirror—with gloves, opera hat and stick—furnish him his mead of our common vanity. He was a man without a country—and for a crime as vain, casual and innocuous as his look at himself in the glass.

Into these gloomy days a ray of white light suddenly penetrated. It was a letter from Ellen.

Dearest Val: I shall be in America almost as soon as this reaches you. I'm going to stay only three days—can you imagine it?—and then coming back to England for Cowes Week. I've tried to think of a way of seeing you and this is the best. The girl I'm sailing with, June Halbird, is having a week-end party at their Long Island house and says I can bring who I want. Will you come?

Don't imagine from this that there'll be any more sappiness like last winter. You certainly were wise in not letting us do an absurd thing that we would have regretted.

Much love,
ELLEN.

Val was thoughtful. This might lead to his social resuscitation, for Ellen Mortmain was just a little more famous than ever, thanks to her semipublic swaying between this titled Englishman and that.

He found it fun to be able to say again, "I'm going to the country for the week-end; some people named Halbird——" and to add, "You see, Ellen Mortmain is home," as if that explained everything. To top the effect he sighed, implying that the visit was a somewhat onerous duty, a form of *noblesse oblige*.

She met him at the station. Last year he had been older than she was; now she was as old as he. Her manner had changed; it was interlaced with Anglicisms—the terminal "What?" the double-edged "Quite," the depressing "Cheerio" that always suggested imminent peril. She wore her new swank as light but effective armor around the vulnerability of her money and beauty.

"Val! Do you know that this has turned out to be a kids' party— dear old Yale and all that? Elsa couldn't get anybody I wanted, except you."

"That's my good luck."

"I may have to slip away to another binge for an hour or so—if I can manage it. . . . How are you?"

"Well—and hopeful."

"No money yet?" she commented with disapproval.

"Not a bean."

"Why don't you marry somebody?"

"I can't get over you."

She frowned. "Wouldn't it have been frightful if we'd torn off together? How we'd loathe each other by this time!"

At the Halbirds' he arranged his effects and came downstairs looking for Ellen. There were a group of young people by the swimming pool and he joined them; almost immediately he was conscious of a certain tension in the atmosphere. The conversation faded off whenever he entered it, giving him the impression of continually shaking hands with a glove from which the hand had been withdrawn. Even when Ellen appeared, the coolness persisted. He began to wish he had not come.

Dinner explained everything: Mercia Templeton turned up as one of the guests. If she was spreading the old poison of the check story, it was time for a reckoning. With Ellen's help he might lay the ghost at last. But before dessert, Ellen glanced at her watch and said to Mrs. Halbird:

"I explained, didn't I, that I have only three days here or I wouldn't do this dashing-off business? I'll join you later in Southampton."

Dismayed, Val watched her abandoning him in the midst of enemies. After dinner he continued his struggle against the current, relieved when it was time to go to the dance.

"And Mr. Schuyler," announced Mrs. Halbird, "will ride with me."

For a moment he interpreted this as a mark of special consideration, but he was no sooner in the car than he was undeceived.

Mrs. Halbird was a calm, hard, competent woman. Ellen Mortmain's unconventional departure had annoyed her and there was a rough nap on the velvet gloves with which she prepared to handle Val.

"You're not in college, Mr. Schuyler?"

"No, I'm in the brokerage business."

"Where did you go to school?"

He named a small private school in New York.

"I see." The casualness of her tone was very thin. "I should think you'd feel that these boys and girls were a little young for you."

Val was twenty-three.

"Why, no," he said, hating her for the soft brutality that was coming.

"You're a New Yorker, Mr. Schuyler?"

"Yes."

"Let's see. You are a relative of Mrs. Martin Schuyler?"

"Why, I believe—distantly."

"What is your father's name?"

"He's dead. My mother is Mrs. George Pepin now."

"I suppose it was through your mother that you met Ellen Mortmain. I suppose Mrs. Mortmain and your mother were——"

"Why, no—not exactly."

"I see," said Mrs. Halbird.

She changed her tone suddenly. Having brought him to his knees, she suddenly offered him gratuitous and condescending advice.

"Don't you agree with me that young people of the same ages should go together? Now, you're working, for example; you're beginning to take life seriously. These young people are just enjoying themselves. They can only be young once, you know." She laughed, pleased with her own tact. "I should think you'd find more satisfaction with people who are working in the world."

He didn't answer.

"I think most of the girls' mothers feel the same way," she said.

They had reached the club at Southampton, but still Val did not reply. She glanced at him quickly in the light as they got out of the car. She was not sure whether or not she had attained her purpose; nothing showed in his face.

Val saw now that after all these years he had reached exactly no position at all. The check had been seized upon to give him a questionable reputation that would match his questionable background.

He had been snubbed so often in the past few months that he had developed a protective shell to conceal his injuries. No one watching him go through his minimum of duty dances that night would have guessed the truth—not even the girls, who had been warned against him. Ellen Mortmain did not reappear; there was a rumor of a Frenchman she had met on shipboard. The house party returned to the Halbirds' at three.

Val could not sleep. He lapsed into a dozing dream in which many fashionable men and women sat at a heaped table and offered him champagne, but the glass was always withdrawn before it reached his lips. He sat bolt upright in bed, his throat parched with thirst. The bathroom offered only persistently lukewarm water, so he slipped on his dressing gown and went downstairs. "If anyone saw me," he thought bitterly, "they'd be sure I was after the silver."

Outside the door of the pantry he heard voices that made him stop suddenly and listen.

"Mother wouldn't have let me come if she'd known he'd be here," a girl was saying. "I'm not going to tell her."

"Ellen made the mess," Val heard June Halbird say. "She brought him and I think she had her nerve just to pass him off on us."

"Oh, let's forget it," suggested a young man impatiently. "What is he—a criminal or something?"

"Ask Mercia—and cut me some more ham."

"Don't ask me!" said Mercia quickly. "I don't like him, but I don't know anything really bad about him. The check you were talking about was only a hundred dollars, not a thousand, like you said; and I've tried a dozen times to shut mother up about it, but last year it was part of her New York conversation. I never thought it was so terrible."

"Just a rubber check? Don't embarrass Bill here. He's left them all over New York."

Pushing open the door, Val went into the pantry, and a dozen faces gaped at him. The men looked uncomfortable; a girl tittered nervously and upset a glass of milk.

"I couldn't help overhearing," Val said. "I came down for some water."

Presence he always had—and a sense of the dramatic. Without looking to right or left he took two cubes from a tray, put them in a glass and filled it from the faucet. Then he turned and, with his eyes still lifted proudly above them, said good night and went toward the door, carrying his glass of water. One young man whom he had known slightly came forward, saying: "Look here, Val, I think you've had a rotten deal." But Val pushed through the door as if he hadn't heard.

Upstairs, he packed his bag. After a few minutes he heard footsteps and someone knocked, but he stood silent until the person was gone. After a long while he opened his door cautiously and saw that the house was dark and quiet; carrying his suitcase he went downstairs and let himself out.

He had hardly reached one outlet of the circular drive when a car drove in at the other and stopped at the front door. Val stepped quickly behind some sheltering bushes, guessing that it was Ellen at last. The car waited tenderly for a minute; then Val recognized her laugh as she got out. The roadster passed him as it drove out, with the glimpse of a small, satisfied mustache above a lighting cigarette.

Ten minutes later he reached the station and sat down on a bench to wait for the early morning train.

III

Princeton had a bad football season, so one sour Monday, Mr. Percy Wrackham asked Val to take himself off, together with the irritating sound of "Hot-cha-cha" which he frequently emitted. Val was somewhat proud of being fired; he had, so to speak, stuck it out to the end. That same month his mother died and he came into a little money.

The change that ensued was amazing; it was fundamental as well as ostensible. Penniless, he had played the young courtier; with twenty thousand in the bank he revived in himself the psychology of Ward McAllister. He abandoned the younger generation which had treated him so shabbily, and, using the connections he had made, blossomed out as a man of the world. His apprenticeship had been hard, but he had served it faithfully, and now he walked sure-footed through the dangerous labyrinths of snobbery. People abruptly forgot everything about him except that they liked him and that he was usually around; so, as it frequently happens, he attained his position less through his positive virtues than through his ability to take it on the chin.

The little dinners he gave in his apartment were many and charming, and he was a diner-out in proportion. His drift was toward the sophisticated section of society, and he picked up some knowledge of the arts, which he blended gracefully with his social education.

Against his new background he was more than ever attractive to women; he could have married one of the fabulously wealthy Cupp twins, but for the moment he was engrossed in new gusto and he wanted to be foot-loose. Moreover, he went into partnership with a rising art dealer and for a year or so actually made some money.

Regard him on a spring morning in London in the year 1930. Tall, even stately, he treads down Pall Mall as if it were his personal pasture. He meets an American friend and shakes hands, and the friend notices how his shirt sleeve fits his wrist, and his coat sleeve incases his shirt sleeve like a sleeve valve; how his collar and tie are molded plastically to his neck.

He has come over, he says, for Lady Reece's ball. However, the market is ruining him day by day. He buys the newspaper thrust into his hand, and as his eye catches the headline his expression changes.

A cross-channel plane has fallen, killing a dozen prominent people.

"Lady Doncastle," he reads breathlessly, "Major Barks, Mrs. Weeks-Tenliffe, Lady Kippery——" He crushes the paper down against his suit and wipes imaginary sweat from his forehead. "What a shock! I was with them all in Deauville a week ago. I might even have taken that plane."

He was bound for the Mortmains' house, a former ducal residence in Cavendish Square. Ellen was the real reason for his having come to London. Ellen, or else an attempt to recapture something in his past, had driven him to withdraw from his languishing art business and rush to Europe on almost the last of his legacy. This morning had come a message to call at their town house.

No sooner was he within it than he got an impression that something was wrong. It was not being opened nor was it being closed, but unaccountably there were people here and there through the corridors, and as he was led to Ellen's own apartment he passed individuals whose presence there would have been inconceivable even in the fantastic swarms of one season ago.

He found Ellen sitting on a trunk in an almost empty room.

"Val, come and get me out of hock," she cried. "Help me hold the trunk down so they won't take it away."

"What is it?" he demanded, startled.

"We're being sold out over our heads—that's what. I'm allowed my personal possessions—if I can keep them. But they've already carted off a box full of fancy-dress costumes; claimed it was professional equipment."

"But why?" he articulated.

"We're poor as hell, Val. Isn't that extraordinary? You've heard about the Mortmain fortune, haven't you? Well, there isn't any Mortmain fortune."

It was the most violent shock of his life; it was simply unimaginable. The bottom seemed to have dropped out of his world.

"It seems we've been in the red for years, but the market floated us. Now we haven't got a single, solitary, individual, particular, specific bean. I was going to ask you, if you're in the art business, would you mind going to the auction and bid in one Juan Gris that I simply can't exist without?"

"You're poor?"

"Poor? Why, we'd have to find a fortune to pay our debts before we could claim to be that respectable. We're quadruple ruined, that's what we are."

Her voice was a little excited, but Val searched her face in vain for any reflection of his own experience of poverty.

No, that was something that could never possibly happen to Ellen Mortmain. She had survived the passing of her wealth; the warm rich current of well-being still flowed from her. Still not quite loving her, or not quite being able to love, he said what he had crossed the ocean to say:

"I wish you'd marry me."

She looked at him in surprise.

"Why, that's very sweet. But after all——" She hesitated. "Who are you, Val? I mean, aren't you a sort of a questionable character? Didn't you cheat a lot of people out of a whole lot of money with a forged check or something?"

"Oh, that check!" he groaned. He told her the story at last, while she kicked her heels against the trunk and the June sun played on her through a stained-glass window.

"Is that the reason you won't marry me?" he demanded.

"I'm engaged to another man."

So she was merely stepping from the wreck of one fortune into the assurance of another.

"I'm marrying a very poor man and we don't know how we'll live. He's in the army and we're going to India."

He experienced a vague envy, a sentimental regret, but it faded out before a stronger sensation; all around her he could feel the vast Mortmain fortune melting down, seeping back into the matrix whence it had come, and taking with it a little of Val Schuyler.

"I hope you didn't leave anything downstairs," Ellen laughed. "They'll attach it if you did. A friend of ours left his golf clubs and some guns; now he's got to buy them back at the auction."

He abandoned her, perched on top of the trunk, and walked solemnly back to the hotel. On his way he bought another paper and turned to the financial page.

"Good Lord!" he exclaimed. "This is the end."

There was no use now in sending a telegram for funds; he was penniless, save for ten dollars and a steamer ticket to New York, and there was a fortnight's bill to pay at the hotel. With a groan he saw himself sinking back into the ranks of the impecunious—like the Mortmains. But with them it had taken four generations; in his case it had taken two years.

More immediate worries harassed him. There was a bill overdue at the hotel, and if he left they would certainly attach his luggage. His splendid French calf luggage. Val's stomach quivered. Then there were his dress things, his fine shirts, the shooting suit he had worn in Scotland, his delicate linen handkerchiefs, his bootmaker's shoes.

He lengthened his stride; it seemed as though already these possessions were being taken from him. Once in his room and reassured by the British stability of them, the ingenuity of the poor asserted itself. He began literally to wind himself up in his clothes. He undressed, put on two suits of underwear and over that four shirts and two suits of clothes, together with two white pique vests. Every pocket he stuffed with ties, socks, studs, gold-backed brushes and a few toilet articles. Panting audibly, he struggled into an overcoat. His derby looked empty, so he filled it with collars and held them in place with some handerkerchiefs. Then, rocking a little on his feet, he regarded himself in the mirror.

He might possibly manage it—if only a steady stream of perspiration had not started to flow from somewhere up high in the edifice and kept pouring streams of various temperatures down his body, until they were absorbed by the heavy blotting paper of three pairs of socks that crowded his shoes.

Moving cautiously, like Tweedledum before the battle, he traversed the hall and rang for the elevator. The boy looked at him curiously, but made no comment, though another passenger made a dry reference to Admiral Byrd. Through the lobby he moved, a gigantic figure of a man. Perhaps the clerks at the desk had a subconscious sense of something being wrong, but he was gone too quickly for them to do anything about it.

"Taxi, sir?" the doorman inquired, solicitous at Val's pale face.

Unable to answer, Val tried to shake his head, but this also proving impossible, he emitted a low negative groan. The sun was attracted to his bulk as lightning is attracted to metal, as he staggered out toward a bus. Up on top, he thought; it would be cooler up on top.

His training as a hall-room boy stood him in good stead now; he fought his way up the winding stair as if it had been the social ladder. Then, drenched and suffocating, he sank down upon a bench, the bourgeois blood of many Mr. Joneses pumping strong in his heart.

Not for Val to sit upon a trunk and kick his heels and wait for the end; there was fight in him yet.

IV

A year later, Mr. Charles Martin Templeton, of Philadelphia, faced in his office a young man who had evidently obtained admittance by guile. The visitor admitted that he had no claim upon Mr. Templeton's attention save that he had once been the latter's guest some six years before.

"It's the matter of that check," he said determinedly. "You must remember. I had a luncheon forced on me that should have been your luncheon party, because I was a poor young man. I gave a check that was really a pretty good check, only slow, but your wife went around ruining me just the same. To this day it meets me wherever I go, and I want compensation."

"Is this blackmail?" demanded Mr. Templeton, his eyes growing hostile.

"No, I only want justice," said Val. "I couldn't make money during the boom. How do you expect me to make it during the depression? Your wife did me a terrible injury. I appeal to your conscience to atone for it by giving me a position."

"I remember about the check," said Mr. Templeton thoughtfully. "I know Mercia always considered that her mother went too far."

"She did, indeed," said Val. "There are thousands of people in New York who think to this day that I am a successful swindler."

"I have no checks that need signing," said Mr. Templeton thoughtfully, "but I can send you out to my farm."

Val Schuyler of New York on his knees in old overalls, planting cabbages and beans and stretching endless rows of strings and coaxing tender vines around them. As he toiled through the long farming day he softly recapitulated his amazing week at Newport in '29, and the Wiener Walzer he had danced with the Hon. Elinor Guise on the night of Lord Clan-Carly's coming of age.

Now another Scottish voice buzzed in his ear:

"Ye work slow, Schuyler. Burrow down into the ground more."

"The idiot imagines I'm a fallen aristocrat," Val thought.

He sat back on his haunches, pulling the weeds in the truck garden. He had a sense of utter waste, of being used for something for which nothing in his past had equipped him. He did not understand why he was here, nor what forces had brought him here. Almost never in his life had he failed to play the rules of the game, yet society had abruptly said: "You have been charming, you have danced with our girls, you have made parties go, you have taken up the slack of dull people. Now go out in the backyard and try it on the cabbages." Society. He had leaned upon its glacial bosom like a trusting child, feeling a queer sort of delight in the diamonds that cut hard into his cheek.

He had really asked little of it, accepting it at its own valuation, since to do otherwise would have been to spoil his own romantic conception of it. He had carried his essential boyishness of attitude into a *milieu* somewhat less stable than gangdom and infinitely less conscientious about taking care of its own. And they had set him planting cabbages.

"I should have married Emily Parr," he thought, "or Esther Manly, or Madeline Quarrels, or one of the Dale girls. I should have dug in—intrenched myself."

But he knew in his sadness that the only way he could have gotten what he really wanted was to have been born to it. His precious freedom—not to be owned.

"I suppose I'll have to make the supreme sacrifice," he said.

He contemplated the supreme sacrifice and then he contemplated the cabbages. There were tears of helplessness in his eyes. What a horrible choice to make!

Mercia Templeton rode up along the road and sat on her horse watching him for a long time.

"So here you are at last," she said, "literally, if not figuratively, at my feet."

Val continued working as if she were not there.

"Look at me!" she cried. "Don't you think I'm worth looking at now? People say I've developed. Oh, Lord, won't you ever look at me?"

With a sigh, Val turned around from the row of cabbages.

"Is this a proposal of marriage?" he asked. "Are you going to make me an honest man?"

"Nobody could do that, but at least you're looking at me. What do you see?"

He stared appraisingly.

"Really rather handsome," he said. "A little inclined to take the bit in your teeth."

"Oh, heavens, you're arrogant!" she cried, and spurred her horse down the road.

Val Schuyler turned sadly back to his cabbages. But he was sophisticated now; he had that, at least, from his expensive education. He knew that Mercia would be back.

On Schedule

(*The Saturday Evening Post*, 18 March 1933)

"On Schedule" was written at "La Paix," on the outskirts of Baltimore in December 1932. The *Post* paid $3000. After Zelda Fitzgerald entered Johns Hopkins Hospital in February, Fitzgerald rented "La Paix." Although he was making his successful effort to complete *Tender Is the Night*, it was necessary for him to write stories for ready income.

This story draws upon Fitzgerald's experiences as a sole parent while his wife was hospitalized and was also a private joke about his own penchant for making schedules. René is a widower; commencing with "On Schedule" the mothers in Fitzgerald's domestic stories are either dead or hospitalized, reflecting his own domestic situation.

In September, René's old house seemed pretty fine to him, with its red maples and silver birches and the provident squirrels toiling overtime on the lawn. It was on the outskirts of a university town, a rambling frame structure that had been a residence in the 80's, the county poorhouse in the 1900's, and now was a residence again. Few modern families would care to live there, amid the groans of moribund plumbing and without even the silvery "Hey!" of a telephone, but René, at first sight of its wide veranda, which opened out into a dilapidated park of five acres, loved it for reminding him of a lost spot of his childhood in Normandy. Watching the squirrels from his window reminded René that it was time to complete certain winter provisions of his own, and laying aside his work, he took a large sheet of paper ruled into oblongs and ran over it once again. Then he went into the hall and called up the front staircase:

"Noël."

"Yes, daddy."

"I wish to see you, *chérie*."

"Well, you told me to put away the soldiers."

"You can do that later. I want you to go over to the Slocums' and get Miss Becky Snyder, and then I wish to speak to you both together."

"Becky's here, daddy; she's in the bathtub."

René started. "In the bath——"

The cracks and settlings of the house had created fabulous acoustics, and now another voice, not a child's, drifted down to him:

"The water runs so slow over at the Slocums', it takes all day to draw a bath. I didn't think you'd mind, René."

"Mind!" he exclaimed vaguely. As if the situation was not already delicate. "Mind!" If Becky took baths here, she might just as well be living here, so far as any casual visitor would conclude. He imagined himself trying to explain to Mrs. Dean-of-the-Faculty McIntosh the very complicated reasons why Becky Snyder was upstairs taking a bath.

At that, he might succeed—he would have blushed to attempt it in France.

His daughter, Noël, came downstairs. She was twelve, and very fair and exquisitely made, like his dead wife; and often in the past he had worried about that. Lately she had become as robust as any American child and his anxieties were concentrated upon her education, which, he had determined, was going to be as good as that of any French girl.

"Do you realize that your school starts tomorrow?"

"Yeah."

"What is that?"

"Yes, daddy."

"I am going to be busier than I have ever been in my life."

"With all that water?"

"With all that water—think of all the baths Becky could take in it. And with the nice cute little power plant of my own the Foundation has built me. So, for you, Noël, I have prepared a schedule and my secretary has made three copies—one for you, one for me and one for Becky. We shall make a pocket in the back of your arithmetic in which to keep your copy. You must always keep it there, for if you lose it, then our whole day is thrown out of joint."

Noël shifted restlessly in her chair.

"What I don't understand," she said, "is why I can't take just like the other girls? Why I have to do a lot of goofy——"

"Do not use that word!"

"Well, why I can't do like everybody else?"

"Then you don't want to continue the piano."

"Oh, yes, piano; but why do I have to take French out of school every day?"

René rose, pushing his fingers distractedly over his prematurely iron-gray hair—he was only thirty-four.

"What is the use of explaining things to you?" he cried. "Listen. You speak perfect French and you want to preserve it, don't you? And you can't study in your school what you already know more accurately than a sophomore in the college."

"Then why——"

"Because no child retains a language unless she continues it till fourteen. Your brain——" René tapped his own ferociously. "It cannot do it."

Noël laughed, but her father was serious.

"It is an advantage!" he cried. "It will help you—it will help you to be an actress at the Comédie Française. Do you understand?"

"I don't want to be an actress any more," confessed Noël. "I'd rather electrolize water for the Foundation like you, and have a little doll's power plant, and I can keep up my French talking to you in the evening. Becky could join in, because she wants to learn anyhow."

Her father nodded his head sadly.

"Very well, then; all right." He brushed the paper schedule aside; being careful, however, that it didn't go into the wastebasket. "But you cannot grow up useless in this house. I will give you a practical education instead. We will stop the school and you can study sewing, cooking, domestic economy. You can learn to help about the house." He sat down at his desk thoroughly disgusted, and made a gesture of waving her away, to be left alone with his disappointment.

Noël considered. Once this had been a rather alarming joke— when her marks were unsatisfactory, her father always promised to bring her up as a fine cook. But though she no longer believed him, his logic had the effect of sobering her. Her own case was simply that she hated running around to extra lessons in the middle of the morning; she wanted to be exactly like the other girls in school.

"All right, then," she said. Both of them stood up as Becky, still damp and pink from her bath, came into the room.

Becky was nineteen, a startling little beauty, with her head set upon her figure as though it had been made separately and then placed there with the utmost precision. Her body was sturdy, athletic; her head was a bright, happy composition of curves and shadows and vivid color, with that final kinetic jolt, the element that is eventually sexual in effect, which made strangers stare at her. Who has not had the excitement of seeing an apparent beauty from afar; then, after a moment, seeing that same face grow mobile and watching the beauty disappear moment by moment, as if a lovely statue had begun to walk with the meager joints of a paper doll? Becky's beauty was the opposite of that. The facial muscles pulled her expressions into lovely smiles and frowns, disdains, gratifications and encouragements; her beauty was articulated, and expressed vividly whatever it wanted to express.

Beyond that, she was an undeveloped girl, living for the moment on certain facets of René du Cary's mind. There was no relation between herself and Noël as yet except that of fellow pupils—though they suspected each other faintly as competitors for his affection.

"So now," René pursued, "let us get this exact, darlings. Here we have one car, no telephone and three lives. To drive the car we have you"—this to Becky—"and me, and usually Aquilla's brother. I will not even explain the schedule, but I assure you that it is perfect. I worked on it until one this morning."

They sat obediently while he studied it with pride for a moment.

"Now here is a typical day: On Tuesday, Aquilla's brother takes me to laboratory, dropping Noël at her school; when he returns to house, Becky takes car to tennis practice, calls for Noël and takes her to Mlle. Ségur's. Then she does shopping—and so forth."

"Suppose I have no shopping?" suggested Becky.

"Then you do 'and so forth.' If there is no 'and so forth,' you drive car to laboratory and catch bus home—in that case, I bring Aquilla's brother—I mean Noël"—he stared at the schedule, screwing up his eyes—"I bring Noël from Mademoiselle's back to school and continue home. Then"—he hesitated—"and then——"

Noël rocked with amusement.

"It's like that riddle," she cried, "about the man who had to cross the river with the goose and the fox and the——"

"Wait one minute!" René's voice was full of exasperated flats. "There is one half hour left out here, or else Aquilla's brother will have to lunch before it is cooked."

Becky, who had been listening with a helpful expression, became suddenly a woman of sagacity and force. The change, expressed in every line of her passionate face, startled René, and he listened to her with a mixture of awe, pride and disapproval.

"Why not let my tennis lessons go this fall?" she suggested. "After all, the most important things are your experiment and Noël's education. Tennis will be over in a month or two. It just complicates everything."

"Give up the tennis!" he said incredulously. "Idiotic child! Of course, you'll continue. American women must be athletes. It is the custom of the country. All we need is complete cooperation."

Tennis was Becky's forte. She had been New Jersey scholastic champion at sixteen, thereby putting the small town of Bingham upon the map. René had followed the careers of his compatriots Lacoste and Lenglen, and he was very particular about Becky's tennis. He knew that already there had been a trickle of talk in the community about himself and Becky—this young girl he had found somewhere or nowhere, and had recently deposited in the keeping of Mr. and Mrs. Slocum on the adjacent truck farm. Becky's tennis had a certain abstract value that would matter later. It was a background for Becky—or rather it was something that would stand between Becky and her lack of any background whatsoever. It had to go into the schedule, no matter how difficult it made things.

René had loved his wife, an American, and after she faded off agonizingly in Switzerland, three years had dragged by before the tragic finality of the fact ceased to present itself at the end of sleep as a black period that ended the day before it began. Curiously crediting the legend that every seven years the human body completely renews itself, she had put a provision in her last sick will that if he married within seven years of her death, the moderate income she bequeathed him should accrue in trust for Noël. What he did after the seven years would be, Edith considered, an act of someone she had never known. The provision had not bothered him. It was rather a convenience to know that marriage was out of the question, and many a trap set for him had gone unsprung during his years as a widower in the college town. The income made it possible for him to stay in research, under the aegis of one of those scientific foundations that gravitated to the university, instead of seeking a livelihood as a pedagogue in a foreign land. In his own line he was a man with that lucky touch. Last year, in cleaning up the junk of someone else's abandoned experiment, he had stumbled upon an entirely new technic in the activation of a catalyst for bringing about chemical reactions. He felt that after another year he would be able to provide for Noël far better than could his wife's shrunken trust fund.

So, for a thousand days he wore his grief down, and eventually he found that his daughter was growing up and that work really was the best thing with which to fill a life. He settled down, and existence became as foreshortened as the rhythm of the college itself.

"My relations with my daughter," he used to say, in those days, "are becoming what you call the Electra complex. If man was an adaptable animal, I should develop a lap and a very comfortable bosom and become a real mother to her, but I cannot. So, how can I put a stop to this father-and-daughter complex we are developing between us?"

The problem solved itself in its own terms. René was in love with youth, and one day he saw Becky Snyder's beauty peering over the back of a cut-down flivver stalled on the Lincoln Highway. It was an old flivver, even for its old-flivverish function of bearing young love from nook to nook. Jokes climbed feebly upon its sides and a great "Bingham H.S. 1932" defaced—if one can call it that—the radiator.

René du Cary, aloof as any university don spending an afternoon on
his bicycle, would have passed it with a shrug of amusement, if he had
not suddenly perceived the cause of the flivver's motionless position
in the road—a deeply intoxicated young man was draped across the
wheel.

"Now, this is too bad," he thought, when, with his bicycle in the
back seat, he was conducting the car toward its destination. He kept
imagining Noël in a like situation. Only when they had returned the
young man and his movable couch to the bosom of his family, and he
sat with Becky and her deaf aunt on the farmhouse stoop, did he
realize how authentically, radiantly beautiful she was and want to
touch her hair and her shining face and the nape of her neck—the
place where he kissed Noël good night.

She walked with him to the gate.

"You must not permit that young man to call on you," he said.
"He's not good for you."

"Then what do I do?" She smiled. "Sit home?"

He raised his hands.

"Are there no more solid citizens in this village?"

Becky looked impatient, as if he ought to know there weren't.

"I was engaged to a nice fellow that died last year," she informed
him, and then with pride: "He went to Hamilton. I was going to the
spring dance with him. He got pneumonia."

"I'm sorry," said René.

"There're no boys around here. There was a man said he'd get me
a job on the stage in New York, but I know that game. My friend
here—a girl, I mean—she goes to town to get picked up by students.
It's just hard luck for a girl to be born in a place like this. I mean,
there's no future. I met some men through playing tennis, but I never
saw them again."

He listened as the muddled concepts poured forth—the mingled
phrases of debutante, waif and country girl. The whole thing
confused him—the mixture of innocence, opportunism, ignorance. It
made him feel very foreign and far off.

"I will collect some undergraduates," he surprised himself by
promising. "They should appreciate living beauty, if they appreciate
nothing else."

But that wasn't the way it worked out. The half dozen seniors, the
lady who came to pour tea on his porch, recognized, before half an
hour had passed, that he was desperately in love with the girl, that he
didn't know it, that he was miserable when two of the young men
made engagements with her. Next time she came, there were no
young men.

"I love you and I want you to marry me," he said.

"But I'm simply——I don't know what to say. I never thought——"

"Don't try to think. I will think for us both."

"And you'll teach me," she said pathetically. "I'll try so hard."

"We can't be married for seven more months because——My heavens, you are beautiful!"

It was June then, and they got to know each other in a few long afternoons in the swing on the porch. She felt very safe with him—a little too safe.

That was the first time when the provision in Edith's will really bothered René. The seven specified years would not be over until December, and the interval would be difficult. To announce the engagement would be to submit Becky to a regents' examination by the ladies of the university. Because he considered himself extravagantly lucky to have discovered such a prize, he hated the idea of leaving her to rusticate in Bingham. Other connoisseurs of beauty, other discerning foreigners, might find her stalled on the road with unworthy young men. Moreover, she needed an education in the social civilities and, much as the railroad kings of the pioneer West sent their waitress sweethearts to convents in order to prepare them for their high destinies, he considered sending Becky to France with a chaperon for the interval. But he could not afford it, and ended by installing her with the Slocums next door.

"This schedule," he said to her, "is the most important thing in our lives; you must not lose your copy."

"No, dearest."

"Your future husband wants a lot; he wants a beautiful wife and a well-brought-up child, and his work to be very good, and to live in the country. There is limited money. But with method," he said fiercely—"method for one, method for all—we can make it go."

"Of course we can."

After she had kissed him and clung to him and gone, he sat looking out at the squirrels still toiling in the twilight.

"How strange," he thought. "For the moment my rôle is that of *supérieure* in a convent. I can show my two little girls about how good work is, and about politeness. All the rest one either has or hasn't.

"The schedule is my protection; for now I will have no more time to think of details, and yet they must not be educated by the money changers of Hollywood. They should grow up; there is too much of keeping people children forever. The price is too high; the bill is always presented to someone in the end."

His glance fell on the table. Upon it, carefully folded, lay a familiar-looking paper—the typewritten oblongs showed through. And on the chair where Becky had sat, its twin rested. The schedules, forgotten and abandoned, remained beside their maker.

"*Mon Dieu!*" he cried, his fingers rising to his young gray hair. "*Quel commencement!* Noël!"

II

With a sort of quivering heave like the attempt of a team to move a heavy load, René's schedule got in motion. It was an uncertain motion—the third day Noël lost her schedule and went on a school botany tour, while Aquilla's brother—a colored boy who had some time ago replaced a far-wandering houseman, but had never quite acquired a name of his own in the household—waited for her two hours in front of the school, so that Becky missed her tennis lesson and Mlle. Ségur, inconvenienced, complained to René. This was on a day that René had passed in despair trying to invent a process for keeping the platinum electrodes nicely blurred in a thousand glass cells. When he came home he blew up and Noël, at his request, had her supper in bed.

Each day plunged him deeper into his two experiments. One was his attempt to develop the catalyst upon which he had stumbled; the second was based on the new knowledge that there are two kinds of water. Should his plan of decomposing electrolytically one hundred thousand gallons of water yield him the chance of studying the two sorts spectrographically, the results might be invaluable. The experiment was backed by a commercial firm as well as by the Foundation, but it was already running into tens of thousands of dollars—there was the small power plant built for his use, the thousand platinum electrodes, each in its glass jar, as well as the time consumed in the difficult and tedious installation of the apparatus.

Necessarily, the domestic part of the day receded in importance. It was nice to know that his girls were safe and well occupied, that there would be two faces waiting for him eagerly at home. But for the moment he could not divert any more energy to his family. Becky had tennis and a reading list she had asked him for. She wanted to be a fine wife to René; she knew that he was trying to rear some structure of solidity in which they could all dwell together, and she guessed that it was the strain of the present situation that made him often seem to put undue emphasis on minor matters. When he began to substitute moments of severe strictness with Noël for the time he would have liked to devote to her, especially to her lessons—which were coming back marked "careless"—Becky protested. Whereupon René insisted that his intensity of feeling about Noël's manners was an attempt to save her trouble, to conserve her real energies for real efforts and not let them be spent to restore the esteem of her fellows, lost in a moment of carelessness or vanity. "Either one learns politeness at home," René said, "or the world teaches it with a whip—and many young people in America are ruined in that process. How do I care whether Noël 'adores' me or not, as they say? I am not bringing her up to be my wife."

Still, and in spite of everything, the method was not working. His private life was beginning to interfere with it. If he had been able to spend another half an hour in the laboratory that day when he knew Becky was waiting discreetly a little way down the road, or even if he could have sent an overt message to her, saying that he was delayed thereby, then the tap would not have been left on and a quantity of new water would not have run into the water already separated according to its isotope, thus necessitating starting over. Work, love, his child—his demands did not seem to him exorbitant; he had had forethought and had made a schedule which anticipated all minor difficulties.

"Let us reconsider," he said, assembling his girls again. "Let us consider that we have a method, embodied in this schedule. A method is better and bigger than a man."

"Not always," said Becky.

"How do you mean, not always, little one?"

"Cars really do act up like ours did the other day, René. We can't stand before them and read them the schedule."

"No, my darling," he said excitedly. "It is to ourselves we read the schedule. We foresee—we have the motor examined, we have the tank filled."

"Well, we'll try to do better," said Becky. "Won't we, Noël? You and I—and the car."

"You are joking, but I am serious."

She came close to him.

"I'm not joking, darling. I love you with all my heart and I'm trying to do everything you say—even play tennis: though I'd rather run over and keep your house a little cleaner for you."

"My house?" he stared around vaguely. "Why, my house is very clean. Aquilla's sister comes in every other Friday."

He had cause to remember this one Sunday afternoon a week later, when he had a visit from his chief assistant, Charles Hume, and his wife. They were old friends, and he perceived immediately the light of old friends bent on friendship in their eyes. And how was little

Noël? They had had Noël in their house for a week the previous summer.

René called upstairs for Noël, but got no answer.

"She is in the fields somewhere." He waved his hand vaguely. "All around, it is country."

"All very well while the days are long," said Dolores Hume. "But remember, there are such things as kidnapings."

René shut his mind swiftly against a new anxiety.

"How are you, René?" Dolores asked. "Charles thinks you've been overdoing things."

"Now, dear," Charles protested, "I——"

"You be still. I've known René longer than you have. You two men fuss and fume over those jars all day and then René has his hands full with Noël all evening."

Did René's eyes deceive him, or did she look closely to see how he was taking this?

"Charles says this is an easy stage of things, so we wondered if we could help you by taking Noël while you went for a week's rest."

Annoyed, René answered abruptly: "I don't need a rest and I can't go away." This sounded rude; René was fond of his assistant. "Not that Charles couldn't carry on quite as well as I."

"It's really poor little Noël I'm thinking of as much as you. Any child needs personal attention."

His wrath rising, René merely nodded blandly.

"If you won't consider that," Dolores pursued, "I wonder you don't get a little colored girl to keep an eye on Noël in the afternoon. She could help with the cleaning. I've noticed that Frenchmen may be more orderly than American men, but not a bit cleaner."

She drew her hand experimentally along the woodwork.

"Heavens!" she exclaimed, awed. Her hand was black, a particularly greasy, moldy, creepy black, with age-old furniture oil in it and far-drifted grime.

"What a catastrophe!" cried René. Only last week he had refused to let Becky clean the house. "I beg a thousand pardons. Let me get you——"

"It serves me right," she admitted, "and don't you do anything about it. I know this house like my pocket."

When she had gone, Charles Hume said:

"I feel I ought to apologize to you for Dolores. She's a strange woman, René, and she has no damn business butting into your affairs like this!"

He stopped. His wife was suddenly in the room again, and the men had an instant sense of something gone awry. Her face was shocked and hurt, stricken, as if she had been let down in some peculiarly personal way.

"You might not have let me go upstairs," she said to René. "Your private affairs are your own, but if it was anybody but you, René, I'd think it was a rather bad joke."

For a moment René was bewildered. Then he half understood, but before he could speak Dolores continued coldly:

"Of course I thought it was Noël in the tub, and I walked right in."

René was all gestures now; he took a long, slow, audible breath; raising his hands slowly to his eyes, he shook his head in time to a quick "tck, tck, tck, tck." Then, laying his cards on the table with a sudden downward movement of his arms, he tried to explain. The girl was the niece of a neighbor—he knew, even in the midst of his evasive words, that it was no use. Dolores was just a year or so older than that war generation which took most things for granted. He knew that previous to her marriage she had been a little in love with him, and he saw the story going out into the world of the college town. He knew this even when she pretended to believe him at the last, and when Charles gave him a look of understanding and a tacit promise with his eyes that he'd shut her up, as they went out the door.

"I feel so terrible," mourned Becky.

"It was the one day the water at the Slocums' wouldn't run at all, and I was so hot and sticky I thought I'd just jump in for two seconds. That woman's face when it came in the door! 'Oh, it's not Noël,' she said, and what could I say? From the way she stared at me, she ought to have seen."

It was November and the campus was riotous once a week with violets and chrysanthemums, hot dogs and football badges, and all the countryside was a red-and-yellow tunnel of leaves around the flow of many cars. Usually René went to the games, but not this year. Instead he attended upon the activities of the precious water that was not water, that was a heavenlike, mysterious fluid that might cure mental diseases in the Phacochœrus, or perhaps only grow hair on eggs—or else he played valet to his catalyst, wound in five thousand dollars' worth of platinum wire and gleaming dully at him every morning from its quartz prison.

He took Becky and Noël up there one day because it was unusually early. He was slightly disappointed because Noël was absorbed in an inspection of her schedule while he explained the experiments. The tense, sunny room seemed romantic to Becky, with its odor of esoteric gases, the faint perfumes of future knowledge, the low electric sizz in the glass cells.

"Daddy, can I look at your schedule one minute?" Noël asked. "There's one dumb word that I never know what it means."

He handed it toward her vaguely, for a change in the caliber and quality of the sound in the room made him aware that something was happening. He knelt down beside the quartz vessel with a fountain pen in his hand.

He had changed the conditions of his experiment yesterday, and now he noted quickly:

Flow of 500 c. c. per minute, temperature 255° C. Changed gas mixture to 2 vol. oxygen and 1.56 vol. nitrogen. Slight reaction, about 1 per cent. Changing to 2 vol. 0 and 1.76 vol. N. Temperature 283° C. platinum filament is now red-hot.

He worked quickly, noting the pressure gauge. Ten minutes passed; the filament glowed and faded, and René put down figure after figure. When he arose, with a rather far-away expression, he seemed almost surprised to see Becky and Noël still there.

"Well, now; that was luck," he said.

"We're going to be late to school," Becky told him, and then added apologetically: "What happened, René?"

"It is too long to explain."

"Of course you see, daddy," said Noël reprovingly, "that we have to keep the schedule."

"Of course, of course. Go along." He kissed them each hungrily on the nape of the neck, watching them with pride and joy, yet putting them aside for a while as he walked around the laboratory with some of the unworldliness of an altar boy. The electrolysis also seemed to be going better. Both of his experiments, like a recalcitrant team, had suddenly decided to function, realizing the persistence they were up against.

He heard Charles Hume coming in, but he reserved his news about the catalyst while they concentrated upon the water. It was noon before he had occasion to turn to his notes—realized with a shock that he had no notes. The back of the schedule on which he had taken them was astonishingly, inexplicably blank; it was as if he had written in vanishing ink or under the spell of an illusion. Then he saw what had happened—he had made the notes on Noël's schedule and she had taken it to school. When Aquilla's brother arrived with a registered package, he dispatched him to the school with the schedule to make the exchange. The data he had observed seemed irreplaceable, the more so as—despite his hopeful "Look! Look!

Come here, Charles, now, and look!''—the catalyst failed entirely to act up.

He wondered what was delaying Aquilla's brother and felt a touch of anxiety as he and Charles walked up to Main Street for lunch. Afterward Charles left, to jack up a chemistry-supply firm in town.

"Don't worry too hard," he said. "Open the windows—the room's full of nitrogen-chloride."

"Don't worry about that."

"Well——" Charles hesitated. "I didn't agree with Dolores' attitude the other day, but I think you're trying to do too much."

"Not at all," René protested. "Only, I am anxious to get possession of my notes again. It might be months or never, before I would blunder on that same set of conditions again."

He was hardly alone before a small voice on the telephone developed as Noël calling up from school:

"Daddy?"

"Yes, baby."

"Can you understand French or English better on the phone?"

"What? I can understand anything."

"Well, it's about my schedule."

"I am quite aware of that. You took away my schedule. How do you explain that?"

Noël's voice was hesitant: "But I didn't, daddy. You handed me your schedule with a whole lot of dumb things on the back."

"They are not dumb things!" he exclaimed. "They are very valuable things. That is why I sent Aquilla's brother to exchange the schedules. Has that been done?"

"I was gone to French when he came, so he went away—I guess on account of that day he was so dumb and waited. So I haven't got any schedule and I don't know whether Becky is coming for me after play hour or whether I'm to ride out with the Sheridans and walk home from there."

"You haven't got any schedule at all?" he demanded, his world breaking up around him.

"I don't know what became of it. Maybe I left it in the car."

"Maybe you left it in the car?"

"It wasn't mine."

He set down the receiver because he needed both hands now for the gesture he was under compulsion to make. He threw them up so high that it seemed as if they left his wrists and were caught again on their descent. Then he seized the phone again.

"— —because school closes at four o'clock, and if I wait for Becky and she doesn't come, then I'll have to be locked out."

"Listen," said René. "Can you hear? Do you want me to speak in English or French?"

"Either one, daddy."

"Well, listen to me: Good-by."

He hung up. Regretting for the first time the lack of a phone at home, he ran up to Main Street and found a taxi, which he urged, with his foot on an imaginary back-seat accelerator, in the direction of home.

The house was locked; the car was gone; the maid was gone; Becky was gone. Where she was gone he had no idea, and the Slocums could give him no information. . . . The notes might be anywhere now, kicked carelessly into the street, crumpled and flung away.

"But Becky will recognize it as a schedule," he consoled himself. "She would not be so formidable as to throw away our schedule."

He was by no means sure that it was in the car. On a chance, he had the taxi drive him into the colored district with the idea that he might get some sort of orientation from Aquilla's brother. René had never before searched for a colored man in the Negro residential quarter of an American city. He had no idea at first of what he was attempting, but after half an hour the problem assumed respectable dimensions.

"Do you know"—so he would call to dark and puzzled men on the sidewalks—"where I can find the house of Aquilla's brother, or of Aquilla's sister—either one?"

"I don't even know who Aquilla is, boss."

René tried to think whether it was a first or a last name, and gave up as he realized that he never had known. As time passed, he had more and more a sense that he was pursuing a phantom; it began to shame him to ask the whereabouts of such ghostly, blatantly immaterial lodgings as the house of Aquilla's brother. When he had stated his mission a dozen times, sometimes varying it with hypocritical pleas as to the whereabouts of Aquilla's sister, he began to feel a little crazy.

It was colder. There was a threat of first winter snow in the air, and at the thought of his notes being kicked out into it, buried beneath it, René abandoned his quest and told the taxi man to drive home, in the hope that Becky had returned. But the house was deserted and cold. With the taxi throbbing outside, he threw coal into the furnace and then drove back into the center of town. It seemed to him that if he stayed on Main Street he would sooner or later run into Becky and the car—there were not an unlimited number of places to pass an afternoon in a regimented community of seven thousand people. Becky had no friends here—it was the first time he had ever thought of that. Literally there was almost no place where she could be.

Aimless, feeling almost as intangible as Aquilla's brother, he wandered along, glancing into every drug store and eating shop. Young people were always eating. He could not really inquire of anyone if they had seen her, for even Becky was only a shadow here, a person hidden and unknown, a someone to whom he had not yet given reality. Only two things were real—his schedule, for the lack of which he was utterly lost and helpless, and the notes written on its back.

It was colder, minute by minute; a blast of real winter, sweeping out of the walks beside College Hall, made him wonder suddenly if Becky was going to pick up Noël. What had Noël said about being locked out when the school was closed? Not in weather like this. With sudden concern and self-reproach, René took another taxi and drove to the school, but it was closed and dark inside.

"Then, perhaps, she is lost too," he thought. "Quite possibly she tried to walk herself home by herself and was kidnaped, or got a big chill, or was run over."

He considered quite seriously stopping at the police station, and only decided against it when he was unable to think what he could possibly report to them with any shred of dignity.

"——that a man of science, has managed, in one afternoon, in this one little town, to lose everything."

III

Meanwhile, Becky was thoroughly enjoying herself. When Aquilla's brother returned with the car at noon, he handed over Noël's schedule with no comment save that he had not been able to give it to Noël because he could not find her. He was finished with European culture for the day, and was already crossing the Mediterranean in his mind while Becky tried to pump further information out of him.

A girl she had met through tennis had wangled the use of one of the club squash courts for the early hours of the afternoon. The squash was good; Becky soaked and sweated in the strange, rather awesome atmosphere of masculinity, and afterward, feeling fine and cool, took out her own schedule to check up on her duties of the afternoon. The schedule said to call for Noël, and Becky set out with all her thoughts in proportion—the one about herself and tennis; the one about Noël, whom she had come to love and learn with the evenings when René was late at the laboratory; the one about René, in whom she recognized the curious secret of power. But when she arrived at the school and found Noël's penciled note on the gatepost, an epidemic of revolt surged suddenly over her.

Dear Becky: Had daddy's schedule and lost it and do not know if you are coming or not. Mrs. Hume told me I could wait at her house, so please pick me up there if you get this?

NOËL

If there was one person Becky had no intention of encountering, it was Mrs. Dolores Hume. She knew this very fiercely and she didn't see how she should be expected to go to Mrs. Hume's house. She had by no means been drawn to the lady who had inspected her so hostilely in the bathtub—to put it mildly, she was not particular about ever seeing her again.

Her resentment turned against René. Looked at in any light, her position was that of a person of whom he was ashamed. One side of her understood the complications of his position, but in her fine glow of health after exercise, it seemed outrageous that anyone should have the opportunity to think of her in a belittling way. René's theories were very well, but she would have been a hundred times happier had they announced the engagement long before, even though every curious cat in the community stared at her for a month or two. Becky felt as if she had been kept in the kitchen, and she was developing a sense of inferiority. This, in turn, made her think of the schedule as a sort of tyranny, and several times lately she had wondered how much of herself she was giving up in the complete subservience of every hour of every day to another's judgment.

"He can call for Noël," she decided. "I've done my best all through. If he's so wise, he ought not to put me in such a situation."

An hour later, René was still unable to think where he had put her at all. He had planned the days for her, but he had never really thought before about how she would fill them up. Returning to his laboratory in a state of profound gloom, he increased his pace as he came in sight of the building, cursed with a new anxiety. He had been absent more than three hours, with the barometer steadily falling and three windows open; he could not remember whether he or Charles was to have spoken to the janitor about continuing the heat over the week-end. His jars, the precious water in his jars——He ran up the icy stairs of the old building, afraid of what he was going to see.

One closed jar went with a cracking plop as he stood panting inside the door. One thousand of them glistened in tense rows through three long rooms, and he held his breath, waiting for them to go off together, almost hearing the crackling, despairing sound they would make. He saw that another one was broken, and then another in a far row. The room was like ice, with a blizzard seeping through eight corners of every window; there was ice formed on the faucet.

On tiptoe, lest even a faint movement precipitate the nine hundred and ninety-seven catastrophes, he retreated to the hall; then his heart beat again as he heard the dull, reassuring rumble of the janitor's shovel in the cellar.

"Fire it up as far as you can!" he called down, and then descended another flight so as to be sure he was understood. "Make it as hot a blaze as possible, even if it is all"—he could not think of the word for kindling—"even if it is all small wood."

He hurried back to the laboratory, entering again on tiptoe. As he entered, two jars beside a north window cracked, but his hand, brushing the radiator, felt just the beginning of a faint and tepid warmth. He took off his overcoat, and then his coat, and tucked them in across one window, dragged out an emergency electric heater, and then turned on every electric appliance in the room. From moment to moment, he stopped and listened ominously, but there were no more of the short, disastrous dying cries. By the time he had isolated the five broken jars and checked up on the amount of ice in the others, there was a definite pulse of heat coming off the radiators.

As he still fussed mechanically around the room, his hands shaking, he heard Noël's voice in a lower hall, and she came upstairs with Dolores Hume, both of them bundled to the ears against the cold.

"Here you are, René," Dolores said cheerfully. "We've phoned here three times and all over town. We wanted Noël to stay to dinner, but she keeps thinking you'd be worried. What is all this about a schedule? Are you all catching trains?"

"What is what?" he answered dazedly. "You realize, Dolores, what has happened here in this room?"

"It's got very cold."

"The water in our jars froze. We almost lost them all!"

He heard the furnace door close, and then the janitor coming upstairs.

Furious at what seemed the indifference of the world, he repeated:

"We nearly lost them all!"

"Well, as long as you didn't——" Dolores fixed her eyes upon a vague spot far down the late battlefield of gleaming jars. "Since we're here, René, I want to say something to you—a thing that seems to me quite as important as your jars. There is something very beautiful about a widower being left alone with a little daughter to care for and to protect and to guide. It doesn't seem to me that anything so beautiful should be lightly destroyed."

For the second time that day, René started to throw his hands up in the air, but he had stretched his wrists a little the last time, and in his profound agitation he was not at all sure that he could catch them.

"There is no answer," he groaned. "Listen, Dolores; you must come to my laboratory often. There is something very beautiful in a platinum electrode."

"I am thinking only of Noël," said Dolores serenely.

At this point, the janitor, effectually concealed beneath a thick mask of coal dust, came into the room. It was Noël who first divined the fact that the janitor was Becky Snyder.

IV

Under those thoroughly unmethodical circumstances, the engagement of René and Becky was announced to the world—the world as personified and represented by Dolores Hume. But for René even that event was overshadowed by his astonishment at learning that the first jar had burst at the moment Becky came into his laboratory; that she had remembered that water expanded as it froze and guessed at the danger; that she had been working for three-quarters of an hour to start the furnace before he had arrived; and, finally, that she had taken care of the furnace for two years back in Bingham—"because there was nothing much else to do."

Dolores took it nicely, though she saw fit to remind Becky that she would be somewhat difficult to recognize if constantly observed under such extremely contrary conditions.

"I suppose it all has something to do with this schedule I hear so much about."

"I started the fire with the schedule," remarked Becky, and then amended herself when René jumped up with a suddenly agonized expression: "Not the one with the notes on it—that was behind the cushions of the car."

"It's too much for me," Dolores admitted. "I suppose you'll all end by sleeping here tonight—probably in the jars."

Noël bent double with laughter.

"Why don't we? Look on the schedule, daddy, and see if that's the thing to do."

More than Just a House

(*The Saturday Evening Post*, 24 June 1933)

"More than Just a House" was written at "La Paix" in April 1933. The *Post* paid $3000. It brought a fan letter from John O'Hara, then a Pittsburgh journalist:

> You've written another swell piece, doing again several of the things you do so well, and doing them in a single piece. Miss Jean Gunther, of the More Than Just a House Gunthers, was one of those girls for the writing about of whom you hold the exclusive franchise. . . . It was all really told when she told Lew Lowrie, 'Well, at least you've kissed one Gunther girl'. . . . the second thing you've done so well: Lowrie the climber; and I wonder why you do the climber so well. Is it the Irish in you? . . . Another thing you did was to take a rather fantastic little detail—the girl wearing bedroom slippers with Jodhpurs—and put it across by timing it just right. You got the old man's madness with the detail of the $20 he borrowed in 1892, and once again you dabbled successfully in death.

Fitzgerald replied with the since widely quoted letter about his own social insecurities: "So if I were elected King of Scotland tomorrow after graduating from Eton, Magdalene to Guards, with an embryonic history which tied me to the plantagonists, I would still be a parvenue."

This was the sort of thing Lew was used to—and he'd been around a good deal already. You came into an entrance hall, sometimes narrow New England Colonial, sometimes cautiously spacious. Once in the hall, the host said: "Clare"—or Virginia, or Darling—"this is Mr. Lowrie." The woman said, "How do you do, Mr. Lowrie," and Lew answered, "How do you do, Mrs. Woman." Then the man suggested, "How about a little cocktail?" And Lew lifted his brows apart and said, "Fine," in a tone that implied: "What hospitality—consideration—attention!" Those delicious canapés. "M'm'm! Madame, what are they—broiled feathers? Enough to spoil a stronger appetite than mine."

But Lew was on his way up, with six new suits of clothes, and he was getting into the swing of the thing. His name was up for a downtown club and he had his eye on a very modern bachelor apartment full of wrought-iron swinging gates—as if he were a baby inclined to topple downstairs—when he saved the life of the Gunther girl and his tastes underwent revision.

This was back in 1925, before the Spanish-American——No, before whatever it is that has happened since then. The Gunther girls had got off the train on the wrong side and were walking along arm in arm, with Amanda in the path of an approaching donkey engine. Amanda was rather tall, golden and proud, and the donkey engine was very squat and dark and determined. Lew had no time to speculate upon their respective chances in the approaching encounter; he lunged at Jean, who was nearest him, and as the two sisters clung together, startled, he pulled Amanda out of the iron pathway by such a hair's breadth that a piston cylinder touched her coat.

And so Lew's taste was changed in regard to architecture and interior decoration. At the Gunther house they served tea, hot or iced, sugar buns, gingerbread and hot rolls at half-past four. When he first went there he was embarrassed by his heroic status—for about five minutes. Then he learned that during the Civil War the grandmother had been saved by her own grandmother from a burning house in Montgomery County, that father had once saved ten men at sea and been recommended for the Carnegie medal, that when Jean was little a man had saved her from the surf at Cape May—that, in fact, all the Gunthers had gone on saving and being saved for the last fifty years and that their real debt to Lew was that now there would be no gap left in the tradition.

This was on the very wide, vine-curtained veranda ["The first thing I'd do would be tear off that monstrosity," said a visiting architect] which almost completely bounded the big square box of the house, circa 1880. The sisters, three of them, appeared now and then during the time Lew drank tea and talked to the older people. He was only twenty-six himself and he wished Amanda would stay uncovered long enough for him to look at her, but only Bess, the sixteen-year-old sister, was really in sight; in front of the two others interposed a white-flannel screen of young men.

"It was the quickness," said Mr. Gunther, pacing the long straw rug, "that second of coordination. Suppose you'd tried to warn them—never. Your subconscious mind saw that they were joined together—saw that if you pulled one, you pulled them both. One second, one thought, one motion. I remember in 1904——"

"Won't Mr. Lowrie have another piece of gingerbread?" asked the grandmother.

"Father, why don't you show Mr. Lowrie the apostles' spoons?" Bess proposed.

"What?" Her father stopped pacing. "Is Mr. Lowrie interested in old spoons?"

Lew was thinking at the moment of Amanda twisting somewhere between the glare of the tennis courts and the shadow of the veranda, through all the warmth and graciousness of the afternoon.

"Spoons? Oh, I've got a spoon, thank you."

"Apostles' spoons," Bess explained. "Father has one of the best collections in America. When he likes anybody enough he shows them the spoons. I thought, since you saved Amanda's life——"

He saw little of Amanda that afternoon—talked to her for a moment by the steps while a young man standing near tossed up a tennis racket and caught it by the handle with an impatient bend of his knees at each catch. The sun shopped among the yellow strands of her hair, poured around the rosy tan of her cheeks and spun along the arms that she regarded abstractedly as she talked to him.

"It's hard to thank a person for saving your life, Mr. Lowrie," she said. "Maybe you shouldn't have. Maybe it wasn't worth saving."

"Oh, yes, it was," said Lew, in a spasm of embarrassment.

"Well, I'd like to think so." She turned to the young man. "Was it, Allen?"

"It's a good enough life," Allen admitted, "if you go in for wooly blondes."

She turned her slender smile full upon Lew for a moment, and then aimed it a little aside, like a pocket torch that might dazzle him. "I'll always feel that you own me, Mr. Lowrie; my life is forfeit to you. You'll always have the right to take me back and put me down in front of that engine again."

Her proud mouth was a little overgracious about being saved, though Lew didn't realize it; it seemed to Amanda that it might at least have been someone in her own crowd. The Gunthers were a haughty family—haughty beyond all logic, because Mr. Gunther had once been presented at the Court of St. James's and remained slightly convalescent ever since. Even Bess was haughty, and it was Bess, eventually, who led Lew down to his car.

"It's a nice place," she agreed. "We've been going to modernize it, but we took a vote and decided to have the swimming pool repaired instead."

Lew's eyes lifted over her—she was like Amanda, except for the slightness of her and the childish disfigurement of a small wire across her teeth—up to the house with its decorative balconies outside the windows, its fickle gables, its gold-lettered, Swiss-chalet mottoes, the bulging projections of its many bays. Uncritically he regarded it; it seemed to him one of the finest houses he had ever known.

"Of course, we're miles from town, but there're always plenty of people. Father and mother go South after the Christmas holidays when we go back to school."

It was more than just a house, Lew decided as he drove away. It was a place where a lot of different things could go on at once—a private life for the older people, a private romance for each girl. Promoting himself, he chose his own corner—a swinging seat behind one of the drifts of vines that cut the veranda into quarters. But this was in 1925, when the ten thousand a year that Lew had come to command did not permit an indiscriminate crossing of social frontiers. He was received by the Gunthers and held at arm's length by them, and then gradually liked for the qualities that began to show through his awkwardness. A good-looking man on his way up can put directly into action the things he learns; Lew was never again quite so impressed by the suburban houses whose children lived upon rolling platforms in the street.

It was September before he was invited to the Gunthers' on an intimate scale—and this largely because Amanda's mother insisted upon it.

"He saved your life. I want him asked to this one little party."

But Amanda had not forgiven him for saving her life.

"It's just a dance for friends," she complained. "Let him come to Jean's debut in October—everybody'll think he's a business acquaintance of father's. After all, you can be nice to somebody without falling into their arms."

Mrs. Gunther translated this correctly as: "You can be awful to somebody without their knowing it"—and brusquely overrode her: "You can't have advantages without responsibilities," she said shortly.

Life had been opening up so fast for Lew that he had a black dinner coat instead of a purple one. Asked for dinner, he came early; and thinking to give him his share of attention when it was most convenient, Amanda walked with him into the tangled, out-of-hand garden. She wanted to be bored, but his gentle vitality disarmed her, made her look at him closely for almost the first time.

"I hear everywhere that you're a young man with a future," she said.

Lew admitted it. He boasted a little; he did not tell her that he had analyzed the spell which the Gunther house exerted upon him—his father had been gardener on a similar Maryland estate when he was a boy of five. His mother had helped him to remember that when he told her about the Gunthers. And now this garden was shot bright

with sunset, with Amanda one of its own flowers in her flowered
dress; he told her, in a rush of emotion, how beautiful she was, and
Amanda, excited by the prospect of impending hours with another
man, let herself encourage him. Lew had never been so happy as in
the moment before she stood up from the seat and put her hand on his
arm lightly.

"I do like you," she said. "You're very handsome. Do you know
that?"

The harvest dance took place in an L-shaped space formed by the
clearing of three rooms. Thirty young people were there, and a dozen
of their elders, but there was no crowding, for the big windows were
opened to the veranda and the guests danced against the wide,
illimitable night. A country orchestra alternated with the
phonograph, there was mildly calculated cider punch, and an air of
safety beside the open bookshelves of the library and the oil portraits
of the living room, as though this were one of an endless series of
dances that had taken place here in the past and would take place
again.

"Thought you never would cut in," Bess said to Lew. "You'd be
foolish not to. I'm the best dancer of us three, and I'm much the
smartest one. Jean is the jazzy one, the most *chic*, but I think it's *passé*
to be jazzy and play the traps and neck every second boy. Amanda is
the beauty, of course. But I'm going to be the Cinderella, Mr. Lowrie.
They'll be the two wicked sisters, and gradually you'll find I'm the
most attractive and get all hot and bothered about me."

There was an interval of intervals before Lew could maneuver
Amanda to his chosen segment of the porch. She was all radiant and
shimmering. More than content to be with him, she tried to relax with
the creak of the settee. Then instinct told her that something was
about to happen.

Lew, remembering a remark of Jean's—"He asked me to marry
him, and he hadn't even kissed me"—could yet think of no graceful
way to assault Amanda; nevertheless he was determined to tell her
tonight that he was in love with her.

"This'll seem sudden," he ventured, "but you might as well
know. Please put me down on the list of those who'd like to have a
chance."

She was not surprised, but being deep in herself at the moment,
she was rather startled. Giving up the idea of relaxing, she sat
upright.

"Mr. Lowrie—can I call you by your first name?—can I tell you
something? No, I won't—yes, I will, because I like you now. I didn't
like you at first. How's that for frankness?"

"Is that what you wanted to tell me?"

"No. Listen. You met Mr. Horton—the man from New York—the tall man with the rather old-looking hair?"

"Yes." Lew felt a pang of premonition in his stomach.

"I'm engaged to him. You're the first to know—except mother suspects. Whee! Now I told you because you saved my life, so you do sort of own me—I wouldn't be here to be engaged, except for you." Then she was honestly surprised at his expression. "Heavens, don't look like that!" She regarded him, pained. "Don't tell me you've been secretly in love with me all these months. Why didn't I know? And now it's too late."

Lew tried a laugh.

"I hardly know you," he confessed. "I haven't had time to fall in love with you."

"Maybe I work quick. Anyhow, if you did, you'll have to forget it and be my friend." Finding his hand, she squeezed it. "A big night for this little girl, Mr. Lew; the chance of a lifetime. I've been afraid for two days that his bureau drawer would stick or the hot water would give out and he'd leave for civilization."

They were silent for a moment; then he asked:

"You very much in love with him?"

"Of course I am. I mean, I don't know. You tell me. I've been in love with so many people; how can I answer that? Anyhow, I'll get away from this old barn."

"This house? You want to get away from here? Why, this is a lovely old house."

She was astonished now, and then suddenly explosive:

"This old tomb! That's the chief reason I'm marrying George Horton. Haven't I stood it for twenty years? Haven't I begged mother and father on my knees to move into town? This—shack—where everybody can hear what everybody else says three rooms off, and father won't allow a radio, and not even a phone till last summer. I'm afraid even to ask a girl down from school—probably she'd go crazy listening to the shutters on a stormy night."

"It's a darn nice old house," he said automatically.

"Nice and quaint," she agreed. "Glad you like it. People who don't have to live here generally do, but you ought to see us alone in it—if there's a family quarrel you have to stay with it for hours. It all comes down to father wanting to live fifty miles from anywhere, so we're condemned to rot. I'd rather live in a three-room apartment in town!" Shocked by her own vehemence, she broke off. "Anyhow," she insisted, "it may seem nice to you, but it's a nuisance to us."

A man pulled the vines apart and peered at them, claimed her and pulled her to her feet; when she was gone, Lew went over the railing with a handhold and walked into the garden; he walked far enough away so that the lights and music from the house were blurred into one entity like a stage effect, like an approaching port viewed from a deck at night.

"I only saw her four times," he said to himself. "Four times isn't much. Eeney-meeney-miney-moe—what could I expect in four times? I shouldn't feel anything at all." But he was engulfed by fear. What had he just begun to know that now he might never know? What had happened in these moments in the garden this afternoon, what was the excitement that had blacked out in the instant of its birth? The scarcely emergent young image of Amanda—he did not want to carry it with him forever. Gradually he realized a truth behind his grief: He had come too late for her; unknown to him, she had been slipping away through the years. With the odds against him, he had managed to found himself on solid rock, and then, looking around for the girl, discovered that she had just gone. "Sorry, just gone out; just left; just gone." Too late in every way—even for the house. Thinking over her tirade, Lew saw that he had come too late for the house; it was the house of a childhood from which the three girls were breaking away, the house of an older generation, sufficient unto them. To a younger generation it was pervaded with an aura of completion and fulfillment beyond their own power to add to. It was just old.

Nevertheless, he recalled the emptiness of many grander mansions built in more spectacular fashions—empty to him, at any rate, since he had first seen the Gunther place three months before. Something humanly valuable would vanish with the break-up of this family. The house itself, designed for reading long Victorian novels around an open fire of the evening, didn't even belong to an architectural period worthy of restoration.

Lew circled an outer drive and stood quiet in the shadow of a rosebush as a pair of figures strolled down from the house; by their voices he recognized Jean and Allen Parks.

"Me, I'm going to New York," Jean said, "whether they let me or not. . . . No, not now, you nut. I'm not in that mood."

"Then what mood are you in?"

"Not in any mood. I'm only envious of Amanda because she's hooked this M'sieur, and now she'll go to Long Island and live in a house instead of a mouse trap. Oh, Jake, this business of being simple and swell——"

They passed out of hearing. It was between dances, and Lew saw the colors of frocks and the quick white of shirt fronts in the window-panes as the guests flowed onto the porch. He looked up at the second floor as a light went on there—he had a conception of the second floor as walled with crowded photographs; there must be bags full of old materials, and trunks with costumes and dress-making forms, and old dolls' houses, and an overflow, everywhere along the vacant walls, of books for all generations—many childhoods side by side drifting into every corner.

Another couple came down the walk from the house, and feeling that inadvertently he had taken up too strategic a position, Lew moved away; but not before he had identified the pair as Amanda and her man from New York.

"What would you think if I told you I had another proposal tonight?"

". . . be surprised at all."

"A very worthy young man. Saved my life. . . . Why weren't you there on that occasion, Bubbles? You'd have done it on a grand scale, I'm sure."

Standing square in front of the house, Lew looked at it more searchingly. He felt a kinship with it—not precisely that, for the house's usefulness was almost over and his was just beginning; rather, the sense of superior unity that the thoughtful young feel for the old, sense of the grandparent. More than only a house. He would like to be that much used up himself before being thrown out on the ash heap at the end. And then, because he wanted to do some courteous service to it while he could, if only to dance with the garrulous little sister, he pulled a brash pocket comb through his hair and went inside.

II

The man with the smiling scar approached Lew once more.

"This is probably," he announced, "the biggest party ever given in New York."

"I even heard you the first time you told me," agreed Lew cheerfully.

"But, on the other hand," qualified the man, "I thought the same thing at a party two years ago, in 1927. Probably they'll go on getting bigger and bigger. You play polo, don't you?"

"Only in the back yard," Lewis assured him. "I said I'd like to play. I'm a serious business man."

"Somebody told me you were the polo star." The man was somewhat disappointed. "I'm a writer myself. A humani—a humanitarian. I've been trying to help out a girl over there in that room where the champagne is. She's a lady. And yet, by golly, she's the only one in the room that can't take care of herself."

"Never try to take care of anybody," Lew advised him. "They hate you for it."

But although the apartment, or rather the string of apartments and penthouses pressed into service for the affair, represented the best resources of the New York sky line, it was only limited metropolitan space at that, and moving among the swirls of dancers, thinned with dawn, Lew found himself finally in the chamber that the man had spoken of. For a moment he did not recognize the girl who had assumed the role of entertaining the glassy-eyed citizenry, chosen by natural selection to personify dissolution; then, as she issued a blanket invitation to a squad of Gaiety beauties to come south and recuperate on her Maryland estates, he recognized Jean Gunther.

She was the dark Gunther—dark and shining and driven. Lew, living in New York now, had seen none of the family since Amanda's marriage four years ago. Driving her home a quarter of an hour later, he extracted what news he could; and then left her in the dawn at the door of her apartment, mussed and awry, yet still proud, and tottering with absurd formality as she thanked him and said good night.

He called next afternoon and took her to tea in Central Park.

"I am," she informed him, "the child of the century. Other people claim to be the child of the century, but I'm actually the child of the century. And I'm having the time of my life at it."

Thinking back to another period—of young men on the tennis courts and hot buns in the afternoon, and of wistaria and ivy climbing along the ornate railings of a veranda—Lew became as moral as it was possible to be in that well-remembered year of 1929.

"What are you getting out of it? Why don't you invest in some reliable man—just a sort of background?"

"Men are good to invest money for you," she dodged neatly. "Last year one darling spun out my allowance so it lasted ten months instead of three."

"But how about marrying some candidate?"

"I haven't got any love," she said. "Actually, I know four—five—I know six millionaires I could maybe marry. This little girl from Carroll County. It's just too many. Now, if somebody that had everything came along——" She looked at Lew appraisingly. "You've improved, for example."

"I should say I have," admitted Lew, laughing. "I even go to first nights. But the most beautiful thing about me is I remember my old friends, and among them are the lovely Gunther girls of Carroll County."

"You're very nice," she said. "Were you terribly in love with Amanda?"

"I thought so, anyhow."

"I saw her last week. She's super-Park Avenue and very busy having Park Avenue babies. She considers me rather disreputable and tells her friends about our magnificent plantation in the old South."

"Do you ever go down to Maryland?"

"Do I though? I'm going Sunday night, and spend two months there saving enough money to come back on. When mother died"—she paused—"I suppose you knew mother died—I came into a little cash, and I've still got it, but it has to be stretched, see?"—she pulled her napkin cornerwise—"by tactful investing. I think the next step is a quiet summer on the farm."

Lew took her to the theater the next night, oddly excited by the encounter. The wild flush of the times lay upon her; he was conscious of her physical pulse going at some abnormal rate, but most of the young women he knew were being hectic, save the ones caught up tight in domesticity.

He had no criticism to make—behind that lay the fact that he would not have dared to criticize her. Having climbed from a nether rung of the ladder, he had perforce based his standards on what he could see from where he was at the moment. Far be it from him to tell Jean Gunther how to order her life.

Getting off the train in Baltimore three weeks later, he stepped into the peculiar heat that usually preceded an electric storm. He passed up the regular taxis and hired a limousine for the long ride out to Carroll County, and as he drove through rich foliage, moribund in midsummer, between the white fences that lined the rolling road, many years fell away and he was again the young man, starved for a home, who had first seen the Gunther house four years ago. Since then he had occupied a twelve-room apartment in New York, rented a summer mansion on Long Island, but his spirit, warped by loneliness and grown gypsy with change, turned back persistently to this house.

Inevitably it was smaller than he had expected, a small, big house, roomy rather than spacious. There was a rather intangible neglect about it—the color of the house had never been anything but a brown-green relict of the sun; Lew had never known the stable to lean otherwise than as the Tower of Pisa, nor the garden to grow any other way than plebeian and wild.

Jean was on the porch—not, as she had prophesied, in the role of gingham queen or rural equestrienne, but very Rue-de-la-Paix against the dun cushions of the swinging settee. There was the stout, colored butler whom Lew remembered and who pretended, with racial guile, to remember Lew delightedly. He took the bag to Amanda's old room, and Lew stared around it a little before he went downstairs. Jean and Bess were waiting over a cocktail on the porch.

It struck him that Bess had made a leaping change out of childhood into something that was not quite youth. About her beauty there was a detachment, almost an impatience, as though she had not asked for the gift and considered it rather a burden; to a young man, the gravity of her face might have seemed formidable.

"How is your father?" Lew asked.

"He won't be down tonight," Bess answered. "He's not well. He's over seventy, you know. People tire him. When we have guests, he has dinner upstairs."

"It would be better if he ate upstairs all the time," Jean remarked, pouring the cocktails.

"No, it wouldn't," Bess contradicted her. "The doctors said it wouldn't. There's no question about that."

Jean turned in a rush to Lew. "For over a year Bess has hardly left this house. We could——"

"What junk!" her sister said impatiently. "I ride every morning."

"——we could get a nurse who would do just as well."

Dinner was formal, with candles on the table and the two young women in evening dresses. Lew saw that much was missing—the feeling that the house was bursting with activity, with expanding life—all this had gone. It was difficult for the diminished clan to do much more than inhabit the house. There was not a moving up into vacated places; there was simply an anachronistic staying on between a vanishing past and an incalculable future.

Midway through dinner, Lew lifted his head at a pause in the conversation, but what he had confused with a mutter of thunder was a long groan from the floor above, followed by a measured speech, whose words were interrupted by the quick clatter of Bess' chair.

"You know what I ordered. Just so long as I am the head of——"

"It's father." Momentarily Jean looked at Lew as if she thought the situation was faintly humorous, but at his concerned face, she continued seriously, "You might as well know. It's senile dementia. Not dangerous. Sometimes he's absolutely himself. But it's hard on Bess."

Bess did not come down again; after dinner, Lew and Jean went into the garden, splattered with faint drops before the approaching rain. Through the vivid green twilight Lew followed her long dress, spotted with bright red roses—it was the first of that fashion he had ever seen; in the tense hush he had an illusion of intimacy with her, as though they shared the secrets of many years and, when she caught at his arm suddenly at a rumble of thunder, he drew her around slowly with his other arm and kissed her shaped, proud mouth.

"Well, at least you've kissed one Gunther girl," Jean said lightly. "How was it? And don't you think you're taking advantage of us, being unprotected out here in the country?"

He looked at her to see if she were joking, and with a swift laugh she seized his arm again. It was raining in earnest, and they fled toward the house—to find Bess on her knees in the library, setting light to an open fire.

"Father's all right," she assured them. "I don't like to give him the medicine till the last minute. He's worrying about some man that lent him twenty dollars in 1892." She lingered, conscious of being a third party, and yet impelled to play her mother's role and impart an initial solidarity before she retired. The storm broke, shrieking in white at the windows, and Bess took the opportunity to fly to the windows upstairs, calling down after a moment:

"The telephone's trying to ring. Do you think it's safe to answer it?"

"Perfectly," Jean called back, "or else they wouldn't ring." She came close to Lewis in the center of the room, away from the white, quivering windows.

"It's strange having you here right now. I don't mind saying I'm glad you're here. But if you weren't, I suppose we'd get along just as well."

"Shall I help Bess close the windows?" Lew asked.

Simultaneously, Bess called downstairs:

"Nobody seemed to be on the phone, and I don't like holding it."

A ripping crash of thunder shook the house and Jean moved into Lew's arm, breaking away as Bess came running down the stairs with a yelp of dismay.

"The lights are out up there," she said. "I never used to mind storms when I was little. Father used to make us sit on the porch sometimes, remember?"

There was a dazzle of light around all the windows of the first floor, reflecting itself back and forth in mirrors, so that every room was pervaded with a white glare; there followed a sound as of a million matches struck at once, so loud and terrible that the thunder rolling down seemed secondary; then a splintering noise separated itself out, and Bess' voice:

"That struck!"

Once again came the sickening lightning, and through a rolling pandemonium of sound they groped from window to window till Jean cried: "It's William's room! There's a tree on it!"

In a moment, Lew had flung wide the kitchen door and saw, in the next glare, what had happened: The great tree, in falling, had divided the lean-to from the house proper.

"Is William there?" he demanded.

"Probably. He should be."

Gathering up his courage, Lew dashed across the twenty feet of new marsh, and with a waffle iron smashed in the nearest window. Inundated with sheet rain and thunder, he yet realized that the storm had moved off from overhead, and his voice was strong as he called: "William! You all right?"

No answer.

"William!"

He paused and there came a quiet answer:

"Who dere?"

"You all right?"

"I wanna know who dere."

"The tree fell on you. Are you hurt?"

There was a sudden peal of laughter from the shack as William emerged mentally from dark and atavistic suspicions of his own. Again and again the pealing laughter rang out.

"Hurt? Not me hurt. Nothin' hurt me. I'm never better, as they say. Nothin' hurt me."

Irritated by his melting clothes, Lew said brusquely:

"Well, whether you know it or not, you're penned up in there. You've got to try and get out this window. That tree's too big to push off tonight."

Half an hour later, in his room, Lew shed the wet pulp of his clothing by the light of a single candle. Lying naked on the bed, he regretted that he was in poor condition, unnecessarily fatigued with the exertion of pulling a fat man out a window. Then, over the dull rumble of the thunder he heard the phone again in the hall, and Bess' voice, "I can't hear a word. You'll have to get a better connection," and for thirty seconds he dozed, to wake with a jerk at the sound of his door opening.

"Who's that?" he demanded, pulling the quilt up over himself.

The door opened slowly.

"Who's that?"

There was a chuckle; a last pulse of lightning showed him three tense, blue-veined fingers, and then a man's voice whispered: "I only wanted to know whether you were in for the night, dear. I worry—I worry."

The door closed cautiously, and Lew realized that old Gunther was on some nocturnal round of his own. Aroused, he slipped into his sole change of clothes, listening to Bess for the third time at the phone.

"——in the morning," she said. "Can't it wait? We've got to get a connection ourselves."

Downstairs he found Jean surprisingly spritely before the fire. She made a sign to him, and he went and stood above her, indifferent suddenly to her invitation to kiss her. Trying to decide how he felt, he brushed his hand lightly along her shoulder.

"Your father's wandering around. He came in my room. Don't you think you ought to——"

"Always does it," Jean said. "Makes the nightly call to see if we're in bed."

Lew stared at her sharply; a suspicion that had been taking place in his subconscious assumed tangible form. A bland, beautiful expression stared back at him; but his ears lifted suddenly up the stairs to Bess still struggling with the phone.

"All right. I'll try to take it that way.... P-ay-double ess-ee-dee— 'p-a-s-s-e-d.' All right; ay-double you-ay-wy. 'Passed away?' " Her voice, as she put the phrase together, shook with sudden panic. "What did you say—'Amanda Gunther passed away'?"

Jean looked at Lew with funny eyes.

"Why does Bess try to take that message now? Why not——"

"Shut up!" he ordered. "This is something serious."

"I don't see——"

Alarmed by the silence that seeped down the stairs, Lew ran up and found Bess sitting beside the telephone table holding the receiver in her lap, just breathing and staring, breathing and staring. He took the receiver and got the message:

"Amanda passed away quietly, giving life to a little boy."

Lew tried to raise Bess from the chair, but she sank back, full of dry sobbing.

"Don't tell father tonight."

How did it matter if this was added to that old store of confused memories? It mattered to Bess, though.

"Go away," she whispered. "Go tell Jean."

Some premonition had reached Jean, and she was at the foot of the stairs while he descended.

"What's the matter?"

He guided her gently back into the library.

"Amanda is dead," he said, still holding her.

She gathered up her forces and began to wail, but he put his hand over her mouth.

"You've been drinking!" he said. "You've got to pull yourself together. You can't put anything more on your sister."

Jean pulled herself together visibly—first her proud mouth and then her whole body—but what might have seemed heroic under other conditions seemed to Lew only reptilian, a fine animal effort— all he had begun to feel about her went out in a few ticks of the clock.

In two hours the house was quiet under the simple ministrations of a retired cook whom Bess had sent for; Jean was put to sleep with a sedative by a physician from Ellicott City. It was only when Lew was in bed at last that he thought really of Amanda, and broke suddenly, and only for a moment. She was gone out of the world, his second— no, his third love—killed in single combat. He thought rather of the dripping garden outside, and nature so suddenly innocent in the clearing night. If he had not been so tired he would have dressed and walked through the long-stemmed, clinging ferns, and looked once more impersonally at the house and its inhabitants—the broken old, the youth breaking and growing old with it, the other youth escaping into dissipation. Walking through broken dreams, he came in his imagination to where the falling tree had divided William's bedroom from the house, and paused there in the dark shadow, trying to piece together what he thought about the Gunthers.

"It's degenerate business," he decided—"all this hanging on to the past. I've been wrong. Some of us are going ahead, and these people and the roof over them are just push-overs for time. I'll be glad to leave it for good and get back to something fresh and new and clean in Wall Street tomorrow."

Only once was he wakened in the night, when he heard the old man quavering querulously about the twenty dollars that he had borrowed in '92. He heard Bess' voice soothing him, and then, just before he went to sleep, the voice of the old Negress blotting out both voices.

III

Lew's business took him frequently to Baltimore, but with the years it seemed to change back into the Baltimore that he had known before he met the Gunthers. He thought of them often, but after the night of Amanda's death he never went there. By 1933, the role that the family had played in his life seemed so remote—except for the unforgettable fact that they had formed his ideas about how life was lived—that he could drive along the Frederick Road to where it dips into Carroll County before a feeling of recognition crept over him. Impelled by a formless motive, he stopped his car.

It was deep summer; a rabbit crossed the road ahead of him and a squirrel did acrobatics on an arched branch. The Gunther house was up the next crossroad and five minutes away—in half an hour he could satisfy his curiosity about the family; yet he hesitated. With painful consequences, he had once tried to repeat the past, and now, in normal times, he would have driven on with a feeling of leaving the past well behind him; but he had come to realize recently that life was not always a progress, nor a search for new horizons, nor a going away. The Gunthers were part of him; he would not be able to bring to new friends the exact things that he had brought to the Gunthers. If the memory of them became extinct, then something in himself became extinct also.

The squirrel's flight on the branch, the wind nudging at the leaves, the cock splitting distant air, the creep of sunlight transpiring through the immobility, lulled him into an adolescent trance, and he sprawled back against the leather for a moment without problems. He loafed for ten minutes before the "k-dup, k-dup, k-dup" of a walking horse came around the next bend of the road. The horse bore a girl in Jodhpur breeches, and bending forward, Lew recognized Bess Gunther.

He scrambled from the car. The horse shied as Bess recognized Lew and pulled up. "Why, Mr. Lowrie! . . . Hey! Hoo-oo there, girl! . . . Where did you arrive from? Did you break down?"

It was a lovely face, and a sad face, but it seemed to Lew that some new quality made it younger—as if she had finally abandoned the cosmic sense of responsibility which had made her seem older than her age four years ago.

"I was thinking about you all," he said. "Thinking of paying you a visit." Detecting a doubtful shadow in her face, he jumped to a conclusion and laughed. "I don't mean a visit; I mean a call. I'm solvent—sometimes you have to add that these days."

She laughed too: "I was only thinking the house was full and where would we put you."

"I'm bound for Baltimore anyhow. Why not get off your rocking horse and sit in my car a minute."

She tied the mare to a tree and got in beside him.

He had not realized that flashing fairness could last so far into the twenties—only when she didn't smile, he saw from three small thoughtful lines that she was always a grave girl—he had a quick recollection of Amanda on an August afternoon, and looking at Bess, he recognized all that he remembered of Amanda.

"How's your father?"

"Father died last year. He was bedridden a year before he died." Her voice was in the singsong of something often repeated. "It was just as well."

"I'm sorry. How about Jean? Where is she?"

"Jean married a Chinaman—I mean she married a man who lives in China. I've never seen him."

"Do you live alone, then?"

"No, there's my aunt." She hesitated. "Anyhow, I'm getting married next week."

Inexplicably, he had the old sense of loss in his diaphragm.

"Congratulations! Who's the unfortunate——"

"From Philadelphia. The whole party went over to the races this afternoon. I wanted to have a last ride with Juniper."

"Will you live in Philadelphia?"

"Not sure. We're thinking of building another house on the place, tear down the old one. Of course, we might remodel it."

"Would that be worth doing?"

"Why not?" she said hastily. "We could use some of it, the architects think."

"You're fond of it, aren't you?"

Bess considered.

"I wouldn't say it was just my idea of modernity. But I'm a sort of a home girl." She accentuated the words ironically. "I never went over very big in Baltimore, you know—the family failure. I never had the sort of thing Amanda and Jean had."

"Maybe you didn't want it."

"I thought I did when I was young."

The mare neighed peremptorily and Bess backed out of the car.

"So that's the story, Lew Lowrie, of the last Gunther girl. You always did have a sort of yen for us, didn't you?"

"Didn't I! If I could possibly stay in Baltimore, I'd insist on coming to your wedding."

At the lost expression on her face, he wondered to whom she was handing herself, a very precious self. He knew more about people now, and he felt the steel beneath the softness in her, the girders showing through the gentle curves of cheek and chin. She was an exquisite person, and he hoped that her husband would be a good man.

When she had ridden off into a green lane, he drove tentatively toward Baltimore. This was the end of a human experience and it released old images that regrouped themselves about him—if he had married one of the sisters; supposing——The past, slipping away under the wheels of his car, crunched awake his acuteness.

"Perhaps I was always an intruder in that family. . . . But why on earth was that girl riding in bedroom slippers?"

At the crossroads store he stopped to get cigarettes. A young clerk searched the case with country slowness.

"Big wedding up at the Gunther place," Lew remarked.

"Hah? Miss Bess getting married?"

"Next week. The wedding party's there now."

"Well, I'll be dog! Wonder what they're going to sleep on, since Mark H. Bourne took the furniture away?"

"What's that? What?"

"Month ago Mark H. Bourne took all the furniture and everything else while Miss Bess was out riding—they mortgaged on it just before Gunther died. They say around here she ain't got a stitch except them riding clothes. Mark H. Bourne was good and sore. His claim was they sold off all the best pieces of furniture without his knowing it. . . . Now, that's ten cents I owe you."

"What do she and her aunt live on?"

"Never heard about an aunt—I only been here a year. She works the truck garden herself; all she buys from us is sugar, salt and coffee."

Anything was possible these times, yet Lew wondered what incredibly fantastic pride had inspired her to tell that lie.

He turned his car around and drove back to the Gunther place. It was a desperately forlorn house he came to, and a jungled garden; one side of the veranda had slipped from the brick pillars and sloped to the ground; a shingle job, begun and abandoned, rotted paintless on the roof, a broken pane gaped from the library window.

Lew went in without knocking. A voice challenged him from the dining room and he walked toward it, his feet loud on the rugless floor, through rooms empty of stick and book, empty of all save casual dust. Bess Gunther, wearing the cheapest of house dresses, rose from the packing box on which she sat, with fright in her eyes; a tin spoon rattled on the box she was using as a table.

"Have you been kidding me?" he demanded. "Are you actually living like this?"

"It's you." She smiled in relief; then, with visible effort, she spurred herself into amenities:

"Take a box, Mr. Lowrie. Have a canned-goods box—they're superior; the grain is better. And welcome to the open spaces. Have a cigar, a glass of champagne, have some rabbit stew and meet my fiancé."

"Stop that."

"All right," she agreed.

"Why didn't you go and live with some relatives?"

"Haven't got any relatives. Jean's in China."

"What are you doing? What do you expect to happen?"

"I was waiting for you, I guess."

"What do you mean?"

"You always seemed to turn up. I thought if you turned up, I'd make a play for you. But when it came to the point, I thought I'd better lie. I seem to lack the S.A. my sisters had."

Lew pulled her up from the box and held her with his fingers by her waist.

"Not to me."

In the hour since Lew had met her on the road the vitality seemed to have gone out of her; she looked up at him very tired.

"So you liked the Gunthers," she whispered. "You liked us all."

Lew tried to think, but his heart beat so quick that he could only sit her back on the box and pace along the empty walls.

"We'll get married," he said. "I don't know whether I love you— I don't even know you—I know the notion of your being in want or trouble makes me physically sick." Suddenly he went down on both knees in front of her so that she would not seem so unbearably small and helpless. "Miss Bess Gunther, so it was you I was meant to love all the while."

"Don't be so anxious about it," she laughed. "I'm not used to being loved. I wouldn't know what to do; I never got the trick of it." She looked down at him, shy and fatigued. "So here we are. I told you years ago that I had the makings of Cinderella."

He took her hand; she drew it back instinctively and then replaced it in his. "Beg your pardon. Not even used to being touched. But I'm not afraid of you, if you stay quiet and don't move suddenly."

It was the same old story of reserve Lew could not fathom, motives reaching back into a past he did not share. With the three girls, facts seemed to reveal themselves precipitately, pushing up through the gay surface; they were always unsuspected things, currents and predilections alien to a man who had been able to shoot in a straight line always.

"I was the conservative sister," Bess said. "I wasn't any less pleasure loving but with three girls, somebody has to play the boy, and gradually that got to be my part. . . . Yes, touch me like that. Touch my cheek. I want to be touched; I want to be held. And I'm glad it's you; but you've got to go slow; you've got to be careful. I'm afraid I'm the kind of person that's forever. I'll live with you and die for you, but I never knew what halfway meant. . . . Yes, that's the wrist. Do you like it? I've had a lot of fun looking at myself in the last month, because there's one long mirror upstairs that was too big to take out."

Lew stood up. "All right, we'll start like that. I'll be so healthy that I'll make you all healthy again."

"Yes, like that," she agreed.

"Suppose we begin by setting fire to this house."

"Oh, no!" She took him seriously. "In the first place, it's insured. In the second place——"

"All right, we'll just get out. We'll get married in Baltimore, or Ellicott City if you'd rather."

"How about Juniper? I can't go off and leave her."

"We'll leave her with the young man at the store."

"The house isn't mine. It's all mortgaged away, but they let me live here—I guess it was remorse after they took even our old music, and our old scrapbooks. They didn't have a chance of getting a tenant, anyhow."

Minute by minute, Lew found out more about her, and liked what he found, but he saw that the love in her was all incrusted with the sacrificial years, and that he would have to be gardener to it for a while. The task seemed attractive.

"You lovely," he told her. "You lovely! We'll survive, you and I because you're so nice and I'm so convinced about it."

"And about Juniper—will she survive if we go away like this?"

"Juniper too."

She frowned and then smiled—and this time really smiled—and said: "Seems to me, you're falling in love."

"Speak for yourself. My opinion is that this is going to be the best thing ever happened."

"I'm going to help. I insist on——"

They went out together—Bess changed into her riding habit, but there wasn't another article that she wanted to bring with her. Backing through the clogging weeds of the garden, Lew looked at the house over his shoulder. "Next week or so we'll decide what to do about that."

It was a bright sunset—the creep of rosy light that played across the blue fenders of the car and across their crazily happy faces moved across the house too—across the paralyzed door of the ice house, the rusting tin gutters, the loose-swinging shutter, the cracked cement of the front walk, the burned place of last year's rubbish back of the tennis court. Whatever its further history, the whole human effort of collaboration was done now. The purpose of the house was achieved—finished and folded—it was an effort toward some commonweal, an effort difficult to estimate, so closely does it press against us still.

I Got Shoes

(*The Saturday Evening Post*, 23 September 1933)

"I Got Shoes" was written at "La Paix" in July 1933. The *Post* paid
$2500—a drop of $1500 in two years. The magazine was having its own
problems. Although circulation held at 2,850,000, advertising was down
drastically as the 200-page issues of the Twenties gave way to 76-page
issues. The year 1933 was given over to work on *Tender Is the Night*, which
Fitzgerald interrupted to write only three stories: "More than Just a House,"
"I Got Shoes," and "The Family Bus." The least successful of these stories is
"I Got Shoes"; but it treats an idea that was much on Fitzgerald's mind and
which he was developing in *Tender*—the price of professionalism.

The Lovely Thing hurried into the hotel, rising on the balls of her
feet with each step, and bumped on her heels before the desk clerk
with an expression of "Here I am!" All the clerks were beginning to
know vaguely who she was—a passed debutante who had done much
dancing in the big ballroom several years before and was now
connected with the city's principal paper.

"Good morning," said the clerk.

"I have an appointment with"—the Lovely Thing paused,
savoring the sweetness of her words—"with Miss Nell Margery."

"Oh." The clerk became more sprightly, but was not properly
overwhelmed. "You're Miss——" He glanced at a card. "Miss
Battles?"

Haughtily, she let the question pass.

"I was to announce you anyhow." And he added familiarly, "If
you knew how many girls've tried to crash her suite in the last twenty-
four hours! We don't even send the flowers up any more. Oh, hello,
this is the desk." Johanna felt the change in his tone. "Miss Battles is
downstairs." And she fumed a little. Of course this young man could
not be expected to know that society in this city still held itself rather
above the stage—even above the best young actress in America.
Nevertheless, her attitude toward Miss Margery underwent a certain
revision, and encountering her friend Teeny Fay near the elevator she
stopped a moment; let the great Nell Margery take a turn at waiting.

"How late were you up last night?" asked Teeny.

"Till two. Then I had to go to the office. How did it come out?"

"Oh, I smoothed her down and somebody smoothed him down. I'll tell you about it if you'll come have a glass of beer—I'm dead on my feet." She groaned and then came alive suddenly. "Say, I just rode down in the elevator with Nell Margery's maid."

"I'm on my way——"

"She's French and she was warm and bothered. She was complaining to the housekeeper because Nell Margery hadn't gotten one of her trunks of shoes! *One* of her trunks of shoes! And I've got three pairs."

"I know," Johanna asserted eagerly. "I read that she was too stingy to throw away any shoes she ever had. There's a warehouse where she has dozens of trunks of shoes, all of them practically new." Johanna paused regretfully. "Still, I suppose they're mostly out of style now."

Suddenly, conscience-stricken, she said, "But she's waiting for me!"—and rushed for a departing elevator.

"What? Why is she?" Teeny cried after her.

"Newspaper!" The gates shut behind Johanna.

Meanwhile, sixteen floors above, Miss Margery was discussing her future with a handsome weatherworn man named Livingstone, just arrived from New York and, also, in the tradition of his famous namesake, recently arrived from parts unknown. His course toward Miss Margery had indeed begun at a station marked only by a Mayan image in the Brazilian jungle, proceeded down an unnamed river into the Branco, thence down the Negro and the Amazon to the sea, and northward in a fruit boat, and southward in a train. But though he had come from strange places, it was upon a familiar quest.

"——so it just occurred to me you might have changed your mind," he was saying.

"I haven't," confessed Miss Margery. "When an actress marries a society man——"

"I object to that phrase."

"——well, whatever you are—they're both taking a chance for the sake of vanity. He wants to parade her celebrity through his world, and she wants to parade his background through hers. 'Vanity Fair, saith the prophet'—or you know what I mean."

Her face was heart-shaped, an impression added to by honey-colored pointed-back hair that accentuated the two lovely rounds of her temples. Her eyes were large almonds, with the curve amended by classically penciled eyebrows, so that the effect during one of her rare smiles was a rakish gleam. At these times it was a face so merry that it was impossible not to smile back into the white mirrors of her teeth— the whole area around her parted lips was a lovely little circle of delight. When she grew grave again she was once more a keyboard, all resonant and gleaming—a generation of theatergoers had formed the habit of concentrating their attention on this face as it reflected the slightest adventures and responses of Nell Margery's heart.

"But we've got more of a basis than that," Livingstone objected. "God knows, I'm only happy working."

"Yes?" she said skeptically.

"I work as hard as you do, young woman!"

"You mean you play as hard as I work."

He smoldered resentfully in the embers of this old quarrel.

"Because I can afford to do things that don't bring in money——"

It was at this point that Miss Johanna Battles was announced.

"I won't be long," Nell promised him. "She's the niece of a great friend of mine. She does some society stuff for the paper here and I promised to see her."

Livingstone nodded moodily and looked about for something to read; Nell opened the door and greeted Johanna in that voice so identical with her beauty that, as far as it chose to reach, her beauty seemed to flow into the intervening space, dominating it, occupying it corporeally by a process of infiltration.

"I'm always glad to talk to a niece of Miss Walters. I think the best thing is for us to go into my bedroom. We can talk better there."

Johanna followed her into the bedroom, took the proffered chair, and Nell sat on the bed.

"You look like your aunt. She told me you wanted to go on the stage."

"Oh, no," said Johanna modestly. "I was in a few Little Theater plays last year, but now I'm a newspaper woman."

"You've given up the other idea?"

"Yes. I still do a little publicity for them—I suppose because I just like to hang around there." She laughed apologetically. "The lure of the stage—I was there till two o'clock last night."

"Have you got a good Little Theater here?"

"I suppose so." Again Johanna laughed. "Off and on. Last night everybody went to pieces again."

Miss Margery stared.

"Went to pieces?"

"Did they! I'll say they did. For two hours. I'll bet you could hear it blocks away."

"You mean a girl got hysterical? I've seen that happen after a forty-eight-hour rehearsal—usually with the girls you'd never suspect of being nervous."

"Oh, this wasn't just girls," Johanna assured her. "This was a woman and two girls and a man. They had to get a doctor for the man. Once they were all yelling together.''

Nell looked puzzled.

"I don't quite understand," she said. "Was this a drinking party?"

"No, no, this was a play." Johanna tried to think of some way to explain more clearly, but gave it up. "They just went to pieces, that's all. I don't think it showed much till the last act, but afterwards in the dressing rooms—zowie!"

Nell looked thoughtful for a moment and Johanna couldn't help wondering why she should be interested in such a thing. In any case she was here to get an interview; so she began.

"Tell me, Miss——" But she was interrupted.

"Why, I thought the Little Theaters—they'd——" Nell broke off. "Of course I can remember lots of cases of people going up in the air—in pictures——"

"Why, I thought it happened all the time. I've seen lots of movies where——"

"I mean really. Still, I have seen it happen. But all the people who 'went to pieces,' as you call it, on duty—well, they're in sanitariums, or hunting for jobs. I suppose that's unfair—but it certainly is one of the real differences between an amateur and a professional."

Johanna was restless. Miss Margery seemed inclined to continue indefinitely on this trivial subject, and she wished she had not mentioned it. Her own duty was to switch the interview back to the victim, and she was possessed with a sudden daring idea:

"Miss Margery——" She hesitated. "Miss Margery—somebody once told me you went in for collecting shoes."

Nell suddenly sat up from the pillow against which she leaned and bent slowly toward Johanna, her eyes like the cut face of jewels.

"Say-ee-ee!" she boomed resonantly, and then in a higher but equally formidable key, with a sudden new tang in the tone that Johanna's friends might have described as common. "Say-ee-ee! Who told you to ask me that? You go back and tell your paper I don't answer questions about my personal life."

Flustered, Johanna fumbled for an apology. Nell jumped up and was suddenly at the window, a glitter of leaves in a quick wind, a blond glow of summer lightning. Even in her state of intimidation Johanna noticed that she seemed to bear with her, as she moved, a whole dream of women's future; bore it from the past into the present as if it were a precious mystery she held in the carriage of her neck and arms.

"This has happened before," she said shortly. "And did I tell them where to get off! Shoes! If anybody wants to save books or postage stamps or diamond bracelets they're not hounded about it. My shoes! If anybody ever again——"

Suddenly Nell was aware of Johanna's stricken face.

"Oh, well, I suppose they told you to ask me." It had simultaneously dawned on her that her little outbreak might make a troublesome story itself, especially since she had just expressed superior surprise at those who behaved badly on duty. She wasn't on duty, but Miss Walters' niece might not make the distinction. Nell sat down on the bed again and everything went out of her voice except the velvet power.

"What did they tell you? That I was very stingy and kept all my old shoes?"

"Well—well, yes—well—well, not exactly——" Johanna stammered.

"Suppose I tell you a little story. It has something to do with that difference between amateurs and professionals I spoke about."

Relieved, Johanna sat back in her chair and with Miss Margery's encouragement lit a cigarette.

I was a stage child, you know, carried on as a baby in arms, nursed between acts on one-night stands, and all that. Until I was seven, I thought all grown people's kisses smelled of grease paint. Father was not an actor, but he was everything else around the theater at one time or another, as long as he lived, and then it was just mother and me. Mother played comedy parts—she did a few bits in New York, and a few seasons in stock, but mostly she toured the little towns with the third- and fourth-string companies they used to put out after a New York success. Plays like *Secret Service* and *The Easiest Way* and *The Witching Hour*—your generation doesn't remember them. She took what she could get—one summer we played *Old Kentucky* in most of the ranch towns of Wyoming and Montana.

We always managed to eat and dress, and when it looked as if we wouldn't I never worried, because I knew mother would fix it all right. I had nice clothes. I have a photograph of myself in some very nice clothes I had—nice clean flounces and ruffles and lace on my drawers, and sashes pressed and all that—like any little girl. I had nice clothes.

One day when I was ten years old—I won't tell you exactly how long ago, but it was before the war—we landed in Richmond, Virginia, in the middle of the summer. It was hot there—not that I minded, but I remember because I remember how the sweat kept pouring down people's faces and wilting men's collars and wetting the rims of women's dresses all through the day. And I remember from something else that I'll come to in a minute.

I knew that things were not going well, though mother tried to scold me around cheerfully as usual. I was worried, for about the first time in my life. Mother had a small part in a road company that had followed a heat wave and stopped paying salaries—that was a familiar story in those days—but enough money had come from New York to take the company back there. Mother was broke, and in debt to most of the company besides, and they were broke too. She didn't like the idea of getting into New York in July, in that condition, so when she heard that the stock company at the other Richmond theater could use somebody of her type she thought of trying for the job. The train that was taking the company to New York wasn't leaving for a couple of hours, so mother and I started across town. We walked— mother had only twenty cents left and we needed that to eat with that night.

I had cardboard in the soles of my shoes; I'd had that before, but, as I told you, mother always kept me very well dressed. Always very well dressed. It was just for a day or so sometimes when things were hard. But everything was so mixed up that last day with packing the trunks that I forgot to cut out a new piece of cardboard. I was just like any other child that age—you know, careless and forgetful.

But when mother took my hand on the street and said we had to hurry I began to be sorry I had been so careless. My old cardboard was worn through; the sidewalk was just a stove lid, and mother was dragging me along in the way older people do in a hurry, in a kind of shuffle that isn't either a walk or a run. I remember passing some colored boys barefoot and thinking that if I could take off my shoes and carry them I could run beside her and touch other parts of the feet sometimes. But I knew from the determined way mother walked that there was no time for that.

The wooden stairs of that other theater felt cool. I wanted to take off my shoes, but mother pulled me into the manager's office with her, and I was afraid that the manager might see the shoes and think we needed the job too bad. He looked like a mean man.

"What can you do?" he asked mother.

"Just about everything; character comedy, comic maids, blackface, heavies, old ladies, comic juveniles——"

He laughed unpleasantly.

"Yes, you can do juveniles."

"I've played Sis Hopkins more than once."

"Not since a long time, I'll bet. And you're not too happy in the face for playing comics."

Mother grinned at him—I knew how worried she was from her breathing and I wondered if he noticed.

"Come back in an hour," he said finally. "I've got somebody I've got to see first. Be here in one hour, sharp." We found out later he didn't have the principal authority after all.

Mother thought quick. The train for New York left in half an hour, and if she didn't get this job—well, it was better for a trouper to be "resting" in New York than in Richmond.

"All right," she agreed.

As soon as we were outside we started off faster than before. "I've got to get to the station before that train goes and have them give me my ticket so I can redeem it."

I said: "Mother, my shoes are worn out," and she answered vaguely, "We'll take care of that tomorrow." So, naturally, I didn't say any more.

I don't remember the walk to the station—not even whether my feet hurt or not, because now I was all worried with her. But I do remember getting there and finding that the train had been gone half an hour; we thought we had been walking faster, but actually we were tired and walking slower.

As soon as mother found that at least her trunk hadn't gone we started back to the stock theater. I hoped we would take a street car, but mother didn't suggest it. I tried to walk on the side of my feet, but it was very difficult and I kept slipping and mother just saved me from falling by jerking me sharply ahead. It was the part of each foot that stuck out—first the size of a half dollar and then the size of a dollar— that made all the trouble. Finally I couldn't bear to touch the ground with it, and after that it was even harder for mother. She got terribly tired and all at once decided we could waste a minute sitting on the steps of the Confederate Museum.

It didn't seem the time to say anything—we had gone so far it didn't seem worth while. It was no use taking off my shoes now— anyhow, I was afraid to see what had happened down there. I was afraid, too, that if it was something awful and mother found out she might look less cheerful in the face and we wouldn't get the job. I guess things had been as bad with her before, but this was the first time I'd been old enough to realize it.

The last part of the walk was not so far, but this time I couldn't feel the stairs of the theater like I had before, except they seemed sticky. There was another much nicer man with the manager; he gave mother the job and a few dollars to go on with, and when we got outside again she seemed more cheerful but, by this time, I was frightened about myself. I had to tell her. I saw a line of blood spots on the landing,that I'd left coming in, so I sat down on the first step of the stairs, and suddenly I saw the blood come out all around my feet until they were islands in the middle of it. I was terribly frightened now and wished I hadn't tried to be mother's brave girl. But I hoped the people inside the office would not hear her when she cried so loud, "Oh, my baby, my baby!"

After that I remember the pillow in the ambulance, because it was the biggest one I ever saw in my life.

The telephone rang and Nell Margery called into the living room: "Answer it, will you, Warren?"

"It's a hospital," he announced after a moment.

"Oh, I want to answer. It's a girl from the cast.... Oh, thanks.... Yes, I do want to know about her. . . . Well, that's perfectly fine. . . . Tell her we're all so glad, and that I'll be out for a minute late in the afternoon."

She bobbed the receiver and called the hotel florist. Meanwhile Livingstone had been leaning with his hands on the door frame between the rooms.

"What's all this about shoes?" he demanded. "Can't I listen in on the finish?"

"Sounds as if you have been listening."

"You left the door half open, and there wasn't much to read and I opened Mr. Gideon at some rather difficult pages."

Nell sat on the bed again and continued, speaking always to Johanna.

After the soles of my feet got well we had better times. But for me the one fine time was the day I put on a brand-new pair of white button shoes. I'd sit down and look at them, then I'd stand up and look at them, then I'd walk a little bit. I took care of those shoes, I'll tell you—I whitened them twice a day. But eventually they got scuffed about, and when I was going to walk on in a one-line bit in Albany next fall mother got me a new pair.

"Give me the others," said she. "They're too small for you, and the doorman's daughter——"

Perhaps she saw the look in my face, because she stopped right there. I picked up the discarded shoes and hugged them as if they were something living, and began to cry and cry.

"All right, all right," mother said. "Keep them then, stingy cat."

I didn't care what she called me. I hid them where she or anybody else couldn't find them, and when the next pair got used up I hid them, too, and the next pair, and the pair after that. Two years later, when I was beginning to play juveniles, a pair got thrown out one day, and then I will admit I—well, what you said: I "went to pieces."

You'll ask why do I want the old shoes, and I'll have to answer, "I don't know." Maybe it's just some terrible fear of ever being without shoes again; maybe it's some repressed stinginess coming out in me, like that article said. But I know I'd rather give away a ring from my finger than a pair of shoes.

When Nell stopped there was an odd silence; she looking at the other two defiantly; Livingstone looking at her as if things weren't so serious as all that; Johanna wondering how soon it would be wise to speak; she chanced it:

"May I make a little story out of that for the paper?"

"Oh, I'd much rather you wouldn't," Nell said quickly. "I'd much rather you wouldn't. I didn't tell it to you for that—I told it to you to illustrate something we were talking about. What was it? Oh, yes, about professionals—after that I was always a professional."

"I don't quite understand," confessed Johanna. "Isn't a professional just—just an amateur who's arrived?"

Nell shook her head helplessly.

"I can't exactly explain—it's something about discipline on duty. We stage children—why, when we were fifteen if a director said to one of us, 'You, third girl from the left, take a dive into the bass drum!' we'd have done it without question."

Johanna laughed but persisted:

"Lots of girls have succeeded on the stage without being brought up to it."

"Then they've made their struggle in sacrifices and heartburns of wriggling out of their backgrounds, and in being able to stand all sorts of hardships and tough contacts that they weren't fitted for or brought up for." Nell shook her head again and got up. "I haven't made it clear. I wish some clever man were here to explain it. I just thought perhaps you'd understand."

They moved into the other room. Nell did not sit down and Johanna, still unsatisfied, yielded to the hint that her time was up. Suddenly, she had support from a new quarter.

"I'm not that clever man you speak of, but I don't follow you either, Nell," said Livingstone. "You seem to be saying that everybody's got to go through misery to accomplish anything. Why, I know lots of them that just take it in their stride."

"Not if you know their real stories," Nell was thinking, but she was tiring herself with argument and she said nothing.

"The most successful explorers I know—why, it's been nuts for them. Most of them were brought up with guns in their hands——"

Nell nodded, breaking him off.

"Good-by, Miss Battles." She flashed the heavenly cataclysm of her smile at her. "Nothing about shoes, remember! It might reflect on mother, and she always dressed me as well as any little girl could be dressed. And remember me to your aunt."

Warren took a step into the doorway after Johanna, as if to atone for Nell's sudden lassitude—her own way of resting—and said with an appreciative eye on Johanna's lovely face:

"I hope you get some sort of story."

When he shut the door after her Nell was already sitting and gazing.

"So I'm an amateur," Warren said dryly. "Nellie, what you mean back of what you say is that if you make money out of your work you're a professional, and if you don't, you're an amateur. If you open a good beer parlor you're a professional, but if you fool with fever, and rocks in rapids that look the wrong color in the dusk, and men like monkeys and monkeys like men, you're an amateur."

Still Nell didn't answer—still resting. She had to go on in three hours.

"I admit I haven't made money, but I think I could if I had to."

"Try it," she whispered.

He wanted to choke her—he wanted to move some part of his body violently; but he was under a social contract to keep most of them still, so he worked with his tongue against the left side of his upper jaw. He said:

"For that crack I'll tell you something. We sold forty-five reels of animal and nature stuff to a movie morgue for a sum that paid for the trip and left a margin." He was freezing more and more, but each time he spoke his voice was gentler; yet she felt the recession: "Only you, Nellie, could irritate me to the extent of making such a statement— you and the peak of Everest and the mouth of the Orinoco if I'd given them three years of absolute unwavering devotion." He paused, taking Nell in. "In fact, I might as well admit they're years in the red." Again he looked at her, but still Nell did not stir. "In fact, coming down here was just a waste of time." He picked up his hat. "In fact, there are, after all, those society girls that chill your shoulder blades who may have standards quite as high as yours." He went to the door. "In fact——" He stood for a moment, utterly disgusted at her failure to be moved, and then stepped out and closed the door after him.

Nell looked up at the closed door as if she expected it to open again; she jumped at a knock, but it was her maid, and Nell ordered

SF—33 **

the car in an hour to go to the hospital. She was tired and confused and she knew that it would tell a little bit in her performance tonight. Never had she tried so hard to put her ideas into words; notions of Warren Livingstone and old shoes were mixed up in her mind.

She looked down at her shoes; the satin fabric had been somehow scuffed open in breaking the seal on that hidden thing of her childhood.

"I'll need a new pair of shoes, Jaccy. These are done."

"Yes, madame."

Jaccy's Savoyard eyes lowered for a moment to the shoes madame wore, then lifted quickly; but Nell had seen. She stared at Jaccy's foot that was the same size as her own.

"Is that why he went away? Because he suddenly saw me as a mean woman with an illogical streak one yard wide?"

And suddenly it seemed to her as if all those dozens and dozens and hundreds and hundreds of shoes made a barrier between him and her, between her and life, and she wanted to push it over or break through it. She jumped up.

"Jaccy!" and the maid turned. "Do you know—did you ever notice—our feet——" She hesitated, fighting through waves of old emotions, running against the stumps of old habits—"our feet are exactly the same size."

"Why, yes, madame," Jaccy's eyes danced and flickered. "Madame, I have often noticed it."

"Well, I thought that it was such a coincidence—my shoes would fit you exactly."

She took off the scuffed shoe quickly and tossed it to Jaccy, who examined it with covetous admiration.

"So I thought——"

Nell paused, breathing hard, and Jaccy, perhaps guessing what was going on inside her mistress, tried to help her over a difficult fence. "In fact—one day I took the liberty of trying on one of madame's used shoes before I added it to the others."

Nell stiffened—Jaccy had dared! Her own shoes—to try one on! The phone rang and Nell took off her other shoe and, carrying it in her hand, crossed to the phone in her stocking feet. As she picked up the receiver she tossed the second shoe; watching her mistress' face, Jaccy caught it and said with obvious disappointment:

"Shall I——"

"Of course, put them with the others." Nell's voice was cold as she picked up the phone; then suddenly her voice was all expectant and doubtful:

"Well, you didn't go far on this latest exploring trip."

"Far enough," said Warren. "Far enough to make a great discovery."

"What was that—that I'm just a sort of shopkeeper after all?"

She heard him laugh over the phone.

"No. It was that I'm condemned to go through life never looking at another woman, except as something unreal, something stuffed and mounted, seeing only you alive. Wherever you are, or whatever you do, I'll always be stalking you in my mind; half a dozen times in these three years I've really seen you around the edge of a copse, or as a kind of shadow darting away from a water hole. I'll always be one of those hunters you read about—you know—saw a vision once and just had to keep going after it—had no choice. Won't that make me a sort of professional in the end?"

An enforced pause while the line crackled with other dissonances or harmonies.

"Where did you make this discovery?"

"Beside the telephone desk in the lobby."

"Come up, Warren!"

Nell leaned back slowly in her chair, not relaxing, but nerving herself.

"Jaccy!" she said, breathing it in, and then, taking it big, feeling her heart pumping it down to the ends of her fingernails, the soles of her feet.

"Madame?"

"If you like, you can have those shoes. We're not saving them any more."

The Family Bus

(*The Saturday Evening Post*, 4 November 1933)

"The Family Bus" was written at "La Paix" in September 1933. The *Post* paid $3000. Again Fitzgerald was trying to respond to the mood of the Thirties with a story that reaffirms the opportunities in American life: the gardener's daughter becomes a lady; the ex-rich boy succeeds on his own after his family loses its money. The car material probably derived from the circumstance that Fitzgerald had bought a venerable Stutz which he drove— always tentatively—on his infrequent forays around Baltimore.

The names of the heroine, Janneken Melon-Loper, and her father Jan came from a chart in a voluminous study of the Sayre family which Zelda's mother, Minnie Sayre, kept in a breakfront cabinet in her living room in Montgomery. Fitzgerald, fascinated by genealogy though often inaccurate about it, obviously became intrigued by one of Zelda's first ancestors in America: Cornelis Melyn, born in Amsterdam, who settled on Staten Island with his wife Janneken in 1634. Janneken's last name may have been Loper, for their daughter Cornelia, who married Jacobus Schellinger and became a pioneer of East Hampton, Long Island, is on the chart as Cornelia Melyn-Loper. Fitzgerald must have stored this information in his mental filing cabinet, for the names come out transposed and the spelling slightly altered. This was not the first time he had dipped into Zelda's family history for a name: Basil Duke Lee, hero of the Basil series he wrote in 1928-1929, was borrowed from Basil W. Duke, brother-in-law and biographer of General John Hunt Morgan, Confederate cavalry leader and first cousin of Zelda's grandmother, Musidora Morgan. This book also was in the Sayre library.

Dick was four years old when the auto arrived at the Hendersons'—it was a 1914 model, fresh from the factory—but his earliest memory of it was dated two years later. Lest younger readers of this chronicle hesitate to embark on an archaeological treatise—about a mummy with doors in the back, gasoline lamps, gears practically in another street, and, invariably, a human torso underneath and a woman all veil and muff perched serene on top—it were best to begin with a description of the vehicle.

This was not that kind of car. It was of an expensive make, low-slung for that period, with electric lights and a self-starter—in appearance not unlike the machines of today. The fenders were higher, the running board longer, the tires more willowy, and undoubtedly it did stick up higher in the air. If it could be stood today beside, say, one of the models of 1927 that are still among us, you would not immediately be able to define the difference. The older car would seem less of a unit—rather like several cars each on a slightly different level.

This was not apparent to young Dick on the day he became conscious of the car; its sole fault was that it didn't contain Jannekin Melon-Loper, but he was going to make it contain her if his voice held out.

"Why ca' I ha' Ja'kin?"

"Because we're going some place," his mother whispered; they were approaching the gardener's cottage, and Jan Melon-Loper, father of the coveted Jannekin, tipped his large straw from a grape arbor.

"Oh, waa-a-a!" Dick wailed. "Oh, waa-a-a! I want Ja'kin!"

Mrs. Henderson was a little afraid of the family retainers; she had grown up in a simpler Michigan where the gardener was known either as "the janitor" or "the man who cuts the grass." The baronial splendor made possible by the rise of the furniture company sat uneasily upon her. She feared now that Jan had heard her son's request and would be offended.

"All right," she said, "all right. This one more time, Dick."

He beamed as he ran into the cottage calling for his love; he beamed as, presently, he led her forth by the hand and embarked her at his side. Jannekin, a lovely little Hollander of five, mouthed her thumb shyly for a minute and then found ease in one of those mysterious children's games which consist largely of the word "Look!" followed by long intervals of concentration. The auto carried them far on the fair day, but they gazed neither at the river, nor the hills, nor the residences, but only at each other.

It was always to be the last time with Jannekin, but it never quite was. Dick grew up to ten and played with boys, Jannekin went to public school and played with girls, but they were always like brother and sister to each other, and something more. He told her his most intimate secrets; they had a game they played sometimes where they stood cheek to cheek for a moment and breathed deeply; it was as near as she would come to letting him kiss her. Once she had seen her older sister kissing a man, and she thought it was "ookey."

So, for the blessed hour of childhood, they eliminated the space between the big house and the small one.

Jannekin never came to the Hendersons'. They met somewhere about the place. Favorite of all rendezvous was the garage.

"This is the way to do," Dick explained, sitting at the gears of the car—it was "the old car" now; the place of honor had since been occupied by a 1917 limousine and a 1920 landaulet—"Look, Janny; look, Jannekin, Howard showed me. I could drive it if they'd let me. Howard let me drive it once on his lap."

"Could I drive it?"

"Maybe," he conceded. "Look, I'll show you how."

"You could drive," she said. "I'd just go along and tell you which way to turn."

"Sure," he agreed, without realizing to what he was committing himself. "Sure, I——"

There was an interruption. Dick's big brother Ralph came into the garage, took a key from behind a door and expressed his desire for their displacement from the machine by pointing briskly at each of them in turn and then emphatically at the cement floor.

"You going riding?" Dick asked.

"Me? No, I'm going to lie under the tank and drink gasoline."

"Where are you going?" asked Dick, as they scrambled out.

"None of your business."

"I mean if you're going out the regular way, would you let us ride as far as Jannekin's house?"

"I can stand it."

He was not pleasant this summer, Dick's brother. He was home from sophomore year at college, and as the city seemed slow, he was making an almost single-handed attempt to speed it up. One of that unfortunate generation who had approached maturity amid the confusions and uncertainties of wartime, he was foot-loose and irresponsible even in his vices, and he wore the insigne of future disaster upon his sleeve.

The Henderson place was on the East Hills, looking down upon the river and the furniture factories that bordered it. The forty acres were supervised by the resourceful Jan, whose cottage stood in the position of a lodge at the main entrance, and there Ralph stopped the car and, to the children's surprise, got out with them. They lingered as he walked to the gate.

"Tee-hoo!" he whistled discreetly, but imperatively. "Tee-ee-hoo!"

A moment later, Kaethe Melon-Loper, the anxiety, if not yet the shame, of her parents, came around the corner from the kitchen, hatted and cloaked, and obviously trying to be an inconspicuous part of the twilight. She shared with Jannekin only the ruddy Dutch color and the large China-blue eyes.

"Start right off," she whispered. "I'll explain."

But it was too late—the explanation issued from the cottage personified as Mrs. Melon-Loper and Mrs. Henderson making a round of the estate. Both mothers took in the situation simultaneously; for a second Mrs. Henderson hesitated, her eyebrows fluttering; then she advanced determinedly toward the car.

"Why, Ralph!" she exclaimed. "Where are you going?"

Calmly, Ralph blew smoke at his mother.

"I got a date—and I'm dropping Kaethe at a date she's got."

"Why, Ralph!" There was nothing much to add to this remark, which she repeated in a distraught manner. That he was not speaking the truth was apparent in his affected casualness as well as in the shifty, intimidated eyes of the girl sitting beside him. But in the presence of Kaethe's mother, Mrs. Henderson was handicapped.

"I particularly wanted you to be at home to-night," she said, and Mrs. Melon-Loper, equally displeased, helped her with:

"Kaethe, you get yourself out of the auto this minute."

But the car broke into a sound more emphatic than either of their voices; with the cut-out open in a resounding "tp!-tp!-tp!" it slid off down the lane, leaving the mothers standing, confused and alarmed, in the yard.

Of the two, Mrs. Melon-Loper was more adequate to the awkward situation.

"It should not be," she pronounced, shaking her head. "Her father will her punish."

"It doesn't seem right at all," said Mrs. Henderson, following her lead gratefully. "I will tell his father."

"It should not be."

Mrs. Henderson sighed; catching sight of the two children, who loitered, fascinated, she managed to assert herself:

"Come home with me, Dick."

"It's only seven," he began to protest.

"Never mind," she said with dilatory firmness. "I need you for something. . . . Good night, Mrs. Melon-Loper."

A little way down the lane, Mrs. Henderson released on Dick the authority she could no longer wield over her elder son.

"That's the end of that. You're never to play with that dirty little girl again."

"She isn't dirty. She isn't even as dirty as I am."

"You're not to waste your time with her. You ought to be ashamed of yourself."

She walked so fast that he had trouble keeping up.

"Why ought I be ashamed of myself? Look, mamma, tell me. Why ought I be ashamed of myself?"

He sensed that Ralph had no business driving off into the twilight with Kaethe, but himself and Jannekin—that was another matter. There was great domestic commotion about the affair during the next few days; Mr. Henderson raged at Ralph around the library and the latter sat at meals with a silent jeer on his face.

"Believe me, Kaethe would go bigger in New York than most of the stuff that turns out at the country club," he told his father.

"I've made inquiries, and she has a bad reputation with the people she goes with."

"That's O.K. with me," Ralph said. "I think a girl ought to know something about life."

"Is dissipation 'life'? Sometimes I think you've got a bad heart, Ralph. Sometimes I think none of the money I've spent on your outside got through to your insides. I think now I ought to have started you in the factory at seventeen."

Ralph yawned.

"A lot you know about anything except tables and chairs."

For a week, though—due largely to the firmness of Jan—there were no more night rides. Ralph spent his leisure sampling the maiden efforts of pioneer bootleggers, and Dick, accustomed to the disorganization that, during the 20's, characterized so many newly rich families in the Middle West, when there was scarcely a clan without its wastrel or scamp, concerned himself with his own affairs. These included finding out as much about automobiles as Howard, the chauffeur, could find time to tell him, and searching for his Jannekin again across the barriers that had been raised between them. Often he saw her—the flash of a bright little dress far away across the lawn, an eager face on the cottage porch as he drove out with his mother—but the cordon was well drawn. Finally, the urge to hear her voice became so insistent that he decided upon the clandestine.

It was a late August day, with twilight early and the threat of a storm in the air. He shut himself noisily in his room for the benefit of his mother's secretary, part of whose duties consisted of keeping an eye on him in this emergency; then he tiptoed down a back stairs and went out through the kitchen. Circling the garage, he made his way toward the cottage following the low bed of a stream, a route often used in "cops and robbers." His intention was to get as close as possible and then signal Jannekin with a bird call they had practiced, but starting through a high half acre of hay, he stopped at the sound of voices twenty feet ahead.

"We'll take the old bus"—it was Ralph speaking. "We'll get married in Muskegon—that's where some people I know did."

"Then what?" Kaethe demanded.

"I've got a hundred dollars, I tell you. We could go to Detroit and wait for the family to come around."

"I guess they can't do anything after we're married."

"What could they do? They're so dumb they don't even know I flunked out of college in June—I sneaked the notice out of the mail. The old man's weak—that's his trouble. He'll kick, but he'll eat out of my hand."

"You didn't decide this because you had these drinks?"

"I tell you I've thought of it for weeks. You're the only girl I——"

Dick lost interest in finding Jannekin. Carefully he backed out of the path he had made through the hay and returned to the garage to consider. The thing was awful—though Dick's parents were very incompetent as parents in the postwar world that they failed to understand, the symbol of parental authority remained. Scenting evil and catastrophe as he never had in his life, Dick walked up and down in front of the garage in the beginning rain. A few minutes later, he ran for the house with his shirt soaked and his mind made up.

Snitching or not, he must tell his father. But as they went in to dinner, his mother said: "Father phoned he won't be home. . . . Ralph, why don't you sit up? Don't you think it looks rather bad?"

She guessed faintly that Ralph had been drinking, but she hated facing anything directly.

"S'mustard for the soo-oop," Ralph suggested, winking at Dick; but Dick, possessed with a child's quiet horror, could not give back the required smile.

"If father will only come," he thought. "If father will only come."

During an interminable dinner, he went on considering.

Howard and the new car were in town awaiting his father; in the garage there was only the old bus, and straightway Dick remembered that the key was kept behind the garage door. After a fragmentary appearance in the library to say, "I'm going up and read in my room," he darted down the back stairs again, out through the kitchen and over the lawn, drenched with a steady, patient stream.

Not a second too soon—halfway to the garage he heard the front door close and, by the light of the porte-cochere, saw Ralph come down the steps. Racing ahead, Dick found and pocketed the key; but he ran smack into Ralph as he tried to escape from the garage, and was grabbed in the darkness.

"What you doing here?"

"Nothing."

"Go back the house."

Gratefully, Dick got a start, not toward the house, where he would be easily cornered, but in the direction of the tall hay. If he could keep the key until his father arrived home——

But he had gone barely fifty feet, slipping on the indistinguishable mud, when he heard Ralph's running footsteps behind him.

"Dick, you take 'at key? Hey!"

"No," he called back indiscreetly, continuing to run. "I never saw the key."

"You didn't? Then what were you——"

His fingers closed on Dick's shoulder, and Dick smelled raw liquor as they crashed across a bed of peonies.

"You give me——"

"I won't! You let me——"

"You will, by——"

"I won't—I won't! I haven't got it!"

Two minutes later, Ralph stood up with the key in his hand and surveyed the sobbing boy.

"What was the idea?" he panted. "I'm going to speak to father about this."

Dick took him up quickly.

"All right!" he gasped. "Speak to him tonight!"

Ralph made an explosive sound that expressed at once his disgust and his private conviction that he had best get from home before his father arrived. Still sobbing on the ground, Dick heard the old car leave the garage and start up the lane. It could hardly have reached the sanctuary of a main street when the lights of another car split the wet darkness, and Dick raced to the house to see his father.

". . . They're going to Muskegon and they're on their way now."

"It couldn't have been they knew you were there and said it to tease you?"

"No, no, no!" insisted Dick.

"Well, then, I'll take care of this myself. . . . Turn around, Howard! Take the road to Muskegon, and go very fast." He scarcely noticed that Dick was in the car beside him until they were speeding through the traffic on Canal Street.

Out of the city, Howard had to pick his way more carefully along the wet highway; Mr. Henderson made no attempt to urge him on, but threw cigarette after cigarette into the night and thought his thoughts. But on a down grade when the single light of a motorcycle came into sight on the opposite up grade, he said:

"Stop, Howard! This may be a cop."

The car stopped; owner and chauffeur waved wildly. The motorcycle passed them, pulled up fifty yards down the road, and came back.

"Officer."

"What is it?" The voice was sharp and hurried.

"I'm T. R. Henderson. I'm following an open car with——"

The officer's face changed in the light of his own bright lamp.

"T. R.," he repeated, startled. "Say, I was going to telephone you—I used to work for you. Mr. Henderson, there's been an accident."

He came up closer to the car, put his foot on the running board and took off his cap so that the rain beat on his vivid young face as it twisted itself into sympathy and consideration.

"Your son's car went off the road down here a little way—it turned over. My relief heard the horn keep blowing. Mr. Henderson, you'll have to get ready for bad news."

"All right. Put on your cap."

"Your son was killed, Mr. Henderson. The girl was not hurt."

"My son is killed? You mean, he's dead?"

"The car turned over twice, Mr. Henderson. . . ."

. . . The rain fell gently through the night, and all the next day it rained. Under the somber skies, Dick grew up suddenly, never again to be irresponsibly childish, trying to make his mother see his own face between herself and the tragedy, voluntarily riding in to call for his father at the office and exhibiting new interest in the purposes of the mature world, as if to say, "Look, you've got me. It's all right. I'll be two sons. I'll be all the sons you ever would have wanted." At the funeral he walked apart with them as the very cement of their family solidarity against the scandal that accompanied the catastrophe.

Then the rain moved away from Michigan into another weather belt and the sun shone; boyhood reasserted itself, and a fortnight later, Dick was in the garage with Howard while the latter worked on the salvaged car.

"Why can't I look up inside, Howard? You told me I could."

"Get that canvas strip then. Can't send you up to the house with oil on your new clothes."

"Listen, Howard," said Dick, lying under the engine with the basketed light between them. "Is that all it did—broke the front axle? It rolled over twice and only did that?"

"Crawl out and get me the wrench on the table," ordered Howard.

"But why wasn't it hurt?" demanded Dick, returning to the cave. "Why?"

"Built solid," Howard said. "There's ten years' life in her yet; she's better than some of this year's jobs. Though I understand that your mother never wants to see it again—naturally enough."

A voice came down to them from the outside world:

"Dick!"

"It's just Jannekin. Excuse me, Howard; I'll be back and help."
Dick crawled out and faced a little figure in Sunday clothes.

"Hello, Dick."

"What do you want?" he asked, abstractedly rather than rudely;
then awakening from mechanical preoccupations, "Say, who got all
dressed up?"

"I came to say good-by——"

"What?"

"——to you."

"Where are you going?"

"We're going away. Father has the van all loaded now. We're
going to live across the river and papa's going to be in the furniture
business."

"Going away?"

She nodded so far down that her chin touched her breast bone,
and she sniffled once.

Dick had restlessly got into the car and was pulling at the
dashboard instruments. Suddenly frightened, he flung open the door,
saying, "Come here," and, as she obeyed, "Why are you going?"

"After the accident—your father and mine thought we better go
away. . . . Oh-h, Dick!"

She leaned and put her cheek next to his, and gave a sigh that
emptied her whole self for a moment. "Oh-h-h-h, Dick! Won't I ever
see you?"

For the moment, his only obligation seemed to be to stop her
grief.

"Oh, shut up! Stop it, Janny Jannekin. I'll come to see you every
day. I will. Pretty soon I'll be able to drive this old bus——"

She wept on inconsolably.

"——and then I'll drive over and——" He hesitated; then made a
great concession, "Look, you can drive too. I'll begin to show you
now, Janny Jannekin. Look! This is the ignition."

"Yes—hp—oh!" she choked forth.

"Oh, stop it. . . . Put your foot here. Now press."

She did so, and almost simultaneously a ferocious howl issued
from the cavern beneath the car.

"I'm sorry, Howard!" shouted Dick, and then to Jannekin: "But
I'll show you how to drive it as soon as they let me take it out myself."

Full in the garage door, the sun fell upon the faces they turned
toward each other. Gratefully he saw the tears dry on her cheeks.

"Now I'll explain about the gears," he said.

II

Dick chose Technical High as the best alternative, when it became plain that he could not return to St. Regis. Since Mr. Henderson's death there was always less money for everything, and though Dick resented growing poorer in a world in which everyone else grew richer, he agreed with the trustees that there was not twenty-five hundred extra to send him East to America's most expensive school.

At Tech he thought he had managed to conceal his disappointment politely. But the high-school fraternity, Omega Psi, which, though scarcely knowing him, elected him because of the prestige of his family, became ashamed of their snobbishness and pretended to see in his manner the condescension of a nobleman accepting an election to a fraternal order.

Amid the adjustments of the autumn he did not at first discover that Jannekin Melon-Loper was a junior in Tech. The thick drift of six years was between them, for she had been right—the separation in the garage was permanent. Jannekin, too, had passed through mutations. Her father had prospered in industry; he was now manager in charge of production in the company that had absorbed the Henderson plant. Jannekin was at Tech for a groundwork that would enable her to go abroad and bring back Bourbon, Tudor and Hapsburg eccentricities worthy of Michigan reproduction. Jan wanted no more shiftless daughters.

Edgar Bronson, prominent member of Omega Psi, hailed Dick one morning in a corridor. "Hey, rookie, we took you in because we thought you could play football."

"I'm going out for it when——"

"It doesn't do the fraternity any good when you play the East Hill snob."

"What is all this?" demanded Dick, turning on him. "Just because I told some fellows I'd meant to go East to college."

"East—East—East," Edgar accused. "Why don't you keep it to yourself? All of us happen to be headed to Michigan, and we happen to like it. You think you're different from anybody else." And he sang as a sort of taunt:

The boys all are back at Michigan,
The cats are still black at Michigan,
  The Profs are still witty,
    Ha-a-ha!
  The girls are still pretty,
    Ha-a-ha!——

He broke off as a trio of girls came around the corridor, and approaching, caught up the song:

——*and the old*
  How do you do?
  How are you?
  Says who?
Goes on—on—and on.

"Hey, Jannekin!" Edgar called.

"Don't block the sidewalk!" they cried, but Jannekin left the others and came back. Her face escaped the pronounced Dutchiness of her sister's, and the coarseness that sometimes goes with it—nevertheless, the bright little apples of her cheeks, the blue of the Zuyder Zee in her eyes, the braided strands of golden corn on the wide forehead, testified to the purity of her origin. She was the school beauty who let down her locks for the arrival of princes in the dramatic-club shows—at least until the week before the performance, when, to the dismay of the coach, she yielded to the pressure of the times, abbreviated the locks, and played the part in a straw wig.

She spoke over Edgar to Dick, "I heard you were here, Dick Henderson."

"Why"—he recovered himself in a moment—"why, Janny Jannekin."

She laughed.

"It's a long time since you last called me that—sitting in the car in the garage, do you remember?"

"Don't mind me," said Edgar ironically. "Go right on. Did what?"

A wisp of the old emotion blew through Dick, and he concealed it by saying:

"We still have that car. It's still working, but I'm the only person left who can do anything with it when it doesn't."

"What year is it?" demanded Edgar, trying to creep into the conversation that had grown too exclusive to please him.

"Nineteen fourteen," Dick answered briefly and then to Jannekin, with a modesty he did not feel about the car, "We keep it because we couldn't sell it." He hesitated. "Want to go riding some night?"

"Sure I do. I'd love it."

"All right, we will."

Her companions demanded her vociferously down the corridor; when she retreated, Edgar eyed Dick with new interest, but also new hostility.

"One more thing: If you don't want to get the whole fraternity down on you, don't start rushing Jannekin Melon-Loper. Couple of the brothers—I mean she's very popular and there's been plenty fights about her. One guy danced the last number with her at the June dance, and the boy that took her beat him up. Hear that?"

"I hear," answered Dick coldly.

But the result was a resolve that he put into effect during his date with her a week later—he asked her to the Harvest Picnic. Jannekin accepted. Hesitantly, not at all sure she liked this overproud boy out of the past, absorbed in his dual dream of himself and of machinery.

"Why do you want to take me? Because once we were——" She stopped.

"Oh, no," he assured her. "It's just that I like to take the prettiest. I thought we could go in this old bus. I can always get it."

His tone irritated Jannekin.

"I had a sort of engagement to go with two other boys—both of them have new cars." Then, feeling she had gone too far, she added: "But I like this one better."

In the interval he worked over the old bus, touching the worn places of its bright cream color with paint, waxing it, polishing the metal and the glass, and tinkering with the engine until the cut-out was calculated to cause acute neurasthenia to such citizenry as dwelt between the city and Reed's Lake. When he called for Jannekin to escort her to the place of assembly, he was prouder of the car than of anything—until he saw whom he was taking to the dance. In deepest rose, a blush upon the evening air, Jannekin bounced rhythmically down the walk, belying the care she had put into her toilet for the night. With his handkerchief he gave a flick to the seat where she was to deposit her spotlessness.

"Good Lord! When I look at you—why, sometimes your face used to be as dirty as mine. Not ever quite—I remember defending you once. Mother said——" He broke off, but she added:

"I know. I was just the gardener's child to her. But why bring that up on an evening like this?"

"I'm sorry. I never thought of you as anything but my Janny Jannekin," he said emotionally.

She was unappeased, and in any case, it was too early for such a note; at the Sedgewicks' house she went from group to group of girls, admiring and being admired, and leaving Dick to stand somewhat conspicuously alone.

Not for long, though. Two youths toward whom he had developed a marked indifference engaged him in conversation about the football team, conversation punctuated by what seemed to him pointless laughter.

"You looked good at half today, Dick"—a snicker. "Mr. Hart was talking about you afterwards. Everybody thinks that Johnson ought to resign and let you be captain."

"Oh, come on," he said as good-humoredly as possible. "I'm not kidding myself about being good. I know he just needs my weight."

"No, honest," said one of the boys, with mock gravity. "Here at Tech we always like to have at least three of the backfield from the East Hills. It gives a sort of tone to the team when we play Clifton." Whereupon both boys snorted again with laughter.

Dick sighed and shook his head wearily.

"Go on, be as funny as you want to. You think I'm high-hat. All right, go on thinking it until you find out. I can wait."

For a moment, his frankness disconcerted them, but only for a moment:

"And the coach thinks maybe he could use that nifty racer of yours for end runs."

Bored by the childishness of the baiting, he searched for Jannekin in the crowd that now filled the living room and was beginning to drift out to the cars. He saw her flashing rose against a window, but before he could reach her, Edgar Bronson stopped him with serious hands on his shoulders:

"I've got something I particularly want to say to you."

"All right, say it."

"Not here; it's very private. Upstairs in Earl's bedroom."

Mystified, and glancing doubtfully over his shoulder to see if this could be a plot to steal Jannekin away, he followed Edgar upstairs; he refused the cigarette that training did not permit.

"Look here, Dick. Some of us feel that perhaps we've misjudged you. Perhaps you're not such a bad guy, but your early associations with a bunch of butlers and all that stuff sort of—sort of warped you."

"We never had any butlers," said Dick impatiently.

"Well, footmen then, or whatever you call them. It warped you, see?"

Under any conditions it is difficult to conceive of oneself as warped, save before the concave and convex mirrors of an amusement park; under the present circumstances, with Jannekin waiting below, it was preposterous, and with an expression of disgust, Dick started to rise, but Edgar persuaded him back in his chair.

"Wait a minute. There's only one thing wrong with you, and we, some of the fellows, feel that it can all be fixed up. You wait here and I'll get the ones I mean, and we'll settle it in a minute."

He hurried out, closing the door behind him, and Dick, still impatient, but welcoming any crisis that promised to resolve his unpopularity, wandered about the room inspecting the books, school pictures and pennants of Earl Sedgewick's private life.

Two minutes passed—three minutes. Exploding into action, he strode out of the door and down the stairs. The house was strangely silent, and with quick foreboding, he took the last stairs six at a time. The sitting room was unpopulated, the crowd was gone, but there was Jannekin, a faithful but somewhat sulky figure, waiting by the door.

"Did you have a good sleep?" she asked demurely. "Is this a picnic or a funeral?"

"It was some cuckoo joke. Some day I'll pull something on those guys that'll be really funny. Anyhow, I know a short cut and we'll beat them to the lake and give them the laugh." They went out. On the veranda, he stopped abruptly; his car—his beautiful car—was not where he had left it.

"My gosh! They've taken it! They took my car! What a dirty trick!" He turned incredulously to Jannekin. "And they knew you were with me too! Honestly, I don't understand these guys at all."

Neither did Jannekin. She had known them to behave cruelly or savagely; she had never known them to visit such a stupid joke on a popular girl. She, too, stared incredulously up and down the street.

"Look, Dick! Is that it down there—beyond the third lamp-post?"

He looked eagerly.

"It certainly is. But why——"

As they ran toward it, the reason became increasingly clear— startlingly clear. At first it seemed only that the car was somehow different against the late sunset; then the difference took form as varicolored blotches, screaming and emphatic, declaratory and exclamatory, decorating the cream-colored hulk from stem to stern, until the car seemed to have become as articulate and vociferous as a phonograph.

With dawning horror, he read the legends that, one by one, swam into his vision:

PARDON MY SILK HAT
WHAT AM I DOING IN THIS HICK TOWN?
ONLY FOUR CYLINDERS, BUT EACH ONE WITH A FAMILY TREE
STRAIGHT GAS FROM THE EAST HILLS
MARNE TAXI—MODEL 1914
WHY BALLOON TIRES WITH A BALLOON HEAD?

And perhaps the cruelest cut of all:

YOU DON'T NEED A MUFFLER WITH A CULTIVATED VOICE

Wild with rage, Dick pulled out his handkerchief and dabbed at one of the slogans, making a wide blur through which the sentence still showed. Three or four of them must have worked on the mural; it was amazing, even admirable, that it had been accomplished in the quarter hour they had passed in the house. Again he started furiously at it with the already green blob of his handkerchief. Then he spied the convenient barrel of tar with the help of which they had finished the job after the paint gave out, and he abandoned all hope.

"There's no use, Dick," Jannekin agreed. "It was a mean trick, but you can't do anything about it now. You'll just ruin your clothes and make it all splotchy and give them the satisfaction of thinking you've been working on it. Let's just get in and go." And she added with magnanimity, "I don't mind."

"Go in this?" he demanded incredulously. "Why, I'd sooner——"

He stopped. Two years ago he would have phoned the chauffeur or rented another car, but now dollars were scarce in his family; all he could muster had gone into cosmetics for the machine.

"We can't go," he said emphatically. "Maybe I can find you a ride out and you can come back with someone else."

"Nonsense!" Jannekin protested. "Of course, we'll go. They're not going to spoil our evening with such a stupid stunt!"

"I won't go," he repeated firmly.

"You will so." She reverted unconsciously to the tone of six years before. "By the time we get there, it'll be almost too dark to read the— to see the things they painted. And we don't have to take streets where there're many people."

He hesitated, rebelling with her at being triumphed over so easily.

"Of course, we could go on the side streets," he admitted grudgingly.

"Of course, Dick." She touched his arm. "Now don't help me in; I don't want to get in the paint."

"When we're there," Dick told himself grimly, "I'll ask Mr. Edgar Bronson aside for a little talk. And I'll do some painting myself—all in bright red."

She sensed his fury as they drove along dusty roads with few street lights, but great roller-coaster bumps at the crossings.

"Cheer up, Dick!" She moved closer. "Don't let this spoil the evening. Let's talk about something else. Why, we hardly know each other. Listen, I'll tell you about me; I'll talk to you as frankly as we used to talk. We're almost rich, Dick. Mother wants to move to a bigger house, but father's very cautious, and he thinks it would look pushing. But anyhow we know he's got more than we know he's got—if you know what I mean."

"That's good." He matched her frankness. "Well, we've got even less money than people know we have, if you know what I mean. I've got as much chance of getting East to Boston Tech as this car has to get into the automobile show." A little bitterly, he added: "So they needn't have wasted all that sarcasm."

"Oh, forget it. Tell me what you are going to do."

"I'm not going to college at all; I'm going to Detroit, where my uncle can get me a place in a factory. I like fooling around cars. As a matter of fact——" In the light of recent happenings, he hesitated before he boasted, but it came with an irrepressible rush: "Over at Hoker's garage they phone me whenever they get a job that sticks them—like some new foreign car passing through. In fact——"

Again he hesitated, but Jannekin said, "Go on."

"——in fact, I've got a lot of little gadgets at home, and some of them may be worth patenting after I get up to Detroit. And then maybe I'll think of some others."

"I'll bet you will, Dick," she agreed. "You could always mend anything. Remember how you started that old music box that father brought from the old country? You—you shook it or something."

He laughed, forgetting his temper.

"That was a brilliant hunch—young Edison in the making. However, it won't work with cars, because they usually shake themselves."

But when the picnic grounds came into sight, at first faintly glowing with many Japanese lanterns upon the twilight, then alive with bright dresses, a hard mood descended upon him. He saw a knot of boys gather at his approach, and looking straight ahead, he drove past the crowd that milled about the laden tables and to the parking place beyond. Voices followed them:

"Who'd have thought it?"

"Must be some Eastern custom."

"Say, that's some jazzy little tank now."

As he swung the car savagely into an empty space, Jannekin's hand fell on his taut arm.

"What are you going to do, Dick?"

"Why, nothing," he answered innocently.

"You're not going to make a scene about this. Wait! Don't get out yet. Remember, you're with me."

"I'll remember that. Nothing'll happen around you."

"Dick, do you know who did this?"

"I know Edgar Bronson had something to do with it. And two others I'm pretty sure of, and——"

"Listen. . . . Please don't get out, Dick." It was the soft voice of pleading childhood. "Listen, Dick. You could beat any of those three boys, couldn't you?"

"Beat them!" he repeated scornfully. "I could mop up the lake with them. I could ruin any two of them together, and they know it. I'm just wondering what part of the grounds they're hiding in—or maybe they're keeping their girls with them for protection."

He laughed with his chin up, and in the sound there was a wild foretaste of battle and triumph that frightened her and thrilled her.

"Then what would be the satisfaction, Dick?" she begged. "You know already you could beat them, and they know it, and everybody knows it. Now, if it was Capone Johnson——" This was an unfortunate suggestion; she stopped herself too late as lines appeared between Dick's eyes.

"Maybe it was Capone Johnson. Well, I'll just show him he's not so big that he can——"

"But you know it wasn't him," she wailed. "You know he's the kindest boy in school and wouldn't hurt anybody's feelings. I heard him say the other day he liked you 'specially."

"I thought he did," he said, mollified.

"Now we're going to get out and take our baskets and walk over as if nothing had happened."

He was silent.

"Come on, Dick; do it for Janny. You've done so many things for Janny."

Had she put it the other way—that she had done so many things for him—he would not have yielded, but the remark made it seem inevitable that he should do one more.

"All right." He laughed helplessly, but his laugh changed to an intake of breath as, suddenly, her young body pressed against him, all that rose color crushing up to his heart, and he saw her face and eyes swimming under him where the wheel had been a minute before.

A minute later, perhaps even two, even three minutes later, she was saying:

"Let me get out by myself. Remember the paint." And then: "I don't care if I am mussed. At least none of them can say they've seen me so mussed before."

Hand in hand, with that oddly inimitable, not-to-be-masked expression on both their faces, they walked toward the tables beside the lake.

III

But after a few months during which Dick laced up Jannekin's skating boots or kissed her lips in the many weathers of the long Michigan winter, they arrived at another parting.

Jannekin, borne up on the wings of the family fortune, was taken from Tech and sent to be fashionably educated in Europe.

There were forget-me-nots, but after a time there were fewer letters. Jannekin in Geneva, Jannekin in Paris, Jannekin in Munich; finally Jannekin at The Hague, being presented to the Queen of Holland—Miss Melon-Loper, the gardener's daughter, a splendid plant of the Netherlands that had taken root in the new world.

Meanwhile there was Dick in overalls, Dick with his face grease black, Dick with his arm in a sling and part of a little finger gone. Now, after five years, there was Dick at twenty-three, assistant to the factory superintendent of one of the largest automobile plants in Detroit. Finally, there was Dick driving to his native city, partly on business and partly because word had reached him that Jannekin had once more set foot upon the shore of the republic. The news came through Edgar Bronson, who worked in a competing factory, but was more in touch with home than Dick. Dick wrote, and in return got a telegram inviting him to dine.

They were waiting for him on the porch of a big Dutch-colonial house—not old Jan, who had broken down under the weight of years and been put in a nursing home, but Mrs. Melon-Loper, a stout patroon now, and proud of the family fortunes, and a scarcely recognizable Jannekin, totally unlike the girl who had lost her voice cheering at the game with Clifton or led her basket-ball team in bloomers. She wasn't merely developed, she was a different person. Her beauty was as poised and secure as a flower on a strong stem; her voice was cool and sure, with no wayward instruments in it that played on his emotions. The blue eyes that pretended a polite joy at their reunion succeeded in conveying only the face value of the eyes themselves, even a warning that an intention of being amused lay behind them.

And the dinner was like too many other dinners; a young man and woman whose names Dick associated with the city's older families talked cards, golf, horses, country-club scandal; and it became evident to Dick that Jannekin herself preferred the conversation to remain on a thin, dehumanized level.

"After Detroit, we must sound provincial, Dick." He resented the irony. "But we happen to like it here, really. It's incredible, but we do. We have almost everything, but it's all in miniature. We even have a

small version of a hunt club and a small version of the depression—
only we're a little afraid at the moment that the latter's going to eat up
the former. Nevertheless, Mr. Meredith here isn't any less of an M. F.
H. because he has two pairs of boots compared to some Meadowbrook
nabob with a dozen."

"Jannekin's subsidized by the Chamber of Commerce."
Meredith said. "Personally, I think the place is a ditch, but she keeps
arranging and rearranging things until we all think we're in Paris."

She was gone. Dick might have expected that. Once they had
recaptured the past after a lapse of six years; it was too much to expect
that it would happen again. There was nothing left of the Jannekin
he had known, and he was not impressed with her as the ringmaster of
the local aristocracy. It was even obvious that she was content to be
top dog here because of a lingering sense of inferiority at having been
born a servant's daughter.

Perhaps to another man her new qualities would have their
value, but she was of no use to him any more. Before the end of the
evening, he had dismissed her from his mind except as a former
friend, viewed in enlightening perspective. But he went down the
steps empty-hearted from the riddance of that face drifting between
the dark and the windows.

Jannekin said, "Come over often, Dick."

With forced heartiness, Dick answered:

"I'm certainly going to!" And to himself he added, "But not to
see you, my dear." He did not guess that she was thinking: "Why did I
do this to-night? Whatever made me think he'd like it?"

On his way to the hotel, he stopped by the entrance to his old
home. It was unoccupied and for sale. Even with part of the property
converted into a real-estate development, there were few families in
the city who could undertake its upkeep. Dick sighed, expressing he
knew not what emotion.

Down at the hotel he could not sleep. He read a magazine for a
while and then bent a long, fine piece of wire that he often carried
with him into a shape that might some day be embodied in a spring.
Once more he recapitulated to himself the impossibility of loving a
girl for the third time, when she was not even the girl he had loved
before; and he pictured himself with scorn as one of those faithful
swains who live perennially in an old hope from sheer lack of
imagination. He said aloud: "This thing is out of my mind for good."
And it seemed to vanish obediently and he felt better; but he was not
yet quite asleep at two o'clock when the phone pounded at his
bedside. It was long distance from Detroit.

"Dick, I want to begin by telling you about McCaffray."

"Who is this speaking?"

"This is Bill Flint calling from the office. But first I want to ask you: Were your father's initials T. R.?"

"What is this, anyhow?" Dick grumbled. "Are you having a party over there?"

"I told you I'm in my office in the drafting building and I've got a stack of files in front of me two yards high."

"This is a fine time of night——"

"Well, this is a damn important business."

"My father's initials? He didn't know an automobile from a velocipede."

"Shut up and I'll tell you the dope. Now, this McCaffray——"

Back in 1914, a pale little man named McCaffray had appeared in Detroit from nowhere, lingered a few weeks and then inconspicuously died. The little man had had a divine foresight about dual carburetion fourteen years in advance of its time. The company experimentally installed his intake manifolds on the first six cars of a series, abandoned the idea, and let Mr. McCaffray, with his unpatented scheme, wander off to a rival factory and thence on to his death. But within the last twenty-four hours it had become highly important to the company engineers to find out exactly what that intake manifold had looked like. One old mechanic remembered it hazily as having been "something like you want." Apparently no drawing of it was in existence. But though five of the six cars had been issued to company executives and long ago vanished, the sixth had gone out on a hurry order to a certain Mr. T. R. Henderson.

"He was my father," Dick interrupted. "The car is here, laid up in a garage kept by an old chauffeur of ours. I'll have the intake manifold tomorrow."

The family bus again—he felt a rush of sentimentality about it. He'd never sell it; he'd put it in a special museum like the coaches at Versailles. Thinking of it warmly, affectionately, he drowsed off at last, and slept until eleven in the morning.

Two hours later, having accomplished the business that had brought him to the city, he drove to Howard's garage and found him filling a gas tank in front.

"Well, there, Dick!" Howard hurried over, wiping his hands on a ball of waste. "Say, we were talking about you. Hear they made you czar of the auto industry."

"No, only mayor. . . . Say, Howard, is the old car still running?"

"What car?"

"The old open bus."

"Sure. She never was any five-and-ten proposition."

"Well, I'm going to take her to Detroit." At Howard's expression, he stiffened with alarm. "She's here, isn't she?"

"Why, we sold that old car, Dick. Remember, you told me if I had an offer I could sell it for the storage."

"My God!"

"We got—let's see—we got twenty-two fifty, I think, because the rubber and the battery——"

"Who did you sell it to?"

Howard scratched his head, felt his chin, hitched his pants.

"I'll go ask my daughter how much we did get for it."

"But who bought it?" Dick was quivering with apprehension lest the company of Edgar Bronson, where Mr. McCaffray once labored, had snatched the thing from under his nose.

"Who?" he demanded fiercely.

"Jannekin Melon-Loper bought it."

"What?"

"Sure thing. She came down a month ago, and had to have that car. If you wait a second, I'll ask my daughter——"

But Dick was gone. Had he not been so excited he would have regarded the time and not rung the doorbell at the Melon-Lopers' before a luncheon party of women had risen from the table. As it was, Jannekin came out on the porch and made him sit down.

"I know you don't want to meet a lot of women, but I'm glad you came, Dick. I'm sorry about last night. I was showing off, I guess."

"Not at all."

"Yes, I was—and in such an idiotic way. Because at dinner it kept running through my head that once your mother had called me a dirty little girl."

He breathed in her sparkling frankness like a draught of fresh air and, as they laughed together, he liked her terrifically again.

"Jannekin, I want to see you soon; we have lots of the past to talk about, you and I. But this is a business call. Jannekin, I want to buy back that old car of ours."

"You knew I had it, then," she said guiltily. "I hated to think of it sitting there so—so aged and so neglected."

It was their old love she was talking about, and he knew it, but she hurried on:

"I hear about you sometimes—from Edgar Bronson. He's done very well, hasn't he? He came down last week and dropped in on me."

Dick frowned, with a resurgence of his old sense of superiority.

"Of all the boys who were at Tech, you two are most spoken of," went on Jannekin innocently.

"Well"—his voice held a touch of impatience—"I musn't keep you from your luncheon."

"That doesn't matter. About the car—if you want it, you can have it, of course. I'll tell the chauffeur to run it around."

A minute later she reappeared, wearing an expression of distress. "The chauffeur says it's gone. He hasn't seen it for weeks."

Dick turned cold inside.

"It's gone?"

"It must have been stolen. You see, I never bought it to use, but only——"

"This is extraordinary," he interrupted. "I really have to have that car. It's of the greatest importance."

At his change of tone, she hardened also:

"I'm sorry. I don't see what I can do about it."

"Can I look around in back myself? It might be behind the garage or somewhere."

"Certainly."

Scarcely aware of his own rudeness, Dick plunged down the steps and around the house. Wild suspicions surged through him—that Edgar Bronson had persuaded her to part with the car, and now Jannekin, ashamed, was lying to him. It was hard to imagine anyone stealing such an automobile; he searched every foot of the place as if it were something that might be concealed behind a dog house. Then, baffled and raging, he retraced his steps and stopped suddenly within the range of a sentence that drifted out the kitchen window:

"She ask me, but I wan't goin' to tell her. The old man sell it to me last week with a old gun and fishing tackle, just 'fore they took him down to that institarium. He not givin' nothin' away. So I pay him eight dollar out of my wages and I sell the car to Uncle Ben Govan over to Canterbury for ten dollar. No, suh. Old man sold me that stuff fair and square, and I pay him for it. I just shet my mouth when Miss Jannekin ask me. I don't tell her nothin' *at* all."

Dick walked firmly in at the kitchen door. Observing the look in his eye, the chauffeur sprang to his feet, a cigarette dropping from his mouth. A few minutes later, Dick rounded the house again, sorry for his wild imaginings. Jannekin was on the veranda speeding a guest; impulsively, he walked up to her and declared:

"I'm going on an expedition, Janny Jannekin, and you're coming with me right away."

She laughed lightly: "These Motor Boys—he mistakes me for a spare part." But as he continued to regard her, she gave a startled sigh and the color went up in her transparent cheeks.

"Well, very well. I don't suppose my guests will mind. After all, they've been telling me for months I ought to have a young man. . . . Go in and break the news, Alice, will you? Say I'm kidnaped—try to get the ransom money together."

Pulled not so much by Dick's hand as by his exuberance, they flew to his car. On the way, across the river and up the hill to the darky settlement, they talked little, because they had so much to say. Yassuh, Uncle Ben Govan's house was that one down there. And in the designated hollow a dark, villainous antique came toward them, doffing, so as to speak, his corncob pipe. After Dick had explained his mission and assured him that they were not contesting his legal rights to the machine, he agreed to negotiate. "Yassuh, I got her roun' back. How much you want pay for her, boss? . . .

"Boss, she's yours." Carefully he requested and pocketed the money, and then led them round to where, resting beside a chicken coop, lay the familiar, cream-colored body of the family bus— cushions, door handles, dashboard and all.

"But where's the chassis?" Dick exploded.

"Chassis?"

"The engine, the motor, the wheels!"

"Oh, that there part." The old man chuckled belittlingly. "That part I done soe a man. This here comfortable part with the cushions, it kept kind of easin' off the wheels when the man was takin' it away, so he lef' it here, and I thought I'd take these cushions and make me two beds for my grandchildren. You don't want to buy it?"

Firmly Dick retrieved ten of the twelve dollars, and after much recapitulation of local geography, he obtained the location of a garage and an approximation of its name.

"The thing sits quiet for five years," he complained as they raced back down the hill, "and then, at the age of about ninety, it begins to bounce around the country like a jumping bean!"

Finally they saw it. It stood in a row of relics back of the garage— a row which a mechanic was about to slaughter.

But one of them was not a junk to Dick and Jannekin as they rushed forward with reprieve in their eyes. There it was, stripped to its soul: four wheels, a motor, a floor board—and a soap box.

"Take it away for twenty-five," agreed the proprietor, "as it stands. Say, you know, for a job nineteen years old, the thing runs dandy still."

"Of course, it does!" Dick boasted as they climbed on and set the motor racing. "I'm turning in my car on the trade."

"That's a joke!" called back the practical Jannekin as they drove away. "We'll be around for it."

They throbbed down Canal Street, erect and happy on the soap box, stared at curiously by many eyes.

"Doesn't it run well?" he demanded.

"Beautifully, Dick." She had to sit very close to him on the box. "You'll have to teach me to drive, dear. Because there isn't any back part."

"We always sat in the front. Once I consoled you beside this wheel and then once you consoled me—do you remember?"

"Darling!"

"Where'll we go?"

"To heaven."

"By George, I think it'll make it!"

Proud as Lucifer, the flaming chariot swept on up the street.

In the Darkest Hour

(*Redbook*, October 1935)

"In the Darkest Hour" was written in Baltimore in April 1934. When it became clear that *Tender Is the Night* (published 12 April 1934) was not going to earn Fitzgerald a respite from magazine work, he turned to the plan of writing an historical novel in the form of a series of connected stories which he could then revise into a book. This series was probably conceived earlier and held in reserve. Harold Ober had difficulty selling the project to editor Edwin Balmer of *Redbook*, who bought the first story—"In the Darkest Hour"—for $1250. *Redbook* supplied the subtitle "A Poignant Romance of Chaos and Leadership." When Fitzgerald pressed for a commitment to publish the series, Ober informed him in December:

> I think we have to remember that you have made a reputation for writing a very modern story. If an editor wants an authentic story about modern society, you are one of the first authors that would come to his mind. The result is that when a reader picks up a magazine with one of your stories in it and finds a story about the ninth century he is going to be shocked. You will remember that I approached several magazines about this series and that is what every editor said. Balmer was the only one who was willing to try the series and he told me yesterday that the owners of his magazine were not yet convinced that he was not partially crazy in buying these stories from you.

Fitzgerald wrote four stories for the series: "In the Darkest Hour" (October 1934), "The Count of Darkness" (June 1935), "The Kingdom in the Dark" (August 1935), "Gods of Darkness" (November 1941). Although the fourth story was submitted in December 1934, it was not published until after Fitzgerald's death because *Redbook* gave up on the series.

The most interesting circumstance about the Philippe or Count of Darkness stories is that the hero was based on Ernest Hemingway, as indicated by one of Fitzgerald's *Notebooks* entries: "Just as Stendahl's portrait of a Byronic man made *Le Rouge et Noir* so couldn't my portrait of Ernest as Philippe make the real modern man." Hemingway's reaction to the series is unknown.

Fitzgerald was an enthusiastic history student who was proud of his history library and kept a "histomap" on his study wall. He devised a game for his daughter which was played with cards bearing the portraits and biographies of French historical figures. But the Philippe series, his only extended attempt at historical fiction, does not succeed because he could not work well with researched materials; the personal quality of his best stories is missing. Moreover, these stories are flawed by linguistic problems because Fitzgerald tried to present ninth-century speech by having Philippe speak like a hard-boiled detective and the peasants like southern sharecroppers. The effect is sometimes inadvertently funny.

Although Scottie Fitzgerald Smith feels that these stories are so inferior to her father's other work that they should remain interred in *Redbook*, "In the Darkest Hour" has been included here as a specimen because the series marks such a departure in Fitzgerald's work and because he had such high hopes for it. Indeed, in 1939 when he began work on his last novel, *The Last Tycoon*, he was uncertain whether to return to Philippe instead.

On a May afternoon in the Year of Our Lord 872 a young man rode a white Arabian horse down a steep slope into the Valley of the Loire, at a point fifty miles west of the city of Tours.

He was lost. He was following directions given him six weeks before in Cordova—directions that were based on a woman's memory of eighteen years before. Since then all this part of France had been ravaged and pillaged by band after band of Northmen surging into the estuary of the Loire with their small Viking galleys; and most of the landmarks Philippe's mother had given him had long disappeared.

He was broad and strong, and well-developed for his twenty years. His hair was tawny and waving; his mouth was firm; his eyes, of a somewhat cruel gray, were shrewd and bright. Though not of Moorish birth, he wore a pointed Oriental headpiece, cloth-covered to keep out the sun, and a travel-stained tunic bordered with gold and held together by a leather belt, from which swung a curved sword. More formidably, a mace was hooked to his saddle; and a light coat of fence-rings sewn upon leather was rolled like a blanket behind it.

During three days Philippe had not seen a human being—only half-burned farmhouses, inhabited here and there by ghostly ill-nourished pigs and poultry prowling among the ruins; now as he stopped to drink from a stream, he started as he saw a youth of his own age engaged in the same function on the other side not fifteen feet away. He was of a type that, for all the Christian prisoners daily paraded through the streets of Cordova, Philippe had never seen before. His hair was straight and red; his eyes were blue with a tough luster over them and a smiling mouth. He wore a coat of interwoven links and carried a straight flat-sword.

For a long moment they stared at each other; then Philippe, after the custom of Moorish Spain, greeted him in the Tourainian dialect that he had learned from his mother.

"Hey, stranger."

The man did not reply.

"Hey, where's this place at?" Philippe demanded; and as the man still remained silent: "What's the trouble—haven't you got any tongue? I'm just asking a friendly question. I'm figuring that my people used to live somewhere about here."

Evidently deciding after his long inspection that Philippe meant well, the stranger then spoke—but unfortunately in a language that Philippe had never heard before.

Philippe shrugged his shoulders and tried once more, in pigeon-phrases this time.

"No speak Lingua Franca?"

The man shook his head, and they both laughed good-humoredly. Suddenly Philippe saw that the man was not alone. As if waiting for him, a little way back from the bank of the stream, a girl stood cleaning her teeth with a twig, and watching. She was of a type more akin to Philippe's than to the other's—she was about sixteen, with large eyes of the kind sometimes described as starry because of a peculiar wet brightness that danced like a reflection along the edge of the upper lid. Seeing her, Philippe felt a desire to assert himself.

He tapped his chest.

"Philippe!" he announced.

Only half understanding, the other repeated the gesture and proclaimed proudly, "Viking!" which Philippe assumed to be his name.

Suddenly the young Northman came to a great decision. He took a wooden bottle from a sack at his belt, raised it to his lips with an expression of enjoyment, and invited Philippe to come over and join him. Welcoming any human companionship, Philippe took from his saddle-bag some flapjacks made that morning, and a flask containing his last ounces of olive oil; with these he went a little upstream till he found a ford, and crossed to the other side. To his disappointment, the girl had disappeared. The two young men, one from the fjords of Norway, one from a city in Andalusia, sat side by side eating and drinking together in an unfamiliar land.

It was stranger then, than it would have been at almost any other time in history. One can think loosely of the Dark Ages as extending from the decline of Rome to the discovery of America; but in the dead middle of those ten centuries, there were two hundred years so brutal, so ignorant, so savage, so dark, that little is known about them. It was the time when Europe was so overrun by Northmen, Moors and Huns that it had fallen into a state of helpless and sub-bestial degradation. Leaderless, the wretched farmers had no protection from the fiercest hordes from the north and the east, or from more skillful and better organized Saracens from the south. The earlier barbarian invasions, those of five hundred years before, had been gradually absorbed by Roman civilization; the barbarians had adopted the customs and manners of those they conquered. But the saturation-point had long been reached. Rome was no more. You could ride for two days across France without meeting a man who could read, write or count to ten; the inhabitants had nothing to offer to the new invaders except their scrawny livestock, their scanty grain, their womenfolk—their lives.

This condition of things was not known to young Philippe as, parting with his Viking acquaintance, he rode wéstward along the Loire. He knew only what his Frankish mother had told him in their native dialect in the long Andalusian evenings—of former glories, of captains great as the old Romans. She would never go north again; she had come to love the chieftain who had slain her husband and carried her with her infant son off to Spain—but it was understood that some day Philippe would return. His stepfather, the Vizier, had approved, and had presented him with a good horse, arms and a fat purse. . . .

Philippe stopped at twilight beside a decayed grange, where, leaving his horse to browse, he sopped the last flapjack in his last drop of olive oil. It was a desolate countryside, the more so, as there was evidence here and there that it had once been highly cultivated. As Philippe finished his meal, he heard voices approaching on the rough road, and recognized with a sharp pang of excitement the tongue that his mother had taught him, the tongue of his native land.

The voices belonged to two weary husbandmen, carrying flails, and followed by a small tired ox pulling a wooden plow on a sledlike drag. They were smallish, bent, bearded men, dressed each in a single coarse garment. Barefooted, their legs were protected by rags secured with laced thongs.

"I heard tell of a thing up to Tours last market-day," one said. "It was when them there yeller devils messed up St. Hilaire."

"I heard some talk of it," said the other man morosely.

"Well, them devils had to leave two hurt ones behind. One killed himself, but the other was hid out by some widow woman. Say, did the town people tear him apart! They chopped him up a little bit at a time with the flayers—the young uns came out and helped. Kep' him alive two hours."

"Hm," grunted the other noncommittally.

"That aint all. Then the townspeople went after that widow woman—lemme tell you what they did. They took a yoke of oxen—"

At this point the men were abreast of Philippe, and he stood up from behind his bush.

"Howdy," he said. "God save you!"

The two men stopped and stepped back; one of them crossed himself. The ox pulled up and waited.

"Don't be afraid—I'm not going to hurt you. I only want to know where I'm at." His tone was placatory.

They eyed him and his clothing suspiciously, and exchanged glances.

"Where do you want to get to?"

"I asked you a question," said Philippe impatiently.

"You're in a place used to be called Villefranche, but they aint no village any more. The church used to stand over there about half a mile. We aint had a market here nigh on to ten years."

This was gloomy news.

"Many people live hereabouts?"

"Used to be a right smart lot of them. But since them yellow devils come through, and them red-headed heathen from the north, it sort of thinned us out a little."

Jacques, the morose farmer, nodded gloomily.

"If you count on finding anything worth while around these parts, you mought as well move along," said the first man. "Aint enough grain in any bin to feed a family one month. Aint a family not short-handed. Aint enough women and children, barrin' men, to tend the fields proper. Jacques and me had six head of oxen between us; this is what we got left—an' a donkey."

"But what about the King—this Charles they call 'Baldy'?"

They both laughed.

"Lot of good he does us! Haven't heard tell of him since my father's time—except he wants to be the Emperor of Rome."

Philippe considered: things were poorly here. He came to his main point: to find who was the responsible man of the community—who, if anyone, sat in the manor hall.

"You had a lord here once—a man of family, who owned these lands."

"Once, yes."

"Where's his house?"

The farmer pointed at the side of the road: "Here it stood."

In the gathering dusk, fraught with a promise of rain, Philippe stared around him, shocked. At first sight neither stick nor stone of the manor remained—only the abandoned granary, through the broken sides of which he could see the sky. Then he made out that a fallen cylinder, which he had taken for a tree-trunk, was part of a pillar. There was no manor house; there was no fine property—there were only some rabbitlike families scattered among the solemn acres.

"I want to see the head man of the community," he said.

They exchanged glances.

"Whoever collects taxes."

The men looked at him blankly.

"They's been little to collect since the wars," Jacques said. "Everything's been took off by the foreigners." He considered. "I guess you'd call Le Poire the head man. But like everybody else, he's got nothin' for you."

Le Poire's house, a superstructure of clay and branches erected upon an old stone foundation, was rather superior to the hovels they passed on their way. Le Poire himself, a bent hatchet-faced man of forty, stooping over a charcoal brazier, sprang to his feet as they came in, and took a step toward a club that lay at hand.

"God be with you!" said Philippe quickly. "Don't get up on your ear."

Reassured by the sound of his own dialect and the sight of Jacques, Le Poire asked:

"What do you want of me?"

The place stank of charcoal and crowded habitation, and Philippe's face creased in disgust. On the way north he had prepared a few phrases in the grand manner of the Vizier his stepfather, but they seemed inappropriate to this verminous hut.

"I've got something to say to you, and to the farmers around here." He turned to Jacques: "You take my nag and round up a few of them."

Something in his voice made Jacques obey, but the other man was not pleased.

"Why?" demanded Le Poire.

"You'll learn soon enough, old boy."

"But why?" he insisted. "What do you want to say?"

Not answering, Philippe reached out carelessly for the young girl who stood regarding him with awe, pulled her toward him and looked into her face.

"You're a pretty little parcel," he said.

She stared up at him, silent and acquiescent. Philippe saw Le Poire's sullen eyes stray again toward his club and he released the girl with a short laugh.

"Your meat's going to burn," he warned Le Poire.

Le Poire's eyes smoldered like the brazier itself.

"You take this for meat! I aint killed a goat since Easter."

"What *is* that you're cooking, then?"

"Who wants to know?" Le Poire grumbled.

Philippe stepped forward and slapped the man's face sharply.

"Answer me like that once more, and I'll let daylight through you."

The passion in Le Poire's expression equaled that in Philippe's, but either from the habit of defeatism or because Philippe was better armed, Le Poire controlled himself and knelt again beside the brazier.

In half an hour Jacques had returned with four other farmers. They were puzzled and ill at ease in the presence of this curiously dressed person who stood taciturn and scornful against the wall.

"Well, men," Philippe said, "here's the line-up: This happens to be my land. I am Philippe, Count of Villefranche, son and heir of Count Charles. I've come here to take over."

They stared at him in astonishment.

"For twenty years you haven't had anybody to tell you what to do, and you've got in a big mess. I'm going to put things to rights."

For a minute he was disappointed at their lack of response; his voice hardened as he continued:

"I hold this land along the Loire for twenty miles in fee simple to Charles, Roman Emperor and King of the West Franks. The title was given my grandfather by the great Charles. I undertake to keep all foreigners and cutthroats off your necks, so you can do your work in peace; and on your part I expect you to give me good service, so long as it doesn't go contrary to your duties to God and the King."

Still there was silence. The young girl edged closer, still staring as if bewildered.

"I've been a prisoner in Spain since I was a kid—" He stopped, realizing that this meant less than nothing to them. "I've been in a country where the people are building churches and forts and palaces such as you couldn't imagine. Like they used to have in Rome. Now, somebody's got to make you people stand up on your hind legs so all these heathen won't ride over you. And Providence in its wisdom has chosen me."

There was another long pause. Le Poire turned away a little, to avoid Philippe's eyes.

"We get along all right," he muttered. "It aint goin' to help if we get us a master to share the little we got."

There was a faint murmur of approbation.

"Stop that talk!" cried Philippe, throwing prudence to the winds as if he had a troupe of horses behind him. "I'm not asking you—I'm *telling* you. You'll be glad enough when you don't get burned out and plundered every few months."

The general opinion swung toward him again, but Le Poire had recovered his courage and his stubbornness.

"Son of the old master—if y'are that, and how do we know—"

"I have proof of who I am."

"Anyhow, you come here and just say all this—how you're goin' to be the boss and this-and-that. But we people got to take time to think."

"*You* think!" Philippe exclaimed. "I tell you this belongs to *me*! It is for *me* to say what you should do."

One of the farmers offered mildly:

"We got to anyhow see how the Church people feel."

"I'll do nothing without the approval of the Church," agreed Philippe cautiously, again remembering a warning from his mother. "I'll take up the matter with the clergy of these parts tomorrow."

He smiled suddenly at the girl, as if to say, "I'll take care of it all, kid." Then he said, "God save you!" to the farmers, and went out. Mounting in a drizzle of rain, he discovered that he was hungry, and wished he had got something from Le Poire, but it was beneath his dignity to go back. There was a wood with protective foliage against the rain a few hundred yards from Le Poire's cottage. Here he camped, and gave his horse an armful of Le Poire's hay to which he had helped himself. Scooping three depressions in the ground to fit his hips and shoulder-blades, he wrapped himself in his cloak and slept. . . .

He awoke in what might have been one hour or six; in the darkness the peasant Jacques was leaning over him.

"Don't speak! They know where you're camped, and they're a-going to kill you. They've been talkin' about it ever since you left—there's ten of them now, all full of wine."

Philippe was on his feet in an instant.

"Where are the dirty dogs?" he demanded furiously. "I'll—"

He saddled quickly and rode, wild with anger, to the shelter of another copse closer to the house. He meant to scatter them once, before he retreated. As they approached through the rain, he drew his sword, and then, leaning forward Moorish fashion, passed his left arm and buckler beneath the horse's neck so that it protected his head and the beast's throat on his combat side. When they were ten feet away, he rode at them, straight along the length of their straggling column, yelling like three men and slashing with his sword. Twice it hit into flesh; once it pierced: the sudden offensive took away what fight there was in the men, and they flinched back on the slippery ground. Wheeling at the end of the line, he briefly considered another foray, but a rivulet of cold blood carried caution to his mind, and instead he cried in a loud voice:

"I'll be back, you rats, I'll be back!"

Turning his horse, he spurred away into the rain.

After five or six miles, Philippe tied up out of sight of the road, and knelt down under a tree to pray, repeating the Latin words with more fervor, more hope of propitiation, than ever he had upon Moslem soil.

He knelt a long time, promising many things to God; he was still on his knees when he tumbled off to sleep.

When he awoke in a still rainy dawn, he heard voices not a hundred feet away—a babel of voices, harsh and guttural, rough and unfamiliar, together with the sounds of much activity—a sharpening of steel, a creak of wooden-wheeled carts, gruff commands, women's voices scolding.

He crawled up to the edge of the leafy hollow in which he lay, and peered out.

Forty-odd men, in appearance like the red-haired youth encountered yesterday, were breaking camp. They were tall, with reddish-yellow hair and ruddy faces. Their close-fitting steel caps were equipped with nose-pieces, which while they worked were worn pointed sidewise. Their baggage-train consisted of half a dozen oxcarts of a type Philippe had noticed throughout Aquitaine; the carts were heaped high with grain, provisions and other goods. The work was shared by half a dozen women of a darker complexion, obviously of a different race.

From what Jacques had said, it did not take Philippe long to identify the cavalcade; this was one of the roving bands of Northmen so dreaded throughout the helpless kingdom, bound upon a raid, or more probably returning from one, and heading toward their galleys concealed in the delta of the Loire. He had spent a night within bowshot of them without knowing it.

At a sound behind he turned quickly, hand on dagger. A woman with a water-jug on her hip was looking down at him, laughing silently. He recognized her immediately as the girl he had glimpsed yesterday across the stream.

"You're on a bad spot, Mister," she volunteered. To his astonishment, her tongue was like his, in spite of a difference of accent.

"What are you hanging around here for?" she inquired. "Suppose I should sing out now? What wouldn't they do to you! Boy!"

"Sing out, then!" he challenged her, calculating the distance to his horse.

With mischief in her eyes, she cupped her hand suddenly to her lips; but Philippe was taking no chances, and in the same instant he was on her, his hand over her mouth; they threshed about in the shrubbery until he pinioned her helpless on the ground.

"I don't want to hurt you," he said. "But don't you sing out. I want you to help me."

Hoping he had said the right thing, he removed his gagging hand cautiously.

"I wasn't going to yell," she protested. "I was kidding. I'm tickled to hear a voice I can understand. I'm from south of here, but this bunch came along last month and carried off five of us, and just about everything in the village. Now I'm the chief's girl." She seemed half resigned, half amused. "Robert the Frog—that's his name. He's nice. We're married—at least we are according to his religion."

"You don't mind their wolfing you off?"

"Not me. After living on stale bread for a couple of years, you don't mind anything—at least these boys eat well."

She picked up her spilled water-jug—then, staring out of the glade, became rigid.

"Here comes a couple of noseys now. You better get out—and get out quick."

Two warriors were approaching the hill rapidly, and Philippe guessed that they had spotted his horse's white coat against the full day. In half a minute he had flung the saddle on him and mounted. Not a second too soon—a spent arrow whirred into the ground beside him as he dashed away.

Riding slowly westward again, he began to realize, aided by an overcast morning and an empty stomach, the difficulties of his situation. For twenty hours he had been on his own land, but neither those in possession nor those strangers now trespassing upon it seemed properly appreciative of the fact. Something must be done, and quickly. With care he circumvented the scene of last night's trouble, and after an hour's touring in a circle through the persistent drizzle, he located the monastery.

It was composed of a group of one-story wooden buildings; yet by all odds it was the most prepossessing establishment he had seen in these parts. A gate of heavy oak made entrance both to the high-fenced fields and to the interior palisade around the buildings, behind which inmates could retire in time of danger. At his hail a panel in the gate slid open, and a wildly impish face topped with wild red hair looked out at him appraisingly.

"So what?" said the man.

"God save you, Father—"

"Brother."

"Brother, then—God save you anyhow."

The man laughed. "Where've you got your gang hid?" he demanded.

"I'm alone."

"I should believe that!"

Philippe took formal oath on the subject. The monk seemed satisfied, and presently pulled the bars on the gate and swung it open.

"So what?" he repeated.

"I want to see the Superior," said Philippe.

The man locked the gate carefully behind them.

"I guess it's all right. I'm Brother Brian—who are you? You've got a Moor's helmet on your head."

"I've been a prisoner in the south."

The Abbot was a handsome and imposing man, but as Philippe perceived, of a timid and querulous temperament.

"I knew your father," he said. "We didn't always agree—he was rather a violent man; still, things went on well enough."

"Better than now; that's certain."

"Yes; but times have changed all around these parts. We've been burned out three times since then, and robbed and what-not. None the less, even the worst of these rough-necks seem to see we're peaceful folk, and spare our lives, thanks be to God—"

"Peaceful folk—nowadays?" cried Philippe scornfully. "Seems to me, Father, I heard my mother tell of bishops who fought out front with battle-axes."

"Times change," insisted the Abbot. "Nowadays it's every group for themselves. If we tried to fight, we wouldn't last long. We return to our industrious ways after they pass, and soon we are managing to exist again."

"He's yellow!" thought Philippe bitterly. Aloud he said: "I'm here for just that—to protect these jakes."

"Maybe they don't want to be 'protected,' " said the Abbot dryly.

They argued back and forth; finally Philippe felt himself becoming increasingly angered, but he knew any outburst would be of small avail. The Abbot offered him dinner and lodging, and was not above accepting the pieces of silver which Philippe proudly tendered in return. After the noon collation Philippe retired to the room assigned him, and stretching out on the straw, thought for an hour.

He thought creatively. There are epochs when certain things sing in the air, and certain strong courageous men hear them intuitively long before the rest. This was an epoch of disturbance and change; all over Europe men were thinking exactly like Philippe, taking direction from the arrows of history that seemed to float dimly overhead. Each of those men thought himself to be alone, but really each was an instrument of response to a great human need. Each knew that the spirit of man was at low tide; each one felt in himself the necessity of seizing power by force and cunning.

By mid-afternoon Philippe had evolved a tentative plan. The rain had ceased temporarily, and he strolled out into the grounds. By the gate, as if by accident, he fell into conversation with the red-headed brother.

As he had already divined, Brother Brian was of a type Philippe could always influence and handle. An Irishman by birth, he had led the life of an itinerant friar, stopping for long periods at any monastery where he could use his talents—cooking, gardening and handicrafts.

He agreed with Philippe that the morale of the countryside was broken indeed, and could only be mended by some strong and properly constituted authority.

"We need a captain and a special trained band of men to protect the farmers as well as the church. There should be a stronghold to rally around—like we hear of the Roman camps and walls in the old days."

Philippe agreed. "But I can't sell the idea to this Abbot," he said.

They talked a long time; finally Philippe unfolded his plan.

When he had done, Brian exclaimed: "By Our Lady, that's a large order!"

"It's a man's job," said Philippe. "How about it—will you come in with me?" As Brian hesitated, he added quickly: "I don't want you to break any vows. I don't want to begin by offending Providence—"

"Never fear! I've taken no vows, except sometimes simple ones that I've always been properly released from."

"How many men could I count on from here?"

"You go fast," said Brian, laughing. He considered. "I'm not sure. After Vespers I'll look around. There're a few brothers who might feel as I do, and there's maybe a few workmen who would do as I say. How of your farmers?"

"There's a guy named Jacques I think I can trust. I'll work through him. I'll go find him now—there's damn' little time."

"You'll find him a mile down the road in a little hut that leads into a cave. And he has twin brothers turned sixteen you could maybe persuade."

Philippe found Jacques working in his field; he thanked him heartily for his service of the night before, and they sat down amidst the ripening wheat while Philippe unfolded his plan.

Jacques' morose discontented eyes showed a spark.

"High time somebody did somethin' around here. Everything's rottin' away. . . . Sure, Master, I'm with you."

"Good. I want eight men from you, and eight from the monastery—no more. When you've signed them up, go and see Le Poire. Tell him about the Northmen, and put the bug in his ear. He'll fall for it—even rats will scrap in a corner. Make him think there's only about twenty Northmen, with all sorts of loot, silver and gold and all. Tell him they've been in a lot of fights lately, and they're discouraged and shot to pieces."

"I get you, Master. To my thinking, Le Poire can get out about sixty folks, countin' men and women. Some of these dames would make better fighters than the men."

"Tell him you know where the Northmen will camp. I've figured it out, and I can't be far wrong, calculating the pace of those oxcarts in a day, and that they'll want to be near a stream. Pass that on to Le Poire, as if you'd found it out yourself."

"Good!" Jacques rubbed his hands together, a man transformed. "I'll meet you at midnight with some lads you can trust."

"And the clubs and axes," Philippe reminded him. "Scythes are too clumsy."

"And the horses."

"*And* the horses. There's maybe three we can round up here on the quiet. But there's other beasts besides horses you can ride on. By God, bring oxen if you can get them in motion. I'm counting on some of the monastery nags."

So all unknown to Le Poire and his neighbors, twenty others—farmers, lay brothers, monastery serfs—met at midnight, riding a strange collection of palfreys, work-horses, spavined skin-and-bones, mules and donkeys—as grotesque a caricature of chivalry as could be imagined. Nevertheless, mounted they all were, after a fashion; and Philippe's idea was a prefiguration of an age already beginning, when mounted men were to take over the shaping of feudal Europe. His chief advantage over the Normans, as well as over the farmers, was just this.

He told them briefly the technique of the charge, the adjustment to the speed of the different animals, the weight of the shock, the ride through, the wheel-around, and return through the enemy to form for a second charge—a technique preserved on the plains of Hungary and south of the Spanish Marche.

They were to wait in ambush until farmers and Northmen were deeply engaged—wait, even, until there had been much blood-letting, until the two forces were reduced and the first energy of combat had been fatigued and dissipated. Then these rustic men of action would strike upon the Norman flank, and put to the proof their right to lead and to command.

Philippe felt it to be a good omen that the rain had drifted off, and uncovered a bright starry night. Riding cautiously by circuitous lanes, they came after a few hours in sight of distant fires. The Northmen were camped upon the spot Philippe had prophesied, a flat clearing beside a stream. Behind them rose an eminence, thickly wooded on its crest, and here Philippe took his station.

His chief worry was not about his own men, but as to whether Le Poire would be there before dawn, and could control his undisciplined company sufficiently to take the Normans by surprise. He paced to and fro impatiently while the last fires of the Northmen smoldered out.

At length Brother Brian came up excitedly.

"From the top of the tree I could see quite a way," he said. "They're coming. I could see movement westward."

"I pray to God that Le Poire don't let them straggle," mused Philippe. A horse whinnied sharply. "See to that. Muzzle them if you have to."

Ten minutes later the attack came with the suddenness of a tidal wave, came as a surprise even to the watchers on the hill—sixty ragged savages, male and female, armed with scythes, bill-hooks, clubs and axes, poured into the clearing with a wild cry; and in a minute all was confusion as men, women and boys flung themselves upon the half-awakened Northmen.

For a minute it looked as though Le Poire would have an easy time of it. The first Northmen to meet the avalanche were cut down before they could draw swords; but the country people, unused to organized combat, tried to atone by a wild, vengeful ferocity, and in consequence got in each other's way and shouted adjurations and warnings that increased the confusion. Within five minutes two nuclei of Northmen had gathered on either side of the wagons, one under Robert the Frog, their swollen bandy-legged leader, the other under his son Goldgreaves. Then the farmers began to feel the prick of steel, and after each rush forward left bleeding, groaning bodies behind, the breath to be quickly extinguished by the Viking swords.

On the side of the wagons held by Goldgreaves the peasants fought at close quarters instead of in rushes—here the casualties were greatest. One by one the Northmen were pulled from their thinning ranks, to disappear amidst the slashing flails and clubs; on the other hand, when a villager fell, their greater number supplied another to take his place.

Still Philippe waited, hoping that some turn of the tide would wash the battle away from the wagons so that his charge would be most effective; and presently his prayer was answered—Robert the Frog, noting a certain diminution of enthusiasm in the farmers, felt that the time had come to crack them up while he still had fifteen warriors on their feet. And now, when Philippe saw the line sway forward, he ordered his cavalry to mount.

Down the slope with a high yell, slow at first to keep the line, then faster, until just as the Normans reached the wavering peasant line, Philippe's men were among them, slashing, slamming and trampling. Out in the clear, they turned about and rode once more over the bewildered platoon. The Northmen fought desperately, but their cohesion was broken; a dozen had lost their footing in the first rush; and the farmers, taking heart, rushed in and dispatched them. Their leader disappeared under a mass of men, and now there were but four fighting back to back, then three; then it was as if a wave rolled over them all, and there were no more Northmen on this side of the wagons.

Following Philippe, the victors turned to the other part of the melee, Philippe trying in vain to keep his own men together as a last bloody struggle took place. In the press he was pulled from his horse, and found himself rolling on the ground with an enemy warrior. The man's arm had been broken; and Philippe pinioning him, felt for his small curved dagger. As the man saw the steel he relaxed, waiting, his eyes looking up pitifully at Philippe, his face set in a faint smile. . . . Suddenly Philippe got to his feet, pulling his man with him, and motioned him to stand where he was; then he swung himself back into the saddle.

"Don't kill any more of them!" he shouted high above the cries of combat. "Jacques! Brian! Take them prisoners!"

Failing to be heard, he spurred angrily into the last flurry of fight, striking at the farmers with the flat of his sword.

"Get back, you dogs! I said kill no more!" He cleared a little space for himself, and shouted again: "These last men are prisoners if they yield!"

A peasant, intoxicated with slaughter, cried back at him:

"Who says we can't? We've beaten these wolves—we'll treat them like they'd of treated us. Who the devil are you to say what we do?"

A faint murmur of approbation ran through the impassioned men. Philippe knew that the crux of his struggle for mastery was at hand.

"Stand by, my men!" he cried; spurring his horse viciously, he galloped directly at the peasant who had spoken, at him and over him, striking him down with the flat of his mace.

"And who else wants to question my word?" Philippe cried. "I am your lord, Philippe of Villefranche, and what I say goes in these parts."

The murmuring died away. The last five Normans were disarmed and bound, and as if the false dawn flushing the east were a signal, the farmers sank exhausted on the ground, or went down to the stream to drink and bathe their wounds.

Philippe's men sat watchfully waiting for orders. He approached the panting prisoners and signed to the first man, the same whom he himself had spared a few minutes before: "Do you want your throat cut—or will you kneel and swear faithful service and allegiance to me?"

After a minute the man understood. He knelt on the ground, and taking Philippe's hand, pressed his forehead against it. The next prisoner, gray-haired and tall, was given the same choice—but he drew himself up proudly, folded his arms and shook his head. Philippe signaled to Jacques, who dismounted, threw himself on the man like a cat, and ripped his throat from ear to ear. With his blood soaking his proud beard, the warrior dropped where he stood.

The next two men followed the lead of the first in doing obeisance to Philippe. The last man to be brought up was Goldgreaves, son of the dead chieftain. Recognizing Philippe, the man uttered an exclamation; then he composed his face stoically, and looked into Philippe's eyes for what he could find there.

Philippe knew that in this case mercy would not avail. This man was the son of a chief, a chief in his own right. Momentarily Philippe hesitated; then he hardened himself—there was no room for two leaders here. He put no questions, but signaled again to Jacques, and turned his own face away in sudden revulsion. An instinct told him that this act would return to haunt him. . . .

The thing was done and Goldgreaves was one with his band again. Of the forty Northmen who had marched into Touraine the day before, only the three prisoners, and two others who had led the women into the woods at the beginning of the fight, remained alive. One-third of the peasants, including Le Poire and several of the women, were killed; many of the others nursed wounds.

The sun was now over the horizon. Facing toward it, in some throwback of memories to Moslem ceremonies, Philippe cried aloud:

"O God, who sent these murderous heathen here so we could wipe them off the face of the earth, we thank Thee. Thy will be done on earth as it is in heaven."

It was a busy day. To begin with, the rations from the Northmen's carts were distributed, and the farmers fell ravenously upon the food. Afterward they collected their own dead, and then after stripping the bodies of the enemies of such clothing and trinkets as they coveted, pulled them into a pile later to be banked with wood and set alight; Philippe took care that the bodies of Robert and his son were placed on top of the prospective pyre. In another regard he had been careful to anticipate the farmers: everything in the nature of a weapon—sword, mace, dagger, bow, shield and helmet—had been collected by his own men, dumped into the empty ration-wagon and carefully guarded.

Before starting back, he spread word also as to the division of the other loot, the goblets, chalices, fabrics, precious vestments and utensils which the raiders had collected in Aquitaine.

On the march Philippe used his time to talk to some of the younger men, several of whom he felt were likely material for a permanent guard. In the late afternoon they came to the first hovels of the community, and families began to drop away, sometimes carrying their dead with the mute resignation of those who have endured much. But Philippe, with the wagons and his weird cavalry, kept on until they reached the site of the manor. There he pitched the tent of the dead chief for his own headquarters.

Half an hour later the Abbot and some of his men rode up. The Abbot was inclined to be sulky at the high-handed use that Philippe had made of members of his community, and more especially of his horses. Philippe heard him in silence. Then he said deferentially:

"I gave you a chance to come in on it, Father, didn't I? And you wouldn't—so I had to do it myself. Hadn't been for us, those devils might be burning your keep by this time."

"What are you going to do next?" demanded the Abbot suspiciously.

"That's my affair," Philippe said. "I do not want to be disrespectful, Father. I've big plans, but I'm working them out slowly. When you want to stand beside me four-square, I'll be glad. Till then I keep my mouth shut."

The Abbot rose testily. "Then I'll take my men and horses and go."

"Wait!" said Philippe. "We've got eight horses of yours, and I want to buy them." He took out his purse.

"But that's an outrage—they're not for sale—we have only ten horses altogether."

"I'll buy five then," said Philippe firmly. "That'll make five apiece. And as for the men, I think some of them would rather stay with me—Brother Brian for instance—"

"I wouldn't take him back under any circumstances."

And the Abbot rode off, dissatisfiedly.

After the strained and bloody day, the night fell easily and gratefully. One by one the men who remained made beds for themselves in the straw from the wagons. Only Philippe's shelter was empty as he walked up and down under the stars. This was his land now, as far as he could see. He picked up two handfuls of the soil and let it dribble through his fingers. Then in a sudden fervor he knelt and thanked God privately for His goodness. Resuming his pacing, he pointed presently toward a stone hill that, on its other slope, descended to the Loire, and whispered: "There I will build my fort and my house. And where the road fords the stream, I will build a bridge—".

His meditations were interrupted by an unexpected apparition— a small figure in white who emerged from nowhere and flung herself suddenly at his feet.

"Noble sire," she said, "forgive me—I followed you."

He pulled her up—it was the girl from the Viking camp with whom he had talked yesterday morning—she who had been consort to the slain Norse leader.

"So what?" he said coldly. "We have no place for girls here—not yet, anyhow."

"What am I going to do?" she wailed. "After the fight the others went off—and I didn't have anybody. The sea-king is dead. I can't starve in the woods, and I'm ten days' march from home."

Again she sank to the ground, clasping his knees desperately.

"Go on in there." He pointed to the tent.

"And where will you go? Aren't you tired?"

"I keep the watch," he said harshly. "Let the others get tired. I keep the watch."

After she had gone, he pursued his slow pace around the perimeter of the camp. Embodying in himself alone the future of his race, he walked to and fro in the starry darkness.

No Flowers

(*The Saturday Evening Post*, 21 July 1934)

"No Flowers" was written in May 1934 after Fitzgerald had given up "La Paix" and moved to Baltimore. The *Post* paid $3000. The sales of *Tender Is the Night* were disappointing, as it sold only 15,000 copies in 1934; and most of the royalties had been consumed by advances. Once again Fitzgerald was compelled to write stories; but of the eight published 1934 stories, only three were bought by the *Post*.

The time in Maryland brought a renewal of Fitzgerald's association with Princeton, which he always loved deeply. He took young Andrew Turnbull (his neighbor, later his biographer) to Princeton football games, volunteered advice to the coach, and even offered a plan for a new library. It was therefore natural for him to turn to his college in his search for story material. During one of his visits at this time Fitzgerald re-arranged the furniture in the Cottage Club, his undergraduate club, the way it had been during his student days. Although Princeton is not identified, "No Flowers" is clearly set there; and this story is informed by Fitzgerald's identification with Princeton.

"Now tell me again about the proms, mother," begged Marjorie at twelve.

"But I've told you, over and over."

"But just tell me just once more, pulease, and then I'll go right to sleep."

"Well, let's see," her mother considered. "Well, I used to be invited to go to proms at certain colleges——"

"Yes, go on. Start at the beginning. Start about how they invited you and everything."

"Well, there was a boy I knew once, named Carter McLane——"

"Yes, go on, I like about that prom," enthused Marjorie, squirming closer to her mother.

"——and he seemed to think I was very nice, so he invited me to be his guest. So, of course, I was very excited——"

"What happened to him later?"

"But I've told you this so often. You know my stories as well as I do."

"I know, but I just like to hear you say the whole thing over."

"Why don't you close your eyes and go to sleep?"

But after her mother left, Marjorie lay awake half the night listening to orchestras playing in a great gymnasium bewitched into a paradise of flowers and banners; all night boy after boy cut in on her, until she could scarcely take a step before adjusting herself to a new rhythm—just like Hotsy Gamble, who was two years ahead of her in school and danced cheek-to-cheek and was Marjorie's current Ideal. All evening she drifted, a bright petal cluster among dark-trunked trees. . . .

Six years later she went to her first prom, at the university where the women of her family had gone dancing for several generations. But she wore no orchids on the shoulder of her pale-blue organdie frock. This was because of Billy Johns' letter:

——don't expect me to send you any, and don't bring any. In these times (famous phrase) there are only a few guys can afford them, so the committee ruled them out altogether. Anyhow, you're flower enough for me—and for too many other people, damn it——

She heard also that there would only be one orchestra—not at all like her mother's stories of 1913, when Jim Europe and his bucks were enthroned at one end of the hall, and some Toscanini of tangos at the other. Lawdy, Lawdy! Next thing they'd be dancing to radio and it wouldn't be worth while going up there. What a break—to grow up into the middle of hard times, when all the luxury and revelry was subdued and everybody was economizing—economizing even on proms. Imagine!

"Probably there'll be champagne punch at the teas," said her mother innocently. "I do hope you won't touch any."

"Champagne punch!" Marjorie's scorn withered the plush in the chair car bearing them northward. "A girl will probably be lucky if she gets a glass of beer. Billy says they're giving the prom on a shoestring. Honestly, mother, sometimes I think father's right when he says that women your age don't know what's happening."

Her mother laughed; she let few things disturb her, and there were scarcely any more lines in her face than when, as Amanda Rawlins, she had ridden north on a similar pilgrimage.

"It may be more fun having it simpler," she said; but she added smugly, "Of course, in my day it was the event of a girl's year—except the year of her debut."

"More fun!" protested Marjorie. "Mother, try and realize you've had your fun, all that luxury and everything, but all we can do is watch it in the movies, and as often as not have to go Dutch treat to the movies."

"Well, Marjorie, we can still get off the train and go home."

Marjorie sighed.

"I'm not really complaining, mother. I've been very lucky. But sometimes I wish boys didn't wear such old suits and have such old cars and worry about how much gasoline they can afford. Do you realize that one of the Chase twins is driving a taxi and John Corliss is a movie usher?"

"Well, then, at least *he* has new suits."

"Do you know what he'd planned to do? The diplomatic service."

"We haven't abolished the diplomatic service, have we?" her mother asked.

"No, but he failed his examinations, and they won't take them any more if they fail in their examinations. And let me tell you he's sore; he thinks there ought to be a revolution."

"I suppose he wants them to turn the examination list upside down.".

Marjorie sighed again.

"All that makes me boil is that you were young in a sort of golden age, and I've got to be young in a sort of tin age. I'm growing plain jealous."

But when the towers and spires of the university town swam into the range of the car windows, Marjorie warmed with excitement. This was *it*. The boys who milled around the station were not the legendary Chesterfields with Bond Street clothes and streamlined cars; nevertheless, the Gothic walls rose from the many acres of fine green grass with as much grace and aspiration as if this were a five-million-share day of the 20's.

All afternoon there were teas, and then dinner at the club where her mother had come as a girl, and where they would lodge that night. Afterwards they went to a performance of the dramatic association and then to an informal dance; the prom took place tomorrow. Sometime during the evening Marjorie's mother repressed a yawn and faded off to bed. Others gave up, retired, but in the great hall of the club a half dozen couples lingered while the hours began their slow growth toward dawn. Billy Johns beckoned to Marjorie and she followed him through the dining room into a parlor beyond.

It was an old-fashioned chamber, Victorian and worn in contrast with the elaborateness of the rest of the club.

"This is called the Engagement Room," he said.

She looked around; there was an odd atmosphere about it, a nostalgia for another age.

"It was part of the old clubhouse on this site, and it meant a lot to some of the alumni members; so they had the architect build the new club building around it.

"The Engagement Room," she repeated.

As if at a signal, Billy took a step toward her. She kissed him quickly, stepping back from his arms.

"You're very handsome tonight," she said.

"Only tonight? Anyhow you can imagine why it's called the Engagement Room. It's haunted, you see. The old love affairs that first clicked here come back and click all over again."

"I can believe it."

"It's true." He hesitated. "I'm awfully glad to be in this room with you."

"Get me a glass of something cool," she said quickly. "Would you be a darling?"

He left the room obediently, and Marjorie, fatigued by the day, sank down in a big Victorian leather chair. Alternately she closed her eyes and pulled herself awake, thinking after a while, "Well, he certainly is taking his time about it." It was just at this moment that she realized that she was not alone in the room.

Across from her, sitting beside the gas fire that burned blue over imitation logs, were a young man and a girl. The man wore a wing collar and a blue bow tie; his coat buttoned high in an archaic fashion. The girl wore a gown voluminous of material, with huge puffed sleeves that were reminiscent of contemporary fashion, yet somehow different. Her hair, molded close to her head in ringlets, served as a perch for a minute bonnet that, like the sleeves, suggested the present without being of it.

"I promised you my answer today, Phil. Are you ready?" She spoke lower and slower, "My dear, I'll be very proud and happy to announce our engagement in June."

There was an odd little silence; the girl continued:

"I would have said yes to you last month, because I knew then that I cared. But I'd promised mother to take a while to think things over."

She broke off in surprise as the young man suddenly got up and paraded back and forth across the room—a look of misery, akin to fear, had come into his face. The girl looked at him in alarm, and as her profile caught the light, Marjorie recognized simultaneously her profile and her voice as the profile and voice of her mother's mother. Only now the voice was younger and more vibrant, the skin was of the texture that Italian painters of the decadence used for corner angels.

Phil sat down again, shading his eyes with his hand.

"I've got to tell you something . . . I don't know how."

Lucy's expression was drawn with apprehension; achieving an outward calm, she spoke in a clipped tone:

"Of course, Phil, if your ideas have changed, you must feel free to——"

"Nothing like that."

Somewhat relieved, Lucy said:

"Then won't you—won't you sit a little nearer while you tell me about it?"

Luther, the hall boy, stood at the door.

"Pardon, Mr. Savage; Mr. Payson would like to speak to you."

Phil nodded.

"All right, tell him I'll be there—very soon—presently. Tell him I'm almost ready."

"Phil!" Lucy demanded. "What is it?"

He blurted it out suddenly:

"I'm leaving college this afternoon, by request."

"You're expelled, Phil?"

"Something like that."

She went to him and put her arm over his shoulder. Watching them, Marjorie knew what was going to happen, because she had heard the story from her grandmother; yet, in the same breath, she was not sure, and she listened, tense with hope.

"Phil, what was it? Did you take too much champagne or something? It doesn't matter to me, Phil, because I love you. Do you think I'm such a light-weight that that could make a difference? Or did you fail some old examination?"

"No," and he added bitterly, "I passed an examination. I felt it was necessary to pass it—at any cost. And I did. It's not the faculty that's asked me to leave; the men waiting outside for me are two of my best friends. Did you ever happen to hear of a thing they've introduced here, the honor system?"

She had heard of it from her brother—a scarcely born tradition of this principality of youth: "I pledge my word of honor as a gentleman that during this examination I have neither given nor received aid."

"Why, Phil——"

"My degree depended on it, and I began thinking that if I flunked out, I'd never have the courage to tell you. Now I've got to tell you, because I happen to have been observed. My dear friends were kind enough to give me twenty-four hours, so that I could meet you and take you to the dance last night, but I'm sentenced to leave this locality forever by six o'clock."

Lucy went slowly back to her own chair.

"You had to know," said Phil. "Sooner or later you'd have found out why I couldn't come here any more—to this place I've loved so much."

"Yes, I suppose I had to know," she agreed; after a pause, she added: "You didn't do it for me, Phil."

"In a way, I did."

"No, Phil. You did it for some part of you I'm not even acquainted with."

The boy came to the door again.

"Beg pardon, sir; Mr. Payson says he must see you right now. He says to tell you it's quarter to six."

Phil nodded miserably.

"I'm coming." And then, harshly, to Lucy, "So what now?"

"That's all, isn't it?" she said in a dead voice. "We couldn't begin to build anything on a foundation of——" She looked at the floor.

"——of dishonor," he supplied. "I suppose not."

He came over and kissed her gently on her high white forehead. After he had gone out, she sat quiet, looking blindly toward the fire. Then suddenly she got up, tore the bouquet of lilies of the valley from her waist and flung it to the hearth.

"I could probably marry a cheat," she muttered, "but I couldn't marry a fool."

Coming into the room with the ice, Billy Johns said:

"So you've come to life again. I didn't like to murder sleep."

"I guess I was dozing," she explained.

"I guess so, either." He stooped beside the fireplace, "Look at the corsage; somebody's been bootlegging flowers against the rules."

II

Marjorie's mother, having retired early, came downstairs at nine o'clock into the deserted lower floor of the club, with French windows open to a gentle, melancholy rain. At the foot of the stairs she turned and looked at herself in a pier glass, momentarily surprised that she knew instinctively where it was; but presently she was not surprised, remembering the day when she had first looked into the same glass. She examined her brown eyes, eyes more beautiful, less alert than her daughter's, examined the lovely shape of her face, her fine figure scarcely changed in twenty years.

She breakfasted in the paneled dining room with another chaperon. Amanda felt a certain impatience in being just another mother at a festival that she had several times come close to ruling. That was the year before she married, when she had been honored by so many bids that she had placed several with less-sought-after girls in town.

After breakfast she began thinking about Marjorie; in the past few years she had realized that she was very far away from Marjorie; her own generation was prewar, and so many things had happened since then. This Billy Johns, for instance. Who was he? Just a boy who had visited in their city, who came from some vague part of the Middle West, and who, Marjorie informed her, was "stripped"—a reference, not to nudist predilections but to his pocketbook. What were Marjorie's relations to him? And what next when a woman hadn't an idea how to guide and direct her own daughter?

She was smoking in what she remembered was called the Engagement Room; she remembered it very well indeed. She had once sat here trying helplessly to think for herself, as she had just now been trying to think for Marjorie.

It had been the more difficult to think for herself because of the intensity of the young man who was with her—not Carter McLane, who was taking her to the prom, but his roommate. She had begun to wonder whether she was wasting time with Carter McLane. Most probably he didn't want to get married; he was too perfect. He had never so much as tried to commandeer a kiss; he went around "respecting" girls because he was afraid of life.

Sometimes she believed this.

In any case, the man beside her was different; he swept you off your feet. In many ways he wasn't up to Carter; he had no particular standards, he wasn't a hero in college, but he was "human"—and he made things so easy.

"Don't sit brooding," he begged. "We have such a short time alone together. That doesn't sound quite right, because Carter brought you, but such things have got to be decided right, because it's forever. When two people are attracted to each other——"

"What makes you think that you attract me more than Carter does?"

"Of course I can't know that. The point is whether he's up to appreciating you."

"He respects me," she said dryly.

"And do you like being respected?"

Someone began playing the piano in the music room across the court; two girls in evening dress ran down the corridor past the door. Howard came closer and whispered:

"Or would you rather be loved?"

"Oh, I'd rather be loved," she said—"I'd rather be loved."

But when he kissed her, she began thinking once more of Carter, with his gallant carriage, his wholehearted, reassuring smile. A melody was pouring in the open windows:

To the Land of
* The Never-never*
Where we
* Can love forever—*

The tune said to Amanda that, despite the enchantment of the weekend, life was flowing by imperfect, unachieved. It was love for love's sake that she wanted. This time she didn't flinch when Howard kissed her.

"I've been waiting for this," he said. "Amanda, there's something I want you to do for me—only a little thing, but it means so much. I won't be seeing you tonight except on the dance floor, and I want to be knowing all the time that you feel like I do."

"What is it, Howard?" This was living, this was better, this was Now.

From a flower carton he took three orchids, the stems bound in silver, a corsage identical with the one she wore at the waist of her evening dress.

"I want you to wear these instead."

She had a moment of uncertainty; then, with Howard's voice, warm and persuasive at her ear, she unpinned Carter's corsage and replaced it with the other.

"Are you satisfied?"

"Almost."

She kissed him again. She felt excited and defiant. Once again the thin sweet notes of the piano surged in out of the spring dusk:

A-pril rain—dripping hap-pily
Once a-gain—catch my love and me
Beneath our um-ber-ella cosy
The world will still be pink and rosy—

Howard put the other orchids out of sight in a vase and they strolled from the room, their hands pulling apart as they reached the lounge.

The evening was in full flower. The street of the clubs echoed to vehicles and voices; the gleaming shirt fronts and the dresses of many girls blended to one melodious pastel in the dusk. At the Musical Clubs' concert, Amanda had a slight reaction. Carter, leading the Glee Club, was very handsome up on the platform, and as forty masculine voices were signaled into sound at a nod of his head, she felt a sudden pride that he had asked her here. What a shame he was such a stick. Nevertheless, she was sufficiently impressed and engrossed to be annoyed when Howard's hand brushed hers purposely, and she would not meet his persistent eyes. When she was away from Carter she was free, since he had never spoken a word or a whisper of love, but in his presence it was somehow different.

With a contagious trembling, a universal palpitation, that was the uncertainty of many girls at their first prom, and the concealed uneasiness of others, who feared that this would be their last, the young crowd poured out of the concert hall and down through the now-starry night to the gymnasium, transformed with bunting and flowers. One of the orchestras was playing Hawaiian tunes as Amanda moved down the receiving line on Carter's arm. Her card, scrawled with the most prominent names in college, dangled from her glove. Formal deference was still paid to the old system, but long before midnight cards were lost or abandoned, and Amanda, whose young loveliness radiated here and there as she wished, swung from man to man in fox trot or *maxixe*, conservative Boston or radical Ballin' the Jack, at the call of the alternating musics.

Carter McLane cut in on her once a dance, Howard more frequently. Swarming dozens followed her, the image of each man blotted out by the next. At the supper hour, the crowd swayed out into the trophy room to scatter along the wide stairs or to run for dusky preempted alcoves; it was in this pause that Amanda realized that she was not particularly happy.

She was glad to be alone and quiet with Carter. He was nicest when one was a little tired and in the clouds. Howard had hinted at joining them, but she discouraged the idea. As they found places in a far corner out of anyone's sight or earshot, she felt the atmosphere change suddenly and surprisingly. A light remark failed to reach Carter; instead of the protective, appreciative smile, he looked at her very seriously and as if he hadn't heard.

"Are you in the mood to listen to something important," he asked, "or are you still hearing the music?"

"What is it, Carter?"

"You," he said, and then, "I love that word. You."

"Doesn't it depend who you're with?"

"Yes."

Her heart had missed a beat and then begun to race. This was Carter, and he was different.

"Here is your hand," he said. "Here is the other hand. How wonderful—two hands."

She smiled, but suddenly she wanted to cry.

"Do you like questions?"

"Some questions."

"They've got to come at the right time, I think. I hope this is the right time, Amanda."

"Well, I don't know——"

"This is an old question. It's been hanging around me a year or so, but it never seemed the time to ask it. Did you ever read Ecclesiastes? 'There is a time to weep, and a time to laugh.' "

"No, I've never read it."

"Well, here's the question: I love you, Amanda."

"That's not a question."

"Isn't it? I thought it was. I thought it was a fine question. What would be a question?"

"Why, I suppose you'd just turn it about."

"Oh, I see. Do I love you? That doesn't sound right either. I never wanted to ask that question."

Her face came closer to him, and she whispered: "I'll just give you the answer without a question."

There was a silence in the corner for a minute and she felt the great difference between two embraces separated only by a few hours.

Presently he said: "I want you to do me a favor—unpin your corsage."

Amanda started; it was the second time that she had been asked this tonight. In a panic, she tried to think whether there was some observable difference in the two corsages, whether she and Howard had been watched in the Engagement Room. With uncertain fingers she obeyed.

"Thank you. I had them sent from New York this morning because the florist's here had been picked over."

As yet, she could detect no irony in his voice.

"Now unwrap the foil," he said.

She untied the ribbon and picked at the silver binding. Carter said nothing; he looked straight ahead with a faint smile, as if he expected her to speak.

"Now what?" she asked.

"Do you see what holds the stems together?"

"Why, nothing. I've taken off the foil."

Quickly he turned, took the orchids from her, staring at them; he picked up the ribbon and the silver paper and spread the latter flat. Then he glanced at the sofa and underneath it.

"Amanda, please stand up and spread out your dress."

She obeyed.

"My Lord, that's funny!" he exclaimed.

"What is it, Carter? I don't understand at all."

"Why, the stems were drawn through a ring under the foil—a diamond engagement ring that once belonged to my mother."

For a moment she stared at him in muted horror. Then she gasped and gave a frightened little cry; Carter, absorbed in his search, did not notice.

"Let me see," he mused anxiously. "I took off the foil and put the ring on the stems myself, after I left the florist's. The box was in my room in plain sight for ten minutes; then I gave it to Luther at the club, and told him to give it direct to you. Did he?"

"Why, yes," she said, regretting the admission immediately.

"And Luther—why, he's straight as a die." Carter brightened up with an effort: "But I wouldn't let the Koh-i-nur diamond ruin this evening. Presently I'll slip out and have a look around."

Miserably she played with her supper, while Carter told her the things she had waited long to hear—how he had started to speak several times, but had wanted to wait until after senior mid-years, when he could look ahead confidently to a start in the world.

And Amanda was thinking that when he left, she must leave, too; she must go back to the club, find the other orchids, possess the ring and account for the matter somehow—somehow.

A quarter of an hour later, with her cloak trying to conceal her face, she hurried toward the gymnasium door, and ran into Howard.

"Where are you going?" he demanded.

"Don't bother me, please, Howard. Let go my arm."

"Let me go with you."

"No!" She tore away and out the door, up a stone walk, a path, past buildings silver with starlight and late-burning yellow windows, over a highway and onto the street of the clubs.

In the great hall, a last sleepy misogynist lounged over a book; she passed him without speaking. In the Engagement Room she ran for the vase in which Howard had concealed the other corsage, grasping blindly with her hand; then she peered, she turned it upside down; the pin that had held the flowers to her waist fell out upon the table, nothing more. The jar was empty.

In despair she rang for the steward and sank down on a sofa fingering the pin. Luther appeared, knuckling weary eyes.

"No, madame, I haven't seen any orchages. Mr. Carter McLane gave me a box this afternoon and I brought it direct to you. I had no other boxes to deliver, so it couldn't have been mixed up."

"I mean in this vase," she begged him.

There was a sound, and they both turned to see Carter standing just inside the door.

"What's all this?" he asked gravely.

Instinctively Amanda put the hand that held the pin behind her back.

"The young lady says there was an orchage in that jar," supplied Luther obligingly.

"All right, you might check up and see what servants might have been in here. That's all, Luther." As the steward withdrew, he demanded again of Amanda's frightened face, "What is all this?"

She was weeping a little in her throat.

"Oh, it was a silly mix-up." Her voice tried to be careless. "Somebody else sent me flowers, some crazy boy—from home—and I must have put them on by mistake."

Carter's face did not change.

"There's something more than that."

Just at this point, with their two pairs of eyes meeting and glinting each on each, Howard came into the room.

"Oh, I beg pardon." He looked at the vase on the sofa; then questioningly, but unprofitably, at Amanda; then, rather defiantly, at his roommate. "I thought Amanda was alone. I followed her to see if I could help in any way."

Carter's eyes were equally inquisitive. He seemed to come to a conclusion, for suddenly he took from his pocket one of the little paper mats used to protect a dress from bouquet stains, and read aloud from the reverse side:

" 'Dahlgrim & Son, Trenton.' Do you deal with that concern, Howard?"

Amanda could no longer keep her face from being aghast and despairing.

"You don't think he took the ring!" she cried.

"Of course not. He didn't even know about it." Carter's voice grew colder and colder word by word. "He took something much more valuable to me than that. I think I understand it all now."

Luther, the steward, returned from his quest.

"I'm pretty certain there's no orchages in the house now, sir. All the under stewards are gone home."

"All right, we'll find it. I might need it again some day."

He nodded to Amanda and went out quickly. In terror, she started after him.

"Carter," she cried, the tears streaming down her face. "Carter! Wait!"

"Carter!"

Amanda Rawlins Clark, with little lines about her eyes, stood in the middle of the empty room. It was still raining outside, so that it was too dark to see if the jar still existed as part of the bric-a-brac in the room. Not that it mattered any more; McLane had been killed five years later on an Army airfield in Texas. It was just that she would always remember a few minutes in a corner of the gymnasium, twenty years ago.

"And just think," she whispered to herself, "that was all I was ever going to have—those few minutes—and I didn't know it until they were over."

III

Marjorie slept late and appeared at luncheon in a vague and floaty state shared by the other night-blooming girls. The rain had stopped and fair weather loomed over baseball game and the prom. Billy Johns appeared and rescued her from the attentions of three young Southerners who had not been asleep at all, and were urging her to fly in a plane with them to a dry state where they could "get a man's drink."

Her mother had decided not to stay for the prom, after all, so the hypothetical supervision of Marjorie was turned over to another chaperon. When Mrs. Clark had embarked on the train, the young people looked very young indeed to her as they waved good-by standing against the sunshine; it made her sad to think how much they expected from life.

"It's now, right now," she wanted to cry out to them. "It's today, tonight; use it well."

Billy and Marjorie went to the game, where they were joined by a club mate known, for all his coal-black hair, as "Red" Grange, just as, a generation before, all Sloans were called "Tod" and all Doyles, "Larry."

"More money than anybody in my class," Billy whispered, "yet he's the guy that put over the rule about no flowers. How's that for democratic? He even gets patches sewed on all his new clothes; a lot of people do—the poverty racket." When the crowd poured lava-like from the stands, Billy and Marjorie strolled to the main street, and she waited for him outside Kurman's tailor shop for an abnormally long while. When he emerged at last, his cheery face was sobered with alarm.

"Whew!" he gasped.

"What's the matter?"

For a moment he hesitated, overwhelmed.

"Why, that lousy Kurman! Say, I've got to dig up something to wear; the dinner coat I had last night was only loaned for the evening. This Kurman's been making me one, but he won't come across except for cash."

"Well, can't you borrow it?"

"Who from? Everybody's hocked their watches to go to the prom."

They strolled along, Billy lost in speculation.

"But can't you find some man who's going to wear his dinner coat and borrow his full dress? Or if he's going to wear his full dress, borrow his dinner coat," she added brilliantly.

"Too many people thought of that weeks ago," he said with regret. "I know one coat that was ripped in two, with one claimant pulling each tail."

What a time! What a state of things! No flowers, one band—the committee had almost decided on an undergraduate band—next they would dance to radio or assign a freshman to wind a phonograph. And now, of all absurdities, to find one's swain unable to release his evening clothes from the clutches of a tradesman. For a moment Marjorie was pervaded with melancholy; then she burst forth with helpless hilarity.

"It's so pre-preposterous," she burbled. "It's like that boy in Seventeen who tried to buy a waiter's suit."

"I'll get me a uniform, all right," he said grimly.

She took his arm, liking him suddenly more than ever, the way he went about things. She knew his story—he had worked his way through with high credits, and managed to play on two minor athletic teams besides. The minor problem of a costume—she had every confidence that he would take it in his stride.

It was after four. His first idea was to borrow, and they made a quick round of the campus possibilities, Marjorie waiting outside the entries while Billy went in, to reappear each time with the news that the man wasn't in or had only his own. Finally he gave this up and seemed to be considering some other plan that he did not reveal.

"I'm dropping you at the Dramat tea," he said. "Red or somebody'll take care of you. When I call for you I'll have a suit."

Marjorie was sure he would; she danced away the late afternoon without a doubt to disturb her pleasure. The initial resentment at having missed an age of exceeding swank faded out in the nostalgic harmonies as Smoke Got in Her Eyes, and she strolled along the Boulevard of Broken Dreams, or wiggled coolly through the Carioca with flushed and panting men. At 6:30 Billy arrived, his face relieved and lit with enthusiasm; after a single dance, he led her out.

"I had a hellish time. Good Lord, what hasn't happened since I left you here. But it came out all right."

"What happened?"

"Well, I was passing by the Students' Pressing Bureau and I looked in the window, and there was one last dress suit on a rack—probably forgotten. The door was locked, so I went in the window and wolfed the suit over to my room across the court to try it on. It was a bust; it would have made a nice suit of short pants for me. So I decided to take it back, and just as I was straddling the window, a proctor came along and I did some tall, quick arguing."

"But you got a suit?" she asked anxiously.

"Oh, I got one." He chuckled ferociously. "After that, my morale began to break down—or maybe it began to build up—survival of the fittest and all that. No pun intended."

"Where did you get it?"

"I went amoral, I tell you—that course in Nietzsche must be getting me. I was walking along sort of morose, if you know what I mean, and I was just about here, where we are now. And right about there was the delivery push wagon of the Students' Pressing with two or three dinner coats on it. I inspected them in an idle way, and what do you think—there was one just made to fit William Delaney Johns—perhaps not quite up to what the court tailor whips together for me but fair enough—fair enough. So imagine my surprise and indignation when I saw the tag pinned to it; it belonged to a particularly obnoxious freshman in my entry. I boiled. Why, in my father's time no freshman would have dared attend a prom. I thought of going to the senior council, the dean, the board of trustees——"

"But instead you took the suit."

"Well, yes," he admitted, "I took the suit. This is no time to shake the university to its foundations, but somebody had to protect that freshman from himself."

Marjorie was a little shocked, but she was amused, too; it wasn't her affair.

Later, dressing at the club, she renewed in herself the anticipatory emotions of many generations, realizing that it was youth itself that was essential here; the casual trappings were shrinking in importance moment by moment. She might some day make her bow before royalty, but nothing would ever be quite such a test of her own unadorned magnetism as tonight.

She thought of Billy, feeling oh, so friendly, almost loving him— or did she love him? If only he had the prospects of Red, what a background, this, for a courtship. Walking beside him, her gown of printed satin swishing close to his purloined dinner coat, she felt a tender satisfaction in his presence. She would be good to him tonight; she would make him feel that never, never, was she so happy; that through him she was realizing the fulfillment of a long, old dream.

"I want to stop by my room a minute," Billy said. "I didn't seem to have any studs, so I just buttoned my union-suit buttons through the dress-shirt buttonholes, and one of them didn't stand the strain. I've got to go up and stitch."

"Shall I come and do it for you?"

"Too dangerous. Wait here."

She sat on the dormitory steps. Just over her head was a lighted window, and after a minute a disconsolate voice floated out into the thickening dusk. It was a girl's voice, full of the kind of false cheer that veils a deep disappointment:

"We can go to the Glee Club concert anyhow. We can sit upstairs, like you said."

Then a man's voice, curdled with wretchedness:

"After you came all the way from Greenstream. I tell you I can find somebody to look after you. I'll make them. You're going to the prom."

"I'm going to stay with you. I'm not going to the prom without you."

"She's right, Stanley," said another woman's voice, Middle Western like the others. "Estelle wouldn't go without you. These other girls got a lot of boy friends and Estelle would feel scared if she didn't have somebody to look after her. Never you mind. We can all walk down and hear the music, and that'll be nice, and I'm sure Estelle doesn't mind a bit."

"Mamma's right," said Estelle. "It wouldn't be nice to go without you."

Stanley sighed.

"If I could only get my hands on the guy who took my tuxedo. I'd knock his back teeth——"

"Don't let it fret you, Stan," urged Estelle. "We can maybe come down again."

Holding her breath, Marjorie mounted the steps of the dormitory. The door of the lighted room was ajar and from the semidarkness of the hall she looked in. A girl, very straw-haired, very young, dressed in an overelaborate satin gown, sat on the arm of the chair occupied by the very miserable young man. The mother, rural and worn, looked on with helpless compassion.

"Don't take on so, Stan," the girl said, her lip quivering. "Honestly, I don't mind at all."

Quietly Marjorie ran up the stairs, looking for the room number to which she had addressed many letters. She went in to find Billy adjusting the secured button with satisfaction.

"Everything but a flower," he said smugly. "I agree it's all right not to send corsages to girls, but there's no rule against a girl sending a man a gardenia now and then."

"Billy," she said abruptly, "you can't wear that dinner coat to the prom."

"I can't, can't I? Why, I'm wearing it."

"There's a girl downstairs—she's that freshman's girl, and now they can't go to the prom. Oh, Billy, it means so much to her—so much more than it could ever mean to me. If you could see her, Billy.

She's dressed all wrong and she must have been so proud of herself, and now she's just heartbroken."

"What? That freshman had the additional nerve to bring a girl?"

"It's no joke, Billy—not to them. This prom is probably the greatest thing that'll ever happen to her in her life."

"Well"—he sat down philosophically—"if the young punk's got a girl, I suppose that does change the face of the situation. Though he might have told me, before I went to all the trouble of stealing his suit."

Ten minutes later he returned the dinner coat to its owner, with the information that it had been delivered to his room by mistake. Watching again from the door, Marjorie saw the girl's face, and for a minute that was just as much fun as any prom.

Outside, Marjorie and Billy sighed together as they strolled over to the Glee Club concert.

"I guess Red takes you, the lucky goat," Billy mused. "And won't he be sorry, the wolf!"

"Oh, I'm not going without you," she exclaimed, her voice like Estelle's.

"Oh, yes, you are. You just don't know it."

After a long argument, Marjorie conceded that she might go in later for one dance.

Later they watched the couples entering the gymnasium and heard the first strains of "Coffee in the Morning," even danced to it for a moment on the grass; but a sort of melancholy stole over them both. On a mutual impulse they turned and began walking away from gayety, away from Marjorie's first prom. The joke that they had good-humoredly built up around the situation had grown flat.

They reached the now-deserted club and he followed her at a mourner's pace into the Engagement Room.

"This is a case of the strong being sacrificed to the weak," he complained—"of everybody being sacrificed. Think of the hundreds of young men on the very threshold—you know what a very threshold is—think of them seeking beauty and finding only the freshman's girl."

"Let's forget it," she said.

"All right," he agreed. "And do you know a better way than this?" He snapped out the lights overhead. . . .

After a while he said: "Strange as it seems, as a matter of fact, I have a future, a real future. I might even ask you to share it with me if you were a little more grown up, if you'd been to a prom, for instance——"

"Oh, be quiet."

"——and absorbed some sophistication, and weren't just"—a brief interlude—"just mamma's girl."

He got up and lit them cigarettes.

"In fact, my mother has a brother with a Horatio Alger complex, and he has said that if I got through college absolutely on my own, he'd do wonders for me. So, if he's alive in June, consider you have a suitor."

Marjorie had almost succeeded in forgetting the prom now; there was only this man with his proud poverty, his defiant gayety. Just as she had always respected her grandmother of the gilded age as being less insulated from realities than her mother of the golden age, so she felt new communions of *noblesse oblige* in this tin age of struggle that her mother would not have understood. Marjorie had come to the university with no illusions; she left with none acquired. But she knew pretty certainly that she loved this man, and that some day she would marry him.

Mr. Luther, the club manager, stood in the doorway of the room.

"Beg pardon, sir. Mr. Grange came in and grew a little—drowsy on the lounge. I thought I might find someone to help me put him in bed before any ladies start coming in."

"Of course."

Suddenly the glow of one possessed by a hunch lighted up Billy's face.

"Of course!" he repeated jubilantly, and then, to Marjorie: "You wait here!"

Minutes later, on the stroke of midnight, Billy reappeared; he was clad in exquisite raiment, cut on Bond Street by a caterer to kings.

"If you loved me before," said Billy, "what do you think of me now?"

"I don't know," she answered doubtfully. "Has Red had patches sewed on the trousers of that too?"

He caught her close for a moment; then, with three good hours before them, they hurried out the door and over the campus toward the melody of "Orchids in the Moonlight."

"No flowers," Marjorie panted.

But Billy could not entirely agree, and they stopped under an elm on President's Walk, so he could reassure himself that there was at least one.

New Types

(*The Saturday Evening Post*, 22 September 1934)

"New Types" was written in Baltimore in July 1934. The *Post* paid
$3000. Fitzgerald, like Dixon, had returned to América from a world almost
totally unrelated to Depression America and was trying to adapt his stories to
the new types of the Thirties—here a seemingly mercenary young woman
who is actually trying to raise money for her husband's medical treatment.

Fitzgerald's heart was not in the stories written after *Tender Is the Night*.
He was now really struggling to write pot-boilers, as distinguished from his
earlier commercial fiction in which he could take a professional pride. At
about this time he wrote in his *Notebooks*: "It grows increasingly harder to
write because there is much less weather than when I was a boy and
practically no men and women at all."

So it was all true then—these places, people, appurtenances,
attitudes, actually existed. Leslie Dixon had never really believed that
they did, any more than one really believes in the North Pole or the
country of the Pygmies. And since he had lived in China through
weird and turbulent years he had had almost as much practice in
believing as the Red Queen.

There was, to begin with, a beach, seemingly the same beach that
he had often regarded in the advertisements. It was a perfect beach,
sand of Egypt, sky of Naples, blue of the Bahamas, sparkle of the
Riviera—and all this not forty minutes from Times Square. Then
there were these new oddly shaped cars that slid along on tiptoe,
glittering. They did not look a bit like cars to Leslie, they just looked
like *something*—very much as German toys often look like the
originals that went out of existence twenty years ago. These cars were
the exact reverse of that; they looked as if they should not have come
into existence for twenty years more. Likewise the bathing suits of the
girl beside him and of the girls in front of him and the girls in front of
them did not look like bathing suits, at least not in Dixon's idea of a
bathing suit. They just looked like *something*. They made him want
to laugh; they made him feel old and rather susceptible. He was
thirty-four.

The girl beside him apparently had no idea of following up the
introduction with anything approaching conversation. Only once
had she surprised him with what was, for her, a perfect babble of talk.

"It's hot," she declared.

She was a rather tall girl. Her ash-blond hair seemed weatherproof save for a tiny curtain of a bang that was evidently permitted, even expected, to stir a little in a mild wind. She was ruddy brown and without visible make-up, yet with an unmistakable aura about her person of being carefully planned. Under minute scallops that were scarcely brows her eyes were clear and dark blue, even the irises were faintly blue and melted into the pupils' darkness. Her teeth were so white against the tan, her lips so red, that in combination with the blue of her eyes the effect was momentarily startling—as startling as if the lips had been green and the pupils white. She was undoubtedly up to all the specifications in the advertisements. About her back Leslie could scarcely guess, not wanting to stare; from the corner of his eye it seemed quite long, and he judged it was much like the backs in front of him.

"Do you want to go in the water?" he asked.

"Not yet," she answered.

After this impassioned argument there was an interruption. Two young men came up, seized the girl by the head and shoulders, twisted her, mangled her, were violently familiar with her, and then stretched themselves on the sand at her feet. During the bout the expression of her face did not change, nor the set of her hair; she only murmured "Don't," in a purely formal way and turned to Dixon:

"Would you like to come to a dance my aunt is giving for me Wednesday?"

"Why, I'd like it very much, unless my cousin has made——"

"No. She's coming. My aunt is Mrs. Emily Holliday and her house is The Eglantine on Holliday Hill. About nine o'clock."

"I think I know her—I think my mother knew her when we lived here."

The girl said without hesitation:

"That was a bad break for your mother. My aunt is the most obnoxious person. I try to stay out of the house as much as possible."

He was somewhat shocked and covered it with a question.

"Do you live with her?"

"I'm visiting her. However, she's so rich that I expect at any minute to be asked to pay board."

He laughed, but the subject had become embarrassing.

"Where do you live?"

"New York."

She said it in a way that has something final about it. New York!

"Where do you live?"

"I've lived a long time in the Far East, but now I think I'm home for good."

The two young men—they were of college age—turned and inspected him briefly during this conversation.

After their violent approach they had spoken no word, but now one of them said to the girl without looking at her:

"I hear Mrs. Holliday feels the same way about you, Paula. Just a shallow, empty girl."

Paula's face was unmoved.

"I know. Inviting me here is the first thing she's done for any of the family in twenty years—when I saw that menagerie of animals she keeps I knew it was going to be the last."

Ellen Harris, Leslie's cousin, came up, dripping from the water. Here was a girl he understood, such a girl as had already been in circulation in 1922 when he left the States. The basis of Ellen's character was still "old-fashioned," something one could prophesy and rely on; she had eaten the salt of the flapper and turned responsive eyes toward the modern world, yet after marriage one was sure she would revert to type and become her mother, even her grandmother.

As if reminded by Ellen's arrival of the Sound's proximity, Paula and the two young men got up to go in, but Leslie lingered, lest Ellen think he had allied himself with them. He was aware dimly that Ellen found him attractive. His long residence in foreign parts, his prominence in the family as an outstanding "success," gave her the feeling that he was valuable.

But Paula Jorgensen, the girl he had been sitting with, achieved no more than half the distance to the beach without being interrupted.

It was a small man, of very gross aspect, and he seemed to have no place in the picturesque surroundings. Evidently, though, he had power, for Paula, after his self-introduction, turned about patiently and led him back to her original camping ground.

Even if their curiosity had not been aroused, Leslie and Ellen would have had difficulty in not hearing the conversation that ensued:

"We all think"—the man uttered in one of those voices that, having achieved all nuances in their early stages, had no choice for emphasis but to talk louder and louder—"that if we pay you this——"

"Don't say 'if,' " Paula interrupted. "You've got to pay me. I've got to have that money."

"Exactly! You got to. So have we. We're all embarked on the campaign. What we want is you got to be seen with your"—he glanced around, managing to sink his voice an octave in deference to Ellen and Dixon—"your swell friends, your society social friends, that's the point. We need first six flash lights to work on. One alone on, say, a staircase——" He paused again and kindly explained with enormous gestures what a staircase was—how it ran up and down. "Then we want groups, the sweller the nicer, some real classy people, you know, nothing cheap, you know, really the classy type. You know?"

Paula did not nod. It seemed to Leslie that she sighed faintly.

"All right," she said, "anything, but no more 'ifs'. I've got to have that money. Now go 'long."

"Thank you," said the man; then doubting the aptness of his phrase he amplified, "Thank you for your coinperation——"

As he stood doubting the validity of this coinage Paula helped him.

"Good-by," she said.

He went, starting, by some curious combination of instincts, to raise his hat, then deciding against it, fading off in a highly bow-legged way, exigent even at a distance, down the beach.

Paula turned and smiled at them, without a trace in her eyes of having been bothered by the encounter.

Her expression seemed to say, "Well, that was that—we all have our troubles."

As she went down for her delayed swim, Ellen turned to Leslie.

"I wonder what Madame Holliday is going to think of that."

"Well, as a matter of fact, I have been thinking," he said, "something."

"Now tell me what you've been thinking about," Ellen said. "You have that brooding look."

"——about the advertisements; it seems they're all true. Everybody here had just the kind of teeth and hair and clothes and cigarettes and automobiles and expressions that the people have in the advertisements."

"Remember, this is a very swanky beach."

"Even allowing for that. The girl you introduced me to——"

He decided not to go on with this, but Ellen urged him.

"You mean Paula Jorgensen?"

"Yes. Why, she's the absolute type of all the girls in the ads—her face, the way she holds herself, what she says, or rather what she doesn't say."

Ellen had a readier explanation.

"As a matter of fact she has modeled for fashion magazines a great deal. But she *is* a very familiar type."

"I guessed as much."

"Oh, yes, the tall indifferent type. Paula could have lots of attention, but she doesn't seem very interested."

"What is she interested in?"

"Nothing, I guess."

But Leslie had decided differently—he had decided that Paula Jorgensen was interested in some form of perfection. It was perhaps a perfection that, in his unfamiliarity with the customs current in his country, he could not understand, a perfection of form, a purely plastic aim, as if toward a motionless movie, a speechless talkie.

"——her aunt invited her here apparently to abuse her," Ellen was saying. "Gave her a luncheon party and regaled half the table with the story of how Paula's father drank himself to death."

"Did Paula just take it?"

"She didn't say a word, didn't turn a hair; you'd have thought Mrs. Holliday was talking about somebody in Africa——Hey! I almost forgot to tell you that you're invited to a dance *chez* there Wednesday, and you'll have a chance to make your own observations. This dance is all Paula's staying for—she never had any kind of a debut or anything like that." After a minute Ellen added: "Paula's an odd girl. She's very correct and all that, but she doesn't live with her family and she hasn't gone around much since she was seventeen. Just when everybody's forgotten her she seems to step out of a band-box from somewhere."

Leslie met her again on the afternoon of that same day. This time she was in specification riding clothes and accompanied by two other young men, scarcely distinguishable from the two at the beach. They joined the group on the porch of the golf club and Leslie watched her as she accepted several introductions—not by a flicker of her face did she seem to see the people she met, or to be conscious of the group with which she stood, yet there was no touch of rudeness in her manner; it was rather an abnegation, the silence in company of a well-bred child.

Suddenly she saw Leslie Dixon, and, leaving the others abruptly, came over to him. Thinking she might have something special to say, to ask, he waited for her to speak, but she merely took up a station beside him, caught his eye as if to report that she was there and then just stood, stood and waited.

Leslie decided that he, too, would just stand. They listened to the chatter that went on around them, they spoke to mutual acquaintances who passed. Once their glance met and they smiled just faintly.

After quite a long while she said:

"Well, I must go now."

And only then did he feel the need of some communication.

"How's your aunt?" he asked abruptly.

"She's awful," Paula reassured him. "By the way, don't forget the dance. Good-by."

She turned away, but he called her back.

"Look, tell me one thing before you go. Just what are you waiting for?"

For a moment her eyes seemed startled. "Waiting?"

"Yes. I mean, what do you want to happen to you? What do you expect to happen to you? Listen to me! I think you're so particularly attractive that I've whooped up the nerve to ask you what you're preparing yourself for. Certainly it isn't for a man."

"A man?"

She spoke the word as if she had never heard it before.

"I mean you don't seem to——" Leslie was becoming embarrassed at his presumption. "I mean you treat yourself as if you were just something to display, fabrics or something. And you're a lot more than that, but what?" He was almost stammering, sorry now that he had spoken. Paula looked past him slowly.

"What do you want me to be?" she asked. "I could be anything they wanted me to be if I knew what it was." Then suddenly she looked him straight in the eye. "A lot of us don't know any more."

Acknowledging no one save with a faint set smile, she flicked her two escorts into motion with her crop and left the club.

II

He did not see her alone again until the afternoon of her aunt's party, when they sat together in a rumble seat driving back from a boxing match in Greenwich.

"What would you say if I told you I was a little in love with you?" he said. He was quite sober and deliberate. A few little unattached sections of her sun-warm hair blew back and trickled against the lobe of the ear closest to him, as if to indicate that she was listening.

"I'd say the usual thing: That you hardly know me and I hardly know you."

"I'm thirty-four," he said gently. "I thought I might be able to dig up a few odds and ends out of the past and make a high ideal, and you could try and shoot at it."

She laughed, cheered, somehow, by his interest.

"I'm not equipped for an idealist. I saw my mother begin by believing in everything and end up with five children and just enough life insurance to pay for the funeral. Up to then I'd been the family orchid, then suddenly I was a telephone girl. Orchids can't turn into telephone girls and still be good idealists."

"Were you a good telephone girl?"

"Terrible. Tried the stage next, but so did a lot of other people. Then I got to be a model. I get along. I'm quite in demand as a matter of fact, but no one could ask me to believe again how kind the world is to everybody and all that. I take what I can get."

"The morality of a gold digger."

"Without any gold," she murmured, "but plenty hard enough, or how could I stay on here with this awful woman who loathes me? If she's rotten to me at a luncheon party, do I let that spoil a nice free meal?"

She swung her knees pressed together in his direction.

"Did I spring up and go through heroics and stomp out of the house on account of a few insults, just when she's giving me a big dance? Not I—I don't let myself get unhappy about the things that would make my mother unhappy. Tonight I have a new dress that an advertiser gave me because I worked overtime and sold a whole series for him; I'm going to be the center of things for the first time in my life in a great big luxurious house; and I'm going to enjoy myself. If my aunt beats me with sticks when I go home, and accuses me of every crime in the dictionary, I'm still going to be gay tonight."

They dropped her at the house, a great spreading wooden mansion of another era, overlooking the sea. A platoon of caterers had been working since morning, turning the extra-wide verandas into corridors of roses and festooning the two great rooms that, thrown open to each other, made the ballroom. Mrs. Holliday was waiting when Paula entered; her little eyes darted around at the caterer's men setting up the long buffets.

"Where have you been?" she inquired, with a false patience. "Since this dance is largely for you, you might have been on hand to give what help you could."

"You told me to go away," Paula said. "You told me I was in the way."

"You were, but I didn't mean to go all afternoon. Who were you with?"

"Since you're interested, I was with the Dixon man."

"Since I'm interested? That's a nice way to address me! What Dixon man?"

"Leslie Dixon."

"Does he understand that you're only a visitor here?"

"He does if he understands English."

"Did you tell him you'd been acting as a model?"

"I told him everything necessary."

"I wouldn't reach too high if I were you—not with your heredity."

"I want to ask you a particular thing about tonight."

"What—about having the party on the lawn? I thought I went into that in detail with you. Older people feel heat and cold much more intensely—and just remember, everybody in my generation wasn't brought up in France."

"It wasn't about that, Aunt Emily. That's all settled. We couldn't have a platform put down at this hour if we had to. It was about——" She hesitated. "It means a great deal to me."

Her aunt interrupted her. "We don't seem to agree at all on what is important and what isn't important."

Paula shifted her foot around impatiently. "Aunt Emily——"

"Your own family have found you so difficult. I don't see why on earth I should ever have——"

"Aunt Emily, our time together is so short now can't you really forget for a minute that you don't like me? Why, maybe—maybe I don't like you."

"What?" Mrs. Holliday leaned forward. Her face was suddenly strained and warped. "You don't like me? You mean that?"

For the moment, in the distortion of Mrs. Holliday's face, Paula wondered if anybody liked anybody. It was a quintessence of hatred she saw in it, as if one wanted to bring hatred into the world as a commodity that could be played around with as harmlessly as one can play with affection. But having her ax to grind, Paula held her tongue. She was going to grind that ax, and a phrase from the recent diary of an explorer haunted her: that "many very different ends are achieved with blood in the ears." The first time she had read the phrase it had offended her, yet fundamentally she believed in "this man's world," and knew that men went through their own particular hells, and respected them, both for the fact itself and for their reticence about it. She recognized the difficulty of what she was trying to put over as one of the sordid businesses life can lay out for you.

But she was wise enough to put the first thing first and the third thing third—a harder alignment than one might think—and her first principle, her secret, called to her overwhelmingly so she knew that to carry out the idea of the advertising firm she would have to be photographed coming down the stairs, then again in the middle of the evening, and then, more especially, with certain prominent people whom she had chosen as being of her generation, people she could go on with in an exigency, people who could cooperate. However, she didn't feel this was the time to explain things to her aunt. There was no time to explain things to her. Mrs. Holliday was one of those people to whom nothing could ever be explained.

"Aunt Emily, there may be strangers around."

Aunt Emily turned to her swiftly. "Men that my husband would not have received?"

The opportunities for comment on this left-handed remark sped by Paula's ear.

"I mean mechanical men, Aunt Emily. Photographers."

Still absorbed in the detail of seeing that the caterer's assistants would not abscond with the silver, Aunt Emily caught only the end of this.

"Well, we've had enough of that around today," she said, watching a man taking a dead bulb from a bank of lights. "Enough so-called mechanical men."

Paula gave up. She backed away.

She went upstairs. Presently Paula came down in a bathing suit for a quick dip in the Sound. Paula liked swimming alone; she had been alone so long that groups often tired her and embarrassed her; her easy reticent manner was a method of concealing this. It had been a long time since she had spoken out as frankly as she had to Leslie Dixon. His interest had surprised her.

After her swim she had a light supper in the breakfast room; her aunt did not come down.

Upstairs she took a quick tub, and then even more quickly she poured herself into her new dress, settling it with almost one motion, and then drew her lips in the mirror. Simultaneously a knock at the door brought a maid with a box of orchids from Leslie Dixon.

"And Mrs. Holliday would like to see you, please," the maid added, "soon as possible."

Paula left the orchids in their box and went to her aunt's room. She came into the room absorbed in her own thoughts with "Yes, Aunt Emily," on her tongue, but she could not have told afterward whether she had actually said it, for immediately she was aware of something unfamiliar and unexperienced about Mrs. Holliday. She took a step forward, paused again, then ran toward her.

She was aware precisely at that moment that all her relations with Mrs. Holliday were changed; her dislike, created automatically by Mrs. Holliday's dislike for her, was vanished. She knew surely that the pale figure collapsed in the armchair was in a world without hatred, without human emotions. She went and listened for the heartbeat, hating the smell of the scent that her aunt used, inseparably associated for her with bullying and cruelty.

"Aunt Emily," she said, "wake up."

Downstairs, as if collaborating with her, the nascent orchestra drew unmotivated tears from the fiddles and piano wires. But the figure in the armchair did not move.

Paula dreaded to wait—she didn't believe it—she had a sharp reversion to a scene in her own childhood and heard repeating in her head:

"Brother made it up—it's a joke."

Then she arose from the armchair where she had taken refuge with the first shock; she approached the body and said in the most sincere outburst of tenderness she had felt in all their relations, "Aunt Emily!"

But still Aunt Emily did not move. A cigarette that Paula had brought in with her expired finally with the faintest of sounds, and as if answering to a signal, Mrs. Holliday's head fell sidewise.

Paula looked, then looked away; she looked sidewise, but in the sweep of her eyes around the room, from the cyclorama of the walls to the object for sympathy, found no help. Only a fat Victorian pincushion filled with an assorted variety of many-colored-headed pins seemed to assure her that a well-brought-up girl would do the right thing.

"Aunt Emily," she said again.

"You——" she began, and stopped. She went over to her and, in a sort of rush, as if making up to her aunt for an early neglect, she said aloud:

"You—well, you hated me, didn't you? And you were the sister of my father. I guess you didn't mean to be so bad." She hesitated, breathing hard, half sobbing, wondering how anybody could be so bad. "You didn't mean to be so bad, did you—did you?"

Her instinct was to shake her aunt impersonally, as if that would galvanize her into life.

"But," she thought, "you did even manage to be bad after you were dead."

Paula sat down again suddenly.

"I hate you," she said. "You're gone now and I'd like to respect you."

The air of a first tentative Wiener waltz climbed up the branches of the wistaria and choked the window. Once more Paula stood up, suffocated.

"All right, Aunt," she said, "you stay here—you be nice to me for once. Oh, I'm sure that you—that even you wouldn't mind, if you knew how important it was. You wouldn't, would you? You——"

Mrs. Holliday's head drooped further.

"Aunt Emily," she said again, automatically.

"But this is so strange," she thought. "This is a cruel woman who might have helped us when we needed help and didn't choose to."

Then suddenly the image of the harassed publicity man who had asked for "coinperation" on the beach appeared to her with the awful "if"—the "if" that he had carried like the reminder of her secret—Paula stood up.

"Aunt Emily," she said, aloud, "you shouldn't have died. I suppose you did your best in your own way, but, but oh my, you shouldn't have died now because I needed tonight."

She was all tied up in her own problem now, and when she went to the gray figure in the chair and picked up the limp left arm to put it decently in the lap, the gesture was automatic. What did this mean to her?

Suddenly she realized the dance was canceled, there was no dance. There was not only no dance, there was no opportunity. No dance, no chance. Nothing. In view of this new happening there would be none of the photographs specified, and no photographs automatically meant no money—and there had to be money; there had to be money. Three hundred, that would do it, that was enough.

"You wouldn't know, you wouldn't care, where you are now."

She stood aloof, detached, questioningly, talking to her as one might talk to a baby.

She leaned suddenly forward and rearranged her aunt's tie.

"There," she said.

She was thinking very fast now; she heard the orchestra change to a fox trot downstairs.

"You wouldn't mind, would you?" she said. "If you knew, if you were the kind of person who cared about people. I mean you wouldn't mind since you're dead, doing something much kinder than you'd ever have done while you were alive?"

Paula had moved toward the door while she was saying this. Now she opened it, then shut it again and turned once more toward the figure in the armchair.

"It's just life against life, Aunt Emily. And you don't seem to have any, any more."

On an impulse, she ran across the room and kissed the still cold brow. Then she went out, turned the key in the door, tried to think of any part of her apparel that would hold a key—nothing; she hesitantly explored the reliability of her bodice, and her sandals. No chance. She raised the corner of a rag rug and slipped the key under it and went down into the white thunderous boom of a flash light pointed at the staircase.

III

Leslie assumed that it was a version of a ball that might have taken place twenty years earlier, but no, there were plenty of people who might have been present at either ball, but they were not the same people exteriorly or in their attitude.

Later he gazed as one of many half-puzzled spectators at the groupings of a dozen young people who posed in the middle of the dance floor. Among them he recognized the two young men from the beach, and again his mind slumped upon the helpless haunches of, "I wonder what this is all about; it wasn't like this in my time."

In the glare of the flash light she had seen Mr. and Mrs. Haggin, whom she knew her aunt had asked to stand in the receiving line; and with a dread that the dancing might start without her being there, she headed for them, perhaps heading for a solid rock, and with the qualification that it might be the rock upon which she would wreck herself.

"How do you do, Mrs. Haggin? I'm Paula Jorgensen."

Suddenly she gave up and made a unit of her personality; and in the making of it realized that what had happened upstairs could not be fitted into the pattern of the evening downstairs. However, she was committed; she had nourished herself for a long time on the idea that courage was everything, so she could not afford to betray such a stand-by.

"——I believe you were to receive with my aunt. She's feeling the weather a little and she'd appreciate it if we'd just go on without her. She expects to be down later."

"I'm so sorry. Shan't I run up and see her first?"

"I think she's trying to sleep at the moment."

When the guests were told at the receiving line that Mrs. Holliday was slightly indisposed, the hostess achieved a factitious popularity from the fact that she had sportingly commanded the dance to go on. There were, however, malicious individuals to wonder how she could have taken any other course. Presently the younger people forgot her, and with the great sweep of the "Blue Danube," the summer ball rocked into motion.

Early in the evening Paula saw Leslie waltzing with his cousin Ellen; later she found her eyes being swayed and pulled here and there and this and that way and she finally settled with herself that they were being pulled toward him. When he cut in she was with him, almost before she knew it, in a niche of the obscure rose-scented darkness of the veranda.

Despite the fact that they were both by temperament on the

romantic side, they had each, in different ways, been living a long time in the face of harsh reality. Irresistibly they picked out the material facts from a given situation. The one that interested him specifically at this time was the soft swaying gowns that for a moment seemed to be the gowns of people that had waited for Jeb Stuart and the gallant Pelham to ride in out of the night; all the people there seemed to have for a moment that real quality which women have when they know that men are going toward death, and maybe will get there, and maybe not; and then that feeling centered in Paula. Not that Leslie belittled such efforts, such unexplored tragedies as might lie below the lacy furbelows swishing the dust from the age-old ballroom; but that all Leslie's thinking of the past, or future, had become embodied in the lovely figure of Paula as she shone out through a cloud of clinging, billowing white.

Thinking as she did about him, she was glad when a chance gave them the intermission together. But it was late and she didn't know whether she wanted to talk frankly to somebody or whether she could ever talk frankly any more, whether in the future everything had to be locked up inside forever, locked into the feminine characteristic quality of patience, of standing and bearing what life had to offer. During the evening she had carried with her a special liking for this man.

She thought then suddenly of what was upstairs!

"Of all times," he was saying, "of all times not to make love to a girl—it's at her own dance."

"Debut," she interrupted. "Do you realize I'm having a debut at twenty-four? Look, I'd like to tell you——"

Someone swung her away from him and Leslie Dixon returned to his vantage point with the impression that there was a new fervor burning in her calm eyes. Wine of excitement—she had promised that she was going to enjoy herself.

With the evening singing on, the impression of her beauty deepening moment by moment, the dance itself gathering around her, dependent on her physical existence there, complete so long as she was on the floor, his desire to have some sort of share in her loveliness increased.

He took his cousin Ellen to supper. Afterward he cut in on Paula as a number came to a close, and he was alone with her. The unrest, the peculiar abstraction remained in her eyes; she followed him out, not speaking when he suggested that they go into the garden.

She shivered.

"Cold," she said, "I'm cold and frightened. I've got to talk to somebody I can—can I trust you?" She looked at him searchingly. "I think maybe I can. Let's go somewhere we can be alone."

But in the seat of a dark car she changed her mind.

"No, not now—afterward—after the dance." She sighed. "I said I was going to have a good time, and since I've gone this far——"

Then, for both of them, it was darkness on Long Island; then for a moment still sitting there close together they faded into the sweet darkness so deep that they were darker than the darkness, so that for a while they were darker than the black trees—then so dark that when she looked up at him saying, "Yes, I love you, too," she could but look at the wild waves of the universe over his shoulder and say, "Yes, I guess I love you, too."

Once more she crushed the puff of her shoulder flat against his shoulder.

"That was so nice," he said presently.

"If you knew how long it has been since I kissed anybody."

"But I told you I loved you."

"What a waste. But if it gives you any satisfaction, go on loving me——"

"Paula, now you can tell me what is bothering you."

"Let's go in. I want to have a whole lot of people telling me that I'm attractive."

She let herself be delivered into the dance and just before she was surrounded, beaten and made dim by an always increasing swarm of men, she heeded a signal from the stairs.

It was her aunt's maid trying to attract Paula's attention, yet afraid to wave at her; she compromised on a broken gesture that consisted of raising the hand as if for a knock-out punch; and then she merely wiggled the second and third fingers. Paula obeyed the summons, steeling herself to what it might imply; but the maid only said: "Miss Paula, I think Mrs. Holliday has locked herself in."

"Well, if she has, nothing can be done about it right at this minute."

"But she has never done that before."

"Please don't worry about that now, I'll go up in a minute and see."

Surprised at the casualness which she had mustered in dealing with the situation, Paula slid out again on one of the many arms available.

The violins hummed, the cello crooned, the kettledrum marched till after two; it was three before the last groups pried themselves away from the last of the champagne.

The publicity man was almost the last to go; Leslie Dixon was the last to say "good-by," and suggested himself he should do a little locking of French windows. She wondered momentarily if she had got much fun out of her "debut"; then once again she became conscious of the reality she must sooner or later face.

Leaving the lights burning she started upstairs, paying a passing deference to the fact that, while she had brought off the party, she had not finished well as an organizer: The caterer's men seemed to have left, and there seemed to be no servants on duty.

"It's over," she thought on the way. "Over. I have the money."

Reluctant to think further than that, Paula recognized there was no denying that Aunt Emily was very dead upstairs, but the forefront of her mind was really occupied by some necessity of explaining to Aunt Emily why she had done as she had.

There was, however, no more explaining to be done to Aunt Emily.

The upstairs maid came out of a patient doze on a big chair in the hall. As Paula started to search for the key with a kick of her heel under the rag rug, and found it was not there, she ran in a sudden hysteria past the maid and over to the edge of the balcony.

"Are you there, Leslie?" she called.

As if by a miracle he still was. He called up, mistaking her for the maid, "I'm trying to turn out these darn lights. Or do you want them to burn all morning?"

Paula could hear him fumbling with the unfamiliar fixtures. In a faint voice she called:

"It's me."

"Who?"

"It's—nobody."

In another panic she tore back past the maid, kicked aside the rag rug and finally found the key tangled in the rug itself.

She went in. Nothing was changed. The dead woman huddled in the chair. The room was close and Paula shoved up another window. Then she sat down on the side of the bed as she had before, and thought the same things, but not in the same way.

It was done now; the outrage—if so it was—was perpetrated. She had the five hundred, she could afford the operation. But all the dislike that had previously lodged in her heart oppressed her now, as she stared at the object of it.

"Aunt Emily," she said aloud, "I wouldn't have done this for no reason. Please believe that, however unpleasant you——"

She paused. It wasn't right to talk to somebody who couldn't talk back, yet in a way she was helping Aunt Emily, explaining to some vague judge that Aunt Emily wouldn't have been the way she was if it were not for the forces that had produced her.

Suddenly as if Aunt Emily was cognizant of what was taking place, her hand fell over the edge of the chair. At the same moment Paula saw that the door was opening and Leslie Dixon was on the threshold.

"I finally got the lights out," he said. "What is going on here? I've got to know."

"All right; come in then. You might as well know the whole story."

She had really been aware for some moments that he was the judge she had been waiting for.

She knew that he loved her—she had begun to love him, not with the love she associated with duty, with having to have five hundred dollars, but with the many lonely hours, long years of hours since she had been taken care of. She allowed for the chance that it might work out; she clutched at any straw and hoped it would turn out to be a girder.

So fixed had been Leslie's concentration on her and what harassed her, that only now did he become fully aware of the still figure in the chair. Then Paula saw his face preparing for an emergency.

In a minute he had grasped the situation, and rushed over to the figure slumped in the armchair, and took the pulse of the arm that had fallen down. Then he turned to Paula.

"She's dead," he said.

"Yes."

"Did you know she was dead?"

"She's been dead since nine o'clock tonight."

"And you knew she was dead all the time?"

"Yes, I knew she was dead."

"And so you went and had the party anyhow."

"Yes, I went and had the party anyhow."

He put his hands in his pockets; then he repeated, "You knew she was dead, and you went and had the party anyhow. How could you do that?"

"Yes, I knew she was dead—but we seem to have covered that."

He took a half step away from her as though he were going to walk up and down the room; changing his mind he turned to her. "I swear I don't understand this."

Paula gave up; she began adapting the tempo of his walk, tapping her heels together.

"Don't complicate things any further!" she exploded. "Why did you come up here anyhow? I thought you'd gone home. I thought everybody had gone home."

As they both strained toward a solution, their eyes fell again upon the tangible presence of Mrs. Holliday.

"Anyhow, that's the way it was," Paula said in an awed way.

"I can't believe it," Leslie said. "I can't believe that anybody could be so——"

"Neither can I," said Mrs. Holliday.

For a moment each of them thought the other had spoken. They exchanged a sharp glance and gasped out a "What!" Then each seeing an embarrassed innocence in the other's face, they were compelled to bend their glances upon the fantastic fact that the word had come from one supposed to be communicating solely with angels.

"Well——"

"Well——"

Still they exchanged a last desperate glance, each hoping the other had spoken.

Leslie was the first to return to reality. He faced the voice and mustered up one helpless and strange word.

"Well."

"Well," said Mrs. Holliday. She took up the arm that he had dealt with so reverently only a few minutes before, leveled it at him like a rifle and repeated:

"Well."

In the miasma of alarm the monosyllable was rapidly becoming sinister, but it was difficult to know what to substitute for it.

"But, Mrs. Holliday, you don't really think——"

As Leslie heard his own voice he decided that this was not at all the remark with which this Lazarus should be greeted upon her resurrection, yet he could think of no other.

"Aunt Emily," Paula said, and stopped. She had said all she had to say to Aunt Emily some time before.

During this conversation Aunt Emily had been gradually taking control of the situation, at least in so far as she guessed that there was any situation. Her eyes fell upon Paula's evening dress, and associating it with something unpleasant she reached back into her own obscure depths to find some unpleasantness that would match it.

"The dance," she said hopefully.

Paula and Leslie fell eagerly on this tangible fact.

"The dance is over," Paula supplied.

"The dance is over. Have you gone crazy, Paula? Answer me at once. Who is this young man and what is he doing upstairs?"

Leslie took up the explanation.

"The dance is just over, Mrs. Holliday. You didn't seem well, so Paula didn't want to wake you up."

"You mean I slept all through the dance?"

"It was impossible to wake you."

"What nonsense! What an outrage!"

It was awful, Paula agreed privately. But there was the five hundred. Nothing could destroy that. There was the five hundred.

"We were just about to phone your doctor," said Leslie.

"I was allowed to sleep through the dance!" Mrs. Holliday sat there panting, so alive now that her vitality minimized their feeling for her.

"Where are the maids? Is there nobody I can count on? Where is Clothilde?"

Leslie went toward where he imagined the servants' quarters to be, and encountered Clothilde on the way.

"Here," he said and found five dollars. "Mrs. Holliday locked herself in; she mustn't know that she did it. Any excitement tonight might——" He said the rest with his shoulders and then hurried to a phone and called a doctor. That much accomplished he waited in the hall until Paula came out of her aunt's room, walking to the rhythm of Mrs. Holliday's furious voice that followed her out the door.

"Well?" she asked.

The folds of her dress were tired but gracious. The orchids were still fresh upon her shoulder.

"Do you want to come over to my cousin's for the night? But maybe it'll make gossip."

"I'll be fine here."

"Your aunt'll have things figured out by tomorrow. At least she'll know there was something wrong."

"I'm going to leave before breakfast."

"Maybe that's wisest. Good night."

As he went down the stairs she saw him hesitate.

"Well," she said.

At the word he turned and looked back at her, and suddenly said "Well," again. The word seemed to have been used before between them; they faced each other, Paula from the top landing. Leslie trying to leave as politely as possible, to let her down easily, yet still with the intensity of feeling about her that had made him linger after the dance, made him be bold enough to push his way into the tragic trouble in which she was involved.

"So what?" he demanded.

"You don't know why I did what I did," she said; "I was fighting for life."

"Apparently, you can handle your own affairs better than I could handle them for you."

Paula put her left heel on the first step, then her right heel on the second step, and her elbow on the balcony railing, not in a casual way, but rather suggesting a compromise.

A physical response to her increasing nearness made Leslie say, "Well then, what? I can't swallow the idea of somebody looking for fun going as far as that."

Paula turned quickly and retraced her two steps up to the landing, throwing behind her: "You can't? Then good night."

"You're going to New York with me," he said.

"No; say good-by now," Paula objected.

"Go and get your clothes."

"I'm not helpless. I'll get them in the morning."

"We're going now."

"Why?"

"Because we are. Go and get your stuff."

At this moment the doctor arrived and Paula in a lightning dash to her room was suddenly equipped.

IV

With the false dawn pushing up the leaves over Long Island they borrowed the doctor's taxi and rode to the station. On the car seat, feeling the five-hundred-dollar check against her heart, safe now, the events of the evening assumed an unimportance. Even Leslie sitting across from her seemed remote and in the past, as compared to the problem of getting the money.

She felt gay. She felt light-headed. She had to express her rebirth of hope in words—now it took the form of teasing him.

"Would you like to know the truth—do men ever sometimes want to know the truth? Even in China?"

They were sliding into the station at the moment; it was a morning pulled ripe and cold, through the mouths of tunnels, breaking with them into New York.

"You told me about your idea of what was pleasure," he said in the taxi. "You said when you were fighting for your life there were no rules."

"I didn't say my life—I said fighting for life." Impatiently, suddenly she turned to him, "Would you like to actually contemplate the low-down?"

She profited by his confusion: "Let me initiate you into the facts of one life——"

Leslie cut through her speech: "You—you have me down for a prig. I don't suppose there is anything much I can do about that——"

"Even if you wanted to," she amended.

"Even if I wanted to." He repeated her phrase slowly. "However, since we seem to keep up this argument I'll try to tell you what, what——"

"Don't bother to do all that," Paula suggested.

"Yes, I'll bother. The very fact that I do, or maybe did care about you deeply"—he paused and repeated—"deeply"—"gives me a right to say what was in my mind, my heart."

"You seem to have a gift for words in China."

"Don't be mean."

"I'm not mean."

"Don't be. Try to think of me as an ignorant visitor to your shores. Let me just wonder. Let me wonder, for instance, why such—such a lovely person as you, that any man would like to know, admire, or be near——" He hesitated. "All right then, why should a girl like that spend all her life preparing to go to some personal moving picture that never comes off? You can't always keep on being Narcissus looking into his pool. You—you can't, you can't go on trying to get ready to fascinate some millionaire, or British nobleman."

"I did get myself a British nobleman. I was pretty precocious. I got him when I was seventeen."

"You mean you're married—no fooling?"

"Very much married."

"Recently?"

"A long time ago, when I was seventeen. My husband is an invalid." She smiled in a surprised way. "Isn't it preposterous? I'm a ladyship. I'm Lady Paula Tressiger, and I've never even been called it."

She leaned forward and tapped the driver.

"Mind stopping at this drug store for a moment?"

"Why?"

"To get some morphine."

"Why do you want to get morphine?" he demanded.

"'Cause till tonight I didn't have any money for a long time, but I've had the prescription in my bag for three weeks."

"I still don't know whether you're fooling——"

In the new-found confidence of the new morning she said: "Well, then you must be slow on the uptake."

She made her purchase hastily, and as she returned, said: "It's so close to my apartment. We might as well not have kept the taxi."

They drew up at a somewhat dingy brick front.

He followed her into a modest suite on the second floor, with a divan that he guessed became a bed on small provocation.

Then Paula opened the door of the other room. As if she was showing him a baby, she motioned him inside.

In the bed lay the thin figure of a man, a man so still that he scarcely seemed to be breathing.

The fact that he was carefully shaven made his extreme emaciation more apparent. Murmuring something in his ear Paula ran her hand through the sparse hair. She adjusted the pillows and led Leslie back into the other room.

"He's been like that for seven years. Since a week after we were married. All right, ask me why I married him. All right, because home was hell. Eric came over to learn the banking business. He was all shot by the war, and shot with drink, too, but I didn't know that then."

"He's paralyzed?"

She nodded.

"We got married secretly—I was too young and mixed up about things, and ashamed and afraid to say anything. So I took care of him myself."

As if he had reproached her, Paula added hastily, "Oh, sometimes I had the very best medical attention for him, whenever I could afford it; once I kept him in a hospital for months."

"Yes, I see—I see."

"When I went to Aunt Emily's I had a woman who did every last thing. He doesn't need very much—he needs very little. Maybe I shouldn't have gone away and left him this time." Paula hesitated, "First you disliked me for what I did there, now you'll dislike me for going at all——

"——hate to tell you any more of the ways. But this money"—she touched her heart—"this is one of the most sordid. This money I got from the publicity agent, it'll give Eric his last chance, it's a pretty poor chance, one out of ninety-nine, but I tried to think the way *he'd* like to think. He'd rather take this chance than lie there forever. Would you want to be like that forever—lie on your back for seven years? Do you know how long seven years can be?"

God, it must have been so long, he thought, so long. . . .

"Now he can have the operation, he can have——"

All he had misguessed, misjudged about her fell away, minute by minute.

"That's why you did that?"

"Did what?"

He could suddenly find no word or phrase for what she had done.

"I can't try to get in touch with the specialist tonight," she said abstractedly. "I'll call the hospital resident in the morning. But it is morning—I should have called long ago."

"If there is anything that I can do to help?"

Leslie realized that this was a false start.

But Paula was suddenly all full of life, and an upsurge of feeling made her cross the room, put her arms around him and kiss him on the lips.

"So, I did it, didn't I?" she said. "I did what I started out to do."

"Well, you seem to have. I'm amazed. I'm——"

"——so you go away," Paula advised him. "You forgive me, don't you?"

There was no answer to make. There was simply the feel of her cheek as he touched it that he knew he would carry with him forever.

V

Eric Tressiger, second baronet, was destined to be one more victim in his race's fight for life. In one moment they thought he was saved, in another he wavered, in a third he died.

At the end Leslie was waiting outside the operating room of the hospital. A nurse who knew him rushed out and said, "You're a relation of Mrs. Tressiger—at least you're the only person that has called here regularly."

"Yes?"

"He died five minutes ago."

"I knew that," he said.

"His wife slapped right down against the floor. I never saw a girl do that before"—she was ripe with gossip—"except an anæsthetist who was taking care of——"

"Where is Mrs. Tressiger now?"

By this time she was following Leslie along a corridor of the hospital. "No, she's not ill now, she——"

Paula was sitting in the waiting-room chair against an imitation of 1880 mosaic work. She looked well—she sat up straight, holding her purse. Leslie went to her so quickly that he brought up before her with a sort of slide upon the marble floor.

"My—Paula——" he began.

She looked up at him brightly, almost cheerfully.

"Now it's over," she said. "Now I'm going to be gay!"

"You mean that?"

"Yes, Leslie. Now it's done, now it's over."

He prepared to revise his opinions. Leslie had been face to face with the terrible floods in the Yangtze River in 1926, the delivering to solemn women of the bodies of brothers, fathers, sisters, children— seeing them taken up into death in the enveloping arms of their religion. . . .

So with Paula now, facing her proud mask, he saw his country all over again. He felt, simultaneously, that awesome loneliness of that which had led them all here, and a pride in the fact that somehow they had done so many of the things they had promised to do in their hearts.

The ambition, of lonely farmers perhaps—but the cloth of a great race cannot be made out of the frayed lint of tired princes. . . .

Instead of saying anything that he had meant to say, he said simply, "I understand."

"You do? Maybe I guess you do. Well then, that helps me to go home."

"What is home?" And he added: "Maybe I'm home."

"I guess you're home now," Paula admitted.

On their way out he said: "Isn't it nice to think of all the things we'll never have to talk over? We can start from scratch, like—like people do in advertisements."

Paula picked up his hand, touching her lips to his knuckles. They had no more to say to each other—only the little bang that did not agree with any weather blew a little in the wind of that sad and happy morning.

Her Last Case

(*The Saturday Evening Post*, 3 November 1934)

"Her Last Case" was written in Baltimore in August 1934. The *Post* paid $3000 for it. As the Thirties increasingly became a time of illness, hospitals, doctors, and nurses for the Fitzgeralds, it was natural for him to turn to this material for fiction. At this time Fitzgerald's alcoholism had reached the stage where he could no longer sober up by himself. He required nurses to help him dry out—partly because he wanted companionship. The setting of "Her Last Case" was suggested by "Welbourne," a mansion in Middleburg, Virginia, where Fitzgerald's editor, Maxwell Perkins, took him to visit his cousin, Elizabeth Lemmon, in July 1934.

Fitzgerald originally planned to include this story in *Taps at Reveille*. He explained to Perkins his reason for dropping it:

> The real thing that decided me about "Her Last Case" was that it was a *place* story and just before seeing it in *published form* I ran across Thomas Wolfe's "The House of the Far and Lost" and I thought there was no chance of competing with him on the same subject, when he had brought off such a triumph. There would inevitably have been invidious comparisons. If my story had anything to redeem it, except atmosphere, I would not hesitate to include it but most of it depends on a mixture of hysteria and sentiment—anyhow, I did not decide without some thought.

When Miss Bette Weaver got off the bus at Warrenburg, there was a storm in the sky, blowing east from the Blue Ridge. Washington had been stifling, and, insulated by the artificially cooled bus, she was unprepared for the sharp drop in temperature; it was not what she expected from Virginia in July.

There was no car in sight to meet her and drops were already splattering the road, so she had time for only the briefest glance at the town before crossing to the drug store for protection. It was an old town—an old church, an old courthouse, old frame or stone houses; over the main street hung the usual iron sign:

HERE A SQUADRON OF STUART'S CAVALRY
FOUGHT A FIERCE ENGAGEMENT WITH——

She read only that far—there had been such signs all along the road, and Bette's interest was as faint as that of most women in the record of old wars. But Virginia, the name itself, thrilled her—real

Virginia, not just the swimming hotels of the shore. She thought of Marion Davies in a hoop skirt dancing the lancers with handsome Confederate officers, and of books about gallant, fierce times, and gracious houses and Negro "ha'nts." It was all a lovely blur—she was pretty sure that George Washington wasn't in the Civil War, and also that Château-Thierry came a little later, but she was sure of little more.

Beyond that she felt suddenly strange and foreign and frightened; it was the arriving at a new lonely place with a storm in the air.

A large car slid into the courthouse circle, rounded it and drew up at the drug store, and a Negro chauffeur got out.

Bette got her change from the hairpins she had bought and met him at the door.

"Miss Weaver?" He touched his hat and took her little satchel. "Sorry I'm late, but I got a flat outside of Warrenburg."

He shut the rear door on her and she felt safer in the big limousine, closed in against the thunder and the rain.

"Is it far?"

"Ten mile to the house."

He seemed a polite Negro, huge and protective, but with an asthmatic whispering voice. After a little way, she asked:

"How is Mr. Dragonet?"

For a moment he didn't answer, he didn't move even the back of his shoulders as an indication that he had heard her, and Bette had the feeling of having been indiscreet. This was absurd, though, in view of the fact that she was here in the capacity of trained nurse, with due credentials from Baltimore authorizing her to take care of Mr. Dragonet. Unmet, he was to her not a person but already a case. He was the last patient she would have—the last case forever and ever.

The thought filled her with a certain sadness. Born and bred in a desolate little streak of wind and rain on the Pennsylvania border of Maryland, her days as probationer, "blue nurse," graduate nurse, had opened a new world to her. They had been happy years—she had had good cases; almost always nice men and women, who lived or died with respect and liking for her, because she was lovely to look at and considered a fine young nurse. She had taken every kind of case in her three graduate years—except infantile paralysis, which she avoided because she had three little nephews in Baltimore.

The Negro decided to speak, suddenly, as if after mature consideration.

"I don't say he is well, I don't say he ain't well. He don't seem to change to me, but they been lot of doctors round——"

As if he had spilled too much, he broke off suddenly, and Bette conceded he was right in saying nothing. Even Doctor Harrison in Baltimore had said very little; though she'd thought at the time it was because he was in a hurry.

It was a pity, he had said, that on her last case she should go so far away. Wouldn't she rather——

"No," Bette answered, "I'd rather do this. I've always taken potluck about cases and my name's at the head of the registry, so I'm going to take this one. I'm sort of suspicious about it."

"Well, I'm sort of relieved. Because this case needs somebody I know I can trust absolutely. You've had some psychiatry work. . . . No, this isn't exactly a psychiatric case. It's hard to say just what it'll turn out to be."

"An old man?"

"Not old. Thirty-five, thirty-six. He was a patient of mine at Walter Reed military hospital just after the war. He got to believe in me, and that's why he wanted me to choose him a nurse from up here."

There were interruptions at this point and Bette had practically to insist on further directives.

"Well, you ask what he's been taking as a sedative, and if it's a coal-tar product, give him that, in slow doses, and if it's paraldehyde, give him that. And if it's liquor, taper him off that. It's sleep he needs—sleep and food, and lots of both. Keep in touch with his doctor down there, and phone me if things get out of hand."

Doctor Harrison was known for a rather sly habit of making all subordinates—junior doctors, internes, nurses—figure out situations for themselves, and Bette suspected that there was going to be nothing more.

So—off then for the last time with the starched white uniforms, the sense of adventure, of being used for some purpose larger than herself, some need greater than her own. The last time—because in one month she would become housewife and handmaiden to young Dr. Howard Carney, of the Mercy Hospital in New York.

The car turned off the road onto a clay pike.

"This is Dragonet land from now on," the chauffeur said. "Plenty bad road; had to fix it up in that dry spell, so it didn't set."

The house floated up suddenly through the twilight of the rain. It was all there—the stocky central box fronted by tall pillars, the graceful one-story wings, the intimate gardens only half seen from the front, the hint of other more secret verandas to face the long southern outdoors.

She waited, rather uncertain, rather awed, in the central hall while he went for the housekeeper. From the hall she had an impression of great rooms on either side, massed with portraits and gilt-framed oil paintings—and books, books everywhere. There were certain houses where one simply jumped into uniform and took over from an anxious and confused family; there were others where the position of a trained nurse was uncertain. She must wait and see.

A worn Scotswoman came in and looked her over quickly.

"Whisper, take Miss Weaver's bag to the left wing. . . . Perhaps you'd like some tea, Miss Weaver. Mr. Ben has got to sleep for once, and I don't suppose you'll wake him up."

"Certainly not," Bette agreed. "I'll be——"

A voice, from somewhere on the dusky stairs that mounted out of the hall, startled and interrupted her:

"I was putting it over on you, Jean."

Mrs. Keith snapped on a hall light against the dusk and the owner of the voice became apparent. He was a handsome man with very dark deep-set eyes; and Bette's first impression was that he was younger than she had expected. He was tall and well-built in a gray flowered dressing gown of Japanese silk; but it was his voice that caught and held her—it was the sort of voice that can "do anything with anybody," a voice that could beg, command, wheedle, storm or condemn. When he spoke, in no matter how low a tone, there seemed to be no other voice than his.

"Jean, you run along and leave Miss Weaver and me alone. Miss Weaver has a face that makes me sure she'll do me no harm. . . . You like sick people, Miss Weaver, don't you? That's why you took up nursing."

Bette laughed, but rather uncertainly.

"Suppose I put on my uniform," she said. She would feel much better in her uniform, far more in armor, more able to cope with any situation. Not that she anticipated any. Doctor Harrison wasn't one to send her into a questionable environment, but Mr. Ben Dragonet's facetious speech and the look of desperation in his eyes put her on guard. She was driven by a need to put on her uniform immediately. But:

"Not yet," Dragonet commanded. "I spent years of my life looking at nurses' uniforms, and I must say there's a certain monotony. Sit down and let me tell you my symptoms while you're still in personal plumage."

She was suddenly glad she had worn her best frock, but professional training made her obdurate, and formally she followed the beckoning finger of Mrs. Keith toward the left wing.

"I won't be five minutes really. Remember, I've been traveling two hours."

He was still there when she returned, leaning against the balustrade in an attitude that changed to quick courtesy as he saw her.

"I didn't mean to be insistent. What I really wanted was not to be alone."

She sat down on a sofa in the hall.

"It's these damn nights," he went on. "I don't mind the days— it's between the first and second sleeps. I spend all day worrying about what I'll think in those hours."

"We'll fix that," she said confidently. "Don't you think I'd better talk to your doctor here right away and see what regime you're on?"

"I can tell you all that. Old Bliss lets me make my own regime. I was hoping you'd have a regime along. Haven't you got a nice regime in that black bag?"

"I must get in touch with your doctor here. Doctor Harrison expects it."

"All in good time. Have you got any clear idea what's the matter with me?"

"I know you've been generally run down and have some old head wound that bothers you."

"And about ten other things. I seem to be something of a wreck, but it's only recently I can't seem to steer myself any more. One man had the effrontery to suggest that I go to a rest cure—as if it wasn't too damn restful here already. By the way, you better get the keys to the wine closet from Jean. This same man had the double effrontery to suggest that I drank too much, and I want to prove to you that has nothing to do with it. I'll want a nightcap this evening because today I have nourished myself a little. But after tonight I won't want anything."

"All right."

"Now we'll go out on the big veranda and watch the rain for awhile—that's one of my favorite stops in my nightly marches. I've found out more about my own house in these last three months than in all the rest of my life."

Bette felt that the time had come to assert her authority:

"Mr. Dragonet, I think the first thing should be for you to get into bed and get some rest. Meanwhile I'll find out what they're giving you to eat, and just what medicines you've been taking. The more tired you get from talking and walking around the harder it's going to be to relax."

"Miss Weaver, I didn't expect you till six o'clock. It's now half-past five. After six o'clock I'm your patient; until then—the veranda."

Reluctantly she preceded him—this was going to be more difficult than she had counted. There were times, professionally, when she had wished her person to have been less appealing.

He glanced at it quickly across the veranda—at a face whose every contour seemed to be formed to catch the full value of light or shadow, so that no angle could be turned far enough aside to obscure the delicate lines along the ridges of cheek bone, brow, chin and throat. A sculptor's, not a painter's face, but warmed and brought back into full life by the bright healthy warm blue eyes.

"You were wounded in the war?" she asked to get his attention off her.

"Wounded? I was killed."

"But you got all well."

"Oh, yes. Up until six months ago I practiced law in Winchester. Then things began to go haywire—other things that had nothing to do with war—and now general deterioration has set in. But remember, up to six o'clock I'm your host, and I want to hear about you."

She took advantage of this to tell him that she was engaged to be married.

"It's always rather awful to hear of a girl who looks like you being engaged," he remarked. "Seems as if there's something unfair about it."

Her face rejected the personal quality of the compliment.

"——so this is my last case," she finished.

"It may be mine too," he said.

Oh, really, things were going too far. She couldn't imagine how she had been so unprofessional as to let it all get started in this direction. She rose quickly.

"Come now, Mr. Dragonet, it's nearly six and we're going to get you to bed."

"Bed?" Obviously, the word revolted him, but he got up wearily. As they went toward the stairs he tried to stave off the eventuality: "But I ought to show you the sights of the house. It's quite a historic house. Do you see that windowpane with the name scratched on it? Well, that was made by a diamond ring belonging to the Gallant Pelham—made on the morning of the day he was killed. You can see the year—1864. You know who the Gallant Pelham was? He commanded Stuart's horse artillery at twenty-three. He was my hero when I was a boy."

The stairs were difficult for him, and once in his big bedroom he threw off the dressing gown wearily and flung himself on the huge bed. Bette looked around with the sense that he had filled the room, up to the dark molding, with his own personal melancholy. She took his pulse and his temperature. Then she picked up a white-capped pin from the table beside the bed.

"Just what I need for my bonnet," she said lightly. "In fact, the regular pin. I bet you've had another nurse."

"I had a nurse from Winchester," he admitted, "but she was frightened; she went away."

"Well, I'm not frightened, but I'm very strict. Now you try and rest, and I'll get things started."

II

She slept deep through the first part of the night, soothed by air softer than the air of the lush over-rich Maryland nights. When she awoke with a start, she saw from her watch that it was three, and realized simultaneously that there was activity in the house. Slipping on her dressing gown, she opened the door that led through a library into the main hall, whence the voices were coming.

"Now be a good boy and go to bed," Jean, the housekeeper, was saying.

"I'd rather wander around, Jean. It's my form of exercise."

"You'll frighten the new nurse and she'll leave like the other one. Pretty soon you won't be able to get a nurse at all."

"Well, there's you to carry on."

"That isn't what you told me the other night."

"I told you that I'd asked Doctor Harrison to send me someone young and beautiful."

"Well, I don't think this one's going to spoil you. But now you musn't frighten her. I know you mean no harm."

"Go and call her," he commanded.

"Now, Mr. Ben——"

"I said, go and call her!"

Bette was already hurrying into her uniform. She left her room with Jean's "Pray God you can do something with him," ringing in her ear.

"Good evening, Miss Weaver," he said. "I came down to suggest an early morning walk around the place. I notice that the false dawn has arrived and the more unsophisticated birds have been fooled into believing it." And as he saw her expressionless face, "Don't get afraid of me; these are just the perambulations of old stock—my father wandered and my grandfather wandered. He is the Confederate brigadier over your head. My grandfather used to wander around cursing Longstreet for not using his flanks at Gettysburg. I used to wonder why he wandered, but now I'm not surprised. I've been weeping a lot over a long time because they sent us up replacements, in 1918, that didn't know a trench mortar from a signal platoon. Can you believe that?"

"You've been drinking, Mr. Dragonet," said Bette distinctly.

"I offered you the keys."

"I thought it would be better for you to keep them, but I'll take them now. In fact, I'll insist on keeping them as long as I'm in this house."

She knew, though, that in spite of having drunk something, he was not drunk. He was not the kind who would ever be drunk. Drink could not remedy whatever had happened to him.

"Old stock in old wars," he brooded. "And after that wandering." His eyes were full of tears. "What is it I've lost? Isn't there some woman somewhere that would know?"

"What do you mean?" she demanded.

"I thought you might know. After wars everything goes out of the men who fought them—everything except the war itself, but that goes on and on forever. Don't you see this house is full of war? Grandmother made it a hospital, and sometimes the Virginia women got here to see their husbands, but the women from farther south usually came too late, she used to say."

He broke off and pointed: "There's the twins, my brothers—the two red-haired kids in the painting over the stairs. They're buried back in the family plot, but they may not even be the twins, because there was a mix-up at Montfaucon. Still—it may be the twins——"

"You must go to bed," she interrupted.

"But listen," he said in a strange, low voice. "I'll go, but first you must listen."

In the hall, dusky now with the real dawn, she felt an electric silence. And suddenly, as he said Listen! again and raised his finger, she felt the little hairs on her neck stand out from it, felt a tingling along her spine. In a split second it all happened. The great front door swung back slowly on its hinges and the hall was suddenly full of young faces and voices. Ben Dragonet sprang to his feet, his voice clear over the young voices, over the many voices:

"Can't you see it now? These were my people, bred to the sword, perished by the sword! Can't you hear?"

Even as she cried out frantically, clinging to the last shreds of reality, "You must go to *bed*! I'm going to give you more sedative!" she saw that the big front door was still open.

III

Bette's intention at seven o'clock that morning—when the sound of life in the kitchen relaxed her enough to read the magazine at which she had stared for three hours—was to leave by the first bus. But as it turned out, she did not leave. She bathed and then went upstairs and tiptoed into Ben Dragonet's room. Under the influence of the heavy sedatives, he was sleeping soundly; the lines of anxiety and nervous pain about his eyes and mouth had smoothed away and he seemed very young, with his neglected hair burrowed into the pillow. Sighing, she went down to her room, extravagantly donned her second clean uniform and waited for Doctor Bliss' visit.

He was an elderly man, with the air of having known all the Dragonets forever, and he told her what she expected: The story of the breakdown of a very proud and stubborn man.

"People think a lot of Ben over in Winchester, and he's had chances to go in big firms in Baltimore and New York. But for one thing, he never got over the war. His two brothers were killed in the same aeroplane, pilot and observer; then he was wounded. Then, when he got well——"

The doctor hesitated, and Bette guessed, from a little trailing motion of his mouth, that he had changed his mind about making some other revelation.

"When did this start?" she asked.

"About Christmas. He walked out of his office one day without a word to his partners and just never did go back." He shrugged his shoulders. "He's got enough to live on, but it's too bad, because his law work *did* keep him from all this brooding. If I didn't have my work to do, I don't think I'd sleep nights either."

"But outside of that, is he absolutely sane?"

"Just as sane as any of us. The other nurse got uneasy about all that night prowling and walked out, but Ben wouldn't be rude to a burglar in his own house."

Bette decided suddenly and defiantly that she was going to stay—defiantly because she had begun to wonder how Dr. Howard Carney up in New York would have approved her being on this case. He was a precise young man who knew what he wanted, and he had not wanted her to go on any more cases at all, as if he feared at the last moment she might become a casualty of her profession. But it was not so easy to sit around twiddling thumbs for two months. It eased her conscience to write him a letter while she waited for Ben Dragonet to wake up.

The sleep did him good. All day he was content to rest in bed, dozing from time to time, taking obedient medicine, eating what was prescribed, talking to her only a little, casually and impersonally. But once she caught his eye unexpectedly and found in it the hungry and despairing look of the night before, the look that said, mutely this time: "I thought perhaps there was a woman somewhere who could tell me. . . ."

That night, with more sedatives, he slept through, though Bette lay awake anxiously between two and five, listening for his voice or his footstep downstairs.

Next day she said:

"I think you'd better dress and we can sit in the garden awhile."

"Good Lord!" he groaned, laughing. "Just as I'm getting my first rest in months, you order me out of bed."

"You'll have to tire yourself out a little in the daytime before you can sleep at night without sedatives."

"Well, you'll stay pretty close, won't you?"

"Of course."

He passed a tranquil day, still a little dazed and abstracted. For Bette it was a happy day with a cool dry wind blowing the Virginia sunshine through the trees and along the eaves of the veranda. She had been in larger houses, but never one so rich in memories—every object she saw seemed to have a significance and a story. And at the same time a new picture of Ben Dragonet himself began to develop. He seemed gentle, uninterested in himself, adept in pleasing her and making her feel at home; and comparing that with the hysteria of the first night, she took his pulse carefully, wondering if it indicated any lesion of vitality.

But as the quiet days passed, she began to realize that this was his natural self, his natural attitude toward the world. Without any reference on his part to the condition in which Bette had found him, she gathered that he was beginning to see his way out and—from a chance remark—that he considered going back to work.

They came to know each other quite well. She told him about Howard and herself, and their plans, and he seemed interested.

Then she stopped telling him, because she perceived that it made him lonely. So they built up private jokes to take the place of personal discussions, and she was glad to see flashes of laughter sometimes in his dark eyes.

As the week waned he grew strong enough to protest at his invalid's regime; they took wider walks and splashed about one afternoon in the small swimming pool.

"Really, if you're getting well this quick, you don't need me any more."

"Ah, but I do though."

Next morning Bette, in borrowed jodhpurs, rode with him upon the pike.

She realized with a sort of surprise that he was no longer her patient—it was he who dominated the days. His fingers rearranged her reins this afternoon instead of her fingers taking his pulse, and with the change a sense of disloyalty to Howard lodged itself in her mind—or was it rather a sense that she should have felt disloyal? Howard was young and fresh and full of hope, like herself; this man was tired and worn and knew a thousand things she had never guessed at; yet the fact remained that he was no longer a patient to her. Divested momentarily of the shield of her uniform, she wondered that she had had the nerve to give him orders.

"——back in '62," he was saying, "grandfather was wounded at Hanover Court House and the family had to go to him——"

"I thought we weren't going to talk about wars."

"This is just about the pike here. They started out at midnight with hoofs muffled and orders not to say a word. Children of ten take things literally; so, when mother's saddle girth, that had been put on badly, slipped and swung her right under the horse, she just hung there for ten minutes—upside down, afraid to open her mouth, until, luckily, somebody turned around and saw——"

Bette was half listening, half thinking that she had never been on a horse before except a plow horse at home, and how easy Ben Dragonet made it for her. And then, halfway home, she let herself say something she would not have said in uniform.

"You can be so nice," she said, and she heard Howard's voice in her ear protesting, and fought through it: "I never knew anyone who could be so nice."

Looking straight ahead, he remarked:

"That's because I'm in love with you." They walked their horses in silence—then he broke out suddenly: "Excuse me for saying that. I know your position has been hard enough here."

"I didn't mind your saying it," she answered steadily. "I took it as a great compliment."

"This insomnia," he continued, "gets a man in the habit of talking aloud to one's self, as if there was nobody there."

"What then?" she thought. "Oh, this is impossible. Am I falling in love with this man, this ruin of a man? Am I risking all that I ever thought was worth while?"

Yet, as she saw him from the corner of her eye, she had to resist actively a temptation to sway over toward him.

There were storm clouds in the west, and they went into a trot; there was a drizzle and thunder when they reached the straight driveway to the house. Bette saw Ben Dragonet's head go up, his eyes peer forward; he spurred his horse twenty feet ahead, pulled up, wheeled, dashed back and seized her bridle. In two minutes his face had changed—the repose of five days had vanished; the lines had creased back.

"Listen to me." His voice was strange and frightened. "There's someone I have to see. It's very important. It may change things here; but you've got to stay on, whatever happens."

The two pair of startled hands on the reins made Bette's horse dance.

"You'd better go in alone," she said.

"Then you'd better get off and let me take the horse in." His eyes were full of a terrible appeal. "You won't leave me."

She shook her head, miserable with apprehension. Then she perched on a fence rail in the increasing rain as he rode toward the house with her horse in tow. Presently, over a bush, she could see two heads on the porch, one Ben Dragonet's, the other a woman's, saw them vanish into the square of the front door. Then she walked thoughtfully up to the house and entered through the separate door of her wing.

IV

A little girl of about nine was in the room, a well-dressed little girl, apparently just walking around looking, a sad-eyed little girl of a lovely flushed darkness.

"Hel-lo," Bette said. "So I have a visitor."

"Yes," agreed the child calmly. "Jean told me this was the room I had when I was a little girl, and now I almost remember."

Bette caught her breath.

"You haven't been here for a long time?" she asked.

"Oh, no, not for a long time."

"And what's your name, dear?"

"I'm Amalie Eustace Bedford Dragonet," said the little girl automatically. "This is my father's house."

Bette went into the bathroom and started the water in the tub.

"And where do you live when you don't come here?" she asked, seeking time to collect her thoughts.

"Oh, we go to hotels. We like hotels," Amalie said without conviction, and added. "I had a pony when we lived here."

"Who do you go to hotels with?"

"Oh, my governess, or once in a while my mother."

"I see."

"Not father ever; father and mother have incability of temperence."

"Have *what*?"

"Incability of temperence. That's just a thing. So we go to hotels."

"Here!" Bette told herself sharply: "I'm coming down with nurses' curiosity. I can't let this child run along like this."

Aloud she said:

"Now, dear, I have to take my bath; I'm all wet, you see. Why don't you sit on a big veranda and see how many things you can remember in the garden?"

But when Amalie had departed, Bette stood silent a moment before she wrestled out of her jodhpurs. What did all this mean? Why hadn't she known that Ben Dragonet was married, or had been married? She felt exploited, exasperated—and then, to her sudden dismay, she realized that how she *really* felt was jealous.

Back in uniform, and feeling upset and confused, Bette went out into the library adjoining, and pulled a dusty volume of Pollard's *War Between the States* from the stacks and sat down to read.

Outside, the storm was crashing about now; from time to time the lights flickered low and the telephone gave out little tinkling protests that were less than rings.

Perhaps the very persistence of the thunder made Bette's hearing more acute in the intervals—or perhaps the position of her chair was in line with some strange acoustic of the house, for she began to be conscious of voices, voices not far away.

First there was a woman's laugh—a low laugh, but a real one with a sort of wild hilarity in it—then Dragonet's voice in a rush of indistinct words; and then, very clear and sonorous and audible in a lapse of the storm, the woman's voice saying:

"——since the day we took the big blind-looking gate together."

The voice was Southern, Bette could even place it as Virginian. But it was not that which made her rise suddenly and pull a chair to the other side of the table; it was the quality of malice in it—of fierce throaty feeling, as if the woman were letting the words slip up in calculated precision to her lips. Bette heard Ben Dragonet's voice once more in the excited tone of the night she had first come here; finally, then, she gave up the library entirely and went back into her bedroom.

She had hardly sat down when Jean was at the door.

"You have a long-distance call from Washington, Miss Weaver. Do you want to take it?"

"From Washington? But—of course I'll take it."

"You're not afraid of a shock in this storm? . . . No? Well, there's a phone in the library."

Bette went back into the library and picked up the receiver.

"Bette! This is Howard. I'm in Washington."

"What?"

"This is Howard, I tell you. Darling, what in heaven's name are you doing down there in Virginia? From what Doctor Harrison says, I gather you're on some psychiatric case."

"Oh, no, it's not that at all. I thought you were in New York."

"My idea was to surprise you; then I found you were nursing at the South Pole. I want to see you."

"I wish you'd told me, Howard. I'm terribly sorry you got there and found me gone. I wanted to take one last case, Howard. I thought you'd——"

"Hello—hello!" Their connection was broken and resumed again: "It makes me uneasy——" Again a break. "——for a little while when you're off——"

The telephone went dead, with more little squeaks and murmurs. Bette bobbed the receiver without response; then gave up. She was somehow annoyed by his unannounced presence in Washington.

But she had no sooner returned to her room when Jean, evidently loitering outside, precipitated herself upon her, went almost to her knees, begging, imprecating

"Oh, good Lord, Miss Weaver, that devil's here again! Can't you help him now? Is there nothing you can do to get rid of her?"

"I don't understand."

"Do you know what a witch is? Do you know what a devil is? Well, this is one. Do you know what appears when the earth opens and gives up things out of damnation? Well, this is one. Can't you do something? You know so much, almost like a doctor."

Vaguely terrified, Bette kept control of herself, shook the woman slightly and stood back from her.

"Now tell me what this is about!"

"His cousin, his wife that was. She's back again. She's there with him. She's breaking him all over again like she always did. I heard them laughing together—laughing awful, like they laughed when they were children and she first got hold of him. Listen! Can't you hear them laughing, as if they hated each other?"

"You'll have to tell me more clearly." Bette was fighting for breath, for time.

"It was she that did it; it wasn't the bullets in the war. I've seen it—I've seen her come and go. Six months past she came here, and six months he walked the floor in the night and turned for the liquor bottle."

"But they're divorced. The little girl said——"

"What's that to her, or to him. She owned him in her black heart when he was no higher than my shoulder, and she comes back to feed on his goodness, like a vampire feeding on his blood to live by."

"Why is she so bad for him?"

"All I know is what I've seen over and over," Jean insisted. "She's his poison, and I guess a man comes to like poison after he's had enough of it."

"But what can *I* do?"

A knock rattled the door at the end of a roll of thunder. It was the Negro butler, speaking in his tone of asthmatic kindness:

"Miss Weaver, ma'am, Mr. Ben send you the message he goin' to have business to talk about at dinner. He says you take little Amalie for dinner here with you in the library."

"Of course."

Bette felt her tension decrease as she found that she was not to meet Ben's wife. When Amalie appeared presently, she was composed and controlled.

"So what did you do this afternoon?" she asked as they sat down at table. "Did you recognize things in the garden?"

Suddenly she perceived that Amalie's eyes were full of tears.

"Or was it raining too much to go out from the veranda?" she said cheerfully.

"Oh, I did," Amalie was sobbing suddenly. "I went out and only got a little wet, and then I came to another veranda, and I heard mother tell father she'd trade me for something."

"Nonsense!" Bette said. "You just thought you heard that."

"No I didn't. I heard her talk about the same thing to the man that's her friend now—before we left New York."

"Nonsense!" Bette repeated. "You heard some joke you didn't understand."

At the misery in Amalie's face, she felt her own eyes filling with angry tears, and she concentrated on distributing the supper.

"Take some beets anyhow. When I was your age, I used to think I heard people say things."

"She hates me!" the little girl interrupted vehemently. "I know. I wouldn't care if she traded me." Her face puckered up again. "But father doesn't want me either."

"Now, Amalie!" Bette's voice was almost harsh to conceal her feelings. "If you don't stop this silly talk and eat your vegetables, I'm going to trade you. I'm going to trade you to a very silly cow who comes and moos outside my window whenever she mislays her calf."

Amalie's smile changed the course of her tears.

"Does she? Why does she mislay it?"

"Ask her. Just careless, I suppose."

Suddenly, even as Bette held out Amalie's plate, lightning flashed by the windows and they were in blackness.

"What is that?" came Amalie's voice, startled, across the dark room.

"Just the silly old storm."

"I don't think I'd like to live here."

"Don't you? I think it'd be wonderful to live here. There'll be candles in a moment. Don't you like candlelight?"

"I don't like the dark," insisted the little girl.

"What a silly idea to get in your head! Did some baby nurse put that idea in your head? Give me your hand while I get my flash light."

Amalie clung close to her while Bette located it. The storm was directly over the house, but even now Bette could hear the woman's voice—it seemed to be coming nearer, coming into the hall.

"——of course I'm leaving. This is weather I like. You ought to know that. . . . I know he can find the way back, and I know every inch of these roads, if he doesn't."

Then, as two candles wavered into the hall, came Ben Dragonet's voice, very cold and rigid:

"You're welcome to stay the night."

"Stay here!" The voice rose in scorn. "It would take a cyclone to keep me here—and you're hardly a cyclone, are you, Ben?"

The electric lights flashed on again for half a minute, and through the bedroom door Bette had a glimpse of a tall, handsome woman facing Dragonet in the hall. She was saying: "——so you won't take Amalie?"

"She'll be taken care of, but no child of yours can have a place in this house."

Quick as a flash, Bette shut her bedroom door and waited in anxiety lest Amalie had heard. Gratefully she listened to a small voice:

"What did daddy say? I couldn't hear."

"He just said he'd be glad to look after you, dear."

A minute later a car crunched away on the wet drive; at almost the same moment the lights flashed on definitely—the storm was over.

"Now you're not scared, are you?" Bette asked Amalie.

"Not if the lights stay on."

"They will, now. So come out into the library and go on with your dinner. Here's Jean with two candles, just in case. Maybe she'll sit with you."

"Where are you going?" demanded Amalie doubtfully.

"I want to speak to your daddy for a minute."

She found him in the big reception room far across in the other wing. He was stretched wearily on a sofa, but he got up when she came in.

"I'm sorry about all that rumpus," he said. "I suppose you couldn't help hearing some of it. My wife's personality is sometimes too large for a private house."

"I was thinking of your daughter."

He dismissed the mention of his daughter impatiently.

"Oh, Amalie is—another matter. Amalie was always timid and anaemic. I tried to sit her on a horse when she was six, and she made a fuss and I somehow lost interest—her mother isn't afraid of anything that moves."

Bette's disgust rose:

"Your daughter is a sensitive little girl."

He shrugged his shoulders wearily and Bette continued, her temper mounting:

"I don't know anything about you and your wife, but you should have the intelligence and kindness to put yourself in the child's place."

She broke off as Jean came in, holding Amalie's hand.

"Miss Weaver, there's another phone call for you." She glanced nervously at Ben Dragonet. "I brought Amalie because she didn't want to be alone."

Bette went to the phone. It was Dr. Howard Carney.

"I'm in Warrenburg," he announced.

"What?"

"I told you I was coming, dear."

"In the storm I couldn't hear a word."

"I thought you said to come down. The idea was you were to slip away and see me for a minute."

She considered quickly, and said:

"You find some driver who knows the Dragonet place and come out here. This has been so strange and I'm so confused that I don't know what to do. Maybe seeing you will clear things up in my mind," she added doubtfully.

She returned to the reception room to find Ben Dragonet, Amalie and Jean sitting in three chairs, far apart, with the air of not having moved, smiled or spoken since she left. Oh, it was all so helpless. What could she do against all this dead weight of the past?

Suddenly Bette made up her mind and asked Jean to take Amalie out of the room. When they were gone, she said:

"Mr. Dragonet, I've decided to go."

"You what?"

"It's too much for me. Your attitude toward Amalie decided me."
He frowned.

"I thought you liked me."

"I was beginning to. But this has put us back where we started.
I've tried to stick it because I hated to quit on my last case, but—
anyhow, I can't. My fiancé happens to be in the neighborhood and
he's coming up to take me away."

"But what'll I do?"

"Get another nurse—a nurse of more robust sensibilities."

There was nothing he could say except: "I'm very sorry. I'll make
out your check." And he added slowly, "In exchange I'd be grateful for
the key to the liquor closet."

Bette went into her room, changed her clothes and packed her
bag. When Howard arrived, she embraced him quickly, and started
into the reception room to say good-by to Ben Dragonet, but he had
heard the doorbell and he came out into the hall.

She introduced the men and examined them as they stood
opposite each other; Howard, young, calm and efficient; Howard
who stood for peace and healing; Ben Dragonet, dark and restive, who
stood for pain and self-destruction and war. Oh, there was no
question which she should choose.

"Won't you come in for a moment?" Dragonet asked; to her
surprise, Howard accepted.

They talked impersonally and amicably, until, in a few minutes,
the butler announced dinner.

"You've got to dine with me, doctor. Don't protest," Dragonet
insisted. "You can't get anything fit to eat this side of Washington—
and your fiancée has been too kind for me to let her starve."

Bette weakened, but Amalie came in and curtsied and stood
uncertainly; looking at her, she hardened again.

Then Ben, catching her expression, somehow understanding it,
capitulated, suddenly, gracefully and entirely.

"I have a little hostess here now," he said, resting his hand on
Amalie's shoulder, "and I'm very glad, because I know she'll do the
honors of the place very well. . . . Amalie, will you be so kind as to take
Doctor Carney's arm and lead the way in to dinner."

After dinner, when Bette had a moment with Howard, she gave
him a censored version of the adventure; when he had heard he
insisted on her staying on.

"——because I'll be very busy for a month, dear. I've got to go
straight up to New York tonight. And since you did take the case,
don't you think it'd be unprofessional to walk out on it?"

"I'll do what you think best."

He took her by the elbows.

"Little girl," he said, "I know I can trust you." Why had he come here, then?—"I know that when you gave me your word, you gave it forever. So I'm going away with every confidence that all your thoughts will be of me, as mine will be of you, while I'm struggling to bring us together."

"Oh, I know. I know how hard you work. And you know I love you."

"I know you do. I have every confidence—and that's why I think it's all right for you to stay on this case."

She thought a minute.

"All right, Howard."

He kissed her good-by—for too long a time, it seemed to her. When Ben Dragonet reappeared, Doctor Carney shook hands and said:

"I'm sure that Miss Weaver will be very—very——"

Bette wished he would say no more, and he didn't. With a last fleeting pressure of her hand, he was gone, and she went to change back into her uniform.

When she returned to the reception room, her patient was sitting with Amalie on his knee.

"When can I have my pony?" she was saying.

"You have him now, only it won't be a pony—you're too big for a pony—it'll be a little horse. We have just the one for you. I'll show him to you in the morning."

He saw Bette and made a formal gesture of rising, arresting it before Amalie slid off his knee.

"You deserve congratulations, if that were a thing to tell a girl," he said. "He seems a mighty fine young man, that doctor of yours."

"Yes," she said absently, and then, with an effort, "He's a fine doctor. He's considered to have a big future."

"Well, frankly, I'm envious of him, but I don't believe you could have chosen better."

Amalie asked her:

"Are you going to marry him?"

"Why—yes, dear."

"And going away?" Her voice was concerned.

"Of course," Bette answered lightly. "But not before a week or so."

"I'm sorry," said Amalie soberly; then she broke out: "It's like hotels—whenever you get to like anybody, they go away."

"That's true," agreed Ben slowly. "Whenever you get to like anybody, they go away."

"I'll leave you two alone," Bette said quickly. "I have a letter to write."

"Oh, no, you won't. We want all of you we can get, don't we, Amalie?"

It was cool after the storm, so they sat in the big room for an hour.

"You look as if you're worrying," Ben said suddenly. "You've been worrying for five minutes."

"But I'm not worrying!" she exclaimed.

"Yes, you are," he insisted. "I knew all that row this afternoon would bother you."

"But I'm not worrying." She drew her face out of the lamplight.

She was worrying, though, in spite of the fact that Ben Dragonet had not yet guessed the reason. She was worrying how she could most kindly break the news to Howard that her last case was going to last forever.

Lo, the Poor Peacock!

(*Esquire*, September 1971)

"Lo, the Poor Peacock!" was written in Baltimore early in 1935. After it was declined by *The Saturday Evening Post* and *Ladies' Home Journal*, Harold Ober withdrew it. In 1971 *Esquire* published this story in a version abridged and revised by one of the magazine's editors. The text printed here is the story Fitzgerald wrote in 1935.

At this time, Fitzgerald was living at 1307 Park Avenue with Scottie, while Zelda was at Sheppard Pratt Hospital. With his magazine earnings shrinking, money became a constant anxiety; and he was compelled to pawn the silver—a detail included in "Peacock" (the Supreme Court bowl had been a wedding present from the Associate Justices of the Alabama Supreme Court, on which Zelda's father, Anthony Sayre, served for many years). Fitzgerald's *Ledger* entry for February 1935 reads: "Wrote story about Peacocks. Very sick. Debts terrible. Left for Tryon Sun 3d. Oak Hall. Went on wagon for all liquor + alcohol on *Thursday 7th* (or Wed. 6th at 8.30 P. M). . . ."

Miss McCrary put the leather cover over the typewriter. Since it was the last time, Jason came over and helped her into her coat, rather to her embarrassment.

"Mr. Davis, remember if anything comes up that I didn't cover on the memorandum, just you telephone. The letters are off; the files are straight. They'll call for the typewriter on Monday."

"You've been very nice."

"Oh, don't mention it. It's been a pleasure. I'm only sorry—"

Jason murmured the current shibboleth: "If times pick up—"

A moment after her departure her face reappeared in the doorway.

"Give my love to the little girl. And I hope Mrs. Davis is better."

At once it was lonely in the office. Not because of Miss McCrary's physical absence—her presence often intruded on him—but because she was gone *for good.* Putting on his coat Jason looked at the final memorandum—it contained nothing that need be done today—or in three days. It was nice to have a cleared desk, but he remembered days when business was so active, so pulsating that he telephoned instructions from railroad trains, radiographed from shipboard.

At home he found Jo and two other little girls playing Greta Garbo in the living room. Jo was so happy and ridiculous, so clownish with the childish smudge of rouge and mascara, that he decided to wait till after luncheon to introduce the tragedy.

Passing through the pantry he took a slant-eyed glance at the little girls still in masquerade, realizing that presently he would have to deflate one balloon of imagination. The child who was playing Mae West—to the extent of saying 'Come up and see me sometime'— admitted that she had never been permitted to *see* Mae West on the screen; she had been promised that privilege when she was fourteen.

Jason had been old enough for the war; he was thirty-eight. He wore a salt-and-pepper mustache; he was of middle height and well-made within the first ready-made suit he had ever owned.

Jo came close and demanded in quick French:

"Can I have these girls for lunch?"

"Pas aujourd'hui."

"Bien."

But she had to be told now. He didn't want to give her bad news in the evening, when she was tired.

After luncheon when the maid had withdrawn, he said:

"I want to talk, now, about a serious matter."

At the seriousness of his tone her eyes left a lingering crumb.

"It's about school," he said.

"About school?"

He plunged into his thesis.

"There've been hospital bills and not much business. I've figured out a budget—You know what that is: It's how much you've got, placed against how much you can spend. On clothes and food and education and so forth. Miss McCrary helped me figure it out before she left."

"Has she *left*? Why?"

"Her mother's been sick and she felt she ought to stay home and take care of her. And now, Jo, the thing that hits the budget hardest is school."

Without quite comprehending what was coming, Jo's face had begun to share the unhappiness of her father's.

"It's an expensive school with the extras and all—one of the most expensive day schools in the East."

He struggled to his point, with the hurt that was coming to her germinating in his own throat.

"It doesn't seem we can afford it any more this year."

Still Jo did not quite understand, but there was a hush in the dining room.

"You mean I can't go to school this term?" she asked, finally.

"Oh, you'll go to school. But not Tunstall."

"Then I don't go to Tunstall Monday," she said in a flat voice. "Where will I go?"

"You'll take your second term at public school. They're very good now. Mama never went to anything but a public school."

"Daddy!" Her voice, comprehending at last, was shocked.

"We mustn't make a mountain out of a mole-hill. After this year you can probably go back and finish at Tunstall—"

"But *Da*ddy! Tunstall's supposed to be the best. And you said this term you were satisfied with my marks—"

"That hasn't anything to do with it. There are three of us, Jo, and we've got to consider all three. We've lost a great deal of money. There simply isn't enough to send you."

Two advance tears passed the frontier of her eyes, and navigated the cheeks.

Unable to endure her grief, he spoke on automatically:

"Which is best—spend too much and get into debt—or draw in our horns for a while?"

Still she wept silently. All the way to the hospital where they were paying their weekly visit she dripped involuntary tears.

Jason had undoubtedly spoiled her. For ten years the Davis household had lived lavishly in Paris; thence he had journeyed from Stockholm to Istamboul, placing American capital in many enterprises. It had been a magnificent enterprise—while it had lasted. They inhabited a fine house on the Avenue Kleber, or else a villa at Beaulieu. There was an English Nanny, and then a governess, who imbued Jo with a sense of her father's surpassing power. She was brought up with the same expensive simplicity as the children she played with in the Champs Elysées. Like them, she accepted the idea that luxury of life was simply a matter of growing up to it—the right to precedence, huge motors, speed boats, boxes at opera or ballet; Jo had early got into the habit of secretly giving away most of the surplus of presents with which she was inundated.

Two years ago the change began. Her mother's health failed, and her father ceased to be any longer a mystery man, just back from Italy with a family of Lenci dolls for her. But she was young and adjustable and fitted into the life at Tunstall school, not realizing how much she loved the old life. Jo tried honestly to love the new life too, because she loved things and people and she was prepared to like the still newer change. But it took a little while because of the fact that she loved, that she was built to love, to love deeply and forever.

When they reached the hospital Jason said:

"Don't tell mother about school. She might notice that it's hit you rather hard, and make her unhappy. When you get—sort of used to it we'll tell her."

"I won't say anything."

They followed a tiled passage they both knew to an open door. "Can we come in?"

"*Can* you?"

Together husband and daughter embraced her, almost jealously, from either side of the bed. With a deep quiet, their arms and necks strained together.

Annie Lee's eyes filled with tears.

"Sit down. Have chairs, you all. Miss Carson, we need another chair."

They had scarcely noticed the nurse's presence.

"Now tell me everything. Have some chocolates. Aunt Vi sent them. She can't remember what I can and can't eat."

Her face, ivory cold in winter, stung to a gentle wild rose in spring, then in summer pale as the white key of a piano, seldom changed. Only the doctors and Jason knew how ill she was.

"All's well," he said. "We keep the house going."

"How about you, Jo? How's school? Did you pass your exams?"

"Of course, Mama."

"Good marks, *much* better than last year," Jason added.

"How about the play?" Annie Lee pursued innocently. "Are you still going to be Titania?"

"I don't know, Mama."

Jason switched the subject to 'the farm,' a remnant of a once extensive property of Annie Lee's.

"I'd sell it if we could. I can't see how your mother ever made it pay."

"She did though. Right up to the day of her death."

"It was the sausage. And there doesn't seem to be a market for it any more."

The nurse warned them that time was up. As if to save the precious minutes Annie Lee thrust out a white hand to each.

As they got into the car, Jo asked:

"Daddy, what happened to our money?"

Well—better tell her than to have her brood about it.

"It's complicated. The Europeans couldn't pay interest on what we lent them. You know interest?"

"Of course. We had it in the Second Main."

"My job was to judge whether a business showed promise, and if I thought so we loaned them money. When bad times came and they couldn't pay, we wouldn't loan any more. So my job was played out and we came home."

He went on to say that the money he had invested in the venture—oh, many thousands, oh, never mind how much, Jo—and now all that money was 'tied up.'

Under the aegis of the old shot tower they slowed by a garage to fill the tank.

"Why do you like to stop at this station, Daddy? Beside that ugly old chimney over there?"

"That's not a chimney. Don't you know what it is? During the Revolution they had to drop lead down to make the bullets to fire at the British. This is a Historical Monument."

. . . They rounded the corner of the Confederate dead. Jo spoke again suddenly:

"Americans have a hard time, don't they, Daddy? Always fights about nothing."

"Oh well, we're a fighting race. That's what brought us here in the first place."

"But it's not happy—like in Europe."

"They have their troubles. Anyhow you were just a child and all shielded." And he added as they stopped in front of their house, "What of it?"

"Mummy has heart trouble, and you lost your money, and—"

"For heaven's sake don't get sorry for yourself!" he said gruffly. "That spoils people for good. We have a nice house, at least." He felt a pang at knowing that they were going to have to give it up, but he did not want to put too much upon her in one day.

But in the hall Jo was still absorbed in her inner story.

"Daddy, we're like the characters in Little Orphan Annie, only we haven't got that dog that says *Arp* all the time. I never heard a dog say *Arp* did you? They always have dogs in the funny papers now that say 'Arp' or 'Woof,' and I never heard a dog say either."

He was relieved at the turn the conversation had taken.

"I only like the Gumps. Except when I feel mean I like Dick Tracy and X-9."

Jo sighed as she started to her room.

"Nothing seems so bad—when you only have to read about it," she said ruefully.

II

Almost before Jo was adjusted to public school the news broke to her of their impending move. It was a far cry from the spacious house with the mutual, free-rolling lawns of the new suburbs, to the little apartment. Into which the big sofa and the big bed simply wouldn't go and had to repose instead at storage, along with many other things. Jo derived a melancholy consolation from being allowed to act as interior decorator. With some difficulty her father restrained his hilarity.

"I think it's *beau*tiful, Baby."

"Oh, I know you don't. But *Da*ddy, I thought I'd get tinfoil at the five-and-ten and make the whole room silver, like a room in the *House Beautiful*. But it *rum*pled. And now it won't come *off*—no matter what I do makes it worse!"

During Washington's Birthday vacation she repainted her furniture. The man from the Cleaning and Dyeing Company looked aghast at the rug he was expected to restore. And that evening at dancing school mothers warned their children away from the violent rashes on her arms—and were appalled—no understatement is possible—by the clearly leprous quality of the green or purple patches that glared like menacing eyes—dull and sinister eyes—from her hair. There had been nothing to do about it; hair is not washed in tears. The patches remained, remained indeed for weeks. After a fortnight they took on a not unattractive hue—attractive, that is to say, to anyone but Jo—of the roofs of many European villages washed down by an avalanche. And mingled. Thoroughly mingled.

The catastrophe discouraged Jo so much that she no longer wanted to go to the Beacon's Barn dancing class.

Jason argued for it—it was not expensive.

"But there's no *use*," she said, "—now I don't go to Tunstall any more. They have secrets. I like a lot of people at school now."

"You'd better," her father said.

"Why do you say I'd *better*?"

In their new isolation these two talked and fought against each other like adults, almost the old sempiternal dispute of man and wife.

Jason hated that it should be that way, hated her to see him in moments of discouragement.

"Let's go out to the farm," he said one Saturday at breakfast. "You've never been there."

"Can we afford to run the car?"

"Jo, can't you forget for a minute that I'm poor? I've explained;

in the textile business there're only three or four accounts that pay commissions. That's like interest. You said you understood that."

"Yes."

"And the brokers who have them are naturally hanging on—they had them before I came here. As long as I have to sell second-class merchandise to—"

"Let's forget it and like the ride."

"It certainly can go fast, Daddy. Can we really afford to run it?"

"It's cheaper running fast. I want to get there before they finish making the first batch of sausage."

It was seventy miles between fields of frosty rubble, between the ever-dividing purple shoulders of the Appalachians, between villages he had never wanted to ask the names of, so much did he cherish the image of them in his heart. . . .

But Jo's heart was still in France. She was less regarding than thinking.

"Daddy—why couldn't we just make a lot of money out of the farm? Like grandmother did. And just live on that. And get rich."

"But there isn't any farm any more, I tell you. There's just a——just a large pig-sty!"

He retreated from his coarseness as he saw her face contract.

"It isn't quite all that, Baby. Young Seneca does a little truck farming—"

"Who's Young Seneca?"

"There was an Old Seneca and now there's a Young Seneca—"

"When it was a big farm how big was it, Daddy?"

"As far as you can see."

"Far as the mountains?"

"Not quite."

"It was a big farm, wasn't it?"

"It was good and big—even for these parts," he answered, falling into the vernacular.

After a time Jo asked:

"How do they make the sausage, Daddy?"

"I kind of forget. I think—let's see—I think the formula is sixteen pounds of lean meat and sixteen of fat meat. And then they grind it all together. Then they knead in the seasoning—nine tablespoons of salt, nine pepper, nine sage—"

"Why *nine*?"

"That's what your grandmother did."

——Jason had fed Jo's insatiable curiosity with as much as he remembered of the process as they turned into the washed-out lane that led to the farm.

Young Seneca, plunged into work, hurried over to greet them.
"How goes?" Jason asked.

"Just startin', Mr. Davis. We butchered last night. Then a couple of boys thought they had a right to sleep all day. Have I got to pay 'em for that time? They just keep the dogs off."

"The *dogs?*" Jo demanded.

He acknowledged her presence.

"That's right, Missy. Dogs down here are up to anything. We say: 'It's a poor dog that can't keep his own self.' "

Getting out of the car they walked toward the smokehouse.

"We pay those hands well," Jason said. "They still get the chitlings and cracklings and hogs' heads?"

"They gets the regular, Mr. Davis. Even them ditchers work right hard. You take now Aunt Rose that worked for your mother-and-law—she's been kneadin' that seasoning till her arms like to fall off."

The Negress in question greeted them cheerfully.

"Day! Mr. Davis. Day! young lady."

She left her job momentarily to inspect the child, wiping her hands of the sharp spices on a big old kitchen towel.

"And *don't* you look like your mother did?"

Jo wandered into the smokehouse. She passed barrels of flour, salt, lard—of brown sugar, of cut sugar, of sugar granulated. Coming out she ran into a colored girl with a bucket of milk on her head.

"I'm sorry."

Without losing a bit of her balance the young woman laughed hilariously.

"Don't need to be sorry. There's chits been threatnin' to push me down three years, and none ov'em ever do it."

. . . Jo emerged from the smokehouse to find her father in argument with Young Seneca, who broke off from time to time to call instructions to his helpers.

"That there's a flour sifter you're using, Aunt Jinnie. You ought to use a cornmeal sifter for getting out them sage stems."

Jo's interest was divided between the sausage grinding and her father's conversation with Young Seneca.

"We're not making a cheap sausage and listen to this."

He took a letter from his pocket and read aloud: " 'We cannot undertake to distribute your product any longer because of the cancellations.' Now I can't believe that's just hard times. This used to be the best-known stuff of its kind in the East. It's fallen off in quality. So where's your pride, man? They didn't use to be able to keep up with the orders. Something's missing."

"Sure I don't know what it is, Mr. Davis."

When they started back a hickory fire flamed against the white sycamores and it was cold.

"Daddy, if the farm was mine I'd try to find out what's the matter about the sausage."

Every day Jo lost a little faith in her father. Father had been "wonderful" once, and she went on, because she had been correctly tuned to the idea that duty is everything. She had been early made to put her back and wrists into that great realization—work isn't all enthusiasm, though that is an essential part of it—in the long stress and strain of life it is more often what one doesn't want to do any longer.

III

At high school Jo was behind in some subjects but in language classes her only difficulty was to bring her accent down to the level of the rest; her weak spot was Ancient History, which she had never studied—her remark that Julius Caesar was King of Egypt, remembered vaguely from a quick reading of *Anthony and Cleopatra*, became a teacher's legend in the school. She made only a few friends at school; she was at the age of existing largely in her imagination.

On Jason's part it was no help in the dull late winter to know that Jo was losing faith in him. Her right to security and to special privilege as well—this, that was as much a part of her as her sense of responsibility—made a friction between them. But something was gone—Jo's respect for the all-wise, all-just, all-providing.

He tried to keep up his morale with exercise, and with ceaseless pursuit of better textile accounts. His thin stream of commission money scarcely sufficed to keep his head above water. With one of the big ones he would be on safe ground; for he was favorably known here. Well disposed wholesalers tried to slant in his direction, but they were prevented by a class of merchandise they did not care to carry.

There came the black day when he cracked—the blue black, the purple black, the green black of those unused to it. In the morning the grocer's wife came; she said loud in the living room that she and her husband did not care to carry the account any longer.

"Be quiet!" Jason warned her. "Wait till the little girl gets off to school."

"Your little girl! What about mine. One hundred ten dollar—"

Jo's feet sounded on the stairs.

"Morning Daddy. Oh! Morning Mrs. Deshhacker."

"Good morning."

Temporarily, Jo's imperturbability disarmed Mrs. Deshhacker, but after she had gone into the dining room, she delivered her ultimatum more firmly. Jason could only say:

"I'll try.... Middle of next week.... Anyhow a partial payment."

There was the silver: Certain pieces were inviolate—the Supreme Court Bowl, the Lee spoons with the crest of his grandfather—

Jason had seen the sign many times. Mr. Cale would take any security—was most generous, most reliable.

"How do you do, sir?"

With the infallible good manners of the Marylander, even of the humbler denominations, he stood waiting. His venality scarcely showed through his mask.

Jason mumbled something with a shamed face. Mr. Cale was used to that and stopped him.

"You want to raise some money?"

"Yes—on some silver."

"What kind?"

"Table silver. Some goblets that have been a long time—" He broke off—the indignity was intolerable— "and a coffee set."

"Well naturally you have to show me."

"Of course. There may be other things—some furniture. A few pieces—I'll redeem them in a month or so."

"Oh, I'm sure you will."

Big chance he will, he added from his own experience. . . .

At the hospital Jason was stopped in the hall and made to sit down by the floor nurse. Doctor Keyster was finishing his rounds and wanted to talk to him before he went into his wife's room.

"About what?"

"He didn't say."

"She's *worse?*"

"I don't know, Mr. Davis. He just wants to talk to you—"

She was cleaning thermometers as she talked.

Half an hour later in a little reception room Dr. Keyster spoke his mind.

"She doesn't respond. There's nothing before her but years of rest, that's all I can say—years of rest. We've all got fond of her here but there'd be no service to you in kidding you."

"She'll never get well?"

"Probably never."

"You don't think she'll ever be well?" Jason asked again.

"There *have* been cases—"

...... Then the spring was gone out of life, April, May and June. That was all gone.

... April when she came to him like a rill of sweetness. May when she was a hillside. June when they held each other so close that there was nothing more except the lashes flicking on their eyes. ...

Dr. Keyster said:

"You might as well make up your mind to it, Mr. Davis."

Going home once more from one of the many pietas to his love, Jason's taxi passed through an agitated meat market; a labor agitator was addressing the crowd; when he saw Jason in his taxi he shifted the burden of his discourse to him.

"Here is one! And here *we* are! We'll turn them upside down and shake them till the dimes and quarters roll out!"

Jason wondered what would roll out of him. He had just enough to pay the taxi.

Up in his bedroom he felt for the third time the balance of the thirty-eight revolver——life insurance all paid up.

"Help me to kill myself!" he prayed. "No fooling now. Put it in the mouth."

——The phone rang sharp and he tossed the gun onto the empty twin bed.

A woman's voice said: "Is this Mr. Davis? This is Principal McCutcheon's secretary. Just one moment."

Then came a man's voice, level and direct.

"This is Mr. McCutcheon at the High School. It's an unfortunate matter, Mr. Davis. We have to ask you to withdraw your daughter Josephine from school."

Jason's tense breath caught in his throat.

"I thought you'd rather know before she reached home. I tried your office. We're compelled, much against our sensibilities, to expel three of the girls for conduct that can't be condoned. When a pupil falls below the tone of the school the individual must be sacrificed to the good of the majority. I called a committee of teachers, Mr. Davis, and they saw eye-to-eye with me."

"What was the nature of the offense?"

"That I don't care to go into on the phone, Mr. Davis. I shall be glad to see you by appointment any afternoon except Thursday between two and four. I must add that we were more than surprised to find Josephine linked up to this matter. She's held herself—well, I must say, a little aloof; she hasn't ingratiated herself with her teachers, but—well, there we are."

"I see," Jason said dryly.

"Good afternoon, sir."

Jason reached for the revolver and began taking the cartridges out of the magazine.

——I've got to stick around—a little longer, he thought.

Jo arrived in half an hour, her usually mobile mouth tight and hard. There were dark strips of tears up and down her cheeks.

"Hello."

"He*llo*, darling." He had been waiting for her downstairs; he waited till she had taken off her coat and hat.

"What's it all about anyhow?"

Furiously she turned to him.

"I *won't* tell you! You can shake me, Daddy! You can beat me!"

"For *God's* sake—what's this all about? When did I ever beat you?"

"They wanted to this morning because I wouldn't say what they wanted."

Jo flung herself into a corner of the big couch and wept into it. He walked around the room, concerned and embarrassed.

"I don't want to know, Jo. Whatever you do is all right with me. I trust you, Baby, all the way. I'm not even making any inquiries."

She turned tired eyes up at him.

"You won't? You promise, word of honor?"

"Yes."

"I've got an idea, a real hunch. Unless—or say till I get the Gehrbohm account, I have lots of time in the afternoon. Suppose I be your private tutor for awhile. I was pretty good once in Latin and Algebra. For the languages we'll get a reading list from the library."

She sobbed again deep into the big cushions.

"Oh Baby! Stop that. We're not defeatists, you and me. Take a bath and then we'll get up some dinner."

When she had gone into her room Jason tried to think of something outside himself. Then he remembered what Annie Lee had said in their short quarter hour this morning.

"I can't understand about the farm—it was all so simple. There was the seasoning—nine tablespoons of salt, then nine of hickory ash, then the pepper and sage. And of course always the tenderloin—"

"Hickory ash?" Jason had exclaimed. "Tenderloin?"

Stirred by his surprise she lifted herself up in bed, so that he had to ease her gently down again. "Don't tell me Young Seneca isn't using tenderloin—isn't putting in the tablespoons of *hick*ory ash?"

——In the living room of the apartment Jason sat down and wrote Young Seneca.

When Jo came downstairs he said, "Take this over to the post office, will you? It's about the farm."

After examining the address Jo demanded:

"Father—do you mean *seriously* you're going to teach me?"

"Am I? You bet! Teach you all I know."

"All right."

But in the grey dusk he was still bent over the ragged text-book.

"Caesar," he said over the first text. "It's addressed to the damn Swiss!"

He translated:

."In Switzerland they necked the Gods and the men—."

"*What*, Daddy?"

"Wait now: In Switzerland they necked the men and then they necked the Gods—This is difficult now—Latin didn't seem like that in *my* day."

Jason turned to Jo with exasperation. "Don't they give you sentences to construe? *Helvetii qui nec Dēos nec hominēs verēbantur*—That means quiver I think—*magnum dolorem*. That means it all ends up very sad. Why did you ask me to translate it in the first place?"

"I *did*n't ask you. I knew that part. It means the Helvetians who feared neither Gods nor men came to great grief because they were restrained on all sides by mountains."

He read again: "*Patiebantur quod ex omnibus partibus*, and that means a rampart of ten feet," he cried exultantly across the lamplight.

"Yah! You saw that in a footnote."

"I did not," he lied.

"Give me your word of honor?"

"Let's talk about something else."

"You fancy yourself as a teacher."

That was the end of the first night's Latin.

Thumbing over the book Jo found her place and read aloud slowly:

"If the government revenue from taxes increased from one billion dollars in 1927 to five hundred billion dollars in 1929, what was the increased percent?"

"Go on," said Jason.

"Go on yourself, Daddy. You're this wonderful mathematician. And try this one!"

"Let me read it myself:

'If the sum of the reciprocals of two consecutive even numbers is zero. Then the sum of two other consecutive numbers is 11/60. What are the numbers?' "

Jason said, "There's always for the X an unknown quantity. You have to have some system—haven't you?"

"Swell system."

"Got to start somewhere." He bent over it again: "If the government revenue increased from five billions in 1927 to—"

He was temporarily at the end of his resources.

"Darling," he said. "In a week I'll know more about this—"

"Yes, Daddy."

"Time for you to go to bed."

There was a pregnant silence between them.

"I know."

She came over to him and pecked briefly at an old baseball scar on his forehead.

VI

To keep the chronicle going one must skip through the days when Annie Lee's farm came to life again—when Young Seneca realized that Mr. Davis *act*ually wanted *tenderloin* put into the sausage—the day he recalled that an important appendage was *nine tablespoons of hickory ash.*

Orders for the buckets began to increase. From merely paying for itself, the farm began to dribble a trickle of profit.

VII

Some nights Jason used to go to her bedside and sit. Not tonight, though. He picked up in the living room the copy of *Caesar's Gaellic Wars.*

The Swiss, who feared neither Gods nor men, suffered. . . .

"Who am I to be afraid?" Jason thought. He who had led eight Ohio country boys to death in a stable in France and come out of it with only the loss of the tip of his left shoulder!

The Swiss who feared neither Gods nor men suffered—

He pulled the lamp closer.

The night wore on in a melange of verbs and participles. Toward eleven the phone rang.

"This is Mr. McCutcheon."

"Oh, yes."

"There's a serious injustice been done your daughter."

It seems that there had been some wild excursion into the boys' locker-room—during which someone was posted as sentry outside. The sentry had run away but Jo was there trying to warn them at the moment when the monitors appeared.

"I'm sorry, Mr. Davis. There isn't much we can do in these cases—except offer our sincere apology."

"I know."

The phone put on the voice of Mr. Halklite.

Here it was! The Pan-American Textile account.

"He*llo*, Mr. Davis! I'm in Philadelphia. We've had some correspondence—I'll be down in your part of the world tomorrow and I thought I'd drop in. Sorry to call so late. . . ."

Breakfast was waiting when, having made a journey to his office and back, Jason went to his bedroom—almost immediately Jo, who had heard him come in, knocked at the door and demanded in alarm:

"What's the matter?"

"I'm just tired. I've been working all night. Say, if you have those girls to lumpshun—" the words seemed extraordinarily hard and long—"then fix up the room afterwards. Very important. Business meeting."

"I understand, Daddy."

Holding to the bed-post he swayed precariously. "Whole future depends on this man. Make it nice for him."

With no more warning he pitched forward across the bed.

VIII

Unexpectedly at eleven o'clock the colored girl admitted Mr. Halklite. On his tour of inspection Mr. Halklite had become, perforce, less and less kind, though he was kindly by nature. Keenness was his valuable business asset—exercising the quality had temporarily become dull—there was the necessity of weeding out the exhausted and the inefficient. Halklite could tell the dead from the living, and that was half of why he had just been elected a vice-president of Pan-American Textile. Only half, though. The other half was because he was kind.

A little girl came into the room.

"Good morning. Is your father in? I think he expected me."

"Won't you come in? Father's got a cold—he's lying down."

In Jason's bedroom Jo shook and shook the exhausted body without result. She went back into the living room.

"Daddy'll be getting up presently," she said. "He's sorry he wasn't dressed to meet you."

"Oh, that's all right. You're Mr. Davis' little girl?" Mr. Halklite said.

Jo crossed as if casually to the piano bench and turned back to him with sudden decision.

"Mr. Halklite, father's had flu, and the doctor doesn't want him to get up. He's going to try to."

"Oh, we can't let him!"

"The doctor didn't want him to. But Daddy's like that. If he says he'll do something, he does. Daddy needs a woman to take care of him. And I'm so busy at school—"

"Tell him not to get up," Halklite repeated.

"I don't even know whether he can."

"Then tell him it doesn't matter."

She went to her father's room and presently returned.

"He sent you best regards. He was sorry not to see you."

Her heart was in agony. Keeping that agony out of her expression was the hardest thing she had ever had to do.

"I'm good and sorry," Mr. Halklite said. "I wanted to talk to him."

"How old is your father, young lady?"

"I don't know. I guess he's about thirty-eight."

"Well a man can be young at thirty-eight," he protested. "Isn't your father still young?"

"Daddy's young. But he's serious." She hesitated.

"Go on," Halklite said. "Tell me about him. I'll leave you to your lessons as soon as I finish my cigarette. But I think you ought to stay out of your father's room while he's ill."

"Oh, I do."

"You're fond of your daddy?"

"Yes—everybody is."

"Does he go around much?"

"Not much—Oh, he does though. He goes out to see Mama once a week. And he goes to walk half an hour when I go to bed. He starts out when I start to bed and then I call down to him when I hear him open the door coming in—pour dire bon soir."

"You speak French?" She regretted that she had mentioned it, but she admitted, "I grew up in France."

"So did your daddy, didn't he?"

"Oh no, Daddy's very American. He can't even speak French much, really."

Halklite stood up, made his decision suddenly, perhaps irrationally.

"You tell your father we want to put our account in his hands. Maybe that'll cheer him up and help him get well. 'Pan-Am-Tex.' Can you remember that? He'll understand."

IX

It was April again and they walked in the zoo.

"It's been a hard year, Jo."

"I know that, Daddy. But look at the peacocks!"

"This is your education, Jo. It's most of what you'll ever know about life. You'll understand later."

"I know we've had bad times, Daddy. Everything's better again, isn't it? Look at the peacocks, *mon pere. They* don't worry."

"Well, if you insist, let's sit on the bench and stare at them."

Jo sat silent for a moment. Then she said:

"We were peacocks once, weren't we?"

"What?"

"They probably have sorrows and troubles sometimes, when their tails don't grow out."

"I guess so. What school do you want to go to next year? You can have your choice."

"That doesn't seem to matter any more. Look at the peacock—Look! the one that's trying to peck outside the cage. I love him—do you?"

Jason said, "After all, considering everything, it wasn't such a bad year."

"What?" Jo turned from the cage where she had gone to try, unsuccessfully, to feed the bird a shelled peanut.

"Daddy, let's stop worrying. I thought we stopped months ago. Mother's coming home next week. Maybe some day we'll be three peacocks again."

Jason came over to the wire.

"I suppose peacocks have their problems."

"I suppose so. Look, *Daddy!* I've got this one eating the popcorn."

The Intimate Strangers

(*McCall's*, June 1935)

"The Intimate Strangers" was probably written in February and March of 1935 in Tryon, North Carolina, where Fitzgerald had gone to recover from what he was convinced was tuberculosis. The story was turned down by the *Post*, but bought by *McCall's* for a desperately needed $3000. Though he described himself at the time as "half crazy with illness and worry"—he was living from story to story while sinking into debt—there were bright moments, such as his new friendship with Nora and Lefty Flynn, a talented couple who had an elegant modern house at the small mountain resort.

This story is loosely based on the Flynns' turbulent romance. Nora was one of the beautiful Langhorne sisters, one of whom married Lord Astor and another Charles Dana Gibson, the creator of "The Gibson Girl." Flynn was a former football star at Yale and sometime cowboy actor—just the sort of people who would fascinate Fitzgerald. He was particularly charmed by the numbers they performed together for friends, which are described in the story—including the imitation of the dancing master teaching the turkey trot, the French woman teaching English, and the Russian gibberish song.

Fitzgerald spent much of the time from 1935 until mid-1937, when he moved to Hollywood for good, in the Tryon-Asheville-Hendersonville area—partly because Zelda was at the Highland Hospital in Asheville. It was in North Carolina that he began the "Crack-Up" series for *Esquire*, baring his soul to the world in what some of his peers, including Hemingway, condemned as exhibitionism.

Was she happy? Her beach slippers felt strange on the piano pedals; the wind off the Sound blew in through the French windows, blew a curl over her eye, blew on her daringly bare knees over bright blue socks. This was 1914.

"The key is in the door," she sang,
"The fire is laid to light
But the sign upon my heart, it says 'To let.' "

Blow, breeze of the Sound, breeze of my youth, she thought, vamping chords to the undercurrent of the melody lingering in her mind. Here I can ask myself the things that I can never ask in France. I am twenty-one. My little girl is on the beach making molds of the wet sand, my lost baby is asleep in a graveyard in Brittany; in twenty minutes my little boy will be fed for the last time from my own self. Then there will be an hour of sky and sea and old friends calling,

"Why, *Sara!* Did you bring your ukelele, Sara? You have to come back sometimes, don't you, Sara? *Please* do the imitation of the old dancing master teaching the Turkey Trot."

Write the embassy in Washington, said a persistent undertone in the melody. Tell Eduard you're coming there to live like a good little wife until you sail. You're beginning to like your native land too much for one who married a Frenchman of her own free choice.

I must ask you, Mr. Agent, 'bout a problem of today
And I hope that you can solve it all for me.
I have advertised with smiles and sighs in every sort of way
But there isn't any answer I can see—

Once again she felt the wind that ruffled the sheet music. She felt life crowding into her, into her childish resourceful body with a child's legs and a child's restiveness, but disciplined in her case to a virtuosic economy of movement, so that whenever she wished (which was often) she could make people's eyes follow every little gesture she made; life crowding into her mind, wind-blown, newly-winged every morning ("Eduard never knew what he married," sighed his relatives in their hide-outs in the Faubourg, predicting disaster. "Some day he will give her too much liberty and she will flit just like that."); life crowded into her voice, a spiced voice with a lot of laughter, a little love, much quiet joy and an awful sympathy for people in it. "To Let" or not, her heart poured into her voice as it soared through the long light music room, finishing the song:

The key is in the door, you'll find
The fire is laid to light
But the sign upon my heart—

She stopped with a period, realizing that suddenly she was no longer alone on the piano bench. A very tall man with a body like the Lyendecker poster of the half-back, and a face as mad with controlled exuberance as her own, had sat down beside her, and now he tinkled off the last notes in the treble with fingers too big for the keys.

"Who are you?" she said, though she guessed immediately.

"I'm the new tenant you mentioned," he answered. "I'm sending over my furniture this afternoon."

"You're Abby's beau. What's your name—Killem Dead or something?"

"Killian. Killian the silver-tongued. Are you the one that's Madame Sans-Gêne or the Queen of France?"

"That must be me," she admitted.

They looked at each other, they stared, their mouths simultaneously fell just slightly ajar. Then they both laughed, bent almost double over the piano—and a moment later they were both playing "To Let" in an extemporized arrangement for two parts, playing it loud in ragtime, singing it, alternating the melody and the second without a shadow of friction.

They stopped, they stared again; once more they laughed. His blue suit was dusty and there was mud and a little blood on his forehead. His teeth were very even and white; his eyes, sincere and straight as he tried to make them, as if he had been trying hard since early boyhood, were full of trouble for somebody. He had edged one of her feet off the treble pedal and she thought how funny her other bathing shoe looked beside this monumental base of dusty cordovan. Two yellow pigskin bags and a guitar case stood behind him.

"Abby's down at the beach with the others," she said.

"Oh, is she? Look, do you know this . . . ?"

. . . Twenty minutes later, she jumped up suddenly.

"Heavens! I'm supposed to be feeding my son—the poor little—see you on a wave!"

She tore for the nursery. Margot greeted her tranquilly at the door.

"You needn't have hurried, Madame. I gave him his bottle and he took it like a glutton. The doctor said it did not matter, today or tomorrow."

"Oh."

But it did matter. Sara knelt beside the crib.

"Goodbye a little bit," she whispered. "Goodbye a little bit, small son. We shall meet."

Her breast felt heavy with more than milk.

. . . I can feed him tonight, she thought.

But no. To be sentimental over such a little milestone. In a sudden change of mood she thought:

I am only twenty-one—life's beginning all over. And in a rush of ecstasy she kissed Margot and tore downstairs toward the beach.

After the swimming, Sara and Killian each dressed quickly, Sara's comb trembling in her hair till she tried three times before achieving a part, till her voice answered Abby with the wrong answers, in the wrong tone, or with meaningless exclamations that to her meant: Hurry! Hurry!

He was waiting on the piano bench. They sang "Not That You Are Fair, Dear," with his baritone following four notes and four words after her little contralto—that was the fad then. Their eyes danced and danced together. When Abby came in, Sara was on her feet clowning for him, and Abby was appalled, yet hypnotized by the pervasive delight they had created around themselves. As soon as they fully realized her presence—it took some minutes—they were very considerate to her. Abby accepted it in a sporting spirit—Sara had the privileged position of a life-long ideal—and her own claim on Killian was only a fond hope. Anyhow Sara was happily married to the Marquis de la Guillet de la Guimpé, and would presently be going back with him to France.

Three days later the Marquis wrote to his wife from the French Embassy in Washington.

"—for two reasons I will be glad to leave, my dear little one; if the situation in Europe becomes more grave I want to be where I can join my regiment and not be tied to a desk in a neutral country."

. . . As he wrote this Sara was giving a last fillip to her red-brown hair with a comb that slipped and wriggled again in her fingers—

"—second, and most important, because I don't want my little American to forget that she is of another country now, that this is only a pleasant excursion into the past—for her future lies ahead and in France."

. . . As he wrote this Sara was not so much afraid of her heel taps on the silent stairs as of the sound of her heart, which anyone must hear since it was swollen to a throbbing drum.

"—twenty years seemed a long time to lie between us when we were married, but as you grow and develop it will seem less and less—"

. . . As he sealed the letter in Washington, the starlight of a Long Island veranda just revealed the dark band of an arm around the shadowy gossamer of Sara; there were two low voices like two people singing in chorus:

"Yes—"

"Oh, yes—"

"Anywhere, I don't care—"

"Nothing like this has ever happened, even faintly."

"I didn't know anything about this."

"I'd read about this, but I didn't think it was real."

"I never understood."

When they made their decision they were walking along the beach with their shoes full of sand and their hands clutched like children's hands.

. . . They were in a train bound for North Carolina. Killian had his guitar and Sara her ukelele. They had at least six concert hours a day from sheer exuberance, sheer desire to make a noise, to cry "Here we are!" They were like a cavalry fleeing back from a raid, with an aroused enemy thundering behind them. Sometimes they laid aside the instruments and "did" the German band, Sara manipulating hands over mouth for a cornet, Killian growling for a deep tuba. They made friends immediately with conductors and brakemen and waiters, and when the door of their drawing-room was open, the people in the car drifted up to the seats just outside. If they had tried they could have left no wider trail, but when they talked of such things they grew confused, incoherent with having so much to say to each other.

"—and then you left Harvard."

"Almost. I had this offer from the Red Sox and I wanted to take it. I wasn't getting any more education. Well, Father said to go ahead and be a fool any way I wanted, but Mother had a nervous breakdown. You can imagine how Mother is—my name's Cedric, you know. Sometime I'll show you my picture in curls and a skirt."

"Fauntleroy period."

"Fauntleroy was a street urchin compared to me. But then I fooled them—I outgrew them. Anyhow, instead of going south with the Red Sox—"

"Shut the door."

He shut it.

When they were really alone they were no age at all—they were one indissoluble commingling of happiness and laughter. Only now did Sara realize the burden of these last four years of difficult adjustment, a burden carried gracefully and gayly because of the discipline of her training, a training in pride.

When they got out at Asheville and began to mount toward Saluda in a wretched bus, over the then wretched roads of slippery red clay, wires were already buzzing behind them. Mrs. Caxton Bisby, eldest of Sara's sisters, summoned a council of war in New York, a famous detective agency began scanning the horizon, a reporter got himself a raise by an unscrupulous scoop, and it took a week before the Austrian ultimatum to Serbia pushed the story onto the second page. There were repercussions in the Faubourg St. Germaine and the Hon. (and indefatigable) Mrs. Burne-Dennison, another sister, wired from London to hold the fort, she was coming.

Meanwhile Killian had wangled a cabin, a wild broken shack above snow level, where they spent a hundred blessed hours making love and fires. Nothing was wrong, the pink light on the snow at five o'clock, the fallings asleep, the awakenings with a name half formed on the lips like a bugle rousing them.

On the other side there was only a torn calendar in the lean-to where the wood was, a calendar with a chromo of Madonna and Child. When she first saw it, stricken and aghast, Sara's face did not change—she simply stood very still—and *rained*. After that she didn't look toward the calendar when she went after wood.

They had no time for plans. They had no excuses, nothing to say. A week after they had left New York Sara was back, sitting silent in highly-charged drawing-rooms, neither denying nor affirming. A question would be asked her, and she would answer "What?" in an abstracted way. Killian was God knew where.

A few days later she embarked with her husband and children for France. That is the first part of this story.

The war to Sara was a long saying of goodbyes—to officers whom she knew, to soldiers whom she tried to make into more than numbers on a hospital bed. Goodbyes to men still whole, at doorways or railroad stations, were often harder than goodbyes to the dying. Between men and women everything happened very quickly in those days, everything was snatched at, infinitesimal pieces of time had a value they had not possessed before—

. . . As when Sara turned the angle of a corridor in the Ritz and stopped momentarily outside an open door that was not her door. Stopped is not quite the right word—rather she hesitated, she balanced. After another step, though, she did stop, for a voice hailed her from the room.

"Where are you going in such a hurry?"

It came from the handsome man tying a civilian cravat meticulously before a mirror.

"Going along a hall."

"Well, look—don't. Come here a minute."

As already remarked, everything happened quickly in those days. In a moment Sara was sitting on the side of a chair in the room, with the door pulled to just enough for her to be unseen.

"How did you happen to look in at me?" the man demanded.

"I don't know. Men are attractive sometimes when they don't know it—you were *so* absorbed and puckered up over your tie."

"I wanted to have it right. I keep buying civilian ties with no chance to wear 'em. Back to the line tomorrow."

"I've got till tomorrow night."

"What are you?"

"A nurse—with the French."

He slipped on a white vest with obvious satisfaction in himself, and sat facing her. The shining, star-like eyes had met his in the mirror, the lithe figure with its air of teetering breezily on the edge of nothing, the mobile lips forming incisively every word they uttered, were immediately attractive. His heart, stimulated by the nearing sea-change of the morrow, went out to her.

"Why not have dinner with me tonight? I've got a date, but I'll call up and break it."

"Can't possibly," said Sara. "What division are you with?"

"Twenty-sixth New England. Practically a Puritan—look, it'd be a lot of fun."

"Can't possibly."

"Then why did you look in at me?"

"I told you. Because of the way you were tying your tie." She laughed. "The first boy I ever fell in love with was a ship's bugler, because his trousers were so tight and smooth when he bent over to blow."

"Change your mind."

"No—I'm sorry."

In her room down the corridor, Sara shifted reflectively into an evening dress. She had no engagement for dinner, though there were many places she could have gone. Her own house in the Rue de Bac was closed; Eduard was with relatives at Grenoble convalescing from a spinal wound which threatened a life-long paralysis of his legs; it was from there that she had just come. The war was four years tired now, and as she walked with many millions through the long nightmare, there were times she had to be alone, away from the broken men who tore ceaselessly at her heart. Once she felt all the happiness of life in her finger tips—now she clung to little happenings of today or yesterday, gay ones or sad ones. If her heart should die she would die.

A little later the American officer came up to her as she sat in the lobby.

"I knew you'd change your mind," he said. "I phoned and broke my other engagement. Come along—I've got a car."

"But I told you—"

"Don't be that way now—it's not like you."

"How do you know what I'm like?"

They drove over the dark "City of Light" and dined—then they went on to one of the few but popular night clubs—this one, run by an enterprising American, moved to a new address every twenty-four hours to avoid the attention of the *gendarmerie*. They danced a lot and they knew many people in common, and, partly because talking to a man going back into the line was like talking to herself, Sara spoke of things she had not spoken of for years.

"No, I haven't been lonely in France," she said. "My mother was very wise, and she didn't bring us up to count on any happiness that we didn't help make ourselves."

"And you've never been in love with your husband?"

"No, I was never in love with my husband."

"Never in love at all?"

"Yes, I was in love once," she said, very low.

"When was that?"

"Four years ago. I only saw him for two weeks. I—understand that he's married now."

She did not add that ever since that two weeks she had heard Killian's voice singing around her, heard his guitar as an undertone to every melody, touched his hand before every fire. All through the war she had dressed his wounds, listened to his troubles, written letters for him, laid his hands straight for the last time and died with him, for he was all men—Killian the archangel, the silver-tongued.

. . . She got up early and went with the officer to the Gare du Nord. He was all changed now, in trench coat, haversack and shining revolver.

"You're very fine," he said tenderly. "This has been a very strange thing. I might have been more—well, more demonstrative last night, but—"

"No, no—it's much better this way."

Then the train went out toward the thunder and left a hollow of gray sky.

In the movies it is so simple to tell of time passing—the film fades out on a dressing station behind the Western Front, fades in on an opera ball in Paris with the punctured uniforms changed into tail coats and the nurses' caps into tiaras. And why not? We only want to hear about the trenchant or glamorous moments in a life. After the war Sara went to balls in Paris and London, and the side of her that was an actress played butterfly for the dull, neophyte for the brilliant, great lady for the snob, and—sometimes was most difficult of all— herself for a few.

Difficult, because it seemed to her that she had no particular self. She had a fine gay time with her children; she walked beside the wheel chair of the Marquis de la Guillet de la Guimpé for his last few years of life, but there was energy to spare that often sent her prying up mean streets or sitting for hours on the fence posts of quirky peasants; simple people said wise or droll things to her that were somehow a comfort. And she made the most of these things in the repeating. It was fun to be with Sara—even people who begrudged her the gayety patronized her for an incorrigible *gamine*.

When the war had been over eight years and the Marquis had lain for twelve months in the tombs of his ancestors, Sara went again to a ball; she went alone, feeling flushed and excited, and very free—in the entrance she came to a stop, her eyes lighting up higher at the sight of a footman.

"Paul Pechard!" she exclaimed.

"Madame has not forgotten."

"Heavens, no! Were you wounded again? Did you marry Virginie?"

"I married, but not Virginie. I married an old friend of Madame's—Margot, who was *bonne* to her babies. She also works here in this house."

"Why, this is wonderful! Listen—I must go up and be polite for a moment—after that I'll go down by a back way and meet you and Margot in the pantry, and we can talk intimately. What?"

"Madame is too generous."

Up the stairs then on little golden slippers, looking years less than thirty-three, looking no age at all, down the receiving line speaking names out of the pages of Saint-Simon and Mme. de Sévigné, with everyone *so* glad to see her back in the world again— though, privately, a year seemed to many a very short mourning— then on quickly, shaking off men who tried to attach themselves to her, and down a narrow back staircase. Sara had felt that something would happen at this ball, which was why she had broken through her sister-in-law's disapproval at her going. And here was Paul Pechard and Margot, redolent of more intense days.

"Madame is more lovely than—"

"Stop it—I want to hear about you and Paul."

"I think we got married because we knew you, Madame."

It was probably true. So many things can happen in the shelter of some protective personality.

"Madame was wounded, we heard, and received a decoration."

"Just a splinter in the heel. I limp just a little when I walk—so I always run or dance."

"Madame always ran or danced. I can see Madame now, running to the nursery and dancing out of it."

"You dears—listen, I want to go up on that high balcony above the dance floor—do all the maids and everyone still watch the balls from there in this house? It always reminds me of when I was a child and used to look at dances in a nightgown through a crack in the door. It always seems so shiny when you watch like that."

They climbed to the shadowy gallery and gazed down at the ambulating jewels and shimmering dresses, dressed hair bright under the chandeliers, and all against the gleaming back drop of the floor. From time to time a face turned up to laugh, or exchange a mute, secret look, breaking the fabric of calculated perfection like round flowers among the straight lines of rooms; and over the kaleidoscope the music mingled with faint powder and floated up to the watchers in the sky.

Margot leaned close to Sara.

"I saw an old friend of Madame's this morning," she said hesitantly. "I brought the oldest child back from England on the channel boat—"

In a wild second Sara knew what was coming.

"—I saw Mr. Killian—the big handsome American."

Often we write to certain people that we "think of you all the time," and we lie, of course; but not entirely. For they are always with us, a few of them, so deep in us that they are part of us. Sometimes they are, indeed, the marrow of our bones, so if they die they live on in us. Sara had only to look into herself to find Killian.

. . . He knows I am free and he has come to find me, she thought. I must go home.

Even as she went down the stairs the strummings of a dozen years ago were louder than the music; they blended with the June wind in the chestnut trees. Her car was not ordered, so she hailed a taxi, pressed it to go faster.

"Has anyone phoned?"

"Yes, Madame—Mrs. Selby and Madame de Villegris."

"No one else?"

"No, Madame."

It was eleven. He had been in Paris all day, but perhaps he was traveling with people. Or perhaps he was tired and wanted to sleep first and be at his best.

She looked at herself in the mirror more closely than ever before in her life. She was all gaudy and a little disheveled with excitement, and she wished rather that he could see her now. But doubtless he would phone in the morning. Morning was his best time—he was an early-to-bed man. Nevertheless she switched a button so that the phone beside her bed would ring.

All morning she stayed in the house, faintly tired around her eyes from a restless night. After lunching she lay down with cold cream on her face, feigning sleep to avoid Noel, her sister-in-law, who wondered whether her early return from the ball did not indicate she had been snubbed for appearing in society so soon.

. . . Surely it was at tea time that he would call, the mellower, sweeter hour, and she took off the cold cream lest she face him with it, even on the phone. She listened with seven-league ears; she heard the teacups being gathered up in cafes on the Champs-Elysées, she heard the chatter of people pouring from the stores at five-thirty, she heard the clink of tables being laid for dinner at the Ritz and Ciro's—then the clack of plates being piled and taken away. She heard black bells strike the hour, then taxis without horns—it was late. Sara tried to be very wise and logical; why should she have expected him—he might have been in Paris a dozen times since the war. At twelve she turned out her light.

At about three the phone woke her. A thick voice said in English: "I'd like to speak to the lady of the house—the Marquise."

"Who is it?" mumbled Sara, and then wide awake, "Is this—is—"

She heard a click as another receiver was taken up in the house. *"Qui parle?"*

"That's all right, Noel," said Sara quickly. "I think I know who it is." But the receiver did not fall into place again.

"Is this Sara?" said the man.

"Yes, Killian."

"Just got here. Sorry call you so late, but been business."

"Where are you?"

"Place in Montmartre—want to come over?"

—Yes, anywhere.

"No, of course not."

"I'll come see you then."

"It's too late." She hesitated. "Where are you staying?"

"Meurice."

Killian, the silver-tongued, fumbling with his words—and Sara hating drunkenness more than anything in her world. She hardly recognized her own voice as it said:

"Drink two cups of black coffee and I'll meet you in the lobby of the Meurice for an hour."

The receiver in Noel's room clicked just before her own.

Sara's mind had already sorted clothes for any time he might call. In the lower hall Noel was waiting for her.

"Of course you're not going."

"Yes, Noel."

"You—my brother's widow to meet a man in a public lobby at three in the morning."

"Now please—"

"—and I know very well who the man is."

Almost absent-mindedly Sara walked past her and out of the door. She found a cab at the corner of the Avenue de Bois and flew down through the city feeling higher and higher, with all the lost months coming back into the calendar with every square they passed . . .

He was handsome and straight as an athlete, immaculate and unrumpled in his dinner coat—he swayed on his feet.

"Haven't you got a suite?" she demanded. "Can't we go up there?"

He nodded. "Nice of you come."

"I'd have come a longer way than this, Killian."

Darkly and inconclusively he muttered: "Whenever there's been a moon—you know—moonlight."

... Two guitars leaned against the sofa—Sara tuned one softly—Killian went to the window, put his head way out and breathed night air.

" 'Tended look you up," he said, sitting in a chair beside the window. "Then got to know too many people on the boat. After that didn't feel fit to see you."

"It's all right. I understand. Don't talk about it. Come over here."

"After while."

The blown curtains fluttered around his head, obscuring it; she released a dry sob that she had held too long in her throat.

"What's the matter?"

"Nothing—except that you've been on a tear. You never used to do that, Killian—you used to be so vain of your beautiful self."

She felt something begin to slip away and in desperation picked up the guitar.

"Let's sing something together. We mustn't talk about dull things after all these years."

"But—"

"Sh—sh—sh!" Low in her throat she sang:

Beside an Eastbound box-car
A dying hobo lay—

Then she said:

"Now you sing *me* something—yes, you can. I want you to—please, Killian."

He touched the strings unwillingly, and then gradually his mellow baritone rolled forth.

—He had a million dollars and
  he had a million dimes
He knew because he counted them
  a million times.

While he sang Sara was thinking: Is this adolescent the man whom I have loved so, that I love still? Now what? She made him sing again, as if to gain time, sing again and again until his fingers were dusting fainter and fainter chords and his voice was a sleepy murmur.

"But I can't," she exclaimed aloud suddenly.

He came to life startled.

"What?"

"Nothing."

Her exclamation was answer to the thought: Can I kill the

memory I have lived by so long? Ah, if he had never come!

"Are you free?" she asked him suddenly. "Did you come to ask me to marry you?"

"That was my idea. Course, you see me in rather bad light. Can't deny I've too much under my belt last week—and it isn't the first time."

"But, of course, that's over," she said hurriedly.

Yet how could she know? Each of them must have changed so, and she had to look at him from time to time to reassure herself even of his good looks. The dark mischief of his eyes gleamed back at her across the room. If it were only that, she sighed.

Yet she could not forget the girl who had known a wild delight in a mountain cabin. . . .

Killian dozed, Sara moved around the room examining him impertinently from various corners, his Rodinesque feet, his clothes made of whole bolts of cloth, his great hand inert on the sounding board of the guitar. He complained faintly in his sleep and she woke him—automatically his voice rolled out of him again, deep and full, and the blunt fingers began to strum.

"Oh, Killian, Killian." She laughed in spite of herself, and sang with him:

> So merry you make me I'm
> bent up double,
> What is it in your make-up that
> drives away trouble—

. . . Dawn came through the windows very suddenly, and she remembered that it was the longest day in the year. As if impatient to begin it, the telephone jingled.

"The *beau-frère* and *belle-soeur* of Madame are below and wish to see Madame at once on a matter of the greatest—"

"I'll be down."

Gently she rocked Killian from a new slumber in his chair, and as his eyes opened unwillingly she laid her cheek alongside his, whispering in his ear.

"I'll be gone for half an hour, but I'll be back."

"That's all right," he murmured. "I'll play guitar."

The callers were in a small reception-room, Noel and the Comte Paul, Eduard's brother. When she saw the agitation in their faces, decomposed by dawn, she knew that the scenes of twelve years ago were to be repeated.

"This is extraordinary—" Paul began, but Noel cut through him.

"To find you here, Sara! You, the widow of a hero, the mother of the son who bears his name, here in a *hotel* at this hour."

"You can't be very surprised," said Sara coldly. "You knew where to find me."

"Once when my brother was alive you dragged his name through the newspapers—now when he is in a hero's grave and cannot speak for himself, you intend to do it again."

"Eduard wanted me to be happy—"

She stopped—she was not happy, only miserable and confused. Weary with her two-day vigil, she wanted sleep most of all. But she did not dare sleep; she could not risk letting this thing slip out of her hand again.

"Would you like some coffee?" she suggested.

Noel refused, but Paul agreed vigorously and went to order it.

"Are you an old woman bewitched, wanting a pretty gigolo?" Noel cried. "Are there not hundreds of men of culture and distinction for you to know—you who have moved in the best society of Europe. Yes, even men to marry if you must, after a decent interval."

"You think that I'm going to marry Killian?"

Noel started.

"Well, aren't you? Isn't that your—"

Paul returned from the lobby.

"What concerns us chiefly is the children," he said. "Henri bears the senior title; he is the only Marquis in France who walks with Dukes, by the graciousness of the *Grand Monarque*."

"I know all that. I am proud of my son's name and I've tried to make him proud of it. But my part is almost done—they go to Brittany next week for the summer, and in the fall Miette will be fifteen and Henri thirteen and they'll go off to school."

"Then you've made up your mind to marry this—this species of six-day-bicycle-racer?" said Paul. "Oh, we've checked up on him from time to time—once he made himself a promoter of prize fights. Guh!"

"I've said nothing about marrying him."

She drank her coffee quickly—it was so confusing to try to think in their presence. Remembering many public scandals and misalliances, she wondered that each one had seemed so clean-cut in a sentence of gossip or a newspaper headline. Doubtless, behind every case, there were trapped and muddled people, weighing, buying a ticket to nowhere at an unknown price.

The porter brought her in a cable—she read it and said to Noel:

"You cabled Martha Burne-Dennison in London."

"I did," said Noel defiantly. "And I cabled New York too, and at what a cost!"

The message said:

YOU CANNOT THROW YOURSELF AWAY ON A WILD MAN FROM NOWHERE THINK OF US AND YOUR CHILDREN I ARRIVE AT THE GARE ST. LAZARE AT FIVE.

As she crumpled it, Sara wondered if the sun upstairs was in Killian's eyes, keeping him from sleep.

"You will come home now," they said. "We will rest; presently you will view your obligations in a different light."

—And it will be too late. In a panic she felt them close in on her. Ah, if Killian had come to her all whole and straight.

"My wrap is upstairs."

"We can send for it."

"No, I'm going myself."

Upstairs Killian cocked a drowsy eye at her.

"You were a long time."

She uttered a sort of groaning laugh.

"Are you under the impression you've been playing the guitar all this time?"

Suddenly he stood up, seemed to snap altogether. He stretched; his clothes fell into place; his eyes were clear as a child's and the color was stealing back into his face. With this change came another. The faint silliness of last night faded out of his expression and all consideration, all comfort, all quintessence of eternal cheer and tireless energy came back into it. He looked at her as if for the first time, took a step—and then her dress crushed into his shirt bosom, and his stud, pressing her neck like a call button, set her heart scurrying and crying. And she knew.

"We've got to hurry," she gasped, breaking from him. "You start packing." She picked up the phone and, waiting for the connection, said in a choking little laugh, "We're running away again—they'll be after us—isn't it fun? We'll get married in Algiers—Abby's husband's consul-general. Oh, isn't it wonderful!

"Hello—is this Henriette? Henriette, pack me the blue traveling suit—shoes and everything—toilet articles—my personal jewels—and your own bag—be at the Gare de Lyon in an hour."

The shower was already roaring in Killian's bathroom. Then it stopped and he called out:

"I forgot I haven't any street suit or any baggage at all, except a couple of used dress shirts. Caught the night boat from Southampton and my things got stuck in the customs—"

"That's all right, Killian," she cried back. "We've got plenty—you and I—and two guitars."

Her beach slippers felt strange on the piano pedals—the wind off the Sound blew in through the lilac trees, blew on her bare brown shoulders, her brown childish legs—this was 1928.

Blow, breeze of America, breeze of my youth, she thought. I am thirty-six; my daughter is almost grown and every morning she rides in the Bois de Boulogne; my son is here in America with me for the summer. Presently there will be an hour of sky and sea, with old friends calling, *"Please* do the imitation of the French woman teaching English, Sara!"

She swung around suddenly on the piano bench.

"You like the pretty picture?" she inquired of Abby.

"Picture of what?"

"Picture of Killian and Sara."

"Why not?"

"You might as well end your visit without any illusions," Sara said. "I haven't any idea where Killian has been these last four days—I didn't know he was going, where he went, when he'll be back—if ever. It's happened twice since we've been married. Anyhow, I've been doing a lot of thinking these last four days—I suppose all the thinking I've ever done in my life has been crowded into a few weeks—and it's just possible I'm not the right kind of wife for him. I've tried to run a civilized house, but he seems to get yearnings for the society of friendly policemen."

"Why, Sara—"

"Killian never grew up—that's all. Sometimes I try to make it funny—Mr. and Mrs. Jiggs."

"But if my husband didn't go away sometimes—"

"It isn't just that, Abby. I thought that at last maybe I'd have the whole loaf I've never had. I've gone to fights with Killian and baseball games and six-day bicycle races, and broken my heart shooting lovely little quail. I've admired his bottle-green hunting coat and played minstrel show with him at parties, but we just don't communicate. I'm getting very well acquainted with myself."

"You love Killian," Abby said.

"Yes, I love him—all I can find of him. Sometimes I say to myself that I'm expiating—there's a nice new word. Killian and I started wrong, so now I'm cast for Expiation. 'The former Marquise de la

Guillet de la Guimpé was lovely in the rôle of Mrs. Expiation.' " She stopped herself as if ashamed. "I've never talked about this before—the pride must be breaking down."

Killian came home just before dinner, looking exactly like the four days he'd been away. Sara had planned her act.

"Darling! I was sure you'd be home tonight." She went on drawing her lips in the mirror. "You go and shave and take a bath right away, because we're going to the opera. I've got your ticket."

Her voice was calm, but in the terrible relief of his return she drew three red mustaches on her upper lip.

He was himself again on the way back in the car, but only in the morning was the matter mentioned.

"You were pretty sweet about this," he said.

If he would only say more—what made him go?—if there was only something between them beyond the old electrical attraction. They lived lately in the growing silence, and intuition told her that this was one of those crucial quiet times when things are really settled. The battle was not joined; the message, if message there was, could still get through.

In the afternoon he went riding and Sara found herself missing him terribly. With the vague idea that they might talk more freely outside of walls—walls whose function is to keep people apart—she drove slowly along the country roads he frequented. After half an hour, she saw him far ahead of her—first a figure that might have been any man on any horse, and then at the next rise was Killian on his great roan mare. The fine figure against the sky fascinated her—she stopped her car until he passed from sight in another dip.

At the next hill he was still invisible, so she drove to a further viewpoint from which she could see for miles, but no Killian—he had turned off somewhere into the country.

Turning herself she drove back slowly—after a quarter mile she saw the mare grazing on the grassy hillside not far from the road. She left the car and walked up the hill. There in a grove of half a dozen trees she found him.

He lay on his side on the ground, cheek in his hand. Reluctant to surprise him in the solitude, Sara stood silent. After a few minutes he got to his feet, shook his head from side to side in a puzzled way, clapped his gloves together several times and turned about. As he moved she saw a gravestone, against which lay a bouquet of fresh flowers.

He came toward her, frowning a little.

"Why, Killian—"

He took her hand and they went down the hill together.

"That's Dorothy's grave," he said. "I bring flowers sometimes."

A vast silence stole over her. Killian had not mentioned his first wife half a dozen times since their marriage.

"Oh, I see."

"She used to like that little hill—I'm almost sure it was that hill—almost—" A touch of worry came into his voice. "—and we talked about building a house on it. So after she died I bought the piece of land."

The old limp from the war made Sara trip suddenly and he caught her by the waist, half-carrying her as they went on. Only when asphalt instead of the grass was underfoot did she say: "You cared for her a lot, Killian?"

He nodded, and she nodded as if in agreement.

"It was long ago," he said. "But she hated my wild times just as much as you do, and it seems to fortify me to come here."

His words fell unreal on Sara's ears—she had assumed always that his first marriage was a rebound, a substitute. Something broke from her heart that she regretted immediately:

"You forgot me right away."

He hesitated; then he said bluntly:

"I love you so much now that I can tell you this—that I wasn't really in love with you when we ran away together. I didn't realize at first how unhappy you were going to be afterward."

She nodded, surprised at her own calmness.

"I'm beginning to understand some things," she said. "It explains about Paris."

"You mean the time during the war."

"The time I found you tying your tie in a mirror in the Ritz, and we acted it out that we were strangers who had picked each other up. I never quite understood why you didn't make love to me that evening. I supposed it was because my husband was wounded and you were helping me to the right thing." She paused thoughtfully. "And all the time you were being in love with your wife at home."

They stood by the car, their hands still clasped.

"She was lovely," Sara said, as if to herself. "Once I saw a picture of her in a magazine."

"I didn't see any advantage in ringing Dorothy's ghost in on our marriage," Killian said. "You thought that you and I had felt the same way all those years—and I let you think so. But I know now I was wrong—if you begin locking things up in a cupboard, you get so you never say half what's in your mind."

Here were her own words come back to her.

"What brought you to me after the war?" she persisted. And then added quickly, "Oh I don't care—you came for me and that was enough."

Her natural buoyancy tried to struggle back, beating against her pride. She had only made the mistake of believing that Killian's heart was a mirror of her own.

"I love you more than I did ten minutes ago," she said.

They hugged each other, cheek to cheek; their slim silhouette might have been that of young lovers vowed an hour before. Presently his attention left her as he exclaimed:

"Look at that darn' mare!"

"It's all right—we can get her—jump in the car."

When they reached the mare Killian got out and caught it, and Sara drove on, turning at the next curve and waving back at him. But at the turn beyond that the road grew blurred for a moment and she stopped again, thinking of the green hill and the flowers.

"Sleep quiet, Dorothy," she whispered. "I'll take care of him."

Throughout a dinner party that night she was still thinking, trying to accept the fact that a part of Killian and a part of herself would always be strangers. She wondered if that were especially her fate, or if it were everyone's fate. From earliest childhood she remembered that she had always wanted some one for her own.

After coffee, they responded to a general demand, moved the piano bench to the middle of the floor, left only the firelight shining in the room. She sat beside Killian, making a special face of hers that was more like laughing than smiling, fingers pressed to a steeple over her heart, as he meticulously tuned his guitar, then at his nod they began. The Russian jibberish song came first—not knowing a word of the language they had yet caught the tone and ring of it, until it was not burlesque but something uncanny that made every eye intent on their faces, every ear attune to the Muscovite despair they twisted into the end of each phrase. Following it they did the always popular German Band, and the Spanish number, and the spirituals, each time with a glance passing between them as they began another.

"You're not sad, are you?" he whispered once.

"No, you old rake," she jeered back at him cheerfully. "Hey! Hey! Scratch a marquise and find a pushover."

No one would ever let Killian and Sara stop, no one ever had enough, and as they sang on, their faces flushed with excitement and pleasure like children's faces, the conviction grew in Sara that they were communicating, that they were saying things to each other in every note, every bar of harmony. They were talking to each other as surely as if with words—closer than any two people in the room. And suddenly she was forever reconciled—there would always be this that they had had from the beginning, music and laughter together, and it was enough—this, and the certainty that presently, when their guests were gone, she would be in his arms.

Zone of Accident

(*The Saturday Evening Post*, 13 July 1935)

"Zone of Accident" was started in the fall of 1932 and put aside until May 1935, when Fitzgerald finished it in Asheville. The *Post* paid $3000. This story was probably intended as a companion to "One Interne," written in August 1932 and also set at Johns Hopkins Hospital in Baltimore. Fitzgerald knew Hopkins from his own stays there and was fascinated by the hospital atmosphere. His *Notebooks* include memoranda on the emergency room. Needing story material, Fitzgerald tried to take advantage of reader interest in medicated fiction, and he wrote six published doctor-nurse stories between 1932 and 1936: "One Interne," "Her Last Case," "An Alcoholic Case," "Zone of Accident," " 'Trouble,' " and "In the Holidays."

Bill missed the usual feeling of leaving her house. Usually there was a wrench as the door closed upon the hall light and he found himself alone again in the dark street. Usually there was a series of light-headed emotions that sometimes sent him galloping half a block or made him walk very slow, frowning and content. He wouldn't have recognized the houses near by going away from them; he only knew what they looked like when he came toward them, before hers was in sight.

Tonight there was this talk of California, the intensity of this talk about California. Half-familiar, suddenly menacing names—Santa Barbara, Carmel, Coronado—Hollywood. She'd try to get a screen test—more fun! Meanwhile he would be completing his second year as an intern here in the city.

"But mother and I would go to the shore anyhow," Amy said.

"California's so far away."

When he reached the hospital, he ran into George Schoatze under the murky yellow lamps of the long corridor.

"What's doing?" he asked.

"Nothing. I'm looking for somebody else's stethoscope, that's how busy I am."

"How's everything out in Roland Park?"

"Bill, it's all settled."

"What?" Hilariously, Bill slapped George's shoulder. "Well, congratulations! Let me be the first——"

"She was the first."

"——let me be the second to congratulate you."

"Don't say anything, will you—not yet?"

"All right." He whistled. "Ink scarcely dry on your medical certificate and you let some girl write 'meal ticket' on it."

"How about you?" countered George. "How about that love life of yours?"

"Obstacles are developing," said Bill gloomily. "Matter of climate."

His heart winced as he heard his own words. Walking along in the direction of the accident room, he had a foretaste of the summer's loneliness. Last year he had taken his love where he found it. But Thea Singleton, the demon anesthetist, was now at the new Medical Center in New York; and gone also was the young lady in the pathology department who sliced human ears thinner than carnation sandwiches, and the other attractive ghoul on the brain-surgery staff who spent her time rushing into people's brains with a sketch pad and pencil. They had been properly aware that, seriously speaking, Bill was nobody's business—that he was in the safety zone. And now, in a fortnight, there was a girl who didn't know centigrade from Fahrenheit, but who looked like a rose inside a bubble and had promised to trade exclusive personal rights with him in another June.

The accident room was in a dull humor. Holidays are the feasts of glory there, when the speed merchants send in their victims and the dusky brand of Marylander exhibits his Saturday-night specimens of razor sculpture. Tonight the tiled floor and walls, the rolling tables packed with splints and bandages, were all for the benefit of a single client, just being unstrapped from the examination table.

"It's been wonderful," he said, humbly drunk. "I'm going to send you doctors a barrel of oysters." Barber by trade, he stood swaying gently in his worn coat. "My father's the biggest fish dealer in Carsontown."

"That'll be fine," the intern said. The patient regarded his bandaged hand proudly.

"I can take it," he boasted, "can't I?"

"You certainly can. But don't push your hand through any more windows."

His friend was summoned from without and, wabbling a little, the injured barber strutted out. The same swing of the door admitted a stout man of fifty who blurted incoherent words to Doctor Moore, intern on duty; Bill turned meanwhile to Miss Wales, who for a decade had been priestess of this battlefield. "Any high comedy?" he asked.

"Mostly regulars," she answered. "Minnie the Moocher turned

up again, carrying her head under her arm and wanting it sewed on
again. She was cut this morning. . . .*

Doctor Moore had meanwhile backed away from his exigent vis-
à-vis; he turned to Bill.

"Here's a mystery for you. This man——"

"You don't understand!" cried the stout man. "We can't let
anybody know! She made me promise!"

"Who did?"

"This lady outside in the car. She's bleeding from her whole
back. I live only two blocks away, so I brought her here."

Simultaneously the interns started for the door and the man
followed, insisting: "It's got to be no publicity. We only came because
we couldn't get a doctor to the house."

In a small sedan in the dark, deserted street slumped a bundled
form that emitted a faint moan as Moore opened the door. It took but
an instant for Doctor Moore to feel the blood-soaked dress.

"Get the stretcher out quick!"

The middle-aged man followed Bill to the door.

"It must be kept quiet," he persisted.

"You want her to bleed to death?" Bill answered sharply.

A few minutes later the patient was wheeled into the white light
of the accident room. A curtain was flung aside from a cubicle which
contained an operating table, and the two interns began untangling
the ravel of dish towels, torn sheeting and broadcloth in which she
was swathed. It was a young girl, the pale color of her own ashen hair.
Pearls lay along her gasping throat, and her back was slit from waist
to shoulder.

"Lost a lot of blood," Moore said. He was looking at the blood-
pressure gauge. "Say, it's low—eighty over fifty! We'll pack the
wound right away. Tell Miss Wales."

Miss Wales faced the father, as he admitted himself to be, and
spoke impatiently, pad in hand: "You've got to tell the name. We
can't take care of your daughter if you won't tell the name."

"Doctor Moore wants to pack the wound right away," said Bill.
To the father he added, "Wait outside. Your daughter's badly hurt.
What did it?"

"It was an accident."

"What did it—a knife?"

At his peremptory voice, the man nodded.

"You didn't do it?"

---

*Fifty words have been omitted.

"No! I can't tell you about it except that it was an accident."

He was talking at Bill's vanishing back; presently, bumped by a hurrying nurse and orderly, he was pushed out the door.

Back in the cubicle, Bill whispered, "How's the pulse?"

"It's thready—I can hardly get it."

He was sponging the wound, exposing the lovely young lines of the back. "This is going to leave a beautiful scar."

He spoke low, but the patient heard him and murmured: "No scar."

Bill called Moore's attention to the pearls, and whispered, "This girl's well off; maybe she cares about her back. You ought to send for a good surgeon."

"And let her bleed to death while we wait?"

"I was thinking of the resident."

"You medical guys!" said Moore disgustedly.

"All right," said Bill. "Anyhow, I'm going to get the father's consent and protect you that much."

"He's not John D. Rockefeller. Or why did he come to the accident room?" Moore dried his hands thoroughly. "How do you know those are real pearls—five-and-ten, maybe."

"I know this woman's well dressed—or was till half an hour ago."

Bill went out in the hall again.

"I want this woman's name," he said to the father. "If you won't tell me, I'll trace it through the car license."

"Labroo!" he breathed, incomprehensibly.

"Who?"

This time Bill heard the name, Loretta Brooke, but it meant nothing to him until the man added, "in the movies." Then Bill remembered it vaguely.

"Our name's Bach—that's German for Brooke. Loretta stopped off here to see me on her way out to Hollywood——" He gulped and swallowed the rest. "I can't say any more. They throw them right out of the movies for any trouble. First thing she said was 'Papa, keep it a secret.' But she kept bleeding and I couldn't get hold of our doctor."

The accident room grew suddenly crowded—there was a boy with a twisted knee; a Jamaica Negro badly cut about the head, but refusing treatment with the surly manners of his island. The usual number of second-year medical students had drifted in and stood about in the way. Pushing through them to the cubicle, Bill closed the curtain behind him; Moore had begun to sew the wound.

"The blood pressure is down to sixty over thirty-five," he muttered. "We'll have to do a transfusion. Better be getting a donor."

Bill went to the telephone; in a few minutes Moore came out, saying anxiously:

"I don't like waiting any longer. I can hardly feel the pulse now." He raised his voice. "Isn't there somebody here that sells blood—a Group Four?"

The second-year medical students moved about uncomfortably.

"I'm Group Three myself," Moore continued, "and I know Boone and Jacoby are Group Three."

Bill hesitated; his own blood was Group Four—the kind it is safe to transfuse to anyone—but he had never given any blood, never had the economic necessity of selling any, as did some interns.

"All right," he said, "I'm your man."

"Let's get them matched up then."

As he arranged matters for his little operation, Bill felt a broad amusement. He felt that part of himself was "going into the movies." Wouldn't the future blushes rising to the cheeks of Loretta Brooke be, in a sense, his blushes? When she cried, "My blood boils with rage," would it not be his blood that was boiling for the excitement of the public? When she announced that the bluest blood in America flowed in her veins, would that not be a subtle tribute to the honorable line of Dr. William Tullivers, of which he was the fourth?

He remembered suddenly that Intern George Schoatze was also Group Four, and thought fantastically of sending for him instead and determining the effect of the placid content of George's veins upon the theatrical temperament.

By the time he had been bled, refreshed himself with a drink, and got up feeling curiously well, Doctor Moore's suture was finished and Bill waited around with more than personal interest to see the case through; elated that before the transfusion was finished, Miss Loretta Brooke's blood pressure had risen and the pulse was stronger. He took the news to the man waiting in the hall. His chief concern was still the concealment of the scandal.

"She'll have to stay here," Bill said. "The hospital authorities must know who she is, but we'll protect her from the newspapers. She'll want a room in a private ward, won't she? And a private nurse?"

"Anything she would need."

The valuable person of Loretta Brooke, strapped face downward to a rolling stretcher, was pushed by an orderly into an elevator and disappeared into the quiet anonymity of the corridors above, and Mr. Bach was persuaded to go home and sleep. By midnight the great hospital was asleep too: The night porter sat in a small-hour daze under the great stone figure of Christ in the entrance chamber, and the night nurses walked lightly along the silent distances of the halls;

only in a few corners people stayed awake to suffer silently or noisily, to die or to return to life; and in the accident room, still brightly gleaming at two, at three, at four, all the processes of life went on repeating themselves to the swing of Miss Wales' starched dress, as the beaten and the broken, the drunken and the terrified trickled in the door.

Bill dreamed about being in Hollywood, parading up and down in a one-piece bathing suit before a stand full of judges; across his breast he wore a sash with red letters on it which spelled "Mr. Baltimore."

II

Doctor Tulliver came into the room at the same moment that a blowing shutter let in a burst of sunshine. The sunshine sought out Miss Brooke, enclosing her still-pale face in a frame and lighting one cheek to a faint geranium. Her eyes were half closed, but as he came in they opened—and opened—until he could scarcely believe there were such eyes, and simultaneously a small tongue tip passed momentarily over her upper lip, changing it to a brighter shade.

She looked him over from his fine, serious face to the white suit, unwrinkled by a new day.

"If it isn't Doctor Tulliver!" she said calmly. "Where've you been these last three days?"

"How do you feel?"

"All right. When can I really lie on my back?"

"Why, you're practically lying on it. A person can *see* you now; you've really got a third dimension."

"I keep worrying about the scar," she said.

"You needn't worry about it," Bill assured her. "In the first place, a better spot couldn't have been chosen if anyone wanted to avoid marking you up."

"Will it show in a low-backed dress?"

"Hardly at all. Moore did a good job and the plastic surgeon improved it. Why, I've seen bigger scars from a chest tap."

She sighed.

"I never thought I'd see the inside of this hospital, though I was born two blocks away from here and I used to go by it on roller skates."

"Very different from me. I always knew I'd see the inside of it. My father was an intern here."

"What do you interns have to do—just stay around here forever, like a monk or something?"

"Until they're no longer afraid to let us practice outside."

"I suppose you make love to the trained nurses. That's what the doctors did in a picture I was in."

"All day long," he assured her. "Every intern has certain nurses assigned to him."

"You look it, Doctor Tulliver."

"What?"

"You look as if you were very good at it."

"Thanks." Bill was pleased. "I certainly will have to grow a pointed beard and get down to business."

"My back itches. Shall I scratch it?"

"And make the scar worse? No, we'll get them to change the dressings oftener."

She shifted restlessly.

"What a thing to happen! How did that half-wit find where my father lived?"

Bill busied himself with a gadget on the blood-pressure machine, but he was listening eagerly. It was the first time she had mentioned the origin of the accident in the three weeks she had been there.

"What do you think he wanted?" Miss Brooke demanded suddenly.

"Who?"

"You might as well know. I like you better than anybody here, and I feel like telling somebody. It was my old dancing partner—a man I danced with at a hotel in New York two years ago. He wanted me to marry him and take him back to Hollywood and get him a job."

"So he took a whack at you?"

"I promised I'd see him in New York when I came East. And when I came to visit my father, he followed me down here. It was terrible; I hate to think about it. He got threatening and I took up a fork and told him he'd better look out, and then he picked up a paring knife." She shivered. "After he cut me, he went right on out and passed my father on the porch without even bothering to tell him what had happened. Can you imagine? I didn't realize what had happened myself for about five minutes."

"Have you heard about him since?"

"There was a crazy note from New York—sorry and all that. Sorry! Can you imagine? But nobody knows and you musn't tell."

"I won't."

It was, indeed, the doctors who protected her from herself in the matter of undesirable publicity, taking a gossipy night nurse off the case and discouraging the visits of hairdressers and manicurists. But the doctors came themselves; there was usually a small visiting gallery of interns, assistant residents and even graying medical men of mark, yielding to the glamour of a calling which the people had pronounced to be of infinitely greater prestige than their own.

"I'm getting started out there for the second time," she told Bill. "I was a sort of Shirley Temple of ten years ago—that's why you all remember my name. Now they're trying to make me a real actress, and the question is: Can they?"

"It's done. We—I mean a girl and I—found one of your pictures at a second-run theater and we thought you were great."

"A girl!—you mean your girl? Have you got a girl?"

He admitted it.

"Oh."

"In fact, her one ambition is to meet you. She's going to California this summer and she wants to hear about Hollywood."

"She wants to go into pictures?"

"I hope not. No, she just talks about it—like every other American girl—about how wonderful it'd be."

"I don't think it's so wonderful," Loretta said.

"You've been in it all your life." He hesitated. "I wish you'd tell her why you don't think it's wonderful. I hate to have her going away with some crazy notion."

"I'd like to meet her."

"To tell you the *ab*solute truth, she's downstairs now. She'd like nothing better than to come up for just a minute."

"Tell her to come up."

"That's mighty kind of you. She's been begging me——"

"It seems a very little thing to do for the man who saved my life."

"What?" He laughed. "Oh, we don't think of that as——"

"Never mind. It's made me feel sometimes as if we were—oh, blood brothers, like Indians, you know. Now that I know you're engaged, I can confess that. You think I'm silly."

Admitting hastily that he did, Bill went to get Amy.

When he introduced them they exchanged an appraising look, and it struck Bill that Amy was the more vivid of the two. It took a moment of looking at Loretta Brooke to realize that there was a constant activity in her face. There was always something going on— some little story, grave or gay, that took a moment to catch up with before it could be followed. After that it was a face that could be looked at almost permanently, with a fear of missing something if one looked away. Amy, on the contrary, was there all at once, darkly and breathlessly pictorial.

They talked of being in pictures.

"I can't imagine not liking it," Amy said.

"It's not liking or disliking. It's just plain work to me; when I was a child, it was play that I didn't quite understand. When I was fifteen, it was worry about whether I'd be pretty. Now it's fighting to catch on or hang on, and there's so little that you can do about it."

"But it's such a wonderful game," Amy said. "And if you do win——"

"There are games where the price isn't so high."

"Like what?"

Bill said lightly:

"Love and marriage, darling."

"Don't be absurd," said Amy. "There's nothing especially distinguished about love." She laughed and turned to Loretta. "Unless it's very good love in a very good picture."

"You've got to have a model somewhere," said Bill.

"We've got to die, too, but why bring it up?"

Loretta drew the onus of the exchange upon herself: "It's a very artificial life. All the time after I was—hurt, I kept thinking of the impression I was making on the doctors."

"And ever since then," Bill said, "the doctors have been thinking about the impression they make on you. I don't know what we'll do when you leave."

Driving home, Amy said:

"She's wonderful, but she just doesn't know how lucky she was to be born in the movies." After a moment's hesitation she added suddenly, "Bill, I've decided to go in the contest after all. You think it's silly——"

He groaned.

"——but it's really a big thing—girls from cities all over the East. I didn't go in the preliminary because you objected so, but Willard Hubbel thinks he can slip me in anyhow. In fact he knows he can, because he's handling the newspaper end."

"Of all the——"

"Wait till I tell you everything. It isn't so much to go in the movies, but I'd get a free trip to California. Oh, Bill, don't look so gloomy."

They rode along in silence for a moment.

"I'm glad I met Loretta Brooke. It'll be something to talk about to this other man."

"What other man?"

"This man who's coming from Hollywood to run the thing. Willard Hubbel's bringing him to see me tonight."

"Oh, he is?"

"You said you had to go to the hospital early, Bill."

"All right, darling," he said grimly, "all right. Have your fun, but just don't expect me to go into a dance about it."

They stopped in front of her house; and as he pulled her lovely head close to his for a moment, it didn't seem to matter what she did as long as he possessed her heart.

Life in a hospital is a long war on many fronts—vigorous offensives are followed by dreary sieges, by inexplicable lulls, by excursions and alarms. An alarm sounded suddenly that week—the dreaded tocsin of influenza. The disease settled like a snowfall on the hospital; members of the staff came down with it and all the wards, public and private, were full. On double duty, then triple duty, Bill had little time for Amy and less for Loretta Brooke, who lingered in bed running a very slight intermittent fever.

He talked for her, though—that is, he answered her long-distance calls from California from her agent and her producer. He affected the tone of a very haughty old doctor, but the producer's questions revealed a persistent suspiciousness:

"We'd like to know when we can expect Miss Brooke."

"We can't exactly say."

"If you tell us what the trouble is, we can figure out ourselves how long it'll be."

"I've told you it was an accident—no more serious than a broken arm. We don't give out medical details except to the patient's family. Miss Brooke ought to be starting West in a week or so, as soon as her temperature is normal."

"Sounds a little phony to me," the voice growled over three thousand miles of wire. "It isn't a broken nose or anything like that?"

"It is not."

When the man concluded, with a vague hint that the hospital might be detaining Miss Brooke for profit, Bill rang off.

Five minutes later, as a sort of postscript, a mild-mannered secretary called up to apologize—Mr. Minska, she said, had gone to lunch.

"You mean supper," said Bill irritably.

"Out here it's one o'clock," explained the secretary.

Bill found time to drop in and tell Loretta Brooke.

"They owe me a vacation," she said. "Anyhow, I like the atmosphere here, now that I can sit up. You've all been so good to me."

"We'll get rid of you as soon as that fever disappears."

"Please sit down for a minute. Lately you've been acting as if I was rather repulsive."

He sat tentatively on the side of the bed.

"Half the men in our service are down with flu," he said. "This is the first time I've had a minute."

He had had no supper, but as her face brightened, he felt a sudden pity for all this youth and loveliness penned up here because of an idiot with a paring knife.

She snuggled into the lace of her negligee.

"Why don't you come out to Hollywood?" she demanded. "I could get you a test. What do they pay you here?"

He laughed.

"Nothing."

"What?" She sat up in bed. "Nothing?"

"We get our board."

"Don't they pay any doctors in hospitals?"

"No. Only the nurses. And the patients are paid after the first three years."

"Why, I never heard of any such thing in my life." Loretta's idea began to grip her really: "Why don't you come to Hollywood? Honestly, you've got more It than Clark Gable."

He winced with embarrassment.

"We make lots of money later," he said lightly.

She considered.

"Now that I think, I never did hear of anybody marrying a doctor."

"I never did either. I don't know a single doctor who got himself a wife."

"But you're getting married."

"That's different. I'm lucky enough to have a little money of my own."

"I suppose I'll end marrying somebody in pictures," she said. "Somebody with a steady future, like a cameraman."

The arrested rhythm of the hospital, the flow of quiet along the corridors, the disparity of their two destinies always made what they said seem more intimate than it was. When he moved to get up from the bed, something happened so swiftly that he was not conscious of any transition—she leaned forward into the circle of his arms and he was kissing her lips.

He was not thinking; too fatigued even to be stirred by her nearness; too fatigued to worry about a position that might compromise his assistant residency. It was only his muscles that held her for a moment; then lowered her gently to the pillows.

She welled over in a little sighing sob.

"Oh, what's the use? You don't care. You saved my life, but you don't——"

The prospect of a long night of work unrolled itself before him.

"I like you enormously," he said, "but after all, we *are* in a hospital."

There were other objections, but for the moment he couldn't think what they were. He knew the attraction of the well for the sick, and such things had happened before, sometimes ludicrously and unpleasantly. But during the next few days, as he moved like a ghost through a maze of cases, he remembered this as having been fun.

He had been forty-nine consecutive hours on his feet, and the nurses coming on duty had begun to feel a sort of crazy awe for his fatigue; they had begun babying him a little, allowing him extra time to leave orders as his mind fumbled with the transition from one case to another. He began to be a little proud of his power of survival. On rounds he found time to ask news of Loretta from the nurse at the desk.

"Is she still running that fever? I don't understand it. It can't be from the wound."

The matter had bothered him as he watched over many graver fevers. He wanted the business of her illness to be cleared up.

"I just this moment gave her the thermometer, Doctor Tulliver. I'm going in now."

"Never mind; I'll see."

He went toward her room quietly, and with a step taken from the rhythm of the dying, half asleep, he paused in the doorway; this is what he saw:

Loretta held the thermometer in her mouth, but simply between tongue and lips, moving her mouth over it and then taking it out and looking at it, returning it, rubbing it, looking at it, frowning— shaking it once very gently. Then, with the air of having achieved her object, she removed it permanently.

At that moment she saw Bill, and simultaneously he grasped the whole matter—the business of faking the temperature by which she had lengthened her stay for two weeks. A current of resentment flowed through his fatigue as her egotism stood out ugly green against the somber blacks and whites of the past fifty hours. He was angry at having spent worry on her in this environment of serious illness and frantic haste, and professionally he felt a disgust at having been fooled. He thought of the phone calls from Hollywood and his answers from the authority of his profession—answers now made into lies.

"I'm afraid that's a pretty delicate instrument to fool with," he said.

She broke into real tears as the thermometer broke into glass ones and Bill left the room.

He drove to Amy's house, forgoing his turn to sleep; he had a sudden need for a world where people were "brought up" so that they could not do certain things. The young doctor, having abandoned more than a fair share of illusions, subscribes instead to a code of ethics more rigid than that of a West Point cadet—subscribes so firmly that he can joke about it, mock at it, blaspheme it and profane it, and do it no more harm than if it were earth itself. That is why a doctor who has lost this thing is nearly the most sinister character of which one can conceive.

He walked into Amy's house without knocking. At the door of the drawing room he stopped, stared . . . then he sat down feeling more tired than he had ever been in his life.

". . . Why, Bill," Amy said, "don't let's make a scene of it."

When the gentleman from Hollywood had taken his departure, Amy cried:

"He asked me to kiss him once, Bill. He's been so good about this, and it didn't mean anything; he's got a real girl in California and he was lonely."

"Aren't you a real girl?"

She came close to him, frightened.

"Bill, I could kill myself right this minute for letting it happen."

She pressed against him and he found himself patting her shoulder absently.

"So we won't make a fuss about one kiss, will we?" she pleaded.

He shook his head.

"That was a hundred kisses; you don't belong to me any more."

"You mean you don't want me?"

"Yes, yes. I guess I want you too much—that's just the trouble."

He drove back to the hospital and, to avoid meeting anyone, went in through the accident-room entrance; from behind the screen door came the murmur of a drunken Negro and as he passed on, Miss Wales came out into the corridor.

"Doctor Tulliver."

"How do you happen to be on day duty?"

"There isn't anybody else. And believe me, I'm glad. Look what Santa Claus brought."

She displayed a ring set with three small emeralds.

"Getting married?"

"Not I. This is from our little patient, the actress—Loretta herself. She stopped by on her way out."

"What?"

"Just ten minutes ago. And was she pretty in her clothes? I hardly knew her."

But Bill was gone, walking fast and feeling very afraid.

At the desk he found that Miss Brooke had gone for good and left no address behind.

III

Amy phoned him three times that night; the third time he answered.

"You've got to know the whole truth," she said. "It may sound commercial and calculating, but at least you'll see it wasn't that I wanted to kiss him, Bill."

"Skip it," he said wearily.

"But I can't skip it," she wailed. "I tried to be attractive to this man because if I don't get this free trip, then mother and I can't go at all. Mother went over her accounts at the bank yesterday and we have literally nothing to spare."

"And the kiss fixed it all up," he said ironically. "Now you're sure to be elected?"

"Not at all. It's much more difficult than that," she said with unconscious humor. "But now I'm in the running, even though I wasn't in the preliminaries. These are the finals; he's slipped me in instead of a girl who won in Washington."

"And now I suppose all you have to do is neck Will Hays, Laurel and Hardy and Mickey Mouse."

"If that's how you feel——"

"I go on duty at twelve," he said. "I'm going to rest now, so I maybe won't fall down in the corridors."

"But, Bill, can't you tell me one sweet thing, so I can sleep? I'll just fret and worry all night long and look terrible the day after tomorrow. Say one sweet thing."

"Kisses," he said obligingly. "Fifty-foot kisses."

The contest was sponsored by Films Par Excellence, a string of newspapers, and the A B C Chain Stores. The main contest—there was also a contest for children—had been narrowed down to thirty girls from as many cities in the North Central States. Each was on hand, her expenses having been paid to the city.

For several weeks all this had been in a newspaper, and each day Bill had gazed unsympathetically at the faces of the three judges, Willard Hubbel, local dramatic critic; Augustus Vogel, a local painter; and E. P. Poole, a chain-store magnate who understood what the public liked. But tonight the paper screamed something new at Bill which caused him to jump and pace his room. The magnate had suffered a collapse, but luckily Miss Loretta Brooke, local product and Wampas Baby Star of a year ago, had consented to take his place.

She was still in town. The city seemed to enlarge, take on color, take on sound, take on life; it stood suddenly erect on its cornerstones, when, twenty-four hours before, it had been flat as a city of cards. He was shocked to find how much her presence mattered. Women were liars and cheats—Loretta's deliberate malingering to remain in the hospital in a time of stress was less defensible than what Amy had done. Nevertheless, Bill got thoughtfully into his dinner coat. He would look over the contest, after all.

When he arrived at the hotel, the lobby was already full of curious ones cloistering the stately passage of slender stately figures. At his first sight of these latter, each one seemed unbelievably beautiful; but by the time he had mounted in the elevator with six of them and squirmed through a crush of a dozen getting out, he decided that Amy might very well hold her own.

He thought so again when he saw Amy, unfailingly lovely and picturesque; she stood in a group watching the preliminary contest for children, which had already started; and when she saw him, the wild excitement in her face made way momentarily for a look of sad wistfulness. She beckoned, but pretending not to see the gesture he made his way to one of the chairs that lined the sides of the hall. On a dais at the end sat the judges, Loretta in the middle. At the sight of her, he wondered that the girls downstairs had caught his eye for an instant, wondered that Willard Hubbel and Augustus Vogel, the painter, who flanked her, could concentrate on the mincing brat who danced and mimed before them. The face that, in the accident room, had been tragically drained of blood, the wan face on the hospital pillow, with its just slightly doubtful smile, was framed now by bright clothes, lighted by converging shafts of attention and admiration. This personage, poised and momentous, was not the girl who had broken the thermometer, and to whom he had spoken bitterly—and suddenly Bill wanted her back there on the quiet ward, away from these terribly inquisitive eyes.

The children's contest progressed slowly. Difficult as it was to nag and coax the candidate into animation, it was harder still to extinguish the flame when time was up. One mother had caught his attention from the first—a thwarted mother, a determined mother with fanatical eyes. While the child spoke, the mother's teeth were set as if she were holding her offspring in her mouth; and as she withdrew reluctantly to wait for the verdict, her gaze searched the judges savagely for any hint of prejudice or collusion. Ten minutes later, when the verdict was announced, Bill did not associate her with the word that slipped down the row of chairs: "Is there a doctor in the audience?" But slipping quietly out into the anteroom, he saw her writhing in the arms of two strong men.

"Let me at them!" she shrieked. "I'll kill them! My baby won! It was fixed! They paid them! That woman! Oh, how could they?"

"Are you a doctor?"

Bill sized up the situation and ducked it.

"You need a psychiatrist," he said.

"Are you one?"

He shook his head and walked back to his seat. He remembered once there had been a string of patients admitted to the nerve clinic of the hospital who were haunted by a horror film.

"Dementia Hollywoodensis. Manifestation X."

The real contest had begun. Singly the girls advanced, making the circuit of a table, then sitting at it, taking something from a pocketbook. Then they answered the questions of the judges:

"I'm a student at the Musical Institute. . . ."

"Of course I'd like to go to Hollywood. . . ."

"I've had little-theater experience. . . ."

"I went to Wellesley for a year. . . ."

There was a dying-swan girl, who denied that she admired Lillian Gish, and a wedding-cake girl, and a full-lipped waitress, and a superior art student. There were three Garbos and a Little Black Hat; there was a girl with overwhelming pep; a young girl with an old complexion; a professional dancer; a neat little Napoleon.

The judges noted on their lists, and in lulls talked among themselves. Bill had the impression that although she did not look in his direction, Loretta knew he was there.

When Amy was nearing the head of the waiting line, it became evident that this part of the contest was to be turbulent also. By the door, the representative of Films Par Excellence was involved in a lively argument with a hard, bright blonde and her escort, a neat, sinister man in a neat, sinister dinner coat, and Bill realized that the argument seemed to concern Amy. Once more he edged his way to the back of the room; the moving-picture man was urging his noisy vis-à-vis toward the door.

"Oh, Bill, this is terrible," Amy whispered. "That's the girl who won in Washington. You see, I lived in Washington once, so they slipped me in instead. And that gunman with her is perfectly furious."

"I don't blame him."

"But she's too tough for pictures."

"She could play tough parts."

For the second time that evening a cry came through the crowd that a doctor was needed immediately.

"Lord!" Bill exclaimed. "Why didn't they hold this in the accident room?"

As he went outside, Amy's name was called; he saw her pull herself together and start toward the judges' dais.

"Good-by to all that," he thought morosely.

The new casualty was stretched on a carpet in the hall. It was the moving-picture man. He had been struck with some weapon which might have been a blackjack or even a railroad tie. His temple was torn open and a curtain of blood was seeping down his face. The neat, sinister young man and his girl were not to be found.

"Needs stitches, and I've got nothing here," Bill said. "I'll put on a temporary bandage and someone better rush him to the hospital."

When the victim had been wheeled into the elevator, Bill phoned the accident room at the hospital.

"I'm shipping over another movie case, Miss Wales. . . . No, you needn't bother how the stitches look this time. And you might send over a fleet of ambulances to the hotel, because now they're going to pick the winner and things may get really rough."

When he re-entered the ballroom, the judges had retired to make their decision; the contestants stood about with families and admirers, some insouciant, some obviously jumpy, some pale with the fatiguing wait, some still fresh and lovely. Among these latter was Amy, who ran over to Bill.

"I was terrible," she said. "Oh, Bill, I know you don't want me to win, but please pray for me."

"I do want you to win," he said.

"Do you think I have a chance? I think Willard'll vote for me; it depends on the other two."

"Your Hollywood boy friend has gone to the hospital," he said.

"Oh, has he?" In her excitement she didn't know what she was saying. "He said he always wanted to be a doctor——"

A newspaperman spoke to Bill in a low voice:

"Miss Brooke would like to see you for a moment, doctor."

"God! She's not hurt, is she?"

"No, she just asked me to find you."

Loretta stood outside the judgment chamber.

"I'm glad you're still speaking to me," she said.

"Of course I am."

"Well, listen. Do you want your girl to go to Hollywood?"

Her eyes, looking into his, were full of the question, as if she had considered a long time before asking it.

"Do I? Why, how can I——"

"Because it's up to me. The vote is one and one. Your girl is more of a stage type. All that coloring won't count out there. But—it's up to you." And now he could not deny there was a question behind the question in her voice. In a turmoil, he tried to think.

"Why—why, I don't seem to care any more," he said. And then suddenly, "Hell, yes, let her go."

She made a mark on the paper she held in her hand.

"Of course, if she makes good she may not come back."

"She doesn't belong to me any more," he said simply.

"Then I'll go tell them." She lingered a moment. "I hope I'll be able to will her my luck. You see, I'm not very keen to stay in pictures—if I can find something else."

He stared after her; then, after what seemed a long time, he was listening to her voice speaking from the dais, and as far as her voice reached her beauty seemed to flow into the intervening space, dominating it:

"——so it seems to us . . . these beautiful girls . . . Miss Amy . . . represent this section of the country . . . others not feel disappointed. . . . You were the most beautiful candidates for screen honors I have ever seen."

To his surprise, no one fainted, no one wailed aloud; there was suddenly a loud boom, like a cannon-shot across the room, and Bill jumped, but it was only the flashlight photographers going to work. Loretta and Amy were photographed over and over, singly and together. They looked very lovely together, and it didn't seem to matter which one Hollywood had—that is, it didn't matter except to Bill. And in the sudden ecstatic joy of meeting Loretta's eye, all his rancor at Amy disappeared, and he wished her well.

"The movies give and the movies take away," he mused, "and it's all right with me."

Fate in Her Hands

(*American Magazine*, April 1936)

"Fate in Her Hands" was written as "What You Don't Know" at the Hotel Stafford in Baltimore during June-July 1935. After the story was presumably declined by the *Post*, the *American Magazine* paid $3000.

This story resulted from Fitzgerald's friendship with Laura Guthrie, a professional fortune-teller in Asheville. It is a competent trick-plot story but reveals none of the characteristic qualities of Fitzgerald's best fiction. Reflecting on the change in his stories during this period, Fitzgerald explained to Zelda in 1940:

> It's odd that my old talent for the short story vanished. It was partly that times changed, editors changed, but part of it was tied up somehow with you and me—the happy ending. Of course every third story had some other ending, but essentially I got my public with stories of young love. I must have had a powerful imagination to project it so far and so often into the past.

When Carol was nineteen years old she went into a little tent set in a corner of a ballroom. There was music playing—a tune called "The Breakaway." All the evening many people, mostly girls, had been going into that tent, where they faced a fiery little blond woman whose business was the private affairs of everyone else.

"You don't really believe in any of this, do you?" she asked Carol surprisingly. "I don't want to worry people about things that they can't help."

"I'm not the worrying sort," Carol said. "Whatever you tell me about my hand, I won't be able to remember it straight in half an hour."

"That's good." The woman smiled reassuringly, not at all offended. "Especially because I wouldn't want to worry such a lovely girl—one with so much consideration—such a gift for people—"

"I won't be worried," Carol repeated, embarrassed at this last. "Go ahead."

The fortuneteller looked once more into the outheld palms and sat back in her camp chair.

"For a beginning: You'll be married this year."

Carol laughed noncommittally.

"Are you engaged?"

"Not exactly. But anyhow we hadn't planned to do anything about it till spring."

The woman looked into her hand again quickly.

"I'm sure it's this year, and I'm seldom wrong about such things. And that means this month, doesn't it? It's already December."

Carol thought that if the question of such early nuptials should possibly arise, this cool prophecy would somehow weigh against her consent. She wasn't taking any brusque commands from fate—not this year.

"All right; go on."

"The second thing I see is great fame, great publicity. Not as if you were the heroine of some amateur play here in the city. Great notoriety all over the country. Headlines!"

"Mercy! I wouldn't like that. We're very—I've grown up in a very conservative family."

The palmist sighed.

"Well, I tell you only what I see. So don't be surprised if you marry Mahatma Gandhi about—let's see—three years from now."

"But if I'm to be married within a month!" Carol laughed. . . . Then she frowned suddenly. "You know, somebody else told me that I'd be notorious that way—with cards or tea leaves, I think—"

The woman interrupted dryly:

"That must have been very interesting. . . . Well—so we come to the third thing." Her eyes had grown very bright—she was restless in her chair.

"This is what I felt at the moment I saw you, even before I'd really studied your hand—but you're going to be a wise girl and laugh at me. Your hand is very oddly marked, very sharply marked—with events, and their time, too. About six years from now, in May, I think, something very dark threatens you and yours. If I'm right you can't beat it—black accident—six years from now—in May—"

She broke off, and her voice rose with sudden passion:

"Let me tell you I hate fate, young woman. I—"

Suddenly Carol was outside the tent, uttering a strange crying sound. "Not on account of what she said. But because she jumped up as if she had frightened herself!" Carol thought.

Outside the tent she found Harry Dickey waiting for her.

"But what did she tell you?" he demanded. "Why do you look like that?"

"She told me some things I've heard before: Early marriage—fame or notoriety—and then something that sounds simply terrible."

"That's probably the early marriage."

"No."

"What was it? Come on—tell Papa."

"No, I won't."

"Then don't tell Papa. Marry him, instead. Marry him tonight."

A few months ago she might almost have considered such a suggestion from Harry Dickey. He was not the man to whom she had confessed being almost engaged, but he had been in and out of her mind for several years, and quite welcome there until Billy Riggs made his first flashing visit to the city several months before. Now she only said:

"She was a spook, that woman. I felt that any minute she was going to vanish."

"She has."

Carol looked around. Where the tent had been there was suddenly nothing.

"Am I crazy—or has it disappeared?"

"It has. She's got it folded up under her arm, and she's just this minute gone out the door."

Billy Riggs and his friend, Professor Benjamin Kastler, swooped down upon the city two days later. When the long yellow car stopped in front of her house Carol's heart bumped and her blood pressure increased.

"And if that isn't love, what is?" she asked herself. "At any rate, life will be exciting with milord."

Billy Riggs was one of those who carry his own world with him. He always seemed less to arrive than to land, less to visit than to take possession, less to see than to conquer. Carol found it difficult to calculate her own position in the scene after they were married. She approved of his arrogance; she managed him by a good-humored nonresistance.

For a few minutes Carol did not connect his sudden change of plans about their marriage with the fortuneteller's prophecy: He wanted them to be married before Christmas. There was nothing seriously against it; she was of an age to know her mind, both of her parents were dead, and only the wishes of the parties concerned need be consulted. Yet—

"I won't do it, Bill," she said.

He had reasons, but to Carol her wedding seemed one matter in which her own slightest whim was of more importance than anyone else's logic.

"You talk to her, Ben," Bill said finally.

By this time they had been arguing for most of twenty-four hours and it was almost necessary to have a third party present as a sort of buffer. The victim was Ben Kastler, the prematurely gray young pedagogue whom Bill had brought with him as a week-end entourage. Now Ben tried:

"If you two love each other, why, then—"

They glared at him.

"Of course we love each other!"

"Then why not each set a date and then flip a coin?" he suggested ironically.

"You're a great help," Bill complained. "This isn't a joke. I've explained to Carol that Grandfather can't live a month. Well, I won't go and get married just after he dies—as if I were waiting for it. So it's either right now or else wait till June."

"We can get quietly married any time," said Carol. "I've always wanted just to drive out to my uncle's, in Chester County, and have him marry me."

"I don't like an elopement."

"It's not an elopement—he's my uncle and he's a minister."

After the next half-hour it scarcely looked as if they would be even engaged much longer. Just before the irrevocable things could be said, Ben dragged his friend from the house. Upstairs, Carol walked her room, weeping angrily—this was not going to be the first of a series of submissions which would constitute her life. Of course, it had started with the fortuneteller—if Carol spoiled the first prophecy, that would break the charm. But now the struggle against Bill's will had assumed even greater importance. She had reconciled herself to ending her engagement, when the phone rang that night. Bill capitulated.

She made it hard for him. When he came next day, bringing Ben along in case hostilities should break out, she laid down her terms. He must agree to put off the wedding until after the first of the year, and also to be married informally by her uncle. Then, sorry for his wounded vanity, she suddenly agreed that he could decide everything else.

"Then it's understood that you'll marry me any time next year?"

"Any time."

"How about New Year's morning?"

"Why—sure, Bill; that'll be fine."

"You give me your word of honor?"

"I do—if Uncle Jim is willing to marry us."

"That ought to be easy to fix." His confidence drained back into him moment by moment. "Ben, you're a witness to the contract— now and next month, too. And as you're a professor of law—"

"Economics."

"—whatever it is, you know what a contract is."

After Christmas, Bill and Professor Kastler arrived. With each day the marriage grew more inevitable—her uncle had no objection to performing the ceremony at five minutes after twelve on New Year's morning. It was to be as small and informal an affair as she could have wished—Bill's best man, the aunt with whom Carol lived, her two closest friends, and two cousins of Bill's.

And on New Year's Eve she felt trapped and frightened. She had given her word and she would go through with it, but at nine o'clock, when Bill went to meet his cousins at the station, it was this feeling that made her say:

"We'll start on—we five. Bill will be there almost as soon as we are—he knows the way."

They started off through the crisp darkness, with Ben at the wheel and Carol beside him. She heard the home of her youth crunch away into the past on the hard snow and she looked at Ben.

"It's sad, isn't it?"

When he did not answer she looked again, finding him as always too silent and too old for his youth, but liking a curious form and set to him, something that came from inside, as if he had constructed it himself, and that made a sharp contrast to Bill's natural buoyancy.

"What's the matter?" she demanded.

Still he did not give her any answer.

"Maybe I should have married *you*," Carol said, talking on faster and faster, "or somebody else. That's the sort of thing that worries me—"

He was speaking, and she was utterly startled at the intensity of his voice:

"Yes. You should have married me, Carol."

She looked at him quickly in the glow of a street lamp, to be sure it was just Ben Kastler.... But it wasn't. It wasn't Ben at all. He wasn't plain; he was handsome. The straight-ahead glitter of his dark eyes sent a sharp sword through her—her own voice was different, too, when she whispered:

"I didn't know you cared about me. I didn't have any idea, I feel terribly—"

"Let's not talk," he said. "It's almost over now. I wouldn't have told you, except—"

"Except what—tell me! I have to know. There's something in all this I have to know. Oh, I feel as if things had been kept back from me—and I've got nobody to ask."

"I'll tell you," he said grimly. "I should have spoken the day you had that quarrel. He lost you then, but neither of you knew it."

She sat silent, heavy, and frightened. They were out of town, and he drove faster, through a long suburb and out on to the state road. Desperately she counted the little townships they passed—till only one remained. Then she said:

"You're right. It was over then, if there was ever anything. But what does it matter?"

"You're going to go through with it?"

"I promised."

"That's right. Your word is your bond—Portia."

He was silent so long now that the last village before her uncle's house rushed up and went by before he spoke:

"But do you happen to remember the exact words?"

Five minutes later the group were blinking under the lights of her uncle's parlor. Ceremoniously arrayed, he greeted them, but there was no time to lose and Carol took her uncle into another room.

"You've got to listen very carefully," she said.

He listened to the storm of old words, new intentions.

". . . It'll be terrible for Bill, but marriage is for life . . . and better now than later . . . my promise was—now, listen—'if Uncle Jim is willing to marry me.' "

"But I *am* willing."

"But you *wouldn't* be willing if I was already married to somebody else."

Carol was very beautiful and convincing, and she had always been a pet of her uncle's. At ten minutes to twelve o'clock, she and Ben Kastler were made man and wife.

Waiting for her husband, Carol Kastler bought the baby daughter a new toothbrush, and then stepped on scales that politely refused to accept her nickel. On one side of the scales was an automatic pin game; she didn't want to play that by herself—the drugstore was just across from the crowded city campus and she was a dean's wife. But the nickel wanted to be spent, and next to the gambling board was a slot machine. Into this she put the coin, receiving in return a small white card:

You're the kind who cuts lots of capers;
Look out you don't get your name in the papers.

She read it and smiled. Then she put in another nickel and pressed a lever:

Don't you worry. Some fine day
Lots of fame will come your way.

This time she did not smile.

"Why, I do believe it's the old curse," she thought. "I wonder what would be the mathematical probabilities of these two cards turning up one after the other."

She was about to put in a third coin when her husband came in.

"Gaze at these, darling. Fate's creeping up on me. Remember, about three years ago that fortuneteller told me I'd be notorious?"

"Oh, you mean that fortuneteller," he said, as they got into their car. "I'm sorry—I was thinking of something else."

"You ought to be grateful to that fortuneteller," Carol reproached him. "If it wasn't for her we wouldn't be us."

"Oh, I'm grateful—but I don't think you've ever gotten over it, the second-sight business, I mean. It was just as accidental as these penny cards."

"Nickel cards. . . . But, Ben, it's due now—three years, she said. And, lo and behold, these funny little cards!"

"It's good I don't believe in signs, then," he said placidly, "because notoriety is the last thing we want right now."

"Have you heard anything?" Carol asked eagerly.

"Too much—I have to pretend to be deaf."

"If it *did* happen—at your age—oh, Ben—"

He slowed down suddenly. "You see the effect on me—I'm excited, I step on it, I get arrested for speeding, the regent sees it in the papers—there's your notoriety for you—and I'm disqualified."

Discouraged from mentioning fate, either in its larger aspects or in the possibility that Ben might be the new president of the university, Carol nevertheless thought a moment longer about the cards. They were a warning—but she couldn't think how any unpleasant notoriety could spring out of the quiet happiness that so far was the story of her marriage.

But the cards had somehow disturbed her, and her last thought that night was that if there were a University of Fortunetellers she might have a talk with the president. She decided to inquire around among her friends at a Junior League committee meeting next day. But in the morning it seemed silly, and going into town she put it out of mind.

The League was sponsoring an infants' health show, and Carol took her child along to see the champion babies. Just as she entered the hall of the civic building an almost theatrically dirty and ragged woman, carrying a child, spoke to her:

"You belong to this Junior League?"

"Yes," said Carol.

"Well, how about this show for healthy babies? I'd like to let them see this one that I can't get enough to feed her."

"Go to Room 312. That's the Welfare Bureau."

"You got something to do with this baby show?"

"A little, but that's another matter—"

Two men had drawn near and were listening with unusual interest to the conversation. The woman was insistent:

"Well, if you're so interested in babies you might look at this baby of mine—"

Impatient at the importunity, Carol peered hastily into her bag, found only a nickel and a ten-dollar bill. Simultaneously one of the men touched his hat.

"Excuse me, lady, but if you're on the baby show committee I'd like to have your name."

Instinctively her lips froze upon her name; to the woman she said, "I'm sorry, I only have a nickel—"

"*Hold it, lady.*"

At that instant she saw the camera, and in a split second more she had whirled away from it—just as the corridor flashed full of light. She grabbed up Jean and darted into an elevator as the gate clanged. A woman she knew spoke to her.

"Were they after you, Mrs. Kastler?"

"I guess so," Carol panted. "What on earth is it?"

"It's a tabloid newspaper stunt—you know: 'Rich Boast Babes While—' That sort of thing. Did they photograph you?"

"They tried to—" Carol paused.

They *had* photographed her—though her back had been to the camera at the flashlight—and she had nearly given her name. They wanted a victim from the Junior League, and she had almost played into their hands. They might have pictured her handing a nickel—a nickel—to a wretched mother with exaggerated reports of her social activities. The headline danced in her brain:

"*Dean's Wife Spares Nickel.*"

And she saw the regents of the university in conclave, each with the impression that Dean Kastler was married to a particularly callous and penurious social light.

Notoriety, indeed! She decided to go home without attending the meeting; she went downstairs by another elevator and slipped through a drugstore into the street. Only when the apartment door closed upon her did she draw a breath of relief.

It was a short breath—in a moment the phone rang and a man's voice asked for Mrs. Kastler.

"I don't think she's in," Carol was on guard again. "Who is this, please?"

"This is for a newspaper society column. Can you tell us if Mrs. Kastler has a hat with a bow of ribbon on it?"

"No, I haven't," said Carol—and immediately could have bitten off her tongue.

"So *this* is Mrs. Kastler. We'd like to get a story about you and that kid of yours. We'll have a man out there—"

"I won't see him!" she cried, and hung up.

After a moment she called the university, but Ben could not be located. Stories and movies that told of tabloid persecutions rushed through her mind—if they were after you they sent reporters down chimneys. Not since the sins of childhood had she so passionately wanted to be far, far away.

With the thought came a quiet inspiration—Mary Kenyon. This was a friend who had many times invited her to spend a week in her boasted Arcady—a cabin not three hours from the city, but totally isolated; without neighbors, newspapers, radios, or telephones.

In a hasty letter Carol explained to Ben what had happened. She gave the envelope to the maid, with instructions about carrying on in her absence.

"I haven't sealed this letter," she added, "because if Mr. Kastler calls on the phone you'd better read it over the phone to him right away." The maid was rather flashy but intelligent enough. "If anyone else calls just say I won't be home for a week and you don't know where I am."

At the moment of leaving Carol took a final precaution: She went all over the apartment gathering up every picture she could find of her baby and herself, and locked them into a closet. Then she ordered a taxi to come to the service door.

That night Carol told Mary every detail, from the palmist to the hat with the ribbon bow on it, and she added:

"I brought that along and I'm presenting it to you."

The four days she had allowed passed tranquilly. There was no fear when Mary started with her and the baby for the station; there was only eagerness to see Ben.

A few miles down the road a farmer neighbor hailed them from beside a stalled automobile.

"Sure hate to bother you, Miss Kenyon, but my car burnt out a bearing—these two gentlemen—"

One of the two men with him spoke up briskly, and in a momentary resurgence of panic Carol wondered if the newspapers had caught up with her.

"We want your car for half an hour. We're from the police department, and we want to make a few inquiries near by."

"Up to Marky's shack, Miss Kenyon. They think—"

"Never mind," said the detective.

Mary drove as she was directed, off the main road and down what was little more than a wagon track, until told to stop.

"You wait here in the car," one of the men said.

When they were out of sight the farmer laughed. "Ain't had the law down here since white-mule days."

"Well, we don't want excitement," Mary said. "What are they after?"

He lowered his voice: "I think it's about the kidnapping of this woman and—"

"Heavens! We haven't seen a paper for four days."

"No? Well, there's nothin' else in the papers—the kidnappers are askin' twenty thousand dollars. Kidnapped the wife and child of the president of the university—name of Kastler."

The idea had been the maid's—with the help of an ambitious boy friend. The maid had a police record herself, and when Mrs. Kastler was so kind as to disappear of her own accord, leaving no trace save a letter which need not be delivered—well, what better opportunity for extortion?

But they bungled the job and were in course of being captured about the time when Carol reached her husband by telephone. Their conversation was long and shaky. It was days before they could talk logically about the matter to each other.

What confused Carol most was the reiterated question of how much it had been predestined. Once again she wondered if the future really was engraved in her hand—or if the prophecy itself, by frightening her, had been responsible for the event. Irresistibly her thoughts swung to the third and most sinister of the predictions, and she tried to remember the exact wording the woman had used: "Six years from now . . . a black accident threatening you and yours . . . look out for the month of May . . ."

Several years after the "kidnapping," when Carol went home for a visit, she determined to locate the woman and ask for another reading. When, after some difficulty, Carol located the woman, she was startled to find herself remembered.

"It was at a dance—nearly six years ago," said the palmist. She looked briefly into Carol's hands.

"I remember—everything. Tell me, do things go well?"

"Very well. That's why I'm frightened. You told me—"

"It's all still in your hands. Do you want me to repeat it?"

"Just the part about the accident—about May. Is it still—?"

"Let me look again."

For a long time she stared into Carol's right palm, then she asked the date of her birth and wrote some figures below it.

"Go along with you," she cried. "I've nothing to tell you."

"You mean it's still there—it's so awful you won't tell me?"

"Just remember this—if I was infallible I'd now be traveling the world in splendor."

"Don't send me away like this," Carol begged. "Would it make any difference if I took very good care of things, of myself, of those I love?"

"Not if it's *really* written there. Oh, best forget it, Mrs. Kastler, and wake up one day and find it's June, and say, 'That old fool! didn't know what she was talking about.' "

The experience of being sentenced is commoner than is generally supposed—it must have been remarked that at the moment of birth one is sentenced to death. But the terror of the dentist's waiting-room, the terror of the death house, depend on clock and calendar. And thus it was with Carol—she was afraid of time.

"After the first of June," she promised herself, "I'll put this out of my head."

At the beginning of May she had erected, to the best of her abilities, a Chinese wall around herself and her two children. There was little she could do without Ben's knowledge, but what she could do she did. Privately she gave his chauffeur ten dollars to drive him always at a moderate rate, even when he objected, and twice she followed in a taxicab to be sure.

Her daughter was five, her son was two. There was a nurse, but, during May, Carol went out only when necessary. Several times during the month she took both children to the doctor for examination.

For herself, her precautions were mostly of a general order, but she crossed streets at intersections only, she cautioned drivers, she did not run downstairs nor undertake labors involving struggles with inanimate objects. And all during the month her restlessness grew till she would have welcomed the prospect of some lion hunting at the month's end.

Ben sensed an increased timidity in her. It was because of this that he told her only a part of the Holland House matter.

Holland House was a frame structure about eighty years old, long used as an administration building, and housing, among other bureaus, the president's office. It was of the federal period and, as far as could be ascertained, it was the first extant college building west of the Ohio. Ben had a special affection for this landmark, and now the question had arisen of sacrificing it to progress. For the city was putting in a subway branch which would run within fifty feet of it.

Would the building survive the blasting? A substantial number of regents wanted it condemned to the woodpile. Ben wanted to preserve it at almost any cost.

This much Carol knew. What she did not know was that, after getting expert advice to back his contentions, Ben had announced his intention of sitting in his office on the afternoon of May thirty-first, when the blasting would occur on a street near by. Mrs. Wheelock, the dean's wife, rang the Kastlers' doorbell early that afternoon.

"You'll think this is an odd time to call, Mrs. Kastler—and I admit I'm on a presumptuous errand."

"Not at all," said Carol ambiguously. "But I was wondering if you see what I see. My daughter is in the act of climbing up that pine."

"Let her climb," said Mrs. Wheelock. "She might be startled and fall down—now I *am* being intrusive."

"Jean, come down!"

A face looked reproachfully from a ten-foot branch of the ladderlike pine.

"Oh, can't I?" it protested.

"I'm sorry; not till you're six. We'll have to call it a 'Big Crime.'"

She sat down again, apologizing and explaining to Mrs. Wheelock about big and little crimes.

"I was saying," resumed Mrs. Wheelock, "that I've come about the Holland House matter. It is a matter between—"

For a moment, watching Jean's descent, Carol only half heard. But suddenly she was listening with her whole body.

"—of course, if these termites haven't eaten out the insides of the lumber, your husband can sit in his office till doomsday. But if they *have*, then this blasting—"

Carol was on her feet.

"Why didn't I know this?"

"Your husband's been argued with, but, as you know, he's a most determined man—"

Carol was already in action, seizing a hat, summoning the maid.

"I won't be gone an hour . . . let the baby sleep—don't disturb him . . . Jean is not to climb trees. . . ."

As they hurried down the walk to Mrs. Wheelock's car Carol took a quick last look at Jean and her three little friends from next door, with their collie.

"They're all right," she thought, and then aloud: "I hope I can get to him in time."

She saw the excavation as they turned in at the university gate— that part of the street was marked off with red flags. In front of Holland House she stared at a placard on the door:

NOTICE

THIS BUILDING TEMPORARILY CLOSED
BECAUSE OF BLASTING
OFFICES MOVED TO McKAY BUILDING

Ben was alone in his office, leaning back thoughtfully in his swivel chair.

"Good heavens, Carol!" he exclaimed. "What do you want?"

"I want you to come out of here."

He groaned disgustedly. "There isn't a bit of real evidence that termites—"

"Come with me now—right away, Ben, before they begin. You've got to—there's a reason you don't know—"

"Darling—I can't believe you've been listening to soothsayers again."

"Ben, what if I have—couldn't you do this one thing for me? I'm not a coward, you know that, but after the other two things how can you laugh at me? I'm trying in every way I know to fight against it— and here, with danger in the air, you run deliberately into it."

"Hush!" he said, and then, after a moment, "I wish you'd get out, Carol."

Darkly she hated him for his obtuseness.

"I won't go without you. If you cared you wouldn't sit there."

"I sit here because I do not believe this building will be damaged. I have given in to the extent of ordering out the personnel and removing valuable records. But it's a point of honor that I remain here myself to vindicate my judgment."

She had never hated him so much, admired him so much; but, as an undertone to his words, other words thundered in her head, mingling with the music of a forgotten dance:

"*—black accident . . . May . . . you and yours—*"

"But I do wish you'd go, Carol," he said. "The ceiling is wood, but a little molding may fall."

He broke off suddenly as the air was split as by a cannon outside. Simultaneously there was a mutter of the windows, a mutter that became a rattle; the frames themselves became faintly blurred and a chandelier was swaying.

Br-rr-rr-rr CLAP! Clipclip WA-A-A-A CLAP!

In a sudden stillness she heard Ben's voice:

"That was the first blast. There'll be three, half a minute apart."

At the second boom the windows took on so hearty a vibration as to compete in sound with the timbers—this time the whole fanfare in joist and molding, the shaking and snapping, endured so long that the third *boom* came before it had ceased. Presently through this, like a new, high motif, they heard the tap of plaster falling in a few rooms above. Then a sound went through the house like a long sigh, a last eerie whistle that ended somewhere in the eaves—the quake was over.

Ben got up and walked quickly about the room. His eyes were flashing with delight.

"Is it over?" asked Carol, dazed.

"All over. The next blasting will be half a mile away."

Only now for the first time did he seem to become truly aware of her presence—he put his arm about her.

"How do things go at home?" he said. "Carol, what is the matter lately? Tell me all about it—you can't go on being afraid of bogies."

"I know, Ben. I'm glad this happened. I'm glad I was here this afternoon."

"You're making the children jumpy, too—you scarcely let them exercise."

"I know. I've been a nut." Impulsively she picked up his phone, called the house and spoke to the servant:

"This is Mrs. Kastler . . . I just wanted you to tell Jean she *can* climb that tree."

Carol hung up and turned to her husband. "You see, I've changed. I won't be such a ninny—honest."

And now she confessed everything—the last interview with the fortuneteller, the bribing of Ben's chauffeur—"But not any more. Take me home in the car now, and we'll have him just tear along."

"I had some work—"

"Not today. I feel released—all that sort of thing."

He was rather silent and thoughtful on the way home.

"People who figure on chance and fate and luck—You know about Napoleon and his star—how he used to figure out whether his generals were 'lucky' generals?"

"I don't know about Napoleon," Carol said; "I never knew the man. I just know about you and me. We're lucky."

"No, we're not—we're logical from now on."

There was an unusual silence about their house as they reached the door. Yet Carol, usually sensitive to such things, did not notice that anything was wrong until the maid rushed at them in the hall.

"Now, don't worry, Mrs. Kastler. The chillen's upstairs and all right."

"What is it, Emma? Now, what is it?" Carol shook her by the shoulders.

"No cause to worry *now*—but we had plenty roun' here the last hour. I tried to call you when that mad dog—"

"What?"

"That collie dog next door. He been actin' funny lately, an' he began actin' funny this afternoon, goin' roun' snappin' at them chillen, and he nipped at that little George an' they took George to the hospital—Say, don't you look so funny, Mrs. Kastler; you sit down there."

"Did he nip Jean—where was Jean?"

"I tell you Jean was all right—I told Jean what you said on the phone—so when it all began to happen she was sittin' way up high in that tree."

When she had taken the spirits of ammonia Carol did not follow Ben upstairs but sat very quiet in the dining-room.

If she had not telephoned home about the tree Jean would probably have been bitten like the other children. On the other hand—if the dean's wife hadn't called. . . .

She gave it up. Ben was right. You could regard the future only in the most general way. She sighed wearily as the phone rang and she lifted the receiver.

"Oh, Mrs. Kastler, I recognize your voice. This is Spillman."

That was his secretary—couldn't Ben be left alone after a day like this?

"Can I take the message?"

"Well, I thought he'd want to know. It's about Holland House. It—why, it collapsed like a house of cards about ten minutes ago. Nobody was in it—"

"Oh, my heavens!" she said. Then, after a long pause, "I'll tell him, Mr. Spillman."

She sat quiet in her chair. Faintly from above she heard Ben saying good night to the baby. And Jean's voice: "Daddy, he snapped so quick you wouldn't know, and the man that took him away said they'd keep him under obligation—"

Carol sat still. She felt no sense of triumph, no desire at all to tell Ben about the house; she would rather that the news be deferred as long as possible.

She looked at the clock; the hands stood at six. It would be the first day of June in exactly six more hours.

Six more hours.

Image on the Heart
(*McCall's*, April 1936)

"Image on the Heart" was written in Asheville in September 1935, with the working titles "Finishing School" and "A Course in Languages." After it was apparently declined by the *Post*, *McCall's* paid $1250. Fitzgerald opened an old wound for "Image on the Heart." The Tudy-Silvé relationship draws on Zelda Fitzgerald's 1924 involvement with French aviator Edouard Jozan—which both Scott and Zelda had used in *Tender Is the Night* and *Save Me the Waltz*. This story documents Fitzgerald's difficulty in producing commercial stories during 1936-1937. It seems padded with sight-seeing to achieve the required magazine length. Fitzgerald's difficulty in finding story material at this time can be seen in "Afternoon of an Author," his 1936 story-essay: "The problem was a magazine story that had become so thin in the middle that it was about to blow away. The plot was like climbing endless stairs, he had no element of surprise in reserve, and the characters who started so bravely day-before-yesterday couldn't have qualified for a newspaper serial."

The train rolled into the little French town as if it were entering a dusty garden. As the floor of the railroad carriage trembled and shifted with the brakes, the stationary human figures outside the window became suddenly mobile as the train itself, and began running along beside it. The passengers seemed to blend right into the countryside as soon as the porters on the platform were running as fast as the train.

She was waiting for him—eight months was a long time and they were shy with each other for a moment. She had fair hair—delicate, shiny, essentially private hair—it was not arranged as blondes preferred at the moment but rather as if it were to be let down for someone alone sometime, somewhere. There was no direct challenge in it, and in her face there were the sort of small misproportions that kept her from being smooth and immediately pretty. But in her nineteen years she had managed to be a standard of beauty to two or three men—Tudy was lovely to those to whom she wanted to be lovely.

They got into one of those old-fashioned victorias that have a last refuge in the south of France; as the horse started off down the cobblestoned street, the man turned to the girl beside him and asked simply:

"Do you still want to marry me?"

"Yes, Tom."

"Thank God."

They interlaced hands and arms. Even though the cab was moving so slowly up a hill of the old town that pedestrians kept pace with them, it didn't seem necessary to let go. Everything seemed all right in this mellow Provençal sunshine.

"It seemed forever till you'd come," Tudy murmured. "Forever and forever. The University closes in another week—and that's the end of my education."

"You finish as a freshman."

"Just a freshman. But I'd rather have had this than any finishing school—especially because you gave it to me."

"I had to bring you up to my standard," he said lightly. "Do you feel improved?"

"Do I! Maybe you think these French universities haven't got standards. It's—" She broke off to say suddenly: "There's you, Tom—don't you see? That French officer coming out of the *magasin de tabac* across the street—he's your double."

Tom looked over toward the sleepy sidewalk, picked out the man, and agreed. "He does look like me, at least like I looked ten years ago. We'll have to look him up if he lives here."

"I know him, he's been here a week on leave. He's a naval aviator from Toulon. I wanted to meet him because he looked so much like you."

Like Tom the man was darkly blond and handsome with a flickering in his face, a firelight over high cheekbones. Not having thought much of the matter for years, he stared curiously at the naval officer—who recognized Tudy and waved at her—and said meditatively:

"So that's what I look like."

A minute later the carriage clattered into a green cove under a roof of poplars; beneath the soft roof slept the Hotel des Thermes, tranquil as when it had been a Roman Bath two thousand years before.

"Of course, you'll stay on at your pension until Mother comes," he said.

"I have to, Tom. I'm still a student. Isn't that absurd—when you think that I'm a widow?"

The carriage had drawn up at the door. The concierge was bowing.

"Mother will be here in ten days—then the wedding—then we're off for Sicily."

She pressed his hand.

"In half an hour at the Pension Duval," she said. "I'll be in the front garden waiting."

"As soon as I snatch a bath," he said.

As the cab started off without him, Tudy squeezed back in the corner. She was trying not to think too much but irresistibly she kept saying to herself:

"I'm a lost soul maybe—I don't feel at all like I ought to feel. Oh, if he'd only come a week ago."

They had known each other for many years before this rendezvous in France. Or rather Tom had known her people, for he had thought of her as a little girl until one day at Rehoboth Beach a year before. Then word had gone around the hotel that there was a bride of a week whose husband had been tragically drowned that morning. Tom took charge of the immediate situation—it developed that she had no one to turn to and that she was left penniless. He fell in love with her and with her helplessness, and after a few months he persuaded her to let him lend her the money to go abroad and study for a year—and put something between herself and the past. There were no strings attached—indeed, nothing had been said—but he knew that she responded to him in so far as her grief permitted, and there was correspondence more and more intimate and in a few months he wrote asking her to marry him.

She wrote him a glowing answer—and thus it was that he was here. Thus it was that she sat opposite him in an outdoor restaurant on the Rue de Provence that night. The electric lights behind the leaves swayed into sight sometimes in a faint wind, making her head into a ball of white gold.

"Oh, you've been so good to me," she said. "And I really have worked hard, and I've loved it here."

"That's why I want to be married here, because I've so often thought of you in this old town—my heart's been here for eight months."

"And I've pictured you stopping here when you were a boy, and loving it so much you wanted to send me here."

"Did you really think of me—like your letters said?"

"Every day," she answered quickly. "Every letter was true. Sometimes I couldn't get home fast enough to write you."

If only he had come a week ago!

Tom talked on:

"And you like the idea of Sicily? I have two months. If you have any other place—"

"No, Sicily's all right—I mean Sicily's wonderful."

Four men, two of them naval officers, and a girl had come into the little cafe. One face among them emerged in the hundred little flashlights and dark patches of leaves—it was that of Lieutenant de Marine Riccard, the man Tudy had pointed out that afternoon. The party settled themselves at a table opposite, grouping and regrouping with laughter.

"Let's go," Tudy said suddenly. "We'll ride up to the University."

"But isn't that my double? I'm curious to meet him."

"Oh, he's very—young. He's just here on leave and he's going back soon, I think—he probably wants to talk to his friends. Do let's go."

Obediently he signaled for the check, but it was too late. Riccard has risen from the table, with him two of the other men.

"—'Sieu Croirier."

"—'Sieu Silvé."

"—*soir.*"

"—*chantée.*"

"Why, we *do* look alike," Tom said to Riccard.

Riccard smiled politely.

"Excuse me? Oh, yes—I see—a little bit of a bit." Then he conceded rather haughtily, "I am the English type, I had a Scotswoman for a grandmother."

"You speak English well."

"I have known English and American people." Fragmentarily his eyes strayed towards Tudy. "You speak French well, I wish I could speak so good English. Tell me," he said intently, "do you know any tricks?"

"Tricks?" Tom asked in surprise.

"Americans all know tricks and I am like an American that way. We have been doing tricks this evening before we came here. Do you know the trick with the fork where you hit it so—" he illustrated with graphic gesturing—"and it lands here in the glass?"

"I've seen it. I can't do it."

"Neither can I mostly, but sometimes though. *Garçon*, bring a fork. Also there are some tricks with matches—very interesting. They make you think, these tricks."

Suddenly Tom remembered that though tricks were no hobby of his, he did happen to have with him something of the sort bought for a nephew and undelivered. It was in his trunk in the hotel, and it was plain that Riccard would consider it a prince among jests. Pleased by the thought, he watched the French people bring their ready concentration, their delight in simple things made complex, to bear upon the forks and matches and handkerchiefs that presently came into play. He liked watching them; he felt young with them; he laughed in tune to Tudy's laughter—it was fine to be sitting beside her in the soft balm of a Provençal night watching French people make nonsense at the day's end. . . .

He was an astute man, but he was so wrapped up in his dream of Tudy that it was not until two nights later that he realized something was not as it should be. They had invited several of her friends from the University and Lieutenant Riccard to dine with them in the same little cafe. Tom did the trick that he had recovered from his trunk, a familiar old teaser that depended on two little rubber bulbs connected by a thin cord two yards long.

One of the bulbs was planted under the table cloth beneath Riccard's plate, and by squeezing the other bulb from across the table, Tom was able to make the Frenchman's plate rise and fall inexplicably, jiggle, bump, tilt, and conduct itself in a generally supernatural manner. It was not Tom's notion of the cream of human wit, but Riccard had asked for it and so far as practical jokes go it was a decided success.

"I don't know what can be the matter with my fork tonight," Riccard said mournfully. "You Americans will think I am barbarian. There! I have done it again! Can it be that my hand is trembling?" He looked anxiously at his hands. "No—yet there it is—I am destined to spill things tonight. It is one of those matters in life that can never be explained—"

He started as the knife on his plate gave a little sympathetic clink.

"*Mon Dieu!*" Once again he attempted a logical treatment of the situation, but he was obviously disturbed and he kept a watchful eye on the plate. "It is because I haven't flown in ten days," he decided. "You see, I am used to currents of air, to adjustments very sudden, and when it does not come I imagine it—"

It was a warm night, but there was extra dew on his young forehead, and then Tudy's voice, very clear and piercing, cut through the tranquil air.

"Stop it, Tom. *Stop* it!"

He looked at her with an amazement as great as Riccard's. In fear of a contagious mirth he had been avoiding her eyes, but he saw suddenly that there was no mirth in her face at all—only an engrossed compassion.

His world tilted like the plate for a moment, righted itself; he explained to Riccard the mechanics of the joke, and then as a sort of atonement, presented him with the apparatus. Riccard, trying to get back at someone, tried immediately to put it into action, inveigling the proprietor of the restaurant to sit down on it, but for the time Tom only remembered the expression on Tudy's face when she had cried out. What did it mean when she could be so sorry for another man? Perhaps it was a general tenderness, perhaps her maternal instinct was so strong that he would be glad later when she felt that way about their children. Oh, she was good, but there was something in him unreconciled to the poignancy, the spontaneity of that cry—and on the way home in the cab he asked her:

"Are you by any chance interested in this French boy? If you are, it's all right with me. We've been apart for a long time and if you've changed—"

She took his face between her hands and looked into his eyes.

"How can you say that to me?"

"Well, I thought that maybe gratitude was influencing you—"

"Gratitude has nothing to do with it. You're the best man I ever knew."

"The point is, do I happen to be attractive to you?"

"Of course you are—other men seem unimportant when you're around. That's why I don't like to see them. Oh, Tom, I wish your mother would hurry so we can get married and leave here—"

As he caught her into his arms, she gave a sob that went through him like a knife. But as the minutes passed and she half lay in his arms in the shadow of the cab's awning, he loved her so much and felt so close to her that he couldn't believe anything could really have gone wrong.

Tudy took her examinations. "Not that they matter, because of course I'm not going on. But that's what you sent me for. I'm now 'finished.' Darling, do I *look* finished?"

He regarded her appraisingly.

"You've probably learned enough French to get you in trouble," he said. "You're a little sweeter, perhaps, but not much—there wasn't very much room for improvement."

"Oh, but French wasn't all I learned. How about Siamese. I sat next to the cutest little Siamese all during one lecture course, and he tried so desperately to make up to me. I learned to say, 'No, I will not climb out the window of the pension tonight' in Siamese. Do you want to hear me say it?"

It was a bright morning—he had called for her at eight to walk to the University. Arm in arm they strolled.

"What are you going to do while I'm being examined?" she asked.

"I'm going to get the car—"

"Our car—I'm wild to see it."

"It's a funny little thing, but it'll take us all over Italy—"

"Then what will you do the rest of the time, after you get the car?"

"Why, I'll try it out and then I'll probably stop in front of the cafe about noon and have a bock, and maybe run into Riccard or one of your French friends—"

"What do you talk about with Riccard?" she asked.

"Oh, we do tricks. We don't talk—not exactly, at least it doesn't seem like talk."

She hesitated. "I don't see why you like to talk to Riccard," she said at last.

"He's a very nice type, very impetuous and fiery—"

"I know," she said suddenly. "He once told me he'd resign his commission if I'd fly to China with him and fight in the war."

When she said this, they had come to a halt engulfed by a crowd of students pouring into the buildings. She joined them as if she had said nothing at all:

"Goodbye, darling. I'll be on this corner at one o'clock."

He walked thoughtfully down to the garage. She had told him a great deal. He wasn't asking her to fly to China; he was asking her to go for a quiet honeymoon in Sicily. He promised her security, not adventure.

"Well, it's absurd to be jealous of this man," he thought. "I'm just getting a little old before my time."

So in the week of waiting for his mother, he organized picnics and swimming parties and trips to Arles and Nimes, inviting Tudy's friends from the University, and they danced and sang and were very gay in little restaurant gardens and *bistros* all over that part of Provence—and behaved in such a harmless, lazy, wasteful summer manner that Tom, who wanted only to be alone with Tudy, almost managed to convince himself that he was having a good time. . . .

. . . .until the night on the steps of Tudy's pension when he broke the silence and told her he wasn't.

"Perhaps you'd better think it over," he said.

"Think what over, Tom?"

"Whether you love me enough to marry me."

Alarmed she cried: "Why, Tom, of course I do."

"I'm not so sure. I like to see you have a good time, but I'm not the sort of man who could ever play—well, call it 'background.' "

"But you're not background. I'm trying to please you, Tom; I thought you wanted to see a lot of young people and be very

Provençal and 'dance the Carmagnol' and all that."

"But it seems to be Riccard who's dancing it with you. You didn't actually have to kiss him tonight."

"You were there—you saw. There was nothing secret about it. It was in front of a lot of people."

"I didn't like it."

"Oh, I'm sorry if it hurt you, Tom. It was all playing. Sometimes with a man it's difficult to avoid those things. You feel like a fool if you do. It was just Provence, just the lovely night—and I'll never see him again after three or four days."

He shook his head slowly.

"No, I've changed ideas. I don't think we'll see him any more at all."

"What?" Was it alarm or relief in her voice? "Oh, then all right, Tom—that's all right. You know best."

"Is that agreed then?"

"You're absolutely right," she repeated after a minute. "But I think we could see him once more, just before he goes."

"I'll see him tomorrow," he said almost gruffly. "You're not a child and neither is he. It isn't as if you were a debutante tapering off some heartsick swain."

"Then why can't you and I go away until he leaves."

"That's running away—that'd be a fine way to start a marriage."

"Well, do what you want," she said, and he saw by the starlight that her face was strained. "You know that more than anything in the world I want to marry you, Tom."

Next day on the Rue de Provence he encountered Riccard; by mutual instinct they turned to a table of the nearest cafe.

"I must talk to you," said Riccard.

"I wanted to talk to you," Tom said, but he waited.

Riccard tapped his breast pocket.

"I have a letter here from Tudy delivered by hand this morning."

"Yes?"

"You must understand that I am fond of you too, Tom—that I am very sad about the whole thing."

"Well, what?" Tom demanded impatiently. "If Tudy wrote that she was in love with you—"

Riccard tapped his pocket again.

"She did not *say* that. I could show you this letter—"

"I don't want to see it."

Their tempers were rising.

"You're upsetting Tudy," Tom said. "Your business is to keep out."

Riccard's answer was humble but his eyes were proud.

"I have no money," he said.

And, of all things, Tom was sorry for him.

"A girl must make her choice," he said kindly. "You're in the way now."

"I understand that, too. I shall perhaps shorten my leave. I shall borrow a friend's plane and fly down, and if I crash so much the better."

"That's nonsense."

They shook hands and Tom duplicated the other's formal little bow, succinct as a salute. . . .

He picked up Tudy at her pension an hour later. She was lovely in an inky blue muslin dress above which her hair shone like a silver angel. As they drove away from the house he said:

"I feel like a brute. But you can't have two men, can you—like a young girl at a dance?"

"Oh, I know it—don't talk about it, darling. He did it all. I haven't done anything I couldn't tell you about."

Riccard had said much the same thing. What bothered Tom was the image on the heart.

They drove southward past cliffs that might have had Roman lookouts posted on them, or that might have concealed barbarians waiting to drop boulders upon the Roman legions if they defiled through some pass.

Tom kept thinking: "Between Riccard and me which is the Roman, and which is the barbarian?"

. . . .Over the crest of a cliff a singing dot came into sight—a dark bee, a hawk—an airplane. They looked up idly, then they were suddenly thinking the same thing, wondering if it were Riccard on his way back to the naval base in Toulon.

"It probably is." Her voice sounded dry and uninterested.

"It looks like an old-fashioned monoplane to me."

"Oh, I guess he can fly anything. He was picked to make some flight to Brazil that they called off. It was in the papers before you came—"

She broke off because of a sudden change of the situation in the sky. After passing over them the plane had begun to circle back, and in a moment its flight resolved itself into a slowly graduated spiral which was undoubtedly intended to center over the road a quarter of a mile ahead of them.

"What's he trying to do?" exclaimed Tom. "Drop flowers on us?"

She didn't answer. During what must have been less than a minute of time, the car and plane approached the same spot. Tom stopped the car.

"If this is one of his tricks, let's get out."

"Oh, he wouldn't—"

"But *look!*"

The plane had come out of its dive, straightened out and was headed straight for them. Tom caught at Tudy's hand, trying to pull her from the car, but he had misjudged the time and the plane was already upon them, with a roaring din—then suddenly it was over them and away.

"The fool!" Tom cried.

"He's a wonderful flier." Her face was still and calm. "He might have killed himself."

Tom got back in the car and sat looking at her for a moment. Then he turned the car around and started back the way they had come.

For a long time they drove in silence. Then she asked:

"What are you going to do—send me home to America?"

The simplicity of her question confused him; it was impossible to punish her for an episode that was no fault of her own, yet he had intended just that when he turned the car around.

"What do you want to do?" he asked, stalling.

Her face had that fatalistic helplessness that he had seen on it one day ten months before when he broke the news to her that her husband had left nothing. And the same wave of protective love that had swept over him then swept over him again now. In the same moment he realized that the tragedy of her marriage—which had come so quickly she scarcely knew what had happened—had not really matured her. And by protecting her from its consequences he had aided the retardation.

"You're just a girl," he said aloud. "I suppose it's my fault."

In that case his responsibility was not over, and deep in his heart he knew that in spite of her inopportune coquetry so obvious under her thin denials, he did not want it to be over. On the contrary he seized upon it as a reason for holding her to him.

"You're making a little trip," he said as they neared town. "But not to America. I want you to go up to Paris for three or four days and shop a little. Meanwhile I'll go down to Marseilles and meet Mother."

Tudy cheered up at the suggestion.

"I'll get my graduation dress and my trousseau at the same time."

"All right, but I want you to leave this afternoon. So pack your bags right away."

An hour later they stood together in the station.

"I miss my exam tomorrow," she said.

"But it'll give you a chance to come down to earth."

He hated the phrase even as it left his lips: To come down to earth—was that an appealing prospect to hold out to any woman?

"Goodbye, dearest, dearest Tom."

As the train started off he ran beside it a moment, throwing into her window a packet of two bright handkerchiefs she had liked in a bazaar.

"Thanks—oh, thanks."

It was a long platform—when he came out at its end into the sunlight he stopped. There was his heart in motion with the train; he could feel the rip when the shadow of the last car broke from under the station roof.

She wrote immediately from Paris.

> Oh, I miss you so, Tom. And I miss Provence, too. (Then a lot of erasing.) I miss everything that I've grown so fond of this last year. But I don't miss any person but you!
>
> There are no Americans in the streets—maybe we belong at home now and always did. They have a life they never take us into. They plan their lives so differently. But our American lives are so strange that we can never figure things out ahead. Like the hurricanes in Florida and the tornadoes and floods. All of a sudden things happen to us and we hardly know what hit us.
>
> But I guess we must like that sort of thing or our ancestors wouldn't have come to America. Does this make sense? There is a man knocking on the door with a package. More later.

Later:

> Darling, it is my wedding dress and I cried on it just a little in the corner where I can wash it out. And darling, it makes me think of my other wedding dress and of how kind you have been to me and how I love you.
>
> It is blue—oh, the frailest blue. I'm getting afraid I won't be able to get the tears out of the corner.

Later:

> I did—and it is so lovely, hanging now in the closet with the door open. It's now eight o'clock—you know *l'heure bleu*—when everything is really blue—and I'm going to walk up to the Opera along the Avenue de l'Opera and then back to the hotel.
>
> Before I go to sleep I'll think of you and thank you for the dress and the lovely year and the new life you're giving me.
>
> Your devoted, your loving,
>
> TUDY.
>
> P. S. I still think I should have stayed and gone with you to meet your mother in Marseilles. She—

Tom broke off and went back to the signature: "Your devoted, your loving." Which was she? He read back over the letter pausing at any erasure, for an erasure often means an evasion, a second thought. And a love letter should come like a fresh stream from the heart, with no leaf on its current.

Then a second the next morning:

I'm so glad for your telegram—this will reach you just before you start down to Marseilles. Give your mother my dearest love and tell her how much I hate missing her and how I wish I could welcome her to Provence. (There were two lines crossed out and rewritten.) I will be starting back day after tomorrow. How funny it is to be buying things, when I never had any money like this to spend before—$225.00—that's what it was, after I'd figured the hotel bill and even thought of keeping enough cash in hand so I won't arrive absolutely penniless.

I've bought two presents, I hope you won't mind, one for your mother and one for somebody else and that's you. And don't think I've stinted myself and that I won't be a pretty bride for you! In fact I haven't waited until my wedding day to find out. I've dressed all up half a dozen times and stood in front of the mirror.

I'll be glad when it's over. Won't you, darling? I mean I'll be glad when it's begun—won't you, darling?

Meanwhile, on the morning after she left, Tom had run into Riccard in the street. He nodded to him coldly, still angry about the airplane stunt, but Riccard seemed so unconscious of any guilt, seemed to think of it merely as a trick as innocuous as the bulb under the plate, that Tom waived the matter and stood talking with him a while under the freckled poplar shadows.

"So you decided not to go," he remarked.

"Oh, I shall go, but not until tomorrow after all. And how is Madame—I mean Tudy?"

"She's gone up to Paris to do some shopping."

He felt a malicious satisfaction in seeing Riccard's face fall.

"Where does she stay there? I would like to send her a telegram of goodbye."

No, you don't, Tom thought. Aloud he lied:

"I'm not sure—the hotel where she was going to stay is full."

"When does she come back?"

"She gets here day after tomorrow morning. I'm going to meet her with the car at Avignon."

"I see." Riccard hesitated for a moment. "I hope you will be very happy," he said.

His face was sad and bright at once; he was a gallant and charming young man, and Tom was sorry for a moment that they had not met under other circumstances.

But next day, driving to Marseilles, a very different idea came to him. Suppose instead of going to the air base at Toulon today, Riccard should go to Paris. There were not an infinite number of good hotels and in a morning's search he might find out which was Tudy's. And in the inevitable emotion of a "last meeting," who could tell what might happen.

The worry so possessed him that when he reached Marseilles he put in a telephone call for the Naval Aviation Depot at Toulon.

"I'm calling Lieutenant Riccard," he said.

"I do not understand."

"Lieutenant Riccard."

"This is not Lieutenant Riccard, surely?"

"No. I want to *speak* to Lieutenant Riccard."

"Ah."

"Is he there?"

"Riccard—wait till I look in the orderly room book. . . . Yes. . . . he is here—or at least he *was* here."

Tom's heart turned over as he waited.

"He is here," said the voice. "He is in the mess room. One minute."

Tom put the receiver very gently on the hook. His first instinct was relief—Riccard could not make it now; then he felt ashamed of his suspicions. Strolling that morning around a seaport where so many graver things had happened, he thought again of Tudy in a key above jealousy. He knew, though, that love should be a simpler, kinder thing; but every man loves out of something in himself that cannot be changed, and if he loved possessively and jealously, he could not help it.

Before he met his mother at the steamer he wired Tudy in Paris, asking an answer with a last thought that she might not be there. Bringing his mother back to the hotel for lunch he asked the concierge:

"Have you a telegram for me?"

It was there. His hands trembled as he opened it.

WHERE ELSE SHOULD I BE STOP LEAVING AT SIX TONIGHT AND REACHING AVIGNON TOMORROW MORNING AT FIVE A. M.

TUDY.

Driving up through Provence with his mother in the afternoon he said:

"You're very brave to try to go around the world by yourself at seventy-eight."

"I suppose I am," she said. "But your father and I wanted to see China and Japan—and that was not to be—so I sometimes think I'm going to see them for him, as if he were alive."

"You loved each other, didn't you?"

She looked at him as if his question was a young impertinence.

"Of course." Then she said suddenly: "Tom, is something making you unhappy?"

"Certainly not. Look what we're passing, Mother—you're not looking."

"It's a river—the Rhone, isn't it?"

"It's the Rhone. And after I've settled you at the Hotel des Thermes I'll be following this same river up to Avignon to meet my girl."

But he had a curious fear as he passed through the great gate of Avignon at four o'clock next morning that she would not be there. There had been a warning in the thin song of his motor, in the closed ominous fronts of the dark villages, in the gray break of light in the sky. He drank a glass of beer in the station buffet where several Italian emigrant families were eating from their baskets. Then he went out on the station platform and beckoned to a porter.

"There will be a lady with some baggage to carry."

Now the train was coming out of the blue dawn. Tom stood midway on the platform trying to pick out a face at a window or vestibule as it slid to rest, but there was no face. He walked along beside the sleepers, but there was only an impatient conductor taking off small baggage. Tom went up to look at the luggage thinking maybe it was hers, that it was new and he hadn't recognized it—then suddenly the train was in motion. Once more he glanced up and down the platform.

"Tom!"

She was there.

"Tudy—it's you."

"Didn't you expect me?"

She looked wan and tired in the faint light. His instinct was to pick her up and carry her out to the car.

"I didn't know there was another wagon-lit," he said excitedly. "Thank heaven there was."

"Darling, I'm so glad to see you. All this is my trousseau, that I told you about. Be careful of them, porter—the strings won't hold probably."

"Put this luggage in the car," he said to the porter. "We're going to have coffee in the buffet."

"*Bien*, Monsieur."

In the buffet Tudy took smaller packages from her purse.

"This is for your mother. I spent a whole morning finding this for her and I wouldn't show it to you for anything."

She found another package.

"This for you, but I won't open it now. Oh, I was going to be *so* economical, but I bought two presents for you. I haven't ten francs left. It's good you met me."

"Darling, you're talking so much you're not eating."

"I forgot."

"Well, *eat*—and drink your coffee. I don't mean hurry—it's only half-past four in the morning."

They drove back through a day that was already blooming; there were peasants in the fields who looked at them as they went by, crawling up on one knee to stare over the tips of the young vines.

"What do we do now?" she said. "Oh, yes, now we get married."

"We certainly do—tomorrow morning. And when you get married in France, you know you've been married. I spent the whole first day you were away signing papers. Once I had to forge your signature, but I gave the man ten francs—"

"Oh, Tom—" she interrupted softly. "Don't talk for a minute. It's so beautiful this morning, I want to look at it."

"Of course, darling." He looked at her. "Is something the matter?"

"Nothing. I'm just confused." She smoothed her face with her hands as if she were parting it in the middle. "I'm almost sure I left something, but I can't think what."

"Weddings are always confusing," he said consolingly. "I'm supposed to forget the ring or something by the best traditions. Now just think of that—the groom has to remember to forget the ring."

She laughed and her mood seemed to change, but when Tom saw her at intervals in the packing and preparations of the day, he noticed that the air of confusion, of vagueness, remained about her. But next morning when he called at her pension at nine, she seemed so beautiful to him with her white-gold hair gleaming above her frail blue frock that he remembered only how much he loved her.

"But don't crush my bouquet," she said. "Are you sure you want me?"

"Perfectly sure."

"Even if—even if I have been rather foolish?"

"Of course."

"Even if—"

He kissed her lips gently.

"That'll do," he said. "I know you were a little in love with Riccard, but it's all over and we won't ever mention it again—is that agreed?"

Momentarily she seemed to hesitate. "Yes, Tom."

So they were married. And it seemed very strange to be married in France. Afterward they gave a little breakfast for a few friends at the hotel and afterward Tudy, who had moved over from the pension the day before, went upstairs to change her clothes and do her last packing, while Tom went to his mother's room and sat with her for a while. She was not starting off with them, but would rest here a day or two and then motor down to Marseilles to catch another boat.

"I worry about your being alone," he said.

"I know my way about, son. You just think about Tudy— remember, you've given her her head for eight months and she may need a little firmness. You're twelve years older than she is and you ought to be that much wiser—" She broke off, "But every marriage works out in its own way."

Leaving his mother's room Tom went down to the office to pay his bill.

"Someone wishes to see Monsieur," said the clerk.

It was a French railroad conductor carrying a package.

"*Bonjour*, Monsieur," he said politely. "Is it you who has just been married to the young lady who traveled on the P. L. M. yesterday?"

"Yes."

"I did not like to disturb Madame on such a morning, but she left this on the train. It is a cloak."

"Oh, yes," said Tom. "She just missed it this morning."

"I had a little time off duty so I thought I'd bring it myself."

"We're very much obliged. Here's a fifty—no, here's a hundred francs."

The conductor looked at the size of Tom's tip and sighed.

"I cannot keep all this. This is too generous."

"Nonsense! I've been married this morning."

He pressed the money into the man's hand.

"You are very kind, Monsieur. *Au revoir*, Monsieur. But wait—" He fumbled in his pocket. "I was so full of emotion at your generosity that I almost forgot. This is another article I found—it may belong to Madame or to her brother who got off at Lyons. I have not been able to figure what it is. *Au revoir* again, Monsieur, and thank you. I appreciate an American gentleman—"

He waved goodbye as he went down the stairs.

Tom was holding in his hands two bulbs of an apparatus that were connected by a long tube. If you pressed one bulb the air went through the tube and inflated the other.

When he came into Tudy's room she was staring out the window in the direction of the University.

"Just taking a last look at my finishing school," she said. "Why, what's the matter?"

He was thinking faster than he ever had in his life.

"Here's your cloak," he said. "The conductor brought it."

"Oh, good! It was an old cloak but—"

"And here's this—" He showed her what he held in his hand. "It seems your brother left it on the train."

The corners of her mouth fell and her eyes pulled her young forehead into a hundred unfamiliar lines. In one moment her face took on all the anguish in the world.

"All right," she said, after a minute. "I knew I should have told you. I tried to tell you this morning. Riccard flew up to Paris in time to meet me in the station and ride south with me. I had no idea he was coming."

"But no doubt you were pleasantly surprised," he said dryly.

"No, I wasn't, I was furious. I didn't see how he knew I was coming south on that train. That's all there was to it, Tom—he rode down as far as Lyons with me. I started to tell you but you were so happy this morning and I couldn't bear to."

Their eyes met, hers wavered away from his out into the great soft-shaking poplar trees.

"I know I can never make you believe it was all right," she said dully. "I suppose we can get an annulment."

The sunlight fell on the square corners of her bags, packed and ready to go.

"I was just getting on the train when I saw him," she said. "There was nothing I could do. Oh, it's so awful—and if he just hadn't dropped that terrible trick you'd never have known."

Tom walked up and down the room a minute.

"I know you're through with me," Tudy said. "Anyhow, you'd just reproach me all the rest of my life. So we'd better quit. We can call it off."

. . . . We can die, too, he was thinking. He had never wanted anything so much in his life as he wanted to believe her. But he had to decide now not upon what was the truth, for that he would never know for certain, but upon the question as to whether he could now and forever put the matter out of his mind, or whether it would haunt their marriage like a ghost. Suddenly he decided:

"No, we won't quit—we'll try it. And there'll never be any word of reproach."

Her face lighted up; she rose and came toward him and he held her close for a minute.

"We'll go right now," he said.

An hour later they drove away from the hotel, both of them momentarily cheered by the exhilaration of starting a journey, with the little car bulging with bags and new vistas opening up ahead. But in the afternoon as they curved down through Provence, they were silent for a while each with a separate thought. His thought was that he would never know—what her thought was must be left unfathomed—and perhaps unfathomable in that obscure pool in the bottom of every woman's heart.

Toward evening as they reached the seaboard and turned east following a Riviera that twinkled with light, they came out of their separate selves and were cheerful together. When the stars were bright on the water he said:

"We'll build our love up and not down."

"I won't have to build my love up," she said loyally. "It's up in the skies now."

They came to the end of France at midnight and looked at each other with infinite hope as they crossed the bridge over into Italy, into the new sweet warm darkness.

Too Cute for Words

(*The Saturday Evening Post*, 18 April 1936)

"Too Cute for Words" was written at the Skyline Hotel, Hendersonville, North Carolina, in December 1935. It was planned as the first in a series of Gwen stories for the *Post*, on the model of the successful Basil (1928-1929) and Josephine (1930-1931) stories about adolescents. It is usually easier for a writer to continue a series of connected stories than to write independent stories, and Fitzgerald was trying desperately to increase his productivity. By this time Harold Ober was acting as both editor and agent—providing lists of suggestions for improving stories, which Fitzgerald tried to act on. On 29 December Ober was able to report that the *Post* had bought the first Gwen story, "Too Cute for Words," for $3000 and was interested in the series. The second story, "Make Yourself at Home," was declined. "Inside the House" was written in Baltimore in February-March 1936, and the *Post* paid $3000 for it. The fourth story, "The Pearl and the Fur," was declined. After the characters' names were changed, "Make Yourself at Home" and "The Pearl and the Fur" were sold to *Pictorial Review*, which did not publish them. "Make Yourself at Home" appears to have been finally published in 1939 as "Strange Sanctuary" in *Liberty*.

Gwen was based on Fitzgerald's daughter Scottie who was fourteen when the stories were written. She had seen *Top Hat*, with Fred Astaire and Ginger Rogers, seven times, and "drove Daddy crazy" playing the record of its hit song, "Cheek to Cheek." "Inside the House" also draws on the occasion when Clark Gable came to lunch at the Baltimore apartment.

Fitzgerald tried to compensate for Zelda's absence, but he was under great personal and professional strain; moreover, his somewhat arbitrary strictness generated father-daughter conflict. In 1939, when he was working on *The Last Tycoon*, he explained to Scottie: "And I think when you read this book, which will encompass the time when you knew me as an adult, you will understand how intensively I knew your world—not *extensively* because I was so ill and unable to get about."

Bryan didn't know exactly why Mrs. Hannaman was there. He thought it was something about his being a widower who should be looked after in some way. He had come home early from his office to catch up on certain aspects of his daughter.

"She has such beautiful manners," Mrs. Hannaman was saying. "Old-fashioned manners."

"Thank you," he said. "We brought up Gwen in the Continental style, and when we came back here, we tried to keep up the general idea."

"You taught her languages, and all that?"

"Lord, no! I never learned anything but waiter's French, but I'm strict with Gwen. I don't let her go to the movies, for instance——"

Had Mrs. Hannaman's memory betrayed her, or had she heard her little niecé Clara say that she and Gwen sat through three straight performances of *Top Hat*, and would see it again if they could find it at one of the smaller theaters.

"We have a phonograph," Bryan Bowers continued, "so Gwen can play music of her own choice, but I won't give her a radio. Children ought to make their own music."

He heard himself saying this, only half believing it, wishing Gwen would come home.

"She plays the piano?"

"Well, she did. She took piano lessons for years, but this year there was so much work at school that we just let it go. I mean we postponed it. She's just thirteen, and she's got plenty of time."

"Of course," agreed Mrs. Hannaman dryly.

When Mrs. Hannaman left, Bryan went back to work on the apartment. They were really settled at last. At least he was settled; it seemed rather likely that Gwen never would be settled. Glancing into his daughter's room now, he uttered a short exclamation of despair. Everything was just as it had been for the past three weeks. He had told the maid that nothing must be touched except the bed, because Gwen should do her own straightening up. She had been to camp this past summer; if this was the system she had learned, that was time wasted. A pair of crushed jodhpur breeches lay in the corner where they had been stepped out of, a section of them rising resentfully above the rest, as if trying to straighten up of its own accord; a stack of letters from boys—a stack that had once worn a neat elastic band—was spread along the top of the bureau like a pack of cards ready for the draw; three knitted sweaters in various preliminary stages of creation and the beginnings of many tidying-ups lay like abandoned foundations about the room. The business was always to be completed on the following Sunday, but Sunday was always the day when the unforeseen came up: Gwen was invited to do something very healthy, or she had so much homework, or he had to take her out with him because he didn't want to leave her alone. For a while it had been a fine idea to let her live in this mess until she was impelled to act from within, but as October crept into November the confusion increased. She was late for everything because nothing could be found. The maid complained it had become absolutely impossible to sweep the room, save with the cautious steps of Eliza on the ice.

He heard his daughter come in, and, with the problem in his mind, went to meet her in the living room.

They faced each other in a moment of happiness. They looked alike. He had been handsome once, but middle age had added flesh in the unappealing places. When he spoke of the past, Gwen was never able to imagine him in romantic situations. She was an arresting little beauty, black-eyed, with soft bay hair and with an extraordinarily infectious laugh—a rare laugh that had a peal in it, and yet managed not to get on people's nerves.

She had thrown herself full length on a couch, scattering her books on the floor. When Bryan came in, she moved her feet so that they just projected over the side of the couch. He noted the gesture, and suggested:

"Pull down your skirt or else take it off altogether."

"Daddy! Don't be so vulgar!"

"That's the only way I can get through to you sometimes."

"Daddy, I got credit plus in geometry. Cute?"

"What's credit plus?"

"Ninety-two."

"Why don't they just say ninety-two?"

"Daddy, did you get the tickets for the Harvard game?"

"I told you I'd take you."

She nodded, and remarked as if absently:

"Dizzy's father's taking her to the Harvard game and the Navy game. And her uncle's taking her to the Dartmouth game. Isn't that cute?"

"What's cute about it? Do you know what you said to Doctor Parker the other day, when he asked you if you liked Caesar? You said you thought Caesar was cute." He walked around the room in helpless laughter. "A man conquers the whole known world, and a little schoolgirl comes along a thousand years afterwards and says he's cute!"

"Two thousand years," remarked Gwen, unruffled.... "Daddy, Mr. Campbell's driving them up to the Harvard game in their new car. Isn't that cu—isn't that fine?"

She was always like this in the first half hour home from school or a party—outer worlds where she lived with such intensity that she carried it into the slower tempo of life at home like weather on her shoes. This is what made her say:

"It'd take forever the way you drive, daddy."

"I drive fast enough."

"Once I drove ninety miles an hour——"

Startled, he stared at her, and Gwen should have been acute enough to minimize the statement immediately. But still in her worldly daze, she continued "——on the way to Turtle Lake this summer."

"Who with?"

"With a girl."

"A girl your age driving a car!"

"No. The girl was nineteen—she's a sister of a girl I was visiting. But I won't tell you who. Probably you'd never let me go there again, daddy."

She was very sorry that she had ever spoken.

"You might as well tell me. I know who you've visited this summer and I can find out who's got a sister nineteen years old. I'm not going to have you mangled up against a telegraph post because some young——"

Momentarily Gwen was saved by the maid calling her father to the phone. As a sort of propitiation, she hung her overcoat in the closet, picked up her books and went on into her own room.

She examined it, as usual, with a vast surprise. She knew it was rather terrible, but she had some system of her own as to what to do about it—a system that never seemed to work out in actuality. She pounced with a cry upon the wastebasket—it was her record of "Cheek to Cheek," broken, but preserved to remind her to get another. She cradled it to her arms, and as if this, in turn, reminded her of something else, she decided to telephone Dizzy Campbell. This required a certain diplomacy. Bryan had become adamant on the matter of long phone conversations.

"This is about Latin," she assured him.

"All right, but make it short, daughter."

He read the paper in the living room, waiting for supper; for some time he had been aware of a prolonged murmur which confused itself in his mind with distant guns in Ethiopia and China. Only when he turned to the financial page and read the day's quotation on American Tel. and Tel. did he spring to his feet.

"She's on the phone again!" he exclaimed to himself; but even as the paper billowed to rest in front of him, Gwen appeared, all radiant and on the run.

"Oh, daddy, the best thing! You won't have to take me to the game, after all! I mean you *will* to the game, but not up to the game. Dizzy's aunt, Mrs. Charles Wrotten Ray, or something like that— somebody that's all right, that they know about, that they can trust, and all that sort of thing——"

While she panted, he inquired politely:

"What about her? Has she made the Princeton team?"

"No. She lives up there and she has some nephews or uncles or something—it was all kind of complicated on the phone—that go to some kind of prep school that are about our age—about fifteen or sixteen——"

"I thought you were thirteen."

"The boy is always older," she assured him. "Anyhow, she——"

"Don't ever say 'she.' "

"Well, excuse me, daddy. Well, anyhow, this sort of person—you know, not 'she,' but this sort of Mrs. Wrotten Ray, or whatever her name is—she wants Dizzy——"

"Now, calm yourself, calm yourself."

"I can't, daddy; she's waiting on the phone."

"Who? Mrs. Wrotten Ray?"

"Oh, that isn't her name, but it's something like that. Anyhow, Mrs. Wrotten Ray wants Dizzy to bring Clara Hannaman and one other girl up to a little dance the night before the game. And Dizzy wants me to be the other girl, and can I go?"

"This is all a little sudden. I don't like such things during a school term, and you know that." He hated to refuse her, though, for, excepting an occasional indiscretion of speech, she was a trustworthy child; she made good grades in school and conscientiously wrestled with her ebullient temperament.

"Well, can I, daddy? Dizzy's waiting; she has to know."

"I suppose you can."

"Oh, thanks. Mrs. Campbell's going to call you up, but Dizzy couldn't wait to tell me. Cute?"

She vanished, and in a moment the low murmur behind the door began again.

Something told Bryan that she'd be leading a simpler life at boarding school, but didn't Helen Hannaman say something today about her old-fashioned manners? He couldn't afford it this year anyhow, and, besides, she was such a bright little thing to have around the house.

But if he'd known that the movies were going to produce this *Top Hat*—— She had broken the record of "Cheek to Cheek," but there was still the one about sitting on his top hat and climbing up his shirt front——

Curiously, he opened the door to the dining room and discovered the phonograph going and his daughter in a crouching posture, arms outspread, head projecting from its proper neck, eyes half closed. When she saw him, she straightened up.

"I thought that this 'Cheek by Jowl' was broken," he said.

"It is, but you can still play the inside a little. See, it's over already. You certainly can't object to that much of a record."

"Let's put it on again," he suggested facetiously, "and we'll dance."

She looked at him with infinite compassion.

"Who do you imagine you are, daddy? Fred Astaire? What I want to know is if I can go to Princeton."

"I said yes, didn't I?"

"But you didn't say it like when you mean it."

"Yes, then—yes. Get enough rope and hang yourself."

"Then I can go?"

"Yes, of course. Why not? Where do you think you're going? To the prom or something? Of course, you can go."

II

Having lunch on the train, the three girls were a little bit mad with excitement. Clara Hannaman and Dizzy Campbell were fourteen, a year older than Gwen, and Clara was already somewhat taller, but they were all dressed alike in suits that might have been worn by their mothers. Their jewelry consisted of thin rings and chains, legacies from grandmothers, supplemented by flamboyant Koh-i-noors from the five-and-ten; and it was true that their coats might once have responded to wheedling calls of "Pussy," "Bunny," or "Nanny." But it was their attacks of hysteria that stamped them as of a certain age.

Clara had asked: "What kind of a joint is this we're going to?" She was temporarily under the spell of Una Merkel and the hard-boiled school, and this question was enough to start a rat-tat-tat of laughter, to the extent that eating was suspended, napkins called into play. One word was usually enough to send them off; frequently it was a boy's name that had some private meaning to them, and for a whole afternoon or evening this single word would serve as detonator. At other times a curious soberness fell upon all of them, a sort of quietude. They faced both ways—toward a world they were fast leaving and a world they had never met—and the contradiction was externalized in the uncanny mirth.

There was a sober moment now when they all looked at the girl across the way, who was the debutante of the year and bound for the fall prom. They looked with respect, even a certain awe, impressed with her ease and tranquillity in the face of her ordeal. It made them feel very young and awkward, and they were both glad and sorry that they were too young for the prom. Last year that girl had been only the captain of the basketball team at school; now she was in the Great

Game, and they had noted the men who came to see her off at the station with flowers and adjurations not to "fall for any babies up there. . . . Be five years before they get a job."

After luncheon, the three girls planned to study—they had conscientiously brought books along—but the excitement of the train was such that they never got any farther than the phrase "jeweled stomacher" from an English-history lesson—which thereafter became their phrase for the day. They reached Princeton in an uncanny, explosive quiet, because Dizzy claimed to have forgotten her jeweled stomacher on the train, but their wild chuckles changed to a well-bred reserve as they were greeted on the platform by Miss Ray, young and lovely and twenty.

Where were the boys? They peered for them through the early dusk, not expecting to be greeted like prom girls, but there might have been someone of their own age, the one for whom they had dressed and dreamed and waved their locks sidewise in these last twenty-four hours. When they reached the house, Miss Ray exploded the bomb; while they took off their coats, she said:

"You're due for a disappointment. I tried to reach you by telegraphing and telephone, too, but you'd already left."

Their eyes turned toward her, apprehensive, already stricken.

"Seems that grandmother's not well, and mother felt she had to go up to Albany. So, before I was even awake, she called off the little dance, and she'd phoned everybody. I tried to fix it up, but it was too late."

Now their faces were utterly expressionless.

"Mother was excited, that's all," continued Miss Ray. "Grandmother'll live to be a hundred. I've been on the phone all afternoon trying to find some company for you girls for this evening, but the town's a madhouse and nobody's available—the boys for the little dance were coming from New York. Lord, if I'd only waked up before eleven o'clock!"

"We don't mind," Dizzy lied gently. "Really we don't, Esther. We can amuse ourselves."

"Oh, darling, I know how you feel!"

"Yes," they said together, and Dizzy asked, "Where's Shorty? Did he have to go to Albany too?"

"No, he's here. But he's only sixteen and——I hardly know how to explain it, but he's the youngest man in his class in college, and very small, and this year he's just impossibly shy. When the party was called off, he just refused to appear as the only boy; said he'd stay in his room and study chemistry, and there he is. And he won't come out."

Gwen formed a mental picture of him. Better that he remained in his hermitage; they could have more fun without him.

"Anyhow, you'll have the game tomorrow."

"Yes," they said together.

That was that. Upstairs they took out their evening gowns, which, according to modern acceptance, were as long and as chic as any adult evening gowns, and laid them on their beds. They brought out their silk hosiery, their gold or silver sandal dancing shoes, and surveyed the glittering exhibit. At that age, their mothers would have worn ruffles, flounces and cotton stockings to brand them as adolescent. But this historical fact, dinned into them for many years, was small consolation now.

After they had dressed, things seemed better, even though they were only dressing for one another; when they went down to dinner, they gave such an impression of amiability and gaiety that they convinced even Esther Ray. It was difficult, though, when Miss Ray's escort called to take her to the Harvard-Princeton concert, and she must have seen it in their eyes.

"I've got an idea," she said. "I think we can get you into the concert, but you may have to stand up in back."

That was something indeed. They brightened. They ran for coats; and Gwen caught a sight of a very hurried young man in the upper hall with a plate in one hand and a cup in the other, but he disappeared into his room before she could see him plainly.

In any event, the concert turned out as precariously as most improvisations—it was jammed, and they were obliged to stand behind rows of taller people and to listen to tantalizing bursts of laughter and fragments of song—while from Clara's superior three inches they gathered such information as they could as to what it looked like.

When it was over, they were washed out with the happy, excited crowd, driven back to the Rays', and dumped almost brusquely on the doorstep.

"Good night. Thanks."

"Thanks a lot."

"It was fine!"

"Thanks. Good night."

Upstairs they moved around in silence, casting stray glances at themselves in the mirror and rearranging, to no purpose now, some bit of awry finery. Dizzy had even taken off her necklace of seed pearls, when Gwen said suddenly:

"I want to go to the prom."

"Who doesn't?" Clara said. Suddenly she looked at Gwen

sharply and asked: "What do you mean, Gwen?"

Gwen was drawing her lips in the mirror with Dizzy's lipstick. She would have had one along herself, save it had melted going through Alabama on the way to the ranch last summer, and she had never since been able to get the top off it. Clara watched her until Gwen said:

"How would you make up if you were going to the prom?"

"Like this," Clara suggested.

In a minute they were all at it.

"Not like that; that looks very ordinary." And: "Remember, that's Esther's eye pencil. That's too much, Dizzy."

"Not with powder, it isn't."

Within half an hour they had somehow managed to age themselves by several years, and crying: "Bring on my jeweled stomacher," they minced, paraded and danced around the room.

"I'll tell you what," Gwen said. "I just sort of want to go to the outside of the prom. I mean I don't want to do anything bad, you know, but I want to see how they work it."

"Esther might see us."

"She won't," said Gwen sagely. "She's probably having herself a time, and that girl on the train too—that Marion Lamb—you know, we used to know her in school. You take a lot of these debutantes," she continued, "and when they get by themselves—pretty cute is what I would say, if you asked me."

Dizzy looked like white-pine shavings; even her eyes were so light and virginal that what she said now came as a sort of shock to the other two:

"We'll do it—we'll go to the prom. We've got more what it takes than most of those girls."

"Of course this isn't like a city," Clara suggested uncertainly. "It's perfectly all right; it's just the same as going out in your yard."

This remark was calming to their consciences, but they were really less concerned with kidnapers or molesters of womanhood than with what Gwen's plan was. Gwen had no plan. She had literally nothing on her mind except a certain disparity between the picture of herself wandering around a college campus at night with rouged lips, and a little scene that had taken place a week before, when she had argued with her father that she wanted to set up her doll's house in her room instead of having it sent to storage.

The deciding factor was that they had been cheated by their elders. Though Bryan had never met Mrs. Ray, he somehow seemed to share in her disastrous excitability of the morning. This was the sort of thing that parents did as a class. The sort of thing for which they had joint responsibility. Before Gwen and Dizzy had agreed to the excursion in words, they bumped shoulders around the mirror, modifying their faces until the theatrical quality yielded to the more seemly pigmentation of an embassy ball. In the last burst of conservatism, for they might run inadvertently into Esther Ray, they cleansed the area around their eyes, leaving only the faintest patina of evening on lips and noses. The ten-cent crown jewels disappeared from ear and wrist and throat so quickly that when they went downstairs all taint of the side show had disappeared. Taste had triumphed.

Issuing into a clear brilliant November night, they walked along a high exuberant street beneath the dark trees of Liberty Place—though that meant nothing to them. A dog panicked them momentarily from behind a hedge, but they met no further obstacle until it was necessary to pass beneath a bright arc on Mercer Street.

"Where are we going?" Clara asked.

"Up to where we can hear it."

She stopped. Figures had loomed up ahead, and they linked arms protectively, but it was only two colored women carrying a basket of laundry between them.

"Come on," Gwen said.

"Come on to where?"

"To where we're going."

They reached a cathedral-like structure which Clara recognized as a corner of the campus, and by a sort of instinct they turned into an archway, threaded a deserted cloister and came out into a wider vista of terraces and Gothic buildings, and suddenly there was music in the air. After a few hundred yards, Dizzy pulled them up short.

"I see it," she whispered. "It's that big building down there with all the lights. That's the gymnasium."

"Let's go closer," said Gwen. "There isn't anybody around. Let's go till we see somebody, anyhow."

Arms linked, they marched on in the shadow of the long halls. They were getting dangerously close to the zone of activity, could distinguish figures against the blur of the gymnasium entrance, and hear the applause in the intervals. Once more they stopped, afraid either to go on or to hold their ground, for there were voices and footsteps approaching out of the darkness.

"Over at the other side," Clara suggested. "It's dark there and we can get really close."

They left the path and ran across the turf; stopped, breathless, in the haven of a group of parked cars. Here they huddled silently, feeling like spies behind the enemy lines. Within the great bulky walls, fifty feet away, a sonorous orchestra proclaimed a feeling that someone was fooling, announced that someone was its lucky star, and demanded if it wasn't a lovely day to be caught in the rain. Inside those walls existed ineffable romance—an orchid-colored dream in which floated prototypes of their future selves, surrounded, engulfed, buoyed up by unnumbered boys. No one spoke; there was no more to say than the orchestra was saying to their young hearts, and when the music stopped, they did not speak; then suddenly they realized that they were not alone.

"We can eat later," a man's voice said.

"I don't care about it at all, when I'm with you."

The three young girls caught their breath in a gasp, clutched at one another's arms. The voices came from a car not five feet from where they stood; it was turned away from the gymnasium, so that under cover of the music, their approach had gone unobserved.

"What's one supper," the girl continued, "when I think of all the suppers we'll have together all through life?"

"Beginning next June, darling."

"Beginning next June, darling, darling, darling."

And once again a clutching went on among the listeners. For the girl's voice was that of Marion Lamb, the debutante who had been on the train.

At this point, because it was a rather cool night and her evening cloak was thin, Dizzy sneezed—sneezed loudly and sneezed again.

III

"But how do we know you kids won't tell?" the man was demanding: He turned to Marion: "Can't you explain to them how important it is not to tell? Explain that it'll absolutely wreck your debut at home."

"But I don't care, Harry. I'd be proud——"

"I care. It simply can't get around now."

"We won't tell," the young girls chorused ardently. And Gwen added: "We think it's cute."

"Do you realize you're the only ones that know?" he asked sternly. "The only ones! And if it slipped out, I'd know who told, and——"

There were such sinister threats in his voice that instinctively the trio recoiled a step.

"That isn't the way to talk to them," said Marion. "I went to school with these girls and I know they won't tell. Anyhow, they know it's not serious—that I get engaged every few weeks or so."

"Marion," cried the young man, "I can't stand hearing you talk like that!"

"Oh, Harry, I didn't mean to hurt you!" she gasped, equally upset. "You know there's never been anyone but you."

He groaned.

"Well, how are we going to silence this gallery?" Distraught, he fumbled in his pocket for money.

"No, Harry. They'll keep quiet." But looking at those six eyes, she felt a vast misgiving. "Listen, what would you three like more than anything in the world?"

They laughed and looked at one another.

"To go to the prom, I guess," said Gwen frankly. "But of course, we wouldn't be allowed to. Our parents wouldn't let us, even if we were invited—I mean——"

"I've got the idea," said Harry. "I'll tell you what I'll do. I know a side entrance that leads up to the indoor track. How would you like to sit up there in the dark and look on awhile without anybody seeing you?"

"Whew!" said Dizzy.

"If I take you up there, will you give me your sacred words of honor that you'll never breathe a word of what you heard tonight?"

"Will we!" they exclaimed together.

IV

Leaving them on the running track, the focusing eye must move down momentarily to the thick of the dance below. Or rather to its outskirts, where a person had just appeared who has hitherto played a small and sorry part in this history, and there he stood uncertainly, his view obscured by a throbbing Harvard-Princeton stag line. If, half an hour before, anyone had told Shorty Ray that eleven o'clock would find him in his present situation, he would not even have said, "Huh!" Some boys of inconsiderable height are compensated by an almost passionate temerity. Not Shorty; since adolescence, he never had been able to face girls with a minimum of dignity. The dance at home was part of a campaign to break him of his shyness, and it had seemed a stroke of luck to him that if his grandmother's health were going to fail anyhow, it should have chosen this particular day.

As if in retribution for this irreverence, a telegram from Albany addressed to his sister had come to the house at the very moment when he had started to turn out his lights.

An older man would have torn open the telegram and read it, but anything sealed was sacred to him, and such telegrams spelled emergencies. There was nothing for it save to get it to Esther in the gymnasium as quickly as possible.

One thing he knew—he would not go upon the dance floor in search of her. After he had argued his way past the doorkeeper, he was simply standing there feeling helpless, when Dizzy spied him from above.

"There's Tommy!" she exclaimed.

"Where?"

"The short boy by the door. Well, that's pathetic, if you ask me! He wouldn't even come out and look at us, and then he goes to the prom."

"He doesn't seem to be having much of a time,"said Clara.

"Let's go down and cheer him up," Gwen suggested.

"Not me," said Dizzy. "For one thing, I wouldn't want the Rays to know we were here."

"I forgot about that."

"Anyhow, he's gone now."

He was gone, but not, as they supposed, into the delirious carnival. Irresolute, he had finally conceived the idea of mounting to the running track and trying to locate Esther among the dancers. Even as Dizzy spoke, he was there at her elbow, to their mutual surprise.

"I thought you were in bed!" he exclaimed, as he recognized his cousin.

"I thought you were studying."

"*I was* studying when a telegram came, and now I've got to find Esther."

He was introduced with great formality; Gwen and Clara immediately adopting the convention that they had not known of his existence in the same town.

"Esther was in one of the boxes a while ago," said Gwen. "No. 18."

Grasping at this, Tommy turned to Dizzy.

"Then I wonder if you'd mind going over and giving her this telegram?"

"I would so mind," said Dizzy. "Why don't you give it to her yourself? We're not supposed to be here."

"Neither am I; they let me in. But I can't just walk across there all by myself, and you can," he said earnestly.

Gwen had been looking at him in a curiously intent way for some moments. He was not at all the person she had pictured—in fact, she decided that he was one of the handsomest boys she had ever seen in her life.

"I'll take it to her," she said suddenly.

"Will you?" For the first time he seemed to see Gwen—a girl who looked like the pictures in the magazines, and yet was smaller than himself. He thrust the telegram at her. "Thanks! Gosh, I certainly am——"

"I'm not going downstairs alone," she interrupted. "You've got to take me part way."

As they descended, he looked at her again out of the corner of his eye; at the big arch he paused.

"Now you take it the rest of the way," he said.

"The best way would be to do it together."

"Oh, no!" he exclaimed. "You didn't say that. I'm not going to walk across the floor."

"I didn't mean walk. If we walked, everybody'd kind of look at us, but if we danced across to the box, nobody would notice it."

"You said you'd take it!" he said indignantly.

"I will, but you've got to take me." And she added innocently, "That makes it easy for us both."

"I won't do it," he declared.

"Then you can take it yourself."

"I never——"

Suddenly, before he realized it, she was in the circle of his arm, his hand was on what was apparently a forgotten seam in her dress just between shoulder blades, and they were moving across the floor.

Through the line of stags and out into the kaleidoscope. Gwen was at home; all hesitancy at the daring of her idea vanishing like the tension of a football player after the kick-off. By some inexorable right, this was her world. This was, perhaps, not the time set for entering it, but, maybe because her generation had ceased to move in the old Euclidian world, her age ceased to matter after a moment. She felt as old as any girl on the floor.

And now, miracle of miracles, the lights dimmed, and at the signal, the divine spark passed from one orchestra to another, and Gwen was dancing onward in a breathless trance to the melody of "Cheek to Cheek."

In the Laurel Club box, the ladies were growing weary. Chaperonage, they decided, was too lightly undertaken, too poorly compensated for. They were tired of the parade of animation, of lovely, confident faces, and one of them said as much to the middle-aged man who sat at her side. He, too, wore the look of speculating upon the texture of cool pillowcases and the beatitude of absolute quiet.

"I had to come," she said, "but I still don't understand why you came."

"Perhaps because I saw in the morning paper that you'd be here, after all these years."

"This is no place to say that to a woman of my age; the competition makes me feel very old. Look at that odd-looking couple—like a pair of midgets. I haven't seen them before."

He looked, but they seemed like just the sort of eccentrics to wander into any doze, so, after vaguely replying, "Aren't they cute?" he glazed his eyes for a while, until she commented: "There they are again. Such little people. That girl—why, she can't be more than fourteen, and she's like a blasé, world-weary woman of twenty. Can you imagine what her parents could have been thinking of, to let her come here tonight?"

He looked again; then, after a long pause, he said, rather wearily: "Yes, I can imagine."

"You think it's all right then?" she demanded. "Why, it seems to me——"

"No, Helen, I just meant I can imagine what they would be thinking if they knew about it. Because the girl seems to be my daughter."

V

It was not in Bryan's nature to rush out and snatch Gwen from the floor. Should she pass near him again, he intended to bow to her very formally indeed and let the next step be hers. He was not angry with her—he supposed her hostess was behind the matter—but he was angry at a system which permitted a baby disguised as a young woman, a marriageable young woman, to dance at a semipublic ball.

At his undergraduate club the next day, he wended his way from group to group, stopping to chat momentarily here and there, but with his eye always out for Gwen, who was to meet him there. When the crowd was drifting out and down to the stadium, he called the Rays' house, and found her still there.

"You better meet me at the game," he said, glad he had given her the ticket. "I want to go down now and see the teams practice."

"Daddy, I hate to say it but I've lost it." Her voice was hushed and solemn. "I searched and searched, and then I remembered I stuck it in the mirror at home with some invitations, to see how it would look, and forgot to——"

The connection was broken, and a male voice demanded if there were rooms at the club tonight and if the steward had delivered a brown lunch basket to Thomas Pickering, '96. For ten minutes more he jangled the receiver; he wanted to tell her to buy a bad seat in the end stand and work her way around to him, but the phone service in Princeton shared the hysteria of the crowd.

People began going by the booth, looking at their watches and hurrying to get to the kick-off; in another five minutes there was no one going by the booth, and there was sweat upon Bryan's brow. He had played freshman football in college; it meant to him what war or chess might have meant to his grandfather. Resentment possessed him suddenly.

"After all, she had her fun last night, and now I have a right to mine. Let her miss it. She doesn't care, really."

But on the way to the stadium he was torn between the human roar that went up at momentary intervals behind that massive wall and the picture of Gwen making a last desperate search for that precious counter that gleamed uselessly in a mirror at home.

He hardened himself.

"It's that disorderliness. This will be a better lesson than any lecture."

Nevertheless, at the very gate Bryan paused once more; he and Gwen were very close, and he could still go after her, but a huge swelling cry from the arena decided him; he went in with the last dribble of the crowd.

It was as he reached his seat that he saw that there was a hand signaling him, heard a voice hailing him.

"Oh, daddy, here we are! We thought maybe you'd——"

"Sit down," he whispered, breathlessly slipping into his place. "People want to see. Did you find your ticket?"

"No, daddy. I had a terrible time—but this is Tommy Ray, daddy. He hasn't got a seat here; he was just keeping your seat till you came. He can sit anywhere because he——"

"Be quiet, Baby! You can tell me later. What's happened on the field? What's on that scoreboard?"

"What scoreboard?"

From the aisle steps whither he had moved, Tommy supplied the information that it was nothing to nothing; Bryan bent his whole attention upon the game.

At the quarter, he relaxed and demanded:

"How did you manage to get it?"

"Well, you see, Tommy Ray"—she lowered her voice—"this boy beside me—he's one of the ticket takers. And I knew he'd be somewhere, because he told me last night that was why he had to go home——"

She stopped herself.

"I understand," Bryan said dryly. "I wondered what you found to talk about in that remarkable dancing position."

"You were there?" she cried in dismay. "You——"

"Listen to that Harvard band," he interrupted, "jazzing old marching songs—seems sort of irreverent. Of course, you'd probably like them to play 'Cheek by Jowl.' "

"Daddy!"

But for a moment her eyes were far off on the gray horizon, listening, not to the band, to that sweeter and somehow older tune.

"What did you think?" she asked, after a moment. "I mean when you saw me there?"

"What did I think? I thought you were just too cute for words."

"You didn't! I don't care how you punish me, but please don't ever say that horrible word again!"

Inside the House

(*The Saturday Evening Post*, 13 June 1936)

When Bryan Bowers came home in the late afternoon, three boys were helping Gwen to decorate the tree. He was glad, for she had bought too big a tree to climb around herself, and he had not relished the prospect of crawling over the ceiling.

The boys stood up as he came in, and Gwen introduced them:

"Jim Bennett, daddy, and Satterly Brown you know, and Jason Crawford you know."

He was glad she had said the names. So many boys had been there throughout the holidays that it had become somewhat confusing.

He sat down for a moment.

"Don't let me interrupt. I'll be leaving you shortly."

It struck him that the three boys looked old, or certainly large, beside Gwen, though none was over sixteen. She was fourteen, almost beautiful, he thought—would be beautiful, if she had looked a little more like her mother. But she had such a pleasant profile and so much animation that she had become rather too popular at too early an age.

"Are you at school here in the city?" he asked the new young man.

"No, sir. I'm at S'n Regis; just home for the holidays."

Jason Crawford, the boy with the wavy yellow pompadour and horn-rimmed glasses, said, with an easy laugh:

"He couldn't take it here, Mr. Bowers."

Bryan continued to address the new boy:

"Those little lights you're working at are the biggest nuisance about a Christmas tree. One bulb always misses and then it takes forever to find which one it is."

"That's just what happened now."

"You said it, Mr. Bowers," said Jason.

Bryan looked up at his daughter, balanced on a stepladder.

"Aren't you glad I told you to put these men to work?" he asked. "Think of old daddy having to do this."

Gwen agreed from her precarious perch: "It would have been hard on you, daddy. But wait till I get this tinsel thing on."

"You aren't old, Mr. Bowers," Jason offered.

"I feel old."

Jason laughed, as if Bryan had said something witty.

Bryan addressed Satterly:

"How do things go with you, Satterly? Make the first hockey team?"

"No, sir. Never really expected to."

"He gets in all the games," Jason supplied.

Bryan got up.

"Gwen, why don't you hang these boys on the tree?" he suggested. "Don't you think a Christmas tree covered with boys would be original?"

"I think——" began Jason, but Bryan continued:

"I'm sure none of them would be missed at home. You could call up their families and explain that they were only being used as ornaments till after the holidays."

He was tired, and that was his best effort. With a general wave, he went toward his study.

Jason's voice followed him:

"You'd get tired seeing us hanging around, Mr. Bowers. Better change your mind about letting Gwen have dates."

Bryan turned around sharply. "What do you mean about 'dates'?"

Gwen peeked over the top of the Christmas tree. "He just means about dates, daddy. Don't you know what a date is?"

"Well now, will one of you tell me just exactly what a date is?"

All the boys seemed to begin to talk at once.

"Why, a date is——"

"Why, Mr. Bowers——"

"A *date*——"

He cut through their remarks:

"Is a 'date' anything like what we used to call an engagement?"

Again the cacophony commenced.

"——No, a date is——"

"——An engagement is——"

"——It's sort of more——"

Bryan looked up at the Christmas tree from which Gwen's face stared out from the tinsel somewhat like the Cheshire cat in *Alice in Wonderland*.

"Heaven's sakes, don't fall out of the tree about it," he said.

"Daddy, you don't mean to say that you don't know what a date is?"

"A date is something you can have at home," said Bryan. He started to go to his study but Jason supplied: "Mr. Bowers, I can explain to you why Gwen won't fall out of the tree——"

Bryan closed his door on the remark and stood near it.

"That young man is extremely fresh," he thought.

Stretched out on his divan for half an hour, he let the worries of the day slip from his shoulders. At the end of that time there was a knock, and he sat up, saying:

"Come in. . . . Oh, hello, Gwen." He stretched and yawned. "How's your metabolism?"

"What's metabolism? You asked me that one other afternoon."

"I think it's something everybody has. Like a liver."

She had a question to ask him and did not pursue the subject further:

"Daddy, did you like them? Those boys?"

"Sure."

"How do you like Jason?"

He pretended to be obtuse.

"Which one was he?"

"You know very well. Once you said he was fresh. But he wasn't this afternoon, did you think?"

"The boy with all the yellow fuzz?"

"Daddy, you know very well which one he was."

"I wasn't sure. Because you told me if I didn't let you go out alone at night, Jason wouldn't come to see you again. So I thought this must be some boy who looked like him."

She shook off his teasing.

"I do know this, daddy: That if I'm not allowed to have dates, nobody's going to invite me to the dance."

"What do you call this but a date? Three boys. If you think I'm going to let you race around town at night with some kid, you're fooling yourself. He can come here any night except a school night."

"It isn't the same," she said mournfully.

"Let's not go over that. You told me that all the girls you knew had these dates, but when I asked you to name even one——"

"All right, daddy. The way you talk you'd think it was something awful we were going to do. We just want to go to the movies."

"To see Peppy Velance again."

She admitted that was their destination.

"I've heard nothing but Peppy Velance for two months. Dinner's one long movie magazine. If that girl is your ideal, why don't you be practical about it and learn to tap like her? If you just want to be a belle——"

"What's a belle?"

"A belle?" Bryan was momentarily unable to understand that the term needed definition. "A belle? Why, it's what your mother was. Very popular—that sort of thing."

"Oh. You mean the nerts."

"What?"

"Being the nerts—having everybody nerts about you."

"What?" he repeated incredulously.

"Oh, now, don't get angry, daddy. Call it a belle then."

He laughed, but as she stood beside his couch, silent and a little resentful, a wave of contrition went over him as he remembered that she was motherless. Before he could speak, Gwen said in a tight little voice:

"I don't think your friends are so interesting! What am I supposed to do—get excited about some lawyers and doctors?"

"We won't discuss that. You have the day with your friends. When you're home in the evening, you've got to be a little grown up. There's a lawyer coming here tonight to dinner, and I'd like you to make a good impression on him."

"Then I can't go to the movies?"

"No."

Silent and expressionless, save for the faint lift of her chin, Gwen stood a moment. Then she turned abruptly and left the room.

II

Mr. Edward Harrison was pleased to find his friend's little girl so polite and so pleasant to look at. Bryan, wanting to atone for his harshness of the afternoon, introduced him as the author of "The Music Goes Round and Round."

For a moment, Gwen looked at Mr. Harrison, startled. Then they laughed together.

During dinner, the lawyer tried to draw her out:

"Do you plan to marry? Or to take up a career?"

"I think that I'd like to be a debutante." She looked at her father reproachfully, "And maybe have dates on the side. I haven't got any talents for a career that I know about."

Her father interrupted her:

"She has though. She ought to make a good biologist—or else she could be a chemist making funny artificial fingernails." He changed his tone: "Gwen and I had a little run-in on the subject of careers this afternoon. She's stage-struck, and I'd rather have her do something about it than just talk."

Mr. Harrison turned to Gwen. "Why don't you?" he asked. "I can give you some tips. I do a lot of theatrical business. Probably know some of your favorites."

"Do you know Peppy Velance?"

"She's a client of mine."

Gwen was thrilled.

"Is she nice?"

"Yes. But I'm more interested in you. Why not go in for a career if your father thinks you have the necessary stuff?"

How could Gwen tell him it was because she was happy the way things were? How could she explain to him what she hardly knew herself—that her feeling for Peppy Velance only stood for loveliness—enchanted gardens, ballrooms through which to walk with enchanted lovers? Starlight and tunes.

The stage! The very word frightened her. That was work, like school. But somewhere there must exist a world of which Peppy Velance's pictures were only an echo, and this world seemed to lie just ahead—proms and parties of people at gay resorts. She could not cry out to Mr. Harrison, "I don't want a career, because I'm a romantic little snob. Because I want to be a belle, a belle, a belle"—the word ringing like a carillon inside her.

So she only said:

"Please tell me about Peppy Velance."

"Peppy Velance? Let's see."

He thought for a moment. "She's a kid from New Mexico. Her name's really Schwartze. Sweet. About as much brains as the silver peacock on your buffet. Has to be coached before every scene, so she can talk English. And she's having a wonderful time with her success. Is that satisfactory?"

It was far from being satisfactory to Gwen. But she didn't believe him.

He was an old man, about forty, like her father, and Peppy Velance had probably never looked at him romantically.

The important thing was that Jason would arrive presently, and maybe two other boys and a girl. They would have some sort of time—in spite of the fact that a sortie into the world of night was forbidden.

"One girl at school knows Clark Gable," she said, switching the subject. "Do you know him, Mr. Harrison?"

"No," Mr. Harrison said in such a funny way that both father and daughter looked at him. His face had turned gray.

"I wonder if I could ask for a cup of coffee."

The host stepped on the bell.

"Do you want to lie down, Ed?"

"No, thanks. I brought a brief case of work to do on the train and the strain on the eyes always seems to affect the old pump."

Being one of those who had made an unwelcome breakfast of chlorine gas eighteen years before, Bryan understood that Mr. Harrison could never be quite sure. As the other man drank his coffee, the world was still swimming and he felt the need of telling this pretty little girl something—before the tablecloth got darker.

"Were you offended at what I said about Peppy Velance? You were. I saw you wondering how an old man like me would dare even talk about her."

"Honestly——"

He waved her silent with a feeling that his own time was short.

"I didn't want to give you the idea that all actresses are as superficial as Peppy. It's a fine career. Lots of intelligent women go into it now."

What was it that he wanted to tell her? There was something in that eager little face that he longed to help.

He shook his head from side to side when Bryan asked him once more if he would like to lie down.

"Of course, it's better to do things than to talk about them," he said, catching his breath with an effort.

He choked on the coffee. "Nobody wants a lot of bad actresses. But it would be nice if all girls were to do *some*thing."

As his weakness increased he felt that, perhaps, it was this pretty little girl's face he was fighting. Then he fainted.

Afterwards he was on his feet with Bryan's arm supporting him.

"No. . . . Here on Gwen's sofa . . . till I can get the doctor. . . . Gently. . . . There you are. . . . Gwen, I want you to stay in the room a minute."

She was thinking:

"Jason will be here any time now." She wished her father would hurry at the phone. Growing up during her mother's illness had inevitably made her callous about such things.

Their doctor lived almost across the street. When he arrived, she and her father retired to his study.

"What do you think, daddy? Will Mr. Harrison have to go to a hospital?"

"I don't know whether they'll want to move him."

"What about Jason then?"

Abstracted, he only half heard her. "I hope it's nothing serious about Mr. Harrison, but did you notice the color of his face?"

The doctor came into the study and held a quiet conversation with him, from which Gwen caught the words "trained nurse," and "I'll call the drugstore."

As Bryan started into the other room, she said:

"Daddy, if Jason and I went out——"

She broke off as he turned.

"You and Jason aren't going out. I told you that."

"But if Mr. Harrison's got to stay in the guest room right next door, where you can hear every word——"

She stopped again at the expression in her father's face when what she was saying dawned on him.

"Call Jason right away and tell him not to come," he said. He shook his head from side to side: "Good Lord! Whose little girl are you?"

III

Six days later Gwen came home, propelling herself as if she were about to dive into a ditch just ahead. She wore a sort of hat that evidently heaven had sent down upon her. It had lit as an ornament on her left temple, and when she raised her hand to her head, it slid— the impression being that it was held by an invisible elastic, which might snap at any moment and send it, with a zip, back into space.

"Where did you get it?" the cook asked enviously as she came in through the pantry entrance.

"Get what?"

"Where did you get it?" her father asked as she came into his study.

"This?" Gwen asked incredulously.

"It's all right with me."

The maid had followed her in, and he said, in answer to her question:

"We'll have the same diet ordered for Mr. Harrison. Wait a minute—if Gwen's hat floats out the window, take a shotgun out of the closet—and see if you can bring it down, like a duck."

In her room, Gwen removed the article of discussion, putting it delicately on her dresser for present admiration. Then she went to pay her daily visit to Mr. Harrison.

He was so much better that he was on the point of getting up. When Gwen came in, he sent the nurse for some water and lay back momentarily. To Gwen he looked more formidable as he got better. His hair, from lack of cutting, wasn't like the smooth coiffures of her friends. She wished her father knew handsomer people.

"I'm about to get up and make my arrangements to go back to New York to work. Before I go, though, I want to tell you something."

"All right, Mr. Harrison. I'm listening."

"It's seldom you find beauty and intelligence in the same person. When you do they have to spend the first part of their life terribly afraid of a flame that they will have to put out someday——"

"Yes, Mr. Harrison——"

"——and sometimes they spend the rest of their life trying to wake up that same flame. Then it's like a kid trying to make a bonfire out of two sticks, only this time one of the sticks is the beauty they have lost and the other stick is the intelligence they haven't cultivated—and the two sticks won't make a bonfire—and they just think that life has done them a dirty trick, when the truth is these two sticks would *never* set fire to each other. And now go call the nurse for me, Gwen." As she left the room he called after her, "Don't be too hard on your father."

She turned around from the door—"What do you mean, don't be hard on father?"

"He loved somebody who was beautiful, like you."

"You mean mummy?"

"You do look like her. Nobody could ever actually be like her." He broke off to write a check for the nurse, and as if he was impelled by something outside himself he added, "So did many other men." He brought himself up sharply and asked the nurse, "Do I owe anything more to the night nurse?" Then once again to Gwen:

"I want to tell you about your father," he said. "He never got over your mother's death, never will. If he is hard on you, it is because he loves you."

"He's never hard on me," she lied.

"Yes, he is. He is unjust sometimes, but your mother——" He broke off and said to the nurse, "Where's my tie?"

"Here it is, Mr. Harrison."

After he had left the house in a flurry of telephoning, Gwen took her bath, weighted her fresh, damp hair with curlers, and drew herself a mouth with the last remnant from a set of varicolored lipsticks that had belonged to her mother. Encountering her father in the hall she looked at him closely in the light of what Mr. Harrison had said, but she only saw the father she had always known.

"Daddy, I want to ask you once more. Jason has invited me to go to the movies with him tonight. I thought you wouldn't mind—if there were four of us. I'm not absolutely sure Dizzy can come, but I think so. Since Mr. Harrison's been here I haven't been able to have any company."

"Don't do anything about it until you've had your dinner," Bryan said. "What's the use of having an admirer if you can't dangle him a little?"

"Dangle how, what do you mean?"

"Well, I just meant make him wait."

"But, daddy, how could I make him wait when he's the most important boy in town?"

"What is this all about?" he demanded. "Seems to be a question of whether this prep-school hero has his wicked way with you or whether I have mine. And anyhow, it's just possible that something more amusing will turn up."

Gwen seemed to have no luck that night—on the phone Dizzy said:

"I'm almost sure I can go, but I don't know absolutely."

"You call me back whatever happens."

"You call me. Mother thinks I can go, but she doesn't think she can do anything now, 'cause there's something under the sink and father hasn't come home."

"The sink!"

"We don't know exactly what it is; it may be a water main or something. That's why everybody's afraid to go downstairs. I can't tell you anything definite until father comes home."

"Dizzy! I don't know what you're talking about."

"We're so upset out here too. I'll explain when I see you. Anyhow, mother's telling me to put the phone down"—there was a momentary interruption—"so they can get to the plumber."

Then the phone hung up with an impact that suggested that all the plumbers in the world were arriving in gross.

Immediately the phone rang again. It was Jason.

"Well, how about it, can we go to the movies?"

"I don't know. I just finished talking to Dizzy. The water main's busted and she has to have a plumber."

"Can't you go to the picture whether she can or not? I've got the car and our chauffeur."

"No, I can't go alone and Dizzy's got this thing."

The impression in Gwen's voice was that plague was raging in the suburbs.

"What?"

"Never mind, never mind. I don't understand it myself. If you want to know more about it call up Dizzy."

"But Peppy Velance is in *Night Train* at the Eleanora Duse Theater—you know, the little place just about two blocks from where you live."

There was a long pause. Then Gwen's voice said:

"A-l-l right. I'll go whether Dizzy can go or not."

She met her father presently with a guilty feeling, but before she could speak he said:

"Put on your hat—*and* your rubbers; feels stormy outside; plans are changed and we're dining out."

"Daddy, I don't want to go out. I've got homework to do."

He was disappointed.

"I'd rather stay here," Gwen continued. "I'm expecting company."

At the false impression she was giving she felt something go out of her. With an attempt at self-justification she added, "Daddy, I get good marks at school, and just because I happen to like some boys——"

Bryan tied his muffler again and bent over to pull on his overshoes. "Good-by," he said.

"What do you mean?" inquired Gwen uncertainly.

"I merely said good-by, darling."

"But you kind of scared me, daddy, you talk as if you were going away forever."

"I won't be late. I just thought you might come along, because someone amusing might be there."

"I don't want to go, daddy."

IV

But after her father had gone it was no fun sitting beside the phone waiting for Jason to call. When he did phone, she started downstairs to meet him—she was still in a bad humor—a fact that she displayed to one of the series of trained nurses that had been taking care of Mr. Harrison. This one had just come in and she wore blue glasses, and Gwen said with unfamiliar briskness:

"I don't know where Mr. Harrison is; I think he was going to meet daddy at some party and I guess they will be back sometime."

On her way down in the elevator she thought: "But I do know where daddy is."

"Stop!" she said to the elevator man. "Take me upstairs again."

He brought the car to rest.

But a great stubbornness seemed to have come over Gwen with her decision to be disobedient.

"No, go on down," she said.

It haunted her though when she met Jason and they trudged their way through the gathering snowstorm to the car.

They had scarcely started off before there was a short struggle. "No, I won't kiss you," Gwen said. "I did that once and the boy that kissed me told about it. Why should I? Nobody does that any more—at my age anyhow."

"You're fourteen."

"Well, wait till I'm fifteen then. Maybe it'll be the thing to do by that time."

They sank back in opposite corners of the car. "Then I guess you won't like this picture," said Jason, "because I understand it's pretty hot stuff. When Peppy Velance gets together with this man in the dive in Shanghai I understand——"

"Oh, skip it," Gwen exploded.

She scarcely knew why she had liked him so much an hour before.

The snow had gathered heavily on the portico of the theater with the swirl of a Chesapeake Bay blizzard, and she was glad of the warmth within. Momentarily, as the newsreel unwound, she forgot her ill-humor, forgot her unblessed excursion into the night—forgot everything except that she had not told the nurse where her father could be found.

At the end of the newsreel she said to Jason:

"Isn't there a drugstore where I could phone home, where we could go out to for just a minute?"

"But the feature's going on in just a minute," he objected, "and it's snowing so hard."

All through the shorts, though, it worried her, so much that in a scene where Mickey Mouse skated valiantly over the ice she seemed to see snow falling into the theater too. Suddenly she grabbed Jason's arm and shook him as if to shake herself awake—though she didn't feel asleep—because the snow was falling. It was falling in front of the screen in drips and then in larger pebblelike pieces and then in a scatter of what looked like snowballs. Other people must have noticed the same phenomenon at the same time, for the projecting machine went off with a click and left the house dark; the dim house lights went on and the four ushers on duty in the little picture house ran down the aisles with confused expressions to see what the trouble was.

Gwen heard a quick twitter of alarm behind her; a stout man who had stumbled over them coming in said in an authoritative voice, "Say, I think the ceiling is caving in." And immediately several people rose around them.

"Hold on," the man cried. "Don't anybody lose their heads."

It was one of those uncertain moments in a panic where tragedy might intervene by an accidental word, and as if realizing this a temporary hush came over the crowd. The ushers stopped in their tracks. The first man to see and direct the situation was the projector operator who came out from his booth and leaned over the balcony, crying down:

"The snow has broken through the roof. Everybody go out the side exits marked with the little red lights. No, I said the side exits—the little red lights." Trouble was developing at the main entrance too, but he didn't want them to know about it. "Don't rush; you're just risking your own lives. You men down there crack anybody that even looks as if they were going to run."

After an uncertain desperate moment the crowd decided to act together.

They filed slowly out through the emergency exits, some of them half afraid even to look toward the screen now only a white blank almost imperceptible through the interior snowstorm that screened it in turn. They all behaved well, as American crowds do, and they were out in the adjoining street and alley before the roof gave way altogether.

Gwen went out calmly.

What she felt most strongly in the street with the others was that the durn snow might have waited a little longer because Peppy Velance's picture was about to start.

V

The manager had been the last to leave and he was now telling the anxious crowd that everyone had left the theater before the roof fell in. It was only then that Gwen thought of Jason and realized that he was no longer with her——

That, in fact, from the moment of the near calamity he had not been beside her at all—but just might have been snowed under by the general collapse. Then—as she joined the throng of those who had lost each other and were finding each other again in the confusion—her eye fell upon him on the outskirts of the crowd and she started toward him.

She ran against policemen coming up and small boys rushing toward the accident and she was held up by the huge drift of snow that still gathered about the fallen portico.

When she was clear of the crowd, Jason was somehow out of sight. But she had a dollar in her pocket, and she hesitated between trying to get a taxi or walking the few blocks home. She decided on the latter.

The snow that had brought down the movie house continued. She had meant to be home surely before her father and had calculated on only one hour of time that she would never be able to account for to herself—but time she knew that sooner or later she would account for to her father.

As she walked along she thought that she had made the nurse wait, too, but now she was almost home and she could straighten that out. As she passed the second block she thought of Jason with contempt, and thought:

"If *he* couldn't wait for me why should I wait for *him*?"

She reached the apartment prepared to face her father with the truth and what necessary result would evolve.

VI

There was a coat of snow on her shoulders as she came into the apartment.

Her father in the sitting room heard her key in the lock and came to the door before she opened it. "I have been worried," he said. "You've never gone out before against my orders. What happened?"

"We went to see Peppy Velance at the small theater just over a couple of blocks from here and, daddy, the roof fell in."

"What roof?"

"The roof of the theater."

"What!"

"Yes, daddy, the roof fell in."

"Was anybody killed?"

"No, they got us all out first. Jason didn't bring me home, but I saw him afterward and I know that he's all right, and the man said nobody was hurt."

"I'm glad I didn't think of all that."

"It was the snow," said Gwen. "I know you're pretty sore, but it's been so dull this whole week, with Mr. Harrison sick and this is the last Peppy Velance was going to be at the Eleanora Duse——"

"Peppy Velance was here. She left ten minutes ago. She was waiting to see you."

"What?"

"You saw her tonight, even if you didn't know it. She flew down from New York to see Mr. Harrison about some business, but you seemed to be in an awful hurry. Mr. Harrison didn't expect her so soon. We brought her back here because I knew that you might like to meet her properly."

"*Daddy!*"

"I suppose you didn't recognize her because she had on blue glasses, but she took them off, and when she's got them off she looks just as human as anyone else."

Stricken, Gwen sat down and repeated, "Was she here, daddy?"

"Well, Mr. Harrison seems to think so and he ought to know."

"Where is Peppy Velance now?"

"She and Mr. Harrison had plans to catch the midnight train to New York. He left you his regards. Say, you haven't caught cold, have you?"

Gwen brushed at her eyes, "No, these are only snowflakes. Daddy, do you mean that she was honestly here all that time while I was out?"

"Yes, daughter, but don't cry about it. She left you a little box of lipstick with her name on it and it's on the table."

"I never thought of her like that," Gwen said slowly. "I thought there were always a lot of—you know—a lot of attractive men hanging around her. I guess why I didn't recognize her was because there weren't any men hanging around her. Go on, daddy; tell me—at least, was she attractive—like mummy was?"

"She wasn't like mummy, but she was very nice—I hope you didn't catch cold."

"I don't think so." She sniffed experimentally, "No, I'm sure I didn't. Isn't it funny I went out and the blizzard came? I wish I'd stayed here where it was safe and warm——" On her way to her room she ruminated aloud:

"I guess most important things happen inside the house, don't they, daddy?"

"You go to bed."

"All right, daddy."

Her door closed gently. What went on behind it he would never know. He wrote her a short note saying:

"Peppy Velance and Mr. Harrison are coming to dinner tomorrow night." He stood it up against the English-history book on the table. Then he moved it to rest against the little tin satchel that the maid would fill with sandwiches for school in the morning.

Esquire

In 1934 Fitzgerald began publishing autobiographical articles in *Esquire*, of which the most significant were the three "Crack-Up" essays in 1936. His first *Esquire* story, "The Fiend," appeared in January 1935. Arnold Gingrich, the editor of *Esquire*, was a staunch admirer of Fitzgerald's prose and would publish virtually anything that he submitted. The flaw in this arrangement was that *Esquire* paid only $250 per contribution, a large cut from the $3000 *The Saturday Evening Post* was paying him in the Thirties. At first Fitzgerald sent Gingrich stories that were not placeable in "family magazines"—"The Fiend" and "The Night Before Chancellorsville." But he soon began writing stories especially for *Esquire*, experimenting with condensed or elliptical forms of 1500-2000 words that were much easier to write than 5000-word *Post* stories. Between 1934 and 1940 Fitzgerald sold forty-four articles and stories to *Esquire*—eight of which appeared posthumously in 1941.

In July 1937 Fitzgerald went to Hollywood where he was on the MGM payroll for eighteen months and then free-lanced at other studios until his death in December 1940. During the time he was working on screenplays he lacked the energy to write extended stories. After 1937 Fitzgerald never again sold a commercial-length story. The talent that had provided more than 100 *Post*-type stories was bankrupt.

Fitzgerald's *Esquire* stories were very uneven. "Financing Finnegan" (1938) and "The Lost Decade" (1939) were first-rate; "Design in Plaster" was selected for *Best Short Stories of 1940*. A few were puzzling—for example, "Shaggy's Morning" and "The Ants at Princeton" (which *Esquire* classified as satire). The most sustained effort he made for *Esquire* was the series of seventeen stories about Pat Hobby, a broken-down Hollywood hack. This collection includes six of the *Esquire* stories: "Three Acts of Music," "An Author's Mother," "The Guest in Room Nineteen," "In the Holidays," "On an Ocean Wave," and "The Woman from Twenty-One."

Fitzgerald's *Esquire* work was important in his career simply because it kept him writing; and during the last three-and-a-half years of his life he sold stories only to *Esquire*. In the summer of 1939 Fitzgerald's movie income had run out, and the $250 *Esquire* checks mattered terribly while he was trying to complete *The Last Tycoon*.

Three Acts of Music

(*Esquire*, May 1936)

"Three Acts of Music" was written in Baltimore in February 1936. Arnold Gingrich, the editor of *Esquire*, has reported how this story was written to cover the advances that had been made to Fitzgerald:

> I said that just to satisfy the auditors, and to be able to say that a script—perhaps needing some revision—had been received on such and such a date so the account wouldn't look like all going out and nothing coming in, Scott should write three purported articles simply saying why he couldn't write. I suggested that he put down anything that came into his head, as automatic writing in the Gertrude Stein manner, or that, if even that were beyond his powers of concentration, he simply copy out the same couple of sentences over and over, often enough to fill eight or ten pages, if only to say I can't write stories about young love for *The Saturday Evening Post*.
>
> I also hoped that there might be a therapeutic value in writing these three non-articles, in that the mere writing about why he couldn't write might in itself prime the pump enough to get him started writing again. Actually that's what happened. The first three articles were: "The Crack-Up," "Pasting It Together," and "Handle With Care"; and then along came a fourth, although the series as such was finished, called "Three Acts of Music" (*The Armchair Esquire*, 1958).

I

They could hardly hear it for awhile. It was a slow gleam of pale blue and creamy pink. Then there was a tall room where there were many young people and finally they began to feel it and hear it.

What were they—no. This is about music.

He went to the band-stand; the piano player let him lean over his shoulder to read:

"From *No, No, Nanette* by Vincent Youmans."

"Thank you," he said, "I'd like to drop something in the horn but when an interne has a dollar bill and two coins in the world he might get married instead."

"Never mind, doctor. That's about what I had when I got married last winter."

When he came back to the table she said:

"Did you find out who wrote that thing?"

"*No!* When do we go from here?"

"When they stop playing 'Tea for Two.' "

Later as she came out of the women's dressing room, she asked the man: "Who played it?"

"My God, how do I know. The band played it."

It dripped out the door now:

Tea . . .

   . . . two

Two . . .

   . . . tea

"We can never get married. I'm not even a nurse yet."

"Well, let's kill the idea—let's spend the rest of our lives going around and listening to tunes. What did you say that writer's name was?"

"What did *you* say? You went over and looked, dint you?"

"*Didn't* you," he corrected her.

"You're so swell all the time."

"Well, at least I found out who wrote it."

"Who?"

"Somebody named Vincent Youmans."

She hummed it over:

And you . . .

      . . . for me

And me . . .

      . . . for you

Al—

   o-

   o-

   n-n . . .

Their arms went about each other for a moment in the corridor outside the red room.

"If you lost the dollar bill and the other nickel I'd still marry you," she said.

II

This is now years later but there was still music. There was "All Alone" and "Remember" and "Always" and "Blue Skies" and "How About Me." He was back from Vienna but it didn't seem to matter so much as it had before.

"Wait in here a moment," she said outside the operating room. "Turn on the radio if you want to."

"You've got mighty important, haven't you?"

He turned on:

Re-mem-ber
>*the night*
>*the night*
>*you said—*

"Are you high-hatting me?" she inquired, "or did medicine begin and end in Vienna?"

"No it didn't," he said humbly. "I'm impressed—evidently you can supervise the resident or the surgeons—"

"I've got an operation of Doctor Menafee's coming in and there's a tonsillectomy that's got to be postponed. I'm a working girl. I'm supervising the operating room."

"But you'll go out with me tonight—won't you? We'll get them to play 'All Alone.' "

She paused, regarding him.

"Yes, I've been all alone for a lot of time now. I'm somebody—you don't seem to realize it. Say who is this Berlin anyhow? He was a singer in a dive, wasn't he? My brother ran a roadhouse and he gave me money to get started with. But I thought I was away from all that. Who is this Irving Berlin? I hear he's just married a society girl—"

"He's just married—"

She had to go: "Excuse me. I've got to fire an interne before this gets going."

"I was an interne once. I understand."

They were out at last. She was making three thousand a year now and he was still being of a conservative old Vermont family.

"This Irving Berlin now. Is he happy with this Mackay girl? Those songs don't sound—"

"I guess he is. The point is how happy are you?"

"Oh, we discussed that so long ago. What do I matter? I matter in a big way—but when I was a little country girl your fambly decided—

"Not *you*," she said at the alarm in his eyes. "I know *you* never did."

"I knew something else about you. I knew three things—that you were a Yonkers' girl—and didn't pronounce the language like I did—"

"And that I wanted to marry you. Let's forget it. Your friend Mr. Berlin can talk better than we can. Listen to him."

"I'm listening."

"No. But *lis*den, I mean."

Not for just a year but—

"Why do you say my friend Mr. Berlin? I never saw the guy."

"I thought maybe you'd met him in Vienna in all these years."

"I never saw him."

"He married the girl—didn't he?"

"What are you crying about?"

"I'm not crying. I just said he married the girl—didn't he? Isn't that all right to say? When you've come so far—when—"

"You are crying," he said.

"No, I'm not. Honest. It's this work. It wears down your eyes. Let's dance."

—o

   —ver

      —head

They were playing.

Blue

   skies

      o

         ver

            head

She looked up out of his arms suddenly.

"Do you suppose they're happy?"

"Who?"

"Irving Berlin and the Mackay girl?"

"How should I know whether they're happy? I tell you I never knew them—never saw them."

A moment later she whispered:

"We all knew them."

III

This story is about tunes. Perhaps the tunes swing the people or the people the tunes. Anyhow:

"We'll never do it," he remarked with some finality.

"*Smoke gets in your eyes,*" said the music.

"Why?"

"Because we're too old. You wouldn't want to anyhow—you've got that job at Duke's hospital."

"I just got it."

"Well, you've just got it. And it's going to pay you four thousand."

"That's probably half what you make."

"You mean you want to try it anyhow?"

When your heart's on fire

"No. I guess you're right. It's too late."

"—Too late for what?"

"Just too late—like you told me."

"But I didn't mean it."

"You were right though. . . . Be quiet:

Lovely

      to look at

    Romantic

      *to know**

"You're all those things in the song," he said passionately.

"What? Lovely to look at and all that? You should have told me that fifteen years ago. Now I'm superintendent of a woman's hospital." She added: "And I'm still a woman." Then she added: "But I'm not the woman you knew any more. I'm another woman."

—lovely to look at

the orchestra repeated.

"Yes, I was lovely to look at when I was nothing—when I couldn't even talk plain—"

"I never knew—"

"Oh let's not go over it. Listen to what they're playing."

"It's called 'Lovely to Look At.' "

"Who's it by?"

"A man named Jerome Kern."

"Did you meet *him* when you went back to Europe the second time? Is he a friend of yours?"

"I never saw him. What gives you the impression I met all these big shots? I'm a doctor. Not a musician."

She wondered about her own bitterness.

"I suppose because all those years I met nobody," she said finally. "Sure, I once saw Doctor Kelly at a distance. But here I am—because I got good at my job."

"And here I am, because—"

"You'll always be wonderful to me. What did you say this man's name was?"

"Kern. And I didn't say it *was*. I said it *is*."

"That's the way you used to talk to me. And now both of us are fat and—sort of middle-aged. We never had much. Did we?"

"It wasn't my fault."

---

*"Lovely to Look At" is misquoted in this story—ed.

"It wasn't anybody's fault. It was just meant to be like that. Let's dance. That's a good tune. What did you say was this man's name?"

"Kern."

They

> *asked me how I*
> *knew-ew-ew—*

"We've had all that anyhow, haven't we?" she asked him. "All those people—that Youmans, that Berlin, that Kern. They must have been through hell to be able to write like that. And we sort of listened to them, didn't we?"

"But my God, that's so little—" he began but her mood changed and she said:

"Let's not say anything about it. It was all we had—everything we'll ever know about life. What were their names—you knew their names."

"Their names were—"

"Didn't you ever know *any* of them in that fifteen years around Europe?"

"I never saw one of them."

"Well, I never will." She hesitated before the wide horizon of how she might have lived. How she might have married this man, borne him children, died for him—of how she had lived out of sordid poverty and education—into power—and spinsterhood. And she cared not a damn for her man any more because he had never gone off with her. But she wondered how these composers had lived. Youmans and Irving Berlin and Jerome Kern and she thought that if any of their wives turned up in this hospital she would try to make them happy.

"Trouble"

(*The Saturday Evening Post*, 6 March 1937)

" 'Trouble' " was written in Baltimore in June 1936. The *Post* paid $2000 for it—half of Fitzgerald's 1931 peak price. This story marks the termination of Fitzgerald's career as a successful magazinist; it was the last story he sold to the *Post*. When he wrote " 'Trouble' " Fitzgerald was again trying to launch a series, but the *Post* was not receptive to the plan. Adelaide Neall of the *Post* informed Harold Ober: "Frankly, I think his story would have been a lot better if he had given it a little more definite ending. We have often found that when writers have a series in mind they sometimes hold over material for a future story that could be used in the one they are working on. . . . if Mr. Fitzgerald says anything to you, you can advise him to create a new heroine."

The annual turtle race at Luke Harkless Hospital once attained considerable celebrity because it was news-reeled and broadcast on an Eastern hookup, but this year the hospital's governing board put its collective foot down. The race gave an undesirable brand of publicity to a great, serious institution, looked like advertising, and so on, and had better remain what it was in the beginning—a June-day diversion organized by some ingenious interns a dozen years ago.

As a result of this decision, Trouble's tumble off the sun deck into the arms of Dr. Dick Wheelock, Resident in Orthopedics, is officially unrecorded. And that is a pity, for it would be nice to have preserved the expression on her lovely face.

It happened like this:

Doctor Wheelock was one of four judges, attired in tail coats and top hats, who were stationed at the four corners of the tennis court where the race takes place. Their business was to see which one among the dozen turtles released simultaneously from a cage in the center first finds its way to the rim of a surrounding chalk circle; a voyage, if navigated in a straight line, of about fifteen feet.

There were other officials: An announcer with a mike, a bookie—for each turtle represents one section of the hospital—and a remarkable jazz band made up of members of the staff and composed that year of The Spirit of Seventy-six, Haile Selassie under an umbrella, a guitar and bass drum, and two colored urchins, who furnished the only real music with lively harmonicas.

But the judges, wilting damply in their finery, were by far the most conspicuous. It was thus that Trouble had been impelled to fix her eyes upon Doctor Wheelock's profile during the intervals between heats; so that by the time she fell into his arms, she was well acquainted with the handsome and rather haughty profile, with the back of his head, and the top of his hat, that glistened in the June sun.

Trouble was a trained nurse, at present on general night duty in the private wards. Her real name was Glenola McClurg, but though she was considered an excellent young nurse, she had somehow acquired the nickname "Trouble" and was never known by any other name. Men encountering her in a corridor often thought they knew why. She was Trouble all right, all right. Starting to smile a hundred feet away, she would breeze along, stop and wheel, smart as the military, and come up to the interns, or whoever it was, and figuratively press against them. All she had to say was: "Good morning, Doctor This; good morning, Doctor That"—and then, knowing she'd registered, lean back for a moment against the wall, conscious—oh, completely conscious—of what she had done to their next hours.

Her face was rather like the autumn page from the kitchen calendars of thirty years ago, vivid October eyes, a hazel canopy full of grief that looked down over a tiny childhood scar to her mouth, as if to shadow its smallest sadness and light up its faintest joy.

But this depth of feeling in her face rather belied her, for she was a light-hearted, sensuous, hard-working girl, with iron nerves and a passionate love of life—one who had grown up in sordid poverty, to whom the hospital was the opening up of a wide radiant world. This was before she fell into Doctor Wheelock's arms.

It was not deliberate, though certain malicious spirits intimated later that it was. The central campus of the hospital was jammed. Two thousand doctors and patients and visitors and nurses and probationers swarmed over the sun deck, packed like cigarettes around the tennis court, or leaned from a hundred windows, while on the old bell tower above, a solitary steeple jack quit his work and looked down precariously, overcome with wonder. Trouble and some other nurses had crawled between two wheel chairs on the sun deck and sat with their feet dangling over the edge, while the voices of the crowd rang around them, cheering on their favorite entry:

"Come on, Pathology!"

"Shake it up, Surgery!"

"Come on, Hick's Memorial!"

"Hey, Eye-and-Ear! Don't turn around! You're at the line! You're at the *line*!"

—as the turtles rushed, wavered, spun, reversed or sometimes settled unconcernedly to sleep.

It was a huge hospital and there were thirty entries, from the offices to the nurses' training school, so that there were numerous heats, and many people had waited for the final before appearing. Now as the afternoon waned they hurried forth from duties in the building and pressed forward upon those in front. Trouble, concealed by the back of the wheel chair, felt it slide suddenly from her grasp, felt what seemed a mighty knee in her back, and then, with a sort of yelp, flung off into space, clawing desperately at unsubstantial air.

Dr. Dick Wheelock was not a stiff man, but he was formidable in rather an old-fashioned way. You might say that at twenty-eight he was already the sort of man to whom no stranger would have shown any familiarity, even if he had entered an Oregon logging camp in a morning coat and spats. This was because he had a certain dignity of heart that went deeper than his proud carriage, and his first concern was to find out if Trouble were hurt. She had, in fact, twisted her ankle, but she scarcely knew it at the time.

"I'm all right!" she said breathlessly. "Oh, for heaven's sakes, how shall I get out of here? Everybody's looking and laughing at me!"

Dick Wheelock laughed himself.

"I guess they're laughing at both of us." He escorted her toward the side line. "I think we've made quite a contribution to the afternoon, don't you?"

She looked at him and her heart went out of her and she adored him.

"Are you sure you're not hurt?" he asked again.

"Oh, no, I'm all right."

And suddenly, for a minute, just before he left her, she looked him in the eye and became Trouble for him—Trouble so white, so lovely that it didn't immediately identify itself as such. It was sheer Trouble. It was the essence of Trouble—Trouble personified, challenging!

Trouble.

"Oh, I'm so much obliged," she said.

He tipped his silk hat.

"I've got to get back to my duties. This is the final heat." He threw back his head with a faint chortle, "Excuse me, but it was funny! An angel dropping out of heaven into my arms!"

All that afternoon she remembered just those words. Somehow they took all the humiliation out of the experience. Trouble was not one to brood, but the absurdity of the situation was extreme, and in half a dozen words he had made it all right. Long before supper, in spite of the kidding to which she was inevitably subjected, she was glad it happened.

She did not get far with supper that night, however. Halfway through the main course, a waitress brought word that a lady wanted to see her in the sitting room.

"A lady? What lady?"

After some concentration, the waitress repeated a name, and a curious expression came over Trouble's face. She threw down her napkin and got up.

Going through the corridor, she took a quick look at her hair in a glass door, and she was glad she had replaced her mussed uniform after the catastrophe of the afternoon.

Her visitor arose to greet her, and the two women exchanged instantaneous appraising glances, but while Trouble's expression continued to hold a touch of suspicion, the older woman's melted into a soft charm, and she spoke in a quiet, cultivated voice:

"I've wanted to meet you, Miss McClurg. My son, Frederic Winslow, has talked so much of you."

"Oh, yes, we've got to be quite good friends."

"Can we sit down for a minute? I hope I'm not too close to your dinner hour."

"Oh, no," lied Trouble.

"I tried to find you earlier, but the field there was so full of people for that potato race."

"It was a turtle race."

"Oh, a turtle race? I didn't know that turtles raced."

"Yes," said Trouble uncomfortably, "they do. Very slowly though."

"It must be interesting. My son told me he considered coming, but I thought he said it was potatoes."

Recovering her poise somewhat, Trouble couldn't help saying: "They'd go even slower than turtles."

"What? Oh, yes." Mrs. Winslow's expression became graver. "Miss McClurg, I've always been in my son's confidence, and many times in the year that Fred's known you, he's talked about you and told me how desperately in love with you he is."

"He just thinks he is," said Trouble.

"Oh, no. He loves you. And you're the only person that can do anything with him—I know that too. The six months he didn't drink were entirely due to you. At first I thought it was just an infatuation, and then, even without seeing you, I began to realize it wasn't. Miss McClurg, why did you throw him over?"

"Why, I didn't!" exclaimed Trouble. "We just had a little quarrel because he didn't want me to see any man but him. Or, he said, he'd start drinking again."

"And you said, 'Go ahead.' "

"Of course, I did!" exclaimed Trouble. "Did he expect me to go down on my knees and beg him? Mrs. Winslow, I'm not in love with your son; I like him tremendously when he—behaves himself, but I'm not in love with him, and I never pretended I was."

"He told me that too."

Liking the woman, Trouble spoke frankly:

"I think Fred thought I'd jump at the chance when he first asked me to marry him, because you're sort of"—a faintly defiant look came into her eyes—"because you're sort of rich, and society people, and all that, but I couldn't marry a man I didn't love."

"I see." Mrs. Winslow hesitated. "I thought maybe it was because you were afraid of us—because you thought we were snobbish and—what is it they say now?—high-hat and all that. I asked him to bring you to see us half a dozen times, but he said you wouldn't come."

"No, it wasn't that," denied Trouble. She, in turn, hesitated. "It's partly because he goes on these bats, and I wouldn't want to be nurse to my husband, and it's partly what I said."

Mrs. Winslow nodded.

"I understand. And I see you've made up your mind—and I see you're a girl after my own heart. But I hope you'll find time to see Fred sometimes, and if things do happen to clear up, I hope some day, perhaps——"

She left the sentence in mid-air.

"Oh, I don't mind seeing him, Mrs. Winslow. I'd love to—any time I'm free."

"Thank you." The older woman rose. "I won't keep you any longer; it must be near your dinner hour. And please don't mention to him that I called. He wouldn't like it."

"No, I won't, Mrs. Winslow."

They shook hands, and Mrs. Winslow went down the corridor thinking that this oddly attractive little country girl with the gorgeous eyes and the square little chin might be just the person for her son, and hoping she would think of him differently later.

But all Trouble was thinking on her way back to her supper was:

"An angel dropping out of heaven into my arms—an angel dropping——"

II

Dr. Dick Wheelock had an odd skepticism about trained nurses—
a skepticism shared by many men in his profession. He thought that a
true scientific vocation would have made them take the extra year to
obtain an M.D.—forgetting that few of them had the necessary
preliminary education and still fewer the necessary money. His
feeling was less than logical and can best be illumined as a facet of the
struggle between the sexes—the man insisting upon mastery and then
being faintly contemptuous of the slave he has made.

So he had tried conquests in that direction, and even those were
several years in the past. The peculiar force of Trouble's personality
had come as a shock on the day of the turtle race, and he had asked her
name, but after that, a press of work drove her from his mind. A few
days later, having occasion to pass through the private wards, he
nearly went by her in the corridor without speaking.

Then he remembered and turned back.

"Hello."

"Hello, Doctor Wheelock. I thought you'd forgotten me."

"Certainly not. I meant to find out if you'd broken anything
when you made that spectacular dive."

"And you were the victim."

"I thought maybe it was the turtles made you do it. You began to
think there was a lake down there."

She laughed.

"Maybe. Or maybe it was just an original way of attracting your
attention."

She looked him straight in the eye, and he smiled, rather attracted
by the boldness of the invitation.

"I did sprain my ankle," she said, "but I didn't realize it till I got
out of bed next morning."

He hesitated, uncertain whether to pursue the acquaintance
further, yet unable to move on down the corridor.

"Have you done anything about it?"

"No, but I ought to."

"Come over to the Orthopedic Clinic when you're off duty and
I'll strap it up for you."

"Now?"

"No. I can't now. Sometime this afternoon or tomorrow
morning."

"That's very nice of you, doctor. I've developed a nice little
limp—and it's a nuisance because I'm the number they always call in
a hurry. There's one on every ward."

She was not boasting. It was always: "Miss McClurg can find it," or "Trouble knows where the key is," or "Trouble, for heaven's sake, go and see what's the matter in B 16 and take care of it yourself." She really was a crack nurse—tireless, quick and resourceful—and they were thinking of shifting her to the accident room, where those qualities were much in demand. But the new superintendent of nurses was a somewhat austere lady who had taken one look at Trouble and decided that no girl that pretty could be very serious.

On warm evenings Doctor Wheelock frequently went out into the campus and stood by the grille gate, smoking a few minutes, and listening to the click and scrape of roller skates on the pavement outside and to the Negro patients singing in their building across the way. Tonight, their spirituals, lying suspended on the sweet June air, seemed to have a peculiar melancholy, and he wondered if they were mourning for someone who had departed that day. He recognized the deep bass of Doofus, who had been there two years, and who, Doctor Wheelock had been told, was about to die; his place in the dark choir would be hard to fill.

He threw away his cigarette and started back toward the Orthopedic Clinic. A nurse was going up the steps as he came near, and he saw, first, that she was limping, and, second, that it was Trouble.

"Hello!" he called out of the darkness. At the sound of his voice, she wheeled on the steps and almost fell.

"Take it easy," he said. "You've got a real limp there."

"I guess I have, doctor. I tried to come over this afternoon, but everything seemed to happen at once. If it gets worse, I won't be fit for duty."

"Well, come on up to an operating room and we'll take a look at it."

The elevator hummed upward. He switched on a light and the room sprang into sparse, sterile whiteness.

"Now, if you'll just hop up on this table and get off your stocking, I'll wash my hands and look it over."

He pulled off the adhesive tape and went over the injured member.

"Does that hurt?"

"No. . . . Ouch! That does!"

"You've got a sprain there, all right. A little one, but a sprain. Why don't you lay off for a day?"

"I can't. Everybody's on vacation."

"Well, make the probationers run around for you and save yourself some steps."

He began tearing large strips from a roll of adhesive and sticking them to the side of the table.

"I'm going to make you a regular plaster cast, anyhow, that'll keep you from running away from us."

"Ouch!"

"That's all right. It'll ease up. I wanted to bind it tight. Haven't you got a friend that wears a big shoe you could borrow?"

Suddenly they were not alone. The door swung open and a figure stood there, white against the darkness of the hall.

"Come in, Mrs. Johnston," he said. "I was just strapping an ankle."

"So I see, Doctor Wheelock," said the new superintendent of nurses in a dry, hard voice. . . . "And since when have you been stationed on the orthopedic ward, Miss McClurg?"

"Why, I didn't——"

"I have stood three or four serious breaches of discipline lately, but I simply am not going to permit my nurses to go up into operating rooms with doctors at night."

"Come now, Mrs. Johnston——" began Dick Wheelock, but her voice cut through his:

"Miss McClurg, you might do me the courtesy to stand up when I come in."

Trouble began to roll from the table, but her ankle, half bandaged, caught in the waiting strips of adhesive tape, tangled for a minute, tripped her, and something snapped as she pitched side-ways on the floor with her foot still caught above. In a moment Dick had disentangled her and helped her to her feet, but the leg gave way beneath her and she exclaimed aloud as a burst of pain shot through the ankle joint.

"Now I have got something!" she exclaimed. "I could feel it snap."

"Get back here." Doctor Wheelock boosted her on to the table and his deft fingers went over the ankle bone.

"You certainly have." He turned swiftly on Mrs. Johnston. "Will you kindly get out of here? You've managed to make the girl hurt herself seriously. It's not your province to interfere with a doctor on duty."

"Oh, she's an old busybody!" exploded Trouble, her eyes filling with tears of pain. "Everybody thinks so."

"Oh, they do, do they?" said Mrs. Johnston.

Without another word, she turned swiftly and left the room.

III

"So then," Mrs. Johnston concluded, "I turned and walked out. With Doctor Wheelock looking after me as if he wanted to shoot me."

"What time last night was it?" the superintendent asked.

"About nine o'clock. But there are definite orders about nurses' whereabouts, and Miss McClurg knew perfectly well she should have applied for permission and had another nurse go along with her. At the Medical Center that never would have been tolerated, Doctor Compson."

"Yes, I understand, I understand," said Doctor Compson meditatively. "And I know we can't have nurses saying things like that or we wouldn't have any discipline at all. She's got to go, all right." He sighed and drummed his fingers on the table. "It's too bad. I've heard she was a good nurse. Someone was suggesting her for the accident room."

"I think that's more her face than her competence," said Mrs. Johnston. "She has the sort of way about her that might be particularly attractive—to young doctors. Perhaps you know that her nickname is 'Trouble.' "

"All right—all right. I understand. Bring her in to me and let her speak a word for herself."

"One more thing, Doctor Compson: It's hard for me to keep my nurses in line unless the doctors co-operate by behaving with propriety. At the Medical Center——"

"That's rather in my sphere of judgment, Mrs. Johnston," he interrupted dryly.

Trouble was half expecting the call, but with no particular apprehension. She knew she had lost her temper, but she had seen nurses do that before; and as for being in the operating room, she had no sense of guilt at all, and she knew that Doctor Wheelock would stand behind her.

But when she entered the office and saw the very serious look on Doctor Compson's face and saw Mrs. Johnston standing beside the desk with the face of a gargoyle, she began to feel a faint uneasiness.

"Sit down, Miss McClurg. You seem a little lame."

Discreetly, Trouble answered, "I turned my ankle at the turtle race, doctor. I fell off the sun deck."

"Oh, yes, I heard something about that, but I didn't know it was you." Again he hesitated. "Miss McClurg, I have a difficult duty to perform. Last night you used some insulting words to your superior when she was engaged in the performance of her duty."

They were going to ask for an apology, Trouble guessed. She hated the idea, but she had undoubtedly spoken out of turn. She was utterly unprepared for what followed.

"I'm afraid we have no place for you here, Miss McClurg. The tradition of this institution is one of the most rigid discipline. An incident of this sort, if it took place under other circumstances, might result in serious harm to patients. You were clearly in the wrong. Even that might be forgiven, but your defiance, in the face of a just rebuke, leaves us no alternative."

She stared at him aghast.

"Oh, my!" she exclaimed.

"We're very sorry."

Then she blundered again:

"Didn't Doctor Wheelock——"

"We won't discuss Doctor Wheelock. He has nothing whatever to do with the supervision of nurses."

"Then you mean I have to leave?"

"I'm afraid I do, Miss McClurg."

"Even if—even if I apologize?"

Mrs. Johnston addressed herself to the doctor: "After this affair, I don't think I could continue to keep discipline with Miss McClurg on my staff."

And now Trouble's eyes did not look like October on a calendar. There was December in them—desolation and bleak hail. She was shaking so that she could scarcely trust herself to speak.

"Is that all?" she asked in a dulled voice.

"Unless you have something you want to say."

She shook her head; then, throwing up her chin so that she could avoid looking at Mrs. Johnston, she walked from the room. She walked very slowly, gritting her teeth so as not to limp.

Whatever her faults, Trouble had never lacked character.

Back on the ward there was a note waiting for her at the desk, and with a quick breath of relief, she guessed from whom it came. It read:

Dear Miss McClurg: I'm going away for a few days on a semi-vacation. If it were a real vacation, I'd have stayed over to look after your ankle. But this is a friend and patient that I long ago arranged to see. However, I've spoken to Doctor Donowska and he will look at the ankle every day, and if you decide to lie up, he will come to you. Yours,

R. H. WHEELOCK.

A wave of panic swept over her. She realized that she had counted on his doing something, though what he could do, she did not know. Holding tight to the note, she hurried as fast as she could down the corridor, down an inclined walk onto the campus and across a short cut to the Orthopedic Clinic.

The girl at the desk yielded her attention with maddening leisure.

"Doctor Wheelock? He left not two minutes ago. He was going away for——"

But Trouble was out the door and hastening to the gate where the doctors parked their cars.

Then, twenty feet from the gate, she stopped suddenly. Doctor Wheelock was there indeed, but not alone. He was far from being alone. A lovely shining girl, all shining with blonde hair under the sort of hat that wouldn't be in the department stores for another month, the very girl for whom such things were made, sat at the wheel of a long, glittering open car, and a purely ornamental chauffeur was stowing Doctor Wheelock's bag in the back seat. As Doctor Wheelock got in beside the girl, Trouble saw them look at each other, and saw that the girl's eyes were starry and expectant; Doctor Wheelock's eyes she could not see.

The car moved off in powerful silence, and Trouble stood for a moment struck motionless by the first doubt she had ever had that life was good. Then she hobbled on across the street toward her room in Nurses' Row. She felt as if she were trailing behind her the ruin of her little career, like a tattered train in the street.

IV

It was not so bad as all that, she thought next morning. The Luke Harkless no longer stood alone as the one inspired hospital of America. In placing herself elsewhere, she had only to say truthfully that she had quarreled with the superintendent of nurses on a personal matter. The former superintendent—oh, many others would speak for her, she felt sure; even Doctor Wheelock; but when the name came into her mind, the world turned dark and incomprehensible. It was as if in the space of a week he had become a symbol of all she loved here; he was the fresh strength of coming on duty in the morning; he was the busy silence of the corridor at night; he was the summer sunlight on the red buildings across from her window, and the thrill of hurrying through the winter night just pleasantly a little cold in her thin nurse's cape. He was the majesty of duty she had seen through her young probationer's eyes; the skill of hands, the strength of nerve; he was all that it meant to be ever fearless and never tired. Even, she thought—with horror at the blasphemy—

he was the great stone Christ in the entrance hall. . . .

But he had turned from her. She had aspired too high.

All afternoon her foot throbbed, but she could not bring herself to go and see Doctor Donowska over the way. When the phone rang at eight o'clock, and it was Fred Winslow, sounding entirely sober and asking her to go riding, she answered:

"Yes, I will," and then, because her voice sounded listless, she raised herself to an effort: "Yes, I would love to, Fred. I certainly will."

V

When she went to dinner at the Winslows' country place two nights later, she did not feel it necessary to explain what had happened; her injured ankle accounted well enough for the few days she was taking off.

"Yes, I heard about it," said Fred, on their way out in the car. "Some doctor caught you when you fell. They mentioned it in the newspaper account of the race."

"Oh, did they? I didn't see it."

"It didn't have your name. It just said it was a very pretty nurse and that the doctor didn't seem to mind it a bit."

"I'd like to have read it."

"Did you ever see the doctor again? Who was he?"

"Oh, he was—he was"—she struggled with the name—"a doctor named Wheelock."

Fred Winslow's eyes narrowed a little as he detected the heightened inflections of her voice.

"I bet he's been rushing you ever since."

Trouble groaned.

"Fred, are you going to start that again?"

"I'm sorry." After a minute he added, "But when you're so crazy about a girl that nothing else in the world matters one bit——"

She was silent. It was pleasant to be out in the rushing night in the long open car, not unlike the car in which Doctor Wheelock had embarked on his semi-vacation two days before. It occurred to her that it might be pleasant to drive up to the hospital sometime as a patient, not a very sick patient, in just such a car, and a hat from Paris, and say, rather aloofly, but without any reproach in her voice:

"I think I should prefer to occupy the room we endowed—the Frederic Winslow room. My own doctor is flying down from New York because I'd heard that methods in other cities have become—well, a little antique. Of course, I wanted to come to this funny old dump for old times' sake."

This didn't sound quite right, and she knew there was no hospital like this in the world, from the moment it was built solidly on men instead of bricks—and another image began creeping into her chain of imaginings, so she broke it off. She was a very practical person, Trouble. She would always rather do a thing than think or talk about it.

That was why she was glad that everything was so matter-of-fact at the Winslows' that night. Mrs. Winslow didn't press her hand, as if Trouble had somehow come around to reason; on the contrary, she was accepted as casually as a guest who had often visited there before.

Trouble had done little private nursing and on only one other occasion had she ever entered such a house—to be treated as a goddess when the patient was very sick and as an upper servant when the patient began to grow well. That was all in the game, she knew, but, anyhow, this was quite different. Mr. Winslow teased her about the incident at the turtle race.

"What I want to know is whether you picked your doctor or whether you just jumped at a whole crowd of them."

He seemed to know one or two of the big doctors quite well, appreciating them, and, looking from father to son, Trouble could not help wishing that Fred was like his father, but as the evening waned, that seemed to matter less and less.

The great rooms blurred into a symphony of a thousand notes that she had never heard and did not understand—notes that no radio ever carried into small Virginia villages—from the flashing moment of a single Florentine to the lifelong labor over warp and woof of a whole Circassian family on a carpet, from the porcelains of Ching-tê Chên, which left their factory fifteen hundred years ago, to the latest magnetic rod which Mr. Winslow played like a violin by merely moving a wand near it.

It was all equally incomprehensible to Trouble in detail, but she was quick, and, as a whole, she understood. Later in the evening, as if at Mrs. Winslow's command, a wild summer storm broke out and ranged in white light and thunder up and down the valley, and they insisted she spend the night; the bedroom and the borrowed clothes and the bathroom all went into the gorgeous blur, like the gardens and pools and stables and trout streams next morning.

It was rather terrible to her; it was not austere, it was not a ship cleared for action, but she wanted to forget something and she let the mist settle, growing thicker and thicker.

Forty-eight hours later, on Trouble's insistence that there should be no big wedding, it was agreed that she and Fred would be married next week.

VI

In general, Trouble had found all attractive men equally attractive—the point of view of a man fancy free. Here was Fred, for instance, the very magazine cover of an athlete—he had, in fact, played baseball in college—with a fresh, boyish and rather wistfully appealing face. Sitting opposite him at breakfast at his parents' house a few days after she had reached her decision, he seemed to her as desirable as the others, even a little more so as she began to identify her destiny with his.

Mr. Winslow had been talking with the butler about terrapin, and the subject raised once more a discussion of the turtle race—a matter that apparently refused to die of itself.

It seemed to haunt Fred especially, and when they were alone together, he said:

"I certainly wish I'd been there to catch you. Maybe I'll be able to save your life sometime and then you'll really fall in love with me."

"You don't fall in love with people that save you."

"Are you sure you don't?" He turned to the butler. "Bring me a bottle of beer, Phillips."

"What?" exclaimed Trouble, rather shocked. "Beer at breakfast?"

"Why not? My grandfather always used to start the day with a snifter, but never anything after that."

"You're not your grandfather," said Trouble. "You wouldn't do that way."

"I won't take it if you don't like."

But she shook her head, declining the suggestion.

"Oh, no. I'm not going to be your schoolteacher. Let's get that straight. It's absolutely up to you."

"Trouble, you'll see I'll never abuse liquor again."

She tried to think so, but when they started to town later in the day, she could not help suspecting that he had had a few more. When he opened the car door for her, he forgot the bad ankle until Trouble exclaimed: "Ouch! Wait a minute!"

And then he was too profusely apologetic.

"Why don't you do something about your ankle?" he demanded.

"I'm going to, if it doesn't get better." She had told him a diluted story of her quarrel with the superintendent of nurses and of quitting the hospital, and now she said, "It's not going to be treated at Harkless, though."

Nevertheless, she was going there today for a few minutes to get her back salary and collect a few articles out of her locker.

"Don't be long," Fred said impatiently, when she left the car. "We've got to meet mother for tea."

"We've got hours."

"You want me to come in with you?"

"Oh, no."

"Well, you stay away from that doctor."

She saw that he was not quite joking, and it annoyed her.

"You'll end by putting ideas in my head," she answered.

Though it had been less than a week, she felt as though she had been away from the hospital for years; crossing the campus, she was rather surprised at seeing the same activities continuing. On the court, two interns played tennis under the supervision of convalescents on the sun deck; the male patients of the Psychiatric Clinic were doing something with a basketball in their yard, and outside the Pediatric Clinic, a mother was playing with her child. The grass on the campus already looked a little baked with the summer, the first fresh green was gone.

Only a single nurse was at the desk.

"Trouble! You're not leaving us?"

"I'm afraid I am."

"But why? Where are you going?"

"I'm not sure yet."

"I thought you were just laid up with your ankle."

She collected her things and stopped at the office for the money due her. Then out past the statue that stretched out its arms for the last time; only when she reached the gate did she realize that there were tears on her cheeks. Trouble had been very happy here, put in so much effort and spent so much youth.

Save for the manner of her leaving, she had no regret for anything that had ever happened to her in that square block of hardship and surcease. The endless hum of it would continue when her faint footsteps had long died away—nurses, interns, doctors would change; only the frailty of human flesh would continue, and the communal intelligence of many generations of men to fight against it.

When she reached the car, Fred was not there. Supposing he had gone down to the drugstore on the corner, she waited a moment; then she went after him. He was not there either, nor was he in the little grill bar next door, but, on an impulse, she described him and was told that he had just left. Trouble knew the waitress by sight, and she asked frankly:

"Did he have anything to drink?"

"Yes, he had three drinks very quick."

Trouble returned to the car. After five more minutes of waiting, it was borne in on her with increasing apprehension that he had gone into the hospital seeking her. His morbid jealousy had come to the fore and it was more than probable that his destination was Doctor Wheelock's office. Relegating the ache of her ankle to the world of unimportant things, she set off once more toward the gates she had thought to leave behind.

At the office in the Orthopedic Clinic she found that a man answering Fred's description had asked for Doctor Wheelock and, on being told he was busy, announced himself as a physician and said that he would wait outside the operating room. In a panic, Trouble hurried to the elevator; she arrived upstairs just a minute too late.

As she paused for breath at the door of the anteroom, she saw Fred arguing violently with an orderly who held him by an arm, while a nurse looked on in shocked surprise. Even as Trouble watched, heart in her mouth, the door of the operating room flung open and a doctor came out, tearing the mask from his face and walking directly up to Fred.

"All right, I'm Doctor Wheelock. I don't know what you want of me, but if you try to force your way into an operating room you're likely to get in difficulties. Now what is it?"

At the moment when she started toward them, she saw a reflex in Fred's shoulder, saw the orderly try to pinion him; then she was between the two men at the instant that Fred broke away, and the force of his rush sent her back against Doctor Wheelock, who caught her— for the second time in their lives. Seeing her, Fred stood dead still, breathing hard, and for just a moment it seemed that anything could happen, when there was a sudden interruption.

The door of the operating room opened again and a nurse came out, preceding a rolling table pushed by another nurse, which bore a recumbent form swathed in white. For two minutes there was not a sound in the room except the faint noise of the rubber wheels; even the gasp of Fred's breathing stopped, and with a slow, soundless movement Trouble leaned out and away from Doctor Wheelock and regained her balance.

The rolling table disappeared out the farther door, and as if it were a signal, they all relaxed at once and the silence was broken.

"I'm very sorry," said Fred in a dull voice.

Doctor Wheelock looked at Trouble, then at Fred, then back again.

"What is this, anyhow, Miss McClurg? Say, I've been looking for you for three days. Do you know this fellow?"

"Yes. He's been drinking." She turned despairingly to Fred. "Will you please get out? Wait for me in the car."

"I'm sorry," Fred repeated.

As soberly as if he had not been a man possessed a few minutes before, he accompanied the orderly out the door.

Doctor Wheelock looked after him for a moment; then he shook his head slowly, astounded and outraged.

"Well, of all the nuts," he muttered. "Come in here. We'll go in a gallery. They'll be cleaned up in a minute and I want to talk to you. Where have you been? Who is this fellow? How's your ankle?"

Trouble couldn't answer his questions all at once. How could she say that the momentary touch of her head against his white gown was the strongest memory she had of the incident, that she had of anything?

"Fired?" he was saying. "Of course, you weren't fired. Why didn't you come to me? I started back two days earlier than I meant to—I got thinking about that crazy ankle of yours—and I heard what happened. It's perfectly all right. I'm sorry that woman ever worried you."

"You mean you fixed it up?" she asked incredulously.

"You bet I did. I said, if you left I left. Mrs. Johnston was simply losing her sense of proportion, and a couple of other doctors who had run up against her went to Compson that same week. She thought she was running the hospital. But the difficulty was trying to find you. Where were you?"

"I was in the country."

They had finished cleaning up down below. He called to one of the nurses to wait a minute.

"I want to look at that ankle right now," he said. "Doctor Donowska said you didn't show up."

"Well, after they fired me——"

"Forget it; you're not fired. Come on down here and let me look you over. . . . That's right; take it slow. . . . Where do you pick up these boy friends who knock you around and try to break into operating rooms? Who is he, anyhow?"

"Oh, he's—nobody," said Trouble. "He's just a crazy boy. I had no idea what he was going to do."

He had helped her onto the table and the nurse was taking off her stocking.

"H'm!" grunted Doctor Wheelock again, after a minute. "Well, young lady, you've played fast and loose with this ankle. I'm going to X-ray you, and then I wouldn't be surprised if we didn't have to go into the joint and replace it."

"Oh, not now," she said quickly.

"We'll take the X ray now. Then you come back late this afternoon. There's no point in delaying any longer. Maybe you'll only need a cast."

"All right. Late this afternoon then. There's something I've got to do now."

"No walking."

"No, not much. What does it matter, since it's got to be fixed?"

The nurse had gone to the other side of the operating room to throw away the old adhesive tape.

"It matters to me," he said. "It matters more than I can tell you right now."

Then she saw in his eyes the same look that had been in the eyes of the girl who had driven him away from the hospital last week; and simultaneously she realized she had only seen the back of his head and had not known whether he had returned it. Just as she had seen little more than the back of his head the day she fell into his arms.

"Let's have the X ray," she said quickly.

VII

Fred sat in the car, leaning forward on the steering wheel. His face was penitent, sobered, boyishly appealing.

"I wasn't sure you'd come," he said humbly.

"Where are we meeting your mother?"

"At Coleman Gardens." And as they started off: "Trouble, I can't begin to tell you about my self-contempt for what I did. For a while when you went in the hospital and didn't come back right away, I hardly knew what I was doing."

"Please don't talk, Fred."

"All right, anything you say. But if I can ever make up to you for this——"

They reached the restaurant, to find Mrs. Winslow already there. Looking from one to the other, she guessed something, and when they sat down in the shade of the poplar trees, she caught Trouble's eyes several times, understanding her because she liked her, and each time a deepening expression of apprehension came into her own eyes. Trouble was the first to break the silence.

"Mrs. Winslow, you've been awfully good to me," she said, "and it's hard to tell you this. But I don't think I want to give up nursing now."

"Why"—Mrs. Winslow looked sharply at her son, the worst of her forebodings justified—"why, then—then you've decided to put things off."

"No," Trouble said, "I want to break everything off definitely."

All in a moment, Mrs. Winslow gave up. She loved her son, but she knew in her heart that this girl was worth ten of him and that all their money could not buy her. Her instinct and her sense of justice struggled for a moment, and then she yielded graciously to the inevitable.

"I suppose that hospital life does get in your blood," she said evenly.

"I guess that's it," said Trouble.

She did not dare look at Fred; she did not want to be disturbed by that appeal, childish and false.

"They've X-rayed my ankle and they may have to cut into it this afternoon," she said. "I've let it go too long."

"Oh, that's too bad! I've been worried about it. I suppose you'll be laid up awhile. . . . Please tell me your favorite thing in a garden."

Trouble stood up.

"I'll run you back to the hospital," said Fred in a lost voice.

"No, please. I'd rather not. I'd rather go by myself"—she smiled with an effort—"and get ready for the ordeal."

Out in the street, Trouble waited for a taxi. She was one who never looked backward, and the Winslow family was already behind her. She was thinking that she wanted the X ray to be bad—so bad that Doctor Wheelock would have to operate, and she would see him every day for a while.

Perhaps it was this wish that made her slip and almost fall as she got into the cab, and feel a keen joy at the throb of pain, thinking, perhaps, that did it.

"Where to, please?"

"Luke Harkless Hospital."

And as Trouble heard her voice saying those familiar words, all the things that made her unique and beloved, a symbol of something greater than herself, came flowing back into her. The rich warm self of Trouble bloomed again—a flower beside the bed of man's distress.

An Author's Mother

(*Esquire*, September 1936)

Molly McQuillan Fitzgerald died September 1936, but this obituary story was written while she was still living. It was the third element in a series of autobiographical sketches for *Esquire*: "Author's House" (July), "Afternoon of an Author" (August), and "An Author's Mother" (September).

Fitzgerald's relationship with his mother had been ambivalent; he blamed his character flaws on her permissiveness, though appreciating the strength of her unquestioning love for him. She died at a time when he was deeply in debt, leaving him approximately $25,000, and he wrote a friend that "it would have been quite within her character to have died that I might live."

Molly Fitzgerald's grandmother was an illiterate Irish immigrant who arrived penniless in America in about 1842 with her six children—what Fitzgerald called the "peasant" side of his family, in contrast to the educated "Old Maryland" side represented by the Scotts and the Keys on his father's side. Though his mother was a voracious reader, it was, as this sketch indicates, of sentimental literature of the romantic era. She was proud of her only son, but it is doubtful whether she understood a word of what must have seemed to her his shockingly modern writing.

She was a halting old lady in a black silk dress and a rather preposterously high-crowned hat that some milliner had foisted upon her declining sight. She was downtown with a purpose; she only shopped once a week now and always tried to do a lot in one morning. The doctor had told her she could have the cataracts removed from her eyes but she was over eighty and the thought of the operation frightened her.

Her chief purpose this morning was to buy one of her sons a birthday present. She had intended to get him a bathrobe but passing through the book department of the store and stopping "to see if there was anything new," she saw a big volume on Niaco where she knew he intended to spend the winter—and she turned its pages wondering if he wouldn't like that instead, or if perhaps he already had it.

Her son was a successful author. She had by no means abetted him in the choice of that profession but had wanted him to be an army officer or else go into business like his brother. An author was something distinctly peculiar—there had been only one in the middle western city where she was born and he had been regarded as a freak. Of course if her son could have been an author like Longfellow, or

Alice and Phoebe Cary, that would have been different, but she did not even remember the names of who wrote the three hundred novels and memoirs that she skimmed through every year. Of course she remembered Mrs. Humphrey Ward and now she liked Edna Ferber, but as she lingered in the bookstore this morning her mind kept reverting persistently to the poems of Alice and Phoebe Cary. How lovely the poems had been! Especially the one about the girl instructing the artist how to paint a picture of her mother. Her own mother used to read her that poem.

But the books by her son were not vivid to her, and while she was proud of him in a way, and was always glad when a librarian mentioned him or when someone asked her if she was his mother, her secret opinion was that such a profession was risky and eccentric.

It was a hot morning and feeling suddenly a little faint after her shopping, she told the clerk she would like to sit down for a moment.

He got her a chair politely and, as if to reward him by giving him business, she heard herself asking: "Have you got the poems of Alice and Phoebe Cary?"

He repeated the names.

"Let me see. No—I don't believe we have. I was just looking over the poetry shelves yesterday. We try to keep a few volumes of all the modern poets in stock."

She smiled to herself at his ignorance.

"These poets have been dead many years," she said.

"I don't believe I know of them—but I might be able to order them for you."

"No—never mind."

He seemed an obliging young man and she tried to focus her eyes upon him, for she liked polite young men, but the stacks of books were blurring up a little and she thought she had better go back to her apartment and perhaps order a bathrobe for her son over the telephone.

It was just at the entrance of the store that she fell. There were a few minutes when she was just barely conscious of an annoying confusion centering around her, and then she became gradually aware that she was lying on a sort of bed in what seemed to be an automobile.

The man in white who rode with her spoke to her gently:

"How do you feel now?"

"Oh, I'm all right. Are you taking me home?"

"No, we're taking you to the hospital, Mrs. Johnston—we want to put a little dressing on your forehead. I took the liberty of looking in your shopping bag and finding out your name. Will you tell me the name and address of your nearest relatives?''

Once again consciousness began to slip away and she spoke vaguely of her son who was a business man in the West and of a granddaughter who had just opened a millinery shop in Chicago. But before he could get anything definite she dismissed the subject as if it were irrelevant and made an effort to rise from the stretcher.

"I want to go home. I don't know why you're taking me to a hospital—I've never been in a hospital."

"You see, Mrs. Johnston, you came out of the store and tripped and fell down some stairs, and unfortunately you have a cut."

"My son will write about it."

"What!" asked the interne rather surprised.

The old woman repeated vaguely: "My son will write about it."

"Is your son in the journalistic business?"

"Yes—but you mustn't let him know. You mustn't disturb—"

"Don't talk for just a moment, Mrs. Johnston—I want to keep this little cut together till we can make a suture."

Nonetheless she moved her head and said in a determined voice: "I didn't say my son was a suture—I said he was an author."

"You misunderstood me, Mrs. Johnston. I meant about your forehead. A 'suture' is where someone cuts themselves a little—"

Her pulse fluttered and he gave her spirits of ammonia to hold her till she got to the hospital door.

"No, my son is not a suture," she said. "Why did you say that? He's an *author*." She spoke very slowly as if she was unfamiliar with the words coming from her tired mouth. "An author is someone who writes books."

They had reached the hospital and the interne was busy trying to disembark her from the ambulance. "—Yes, I understand, Mrs. Johnston. Now try and keep your head quite still."

"My apartment is three-o-five," she said.

"We just want you to come into the hospital a few hours. What sort of books does your son write, Mrs. Johnston?"

"Oh he writes all sorts of books."

"Just try to hold your head still, Mrs. Johnston. What name does your son write under?"

"Hamilton T. Johnston. But he's an author, not a suture. Are you a suture?"

"No, Mrs. Johnston, I'm a doctor."

"Well, this doesn't look like my apartment." In one gesture she pulled what was left of her together and said: "Well, don't disturb my son John or my son-in-law or my daughter that died or my son

Hamilton who—'' She raised herself to a supreme effort and remembering the only book she knew really in her heart announced astonishingly, ''—my son, Hamilton, who wrote 'The Poems of Alice and Phoebe Cary—' '' Her voice was getting weaker and as they carried the stretcher into the elevator her pulse grew feebler and feebler and the interne knew there would not be any suture, that nature had put its last stitch in that old forehead. But he could not know what she was thinking at the last, and would never have guessed it was that Alice and Phoebe Cary had come to call upon her, and taken her hands, and led her back gently into the country she understood.

The End of Hate

(*Collier's*, 22 June 1940)

"The End of Hate" had the most vexed history of any Fitzgerald story, as he rewrote it over a three-year period. The lost first version—called "Thumbs Up"—was dictated in Asheville in August 1936 when Fitzgerald's right arm was in a cast. While trying to salvage the story he explained to Harold Ober: "I think I told you that it's shifting around was due to my poor judgement in founding it arbitrarily on two unrelated events in father's family—the Thumbs Up and the Empresses Escape. . . . Its early diffuseness was due, of course, to my inability to measure the length of dictated prose during the time my right arm was helpless—that's why it strung out so long." Although Fitzgerald was a Civil War buff with Southern sympathies derived from his father, and as a boy had written two stories and a play about the war, his only other professional Civil War story is "The Night Before Chancellorsville." "Thumbs Up" was declined by *American, American Cavalcade, Cosmopolitan, Country Gentleman, Delineator, Ladies' Home Journal, Liberty, McCall's, Pictorial Review, Redbook, The Saturday Evening Post, Woman's Home Companion,* and *This Week.* Harold Ober explained to Fitzgerald that the story "is not what editors expect from you," and that the thumbs material was considered too harrowing for women readers. Fitzgerald cut it from 8,800 to 5000 words in 1937. Along the way it was retitled "Dentist Appointment" and "When this Cruel War—." In May 1937 Kenneth Littauer, the fiction editor of *Collier's,* paid $1500 on account against $2500 for an acceptable revision. After rejecting at least two more rewrites, *Collier's* finally accepted "The End of Hate" in June 1939. When the story appeared in 1940 Fitzgerald wrote to his cousin, Ceci Taylor: "Did you see a very poor story of mine that was in Collier's a few weeks ago? It was interesting only in that it was founded on a family story—how William George Robertson was hung up by the thumbs at Glen Mary or was it Locust Grove?"

The buggy progressed at a tired trot and the two occupants were as warm and weary as the horses. The girl's hair was a crackly yellow and she wore a dress of light blue bombazine—the first really grownup dress she had ever known. She was going to be a nurse in a wartime hospital, and her brother complained that she was arrayed like a woman of the world.

"We're now almost in the District of Columbia," said Captain Doctor Pilgrim. "We will stop and get water at the next farmhouse."

The two Pilgrims were probably the only adults thereabout who did not know that southern Maryland was suddenly and surprisingly in Confederate hands. To ease the pressure on Lee at Petersburg, General Jubal Early had marched his corps up the valley in a desperate threat at the capital, had thrown shells into the suburbs, and then unwillingly turned back toward the west. His last infantry columns had scarcely slogged along this road, leaving a stubborn dust behind.

The Pilgrims, who had driven down from Ohio, were unaware of the situation; and as the buggy turned into the Washington Pike, Josie was puzzled by a number of what seemed to be armed tramps who limped past. And there was something about two men who galloped toward the buggy from the farmhouse that made her ask alertly, "What are those people, Brother? Secesh?"

To anyone who had not been at the front, it would have been hard to place the men as soldiers—Tib Dulany, who had once written verse for the *Lynchburg Courier*, wore a planter's hat, a rag of a coat, blue pants originally issued to a Union trooper, and a cartridge belt stamped C.S.A. The riders drew up beside the buggy and Tib saluted Pilgrim.

"Hi there, Yank!"

"Tell us where we can get water—" began Josie haughtily. Suddenly she saw that Captain Doctor Pilgrim's hand was at his holster—but it stayed there—the second rider held a carbine at his heart.

Captain Pilgrim raised his hands.

"Is this a raid?" he demanded. "Are you guerrillas?"

"Turn in yonder at the farmhouse," said Tib politely. "You can get water there."

He addressed Josie, who was driving. He observed that her skin had a peculiar radiance as if phosphorus had touched it, and around her eyes was that veiled expression sometimes described as starry.

"Nobody's going to hurt you," he said, "you're inside Lee's lines."

"Lee's lines!" Captain Pilgrim cried indignantly as he turned the carriage. "Every time you Mosby cutthroats come out of your hills and cut a telegraph—"

The team jolted to a stop—the second trooper had grabbed the reins, and turned white eyes upon the doctor.

"One more peep about Mosby—"

"He just doesn't know the news, Wash," said Tib. "He doesn't recognize the Army of Northern Virginia."

Wash released the reins and the buggy drove up to the farmhouse. Only as the doctor saw a dozen horses tied by the porch did he realize that he was several days behind the times.

"Right now," continued Tib, "Grant is washing the dishes and

Old Abe is upstairs making the beds." He turned to Wash: "I sure would like to be in Washington tonight when Mr. Davis rides in. That Yankee rebellion didn't last long, did it?"

Josie suddenly believed it and her world crashed around her—the Boys in Blue—the Union forever—Mine eyes have seen the glory . . .

"You can't take my brother prisoner—he's not really an officer, he's a doctor."

"Doctor, eh? Don't know about teeth, does he?" asked Tib, dismounting at the porch.

"That's his specialty."

"He's just what we're looking for. Doctor, if you'll be so kind as to come in you can pull a tooth of a Bonaparte, a cousin of Napoleon the Third. He's attached to General Early's staff and he's been carrying on for an hour but the ambulances have gone on."

An officer came out on the porch, gave a nervous ear to a crackling of rifles in the distance, and bent an eye upon the buggy.

"We found a tooth specialist, Lieutenant," said Tib. "The Lord sent him into our lines and if Napoleon still needs help—"

"Bring him in," the officer exclaimed. "We didn't know whether to take the prince along or leave him."

Suddenly Josie had a glimpse at the Confederacy on the vine-covered veranda. There was an egress from the house: a spidery man in a shabby riding coat adorned with faded stars, followed by two younger men cramming papers into a canvas sack. Then a miscellany of officers, one on a crutch, one stripped to his undershirt with the gold star of a general pinned to a bandage on his shoulder. There was disappointment in their tired eyes. Seeing Josie, they made a single gesture: their dozen right hands rose to their dozen hats and they bowed in her direction.

Josie bowed back stiffly. In a moment they swung into their saddles and General Early looked for a moment toward the city he had not taken. Then he spoke to the aide at his stirrup: "I want couriers from Colonel Mosby every half hour till we reach White's Ford."

"Yes, sir."

The general's sun-strained eyes focused on Dr. Pilgrim in the buggy.

"I understand you're a dentist," he said. "Pull out Prince Napoleon's tooth or whatever he needs. Do well by him and these troopers will let you go without parole."

The clop and crunch of mounted men moved down the lane, and in a minute the last sally of the Army of Northern Virginia faded into the distance. A French aide-de-camp came out of the farmhouse.

"The prince is still in agony," he announced.

"This Yank is a doctor," Tib said. "One of us'll go along while he's operating."

The stout invalid in the kitchen, a gross miniature of his world-shaking uncle, tore his hand from his mouth and sat upright.

"Operation!" he cried. "Quel horreur!"

Dr. Pilgrim looked suspicious.

"My sister—where will she be?"

"In the parlor, Doctor. Wash, you stay here."

Prince Napoleon groaned again.

"I am a trained surgeon," Pilgrim reassured him stiffly. "Now, sir, will you take off that hat?"

The prince removed the white Cordoba which topped a costume of red tail-coat, French uniform breeches and dragoon boots.

"Prince, if he doesn't do well we got some apple trees outside and plenty rope."

Tib went into the parlor where Miss Josie sat on the edge of a sofa.

"The general said not to harm my brother," she reminded him.

"I'm more worried about what he's about to do to the prince," said Tib, sorry for her lovely anxious face.

An animal howl arose from the library.

"You hear that?" Tib said. "Napoleon's the one to worry about. And then, after our cavalry pickets pass, you and your brother can resume your journey."

Josie relaxed and looked at him with a certain human interest.

"What did my brother mean when he said you were a gorilla?"

"It's '*guer*rilla,' not '*go*rilla,' " he objected. "When a Yankee's on detached service they call him a scout, but they pretend we're only part-time soldiers, so they can hang us."

"A soldier not in uniform is a spy, isn't he?"

"I *am* in uniform—look at my buckle. And, believe it or not, Miss Pilgrim, I was a smart-looking trooper when I rode out of Lynchburg four years ago."

He told her how he had been dressed that day, and Josie listened—it wasn't unlike the first volunteers leaving Youngstown, Ohio.

"—with a big red sash that belonged to my mother. One of the girls stood in front of the troop and read a poem I had published."

"Say the poem," Josie urged him. "I would so enjoy hearing it."

Tib considered. "All I remember is: 'Lynchburg, thy guardsmen bid thy hills farewell.' I—"

Came a scream from across the hall and a medley of French. Wash appeared in the door.

"Say, Tib—the Yank got the tooth."

"Fine," said Tib. He turned back to Josie.

"I certainly would like to write a few lines sometime to express my admiration of you."

"This is so sudden," she said lightly.

She might have spoken for herself, too.

Presently Wash turned from the window:

"Tib, the patrols have started shootin' back from the saddle."

"Will you leave without *us*?" the French aide demanded suspiciously.

"We sure will," said Tib. "The prince can observe the war from the Yankee side for a while. Miss Pilgrim, I bid you a most unwilling goodby."

Peering hastily into the kitchen, Tib saw the prince so far recovered as to be sitting upright.

Now Wash called from outside:

"Hey, Tib!"

There were shots very near. The two scouts were unhitching their horses when Wash muttered, "Hell's fire!" and pointed down the drive where five Federal troopers were in view at the far gate. Wash swung his carbine one-handed to his right shoulder.

"I'll take the two on the left."

"Maybe we could run for it," Tib suggested.

"They got seven-rail fences."

Leisurely the file of cavalry trotted up the drive. Even after four years, Tib hated to shoot from ambush, but he had no choice.

"Get your mark, Wash. When they break we'll ride through 'em."

But the ill luck of Southern arms that day was with them. Before they could loose a shot a man's body flung against Tib and pinioned him—a voice shouted beside his ear:

"Men! There're rebels here!"

As Tib wrestled desperately with Pilgrim, the Northern patrol stopped, drew pistols. Wash was bobbing from side to side trying to get a shot at Pilgrim but the doctor maneuvered Tib's body in between.

In a few seconds it was over. Wash fired once, but the Federals were around them before he was in his saddle. Panting, the two young men faced the Federals. Dr. Pilgrim spoke sharply to their corporal: "These are Mosby's men."

Those years were bitter on the border. And nothing was more bitter than Mosby's name. Wash dodged suddenly, ran and sprawled dead on the grass in a last attempt to get away. Tib, still struggling, was trussed up at the porch rail.

"There's a good tree," said a soldier.

The corporal glanced at Dr. Pilgrim.

"You know he's one of Mosby's men?"

"I'm in the Seventh Virginia Cavalry," said Tib.

"Are you one of Mosby's men?"

Tib didn't answer.

"All right, boys, get the rope."

Dr. Pilgrim's austere presence asserted itself again.

"I don't want to hang him, but this type of irregular must be discouraged."

"We string 'em up by their thumbs sometimes," suggested the corporal.

"Then do that," said Dr. Pilgrim.

By seven that evening the road outside was busy again. Mail and fresh vegetables were moving toward the capital—the diversion was over, except for the stragglers along the Pike.

In the farmhouse it was quiet. Prince Napoleon was waiting for an ambulance from Washington. There was no sound—except from Tib, who, as his skin slipped off his thumbs, repeated aloud to himself fragments of his own political verses.

When it was late and the provost guard was dozing on the porch, someone came who knew where the stepladder was—she had heard them dump it after they strung up Tib. When she had half sawed through the rope she went back to her room for pillows and moved the table under him and laid the pillows on it. She did not need any precedent for what she was doing. When Tib fell with a grunting gasp, murmuring deliriously, "Nothing to be ashamed of," she poured a bottle of sherry over his hands.

It was a hot, sultry morning, with sleeping dust from the fields and leaves. Since midnight Josie had been driving in the direction that Tib indicated before he lapsed into a broken sleep beside her; but as they approached the village she reined in and woke him gently.

Tib sat up with a jerk, stared at his hands wrapped in the tearings of a petticoat, and remembered.

"We've got to find a doctor," Josie said. "I think we're in Virginia."

Tib stared around. "It looks like Louden County. Leave me anywhere."

"Not before we find a doctor."

That was the last thing he heard as his tired heart tried once more to leap out of his body. His knees buckled. . . .

When he awoke hours later, everything was changed—they were in a glade of trees, with the horses hitched and standing. His hands burned like fire.

"I know a doctor—" he murmured.

"We found a doctor and he fixed your hands. I wanted him to put you to bed—it seems that our cavalry—the Union cavalry are all over here. He didn't dare hide one of Mosby's men."

Her hand touched his hot forehead.

"You're exactly like an angel," he whispered drunkenly. "That's a fact."

"You don't know me," said Josie, but her fingers stayed on his forehead, pushed back the damp strands.

"If I could just get to one of our houses—" Tib fretted indiscreetly. "We have a chain of sympathizers' houses right through the Yankee lines. Or else I could go due east to Georgetown."

"Georgetown!" Josie exclaimed. "That's part of Washington."

"If you think I haven't been in Washington often enough—" He stopped himself and added cryptically. "Not as a spy, mind you—as a dispatch carrier."

"It seems so risky to go there."

"Longest way around, shortest way home."

He closed his eyes—then surprisingly he added: "We can get married in Lynchburg."

In the dim world of the journey it seemed to him that he had proposed to Josie somewhere and she had accepted.

"Try to sleep until it's dark," she whispered.

As he slept she watched him. Then, exhausted herself, she lay down beside him, moving his head till it rested on her shoulder.

When she awoke it was dark; she felt that he was awake, too, but she did not speak. Why not wait a while—wait like this—alive through the very recklessness of her protest and its unknown consequence. Who was she now? What had she done with herself in twenty hours?

After an hour a faint chill from the uplands sifted through the glade.

"What are you?" he demanded suddenly. "You're a good girl, I know—"

"Just another human being."

He considered for a moment. "You're coming on South with me. When we get to our lines we can be married."

"That's not a good idea. I must go to Washington. My brother'll understand—in his own way."

They got up and walked to where the horses had stood patiently through the hours. Before they got into the buggy, Josie turned to him suddenly and for a moment they faded into the sweet darkness, so deep that they were darker than the darkness—darker than the black trees—then so dark that when she tried to look up at him she could but look at the black waves of the universe over his shoulder and say, "Yes, I'll go with you if you want—anywhere. I love you too."

It was a long night. Somewhere outside the first ring of Washington forts they stopped the horses; Tib went into a farmhouse he knew and came out in civilian clothes with the papers of a Kentucky deserter. Josie gave her own name at the barriers and showed a letter from the hospital where she was to nurse.

Then along the sleeping streets of Georgetown with the horses nodding and drowsing in their traces.

"That house on the corner," he said. "This is the only possible danger. Sometimes they get on to the Southern stations and set traps. I'll go in alone first—"

He pulled with his teeth at the bandage on one hand and she cried out in protest.

"I'll just free this one. In case of any trouble I'd like to be able to use one hand. It won't hurt."

"It will!" she said in agony. "I wanted to wait till you were safe before I told you—the doctor had to amputate your thumbs."

"Oh."

With an odd expression, Tib stared down at the bandages.

"In order to save your hands."

"I can feel my thumbs."

"It's the nerves you feel."

Tib was out of the buggy like a flash—stood beside it trembling. "Drive on," he said in a strange voice.

"What?"

"You were trying to pay for what your brother did. Drive on!"

In the brightening dawn she looked at him once more, all other feeling washed by a great surge of compassion. Then he was no longer there—and a sense of utter ruin crept slowly over her. She slapped the reins on the horse and drove down the street, aghast and alone.

April, 1865. And Tib Dulany—by two days an ex-trooper of Confederate cavalry—looking into the bar of the Willard Hotel—in Washington, now a busy, noisy world. He had come on a desperate chance—turned his back on the dark years—to get a job in the West. It was for a test of his ability to forget the past that he had ridden penniless into the capital—the day after Lee's surrender. His story was the story of men who have fought in wars—at the newspaper offices:

"We're saving our jobs for our own men." In the printing shops they stared at his thumbs: "How do you set type with a mutilation—"

Tib went into a shop and bought gloves, as a sort of disguise; he got a trial at one place—but he was no good now as a journeyman printer. No good as a printer—no good now.

The atmosphere of the Willard bar—a boom-town atmosphere—depressed him. Upstairs, in the plush corridors, he quivered at the sight of women in fine clothes; he became conscious of his hand-me-down suit, bought in Alexandria, Virginia, that morning.

Then he saw Josie Pilgrim coming out of a dining room on the arms of two officers—more beautiful than he had remembered. She was a ripe grape, she was ready to fall for the shaking of a vine. . . .

But it wasn't quite this that made him turn around and walk blindly in the other direction—it was rather that she was the same, she was the girl of those old nightmare hours, the girl whose brother's face he had conjured up in the last cavalry action.

And this had made her beauty a reminder of cruelty and pain.

In the past months, Tib had been trying to belittle her into a species of impressionable gamin—a girl who might have ridden off with *any* man. To certain people the symbolism of women is intolerable. Because Josie's face represented a dream and a desire it took him back to the very hour of his torture. . . .

Later when a fellow boarder in Georgetown buttonholed him on the stairs, he shook him off.

"Mr. Dulany, I ask only a little of your time," the man said. "I know you were one of Mosby's men—a true Southerner—that you came to this house several times during the war—"

"Very busy," Tib said.

They were a ruined lot—Tib hadn't liked the spies with whom he had been in contact during the war—now, anyhow, he was absorbed in an idea of his own:

To get a fresh start one had to even things up. Spew forth in a gesture the hate and resentment that made life into a choking muddle. He went upstairs and took a derringer out of his haversack.

An hour later Josie Pilgrim's carriage drew up in front of the boarding house. A woman held the front door half open and looked at her suspiciously.

"I saw a friend, Mr. Tib Dulany, in the Willard," she said.

She kept looking at the flounce on her French skirt.

"You want to see him?" the woman asked. "Please step inside." She took Josie by the arm like a doll, spinning her into the hall.

"Wait," she said.

As Josie waited obediently she was conscious of a scrutiny from the parted double doors of a parlor—first one pair of eyes, then another.

The woman came down the stairs.

"He's gone," she said. "Maybe he's gone for good."

Josie went back to her carriage—back to the state of mind where she lived between two worlds. Her beauty had not gone unnoticed in Washington. She had danced at balls with young men on government pay, and now in this time of victory she should be rejoicing—but she had seen the Glory of the Lord hung up by the thumbs—and then left her heart in the street in front of this house eight months ago.

Dr. Pilgrim was busy packing when the housekeeper told him he had a patient below.

"Tell him I'm busy. Tell him I'm leaving the city—tell him it's nine o'clock at night."

"I did tell him. He said he was from another town—that you once operated on him."

The word operate aroused Pilgrim's curiosity. Patients seldom spoke of the new dental work as "operating."

"Tell him I'll be right down."

He did not recognize the young man wearing black gloves who sat in his parlor. He did not remember any previous transaction—moreover he didn't like the young man—who took some time getting to the point.

The doctor was starting next day for France, on a special invitation from a cousin of Napoleon the Third, to take up plutocratic practice in Paris.

"You're a Southerner," he said, "and I have never practiced my profession in the South."

"Yes, you have," Tib reminded him. "Once you practiced within the Southern lines."

"That's true! I did. Thanks to that I am going to France—" He broke off suddenly—he knew who Tib was—he saw death looking at him from across the room.

"Why—it's you!" he said. "You're that rebel."

Tib held his pistol loosely in his hand pointing at the floor. He slipped off his right-hand glove.

"There are servants in the house—and my sister—"

"She's at the theater."

"What are you going to do?"

With a sudden surge of hate up into his throat:

"I'm going to shoot your thumbs off. You won't be much use in your profession, but you may find something else to do."

"They'll hang you—whatever I did to you was in discharge of my duty. Why—the war's practically over—"

"Nothing's over. Things won't begin till you and I start life on the same terms. Even this won't be as bad as what you did to me. . . . I think we'll close the windows."

He got up without taking his eyes off Pilgrim. There were loud voices in the street now but in his preoccupation Tib did not at first hear what they were calling. A window was flung up across the street and someone shouted from a passing carriage.

"The President's been shot! Lincoln's been shot!"

The carriage went on—the shouting voices multiplied—the quality of panic in them chilled Tib before he realized the import of the words.

"Abe Lincoln has been shot," he repeated aloud. Automatically he pulled down the last window.

"Oh!" groaned Pilgrim. "You people allowed to run loose in Washington!"

Into Tib's bedeviled head came the thought that the plot had been formed in the boardinghouse where he had laid his head last night—half-heard conversations became plain to him—that must have been the private business of the man who tried to speak to him on the stairs.

On the porch outside there were footsteps—Tib had scarcely put away his gun when Josie Pilgrim, a young officer by her side, hurried into the room.

"Brother, have you heard?" Seeing Tib, Josie's voice looped down: "The President was shot and killed in the theater—" Now her voice was high, flicking at the lower edge of panic.

Dr. Pilgrim stood up, trembling with relief at the interruption.

"It's a reign of terror!" he said. "This man—"

Josie crossed the room and stood beside Tib.

"So glad you're here," she said.

"So am I," Dr. Pilgrim said. "Perhaps Captain Taswell will put him under arrest."

Confused, the officer hesitated.

"Captain Taswell," Josie said, "when you asked me to marry you I told you there was someone else, didn't I?"

He nodded.

"This is the man. He and my brother have quarreled. Nothing that my brother says about him can be believed."

"He came here to kill me!" Pilgrim announced with certain civility—sobered way down. He walked to the window, came back, sat down, and listened to Tib's voice speaking loud and fierce:

"No. Not to kill you."

"My brother is afraid," Josie said, with calculated scorn. "He's bothered by something he did months ago."

Dr. Pilgrim made himself speak coolly:

"This man happens to be a Mosby guerrilla."

As Captain Taswell's belief wavered between brother and sister, Josie did something irrevocable, crossed a bridge as definite as the rivers that mark the Virginia border.

"We ran away together," she said to Captain Taswell. "We were going to get married, but it seemed better to wait till the war was over."

Captain Taswell nodded.

"In that case, I'm afraid I'm in the way."

As he went out, Dr. Pilgrim started to call after him, but his lips closed without sound. Josie looked earnestly at Tib. "I guess now you've *got* to marry me."

"You seem to be doing things for me always," Tib answered.

It has been whispered that there are only two kinds of women—those who take and those who give—and it was plain which kind Josie was. Even though his country was a desert of hate Tib was no longer a soul lost by wandering in it.

The shocking news of the evening—still only faintly appreciated—had made a sea change. The strongest man had taken the burden upon his great shoulders, given life its impetus again even in the accident of his death.

Dr. Pilgrim realized something of the sort, for in the silence that ensued he made no comment; nor did he voice any objection when Josie made another decision:

"Tib, dear, I don't know where you're going—I don't know where we're going, but Brother and I would be awfully happy if you'd sleep in this house tonight."

In the Holidays

(*Esquire*, December 1937)

The hospital was thinly populated, for many convalescents had taken risks to get home for the holidays and prospective patients were gritting their teeth until vacation was over. In the private ward one interne took on the duties of three, and six nurses the duties of a dozen. After New Year's it would be different—just now the corridors were long and lonely.

Young Dr. Kamp came into the room of Mr. McKenna, who was not very ill, and snatched rest in the easy chair.

"How's back feel?" he asked.

"Better, Doc. I thought I'd get up and dress tomorrow."

"All right—if you haven't any fever. The X-ray plates didn't show a thing."

"I've got to be out of here day after tomorrow."

"When you get home you better see your own doctor, though I never have felt you were seriously ill—in spite of the pain. We've got a patient downstairs with a dizzy head that we can't find a thing the matter with—there's probably faulty elimination of some kind, but he came through every test sound as a dollar."

"What's his name?" McKenna asked.

"Griffin. So you see sometimes there just isn't any diagnosis to be made. Say, were you in the war?"

"Me? No, I was too young."

"Did you ever get shot?"

"No."

"That's funny—the X ray showed a couple of things that looked like slugs in your buttocks."

"Oh, that was a hunting accident," said McKenna.

When the doctor left the nurse came in—she was the wrong one, not the beautiful little student nurse, dark and rosy, with eyes as soft as blue oil. Miss Hunter was plain and talked about the man she was marrying next month.

"That's why I'm here on New Year's Eve. We need the money and a girl gave me five dollars to take her place over the holidays. I can't see him but I write him a whole book every night."

"It certainly is some life in here," said McKenna. "The food makes me sick."

"Aren't you ashamed—it's better than we get. You ought to see that little student nurse go for the dessert you left today."

He brightened momentarily.

"The pretty one?" Maybe this was an angle.

"Miss Collins." She proffered him a vile liquid. "You can drink her health with this cocktail."

"Oh, skip it. This doctor thinks I'm just bluffing—me and some other fellow that's dizzy in the head. Name's Griffin—do you take care of him?"

"He's down on the first floor."

"What does he look like?"

"Well, he wears glasses, about your age."

"Is he handsome like me?"

"He's very pale and he's got a big bald place in his mustache. What's the use of having a mustache if you have a bald place in it?"

He shifted in bed restlessly.

"I think I'd sleep better if I got up for awhile—just around the corridors. I could get a paper in the office and all that."

"I'll ask the doctor."

Without waiting for permission McKenna got up and dressed. He was tying his tie when the nurse returned.

"All right," Miss Hunter said, "but come back soon and wear your overcoat. The corridors are cold. And would you please drop this letter in the box for me?"

McKenna went out and downstairs and through many halls to the main office. He stopped at the registry desk and asked a question, afterwards writing down something on the back of an envelope.

Out in the damp, snowless night he inquired the way to a drugstore; he went directly to the phone booth and closeted himself for some minutes. Then he bought a movie magazine and a hip flask of port, and asked for a glass at the fountain.

All around the hospital the streets were quiet and the houses, largely occupied by medical people, were dark and deserted. Across the street the dark fortress of the hospital was blocked out against a pink blur in the downtown sky. There was a mailbox on the corner and after a moment he took out the nurse's letter, tore it slowly into four pieces, and dropped it in the slot. Then he began thinking of the little student nurse, Miss Collins. He had a vague idea about Miss Collins. She had told him yesterday that she was sure to be flunked from her class in February. Why? Because she had stayed out too late with boy friends. Now, if that wasn't a sort of come-on—especially when she added that she wasn't going back to the old homestead and had no plans at all. Tomorrow McKenna was leaving town but in a couple of weeks he could ride down again and keep her out late in a big way, and if he liked her get her some clothes and set her up in Jersey City where he owned an apartment house. She was the double for a girl he once went with at Ohio State.

He looked at his watch—an hour and a half till midnight. Save for several occasions when he had been deterred for reasons contingent on his profession, all his New Year's were opaque memories of whoopee. He never made resolves or thought of the past with nostalgia or regret—he was joyless and fearless, one of the stillborn who manage to use death as a mainspring. When he caused suffering it made his neck swell and glow and yet he had a feeling for it that was akin to sympathy. "Does it hurt, fella?" he had asked once. "Where does it hurt most? Cheer up—you're almost out."

McKenna had intended to leave the hospital before the thing came off, but the interne and nurse had only just spilled what he wanted to know into his lap and it was too late at night to leave without attracting attention. He crossed the street in order to re-enter the hospital by the door of the dispensary.

On the sidewalk a man and a woman, young and poorly dressed, stood hesitating.

"Say, mister," the man said, "can you tell us something—if doctors look to see what's wrong with you is it free? Somebody told me they sting you."

McKenna paused in the doorway and regarded them—the woman watched him breathlessly.

"Sure they sting you," McKenna said. "They charge you twenty bucks or they take it out on your hide."

He went on in, past the screen door of the dispensary, past the entrance to the surgical unit where men made repairs that would not wait for the year to turn, past the children's clinic where a single sharp cry of distress came through an open door, past the psychiatric wards, exuding a haunted darkness. A group of probationers in street clothes chattered by him, an orderly with a wheel chair, an old Negress leaning on a grizzled man, a young woman weeping between a doctor and a nurse. Through all that life, protesting but clinging, through all that hope of a better year, moved McKenna, the murderer, looking straight ahead lest they see death in his eyes.

II

In his room he rang for the nurse, had a quick drink and rang again. This time it was Miss Collins.

"It took you long enough," he said. "Say, I don't think I'll go to bed yet. It's so near twelve I think I'll stay up and see the New Year in and all that stuff; maybe go out on the porch and hear the noise."

"I suppose it's all right."

"You'll stick with me, won't you? Want a little port wine?"

Miss Collins wouldn't dare do that but she'd be back presently. She was the prettiest twitch he had seen in a year.

After another glass of port he felt a growing excitement. He pictured "Mr. Griffin" on the floor below, feeling so hidden and secure, possibly asleep. He pictured Oaky and Flute Cuneo and Vandervere strapping on the arsenal; he wished he could be in on the finish but that was no play for a front man.

At a quarter of twelve Miss Collins came back and they went down the corridor to a glassed-in porch overlooking the city.

"I'm afraid this is my last New Year's here," she said.

"What do your care—you've got too much on the ball to go around washing mummies."

At a minute before twelve a din started—first thin and far away, then rolling toward the hospital, a discord of whistles, bells, firecrackers and shots. Once, after a few minutes, McKenna thought he heard the pump sound of a silencer, once and again, but he could not be sure. From time to time Miss Collins darted in to the desk to see if there was a call for her, and each time he kept carefully in her sight.

After fifteen minutes the cacophony died away.

"My back hurts," McKenna said. "I wish you'd help me off with my clothes and then rub me."

"Certainly."

On the way to his room he listened carefully for the sounds of commotion but there was nothing. Therefore, barring the unforeseen, all had gone off as planned—the State of New York's intended witness was now with his fathers.

She bent over the bed, rubbing his back with alcohol.

"Sit down," he ordered. "Just sit on the bed."

He had almost finished the flask of port and he felt fine. There were worse ways to spend New Year's—a job all mopped up, the good warming wine and a swell girl to rub his back.

"You certainly are something to look at."

Two minutes later she tugged his hand from her rumpled belt.

"You're crazy," she exclaimed, panting.

"Oh, don't get sore. I thought you kind of liked me."

"Liked you! You! Why, your room smells like a dog's room. I hate to touch you!"

Then was a small knock and the night superintendent called Miss Collins who went into the hall, hastily smoothing her apron. McKenna got out of bed, tiptoed to the door and listened—in a minute he heard Miss Collins' voice:

"But I don't know how to do it, Miss Gleason. . . . You say the patient was shot. . . ."

And then the other nurse:

". . . then you simply tie the hands and feet together and. . . ." McKenna got back into bed cautiously.

"Last rites for Mr. Griffin," he thought. "That's fine. It'll take her mind off being sore."

III

He had decided to leave next afternoon, when the winter dusk was closing down outside. The interne was uncertain and called the resident, just back from vacation. The latter came in after lunch when the orderly was helping McKenna pack.

"Don't you want to see your doctor tomorrow?" he asked.

He was big and informal, more competent-looking than the interne.

"He's just a doctor I got at the hotel. He doesn't know anything about it."

"Well, we've got one more test to hear from."

"I haven't got any fever," said McKenna. "It must have been just a false alarm."

The resident yawned.

"Excuse me," he said—"they called me at two o'clock last night."

"Somebody die?"

The resident nodded.

"Very suddenly. Somebody shot and killed a patient on the floor below."

"Go on! You're not safe anywhere now, are you?"

"Seems not."

McKenna rang the bell at the head of the bed.

"I can't find my hat, and none of those nurses have been in here all day—only the maid." He turned to the orderly. "Go find a nurse and see if they know where my hat is."

"And oh—" the resident added, "tell them if they have that test ready to send it in."

"What test?" McKenna asked.

"Just a routine business. Just a part of your body."

"What part?"

"It ought to be here now. It's hard to get these laboratory tests on a holiday."

Miss Hunter's face appeared in the doorway but she did not look toward McKenna.

"The message came," she said. "It was just to tell you that the test was positive. And to give you this paper."

The resident read it with interest.

"What is it?" demanded McKenna. "Say, I haven't got—"

"You haven't got anything," said the resident, "—not even a leg to stand on. In fact, I'd be sorry for you—if you hadn't torn up that nurse's letter."

"What nurse's letter?"

"The one the postman put together and brought in this morning."

"I don't know anything about it."

"We do. You left your finger prints on it—and they seem to belong to a man named Joe Kinney who got three slugs in his bottom in New York last June."

"You got nothing on me—what do you think you are, a tec?"

"That's just what I am. And I know now that you work out of Jersey City and so did Griffin."

"I was with Miss Collins when that happened."

"What time?"

Catching his mistake McKenna hesitated.

"I was with her all evening—till one o'clock."

"Miss Collins says she left you after five minutes because you got tough with her. Say, why did you have to pick a hospital? These girls have work to do—they can't play with animals."

"You got nothing at all on me—not even a gun."

"Maybe you'll wish you had one when I get done with you down at the station. Miss Hunter and I are engaged to be married and that letter was to me."

By nightfall the hospital showed signs of increasing life—the doctors and nurses back early to go to work in the morning, and casualties of riot and diet, victims of colds, aches and infections saved since Christmas. Even the recently vacated beds of Messrs. Griffin and McKenna would be occupied by tomorrow. Both of them had better have celebrated the holidays outside.

The Guest in Room Nineteen

(*Esquire*, October 1937)

Mr. Cass knew he couldn't go to sleep so he put his tie on again and went back to the lobby. The guests were all gone to bed but a little aura of activity seemed to linger about a half-finished picture puzzle, and the night watchman was putting a big log on the fire.

Mr. Cass limped slowly across the soft carpet, stopped behind him and grunted, "Heavy?"

The watchman, a wiry old mountaineer, looked around sharply.

"A hundred pound. It's wet—it'll be one o'clock before it's burning good."

Mr. Cass let himself into a chair. Last year he had been active, driving his own car—but he had suffered a stroke before coming South last month and now life was like waiting for an unwelcome train. He was very lonely.

The watchman built burning chunks about the wet log.

"Thought you was somebody else when you came in," he said.

"Who did you think I was?"

"I thought you was the fella who's always coming in late. First night I was on duty he came in at two without any noise and give me a start. Every night he comes in late."

After a pause Mr. Cass asked:

"What's his name?"

"I never did ask him his name."

Another pause. The fire leapt into a premature, short-lived glow.

"How do you know he's a guest here?"

"Oh, he's a guest here." But the watchman considered the matter for the first time. "I hear him go down the corridor and around the corner and then I hear his door shut."

"He may be a burglar," said Mr. Cass.

"Oh, he's no burglar. He said he'd been coming here a long time."

"Did he tell you he wasn't a burglar?"

The watchman laughed.

"I never asked him that."

The log slipped and the old man adjusted it; Mr. Cass envied his strength. It seemed to him that if he had strength he could run out of here, hurry along the roads of the world, the roads that led back, and not sit waiting.

Almost every evening he played bridge with the two clerks, and one night last week he simply passed away during a bridge hand, shrinking up through space, up through the ceilings like a wisp of smoke, looking back, looking down at his body hunched at the table, his white fist clutching the cards. He heard the bids and his own voice speaking—then the two clerks were helping him into his room and one of them sat with him till the doctor came. . . . After awhile Mr. Cass had to go to the bathroom and he decided to go to the public one. It took him some time. When he came back to the lobby the watchman said:

"That fella came in late again. I found out he's in number nineteen."

"What's his name?"

"I didn't like to ask him that—I knew I could find out from his number."

Mr. Cass sat down.

"I'm number eighteen," he said. "I thought there were just some women next to me."

The watchman went behind the desk to the mail rack. After a moment he reported.

"Funny thing—his box ain't here. There's number eighteen, that's Mr. Cass—"

"That's me."

"—and the next one is twenty, on the second floor. I must of understood him wrong."

"I told you he was a burglar. What did he look like?"

"Well, now he wasn't an old man and he wasn't a young man. He seemed like he'd been sick and he had little holes all over his face."

Despite its inadequacy the description somehow conjured up a picture for Mr. Cass. His partner, John Canisius, had never looked old or young and he had little holes in his face.

Suddenly Mr. Cass felt the same sensation stealing over him that he had felt the other night. Dimly he was aware that the watchman had gone to the door and dimly he heard his own voice saying: "Leave it open"; then the cold air swept in and his spirit left him and romped around the room with it. He saw John Canisius come in the open door and look at him and advance toward him, and then realized it was the watchman, pouring a paper cup of water into his mouth and spilling it on his collar.

"Thanks."

"Feel all right now?"

"Did I faint?" he muttered.

"You fell over kind of funny. Reckon I better help you get back into your room."

At the door of number eighteen Mr. Cass halted and pointed his cane at the room next door.

"What's that number?"

"Seventeen. And that one without a number is the manager's rooms. There ain't any nineteen."

"Do you think I'd better go in?"

"Sure thing." The watchman lowered his voice. "If you're thinking about that fella, I must of heard him wrong. I can't go looking for him tonight."

"He's in here," said Mr. Cass.

"No, he ain't."

"Yes, he is. He's waiting for me."

"Shucks, I'll go in with you."

He opened the door, turned on the light and took a quick look around.

"See—ain't nobody here."

Mr. Cass slept well and the next day was full Spring, so he decided to go out. It took him a long time to walk down the hill from the hotel and his progress across the double tracks took a good three minutes and attracted solicitous attention, but it was practically a country stroll compared to his negotiation of the highway which was accompanied by a great caterwauling of horns and screech of brakes. A welcoming committee waited him on the curb and helped him into the drug store where, exhausted by his adventure, he called a taxi to go home.

Because of this he fell asleep while undressing and waking at twelve felt dismal and oppressed. Finding it difficult to rise he rang, and the night watchman answered the bell.

"Glad to help you, Mr. Cass, if you'll wait five minutes. It's turned cold again and I want to get in a big log of wood."

"Oh," said Mr. Cass, and then, "Has the guest come in yet?"

"He just got in now."

"Did you ask him if he's a burglar?"

"He's no burglar, Mr. Cass. He's a nice fella. He's going to help me with this big log. I'll be right back."

"Did he say what room—" But the watchman was gone and Mr. Cass could only wait.

He waited five minutes, he waited ten. Then he gradually

realized that the watchman was not coming back. It was plain that the watchman had been sent for.

Everyone tried to keep distressing things from Mr. Cass, and it was not until the following evening that he heard what had happened from some whispering at the desk.

The man had collapsed trying to lift a log too heavy for him. Mr. Cass said nothing because he knew that old people have to be careful what they say. Only he knew the watchman had not been alone.

After Easter the hotel's short season faded out and it was not worth while to hire a new watchman, but Mr. Cass continued to have lonely nights and often he sat in the lobby after the other guests went to bed. One April night he dozed there for awhile, awakening to find that it was after two and he was not alone in the lobby.

The current of cooler air might have roused him, for a man he did not know had just come in the door.

The man was of no special age but even by the single light left burning Mr. Cass could see that he was a pale man, that there were little holes in his face like the ravages of some disease and he did not look like John Canisius, his partner.

"Good evening," said the stranger.

"Hm," said Mr. Cass, and then as the man turned down the corridor he spoke up in a strong voice:

"You're out late."

"Yes, quite late."

"You a guest here?"

"Yes."

Mr. Cass dragged himself to his feet and stood leaning on his cane.

"I suppose you live in room nineteen," he said.

"As it happens, I do."

"You needn't lie to me," said Mr. Cass, "I'm not an ignorant mountaineer. Are you a burglar—or did you come for some one?"

The man's face seemed to grow even whiter.

"I don't understand you," he said.

"In any case I want you to get out of here," said Mr. Cass. He was growing angry and it gave him a certain strength. "Otherwise I'm going to arouse the hotel."

The stranger hesitated.

"There's no need of doing that," he said quietly. "That would be—"

Mr. Cass raised his cane menacingly, held it up a moment, then let it down slowly.

"Wait a minute," he said, "I may want you to do something for me."

"What is it?"

"It's getting cold in here. I want you to help me bring in a log to put on the fire."

The stranger was startled by the request.

"Are you strong enough?" he asked.

"Of course I'm strong enough," Mr. Cass stood very upright, throwing back his shoulders.

"I can get it alone."

"No, you can't. You help me or I'll arouse the house."

They went out and down the back steps, Mr. Cass refusing the stranger's arm.

He found, in fact, that he could walk much better than he thought and he left his cane by the stoop so that both hands were free for the log.

It was dark in the woodshed and the stranger lit a match. There was only one log, but it was over a hundred pounds, quite big enough to amply fill the small fireplace.

"Hadn't I better do this?" said the stranger.

Mr. Cass did not answer, but bent and put his hands on the rough surface. The touch seemed to stimulate him, he felt no pain or strain in his back at all.

"Catch hold there," he ordered.

"Are you sure—"

"Catch hold!"

Mr. Cass took a long breath of cool air into his lungs and shifted his hands on the log. His arms tightened, then his shoulders and the muscles on his back.

"Lift," he grunted. And suddenly the log moved, came up with him as he straightened, and for a triumphant moment he stood there squarely, cradling it against him. Then out into space he went, very slowly, carrying the log which seemed lighter and lighter, seeming to melt away in his arms. He wanted to call back some word of mockery and derision to the stranger, but he was already too far away, out on the old roads that led back where he wished to be.

Everyone in the hotel was sorry to lose Mr. Cass, the manager especially, for he read the open letter on Mr. Cass' desk saying that no further money could be remitted that year.

"What a shame. He'd been here so many years that we'd have been glad to carry him awhile until he made arrangements."

Mr. Cass was the right sort of client—it was because of such guests that the manager had tried to keep his brother out of sight all winter.

The brother, a tough number, was considerably shaken by what had happened.

"That's what I get for trying to be a help," he said, "I should have known better. Both those old guys looked exactly like death itself to me."

Discard [Director's Special]

(*Harper's Bazaar*, January 1948)

This story was written in Hollywood in July 1939 and led to Fitzgerald's break with Harold Ober over the agent's refusal to resume the policy of making advances against unsold stories. At this time Fitzgerald was hoping to underwrite work on *The Last Tycoon* by returning to the high-paying magazines. Apart from the Pat Hobby series, he was cautious about writing Hollywood stories because he was saving the best material for his novel. He submitted "Director's Special," the first version of this story, to *The Saturday Evening Post*, which declined it because the ending was not clear. He revised it in August, but the *Post* declined it again. Fitzgerald admitted to Ober: "It is not quite a top story—and there's nothing much I can do about it. The reasons are implicit in the structure which wanders a little. . . . It simply couldn't stand any cutting whatsoever and one of the reasons for its faults is that I was continually conscious in the first draft of that *Collier* length and left out all sorts of those sideshows that often turn out to be highspots."

Hoping to establish a connection with *Collier's* in the summer of 1939, Fitzgerald submitted several stories to fiction editor Kenneth Littauer—all of which were declined. With one of these stories Fitzgerald sent an assessment of his situation:

> . . . it isn't particularly likely that I'll write a great many more stories about young love. I was tagged with that by my first writings up to 1925. Since then I have written stories about young love. They have been done with increasing difficulty and increasing insincerity. I would be either a miracle man or a hack if I could go on turning out an identical product for three decades.
>
> I know that is what's expected of me, but in that direction the well is pretty dry and I think I am much wiser in not trying to strain for it but rather to open up a new well, a new vein. You see, I not only announced the birth of my young illusions in *This Side of Paradise* but pretty much the death of them in some of my last *Post* stories like "Babylon Revisited." Lorimer seemed to understand this in a way. Nevertheless, an overwhelming number of editors continue to associate me with an absorbing interest in young girls—an interest that at my age would probably land me behind the bars.

After *Collier's* and *Cosmopolitan* declined it, Fitzgerald withdrew the story. *Harper's Bazaar* supplied the weak title "Discard" when the story was salvaged from Fitzgerald's papers and published posthumously in 1948.

The man and the boy talked intermittently as they drove down Ventura Boulevard in the cool of the morning. The boy, George Baker, was dressed in the austere gray of a military school.

"This is very nice of you, Mr. Jerome."

"Not at all. Glad I happened by. I have to pass your school going to the studio every morning."

"What a school!" George volunteered emphatically. "All I do is teach peewees the drill I learned last year. Anyhow I wouldn't go to any war—unless it was in the Sahara or Morocco or the Afghan post."

James Jerome, who was casting a difficult part in his mind, answered with "Hm!" Then, feeling inadequate, he added:

"But you told me you're learning math—and French."

"What good is French?"

"What good—say, I wouldn't take *any*thing for the French I learned in the war and just after."

That was a long speech for Jerome; he did not guess that presently he would make a longer one.

"That's just it," George said eagerly. "When you were young it was the war, but now it's pictures. I could be getting a start in pictures, but Dolly is narrow-minded." Hastily he added, "I know you like her; I know everybody does, and I'm lucky to be her nephew, but—" he resumed his brooding, "but I'm sixteen and if I was in pictures I could go around more like Mickey Rooney and the Dead-Ends—or even Freddie Bartholomew."

"You mean act in pictures?"

George laughed modestly.

"Not with these ears; but there's a lot of other angles. You're a director; you know. And Dolly could get me a start."

The mountains were clear as bells when they twisted west into the traffic of Studio City.

"Dolly's been wonderful," conceded George, "but gee whizz, she's arrived. She's got everything—the best house in the valley, and the Academy Award, and being a countess if she wanted to call herself by it. I can't imagine why she wants to go on the stage, but if she does I'd like to get started while she's still here. She needn't be small about that."

"There's nothing small about your aunt—except her person," said Jim Jerome grimly. "She's a *'grande cliente.'* "

"A what?"

"Thought you studied French."

"We didn't have that."

"Look it up," said Jerome briefly. He was used to an hour of quiet before getting to the studio—even with a nephew of Dolly Bordon. They turned into Hollywood, crossed Sunset Boulevard.

"How do you say that?" George asked.

" '*Une grande cliente*,' " Jerome repeated. "It's hard to translate exactly but I'm sure your aunt was just that even before she became famous."

George repeated the French words aloud.

"There aren't very many of them," Jerome said. "The term's misused even in France; on the other hand it *is* something to be."

Following Cahuenga, they approached George's school. As Jerome heard the boy murmur the words to himself once more he looked at his watch and stopped the car.

"Both of us are a few minutes early," he said. "Just so the words won't haunt you, I'll give you an example. Suppose you run up a big bill at a store, *and* pay it; you become a '*grand client.*' But it's more than just a commercial phrase. Once, years ago, I was at a table with some people in the Summer Casino at Cannes, in France. I happened to look at the crowd trying to get tables, and there was Irving Berlin with his wife. You've seen him—"

"Oh, sure, I've met him," said George.

"Well, you know he's not the conspicuous type. And he was getting no attention whatever and even being told to stand aside."

"Why didn't he tell who he was?" demanded George.

"Not Irving Berlin. Well, I got a waiter, and he didn't recognize the name; nothing was done and other people who came later were getting tables. And suddenly a Russian in our party grabbed the head waiter as he went by and said 'Listen!'—and pointed: 'Listen! Seat that man immediately. *Il est un grand client—vous comprenez?—un grand client!*' "

"Did he get a seat?" asked George.

The car started moving again; Jerome stretched out his legs as he drove, and nodded.

"I'd just have busted right in," said George. "Just grabbed a table."

"That's one way. But it may be better to be like Irving Berlin— and your Aunt Dolly. Here's the school."

"This certainly was nice of you, Mr. Jerome—and I'll look up those words."

That night George tried them on the young leading woman he sat next to at his aunt's table. Most of the time she talked to the actor on the other side, but George managed it finally.

"My aunt," he remarked, "is a typical '*grande cliente.*' "

"I can't speak French," Phyllis said. "I took Spanish."

"I take French."

"I took Spanish."

The conversation anchored there a moment. Phyllis Burns was twenty-one, four years younger than Dolly—and to his nervous system the oomphiest personality on the screen.

"What does it mean?" she inquired.

"It isn't because she *has* everything," he said, "the Academy Award and this house and being Countess de Lanclerc and all that. . . ."

"I think that's quite a bit," laughed Phyllis. "Goodness, I wish *I* had it. I know and admire your aunt more than anybody I know."

Two hours later, down by the great pool that changed colors with the fickle lights, George had his great break. His Aunt Dolly took him aside.

"You did get your driver's license, George?"

"Of course."

"Well, I'm glad, because you can be the greatest help. When things break up will you drive Phyllis Burns home?"

"Sure I will, Dolly."

"Slowly, I mean. I mean she wouldn't be a *bit* impressed if you stepped on it. Besides I happen to be fond of her."

There were men around her suddenly—her husband, Count Hennen de Lanclerc, and several others who loved her tenderly, hopelessly—and as George backed away, glowing, one of the lights playing delicately on her made him stand still, almost shocked. For almost the first time he saw her not as Aunt Dolly, whom he had always known as generous and kind, but as a tongue of fire, so vivid in the night, so fearless and stabbing sharp—so apt at spreading an infection of whatever she laughed at or grieved over, loved or despised—that he understood why the world forgave her for not being a really great beauty.

"I haven't signed anything," she said explaining, "—East or West. But out here I'm in a mist at present. If I were only *sure* they were going to make *Sense and Sensibility*, and meant it for me. In New York I know at least what play I'll do—and I know it will be fun."

Later, in the car with Phyllis, George started to tell her about Dolly—but Phyllis anticipated him, surprisingly going back to what they had talked of at dinner.

"What was that about a *cliente*?"

A miracle—her hand touched his shoulder, or was it the dew falling early?

"When we get to my house I'll make you a special drink for taking me home."

"I don't exactly drink as yet," he said.

"You've never answered my question." Phyllis' hand was still on his shoulder. "Is Dolly dissatisfied with who she's—with what she's got?"

Then it happened—one of those four-second earthquakes, afterward reported to have occurred "within a twenty-mile radius of this station." The instruments on the dashboard trembled; another car coming in their direction wavered and shimmied, side-swiped the rear fender of George's car, passed on nameless into the night, leaving them unharmed but shaken.

When George stopped the car they both looked to see if Phyllis was damaged; only then George gasped: "It was the earthquake!"

"I suppose it was the earthquake," said Phyllis evenly. "Will the car still run?"

"Oh, yes." And he repeated hoarsely, "It was the earthquake—*I* held the road all right."

"Let's not discuss it," Phyllis interrupted. "I've got to be on the lot at eight and I want to sleep. What were we talking about?"

"That earth—" He controlled himself as they drove off, and tried to remember what he had said about Dolly. "She's just worried about whether they are going to do *Sense and Sensibility*. If they're not she'll close the house and sign up for some play—"

"I could have told her about that," said Phyllis. "They're probably not doing it—and if they do, Bette Davis has a signed contract."

Recovering his self-respect about the earthquake, George returned to his obsession of the day.

"She'd be a *'grande cliente,'* " he said, "even if she went on the stage."

"Well, I don't know the role," said Phyllis, "but she'd be unwise to go on the stage, and you can tell her that for me."

George was tired of discussing Dolly; things had been so amazingly pleasant just ten minutes before. Already they were on Phyllis' street.

"I would like that drink," he remarked with a deprecatory little laugh. "I've had a glass of beer a couple of times and after that earthquake—well, I've got to be at school at half past eight in the morning."

When they stopped in front of her house there was a smile with all heaven in it—but she shook her head.

"Afraid the earthquake came between us," she said gently. "I want to hide my head right under a big pillow."

George drove several blocks and parked at a corner where two mysterious men swung a huge drum light in pointless arcs over paradise. It was not Dolly who "had everything"—it was Phyllis. Dolly was made, her private life arranged. Phyllis, on the contrary, had everything to look forward to—the whole world that in some obscure way was represented more by the drum light and the red and white gleams of neon signs on cocktail bars than by the changing colors of Dolly's pool. He knew how the latter worked—why, he had seen it installed in broad daylight. But he did not know how the world worked and he felt that Phyllis lived in the same delicious oblivion.

After that fall, things were different. George stayed on at school, but this time as a boarder, and visited Dolly in New York on Christmas and Easter. The following summer she came back to the Coast and opened up the house for a month's rest, but she was committed to another season in the East and George went back with her to attend a tutoring school for Yale.

Sense and Sensibility was made after all, but with Phyllis, not Bette Davis, in the part of Marianne. George saw Phyllis only once during that year—when Jim Jerome, who sometimes took him to his ranch for week-ends, told him one Sunday they'd do anything George wanted. George suggested a call on Phyllis.

"Do you remember when you told me about 'une grande cliente?' "

"You mean I said that about *Phyllis?*"

"No, about Dolly."

Phyllis was no fun that day, surrounded and engulfed by men; after his departure for the East, George found other girls and was a personage for having known Phyllis and for what was, in his honest recollection, a superflirtation.

The next June, after examinations, Dolly came down to the liner to see Hennen and George off to Europe; she was coming herself when the show closed—and by transatlantic plane.

"I'd like to wait and do that with you," George offered.

"You're eighteen—you have a long and questionable life before you."

"You're just twenty-seven."

"You've got to stick to the boys you're traveling with."

Hennen was going first-class; George was going tourist. At the tourist gangplank there were so many girls from Bryn Mawr and Smith and the finishing schools that Dolly warned him.

"Don't sit up all night drinking beer with them. And if the pressure gets too bad slip over into first-class, and let Hennen calm you."

Hennen was very calm and depressed about the parting.

"I shall go down to tourist," he said desperately. "And meet those beautiful girls."

"It would make you a heavy," she warned him, "like Ivan Lebedeff in a picture."

Hennen and George talked between upper and lower deck as the ship steamed through the narrows.

"I feel great contempt for you down in the slums," said Hennen. "I hope no one sees me speaking to you."

"This is the cream of the passenger list. They call us tycoon-skins. Speaking of furs, are you going after one of those barges in a mink coat?"

"No—I still expect Dolly to turn up in my stateroom. And, actually, I have cabled her *not* to cross by plane."

"She'll do what she likes."

"Will you come up and dine with me tonight—after washing your ears?"

There was only one girl of George's tone of voice on the boat and someone wolfed her away—so he wished Hennen would invite him up to dinner every night, but after the first time it was only for luncheon and Hennen mooned and moped.

"I go to my cabin every night at six," he said, "and have dinner in bed. I cable Dolly and I think her press agent answers."

The day before arriving at Southampton, the girl whom George liked quarreled with her admirer over the length of her fingernails or the Munich pact or both—and George stepped out, once more, into tourist class society.

He began, as was fitting, with the ironic touch.

"You and Princeton amused yourself pretty well," he remarked. "Now you come back to me."

"It was this way," explained Martha. "I thought you were conceited about your aunt being Dolly Bordon and having lived in Hollywood—"

"Where did you two disappear to?" he interrupted. "It was a great act while it lasted."

"Nothing to it," Martha said briskly. "And if you're going to be like that—"

Resigning himself to the past, George was presently rewarded.

"As a matter of fact I'll show you," she said. "We'll do what we used to do—before he criticized me as an ignoramus. Good gracious! As if going to Princeton meant anything! My *own* father went there!"

George followed her, rather excited, through an iron door marked "Private," upstairs, along a corridor, and up to another door that said "First-Class Passengers Only."

He was disappointed.

"Is *this* all? I've been up in first-class before."

"Wait!"

She opened the door cautiously, and they rounded a lifeboat overlooking a fenced-in square of deck.

There was nothing to see—the flash of an officer's face glancing seaward over a still higher deck, another mink coat in a deck chair; he even peered into the lifeboat to see if they had discovered a stowaway.

"And I found out things that are going to help me later," Martha muttered as if to herself. "How they work it—if I ever go in for it I'll certainly know the technique."

"Of what?"

"Look at the deck chair, stupe."

Even as George gazed, a long-remembered face emerged in its individuality from behind the huge dark of the figure in the mink coat. And at the moment he recognized Phyllis Burns he saw that Hennen was sitting beside her.

"Watch how she works," Martha murmured. "Even if you can't hear you'll realize you're looking at a preview."

George had not been seasick so far, but now only the fear of being seen made him control his impulse as Hennen shifted from his chair to the foot of hers and took her hand. After a moment, Phyllis leaned forward, touching his arm gently in exactly the way George remembered; in her eyes was an ineffable sympathy.

From somewhere the mess call shrilled from a bugle—George seized Martha's hand and pulled her back along the way they had come.

"But they *like* it!" Martha protested. "She lives in the public eye. I'd like to cable Winchell right away."

All George heard was the word "cable." Within half an hour he had written in an indecipherable code:

HE DIDN'T COME DOWN TOURIST AS DIDN'T NEED TO BECAUSE SENSE AND SENSIBILITY STOP ADVISE SAIL IMMEDIATELY

GEORGE
(COLLECT)

Either Dolly didn't understand or just waited for the clipper anyhow, while George bicycled uneasily through Belgium, timing his arrival in Paris to coincide with hers. She must have been forewarned by his letter, but there was nothing to prove it, as she and Hennen and George rode from Le Bourget into Paris. It was the next morning before the cat jumped nimbly out of the bag, and it had become a sizable cat by afternoon when George walked into the situation. To get there he had to pass a stringy crowd extending from one hotel to another, for word had drifted about that *two* big stars were in the neighborhood.

"Come in, George," Dolly called. "You know Phyllis—she's just leaving for Aix-les-Bains. She's lucky—either Hennen or I will have to take up residence, depending on who's going to sue whom. I suggest Hennen sues me—on the charge I made him a poodle dog."

She was in a reckless mood, for there were secretaries within hearing—and press agents outside and waiters who dashed in from time to time. Phyllis was very composed behind the attitude of "please leave me out of it." George was damp, bewildered, sad.

"Shall I be difficult, George?" Dolly asked him. "Or shall I play it like a character part—just suited to my sweet nature. Or shall I be primitive? Jim Jerome or Frank Capra could tell me. Have you got good judgment, George, or don't they teach that till college?"

"Frankly—" said Phyllis getting up, "frankly, it's as much a surprise to me as it is to you. I didn't know Hennen would be on the boat any more than he did me."

At least George had learned at tutoring school how to be rude. He made noxious sounds—and faced Hennen who got to his feet.

"Don't irritate me!" George was trembling a little with anger. "You've always been nice till now but you're twice my age and I don't want to tear you in two."

Dolly sat him down; Phyllis went out and they heard her emphatic "Not now! Not now!" echo in the corridor.

"You and I could take a trip somewhere," said Hennen unhappily.

Dolly shook her head.

"I know about those solutions. I've been confidential friend in some of these things. You go away and take it with you. Silence falls— nobody has any lines. Silence—trying to guess behind the silence— then imitating how it was—and more silence—and great wrinkles in the heart."

"I can only say I am very sorry," said Hennen.

"Don't be. I'll go along on George's bicycle trip if he'll have me. And you take your new chippie up to Pont-à-Dieu to meet your family. I'm alive, Hennen—though I admit I'm not enjoying it. Evidently you've been dead some time and I didn't know it."

She told George afterward that she was grateful to Hennen for not appealing to the maternal instinct. She had done all her violent suffering on the plane, in an economical way she had. Even being a saint requires a certain power of organization, and Dolly was pretty near to a saint to those close to her—even to the occasional loss of temper.

But all the next two months George never saw Dolly's eyes gleam silvery blue in the morning; and often, when his hotel room was near hers, he would lie awake and listen while she moved about whimpering softly in the night.

But by breakfast time she was always a *"grande cliente."* George knew exactly what that meant now.

In September, Dolly, her secretary and her maid, and George moved into a bungalow of a Beverly Hills hotel—a bungalow crowded with flowers that went to the hospitals almost as fast as they came in. Around them again was the twilight privacy of pictures against a jealous and intrusive world; inside, the telephones, agent, producers, and friends.

Dolly went about, talking possibilities, turning down offers, encouraging others—considered, or pretended to consider, a return to the stage.

"You *darling*! Everybody's *so* glad you're back."

She gave them background; for their own dignity they wanted her in pictures again. There was scarcely any other actress of whom that could have been said.

"Now, *I've* got to give a party," she told George.

"But you *have*. Your being anywhere *makes* it a party."

George was growing up—entering Yale in a week. But he meant it too.

"Either very small or very large," she pondered, "—or else I'll hurt people's feelings. And this is not the time, at the very start of a career."

"You ought to worry, with people breaking veins to get you."

She hesitated—then brought him a two-page list.

"Here are the broken veins," she said. "Notice that there's something the matter with every offer—a condition or a catch. Look at this character part; a fascinating older woman—and me not thirty. It's either money—lots of money tied to a fatal part, or else a nice part with no money. I'll open up the house."

With her entourage and some scrubbers, Dolly went out next day and made ready as much of the house as she would need.

"Candles everywhere," George exclaimed, the afternoon of the event. "A fortune in candles."

"Aren't they nice! And once I was ungrateful when people gave them to me."

"It's magnificent. I'm going into the garden and rehearse the pool lights—for old times' sake."

"They don't work," said Dolly cheerfully. "No electricity works—a flood got in the cellar."

"Get it fixed."

"Oh, no—I'm dead broke. Oh yes—I am. The banks are positive. And the house is thoroughly mortgaged and I'm trying to sell it."

He sat in a dusty chair.

"But how?"

"Well—it began when I promised the cast to go on tour, and it turned hot. Then the treasurer ran away to Canada. George, we have guests coming in two hours. Can't you put candles around the pool?"

"Nobody sent you pool-candlesticks. How about calling in the money you've loaned people?"

"What? A little glamor girl like me! Besides, now they're poorer still, probably. Besides, Hennen kept the accounts except he never put things down. If you look so blue I'll go over you with this dustcloth. Your tuition is paid for a year—"

"You think I'd go?"

Through the big room a man George had never seen was advancing toward them.

"I didn't see any lights, Miss Bordon. I didn't dream you were here, I'm from Ridgeway Real Estate—"

He broke off in profound embarrassment. It was unnecessary to explain that he had brought a client—for the client stood directly behind him.

"Oh," said Dolly. She looked at Phyllis, smiled—then she sat down on the sofa, laughing. *"You're* the client; you want my house, do you?"

"Frankly, I heard you wanted to sell it," said Phyllis.

Dolly's answer was muffled in laughter but George thought he heard: "It would save time if I just sent you all my pawn checks."

"What's so very funny?" Phyllis inquired.

"Will your—family move in too? Excuse me; that's not my business." Dolly turned to Ridgeway Real Estate. "Show the Countess around—here's a candlestick. The lights are out of commission."

"I know the house," said Phyllis. "I only wanted to get a general impression."

"Everything goes with it," said Dolly, adding irresistibly, "—as you know. Except George. I want to keep George."

"I own the mortgage," said Phyllis absently.

George had an impulse to walk her from the room by the seat of her sea-green slacks.

"Now *Phyllis!*" Dolly reproved her gently. "You know you can't use that without a riding crop and a black moustache. You have to get a Guild permit. Your proper line is 'I don't have to listen to this.' "

"Well, I *don't* have to listen to this," said Phyllis.

When she had gone, Dolly said, "They asked *me* to play heavies."

"Why, four years ago," began George, "Phyllis was—"

"Shut up, George. This is Hollywood and you play by the rules. There'll be people coming here tonight who've committed first degree murder."

When they came, she was her charming self, and she made everyone kind and charming so that George even failed to identify the killers. Only in a washroom did he hear a whisper of conversation that told him all was guessed at about her hard times. The surface, though, was unbroken. Even Hymie Fink roamed around the rooms, the white blink of his camera when he pointed it, or his alternate grin when he passed by, dividing those who were up from those coming down.

He pointed it at Dolly, on the porch. She was an old friend and he took her from all angles. Judging by the man she was sitting beside, it wouldn't be long now before she was back in the big time.

"Aren't you going to snap Mr. Jim Jerome?" Dolly asked him. "He's just back in Hollywood today—from England. He says they're making better pictures; he's convinced them not to take out time for tea in the middle of the big emotional scenes."

George saw them there together and he had a feeling of great relief—that everything was coming out all right. But after the party, when the candles had squatted down into little tallow drips, he detected a look of uncertainty in Dolly's face—the first he had ever seen there. In the car going back to the hotel bungalow she told him what had happened.

"He wants me to give up pictures and marry him. Oh, he's set on it. The old business of *two* careers and so forth. I wonder—"

"Yes?"

"I don't wonder. He thinks I'm through. That's part of it."

"Could you fall in love with him?"

She looked at George—laughed.

"Could I? Let me see—"

"He's always loved you. He almost told me once."

"I know. But it would be a strange business; I'd have nothing to do—just like Hennen."

"Then don't marry him; wait it out. I've thought of a dozen ideas to make money."

"George, you terrify me," she said lightly. "Next thing I'll find racing forms in your pocket, or see you down on Hollywood Boulevard with an oil well angle—and your hat pulled down over your eyes."

"I mean honest money," he said defiantly.

"You could go on the stage like Freddie and I'll be your Aunt Prissy."

"Well, don't marry him unless you want to."

"I wouldn't mind—if he was just passing through; after all every woman needs a man. But he's so *set* about everything. Mrs. James Jerome. No! That isn't the way I grew to be and you can't help the way you grow to be, can you? Remind me to wire him tonight—because tomorrow he's going East to pick up talent for *Portrait of a Woman.*"

George wrote out and telephoned the wire, and three days later went once more to the big house in the valley to pick up a scattering of personal things that Dolly wanted.

Phyllis was there—the deal for the house was closed, but she made no objections, trying to get him to take more and winning a little of his sympathy again, or at least bringing back his young assurance that there's good in everyone. They walked in the garden, where already workmen had repaired the cables and were testing the many-colored bulbs around the pool.

"Anything in the house she wants," Phyllis said. "I'll never forget that she was my inspiration and ideal, and frankly what's happened to her might happen to any of us."

"Not exactly," objected George. "She has special things happen because she's a *'grande cliente.'* "

"I never knew what that meant," laughed Phyllis. "But I hope it's a consolation if she begins brooding."

"Oh, she's too busy to brood. She started work on *Portrait of a Woman* this morning."

Phyllis stopped in her promenade.

"She did! Why, that was for Katharine Cornell, if they could persuade her! Why, they swore to me—"

"They didn't try to persuade Cornell or anyone else. Dolly just walked into the test—and I never saw so many people crying in a projection room at once. One guy had to leave the room—and the test was just three minutes long."

He caught Phyllis' arm to keep her from tripping over the board into the pool. He changed the subject quickly.

"When are you—when are you two moving in?"

"I don't know," said Phyllis. Her voice rose. "I don't like the place! She can have it all—with my compliments."

But George knew that Dolly didn't want it. She was in another street now, opening another big charge account with life. Which is what we all do after a fashion—open an account and then pay.

On an Ocean Wave
by Paul Elgin

(*Esquire*, February 1941)

"On an Ocean Wave," written in the summer of 1940, was the only Fitzgerald story published under a pseudonym. The disguise was his idea, and he originally proposed it to Arnold Gingrich in February 1940 for "Three Hours Between Planes": "Why don't you publish it under a pseudonym—say, John Darcy? I'm awfully tired of being Scott Fitzgerald anyhow, as there doesn't seem to be so much money in it, and I'd like to find out if people read me just because I am Scott Fitzgerald or, what is more likely, don't read me for the same reason. In other words it would fascinate me to have one of my stories stand on its own merits completely and see if there is a response." It is likely that the real reason was Fitzgerald's suspicion that the Pat Hobby stories had typed him. Moreover, he wanted to accelerate publication of the stories *Esquire* was holding until the Hobby series was completed. Although "On an Ocean Wave" was published posthumously, it had been scheduled before Fitzgerald died and appeared in the same issue as "Fun in an Artist's Studio."

"On an Ocean Wave" was not a new departure for Fitzgerald. The treatment of Scheer is uncharacteristically hard-boiled; but the style is recognizable, as in the final paragraph which might have been written for one of Fitzgerald's Twenties stories.

Gaston T. Scheer—the man, the company, the idea—five feet eight, carrying himself with dash and pride, walking the deck of the ocean liner like a conqueror. This was when it was something to be an American—Spring of 1929.

O'Kane, his confidential secretary, met him in the morning on the open front of the promenade deck.

"See her?" Scheer asked.

"Yes—sure. She's all right."

"Why shouldn't she be all right?"

O'Kane hesitated.

"Some of her baggage is marked with her real initials—and the stewardess said—"

"Oh, hell!" said Scheer. "She should have had that fixed up in New York. It's the same old story—girl's not your wife, she's always sensitive, always complaining about slights and injuries. Oh, hell."

"She was all right."

"Women are small potatoes," said Scheer disgustedly. "Did you see that cable from Claud Hanson today that said he'd gladly die for me?"

"I saw it, Mr. Scheer."

"I liked it." Scheer said defiantly, "I think Claud meant it. I think he'd gladly die for me."

Claud Hanson was Mr. Scheer's other secretary. O'Kane let his natural cynicism run riot in silence.

"I think many people would, Mr. Scheer," he said without vomiting. Gosh, it was probably true. Mr. Scheer did a lot for a lot of people—kept them alive, gave them work.

"I liked the sentiment," said Scheer gazing gravely out to sea. "Anyhow Miss Denzer oughtn't to grouse—it's just four days and twelve hours. She doesn't have to stay in her cabin, just so she doesn't make herself conspicuous or talk to me—just in case."

Just in case anyone had seen them together in New York.

"Anyhow—" he concluded. "My wife's never seen her or heard of her."

Mr. O'Kane had concluded that he himself would possibly die for Mr. Scheer if Mr. Scheer kept on giving him market tips for ten years more. He would die at the end of the ten—you could cram a lot into ten years. By that time he himself might be able to bring two women abroad in the same load, in separate crates so to speak.

Alone, Gaston T. Scheer faced a strong west wind with a little spray in it. He was not afraid of the situation he had created—he had never been afraid since the day he had forced himself to lay out a foreman with a section of pitch chain.

It just felt a little strange when he walked with Minna and the children to think that Catherine Denzer might be watching them. So when he was on deck with Minna he kept his face impassive and aloof, appearing not to have a good time. This was false. He liked Minna—she said nice things.

In Europe this summer it would be easier. Minna and the children would be parked here and there, in Paris and on the Riviera, and he would make business trips with Catherine. It was a willful, daring arrangement but he was twice a man in every way. Life certainly owed him two women.

The day passed—once he saw Catherine Denzer, passing her in an empty corridor. She kept her bargain, all except for her lovely pale head which yearned toward him momentarily as they passed and made his throat warm, made him want to turn and go after her. But he kept himself in control—they would be in Cherbourg in fifty hours.

Another day passed—there was a brokerage office on board and he spent the time there, putting in a few orders, using the ship-to-shore telephone once, sending a few code wires.

That evening he left Minna talking to the college professor in the adjoining deck chair, and strolled restlessly around the ship, continually playing with the idea of going to Catherine Denzer, but only as a form of mental indulgence because it was twenty-four hours now to Paris and the situation was well in hand.

But he walked the halls of her deck, sometimes glancing casually down the little branch corridors to the staterooms. And so, entirely by accident, in one of these corridors he saw his wife Minna and the professor. They were in each other's arms embracing, with all abandon. No mistake.

II

Cautiously Scheer backed away from the corridor. His first thought was very simple: it jumped over several steps—over fury, hot jealousy and amazement—it was that his entire plan for the summer was ruined. His next thought was that Minna must sweat blood for this and then he jumped a few more steps. He was what is known medically as a "schizoid"—in his business dealings, too, he left out intermediate steps, surprising competitors by arriving quickly at an extreme position without any discoverable logic. He had arrived at one of these extreme positions now and was not even surprised to find himself there.

An hour later there was a knock on the door of Mr. O'Kane's cabin and Professor Dollard of the faculty of Weston Technical College came into the room. He was a thin quiet man of forty, wearing a loose tweed suit.

"Oh yes," said O'Kane. "Come in. Sit down."

"Thank you," said Dollard. "What do you want to see me about?"

"Have a cigarette."

"No thanks. I'm on my way to bed, but tell me, what's it about?"

O'Kane coughed pointedly—whereupon Cates, the swimming-pool steward, came out of the private bathroom behind Dollard and went to the corridor door, locking it and standing in front of it. At the same time Gaston T. Scheer came out of the bathroom and Dollard stood up, blushing suddenly dark as he recognized him.

"Oh, hello—" he said, "—Mr. Scheer. What's the idea of this?" He took off his glasses with the thought that Scheer was going to hit him.

"What are you a professor of, Professor?"

"Mathematics, Mr. Scheer—I told you that. What's the idea of asking me down here?"

"You ought to stick to your job," said Scheer. "You ought to stick there in the college and teach it and not mess around with decent people."

"I'm not messing around with anybody."

"You oughtn't to fool around with people that could buy you out ten thousand times—and not know they spent a nickel."

Dollard stood up.

"You're out of your class," said Scheer. "You're a school teacher that's promoted himself out of his class."

Cates, the steward, stirred impatiently. He had left the two hundred pounds in cash in his locker and he wanted to have this over with and get back and hide it better.

"I don't know yet what I've done," Dollard said. But he knew all right. It was too bad. A long time ago he had decided to avoid rich people and here he was tangled up with the very worst type.

"You stepped out of your class," said Scheer thickly, "but you're not going to do it any more. You're going to feed the fishes out there, see?"

Mr. O'Kane, who had bucked himself with whiskey, kept imagining that it was Claud Hanson who was about to die for Mr. Scheer—instead of Professor Dollard who had not offered himself for a sacrifice. There was still a moment when Dollard could have cried out for help but because he was guilty he could not bring himself to cry out. Then he was engrossed in a struggle to keep breathing, a struggle that he lost without a sigh.

III

Minna Scheer waited on the front of the promenade deck, walking in the chalked numbers of the shuffle-board game. She was excited and happy. Her feet as she placed them in the squares felt young and barefoot and desperate. She could play too—whatever it was they played. She had been a good girl so long, but now almost everybody she knew was raising the devil and it was a thrilling discovery to find that she could join in with such pleasure. The man was late but that made it all the more tense and unbearably lovely, and from time to time she raised her eyes in delight and looked off into the white hot wake of the steamer.

The Woman from Twenty-One
(*Esquire*, June 1941)

Ah, what a day for Raymond Torrence! Once you knew that your roots were safely planted outside megalopolitanism what fun it was to come back—every five years. He and Elizabeth woke up to the frozen music of Fifth Avenue and Fifty-ninth Street, and first thing went down to his publishers on Fifth Avenue. Elizabeth, who was half Javanese and had never been in America before, liked it best of all there because her husband's book was on multiple display in the window. She liked it in the store where she squeezed Ray's hand tensely when people asked for it, and again when they bought it.

They lunched at the Stork Club with Hat Milbank, a pal of Ray's at college and in the war. Of course no one there recognized Ray after these years but a man came in with the Book in his hands, crumpling up the jacket. Afterwards Hat asked them down to old Westbury to see the polo in which he still performed, but they went to the hotel and rested as they did in Java. Otherwise it would all be a little too much. Elizabeth wrote a letter to the children in Suva and told them "everyone in New York" was reading father's book and admired the photograph which Janice had taken of a girl sick with yaws.

They went alone to a play by William Saroyan. After the curtain had been up five minutes the woman from Twenty-one came in.

She was in the mid-thirties, dark and pretty. As she took her seat beside Ray Torrence she continued her conversation in a voice that was for outside and Elizabeth was a little sorry for her because obviously she did not know she was making herself a nuisance. They were a quartet—two in front. The girl's escort was a tall and good-looking man. The woman leaning forward in her seat and talking to her friend in front, distracted Ray a little, but not overwhelmingly until she said in a conversational voice that must have reached the actors on the stage:

"Let's all go back to Twenty-one."

Her escort replied in a whisper and there was quiet for a moment. Then the woman drew a long, long sigh, culminating in an exhausted groan in which could be distinguished the words, "Oh, my God."

Her friend in front turned around so sweetly that Ray thought the woman next to him must be someone very prominent and powerful—an Astor or a Vanderbilt or a Roosevelt.

"See a little bit of it," suggested her friend.

The woman from Twenty-one flopped forward with a dynamic movement and began an audible but indecipherable conversation in which the number of the restaurant occurred again and again. When she shifted restlessly back into her chair with another groaning "My God!" this time directed toward the play, Raymond turned his head sideways and uttered a prayer to her aloud:

"Please."

If Ray had muttered a four-letter word the effect could not have been more catalytic. The woman flashed about and regarded him— her eyes ablaze with the gastric hatred of many dying martinis and with something more. These were the unmistakable eyes of Mrs. Richbitch, that leftist creation as devoid of nuance as Mrs. Jiggs. As they burned with scalding arrogance—the very eyes of the Russian lady who let her coachman freeze outside while she wept at poverty in a play—at this moment Ray recognized a girl with whom he had played Run, Sheep, Run in Pittsburgh twenty years ago.

The woman did not after all excoriate him but this time her flop forward was so violent that it rocked the row ahead.

"Can you bel*ieve*—can you im*agine*—"

Her voice raced along in a hoarse whisper. Presently she lunged sideways toward her escort and told him of the outrage. His eye caught Ray's in a flickering embarrassed glance. On the other side of Ray, Elizabeth became disturbed and alarmed.

Ray did not remember the last five minutes of the act—beside him smoldered fury and he knew its name and the shape of its legs. Wanting nothing less than to kill, he hoped her man would speak to him or even look at him in a certain way during the entr'acte—but when it came the party stood up quickly, and the woman said: "We'll go to Twenty-one."

On the crowded sidewalk between the acts Elizabeth talked softly to Ray. She did not seem to think it was of any great importance except for the effect on him. He agreed in theory—but when they went inside again the woman from Twenty-one was already in her place, smoking and waving a cigarette.

"I could speak to the usher," Ray muttered.

"Never mind," said Elizabeth quickly. "In France you smoke in the music halls."

"But you have some place to put the butt. She's going to crush it out in my lap!"

In the sequel she spread the butt on the carpet and kept rubbing it in Since a lady lush moves in mutually exclusive preoccupations just as a gent does, and the woman had passed beyond her preoccupation with Ray, things were tensely quiet.

When the lights went on after the second act, a voice called to Ray from the aisle. It was Hat Milbank.

"Hello, hello there, Ray! Hello, Mrs. Torrence. Do you want to go to Twenty-one after the theatre?"

His glance fell upon the people in between.

"Hello, Jidge," he said to the woman's escort; to the other three, who called him eagerly by name, he answered with an inclusive nod. Ray and Elizabeth crawled out over them. Ray told the story to Hat who seemed to ascribe as little importance to it as Elizabeth did, and wanted to know if he could come out to Fiji this spring.

But the effect upon Ray had been profound. It made him remember why he had left New York in the first place. This woman was what everything was for. She should have been humble, not awful, but she had become confused and thought she should be awful.

So Ray and Elizabeth would go back to Java, unmourned by anyone except Hat. Elizabeth would be a little disappointed at not seeing any more plays and not going to Palm Beach, and wouldn't like having to pack so late at night. But in a silently communicable way she would understand. In a sense she would be glad. She even guessed that it was the children Ray was running to—to save them and shield them from all the walking dead.

When they went back to their seats for the third act the party from Twenty-one were no longer there—nor did they come in later. It had clearly been another game of Run, Sheep, Run.

Editorial Note

These stories are reprinted from their magazine appearances. Spelling errors have been silently corrected, but acceptable variants have been retained. Punctuation has been conservatively emended, also silently. Since the several magazines had different house-styles, a certain amount of regularization was necessary—for example, in the treatment of song titles and newspapers. Some of the magazines—notably *Woman's Home Companion*—introduced space breaks into the stories for make-up reasons. These breaks have been removed where they are non-structural. Deletions—identified with word counts—have been made in two stories.